David Plunkett is an Australian, who lives in the Yarra Valley, situated in Victoria. He has a wife of 34 years and has three adult children. After many years of various jobs, David has now settled as a school bus charter driver, which he has enjoyed for the last 13 years. His favourite hobbies are horse racing and golf, along with anything sport. He has always been an avid reader of fiction, history, and biographies. David loves nothing more than taking hikes in the pristine mountains near his home or sharing a cold beer and fine food with close family and friends. Despite leaving school at an early age and with no formal education, David's passion for history and literature always came to the fore, culminating in his debut novel.

David J Plunkett

To Heaven or to Hell

Bull Ants and Scorpions

AUSTIN MACAULEY PUBLISHERS™
LONDON • CAMBRIDGE • NEW YORK • SHARJAH

Copyright © David J Plunkett 2023

The right of David J Plunkett to be identified as author of this work has been asserted by the author in accordance with sections 77 and 78 of the Copyright, Designs and Patents Act 1988.

All rights reserved. No part of this publication may be reproduced, stored in a retrieval system, or transmitted in any form or by any means, electronic, mechanical, photocopying, recording, or otherwise, without the prior permission of the publishers.

Any person who commits any unauthorised act in relation to this publication may be liable to criminal prosecution and civil claims for damages.

This is a work of fiction. Names, characters, businesses, places, events, locales, and incidents are either the products of the author's imagination or used in a fictitious manner. Any resemblance to actual persons, living or dead, or actual events is purely coincidental.

A CIP catalogue record for this title is available from the British Library.

ISBN 9781398426269 (Paperback)
ISBN 9781398426276(ePub e-book)

www.austinmacauley.com

First Published 2023
Austin Macauley Publishers Ltd®
1 Canada Square
Canary Wharf
London
E14 5AA

To my beautiful wife, Gabrielle, for her endless patience, support, and encouragement from the very first word that was written. Love you dearly.

To Rob and Joe. Your guidance, advice and learned wisdom was invaluable and gave me the confidence to persist.

To all my family and friends who contributed with feedback and critique as I took this journey, many thanks to you all.

Synopsis

In a time in the not-too-distant future, where mankind—through greed and stupidity—had all but used up the earth's fuels and commodities and people's living standards had been plummeted back to over more than a century, comes a story of one man's fight for survival.

Danny Pruitt is an ordinary family man trying to eke out a living in the harshest of times but when a visit from overzealous police turns deadly, Danny's life is turned upside down. With no choice but to escape corrupt authorities, he heads to the nearby mountains and soon embarks on a journey of love, murder, betrayal, tragedy, mate-ship and revenge whilst fighting his inner torment and whatever nature's fury can throw at him.

As Danny tries to elude his relentless pursuers, he finds an unlikely haven in the forest on his quest to arrive at a northern property—named Heaven. Will he find his freedom and reunite with his cherished wife and two young sons and make it to his Heaven, or will the deeds of his committed sins deem him to hell?

Chapter 1

With every swing of the axe, the bitterness and anger he held within forged down on the defenceless blocks of firewood. It was another hard chore that had to be done, however; this was Christmas night and it was supposed to be warm, after all, it was a month into summer and to reignite the fireplace only added to the burdens and frustration.

He reluctantly returned to the house with a full load of wood in his arms and began to stoke the open fire. His wife gave him a glance, then, sensing his mood, turned to the two boys who were playing on the floor.

'Come on, kids,' she said tiredly, 'it's time for bed. Say goodnight to daddy.'

He gave his six-year-old twin sons, Darcy and Daniel, a light squeeze and said goodnight before Greta led them to their bedroom.

Danny stared into the embers and flames that flickered before him, silently stressing over what lay ahead for him. He didn't notice Greta had returned to the lounge room until she wrapped her arms around him from behind and laid her chin upon his shoulder.

'It's alright, Danny,' she comforted. 'We'll get through this, no matter how long it takes.'

'Not so sure anymore, babe!' he sombrely replied as he stood to his feet.

'We will be alright,' Greta confidently said. 'They say that the country is recovering, and that the government is—'

'Don't believe it,' he interrupted her mid-sentence in angry tones. 'They lied back then, and they will lie again; it's all bullshit, Greta. They're only saying it to try and stop all the protests and riots in the streets. It's the same when they said we wouldn't run out of fuel; now look, there's hardly a car on the road. It's the same when they said we wouldn't run out of electricity; now we can't even flick a switch on. We have to use candle-lit lanterns to see at night. Look at all our appliances, they just sit there gathering cobwebs. It's all false hopes. I've had enough, Greta, I've really had enough.'

Danny broke away from his wife and began to walk out the front door, cursing to himself over the life that was now forced upon them. Greta followed and grabbed him by the arm and turned him around, looked deeply into his hazel coloured eyes and with tears welling in hers asked what had happened to her man.

'Don't let it get to you, Danny,' she said soothingly. 'You have always made the right decisions for us, and you will again. Where is my man who never lies down for anything, the man who has always ridden the storm no matter what has been thrown at him? You're a strong man, Danny,' she continued as her voice lowered. 'I need you to be strong, the kids need you to be strong. Come back inside, it's getting dark.'

Danny gritted his teeth as he took a deep breath. 'I can't even give my children Christmas presents,' his choking voice relayed.

'It doesn't matter,' replied Greta. 'They have a roof over their heads, a warm bed and two parents who love them very much, that's all they ask for, Danny, that's all any child asks for.'

Danny looked into Greta's almond-shaped deep brown eyes. They always had the power to soothe the festering beast inside of him. They had done it many times over when he threatened to do things that he would regret later. It was what he fell in love with the first time his own eyes were laid upon her. He ran his right palm over her long dark crinkled hair then slumped into her arms, holding back his wretched emotions. He succumbed to her wisdom and arm in arm, they slowly walked back inside; yet, the strain of everything that was around left a deep hole in Danny's stomach, which to him was irreparable.

He yearned for the return of the good times, the days when he had a steady job as a landscape gardener and home maintenance man, the days when his life was carefree and full of happiness, the days when he could afford to buy his wife and children Christmas presents.

This was not the life he had dreamed and worked so hard for as he continually thought of what might have been. Danny Pruitt was never going to become a millionaire but the money he had been making was more than enough for him and his family to live comfortably. He thought he was doing the right thing by saving for a rainy day, putting time and money into small property investments and planning for a future that in his mind looked bright and prosperous; however, today, it seemed another lifetime away.

Danny and Greta fought desperately hard to keep their house and half-acre property at the northeast tip of the semi-rural town of Graceville. The picturesque town was known as the gateway to the mountains and lay in the Shire of the Hexagon Valley, 70 kilometres northeast from the main city of Marlboro, the second largest city in the nation and the coastal capital of the southern state of Venturia. The shire was aptly named because of the six tall mountain peaks that enveloped her starting from the North West of Graceville where the closest mountain range sat, then stretching far across the expanding valley's and dales around to the South. The Hexagon Valley took in over 5,000 square kilometres and was a mecca for tourists in its heyday because of its flourishing wineries and the beautiful assorted forests and rivers close by. The town Danny had called home for the last ten years boasted a population of nearly 16,000; however, that had increased dramatically as people from nearby smaller towns and villages who had forfeited on their properties and lost employment congregated to Graceville to try and eke out a living on the vacant lands that now surrounded the town.

The seven-year married couple had been able to keep their own roof above their heads through the forced selling of their assets and now Danny got by supplying firewood whilst Greta was lucky enough to remain employed through her primary school teaching. Nevertheless, the hounds were closing in quickly amid the global and domestic disaster and their little oasis on the planet was not immune. The day Danny dreaded was not far away and the life he once treasured was slowly but surely being torn apart.

They awoke to a much milder day the following morning, the sun was shining, and it looked like summer was quickly going to re-join them. His mood was brighter thanks to some reassuring from Greta who was praying things would turn around quickly for her family's sake. Danny devoted the public holiday spending quality time with his children, he knew he had been neglecting their needs over recent weeks as he was so caught up in his own thoughts. It was a day of relaxing and forgetting about their troubles and by the time evening came around he was feeling at ease with himself. With Greta's lead, they immersed themselves in conversation by candlelight under the roof of their veranda, chatting about happier times and focusing on what they could control instead of the hardship that had been bestowed upon them.

All the same, as much as he felt at ease as Greta snuggled into his arms when they bedded down for the night, it was to be another worried night of broken sleep for Danny. In return, he woke up tense the following morning, knowing he had an order of firewood that was to be picked up by lunchtime.

It was 6.30 am and he had scarcely started splitting when he heard a voice he knew so well. He couldn't hear what he was saying, but he recognised it instantly.

Ricky De Graaf had arrived in the Graceville at Danny's request. He was a lifelong friend, best man at his and Greta's wedding. Both grew up together from childhood in the same suburb on the eastern fringes of the big city of Marlboro and although their lives took separate paths, when times were tough, they could always count on each other for help.

'How are ya, Danny?' another voice resonated from behind Ricky.

Danny left his razor-sharp axe in the already cut to size box gum which stretched half the length of the eastern side of his fence line. 'Good to see ya, Barny. Long-time no see, mate,' Danny answered, shaking his hand vigorously before he could dismount.

'Ricky says ya need a hand so here I am. I hear ya paying cash too,' Barny gibed as he tried to playfully turn Danny's hand over in the handshake.

'Can't do that, my friend, but if you help me get this order out of the way, I'll feed and groom your horse and shout you a few beers down the pub later. That's the best I can do. What do ya reckon?' Danny offered.

'Ah, the old bartering system, hey!' joked Barny.

'It's what everybody uses these days, isn't it?'

'You got that right,' Ricky chimed in.

'That's if they haven't got the cash, of course, and if I don't get this order out, I won't have any in my pocket to shout those beers,' Danny added, grinning.

'Yep, can't get any cash out of a hole in the wall these days,' Barny agreed.

'Anyways! I'm glad to see you guys. I doubt if I could get it all done by myself,' Danny said thankfully.

'Why ya bothering to chop wood for anyway? It's bloody summer, mate! Who needs wood this time of year?' Barny asked.

'It's for my regulars. I promised them I'd get it out to them today. The cold snap's caught people by surprise. Anyway, they still need it for their combustion stoves, their hot water tanks, you know, stuff like that. It's the only thing that's keeping me going this time of the year and you guys know I keep my word, so I'm glad you're here to give me a hand,' Danny said.

Within minutes, the men were into it, splitting and throwing the wood aside as if it were balsa. The quicker they would get the job done meant the more time for themselves in the afternoon and in these tough times, the opportunities to catch up were few and far between.

No more than ten minutes into splitting, all three men knew it had become a competition. Danny looked across at Ricky who was a good three inches smaller in height than him but of the same age. His short spiky blond hair was already darkened in sweat... He may have looked on the slim side, but the well-put-together sinewy arms belied the strength that they possessed.

'You're getting a bit lazy in ya old age, Ricky, come on, lift the pace, I'm about a half ton in front of ya already,' Danny quipped, hoping that his best man would take the bait and lift the tempo.

'Hang on, Danny. I've hardly broken a sweat and you're already drenched,' Barny interrupted, tongue-in-cheek before Ricky could reply. 'Looks like you're a bit out of form too, mate.'

It was the way the three lads had always interacted since the day their friendship had bonded. Trying to get one up on each other, happily pushing the wrong buttons until they would get a negative or aggressive reaction. For those around them, it never covered up the respect and tight-knit friendship they shared.

The light-hearted bantering between the three continued until the entire firewood quota had been reached, a good hour before it was to be picked up by cart at midday. They sat around on wooden stumps under one of the five 100-year-old cypress pine trees that stood tall on Danny's property fence line when Greta, who could see that the men had finished their work, arrived with a plate full of sandwiches and soft drinks. She was met with grateful thank yous from the men as she took time to say her hellos to Ricky and Barny, happy to see them again with her husband.

'Where's the beers?' Ricky cheekily gestured after Greta returned to the house.

'Just take what ya given,' said Danny firmly as he leant back against the pine tree, munching down on his sandwich.

'Don't want to start too early on the drink, Ricky, you won't last the distance, mate,' said Barny, as he too relaxed against the pine tree. 'Remember that time when we had to carry you home!'

'More than once, hey Barny!' Danny laughed.

'Yeah!' Barny agreed. 'We're no spring chickens anymore, Ricky. It's hard enough getting ourselves back home, let alone lugging you on our backs.'

'Geez fellas. We're only in our early thirties. You've still got a few good years left of helping me out yet! Don't put yourselves down like that,' mocked Ricky.

Drinking sessions among most men was rampant as the times were brutally tough. It was an excuse to try and forget about the hardship they were all now facing and with unemployment at epidemic proportions they had the time in which to do it. Greta disliked it when Danny would go out on a binge, but she knew if it let off a bit of steam and help release some of the demons that he carried with him, she accepted it.

Further, if it didn't interfere with what little work he had, and what times he could spend with her and the children, she begrudgingly afforded Danny that small luxury. Unfortunately, Greta had seen a lot of her close friends' husbands fall victim to alcohol in recent years that ultimately destroyed their marriages and lives altogether, and she trusted that Danny would never let her down.

'Midday, right on time,' Danny said as he perused his watch after hearing a far-off rattle at the top of his drive. The cart, with two Clydesdale horses at the ready to haul the three-ton of split wood to its destinations, had arrived. Danny introduced the lads to the two men while they loaded. One of the men was a portly gentleman named Alby who everyone around town guessed to be in his early sixties. No one really knew for sure, old Alby had been logging in the area since no one can remember, and he was thriving in this new environment. Danny had met him through mutual acquaintances and would buy discarded logs off him at a small price then cut and split it himself then sell it back to whoever needed cut firewood. With big orders like this one, he would get Alby to deliver it on his behalf as he had no cart big enough or the so-called horsepower to do it himself. Old Alby would then settle payment at the end of the deliveries at the local drinking hole that the lads were about to venture to.

The cart was finally loaded and heading up Danny's gravel drive that met the highway above, Alby giving the Clydesdale's an aggressive heave-ho as they exited. It was now time for the men to grab their wallets and smokes and head off for an afternoon of drink and good times.

'Taking the horses,' Ricky proposed, concerned about the five-kilometre walk to the hotel.

'Always in a bloody hurry, aren't ya, Rick,' Barny snapped.

'Yeah Ricky,' Danny huffed. 'We'll go by foot. You can leave your horses here and pick them up later. Greta will tend to them.'

Riding a horse was a thing which Danny took time to adjust to. One of his mottos in life was to never trust anything that can't talk back, and never trust an animal that's bigger than you, so in Danny's case, the horse fitted this category perfectly. It was through necessity rather than preference that he gained more of an understanding of this majestic animal. As such, his respect for the beast grew and grew, and his riding skills became a lot better over time. Irrespective of his growing admiration, if Danny had the chance to walk rather than ride, he would use leg power every time.

Dressed in T-shirts, jeans and boots, the men set off on foot to the hotel for their long-awaited drinking session. As the temperature was heading towards the 30-degree Celsius mark, they were as thirsty as could be.

Danny led the boys through the streets that locals now called the slums, a route he didn't have to take to get into town. Usually, Danny would take the highway southwards; however, he wanted his friends to see the devastation and despair on the poorer side of town.

The roads were in a shameful state. There simply wasn't enough money in the shire budget to maintain them. Chunks had been eroded away from the bitumen, some large enough to swallow a car itself which once travelled down the same route a thousand times a day. Other than what was deemed essential services such as police, ambulances and fire trucks, vehicles were hardly seen on the roads anymore, particularly through the side streets due to chronic fuel shortages.

Nasty potholes were there to negotiate at every corner as people on horseback mostly trekked on the nature strips or sides of roads, rather than trying their luck on the tar and risking injury to their now valuable equines. The other form of transport that was just as popular were pushbikes as people quickly discovered that riding their bikes was sometimes quicker than getting around town on horseback.

'These people are on their last legs, boys, there's no hope or spirit amongst them,' Danny ranted to Barny and Ricky. 'You know, there's up to four families living in the one house. One family for each bedroom. They can't afford anything else. They've gotta pay rent and the more families under the one roof, the less each family is out of pocket. It's totally fucked, isn't it? What they've done to people!

'Look at the houses,' he continued as he pointed. 'They're just about fallen down. Look at the windows here, the gaping holes in the brickwork and cladding!'

'You reckon they would get off their butts and try and repair them. At least have a crack,' Ricky said as he assessed the surroundings.

'It's not as easy as that, Ricky. They can't afford it, mate! Most of it is caused by vandalism. The landlords don't give a shit. No one ever gets held accountable. Look at all the broken roof tiles and rusted sheeting.'

As the boys passed, a lady was on her front deck, hand rinsing clothes across her washboard. Children with bare feet and torn clothing badgered a stranger for money. Overgrown front yards and nature strips that were infested by weeds and blackberry bushes that grew unabated were to the fore. Household garbage was stacked to the hilt that stunk on hot days and being summer, it was becoming a familiar odour around the slums. Old car bodies lay around the front yards and paddocks where the hardest hit people would make their home and with the poverty came desperation, and with the desperation came violence, and it occurred on a regular basis as every night passed, domestically and publicly.

'Look at this mess, will ya,' Danny said. 'It's a disgrace, look at these people, how do they live like this? There's no way I will end up here, man, no bloody way,' he flustered, shaking his head in disgust while flicking another cigarette butt away.

'You wonder how it all got to this, don't you!' Barny sighed. 'What's it been, four, nearly five years since the energy crisis hit?'

'Through greed and stupidity, Barny,' Danny said scornfully. 'They could foresee what was going to happen and did nothing about it. They even went to war to see who could control what was left of the oil and mining resources, didn't they?'

'Here we go, Barny, we're in for one of Danny's lectures again,' Ricky said, rolling his eyes.

'Mate, the bastards ignored every warning sign, and this is the result, and people like us are paying the penalty for their self-saving incompetence. We may as well be living like our forefathers were 150 years ago the way it is now.'

'It's been a quick downward spiral, hasn't it?' Barny agreed. 'It's ten times worse in the city though, you know that, don't you, Danny.'

'Yeah, I do. I just hope it doesn't get any worse. If it does, everything will turn to anarchy and what will be left then?'

'At least those scumbags who put us here lost all their money when the stock markets crashed,' Ricky added.

'Yeah, they can't hobnob around the world anymore, can they! When was the last time you saw a plane in the air? What's it been, three, four years since commercial airlines stopped travelling?' Danny spurned. 'It kills me not being able to fly up north during winter to step on my Heaven.'

'Heaven? What's this heaven?' Barny asked with fascination.

Barny had found religion recently. It gave him peace and tolerance in these dark times, although Danny didn't know this. Like droves of people around, it was just too hard to catch up with friends anymore who lived a distance away. The times that he had seen him, the conversation was never floated. He knew Danny was a non-believer and thought it would be a waste of time raising the subject, but curiously for Barny though, any talk of heaven, no matter what it may be, would spike his interest.

'Don't you know about Danny's heaven?' Ricky asked surprised.

'No. I don't. Enlighten me,' said Barny.

'Sorry Barny. I thought you knew.'

'No problem, Danny,' Barny accepted. 'But I want to hear more of this Heaven.'

'You should see it, Barny! It's up on the Amber Coast. Do you know where that is?'

'Of course, I do. Up in Northern Capricornia in the tropics,' Barny quickly answered.

'That's right! I've got a magnificent twenty-acre property up there. It's got a four-bedroom ranch style house sitting atop a slight hill. The house has got a raised balcony around the entire circumference with slatted balustrade and capped handrails that start at the top of the staircase to the front door. It's got beautiful green rolling pastures that flow into the rainforests, and it's all twenty-minutes from the ocean.'

'Sounds great! So why do you call it Heaven?' Barny asked intrigued.

'Because that's exactly what the cast-iron arched sign reads above the driveway as you enter the property—Heaven!' Danny excitedly informed him.

'How did you come across that?' Barny asked sounding impressed.

'I had a mate called Steve Goulding. Ricky knows him, don't ya?'

'Yeah, top bloke,' Ricky nodded.

'He moved north there about twelve years ago. He made a success of himself as a bloodstock agent, you know, breeding and selling of brood mares in the horse racing industry. When I was around twenty-one, I went and visited him and saw the area and fell in love with the place. Steve offered the place next door to his stud which he owned, so I loaned and pieced together just about every coin I had and put down a large deposit on it. I was going to move there but then I met Greta.'

'So, you don't own it outright then,' Barny asked.

'Not yet! I still owe 51% on it, but Steve says that he will accept a hell of lot less than what the deal was. I haven't been up there since I married Greta, but we write regularly. He says that he's had to sell off a lot of his stock and property, he's really struggling financially like everyone else. He reckons the house is ready anytime I want to move in, but as much as I want it, I've got no bloody way of getting up there.'

'What's Greta think of it?' Barny quizzed.

'She knows about it, but she's never been there. When I first met her, I planned to take her up but then her mother got sick and she didn't want to leave her. That went on for a few years before she passed away. Every time after that when we would plan to go up, something would get in our way, work or family or some other thing and then she fell pregnant and had the boys and here I still am today.

'I don't talk about it much to her, although she does try to raise it when I'm down on things. It depresses me though; it just reminds me of another thing I've missed out on. She knows I call it Heaven. I was hoping to move up there when the kids got a bit older. Not that I ever told Greta that. She still doesn't know I own part of it. I was going to surprise her; I know she would love the lifestyle up there but that's before the world turned on its head, hey!' Danny lamented.

'I would love to see it one day,' Barny smiled.

'One day, Barny. One day I'll get there, and you'll be the first invited,' patted Danny.

After a good hour's walk, they finally arrived at the Depot hotel with a thirst that needed to be quenched and being a Saturday, the establishment was already well patronised.

'About bloody time,' Ricky tongued.

'Geez! It hasn't changed much, has it,' Barny said surprised.

'Nah, not much, it's kept up its appearance pretty good, hasn't it?' said Danny. 'Out of the five pubs here, it's the only one that's still got lots of money coming through the doors. They've got heaps of gambling tables all over the joint now.'

'I don't care about that, as long as the beer's cold,' Ricky nagged.

'Coldest in town,' Danny excitedly replied. 'See those solar panels on the roof?' He pointed. 'They've got a huge battery storage underneath from the power it gains. It keeps the refrigeration and beer lines nice and chilled. That's why it's my favourite drinking hole, lads.'

'Lot of places in the city and suburbs do the same thing, including private homes,' Barny added.

'Except the ones who didn't have a battery storage,' cackled Ricky.

'Yeah, a lot of people who had solar panels on their roofs got a rude surprise when they realised their power went straight into the grid, hey! Bet they're kicking themselves now for not putting in battery storage, instead of the panels sitting on their roofs just reflecting the sun back,' Danny mused.

'Just like you, hey Danny.'

'Yes Ricky, just like me.'

Chapter 2

'Guns and weapons on the table, boys,' the Depot Hotel doorman ordered.

'Didn't you see the sign?' Danny jovially asked his friends.

Barny and Ricky looked above them.

STRICTLY NO GUNS OR WEAPONS ALLOWED INSIDE PREMISES, the large sign read.

'Sorry Tony. They haven't been in Graceville for a while.'

'No worries, Danny, honest mistake,' replied Tony.

'This is Ricky and Barny, boys, meet Tony and Jacko. They're here to keep the peace inside,' said Danny.

The boys tentatively shook the hands of the nasty-looking tattooed fellows then watched their handguns be put under lock and key, surprised that the men knew that they were carrying.

'Found those batteries you were after, Tony?' Danny enquired.

'Nah mate. Still looking! There's bugger all around these days. Can't even find a car battery. There either all flat or people have sold them off. Even if I got my hands on one, I haven't got the fuel for my generator to charge them up anyway. So, sticking to wax for lighting at the moment,' laughed Tony.

'Join the club,' said Danny. 'Have a good day.'

'You too, Danny, catcha later.'

Danny never knew the doormen well, probably too much trouble if he did, he surmised, nevertheless, it didn't bother him either way. He gave them respect and courtesy and was given it back in return.

'How did they know we had our guns on us?' Ricky asked as the men walked to take their seat at the bar.

'Everyone carries in the Hexagon Valley these days, Ricky.'

'Since when?'

'About twelve months ago,' replied Danny. 'The police force up here mostly turn a blind eye if you are. They never made it official, but they reckon if they arrested everyone for carrying a gun or knife, there would be no man left on the street. The prisons wouldn't be able to hold them anyway. It takes about a year to get to court these days anyhow because they're so backlogged. That's right, isn't it, Barny?'

'Sure is!' he agreed.

'They respect the right to protect ourselves from all the drunk and desperate, you know how violent it can get now. It's funny though! Since they've stopped arresting people for it, there's hardly been a shooting,' Danny chuffed.

'They should bring in the same policy down in the city,' Ricky said.

'That's just it, Ricky. They probably don't even know what our Minister does or doesn't do up here,' Danny flustered.

'Where's your gun anyway?' Ricky asked surprised that he wasn't carrying. 'Don't you have it on ya?'

'My .22 rifle is at home. I don't trust myself with it. I'm liable to put a hole in someone the way I'm feeling nowadays,' he replied tersely. 'Maybe you if you piss me off this arvo…' He then jested.

'I'd be too quick for you anyway,' jibed Ricky.

Until recent times, Danny had had no interest in guns. He never owned one, he never pulled the trigger on one, other than the odd air rifle when he was growing up as a teenager but with guns a common accessory these days, his interest was increasing with every conversation he had about them. Although his sawn off .22 rifle was his favourite, unbeknown to Greta, he had plenty of other guns in perfect order hidden away from her and the children, guns he had easily accumulated over the past twelve months through the soaring black market trade or the man on the street corner. If you knew the right contacts, you were armed within 48 hours.

The men took their seat at the bar and for the next couple of hours reminisced about the times they spent together in their younger days as they downed their beers, only interrupted by Danny introducing some of the locals to his friends as they passed by, including old Alby with Danny's settlement when the conversation swung around to the present.

'Hey Danny! You probably don't want to hear it, but have you heard the rumours about the government re introducing fuels and electricity? We're hearing a lot of shit about it down in the city. They say we're not far away from getting things up and running again,' Ricky excitedly relayed.

'There's a lot of truth in what they're saying,' Barny supported.

'You sound like Greta. Don't believe it. You know my opinions on society's rulers. All they do is lie,' dismissed Danny.

'You've always had a bee in your bonnet when it comes to anything government or authority, haven't ya. It's not all doom and gloom, Danny,' Ricky retorted.

'With good reason, Ricky. We've always lived in the most over-governed, overtaxed country in the world. There were too many people ruling our lives before the energy crisis. Can't remember when I found a politician I liked or respected enough to give my vote to. And look what's happening today. I've now got more mistrust of those in charge than I ever have.'

'Yeah, you're right there,' Barny replied. 'The politicians a half decade ago are looking like angels compared to the ones that make the decisions today.'

'Cheers to that, my friend,' Danny said with vigour as they raised their glasses. 'Don't get me started on our beloved Minister Johnston up here,' he added with scorn.

'Yeah. What a prick he his. We've heard all sorts of shit about him,' Ricky cursed.

'As I said earlier, we probably don't know half of it either. He's as corrupt as they come, believe me,' added Danny. The conversation was continuing when the men's attention was suddenly taken away by a loud argument over by a table where one of many poker games took place. In the middle of the fracas was a man Danny disliked.

Billy Devlin had just turned twenty-one and had recently become a member of the Hexagon Valley police force. Twenty-one was the minimum age limit in the force and most young men who had no job or no hope, joined up for the money after former members quit on mass over numerous issues that government refused to address. Authorities didn't care who was hired as long as they put numbers back on the street and the force had grown tenfold because of the lax entry protocols.

The fortnightly pay was meagre, but it meant the new recruits could have a roof over their heads and a bit of security. Most of the young cops recently recruited had an attitude problem as they flaunted their newfound authority but none bigger than Constable Billy Devlin.

The second youngest of five brothers, he came from a family who loved nothing better than making other people's lives a misery and Danny had plenty of run ins with them recently. Danny was the type who never suffered fools, more so in today's unforgiving rule and the Devlin brothers annoyed him no end.

Danny looked closer at the disturbance and noticed that the young guy Billy Devlin had in his sights was the son of one of his elder friends. Jarryd was an eighteen-year-old who Danny thought to be a nice kid. He was an honest young man who mostly stayed out of trouble but as Danny surveyed the fracas, it looked as if Jarryd was in more trouble than he could handle as the Devlin's had a liking for finishing their arguments violently.

He abruptly left his stool at the bar and approached the duo.

'Everything okay here, Jarryd?' he asked.

'Piss off, Pruitt, mind your own business,' the off-duty constable snarled.

'Move away, Jarryd. Take a seat over there if you want,' Danny calmly advised the now timid teenager as he stood in between.

'Get out of the way, Pruitt.' Billy smarted as he tried to push through him.

Danny grabbed a fistful of Billy's shirt in return.

'You know you can't touch me now,' Billy mocked. 'Get your hands off me.'

Danny ignored Billy's taunts, he stood there defiantly with a broad smile, refusing to move and let Billy past. Ricky and Barny were out of their seats also and moved closer to give Danny a hand if needed. As the floor started to gather around, the young renegade constable quickly comprehended that he was in a no-win situation. Just about everyone nearby the commotion had begun throwing sneers and jeers Billy's way.

'Finish the little prick off, Danny.'

'Punch his lights out, Danny.'

'Leave some for me,' were some of the comments echoing across the bar room floor. Billy and his brothers were about as popular as a bull ant in a pair of underpants. Just as the patrons were getting louder in their enthusiasm to see young Billy Devlin take a hiding, a loud voice echoed across the hotel before Tony and Jacko could leave their posts at the entrance.

'Let it go, Danny,' it resonated.

Still with an iron clad lock on Billy's shirt, he turned around to face where the voice had come from.

'Just let him go, Danny,' he repeated, this time in a calmer manner.

Danny released his grip and pushed Billy away, adhering to the order.

The robust man giving the order was a person who Danny had a lot respect for. Sgt Dane Grainger had a strong presence about him whenever he walked or talked and was known around town as Sarge Dane but to Danny, he was just simply called Dane. Danny had met him when he first moved to Graceville and he became a close and central character amongst his circle of friends, but like everyone else, hardship fell upon him. He was another who joined the police force to keep his house and land he lived on with his elderly parents and younger cousins.

Dane had control over most of the young recruits in town and had the respect of the townsfolk through his decent demeanour and common sense, which in turn quickly put him in a role of responsibility in the police force around the Valley.

'Arrest him, Sarge,' Billy yelled at Dane. 'You saw him assault me.'

'Just get the hell out of here, and it's Sergeant Grainger to you, Constable Devlin,' Dane cursed with authority.

Billy was a loose cannon that Dane knew he and his colleagues could do without on the force. It was hard enough for policemen like himself to keep the peace and confidence of the community without the likes of the Devlin's stirring up trouble everywhere they went. Billy started to exit the hotel with his tail between his legs, he knew it best not to upset the Sergeant any further after he threatened to report him to his superiors. He also knew he didn't have the security of his elder brothers to help him out either. That didn't stop him from giving Danny a warning on his way out that his time was coming and threatened that he'd better watch himself. Danny responded with a sniggered laugh as young Billy was always full of threats that were very rarely followed through.

'All right everyone, back to what you were doing, the fun's over,' the Sergeant requested the patrons. 'What's going on, Danny?' Dane asked as he took him aside.

'Just protecting Jarryd, mate. You know what Billy's like.'

Dane accepted Danny's response and nodded his head in approval.

'I advise you to stay out of trouble in the future though, mate,' Dane said. 'You know, the Minister has already made it public that any violence or disrespect towards his officers would now mean jail time. He's apparently getting heat from above to start protecting his employees better. You know he doesn't give a shit about the hardship everyone's facing but I agree with him on this one. There's been to many bashings on his police lately so be careful please.' Dane finished with authority.

Danny resumed his seat at the bar taking in the advice that his good friend had passed on, quickly forgetting about the antics of Billy Devlin. Another hour had passed, and the boys had just finished dinner, quickly demolishing a large plate of hot fish and chips topped with gravy and the mood inside the noisy and busy pub was jovial. They were having a last round of drinks before heading home and as they were about to take their last sips; a young man came racing into the hotel.

'It's the re-po squad!' he shrieked towards the bar, panic-stricken. 'They're at Tom Potter's, they're trashing the joint,' he continued between distressed deep breaths.

Danny left his stool immediately. He knew the teenage neighbour of Tom's who was alarmed and frightened and without warning to his friends, was running towards the door in a flash.

'What the hell's going on, Danny?' called Ricky.

' Just follow me. I'll explain later,' he replied running.

'Wait up, will ya!' hollered Ricky, after he and Barny had to wait a moment to retrieve their revolvers.

'No time, fellas. Just keep moving!' Danny turned and yelled. The men raced up the road then crossed the railway line before the bridge that the Watkins River flowed under. A few hundred meters downstream was where Ricky and Barny had set up camp. They continued past the entrance to the Graceville Country Club until they veered right at a Y-intersection then turned left at the next road where Tom's house was situated atop of the crest. Ricky and Barny finally caught up to Danny whilst more men passed them, angry, yelling abuse at those who would listen as they descended upon Tom's house. Barny and Ricky impatiently asked again what was happening to get people in such an angry mood so quickly, with still no response from Danny.

After a 15-minute sprint, the trio arrived at Tom's place, still gasping for air. They panned around the area. Danny turned to see if he could find Tom between all the onlookers and horses that had arrived. A woman in hysterics, crying and yelling words that could hardly be understood, had grabbed the attention of those around. 'Check her out,' Barny worried. 'She doesn't look happy at all.'

'Oh shit, that's Linda, Tom's wife!' answered Danny.

'Do you know who this Tom is?' Barny asked Ricky as Danny took off.

'Nah.' He shrugged. 'I think he used to work with Danny or something,' Ricky guessed as Danny pushed his way through the masses in his search for Tom, looking hard from left to right as he avoided household belongings which had been strewn across the roads and front lawn of the house. After a few minutes, he noticed a single figure sitting up against a fence post outside of the property away from the commotion. It was Tom, hiding in the long evening shadows under a branch of an overhanging tree.

'Tom, Tom. It's me, Danny. Are you okay?' Tom kept his head bowed to the ground. He was emotionless and frozen.

'Tom, Tom, speak to me!' Danny pushed at his shoulder.

His friend looked up and shook his head in bewilderment; he was in another world, crushed, his eyes gazed into space, a look of a man whose soul had been destroyed, a man without an ounce of fight left in him.

Danny was fuming at what was happening, it was a sight he was sick and tired of. He looked around and saw Sgt Dane Grainger who had arrived on horseback following the commotion. Danny raced up to his friend and grabbed him by the arm and with an agitated voice hammered in concern.

'This is wrong, Dane, it's fuckin wrong.'

'There's nothing I can do, Danny, it's out of my hands, I hate it as much you do, mate,' he replied.

Danny gave Dane a stern look and asked him again if he could put a stop to it. His friend Tom needed help, but as much as Dane wanted to act, it wasn't in his jurisdiction to interfere with matters of this kind. The Sergeant painfully turned his head away, much to Danny's disgust, who then gave an undertone tirade of abuse towards all the police who had overseen the repossession.

With the help of empathetic bystanders, Danny did as much as he could to help Tom and his family. They assisted by getting their belongings together, loading them on to carts to be taken to a nearby friend's property who offered to take them in for the night. Tom was the last person Danny thought would in debt to the banks, he came across as a person that was secure and happy in his life, but as it was, more and more people were losing their land as the months went on. The ordinary person was getting sick and tired of what was occurring. Minor protests had gathered momentum outside the Ministers office over recent weeks, all to no avail as the Minister would never talk to anyone from the public. After all, he and his offsiders were making a nice little profit from the belongings of the families thrown out on the streets, taking a percentage of the proceeds after they were sold off.

There was nothing more the men could do for Tom. Frustrated and angry, Danny re-joined his buddies and decided to make their way to where Ricky and Barny were camping, an easy 30-minute walk away and with persistent grilling from his friends, Danny finally divulged what the boys had just witnessed.

'What you just saw, boys, was the aftermath of what we call the re-po squad,' Danny seethed. 'Their official name is the Repossession office. The banks employ them with the full blessing of the Minister's office to repossess land and property off people who have forfeited on their mortgages. Those bastard banks are merciless. Once anyone gets the slightest bit behind in repayments, they move in, and as you saw, once there, they show no fuckin respect. By law they have to give at least seven days' notice before they act, but not here, not in the Hexagon valley, not in Johnston's territory.'

'Who are the men they hire?'

'Faceless men, Barny, faceless men. When they strike, they shield their identities however they can, balaclavas, full face helmets, anything that hides their faces. No one really knows who is amongst them. Rumours are that they're led by specially selected police but the rest you don't know. They could be men from the other side of the valley, from the city or suburbs, or it could be your next-door neighbour,' shrugged Danny. 'Only the Minister's office truly knows who's on their payroll. They arrive at any time of day without warning. They grab furniture, chairs, tables, beds, anything that isn't bolted down and throw it out on the street along with its occupants. And all this done under the supervision and protection of the fuckin police,' Danny finished as he flicked another cigarette butt away.

'I wouldn't want to be in their shoes if anyone found out if you were one of them from what I heard at your friend's house,' said Ricky.

'A few have been found out, you can imagine what happened to them, scumbags!' Danny growled.

Barny and Ricky could feel Danny's anger, it was building inside of them as well after hearing what he had to say, and witnessing it first-hand themselves.

They arrived at their campsite along the banks of the Watkins River where passing travellers would pitch tents and set up camp for the night. Some folks were living in their tents on a permanent basis, evicted with nowhere else to go. As they neared their site, they were happy to see that they had company. Harry Mitchell was a nearby neighbour of Ricky's whose friendship had grown over the years and when he heard that Ricky and Barny were heading to Graceville to see Danny, Harry, having no job and now separated from his girlfriend decided to follow. He was a clean shaven, well-groomed dressed fellow who kept his thick brown hair neatly combed.

Danny reacquainted himself with him. It had been a few years since he had seen his likeable gentle souled friend but his time with him would be brief as it was time for him to make his way home to Greta before the dark set in.

'What about our horses?' Barny asked? 'They're still back at your house, Danny.'

'Don't worry, Greta would've taken care of them. You may as well stay here and come get them in the morning. What do ya reckon, around ten o'clock?' Danny suggested.

'Yeah, good idea. We'll see you then. Good luck,' they said, shaking hands with their goodbyes.

Still consumed with anger over what had happened to Tom, Danny's walking pace was solid as he made the trek back home. Through the main street he strode, looking at all the boarded-up shopfronts. At least 25% of the small business that traded had closed their doors permanently and the ones that remained trading mostly shut after daylight hours. He walked further into the main street past its major intersection to see the fighting drunks outside the corner pub. Others sat in the alleyways between shops, passing their beers and flagons around, abusing anyone who came near them.

A group of teenagers threw rocks at the disused traffic and light poles, bored and unhindered. He then made his way up through the slums once more, a sight that made him cringe inside every time he passed by. Danny could have easily bypassed the slums, it was a longer way home for him to traverse, walking straight up the highway would cut 30 minutes off his journey.

Curiously, something would draw Danny to the worst part of town almost every time he was near. Night was falling as the streetlamps began to flicker on to guide him along the way. The overhead pole lamps were staggered 200m apart on either side of the roads and were powered by an attached solar panel. A battery source was stored in a small metal strongbox at the base only accessible by shire employees who adjusted the timer settings for the appropriate season. As it was now summer, the streetlights would come on at 9.00pm and switch off at 6.00am.

As he trudged through the poverty-stricken area, domestic arguments were easily heard bellowing out from the run-down houses. The odd cry of an infant screaming for some food and the local hungry dog life, barking, yapping at anything that moved added to the miserable sounds. Nearly two hours had passed since he had left his mates camp site, the last kilometre of his journey would be walked in darkness as he made his way up the highway and finally to the front door of his house.

Greta had been arguing to herself, concerned about the time it was taking for her husband to arrive home. She had just put her sons to bed and sat under the candlelit lanterns that brightened her loungeroom when she heard a familiar shuffling of feet arrive at their doorstep. She rushed to meet Danny at the door.

'I heard what happened to Tom and Linda,' she relayed, concerned 'Are you alright?'

'Yeah, I'm bloody fantastic, everything's wonderful, Greta,' came the sarcastic retort.

He passed by her, cursing at the world then slumped into his chair.

Moments of silence passed before Greta sat on Danny's lap and faced him. She began to kiss him on his forehead as she gently stroked his hair through her fingers.

She knew there was no sense in trying to talk things through while her husband was in the mood he was; she would just gaze into his eyes. Greta didn't need to say anything; her touch and stare was enough. They never spoke a word as Danny stood up and led Greta to the bedroom. It was another long day for Danny, he was angered, he was frustrated, and he was tired. All he wanted to do now was to take his wife to bed, to hold her, to make love, to forget about what was happening in this screwed up world they now lived in.

Chapter 3

The day dawned as beautiful as ever in the valley as the sun rose over the eastern mountain peaks, a sprinkle of low-lying mist added to the ambience. Greta thought it a wonderful idea to have breakfast on the veranda as she could never get enough of the views their property offered. Their beloved home and land backed onto nearby parklands with the mountains close by as a beautiful back drop.

Inside were three modest bedrooms and a spacious loungeroom along with a playroom for their young sons. The rear of the house had a large decking that overlooked the spacious backyard below which kept their chickens and sheep behind fenced off sections. Further beyond was a small valley where the Watkins River meandered along behind the distant tree line, their view extending across the tree lined parklands then over the never-ending mountain ranges where Greta would often take long walks to keep herself fit and toned.

After some quality time joking and playing with his sons over breakfast, Danny thought it best that he split the remaining logs that lay in his yard. He liked to get the entire cutting out of the way as quickly as possible so when orders came, all was ready to go, he hated delaying his customers. Before he could start on the wood splitting though, he had to go his carport which had been converted into stables and harness up the single open horse drawn carriage for Greta and the kids. After the labour of love was done, he enjoyed his morning cigarette taking in the views and then began to get to work while Greta dressed the children for the ride down to the market.

The outdoor Graceville market was a hub of activity held every Tuesday, Thursday and Sunday where people would sell, buy and trade almost anything that was of use to anyone. It was where Greta would buy most of her fruit and vegetables if her own patch wasn't producing at the time, along with plants and flowers as Greta loved to spend time showing off her talents in the garden. She preferred the market rather than the sole supermarket still operating that was amongst the few buildings in Graceville that had access to the restricted electricity. If you weren't through their doors at the earliest, the shelves would often be bare, and the rationed stock of frozen foods would all be sold out she often complained.

As she sifted through her wardrobe for something to wear, she came across a dress that she hadn't worn for years. Danny had bought the dress six years previously for her 25th birthday and it was the one she wore out for special occasions. Sadly, it had been a long time since they've been able to go out on the town together due to the severe money restraints. Greta's smile stretched from ear to ear as the thought of wearing the dress again engulfed her. Without hesitation she slipped into it with the anticipation of Danny seeing her in it once more. The dress was gypsy like, made of crushed black velvet and laced up around the chest with a hint of cleavage; it fell just below her calves and the dress still hugged the beautiful contours of her body.

Greta proudly walked outside, passed her children who gave off a silent 'wow' then slowly made her way down to the yard where Danny was hard at it splitting firewood.

'I'm ready to leave, going to kiss me goodbye?' she said seductively, holding back her bursting smile.

Danny turned to see his wife standing there; the morning sun showing off her silken tanned skin that had darkened even further during the summer months. The grace and aura she exuded was beacon-like. He dropped his axe, proudly knowing how fortunate he was to have her. He slowly walked towards her, admiringly looking her up and down as he wiped his dirty hands down the front of his singlet.

'Nice look for the market,' he quipped.

'Yep.' Greta smiled agreeingly.

'You're still as stunning as the day I met you, did you know that?' Danny complimented as he backed off for a better look.

'I'm glad you still think that way,' Greta replied.

'You're still the most gorgeous woman I've ever met, you never cease to amaze me,' Danny remarked as he began to give her a passionate embrace.

He tilted his head to the side as the children hurried their mother to get into the carriage. With a twinkle in his eye, he whispered in her ear, 'You just get back here soon, and I will have great pleasure in exploring that dress a little further.'

Greta amorously smiled in return then was buzzing with excitement as she left, waving goodbye with her kids as they slowly made their way off. She was so pleased to see her husband at ease and with a genuine smile on his face after months of worrying about her man. She sympathised deeply about his feelings on matters, however, the continual effort to provide, support and remain patient with him was beginning to put a strain on her own mental health.

It was the best she had felt for some time as she blew kisses to her husband while the children enthusiastically waved goodbye to their father as they sauntered off to the market behind the old placid mare. Unbeknown to them both, the morning happiness and contentment Greta felt as she left Danny was about to be shattered to pieces.

As the large cypress pines cast the morning shadows of the sun over his side yard, Danny was about a half hour into his work, thinking of the way Greta had looked with a contented inner smile. He was forgetting about what had happened to Tom the night before, his spirits were good, throwing aside any self-pity when he was unexpectedly paid a visit by three of the Devlin brothers.

One of them was young Billy, with him was the second eldest Ross, Rosco to those who knew him. Both were on duty and in uniform. Dark blue T-shirts, black leather vests, black pants and holsters around their waist's carrying side arms and batons, while the youngest of the brothers, seventeen-year-old Mickey waited atop of Danny's property on horseback.

Danny looked up and saw the two approaching down his gravel driveway then dismount from their horses. He held his axe in both arms as he turned.

'What are you doing on my property?' he asked patiently.

'Come to give you a lesson in manners, Pruitt,' the eldest replied.

'Too late for that, Rosco,' Danny said as he leant his axe against the woodpile.

Rosco slowly walked closer towards where Danny was standing, advising that he shouldn't make fools out of his family as he did yesterday with Billy.

'He doesn't need me to make a fool of himself,' Danny smugly replied.

'Yeah well, you've done it for the last time Pruitt,' Rosco warned.

The brothers continued to antagonise him with a lot of tough talk. Danny did his best to brush it off; he thought if he just took some insults for a while, they would move on without anything escalating. He turned his back and grabbed his axe and resumed his wood splitting, ignoring the trash and goading coming from their mouths.

' I've seen the list, Pruitt,' Billy smarted.

'Oh yeah, what list might that be, Billy?' Danny replied with contempt.

'The re-po squad list, you're on it, mate. I snuck a gander at it while I was in the shire offices, your name was up there in bright lights,' Billy sniggered.

'Running out of money now, are we, Danny boy,' Rosco added.

Danny knew he had nothing to worry about, yesterday's order would put any doubts to rest. He laughed off the suggestion knowing that he was lying, although his temper was starting to rise as the barbs continued his way. He wanted them off their property. 'If you're not going to arrest me for anything, just fuck off. I've got work to do.'

'We're going to take great pleasure watching your belongings get thrown out on to the road. You'll probably end up living with some of your no hoper mates in the slums,' Rosco continued, ignoring Danny's animated pleas.

'You know what, Rosco,' Billy interrupted. 'I can't wait to wrap my arms around his pretty little wife and drag her up onto the road when they evict them, I can't guarantee my hands will be where they're supposed to be either,' Billy boasted with gestures to go along with his sniggering laugh.

Danny's rage at the men was overflowing. The insinuations about his wife was the last straw. Without a word, he lunged at young Billy. Rosco drew his revolver in retaliation before he could strike.

'Back off, Pruitt,' he yelled, 'or I'll shoot you right here and now.'

Danny halted immediately. 'Just get the hell off my property,' he demanded.

'Oh, we're not going yet, Danny boy,' Rosco assured. 'That's enough to have you arrested after what you just tried to do to Billy.'

As Rosco arrogantly cited the law, Billy noticed a lamb grazing close by in the fenced off yard below where they were. Danny and Greta had it since birth and it was their children's pride and joy; the kids had bottle-fed it when it was born and had raised it themselves ever since.

'Looks like we've found dinner for tonight, Rosco,' Billy commented, licking his lips while nodding his head over the post and wire fence where the lamb was grazing.

'You might be bloody well right, Billy,' chortled Rosco.

Rosco raised his revolver then aimed directly at the children's pet.

' Don't you dare!' Danny nervously warned.

Rosco was taking better aim, ignoring Danny's repeated requests to leave it alone. Every muscle and tendon in Danny's body began to tighten, he could see Rosco's finger squeezing at the trigger, he was about to shoot. Danny leapt forward and grabbed Rosco's shooting hand, trying to point it away from the target. BANG, the gun discharged, the sound echoing around the windless neighbourhood.

Both fell to the ground through the weight of the attempted saving tackle. Danny broke free and rolled over onto his knees and looked in the direction the lamb was. It couldn't be seen; Danny's lunge was to no avail. The bullet had hit its intended target; the family's pet lamb lay motionless on the ground. Danny stood and walked towards the fence line, seeing the neck of the now blood-soaked lamb.

What next, he thought. The chickens he had further down the yard? The other sheep he had? The cats? In the mood they were in, he thought they might open fire on all his animals.

Danny was about to explode. He quickly turned and charged at Rosco to relieve him of his gun. Both fell to the ground again in the wrestle. Another struggle ensued then a further shot was discharged from Rosco's gun. Suddenly, everything went deathly quiet and Danny could no longer feel any resistance. He pushed Rosco off him and thrust himself away.

The accidental bullet had entered the chest of Senior Constable Ross Devlin; he lay on the ground gasping for air, eyes wide open in shock, oozing blood starting to seep out of the entrance wound. Danny stood over him with the gun now in his hand with Rosco's blood stained on the front of his own singlet.

Billy looked at his brother in disbelief; he was standing no more than ten meters away from the two men. He jumped to Rosco's aid. It didn't take him long to comprehend that his brother was in big trouble. Still on his knees, he turned his attention to Danny and started to draw his revolver from his holster.

' You just shot my brother; you shot my brother!' the hysterical screaming began.

Billy was now at his unpredictable worst; he raised his arm in an action ready to shoot.

Danny's reaction was quick, he was sure he was about to be shot. He barely had time to aim the revolver that he had in his own hand and in a reactive instant fired two shots before Billy could shoot at him, one bullet striking Constable

Billy Devlin in the neck, the other into his chest. Billy slumped to the ground, killed instantly, blood beginning to gush out of the entry wounds with every dying heartbeat.

Danny lowered his arm and dropped the gun to his feet. He stood there silent, aghast at what damage the bullet had caused to the neck of Billy. He panned around at the bodies of the two men, trying to make sense of what had just happened. He saw that Rosco was still alive, gargling on his own blood as he tried in vain to breathe. Sounds of scraping hooves then grabbed his attention, he looked up and saw the youngest brother Mickey atop of the property.

'Get down here, I need your help!' Danny yelled.

Mickey panicked; he was in shock with what he had just witnessed, he thought that he was going to be Danny's next victim. In fright he turned his horse and rode off as fast as his animal could carry him.

'Where the hell are ya going, get down here and help your brothers!' Danny screamed. His demands were to no avail; within seconds, young Mickey had disappeared.

Danny raced inside his home to grab pressure bandages and water to see if he could keep Rosco alive. Several moments passed before Danny got back to help him. He pushed the bandages into the wound to try and stop the bleeding, within the minute, Snr Constable Ross Devlin had taken his last breath.

The idyllic morning that started for Danny had now turned into his worst possible nightmare. He had never shot anyone before. He had never even pointed a loaded gun at another human being, nor ever seen a dead body, but now, in his yard lay two dead bodies that came from his own hands.

Danny repeatedly cursed to himself, spitting and jumping around from the adrenalin surging through his body. He turned his anger at the brothers lying motionless in a pool of blood, swearing at them profusely. 'What have you done. What have you done!' he yelled. 'Why did you come here?'

What seemed an eternity was only minutes in real time. A million thoughts raced through his trembling body, but one thing was crystal clear, self-defence or accidental shooting was not going to hold up, not in this present climate. He knew it was going to be his word against young Mickey Delvin's, and he knew that the truth of the matter wouldn't be coming out of the youngest sibling.

He had no doubt in his panic-stricken mind that he would be arrested and slammed in jail no matter what he said. He was now in a petrified panic, looking from side to side trying to get his mind straight. The one thing he did know was that he could no longer stay where he was anymore. He knew the youngest Devlin was riding back into town to raise the alarm. No time to bury two bodies and clean up a blood-soaked yard and act as if nothing ever happened. Danny guessed he had about fifteen minutes to get out of there before his property would be swarming with the law.

With irrational thoughts stampeding through his mind, he dashed inside his house and grabbed his camping gear and old sports bag. He raced from room to room filling the bag with anything he thought that would allow him to live off the grid for a short period. He donned his favourite green khaki jacket off the loungeroom chair, deep zipped pockets inside and out. In a state of confusion, he hurried back through the yard on his way to his shed to pack some essential items. He stopped to have one last look at the dead bodies lying in their respective pools of blood, cursedly trying to fathom what had just happened.

He made his way to the converted stables and saddled his horse after grabbing his guns out of his secret hiding place in the tool shed, he fumbled with the key that opened the steel cabinet behind his shadow board. He had his trusty old sawn off .22 rifle, the one he had to cut to fit in his pigskin sling. He grabbed his small array of handguns and put boxes of spare ammunition in a leather bag which was hanging over his horse.

Danny had no idea where he needed to go. His first thought was to head for the mountains, but the overwhelming urge to see Greta engulfed him. He had to tell her what had happened before the predicted untruths would surface. As he was about to ride off, he looked at his watch and saw it was still an hour before Ricky and Barny were to pick up their horses. He quickly dismounted, saddled both his friend's horses and took off leading them by the reins. He had to try and get the horses back to them. The police would probably seize everything on his property and the boys would be stranded without transport, that was how it worked, and Danny knew there would be no exception in this case.

He rode hastily down through the parklands adjacent to his property until he arrived at the little creek at the base of the valley leading the other horses with him. There was a track he often used for short cuts. It would snake along the side of the creek until it flowed into the Watkins River, from there, the river would continue through the back edge of town then right past where his mates were camping.

It was a difficult ride for Danny, he didn't have much experience leading other horses, especially riding at the pace he was and at times he would have to stop, dismount, and adjust the tangling reins which were leaving burn marks around right left hand. He took this route reasoning that young Mickey Devlin would lead the police back to his property using the main highway being the quickest way of getting there from town. Just as Danny was riding hard to get to Ricky and Barny, Mickey Devlin had already arrived at the police station in town.

'My brothers are dead, Pruitt shot 'em,' he rambled as he stumbled into the foyer of the police station.

Sergeant Dane Grainger was behind his desk when Mickey arrived.

'Calm down,' he yelled. 'I can't understand what you're saying, slow down'

'It's Danny Pruitt, he shot my brothers in cold blood, they're both dead,' Mickey said, shaking and stuttering.

'What the hell are you talking about? Where?'

'At Pruitt's house, you've got to go after him, he shot them for no reason, he's gone mad, he just walked up and shot 'em,' Young Mickey continued in a frightened frenzy.

Dane didn't believe what young Mickey was telling him. He knew Danny had a short fuse if pushed too far and sometimes talked big on occasions, however, he also knew that Danny would never kill anybody in cold blood, even if it were the Devlin brothers he loathed so much. The Sergeant, now unsure of what he was hearing, decided that the only way he could make sense of it all was to ride up to Danny's house himself. He assembled two of his constables, informed his superior by radio of what was transpiring who instantly sent officers out to search for Danny, and with Mickey, hurriedly made his way to the scene.

Ricky, Barny and Harry had already left their campsite on their way to Danny's, oblivious to what had happened. After riding desperately for 15 minutes, Danny spotted his friends from a distance walking through a paddock. Harry was leading his own horse behind them. Danny had to get to them quickly before they would disappear on him. He turned the horses at right angles and began to approach them. Riding through thick pockets of Tea Tree and wattles that sporadically grew near the banks of the river, then across the open paddock, he neared his friends.

'That's Danny, isn't it?' said Barny surprised. 'What's he doing here?'

'Don't know, but it looks like he's in a hurry, he's got our horses with him too,' Ricky replied.

'Saving us the walk, are ya, mate?' Barny yelled as Danny came within hearing distance.

There was no reply from him as he made his way to their side, handing the reins of the horses over to them. The men immediately could see there was something wrong as they investigated his worried and frightened face. It was a face that none of them had ever seen before.

'What's up, Danny? You look like you've seen a ghost or something,' Ricky said as Danny remained in the saddle.

Danny gasped deep breaths, trying to get some air back into his lungs. 'Here's ya horses, I've got to go and see Greta.'

'What's going on? Are you alright?' Barny asked again, concerned for Danny's wellbeing.

'Oh mate, everything's gone crazy.' He slumped his shoulders. 'I've just shot two cops.'

'What do you mean, you shot two cops! Are they alright?' a confused Ricky asked.

'They're both dead, Rick, they're lying in my yard dead,' Danny chastised shaking his head, still trying to come to terms with what had happened.

'What the hell happened?'

'It was an accident, self-defence, they pushed me too far, they kept at me and at me. They shot the kids' lamb; everything just went crazy from there.'

Danny had no time to hang around explaining everything in detail. He was still in a massive confused state of mind and told them that he would fill them in later. All he wanted now was to try and find Greta over at the market.

'Wait up, we're coming with you,' Ricky said, climbing onto his horse.

'No you're not, this has got nothing to do with you guys, stay out of it,' Danny replied pointing his finger at them.

'Bullshit Danny, we're coming with you,' Ricky demanded.

'You need our help, Danny,' Barny interrupted. 'Besides, there's nothing else to do around here,' he added whilst raising his eyebrows and tilting his neck to one side as if to say you've got no say in it anyway.

'Please yourself, I haven't got time to argue, but if anything goes down, you guys piss off out of here, you got that,' Danny ordered.

The four men took off towards the market at full steam, crossing the paddock then roads and grassy parklands, a five-minute ride at best with Danny leading them in search of Greta and his children. Frightened and anxious, they arrived at the market in search of Greta. They slowly rode around the outskirts trying to spot her through the moving bustling crowd.

Painstaking minutes passed before they saw her and the children on the other side of the large run-down bitumen carpark where the market was being held. She had already loaded the children onto the horse-drawn carriage and was about to make her way home when she was approached by two police officers. Danny looked on helplessly through the silver birch trees lining the outskirts of the market.

'Bloody hell!' he cursed. 'They know what's happened already.'

'Do you know any of the coppers with her?' asked Ricky.

'The taller one. I think he goes to the same church as Greta. He patrols the market.'

'What do we do now?'

'Don't know, let's just sit tight and see what happens with them,' Danny replied quietly.

The men watched on waiting for the police to move on, but as the minutes passed, it was becoming obvious they weren't going to leave her at all.

'Why all the questions?' Greta was asking in curiosity. 'What's happening with my husband? The last I saw of him he was back at home chopping firewood,' she said when asked of his whereabouts.

The officers wouldn't divulge anything other than the Inspector would like to talk to her at the station. As Greta and the children departed with the officers, Danny was at his wits end, becoming angrier by the second.

'Where in the hell are they taking her?' he gritted out.

'Let's follow them,' Ricky suggested. 'We can cut back up around the market here and up to the main street if we hurry,' he added pointing his finger in the direction he was indicating.

Danny agreed. The men then turned their horses around and steadily made their way around the marketplace to see if they could get to Greta, carefully avoiding the large gathering of pedestrians in the process. By the time they could see her again through the busy main street, Danny knew exactly where the police officers were taking her. He was beside himself, he pulled out his small binoculars from his sports bag and was able to see the frightened and worried look upon Greta's face as the officers led her towards the police station.

'I've got to get to her,' Danny said, loosening the reins on his horse.

Ricky grabbed on to his arm and held him back. 'No way, Danny, you'll be committing suicide if you do. I wouldn't be sacrificing your freedom just yet.

We'll try and talk to her later and arrange something, just let it be for now mate, just let it be,' Ricky pleaded.

Danny knew Ricky was right, it would be too risky for him to show his face anywhere. All he could do was sit back with a truckload of anxiety and watch his wife and children disappear into the distance with the police officers. He wanted to protect her, protect his sons, his mind was full of mixed feelings and irrational thoughts. Be a man, stand up, don't leave your wife alone his conscious berated. He so much wanted to go to her, but something held him back, selfishness? Self-preservation? Whatever it was, he felt a tsunami of emotions, none of which gave clarity on what he should do.

Barny, ever the pragmatist, knew it was becoming risky for him and the lads as well if they stayed anywhere near town.

'I think we should get out of here and head back to the river until we can figure out what you should do next, Danny,' he proposed.

The boys didn't need any convincing and without a word turned their horses and followed Barny's lead and nervously headed back to their campsite.

Chapter 4

'Why Danny, why would he do this? It was the first thought that went through Sgt Dane Grainger's mind when he arrived at Danny's house. He was plainly in shock of what he saw there. He couldn't believe that his friend was responsible for what lay in front of him. Straight away he canvassed the area. It didn't take long for him to discover the dead lamb; he knew it was the children's pride and joy and something was very wrong with the story that young Mickey Devlin was telling.

He radioed the Inspector once more confirming the deaths and requested he call the Crime Scene Department (CSD) to get to the truth of what really happened. The C.S.D was still operating with whatever technology left at their disposal which was a far cry from what they had previously. With a lack of instant information computers at their whim, and with every police department in the state queuing up to make use of the ones available, it made for slow progress in crime fighting.

Most times those in charge with investigating violent crimes had to rely on physical and hard evidence and their own experience. Without the ready availability of a well-resourced forensic department it was often difficult to achieve a speedy resolution and determine exactly what took place. The closest C.S.D was in the eastern suburbs of the city, at least half a day travel by train.

Dane's immediate supervisor was Inspector Noel Vaccaro, a career policeman who had served nearly forty years in the force. He was a tall, rangy balding man who wore a dark well-groomed beard and moustache who made his way up to the rank of Inspector through sheer hard work. He had seen the good times and the bad. It also helped knowing the right people in the right places. One of those people was Minister Colin Johnston, whose political pull kept Inspector Vaccaro in a job after the police force was privatised and Johnston was all too aware of Vaccaro's gratitude and used it to his benefit on more than one occasion, much to the disdain of the Inspector.

Immediately after hearing from the Sergeant what lay at the Pruitt's property, Inspector Vaccaro quickly traipsed his way to the Minister's office. The Minister's two-storey office building was situated on the high side of the main street of Graceville, opposite the shire office building and post office. It was where Johnston could oversee the comings and goings of *his* town by looking out of his plush top storey private office.

Upon arrival, Vaccaro made his way up the red-carpeted stairs that led to the Johnston's office and with a knock on the door, he opened it and entered once he was bade to do so.

'Sorry to interrupt, Minister: I have some news I think you don't want to hear.'

Pushing his paperwork aside, the Minister looked up.

'You've got a worried look on your face, Noel, sit down and tell me all about it.'

Vaccaro took his place in the seat opposite and with trepidation continued, 'We have two officers shot dead, Sir.'

'Which officers?'

'Senior Constable Rosco Devlin and his brother Billy.'

'Fuckin Devlins. Nothing but trouble those fuckin idiots,' Johnston sneered. 'What happened?' he asked.

'At this stage we can't tell how or why, but we do know who it was that pulled the trigger. A man named Danny Pruitt.'

'Well, if you know who it is, I expect you have him in custody? The Minister confidently predicted.

'Afraid not Sir, he can't be found at this stage. His wife is on her way to the station as we speak, I'm ready to interview her on his whereabouts but at this stage I've been told she's been down the market all morning, but I imagine he won't get far. If we don't apprehend him ourselves, he'll probably turn himself in in the next 48 hours like they always do,' the Inspector confidently replied.

'Who's this Danny Pruitt? Do you know of him?' The Minister's close-set blue eyes squinted as he delved. 'I want to know about the man who has just disobeyed my new order.'

'Nothing much to tell Sir. I don't know who he is myself. He's never been in trouble with law before, that's for sure. From what I've quickly gathered, he pretty much keeps to himself.'

'I want you call on all your officers and start hunting for this Danny Pruitt immediately,' the Minister angrily demanded.

To Johnston, this was the last straw.

'I'm going to make an example of this man. Do you hear me, Noel? Now fuckin' find him. The next time I hear from you, I expect you to have him custody.' The Minister resumed his seat in deep thought. 'Noel,' he called before the Inspector could leave his office, 'I need you to keep this situation amongst us for the time being. Nothing to be said to anyone,' he ordered in quieter tones.

Johnston didn't want the police chief or the head of crime scene in Marlboro to know what was going down in his region. Pressure was mounting on the Minister regarding shootings involving his police officers amongst other things and needed to make sure everything was looking and smelling like roses without giving anyone inside the Government reason to question his stability in the region. His ambition was to someday lead the party in his own right, and he needed a clean slate to achieve it.

He was aware his officers regularly went outside the boundaries of proper policing, although politically he could not be seen to encourage the practice, neither did he discourage it. The last thing he needed was to be quizzed over his law and order tactics. Johnston may have been small in stature, but he held a lot of sway in the halls of power. His political ambitions were no secret and would cross the boundaries to achieve them since he had been allocated the newly formed Shire of the Hexagon Valley.

He was one of the main figures behind privatising the police force when the government in their wisdom thought it a good policy. They had enough problems to handle and one less responsibility the better. The government still had the powers to intervene on serious matters, however, the everyday running of the force was left to others. Johnston was a high sitting member on the board of the new privatised force, but as it is with privatisation, profit became the goal rather than services to the public and corruption was rife within its ranks, with the Minister at the top of the tree.

Greta had been seated at the police station for over 30 minutes, her sons sat next to her, worried and not understanding what was going on, the same as their concerned mother when Inspector Vaccaro arrived and introduced himself.

'Do you know your husband's whereabouts, Mrs Pruitt?' he politely asked.

Greta's answer was short and aggressive. 'As I told the other officers, the last I saw him was at home. Why? What's going on. No one is telling me anything. Why are you looking for him?'

The Inspector ignored her requests. He continued to question as diligently as he could. 'Do you know any place he could be?'

'He has friends camping down the river. They've been in town visiting him. He may have gone to return their horses. I don't know! It's the only thing I can think off. Is he alright?' Greta asked.

'We need to talk him over an incident we've been made aware of,' the Inspector said, trying not to alarm her.

Greta's mind was racing. Did something happen down the pub last night that he didn't tell me about? Did something happen at Tom's? Did he see something on his way home? 'Do you know which part of the river?' the Inspector continued.

'I think they said between the Depot hotel and the Country Club. Down behind the racetrack.' She inadvertently divulged.

The Inspector left Greta's side and discreetly dispatched three of his officers to the campsite on the chance that Danny might be there.

Sgt Dane Grainger arrived back at the police station and immediately sought out Greta who stood to confront him.

'What's going on, Dane?' she asked confused. 'What is this all about? They're not telling me anything. What's Danny done, why are they looking for him?' she continued as she comforted her worried children by her side.

Sgt Dane asked Greta to sit back down. Her sons were led away by the female officer desk clerk and, with the permission of the Inspector, began to inform Greta of the morning tragedy.

'Two policemen are dead, Greta,' he said calmly. 'Their bodies lay in your yard; we believe Danny shot them.'

Greta's body started to shake; she couldn't believe what she had just heard. Dane continued to tell her what he knew of the events so far.

'This has to be a mistake, Dane,' Greta said. 'I know he's been under a lot of stress lately but shooting two police officers, I don't think so. He was fine this morning, I was with him no more than two hours ago, this has to be wrong, Danny would never do such a thing.'

'I promise I'll get to the bottom of this, Greta. In the meantime, I don't think you should go home. There will be police everywhere and I don't want you to see what's there. I don't think they will allow you in anyway. Do you have anywhere go? Anyone that will take you in for the time being?' he asked, concerned.

'Uhmm, yeah, of course. I'll go to Sarah and Corey's,' Greta replied with numbness.

'Good choice. I'll inform you as soon as I know of Danny's whereabouts or any other news regarding him,' Dane promised.

Confused and greatly worried, Greta took her sons and made her out way of the station then around to her and Danny's close friends. Corey and Sarah Porter had two children around the same age and regularly visited one another's house. The two families had a great deal in common and would share all their highs and lows together. Greta saw it as the perfect sanctuary for her and the children until she could get a clearer picture of what was happening with her husband, still in denial of what Dane had said.

The first of the three officers Inspector Vaccaro sent to the river in search of Danny was 28-year-old Senior Constable Steve Sandilands. He was a long-haired, pony-tailed bearded man, who was learning the trade under Vaccaro. The Inspector took Sandilands under his wing three years earlier as a favour to his widowed dying sister. She had asked her brother to look over her son and try and lead him in the right direction in life.

Sandilands' partners were two newly appointed constables by the names of Bourke and Dawson and the men were now at the campsite. Ricky, Barny and Harry were packing their belongings as they spoke about what their next step should be, whether Danny should give himself up and let the law take its course; after all, it *was* self-defence they were convincing themselves. But any thought of spending a single night in jail was not an option for Danny, just the thought of it would almost make him physically ill and told his buddies of his fears in no uncertain terms. He would work things out his way, with or without their help.

The trio took heed of what Danny had to say, they wanted no argument in the fearful mood he was in. Ricky and Barny went to collect their fishing lines they had cast downstream earlier in the morning as Harry and Danny remained at the river's edge. They were sitting down below the embankment which dropped about six feet from the river flats as the stream was running low at this time of year. It enabled campers to get by the river's edge while enjoying the sandy banks that emerged over summer. A few minutes of silence passed between them before Danny began to offer his apologies.

'Sorry I've dragged you into a mess, Harry,' he said with sincerity.

'Ah, shit happens, mate,' Harry responded with a smile as he put his hand on his shoulder.

'If I were you, I would just get the hell out of Graceville now. I mean it, you hang around me from now on, it will only mean trouble for you,' cautioned Danny.

'Can you tell me what happened?' Harry sheepishly asked.

Harry was an inquisitive man and once Danny started to confide in him, the questions came at a fast rate—who he shot, did he know them, how he shot them—he wanted to know all of the events that had occurred.

As the two spoke, Sandilands and the two constables were closing in on the boys' now packed up campsite. Officer Sandilands was no stranger when it came to confronting alleged criminals. In his short time as a policeman, he had already received a commendation for detaining and arresting two armed robbers on the other side of valley in which he wounded one seriously. He was a confident and arrogant man who often went outside the law by taking advantage when the re-po squad struck, grabbing quick ownership of belongings or forcing sex on any vulnerable woman whose place was being victimised, a heinous crime which was now becoming all too common among the young police officers with no fear of repercussions. He knew Danny well enough to say hello when their paths had crossed, but that was where it stopped.

'I think that's them, where those horses are,' Sandilands quietly said as his heartbeat began to increase.

Horses were grazing just above the embankment on the river flats tethered to a low branch from a nearby willow tree. He was sure they belonged Pruitt and his friends. Constable Dawson suggested they radio back to the station as requested by the Inspector if they spotted them.

'No, I'll handle this one myself,' insisted Sandilands. He drew his revolver and quietly rode to the edge of the embankment with the two constables following. Danny and Harry were losing themselves in conversation when the chat was suddenly broken by the sound of a cocking barrel. Looking hurriedly up to the edge of the embankment, they saw the three officers on horseback staring down on them with guns aimed.

'Danny Pruitt, you are under arrest for the murders of Snr Constable Ross Devlin and Constable Billy Devlin,' Sandilands said confidently as his eyes fixed on the wanted man. 'Now stand up slowly and move backwards towards the river.'

Danny and Harry slowly rose to their feet as Sandilands ordered Constable Bourke down off his horse. 'Check for weapons,' he said with purpose.

Sandilands was smiling inside. He could see another commendation coming his way.

'Didn't get far, Pruitt, did we now! You're going away for a long time, mate, hell, you might even get the death penalty; they're talking about legislating again. I hear they might be bringing back the rope,' Sandilands smugly conveyed, all the time never dropping his aim.

As the constable was about to pat down Danny looking for weapons, unbeknown to the Senior Constable, he was about to get a surprise of his own.

A loud voice bellowed out from behind the officers.

'Drop your weapons, drop 'em now.'

Sandilands instantly grasped the demand was directed solely at him and his partners.

'We are police officers in the middle of an arrest, so I advise you not to interfere,' he retorted.

'I mean it. Drop your fuckin guns now,' the voice reiterated louder.

Danny and Harry couldn't see what was going on behind Sandilands. The embankment was too high for them to see over, but one thing they did know for sure was that the voice they were hearing was Ricky's. Danny turned his head to the side when he heard another voice directed at the Constable beside him and Harry.

'That means you too, mate,' said Barny.

He had emerged from behind an old fallen tree that laid halfway across the river, pointing his revolver at the now frightened Constable. Terrified and shaking, Ricky and Barny had to make a stand. They couldn't sit by and watch Danny and Harry get taken away without intervening in some way, and the way they chose would now involve all of them.

Sandilands had no choice but to surrender his arms, he now knew the voice he was hearing was deadly serious and didn't want to risk a shootout. He held out his revolver in his right hand and dropped it to the ground, at the same time telling his partners to do the same.

Danny's heart was pounding like a jackhammer. He thought his life and freedom was about to be taken away. His emotions were to do another abrupt turnaround, quickly changing from anxiety and terror to one of resentment and anger. He and his pals now had control of what was a life-threatening situation for all concerned and with adrenalin pumping through his veins at an insurmountable speed, he raced up the embankment and forcefully pulled Sandilands from his horse, punching him to the side of the head as he fell to ground.

'Who the fuck do you think are?' he roared. 'You think you can waltz in here and take my life away?' Danny drew his gun from inside the front of his jeans and shoved it in the face of a petrified Sandilands. 'I'm sick of you bastards thinking you can stand over everyone, well not me, you've pushed the wrong man too far this time,' he continued to shout.

Danny was beyond fury; it was looking like he was about to lose control. Barny was nearest to him.

'Stop it, Danny,' he yelled. 'Let him go,' he appealed in a softer tone. 'He can't do nothing now, you've already got two hanging over your head, don't make it a third,' Barny pleaded, knowing now that all of them were now in it up to their ears as much as Danny was. 'Let's just get the hell out of here, Danny,' he instructed.

The tension was electric as unpredictable, no one knew what Danny was about to do. Sandilands was adamant he was going to die, one of the young constables urinated in his pants in fear. Danny's mates had never seen him lose control in anger like this before, his eyes were rolling around in the back of his head, it was a situation that could explode any second.

Danny paused for a moment, a sign that relieved the tension slightly to everyone concerned. He looked into the eyes of a panic-stricken Sandilands and unleashed his grip on him and stood him up, as a nervous Harry passed by collecting the officer's weapons laying on the ground.

Danny grabbed the two-way radio that Sandilands had strapped to his side.

'I'm taking this with me,' he said, pointing it in Sandilands' face. 'The only person I want to hear trying to contact me through this is Sgt Dane Grainger, you got that. Do you understand?' he firmly said to the now timid officer.

Sandilands nodded his head in agreement. 'Okay, okay. I'll make sure that happens,' he replied.

Danny thought the only person that he could trust on the force would be Dane. If he contacted him, he would be able tell the truth on what had happened and maybe he could arrange something that would see him get a fair hearing without any rogue police gunning him down on the spot.

The other men were getting nervous; they thought they had been around in the one spot long enough.

'C'mon Danny, let's go, if these three came here, there's sure to be another group coming,' Barny said while scouring a nervous eye over the river flats.

The four men gathered whatever belongings they had left on the ground. Crossing the river at its lowest point they began to ride off at breakneck speed, leaving the three officers tied up against the old willow tree, knowing that they would be seen soon enough for someone to free them.

The men were no more than ten minutes upstream and still hadn't decided where they were heading when Barny's fear was realised. Two police officers were making their way on a path downstream on the town side of the river. On seeing the men riding at full speed towards them, the officers ordered them to stop, not yet knowing the man they had been instructed to arrest was amongst them. By now most police officers in Graceville had been radioed on the situation and were involved in the manhunt.

Drawing their revolvers, the policemen bellowed at the men to pull their horses up and dismount. Danny had no intention of adhering to the officers' demands. He knew the reputations of some of the officers in the valley, and other than ones he knew, had no trust in them whatsoever. He certainly didn't recognise these officers that he was now encountering. Afraid he was about to take a bullet, he suddenly turned his horse sideways left and charged up a slight hill with his three buddies following hastily. The hill was densely populated with razor sharp saw grass at their feet and dotted with thick tea tree, at least ten-foot-tall in parts which in turn stood below the young eucalypt gums which gave the fleeing men camouflage as they tried to escape from the now agitated officers.

'Stop or I'll shoot,' one of the officers commanded loudly from afar, feeling that the man they were looking for was within the group of riders. To the officers, he was a cop killer and nothing else and had to be stopped along with anyone else who rode with him.

Danny and the boys took no notice of the demands and continued to ride hard up the hill, dodging and ducking at low branches as the officers crossed a shallow part of the river in pursuit. The boys were riding low in the saddle when they heard the first gunshot go off. The wayward bullet narrowly missed Harry, who was the slowest getting up the hill. Another shot went off directed at them, tearing the bark off a tree close by. Harry was terrified, never in his wildest dreams had anything like this happened to him.

'They're shooting at us!' he screamed.

'Keep riding,' Danny roared back.

Ricky was third in line of the four riders. He looked back at Harry and saw he was in grave danger. He stopped his horse, turned around and remaining in the saddle, took aim with his revolver at the officer coming up the hill as a terrified Harry rode past. It was pure instinct for Ricky; he feared for his own life and that of his buddy. He had read and heard about the police shootings over the past twelve months, particularly in the Hexagon Valley, and Ricky didn't want to become another victim. In an unforgiving moment, he opened fire at the oncoming officer coming up the steep slope who was now discharging bullets at will. BANG, BANG, BANG, BANG, BANG. Ricky emptied all the rounds out of his revolver in a procession of bullets, striking the pursuing policeman down off his horse.

In an instant, the officer lay dazed and moaning on the ground having taken several shots to the body. Ricky stared down the hill through the thick Tea Tree at the wounded officer; he was almost in a state of suspended animation, shocked at what he had done, only to be awoken by the shouting of his stunned colleagues to hurry up and keep riding.

The second officer arrived minutes later to see his partner on the ground. He looked up, only to see the four men were already out of sight. They were across the top of the hill heading through a clearing to another ridge in which they would climb before riding across several roads and properties then into the foothills of mountain ranges.

The second officer saw that his colleague was wounded and in need of medical care in a hurry and with a panic-stricken voice, immediately radioed the station of their location and of the terrifying incident that had just taken place, naming Danny Pruitt as the shooter. The officer never saw who was responsible for the gun burst, he couldn't even identify the riders, he was a long way behind his partner and couldn't get a proper look, the thick tea tree and shrubs blocked whatever view he had and in his panic and haste reporting back to the station, he simply, and wrongly assumed it was Danny who fired upon his partner.

The police station was abuzz with talk and trepidation on hearing not only the news of the shooting but the embarrassing fortunes of Sandilands and his two constables being tied up to a tree. They were freed by a passer-by not long after Danny and the boys had left them. Inspector Vaccaro was in his office with Sgt Dane and was livid on hearing about Sandilands and the wounded officer.

Dane was suggesting to the Inspector that when the Crime Scene Department arrived, they would get to the truth of what happened at Danny's house on the premise that they were already on their way.

'They will be no CSD coming,' Vaccaro stated.

'What! What do you mean?' Dane asked, astonished.

'No one else is to know what is happening. It's a ministerial decision. It stays within these walls,' the Inspector informed him.

Dane couldn't believe what he was hearing. 'Why?' he argued strongly.

'Enough questions, Sergeant,' Vaccaro furiously said. 'You just obey orders. Now get on with your fucking job.'

Dane was bewildered and angry at the Inspector's stance; he determined that the Minister and Vaccaro must have some sort of hidden agenda but was unable to establish what agenda it could be. The Sergeant was overwhelmed with frustration; he wanted to know the truth, but without the help of his superiors, had little chance if any, of finding it.

For the time being, all he could do was to take his orders and trust that Danny and his mates would come to their senses and give themselves up, and soon. Dane was now hoping beyond hope for a quick resolution to the matter. But he knew Danny well, and deep down inside he also knew that the storm that had been brewing inside his friend's body for some time had already been unleashed, and it would take nothing short of a miracle to calm it.

Chapter 5

More than six hours had passed since the confrontation between Danny and the Devlin brothers and by now most of the townsfolk had heard that two of the Devlin's had been killed. Although the rumour mill was running rife regarding the details leading to their deaths, most of the sentiment around town was that they got was coming to them.

Only a handful of police knew exactly what had happened, but the public knew something big was going down, for they had never seen such large mounted police presence assembled so quickly in Graceville before. Those who knew had been instructed not to say anything to anyone about the dead officers or the shooting down by the river. But to keep things hush hush in this police force was asking way too much. Nonetheless, Minister Johnston was adamant that he wanted it kept quiet at all costs, he believed that Danny and his gang would be found soon enough, and all would be told publicly in his words, and in his words only.

It was late afternoon when after a gruelling ride up through the foothills and into the base of the mountain ranges the four men decided it was safe enough to stop and have a breather. Hardly a word was spoken between the men since Ricky opened fired on the officer. While Barny handed his canteen of water around to his buddies, Harry finally broke the silence by asking where they were heading.

'Up there,' Danny responded, pointing his finger to the top of the mountain. 'That's Mt St Lucia. It's the highest peak this side of Graceville. We need to get to it. It's got great views over the valley and the mountain ranges. There's a large communications tower with all sorts of dishes and satellites discs attached to it. It doubles as a fire watch tower in the summer. We'll join up to a track about a mile and a half from here which will take us up to an old logger's hut just below the tower, it's about an hour and a half away if we keep riding hard,' Danny estimated while slurping down a much-needed drink.

'Do you reckon it's safe?' Harry asked inquisitively,

'Don't worry, we'll be safe there, for a little while anyway,' Danny reassured. 'By the way, boys, I never thanked you for saving my hide down at the campsite,' he gratefully said as he lit up a cigarette.

He knew the men had just thrown away any chance they had of living a normal life from that point on and would be forever in their debt.

'Don't worry about it, Danny,' Barny said. 'I've got a feeling you're going to get a chance to pay us as back somehow.'

Danny raised his eyebrows as he took another puff on his cigarette. 'Yeah, you might be right,' he replied.

The men continued their ride up to the hut. They trekked single file along the winding paths and tracks through overgrown branches, tree ferns and vines that overhung the trails. Looking over his shoulder, Danny could see that Ricky's mind was troubled; he hadn't spoken a word for some time.

'What's wrong, Ricky, you think you're the only bloke that's shot someone today?' Danny heckled, trying to get some sort of reaction from him to break the silence.

Ricky snarled his lip at him, not impressed with what was said.

'C'mon Rick, what's done is done, it couldn't be helped, you saved Harry's life, for Christ's sake. The bloke's not dead, don't be so hard on yourself, lighten up.'

Ricky stopped his horse. He had had enough of Danny's remarks. With explosive aggression, he yelled, 'Two coppers are dead, another wounded, we've threatened another three at gunpoint. We've probably got every copper in the entire valley after us, not to mention the big boys in the city when they hear of all this shit. We've got nowhere to go, and you tell me to lighten up! Well, you can go to hell, Danny. You've stuffed our lives up forever!' he lambasted. 'There's no way out of this, you moron, we're totally fucked, we're as good as dead.'

Danny was taking in the tirade. His mate was letting out all his anger, however, he was getting impatient with the continued abuse and threw back a few retorts of his own. He too was feeling all that Ricky's gut was letting out.

Barny had enough of the slugging match and shouted at the two to shut up and settle down.

'We've got enough to worry about without you two ripping at each other's throats,' he complained loudly.

Danny and Ricky stopped the abuse at each other and looked at a pleading Barny.

'Danny's right, Rick,' Barny continued in a calmer tone now that the shouting had ceased. He rushed his hand through his whispery thin blond hair and over his matching moustache. 'What's done is done, we've got to stick together, now more than ever, otherwise we won't see the night out.'

'I'm sorry, Ricky. This is the last thing I would wish upon you guys. If I could turn things around, I would do it an instance,' Danny apologised.

Ricky quickly calmed down and acknowledged his sentiments as Barny suggested they keep moving and get to up to the shack so they can rest.

Barny was a tolerant man. He would rather settle his differences by talking them through and would try to avoid any sort of violence if he could. He hated to see his mates going at each other in any form. He had gone through his schooling days with both Danny and Ricky which formed the basis of their friendship. He had done his four-year stint in the Army before he plied his trade as a carpenter. He was a tough man inside with an iron will and had the full respect of both Danny and Ricky as it had been proven time and again, that if they needed help, whichever way, Barny was their unconditionally.

The men continued up the track with Danny leading until they finally neared the old shack that he informed them about. To get up to it though, the men had to negotiate a steep granite rock cliff face. As everybody would do, Danny had always approached the tower and logger's hut via four-wheel drive or fire tracks from the east but more predominantly from the western side where the little township of Tangiloo lay just below Mt St Lucia. It offered a much smoother entry to the peak of the mountain because of its gentler uphill gradient.

On this occasion, the men had made their way straight up the southern side of the mountain. They could have taken an easier route, but it would have doubled the time had they followed the winding road that climbed from Graceville to Tangiloo. However, since people still occupied house and land along its route, Danny thought it best not to risk being seen. Instead, they approached the mountain peak in a direct line through the bush where it was at its steepest and treacherous for both horse and rider. If they were to come in from the west or east from where they were now, it meant another hour or more ride around the giant rock face.

'You're kidding,' Harry gasped, looking up the face of the rock, not believing that they were about to climb it.

'It's gotta be done, Harry, just follow the leader,' Danny implored.

Harry shook his head in beleaguered astonishment.

Danny knew it was as dangerous as it could get. He himself had never attempted anything like it, nothing had even came close, and he was sure his mates had neither, but he was desperate and it needed to be done if they were to give the ensuing captors the slip.

The men looked at each other, shrugged their shoulders and decided with great trepidation to begin the climb. They subtly coaxed their horses dangerously up the only rising flat part of the giant granite rock. The partitions of the boulders intertwined over itself, giving the appearance of a molten lava eruption that had baked solid. Narrow slips of dirt gave life to grasses growing out between snaking tree roots.

With every step, the horses struggled for balance. The men were desperately holding the reins on their slipping and unbalanced horses, hunching tightly over their necks. He knew it was a huge risk, if a horse were to slip it could send both it and rider on a spiralling fall off the face of the rock and down the steep bush ravine below which certainly meant severe injury or even death. With a careful watch and desperation overcoming fear, soon the three harrowing minutes was over. Danny was first to get his horse up onto stable ground, avoiding the giant tree roots that protruded through the floor of the giant boulder. He cajoled and encouraged Barny next up the rock.

Danny dismounted and leant over the top edge.

'Take it easy, mate, don't hurry it,' he warned as Barny neared the top.

A few more minutes passed and Barny had made it safely up, letting off a huge sigh of relief, hugging and kissing his horse as if it were a long-lost lover.

Ricky was not far behind in conquering the climb and so it was left to Harry to put his fears behind him. The boys assured him that they were not coming down to get him. Harry gave his trusted bay mare a pat on the neck and muttered that they could ride up this cliff face without a problem.

With the encouragement of the men already atop of the rock, Harry commenced the most terrifying three-minute ride of his life. He never looked more than a metre ahead of him throughout the climb as he and his horse slowly but surely made it to terra firma.

The men all let off an excited cheer, they had climbed where no man had climbed before they were telling themselves as the high fives landed with excitable force. It was a brief moment of joy for the lads as they momentarily forgot what put them through the climb in the first place. After sharing a cigarette and jokingly telling one another how great a rider each of them were, and what the fear upon each other's faces looked like, it was time to move on towards the loggers hut now clearly within their sights where the massive tower looked down on them.

Considering the circumstances, the mood was as good as it could have been between the now four fugitives as they entered the hut to slump their weary bodies down. Inside the hut lay two separate bunks, one of which Barny was to quickly test the comfort of, not complaining at all about the dust infested mattress that lay upon it. Their bodies were so bruised and battered by their arduous ride they could have laid on a concrete slab and thought it good enough. In the middle of the one roomed shack sat a table with six rickety chairs around it, where Danny, Ricky and Harry decided to put their feet up and relax.

'If we're feeling this sore, imagine how the horses are going,' Danny commented after they complained of the injuries each had received.

A few seconds passed before the men realised the seriousness of his comment.

Harry was the first out the door of the old hut. He loved his animals and had some experience in veterinary science and was angry with himself for not once thinking of the welfare of his horse. In all the confusion and the hurriedness to get to the shack and safety, it had never crossed his mind.

Harry went to the horses to give them the once-over as the rest of the men looked on sharing some apples and oranges that Ricky had packed away in the swag that he had untied from his horse.

'How are they looking, Harry,' Danny asked with genuine concern, already seeing the noticeable cuts along the legs of three of the horses, the deepest being in his own.

'Not good, Danny,' was his short response.

'Well, are they going to be alright or what?' Danny impatiently asked again, knowing full well that without their horses, they may as well give themselves up there and then.

'Just let Harry do his stuff and hang off a bit, Danny,' interjected Ricky while rolling a cigarette. 'He knows what he's doing, be patient, will ya.'

The men looked on for another ten minutes, eating away at what fruit they had, as Harry led the horses around trying to get a gauge on their injuries.

'What's the verdict, Harry?' Ricky asked.

Harry turned and faced the men to give them the news they didn't want to hear.

'Well, they're all lame in their front legs except for Barny's. They all have cuts to their legs as well as stone bruises. Your horse is the worst, Danny, looks like he's pulled the muscles down his rear flank. They're all bruised to just about every part of their body so basically, they're not going anywhere in a hurry,' Harry summarised in his analytic way.

'Anything else you want to add to that, Harry?' Danny enquired in a sarcastic tone.

'Yes Danny, as a matter of fact there is. The ones who haven't lost their shoes already, will have to be re-shod,' Harry snarled back.

'You know what?' Danny began to say, looking around at his mates. 'Today is really starting to piss me off.'

Harry was bewildered; he couldn't believe a comment like that could from a man whose life had just been turned upside down. But that was one of Danny's personality traits. Every time he would find himself in a tight situation or became threatened by something, he would use sarcasm or try to make fun of what was happening with one liners or cliché's, even though inside he would feel totally afraid. It was his way of dealing with things.

For those who didn't know him, it came across as total arrogance and disrespect for those around. Ricky and Barny knew his behaviour well and gave off a slight smirk as they shook their heads in good-humoured nature and reassured Harry not to worry too much about what Danny said.

Harry just couldn't get a handle on Danny; most of the time he thought him to be a great bloke, a leader of men, someone he looked up to, but other times he thought Danny had a few marbles loose, which at times scared him, but whatever he thought, Harry knew he could do a lot worse in this world when it came to friendship.

'Do what you can, and we'll look at them again in the morning,' Danny said. He put his arm around Harry's shoulder and led him to a tap that had to be hand-pumped to get cold water from an underground well as Ricky and Barny sat silently pondering their ever-increasing grave situation.

Harry tended the horses as best he could, using old bandages and rags from his saddled bag, drenching them in cold water to try and bring the swelling down and take care of the lacerations they had received. Danny pulled out his binoculars and walked over to the edge of the rock they had just climbed and began to search for any movement coming their way.

From the view he had through the broken canopy of the forest below, he had a clear look down the mountain from the east all the way around to the northwest, and although he was confident of not seeing anything he didn't want too, he needed to be sure.

'I reckon it's unlikely that anyone would come up the route that we took,' Danny said as Barny and Ricky joined him by the cliff face. 'If they're coming after us, they would come in from the West through Tangiloo, so that means they probably won't be near us until mid-morning tomorrow by the time they figure out where we went.'

'I hope you're right,' Barny expressed with hope, who was given a confident wink in return.

It was just after 8.00 pm as the sun began to set over the valley when the Inspector radioed all his officers back to the station for a debrief on the situation, hoping that all who had been summoned had their units by their side. Police had been searching for any sign of Danny and his gang in and around the outskirts of Graceville and as it was getting on towards darkness the Inspector knew it was a waste of manpower and too dangerous to keep looking throughout the night without any leads on their whereabouts. He suspected Danny had gone into the mountains and it would be far too unsafe for his officers to be tracking at night without a lot of planning first, despite the use of the police vehicles who could only make use of the tracks and roads.

Communication between through large parts of the police force was through the battery powered two-way radio system. Connecting through mobile phones had become almost obsolete to the typical person, including large parts of the police force. People struggled to find power sources to recharge what they had, further, many of the towers that carried the signal had been damaged through vandalism or left with no maintenance upgrades. Most service providers had gone to the wall and supply for any kind of electronic goods from overseas had all but dried up.

There were still some in existence through limited stock of the scarce providers but only the privileged minority had them and they were heavily protected. The only phones still in use on a wide scale were landline phones. Nonetheless, there wasn't enough electrical power for the exchange to cope with demand, so telephone communication only went out to certain sections of the metropolitan area. Only a handful of lines went out to towns like Graceville where people had to pay a steep price for the service. Besides the lucky and privileged wealthy at their private abodes and buildings, only public serving organisations such as the police force, fire department, hospitals and the Minister's and shire offices had access to it.

Dane was still at pains over what had happened at Danny's house. Before the sun set on the day's shocking proceedings, he snuck off from the police station to see if he could make more sense of the shootings. Upon arrival at the Pruitt property, he was halted by four officers standing guard over the property who he had never met before.

'Sorry sir, no one is to enter this property,' one of the officers said.

'I'm Sergeant Dane Grainger. Any reason as to why?' he demanded from behind the police barriers that had been installed.

'Minister's orders, sir,' came the calm reply.

He persisted with his enquiries in attempts to enter the property but was met with repeated refusals, only being told that they were under strict instructions not to allow anyone onto the property under any circumstances. The Sergeant's frustration was again growing as he peered over the officer's shoulders as twilight descended. He noticed the bodies of the Devlin brothers had been removed and the whole yard where the shootings took place had been cleaned up. There appeared to be no sign of the blood that had soaked into the dirt, no sign of a struggle, even the lamb that the Rosco had shot was gone.

In fact, the place looked a whole lot cleaner than Danny had ever kept it. Dane was curious to say the least; he couldn't work out why everything had been cleaned up so soon, and more importantly, why he wasn't informed. He was pondering these questions and more as he made his way back to the station to see if he could find some answers.

Dane was riding at a brisk pace as he worried deeply over Danny and the reasons why all this had happened. Some of the answers he was looking for lay behind the hospital walls he had just passed on his way back to town. The Minister had the bodies of the dead officers sent to the hospital morgue. He wanted proof that Danny Pruitt had shot them down in cold blood. He could then issue a statement and inform his superiors from the big city without any pressure coming back on him or his police force. However, it was soon becoming clear to those in the room, including the Minister, that it was far from the case.

After the doctor had removed the bullets from the bodies, along with the one from the dead lamb, it became apparent to them all that the bullets had all come from the same gun, Rosco's. They also had the pressure bandages that were laying across Rosco's stomach which proved that someone had tried to save his life, and that someone had to be Danny Pruitt. As they continued to piece together what evidence they had in front of them, it soon became clear to everyone in the room that this was no random killing as young Mickey Devlin claimed.

The Minister had heard enough; it wasn't the news he had come to hear.

'This is to remain confidential. It's never to leave these four walls. Do you understand?' He cautioned everyone in the room. His jet-black hair shone off the single overhead large lighting, illuminating the greying streaks that ran down the side. His eyes darted around the room, enhancing his natural frowning eyebrows as he warned the congregation that he would make their lives uncomfortable if any of this were to get out.

If the truth of the shootings were to surface, Johnston was paranoid he would have officials swarming from everywhere investigating, not only this shooting but every suspect shooting in his district over recent times. Even more disturbing for him is that they might also uncover some, if not all the other shady dealings he was up to his neck in was his mistrustful mindset. He wanted Danny Pruitt and his gang caught, and quickly.

After consultation with Inspector Vaccaro, Minister Johnston immediately summoned Sgt Grainger to his office at 10.00 pm. On arriving, Dane was told that he was the man that they wanted to lead the search to apprehend Danny. Dane flatly refused.

'No way! Find someone else,' he said.

'This is a direct order, Sgt Grainger,' the Inspector insisted. 'You will do as you're requested.'

'I can't hunt him down, he's a good friend of mine,' Dane rebuked.

'That's exactly why we want you to do the job,' Johnston said, knowing that Dane was the man to do his dirty work. 'Apparently, you know him better than anyone on the force. You know his thinking pattern, his personality, the places he might be. You also know the mountains Sgt Grainger. That's if your friend is there, of course.'

Dane continued his verbal resistance; however, after several minutes of arguing the point, the Minister interjected and gave Dane a brutal ultimatum.

'If you don't do this, Sgt Grainger, you will be dismissed from the force as of now. And I will make sure your family feels the heat from me and the banks as well. I know your family is living on a knife's edge,' he threatened.

Dane was backed into a corner; he knew the Minister would carry through his threats and the last thing he wanted was to bring any grief to his family.

'Anyway!' Johnston coaxed as Dane refrained his anger. 'If you say he's your good friend, I'm sure you would want to get to him first, because I'm going to send out other parties to try and find him, and you know how trigger-happy my police force is at the moment, don't you, Sgt Grainger?' Johnston smugly warned while leaning back into his leather chair.

Dane had no choice but to reluctantly accept. 'I'll do it on one condition.'

'And what might that be, Sergeant?'

'I handpick my own men to go with me. Men who I can trust and aren't trigger happy.'

The Minister grudgingly agreed then ordered Dane to be at the police station with his men at midday tomorrow for further instructions. 'That's of course, if we haven't got your friend first,' he added teasingly.

At the same time Sgt Dane Grainger left the Minister's office, Danny and the men were about to bed down for the night as each of them gathered their thoughts. It had been one hell of a day for the lads; a day that had changed their lives forever. They were sore, they were tired and they were frightened. Danny was leaning his head against his rolled up sleeping bag looking up at the stars that filled the night sky when his attention was grabbed by a whispering voice a few meters away.

Barny was saying his prayers with his head bowed against his chest. Danny couldn't believe it, he had no idea Barny was a religious man, quite the opposite, Danny thought, and in his curiosity walked up to Barny and asked him inquisitively what he was doing.

'I'm praying, Danny, what's it look like!' Barny retorted.

'Yeah, I know that, but why?' Danny persisted.

'I pray every night, Danny, have been for the last five years,' Barny stated, then relayed how he had found god and what a difference it had made to his life.

'Well, bugger me, never would have thought you would go that way,' Danny confessed, still amazed at what he didn't know about his mate.

'You ought to give it a go, I think you could use a bit of the Lord's wisdom and kindness,' Barny quipped.

'Not much kindness in this world anymore, Barny,' Danny sighed back.

'I'm saving a prayer for you especially, Danny. Would you like to join me?' Barny said as he looked up at Danny walking away.

'Thanks, but no thanks,' he refused politely.

Danny was not a religious man. It's not that he knew nothing about it, he married into a family that was religious, he just couldn't see the sense in it all. He would say he finds his own strength and faith from within himself and those closest to him. However, as he always said, each too their own, and would neither ridicule nor question it.

The talk of God and religion quickly turned his mind to Greta and his children. He looked down upon Graceville and wondered how she was coping, if she knew anything at all. He missed her terribly already and wanted to hold her close and tell her everything would be alright. But as it stood now, Danny knew it might be sometime before he will see his family again, if at all.

Greta was coping the best she could; she had just spent the last hour trying to get her children to sleep in the spare bedroom of Corey and Sarah's house. The children were asking Greta a lot of questions in their own innocent way.

What's happened to daddy? Why are we staying at Uncle Corey and Auntie Sarah's place? When is Daddy coming home? Greta did her best to put her son's minds at ease, telling them that Daddy had gone fishing for a while and would be home soon and there was nothing to worry about. But the same questions that her children were asking were the same ones that Greta needed an answer to.

She had been putting on a brave face, despite the aching inside. It was the unknown that was eating away at her; the emotions were running wild within her. One moment she would feel completely helpless and worry for Danny's safety, while the next instant she would direct anger at him. How dare he put his family at risk like this, she would curse to herself.

She entered the loungeroom and sat next to Sarah on the couch. Greta was not alone in feeling the anguish and shock of what was happening, Corey and Sarah were feeling it too. They shared a tight bond with Danny; they had known each other for a long time, grew up not far from one other and were good friend's before Danny had even met Greta.

Sarah was an attractive lady of the same age. Today her blonde hair was flowing with a low fringe. She had attentive soft blue eyes and preferred denim jeans to a skirt or dress. She loved her makeup and would change eyeshadow on a regular basis which became the friendly butt of jokes between those who knew her well, along with her many changes of hairstyle. She had a touch of shyness about her but to those who knew her closely, such as Danny, she was a fun-loving woman who was always there when needed.

Sarah asked how the kids were coping, concerned about their well-being.

'They're asleep now, I don't think they realise what's going on, thank god,' Greta said as she put her head between her hands.

Sarah comforted Greta as best she could, but Greta was unable to hold her emotions any longer. She began to sob uncontrollably. She couldn't understand it, how could Danny shoot two police officers like they say. But the news wasn't about to get any better for her as Corey entered his home through the front door. He had been out and about trying to find any information regarding Danny and the shootings.

'What have you found out?' the women asked in anticipation.

Corey had a glum look on his face as he looked at Greta.

'It's bad,' he conceded.

The women had been at home all afternoon and evening and knew nothing of the Sandilands incident or about the wounded officer. Corey did his best to tell them what he knew of both. Although his details were sketchy to say the least, it was enough to let the women know that things were as desperate as they could be. Greta couldn't believe what she is hearing,

'Danny's not responsible for these things!' she insisted, as she wiped the tears from her eyes. 'Tell me he's not responsible, please Corey, tell me he didn't do these things,' Greta demanded.

Corey was at a loss on what to say, he thought his information was solid. He turned to Sarah for silent help. Greta also turned her attention towards Sarah and pleaded, 'You've known him longer than me; we both know he wouldn't do this…would he?'

All Sarah could do was hold a quivering Greta in her arms; both she and Corey knew that whatever they said, nothing was going to take away the fear and shock that now consumed their friend. Peering over Greta's shoulder as she held her tightly, Sarah looked at her husband knowing it was going to be a long sleepless night for all concerned, including for Danny and the boys.

Chapter 6

The sun peered over the eastern peaks of the mountains surrounding Graceville and Sgt Dane Grainger had awoken at the crack of dawn. He needed men of special quality to help track down Danny and knew exactly who to call on. His first port of call was to a man called Karl Turner. Karl, a tall man with straight light brown hair and a stubbly beard, had a reputation of being the best tracker in the district; he never failed to catch his prey, whether it be man or beast. Dane had previously used Karl's talents to track down missing persons in the bush; he was perfect man to help him on his mission.

On hearing what Dane was about to embark on, Karl had no hesitation in joining him on his quest. Dane would find the same commitment and concern from the second man he wanted with him in the search. Ryan McCulloch, a ginger-haired man with a goatee beard of the same colour, was a great horseman who knew the surrounding mountains as good as anybody. But the most important reason Dane wanted these men with him was what the three all had in common, a very good friendship with Danny, with Ryan being Danny's brother-in-law.

The two men didn't need much convincing to help after Dane explained the circumstances of his request and organised for them to meet him at the police station at midday after they sorted out their home front first, as both were married men, Karl with with children.

Dane finalised his party of five by taking along two young constables he knew well, trusted fully, and had a good understanding of life in the mountains.

It was mid-morning by the time the Sergeant had all his needs under control. He had a couple of hours up his sleeve before meeting the members of his party and beginning the search. He thought it best to pay Greta a visit and let her know what was happening at his end and to answer any questions she might have for him.

Greta was still shaken and tired when she met him at the door of Corey and Sarah's house. She invited him in as Dane confided what his suspicions were over the shootings at her house and promised he would do everything within his power to find the truth and bring this whole tragedy to an end as quickly as possible. Corey stood by as Sarah comforted Greta on the couch as Dane began to ask Greta if she knew of any hiding places Danny might go. She gave it deep thought but couldn't give Dane anything solid to go on. Although she considered Dane a good friend, she honestly didn't know where Danny could be.

'You would probably know better than me,' she said.

Upon exhausting his line of enquiry, Dane was bombarded with a barrage of questions from the trio, all of whom were understandably showing signs of tiredness and emotion from all the strain. Dane tried as best he could but didn't have the answers to all the questions being thrown at him. In the end, all he could do was promise Greta that he would find Danny and do his best to bring him home safely.

About an hour had passed before Dane was on his way; he thanked Sarah for the cup of tea and guaranteed to get word to them as soon as he knew anything about Danny's whereabouts and wellbeing. Greta was thankful for the help and care that Dane was giving and walked with him to the road where his horse was tethered at the front fence.

He was about to mount his horse to return to the police station when Greta had one more request. As she tried her hardest to hold back the tears, she grabbed Dane by the arm and asked with a stammer in her voice, 'If you find him, Dane, tell him I love him, tell him I need him home.'

The burly Sergeant took her hand and gave her a confident nod of the head.

'I will find him, Greta, if it's the last thing I do,' he assured her.

At the top of Mt St Lucia, Danny continued to cast an eagle eye below him through his binoculars, only pausing to wipe his dreary eyes. He was looking for any sign of movement that could be coming his way, but like the morning he and his buddies were having, there was a lot of nothing happening, which pleased Danny no end. They were all in a sombre mood as little sleep had been had the previous night. The early morning hours were spent helping Harry attend the horses; however, things weren't looking good on that front either. The horses were nowhere near fit to go through anything like they had to endure the day before, so as it was, all they had been doing since daybreak was sitting around idly and keeping to themselves.

The silence was broken when Ricky asked Danny for the radio that he had taken from Sandilands down at the river. He was desperate in his angst to find some news on anything that might concern them.

'Where's the radio?' Ricky repeated.

'I haven't got it!'

'What do ya mean you haven't got it?'

'I lost it, it must have fallen off my gear coming up here yesterday,' Danny said calmly as he turned to peer back down the mountain.

Ricky was again angry with Danny; he thought the radio was the only possible way of getting any information regarding their situation. It could have only helped them, Ricky surmised, a possible way of knowing what plans the police were employing to apprehend them. He let Danny know his feelings, least of all calling him careless and stupid.

'You should have had it in your saddlebag, you idiot,' Ricky blasted after Danny said he only had the radio clipped to his jeans pocket.

Barny stood up from his position sitting against the cabin door, wiping the dust off his torn T-shirt. He had to play the peacemaker again between the feuding mates before it would escalate further. Within seconds, he had both the lads calmed down, as Harry looked on bewildered at the viciousness of the insults traded between the two so-called best mates.

Danny didn't seem too perturbed about the argument as he walked away back to his lookout point on the ridge, shrugging his shoulders at Barny with a wry smile. He was used to Ricky going off at the deep end. To him, losing the radio didn't seem to be big deal, but to Ricky, losing the radio could be a monumental mistake which could cost them dearly down the track.

Danny resumed looking through his binoculars over the ridge for any sign of movement while the others sat around on tree stumps surrounding the cabin passing cigarettes around considering their options. They were keeping their voices low away from Danny when Harry suggested that they make their way back to the city.

' At least there, we could be around friends and family. Maybe they could protect and hide us from the law or something.'

'Yep, we're wasting our time sitting around here,' Ricky agreed. 'Doing nothing is only inviting trouble. It's probably our worst option. What do you reckon, Barny?'

'It's a good idea, but we don't know our way out of here, boys. Who knows what we will run into? We are going to have to ask Danny what's the safest route out of here if we do,' Barny wisely advised.

They turned to Danny and asked him to join them then explained their concerns.

Danny glared at them then turned his old faded black cap around his head the opposite way and shook his head in an objectionable manner. He lit up another cigarette and began to tell the men what he thought.

'There is no safe way out of here, not unless you go North and cut back around the ranges to the West, which would take about a two days on fit horses, and in case you haven't noticed, our horses wouldn't outrun a bloody wombat the way they are at the moment. Listen,' Danny reasoned, 'I know you can't see them, but the coppers are on their way, make no mistake about that. There's no way we can go back down to Graceville, but you're right in one thing, we need to keep moving, which means we need new horses and I know exactly where to get them.'

The men were all ears as Danny began to tell them of a good friend of his who lived just outside of Tangiloo. It was only an hour's ride from where they were now. Danny knew he had fresh horses on his property and since his friend owed him a few favours from times gone by, he deduced that he would have no hesitation in helping him and the boys out.

His three buddies weren't too keen on the idea of having to rely on someone they didn't know, but Danny assured them that he trusted this guy to the hilt. A few minutes convincing followed before satisfying the trio's apprehension before the men packed up their gear and started making tracks towards Tangiloo. Danny's horse was in a bad way, still bleeding through the makeshift bandages from the deep laceration on his near hind leg and limping noticeably, and he would nurse his mount as best he could to their destination.

It had just passed noon and the temperature in the valley was already nudging 30 degrees without a cloud in the sky when Sgt Dane Grainger arrived at the Police Station to see Karl and Ryan ready and waiting for the task ahead. Dane introduced the two young constables to his good friends who were by his side.

Johnny Hayes and Brad McNamara were two 23-year olds that Dane had known since they were toddlers. Both were level-headed sensible young men who looked up to Dane as a big brother. They both had lost their own fathers who Dane was close to nearly ten years ago because of a car accident. Dane was around for most of their teenage years and with the blessing of the mothers would help whenever he could.

Dane left his colleagues and was on his way to enter the police station, passing the hordes of fellow police who were gathered around familiarising themselves with the names, identikit sketches and available photos of Danny and the boys. On his way through, he noticed that two of the surviving Devlin brothers appeared to be preparing to join in on the search, along with half a dozen other parties that had been formed. Dane was far from happy with that scenario and sought out Inspector Vaccaro to voice his disapproval.

As far as he was concerned, the Devlin brothers would only be seeking revenge for the death of their two brothers. Although Matt, who was the eldest of the five brothers, was more sensible than the rest of his siblings, Dane fathomed, along with the other brother Eddie, that given the chance they would try to take Danny down without batting an eyelid.

The Sergeant found Vaccaro on his way out of the station as he was entering. He started to explain his agitated concern over the Devlin brothers' involvement when the Inspector pulled him aside away from the masses to a place where they couldn't be heard. Vaccaro had a worried look upon his face. The previous night he had been doing a bit of sleuthing himself and was now convinced he knew why the shootings had happened.

The Inspector had been talking to the doctor, a reliant friend of his who performed the autopsy on Rosco and Billy. He had also questioned young Mickey again; this time alone and with his experience had no doubt that the youngest Devlin had been lying through his teeth about what had occurred. But the worried look upon Inspector Vaccaro's face had nothing to do with the truth of the shootings; it was what he had overheard in Minister Johnston's office only an hour before.

'Just shut up for a second and listen to me,' Vaccaro ordered Dane, who was still protesting over the Devlin brothers being involved in the search. 'The Devlins are the least of our problems now.'

'What do you mean, Sir?'

The Inspector discreetly pointed over to where a group of men were gathered at the foot of the police station steps.

'See those men?'

'Yeah, what about them?'

'That's John Pringle, have you heard of him?'

'No, I don't think so.'

'Well, you should have! He's not good news, Sergeant,' Vaccaro warned. 'About an hour ago, I was about to enter the Minister's office with the names of those involved in the search and the directions of where they were heading. I heard voices coming from inside before I entered. I knew one was Johnston's but couldn't identify the other. I hid in the hallway until he left and that's when I saw him. I recognised him straight away.'

Vaccaro discreetly pointed his finger in Pringle's direction. 'I was on the force with him years back down in Marlboro long before the crisis hit. A lot of us once testified against him on corruption charges. He was the worst of all the crooked cops. He was dismissed from the force long ago. He makes his living now as a gun for hire and problem solver. Politicians, businessmen, crime bosses, you name it, they all use him when they need to silence someone or retrieve debts. Him and his comrades had been charged countless times over the past decade, but nothing ever gets proven.

'Witnesses go missing or are too scared to testify. He's got the protection of the dirty politicians who he's work for in the past. They fear that if he ever faced conviction, he would expose all his dealings with them as part of a plea bargain, so he's had a free rein to do what he pleases.'

'I think you've jolted my memory,' Dane said. 'He was all over the media a while back, wasn't he?'

'That's right, Sergeant. Whatever you've heard about his reputation, you only know the half of it. He's a fuckin psychopath!'

'So, what's he doing here?' Dane asked.

.'I don't know. But what I do know is that Johnston's putting him on the search for your mate, so we've got to expect the worse,' Vaccaro forewarned.

Dane was shocked. 'What? That can't be right!' However, the seriousness on the Inspector's face told him otherwise.

'Whatever you do, Sgt Grainger, make sure you watch your back. If Pringle's here, it can only mean one thing. Just make sure you get to Pruitt before he does.'

Although he had his grave suspicions, what the Inspector wasn't privy to that was that Johnston never planned for Danny to tell his side of the story, even if it meant prison time for him. He wanted him dead.

The Minister's reasoning behind his irrational planning was that if Danny Pruitt were to testify at his own trial, the truth could possibly come out on the shootings, and in return, potentially open a Pandora's box over his police force which may lead to further investigations unearthing more suspect fatal shootings that were shoved under the carpet on his behalf.

Johnston was cunning, he knew the easiest and quickest way to get to Danny was to let Dane find him for them. His secreted hired help had little knowledge of the surrounding ranges. The Minister was banking on Dane's knowledge of the mountains to lead them to him. He offered John Pringle a large pay packet, half now, and half on completion which was happily accepted by the present-day mercenary.

John Pringle was a man that Inspector Vaccaro loathed, and he was astounded and angry that he was in the Hexagon valley at the Minister's request.

What was further astonishing was that he had no idea that Minister Johnston even knew of this murderous bastard.

The presence of John Pringle and his two offsiders was the last straw for the Inspector. He had watched Minister Johnston over the past five years slowly destroy and corrupt everything he stood for as a police officer. He had seen all the cover-ups, the embezzlements, the fraud, and the stand over tactics used against innocent people and the situation in the valley had been eating at his conscious for some time.

Vaccaro was going to try and put a stop to it any way he could, he no longer cared about what might happen to him personally, he wanted to blow the whistle on Johnston and his dealings, even if it meant losing the badge he so proudly wore upon his chest for so long. Although he was unhappy with what had happened to his nephew, Steve Sandilands, by the river, he wasn't about to let Danny Pruitt and his friends be hunted down like wild animals with a bounty on their heads.

Dane took heed of what Vaccaro had earnestly relayed. He thanked him for his honesty and took the Inspector's advice to get moving before the final instructions went out to the search parties, fearfully for Dane however, he was suddenly nervously wondering what he had got himself into. Nevertheless, despite the threat that now hung over them, it only gave him more motivation to track down his friend and bring him to safety.

There were six separate search parties, each of seven men led by a senior police officer. This included John Pringle's party who had the assistance of Matt and Eddie Devlin, and the brothers had no hesitation in helping with their knowledge of the surrounding mountains. Knowing how eager they were to extract revenge for their brother's deaths, Johnston ensured the brothers would ride in the search with Pringle and his men.

The two brothers had no idea who they were about to go bush with. To them, they were just another group hired by the Minister to find the four fugitives. Truth be told, the brothers didn't care who they rode with, they just wanted the chance to reel in Danny and bring him to justice. A perfect combination and Minister Johnston knew as much.

The search parties were getting their final instructions from the senior coordinator before they embarked on their mission to locate and apprehend who they believed to be vicious cop killers. Each party was given different routes to search when heading up into the nearby mountains, all with radio contact to the police vehicles who were already scanning the backroads of the mountains. Each member was issued with UHF radios with a specific channel and instructed to report their progress back to base in Graceville every hour. As would be expected, all men were well armed, had bulletproof vests at the ready and had enough field rations to last three days, confident that was more than enough time to capture the now outlaws with the manpower available.

'Let's go,' Dane hurriedly said to his men while mounting his horse.

'Aren't we supposed to hang around until we get our orders?' Constable Johnny Hayes enquired.

'We've already gotten ours, now let's get the hell out of here.'

Ryan and Karl looked at each other with concern. They knew something was disturbing Dane but weren't about to ask yet what was troubling him. They would wait until later that day when they had the chance to speak to him away from the two younger constables.

The men were almost out of sight heading beyond the railway station which ran parallel to the Watkins River when Eddie Devlin spotted them by chance.

'I wonder where they're heading. Aren't they supposed to wait like us?' he mused, nudging his brother and nodding his head in the direction of where the group was riding.

Pringle looked up to see what Eddie meant by his comment and immediately jumped upon his horse and with his group following, stealthily tailed behind Dane and his posse.

'What's happening? Why are we following them for?' Eddie pestered.

'We're going to let Sgt Grainger find Pruitt for us,' Pringle said as he turned to both Matt and Eddie Devlin with a smug smile.

'Why should we do all the hard work?' one of Pringle's men added as they began to snigger amongst themselves.

Pringle's two partners were also ex-police who decided it was easier to make money on the other side of the law. Max Miller and Stewie Morris had been aiding Pringle for the last five years and didn't care too much for other people if the price was right. Along with Pringle's sentiments, they thought this was a simple put in, take out job, and would be easy money, and besides, they thought they were going to get a good look at the countryside to boot.

Like their boss, they had never heard of Danny Pruitt or his friends, they convinced themselves that he would be just a scared son of a bitch who was hiding from the law and would be easy pickings for men of their experience and prowess. The Devlin Brothers also gave them none to the otherwise by telling them that Danny was just an average simple law-abiding bloke who they always stood over.

Pringle and his men had a lot more firepower than the other search parties. The latest in semi-automatic handguns and rifles, with telescopic sights and ample ammunition was available to them. They also had night vision goggles, which would give them the edge if needed after the sun went down as well as tracking devices fitted with all the latest technology. Unsurprisingly, all this weaponry and hardware impressed Matt and Eddie Devlin who were just carrying .22 rifles accompanied by a 9mm pistol.

Sgt Dane Grainger and the men he entrusted to ride with him only packed rifles and shotguns with limited stocks of ammunition. The Sergeant held the firm view they didn't need an arsenal of weapons because neither of them believed Danny would ever fire upon them. In fact, Dane's only cause for concern about their safety would only be the occasional wild animal they may encounter, chiefly the wild dogs and feral cats that now roamed the hills, the once loved pets dumped by the less fortunate who could no longer feed them which were morphing into frenzied numbers. Disturbingly for Dane, that was before his discussion with Inspector Vaccaro and he was regretting that maybe, he should have equipped himself a bit better than what was at his disposal.

It was late morning when the four fugitives came out of the thickness and cover of the ranges and apprehensively began to cut across open paddocks, carefully looking in all directions not to been seen. Danny provided a good espy through his binoculars and gave the all clear before they had to expose themselves in the clearing. They had no alternative but to ride the kilometre across the wide-open weed-infested paddocks. Ragwort, tall thistle and dandelion dominated the undulating uncut grassy slopes; however, it was the possibility of encountering something they couldn't see that worried the lads the most, and the slithering venomous adders had to be put at the back of their minds if they wanted to reach Damien's homestead sitting on the outskirts of Tangiloo.

Damien Lewis was the man Danny had told his nervous mates about. He was the one who would help them out with fresh horses and maybe a chance to get some decent food in to them, they hadn't had anything solid in their stomachs since yesterday morning and the boys were mighty hungry.

The friendship between Danny and Damien was, through most people's eyes a strange one to say the least. They were complete opposites in the way of lifestyle. Where Danny liked nothing better than to get his chops into a big T-bone steak, Damien was no go when it came to red meats, a staunch vegetarian. Danny never grew his hair past collar length; Damien had hair in a ponytail reaching down the middle of his back. Danny was a beer drinker; Damien would always prefer bourbon or wine. Danny was a smoker; Damien couldn't stand the smell of burnt tobacco. Danny was a strong believer in marriage; Damien had been with the same woman for thirteen years but never once thought of tying the knot. Danny had broad shoulders while Damien was tall and lean and so the list went on with differences in the way they lived and acted.

He had met Damien nearly ten years ago through the large plant nursery that he ran on his property. Danny would buy plants off him at a good price when he was doing landscaping jobs and was up at the nursery quite often and as time went on, they became close friends, even more so when the world's crisis deepened.

The one thing they did have in common was the paranoia and mistrust of governments and those in authority. They would often discuss the issue with much vitriol and venom, but most people thought they enjoyed each other's company because of the curiosity they had for one another's lifestyle, but whatever the reason, they never stopped learning from each other.

Although he never took a backward step when voicing his opinions, Damien was a pacifist. Never once had Danny seen him lose his temper, maybe it had something to do with all the home-grown herbs and vegetables he grew and consumed, along with his lifelong passion for the environment. Whatever it was, Danny liked him a lot, and always offered his services to him without hesitation when needed.

The men arrived at Damien's property to see that there was no one home. They carefully looked around for any sign of life, but none was to be found.

Damien's cart was missing with a couple of empty spaces in his stable which told the boys that he was out for the day, probably down in Graceville, Danny assumed. The boys were hungry as they peered through the kitchen window of Damien's modest three-bedroom abode to see if they could lay their eyes on anything to eat.

'Well, we're not going fill our guts from out here,' Ricky decided 'Any way of getting in?' he asked as he disappeared around the side of the house.

Harry and Danny unsuccessfully began to lift the kitchen window while Barny tried the window on the other side of the house when they heard footsteps entering the kitchen from the inside. The boys ducked under the sills of the windows in panic.

'Come on, fellas, what's taken ya so long?' The voice giggled from within.

'How the hell did you get in there?' Danny marvelled.

'I broke in through the bedroom window. Do you want some of these?' Ricky boasted, already scoffing down some freshly baked bread rolls that Damien's partner Nicki had cooked up in the morning. Ricky unclipped the latch of the kitchen window to let the boys climb through and soon they cleaned out what was left of the bread, helping themselves to any type of spread they could find to go with it. Danny was hesitant at first; however, the hunger he felt overpowered any guilt he carried about breaking into a friend's house.

Thirty minutes had passed before the men decided that they couldn't fit another mouthful into their now contented stomachs when they decided to go and check the stables out.

Harry was impressed with what he saw. The stables contained all he needed to tend their own horses. Bandages, antiseptics, fresh feed and water was ready and available to care for the horses. At the same time, the other three slowly walked around the property admiring Damien's belongings and what he had stored away in the stables and nearby shed.

When Harry had finished and was satisfied he had done all that he could with their horses, Ricky suggested that they leave their horses behind and take their pick of any of the of five horses that Damien had stabled and move on.

'We're not going anywhere until Damien gets home,' Danny objected.

'What do ya mean?' Ricky asked, surprised at Danny's remark.

'I'm not taking his horses without him knowing who took them.'

'Since when have you had a conscience, leave him a fuckin note,' Ricky insisted as he began to saddle up his choice of horse.

'We're not taking his horses, Rick, until he gets home,' argued Danny. 'Shit mate, we just about ate everything in his kitchen, we broke into his house, I think he needs to have an explanation why, don't you!'

'We need to get out of here *now*, Danny,' Ricky protested.

'You can go if you want, but you're not taking any of his *horses*,' Danny said as their voices started to rise at one another again.

'Shut up, both of you, do you want the bloody world to know where we are?' Barny interrupted underneath his breath.

The two were at each other's throats again and for a moment it looked like the argument would be decided with their fists. More minutes passed arguing the point.

'Where are you going to go anyway?' Danny barked. 'None of us have got any bright ideas of what we're going to do. So if you've got any, we would love you to share it with the rest of us!'

The men were all on tenterhooks, the pressure was eating away at them, what to do, where to go, who can they trust, they just couldn't make their minds up. It was a decision they had to get right otherwise if they chose the wrong option, they would pay for it with their freedom, even worse, their lives.

There was no reply from Ricky as he threw the saddle forcefully down to the ground then walked away, cursing to himself over their plight.

'We sit and wait until Damien gets home; it will give us time to think things through properly,' Danny softly ordered. 'If you want to try and make a run for the city later, then so be it. I can't stop you; at least we're safe here for the time being, no one knows where we are and anyway, Damien might be able to help us.'

Danny got his way and as the clock ticked into early afternoon, they mulled over their limited choices. Despite stewing over endless probabilities, including giving themselves up, they couldn't decide what the right course of action was. In the meantime, all they could do was wait for Damien to get home and get as much rest as they could.

Chapter 7

'G'day Dane, what's happening?' the lone rider inquired.

'Nothing much, Franky, how about you?' Dane replied, leaning forward on his horse.

'Been away in the bush fishing the last couple of days, mate,' he said.

'Where abouts?' Dane asked.

'Up at Cratske's,' he enthusiastically replied, showing off his small catch.

'Not a bad couple of days work,' Dane congratulated. 'Hey, listen Frank, you know Danny Pruitt, don't ya?'

'Yeah, why's that?' Frank asked.

'You wouldn't have seen him in the last day or so, have ya?' Dane enquired, thinking he would get the same response as he had received from the previous people he had asked along Mason's road.

'Matter of fact, I have, Dane,' he confessed.

'Yeah, that's great, where did you see him?' Dane asked as his demeanour turned serious.

'At Manning's bridge about a hundred meters from where I was fishing.'

'When did you see him?'

'I don't know, about mid-afternoon yesterday, I suppose. He had three mates with him, and they were going like the clappers too. Why, what's up?' Frank asked.

Danny and his buddies had crossed Cratske's Creek on their way up to Mt St Lucia and in their haste didn't notice Frank sitting on the forested bank fishing. Frank didn't take much notice of them either; he just assumed that Danny was taking a few mates for a cross-country ride, although he did think to himself that were going a bit too hard for a leisurely ride in the mountains.

He had no idea of what Danny had done; Frank had been isolated; Dane was the first person he had spoken to in days and before he could get an answer out of him, the Sergeant and his partners were high tailing it up the track that Frank had come out of and heading for Manning's bridge. Dane had led his men up the bitumen laid road of Mason's Creek which climbed and twisted the 15km between Graceville and Tangiloo. Dane thought that this was the most likely route that Danny would've taken going on the last reported sighting and the history of traveling along the places he knew best.

With Ryan leading the group and Dane bringing up the rear, the five men decided to ride as hard as they possibly could. They knew Pringle and his men were following thanks to Karl's uncanny ability to detect anything untoward, whether behind or ahead of him, and once again he was proven right in his judgment.

Dane's belief was that if ever they had the chance to give Pringle the slip, this was it. They charged down a slight decline overgrown with large tree ferns and grasses in amongst the Mountain Ash trees that doubled in size the further you tracked into the mountain. Once at the bottom of the gully they rode east until they came across Cratske's creek which was one of many little crystal-clear streams that flowed down from the mountain ranges that joined the Watkins River at the foot of the mountains.

The men were asking everything of their steeds, all five men were very experienced when it came to horsemanship, a valuable asset they had over, not only Pringle and his offsiders, but also Danny and his crew and they would use the advantage to its full extent. Dane saw this as the perfect chance to show their skill and show it they did. Within a short space of time, they were confident that they had lost the tail much to Dane's relief.

The men could now concentrate on getting up to Manning's bridge, two kilometres upstream. It was there they hoped to catch onto Danny's trail and finally make some inroads into their mission. They took their horses directly up the shallows of the stream to throw any pursuer off their tracks. They arrived at Manning's bridge, an old barrierless river crossing for forestry workers and fire crews, then dismounted off their horses and looked for any sign of what direction Danny might have gone.

As the horses stretched their neck to the water's edge, Karl called Dane over while he was sifting through what he thought maybe a lead. He lifted some undergrowth away with a stick he had in his hand and pointed down at some hoof prints.

'Looks pretty fresh, yesterday I reckon,' Karl summarised as Ryan and the two young constables joined them.

'Four horses, and they were in a hurry,' he added as he began to explain his findings.

'One's definitely Danny's,' he divulged.

'How do you know that?' Constable Brad McNamara asked.

'It's the horseshoe print, we all get our horses shod by the same farrier, Danny included. I know the farrier's personal etchings on the plates. He only does it for a handful of us,' Karl replied.

'Where does this track head to?' Dane asked, looking Northwood in the direction of where the hoof prints were going.

'Straight up to the old fire and communications tower at St Lucia,' Karl answered.

Karl looked surprised, he knew that the track was probably the most treacherous one around and with Danny's lack of riding skills…he was bewildered to say the least and told the other men so.

'He came this way because he didn't want to be seen,' Dane said.

'Well,' Karl said, concerned for Danny's safety, 'let's just hope wherever he wanted to go, he got there in one piece.'

The men quickly remounted following the trail with Karl at the helm. Danny and the lads had left plenty behind on their travels for Karl to pick up on. The further they moved up the mountain trail, the more clues they would find. Other than the hoof prints and more signs that only Karl could distinguish, there was the obvious. Cigarette butts, the same brand that Danny smoked, a drink canteen that Danny had borrowed off Dane not long ago, not to mention the radio that Danny had lost, which Dane was fully aware of how it had ended up in his hands.

After ascending through the steep rough terrain of the mountain track where the desperate and frightened four had been before them, they arrived below the giant rock face.

Karl was at a loose end, the tracks they were following looked like they had disappeared into thin air. A huge bunch of blackberries overgrown with vines had covered the track, there was no sign that anyone had pushed through it. He looked in all directions, including down the edge of the ravine. It would take him several minutes to work out which direction they took and once he realised, he couldn't believe his eyes.

Karl stood upright, looking up at the rock face in astonishment.

'That crazy bastard,' Karl whispered loud enough for the others to hear.

'What's up, where do you reckon they've gone?' Ryan asked.

Karl didn't need to explain in words, and on closer inspection of the route the boys had gingerly started off on, all he needed to do was point his finger up the rock face.

'You're fuckin joking,' Dane said in disbelief.

'Somehow, someway, the stupid bastards made it up there,' Karl replied.

The great tracker was in awe. Never in his wildest moments would he ever contemplate an incline like that, and to think that relatively modest riders like Danny and his buddies could even achieve such a task was beyond Karl's comprehension. Nevertheless, he was adamant that they had done just that and after discussions amongst themselves as to whether they would attempt the same life-threatening risk, they concluded common sense should prevail and put safety before bravado. They would ride the extra hour around the blocked track and below the rock face and hope to pick up the trail when they arrived at the top.

It was almost nightfall when they came across the old logger's hut and soon discovered there was plenty of proof that Danny and his partners had made camp the previous night.

Fresh fruit skins, footprints in the powder like dust were some of the hints that humankind had been there. The blood-stained rags left behind was proof to Karl that their horses suffered injuries and that they would be not moving nearly as fast as they had been. As there wasn't much daylight left and feeling down right exhausted themselves, Dane and his men decided that they too would set up camp for the night at the hut, safe in the knowledge through the radio's comms that no apprehension had been made yet. They were certain that they were hot on the heels of their fugitive friend and an early start in the morning was paramount.

'There's someone coming,' Harry whispered aloud.

The sun was setting behind the stables when Harry and Ricky took their positions close to the window to see who was coming through the gates. There was only enough room for two sets of eyes as they clamoured for a better view.

'Describe them to me,' Danny asked Ricky.

Ricky gave him as best a description as he could of both the man and the woman at the helm of the reins that controlled the carriage driven by two Chestnut geldings and Danny was left in no doubt that it was Damien and his lady finally arriving home.

'There's another bloke with them,' Harry said anxiously.

It's your other mate, Danny!' Ricky turned and said.

'Which mate?'

'You know, the bloke from the other night.'

'Jesus Christ, Rick, can you be a bit more specific?' Danny retorted, frowning and shaking his head.

'The bloke who got his house trashed.'

'Who, Tom?'

'Yeah, that's him.'

The boys took their positions hiding in and around the stables with Danny at the entrance. They watched on as Damien and Tom unharnessed the horses and started leading them towards the stable as Damien's partner proceeded to the house. They were deep in conversation, unaware of what they were about to get drawn into.

'How are ya, boys?' Danny said calmly as they entered the stables.

'Shit, Danny, you scared the crap out of me,' Damien cursed, taken aback to see him standing there. 'What the hell are you doing here?' he demanded as the other three came out of their hiding places.

'Excuse the intrusion, mate. This is Ricky, Barny and Harry,' he introduced.

'Yeah, nice to meet you all,' Damien acknowledged in a sarcastic tone. 'You still haven't told me what you're doing here,' he rumbled as he started to regain his composure, turning his attention back to Danny who was still amused at their surprised reaction.

'We need fresh horses. I was hoping you might be able help us out,' Danny asked. 'We've gotten ourselves in a bit of a predicament.'

'From what I've heard down in Graceville this morning, I think you're in a bit more than what you call a predicament,' Damien scoffed before Danny could elaborate.

'What are they saying?' he asked intrigued.

Damien told the lads about a press release issued on the steps of Minister Johnston's offices through a spokesman late in the afternoon. On the recommendation of his sycophant advisors, Johnston was convinced to release a statement early in the evening to quash any public rumours that were escalating around town. The press release was also designed to placate the hounding the Minister's office was receiving from local journalists wanting to know what was going on.

Where nearly five years ago the whole of the Hexagon valley had only one local newspaper to peruse through along with the city's publications, today there were four different publications distributed throughout the valley alone. With television no longer transmitting, government owned radio stations took over broadcasted events and you only heard what the authorities aired.

Newspapers were the primary medium available for the ordinary man in the street to receive current affairs of the day and it was a cutthroat business. Reporters would often cross the line to get the scoop on what was happening, and it was a case of not letting the truth get in the way of a good story. If their paper could get the exclusive, it meant big rewards for journalists from the editor and as times were tough financially, they would stop at nothing to get that big story.

The four newly dubbed outlaws gathered closer to hear what Damien was saying and they were shocked to hear was said about them a few hours before.

The press statement in full read.

On Wednesday, the 27th of December at approximately 10.30 am, Senior Constable Ross Devlin and Constable William Devlin of the Hexagon Valley police force arrived at the property of one Mr Danny Pruitt, for routine questioning over an incident at the Depot Hotel the previous day.

After a brief altercation, according to witnesses, the police officers were deliberately and cold-bloodedly shot and killed by Mr Pruitt for no reason. Since this incident, he has shot and wounded another officer of the law, Senior Constable Robert Dukes who lie in hospital in a critical condition. With other numerous charges to be laid against Mr Danny Pruitt, this man along with his accomplices, Mr Rick De Graaf, Mr David Barnard and Mr Harry Mitchell, are now wanted by the Shire and state of Venturia to face these charges.

At the Minister's request, we have all available manpower at our disposal searching for the armed and dangerous criminals. A reward will be allocated to persons with information that will lead to arrest and conviction of these men.

'Do you believe what they are saying?' Danny asked when Damien had finished.

'I know you can be a crazy bastard sometimes, Danny, but I reckon even that's beyond you; I know you wouldn't shoot them deliberately,' Damien reassured him.

Ricky and Barny sat quietly against some saddles while Harry was about to hit panic mode.

'Wanted for murder, we are wanted for murder! We're fucked, I tell ya, we are goners,' he kept repeating as he walked around in circles.

'Calm down, Harry. Get a grip on yourself,' the boys chastised in unison. Harry was almost in tears through pure fear and as Ricky and Barny continued to try and calm him down, Danny informed Damien and Tom of the real circumstances that led to the shootings. As they began to sympathise with their predicament, Damien's partner Nicki entered the stables.

She panned her eyes across the men then drolly commented, 'Well, this explains why all of our bread is missing. What are they doing here?' she asked.

'Don't worry, they won't be here long,' Damien replied, still looking at Danny. 'Go back into the house and let me handle this.'

Nicki began to walk away, then stopped and coolly gave them an ultimatum before she exited, 'Please leave my property before breakfast tomorrow or I will tell the police,' she said.

Nikki was not going to risk their stable lives by helping so-called criminals of any kind and was not going to be compromised by anyone, no matter what Damien would say.

For the next few hours, all six men talked through what may lay ahead of them. The only firm conclusion they agreed on was that Damien would give them the horses they needed on the basis that they would be gone by the time Nicki had said.

Damien left the men just before midnight to return to his wife inside their home. The boys made their beds upon loose hay bales and old blankets and soon silence would echo through the air as the moon's gleam shone through the windows of the barn, the stillness only broken by the whispering prayers reciting out of Barny's mouth.

Tom was left to bunk with the lads, he had nowhere else to go. His wife had taken his children and left to her parent's place after blaming him for losing their home to the Re-po Squad. Tom had met Damien down in Graceville and after hearing his plight; Damien, who had known Tom for as long as Danny, offered him shelter and food until he could get back on his feet up again; however, the problems that Tom faced was about to look like a little storm in a teacup compared to what lay ahead. For, unbeknown to him, he was about to be unwittingly sucked into the whirlwind that would become Danny Pruitt.

Chapter 8

It was early morning, just a hint of daylight was beginning to appear, signalling the start to a new day, when the clinkering of metal stirrups awakened Danny.

'What are ya doing?' he asked, rubbing his tired eyes.

'We're leaving, Danny,' said Ricky.

His friends had just finished saddling up their horses. Ricky, Barny and Harry had decided late last night that they would make an early morning dash towards the city. They didn't want to be shot at again; they didn't want to be arrested and they sure as hell didn't want to hide away in the mountains living like some wild animal.

They explained their edgy feelings, which Danny understood completely. He knew they had done more than enough in helping him and thanked them accordingly. It was a tough decision for the lads, to leave Danny in the position he was in, it hurt them immensely.

'Come with us,' they collectively said.

'Thanks, but no thanks. I have to get in contact with Greta somehow before I do anything.'

The boys could see that he missed his family terribly as he spoke about them. They had no immediate family to tie them down like Danny did, part of which was why they came to Graceville in the first place, a decision they were now deeply regretting.

'Which way are ya going?' Danny asked.

'We're heading northwest up along old Tangiloo road, past the junction and up to Lake Yalumba; from there, we'll follow the Queens River down,' Ricky summarised.

The Queens River flowed down from the next mountain range over to the west. If followed downstream it would take you through to the north-eastern suburbs of Marlboro. It was the route the men found to be the most attractive to them, it would keep attention away from themselves and although it would be the longest way home for them, there was no doubt in their minds that it would be the safest, as they hoped there would be little local police presence in that direction if any.

The pre-dawn conversation awoke Tom and before he could get his faculties together, Danny was bombarding him with questions and demands.

'You're taking the long way around, aren't they, Tom,' Danny asserted. 'Cut through where the old timber mill is, you'll save nearly an hour, Tom will take you there, won't ya, Tom.'

Tom only just understood what Danny was saying, he was still half asleep. Danny had to repeat what he was suggesting and was hurrying up Tom to get going and show his mates where the old timber mill was situated.

Tom didn't want to get involved. 'Why don't you take them?' he replied.

'I've got no time, I can't waste a two-hour round trip, I'm heading into Kensington to the cascades until I can work out what I'm going to do, I've got to get out of here,' Danny responded forcefully to a now wide-awake Tom.

'Alright, but that's as far as I'm going to take 'em—to the mill and that's it.'

The men quickly gathered their belongings and were heading off. Harry and Barny with their own horses who had recovered sufficiently enough; Ricky had to take one of Damien's as his horse was still lame from yesterday's expedition.

The boys were greatly apprehensive in their goodbyes. They didn't want to leave him in these circumstances, but they had to protect their own self-interests and again sympathetically explained their sentiments.

Danny brushed it off, after all, it was him who put them in this situation in the first place and duly respected their troubled sentiments.

'Don't worry about me, I'll be alright' he determinedly said. 'You just get the hell out of here and I will see you downstairs.'

The boys didn't know exactly what he meant by downstairs; they didn't want to know. It was an endearing saying that Danny often used when parting ways with friends. He would often say things that people couldn't fully comprehend because of his offbeat humour and hidden nerves. Although most would have some inkling as to what he was saying, over time they knew best not ask what his real thoughts were because sometimes clarifying what he was saying simply just scared the crap out of them.

The trio didn't push him on this one as Danny reached up to the men now on horseback and shook their hands firmly. Without saying another word, he nodded his head, slowly turned away and let the boys ride out of sight.

Half an hour had passed since Tom and the men had left, the sun was slowly rising over the ranges in the East and after giving himself a quick wash from the water trough that sat next to the stables, Danny had his horse all saddled up and ready to leave Damien's property.

Struggling to rein in his new ride, he casually rode up to Damien's front door to be met by his tall lanky friend. Danny thanked him for his help and then pulled out a letter from one of the deep pockets in his jacket.

'What's this?' Damien inquired, as he held out his hand to accept it.

Danny's voice was full of sincerity. 'I've just written a letter to Greta, I want you to give it to her, it's just to explain what's gone on with me.'

'No worries, I'll try and get it to her today,' Damien confidently replied.

'I've told her to reply to me, so I need a big favour from you.'

'What's that?'

'I need you to hang around and get her reply then get it back to me. There's an old rotten hollow log near Tambourine bridge on Syrian creek road. Do you know where that is?'

'Yeah, pretty much,' Damien nodded.

'The logs about ten meters past the bridge on the south side of the road lying about 20 meters in, put the letter in the log and I will try and get there sometime tomorrow to pick it up, I just need to hear from her, do you know what I mean?' Danny pleaded.

Damien had no hesitation in helping him out; he said he would do his best and try and get the letter there as soon as he could.

He wished him luck and told him to take care of himself, but before Danny could exit through the gates of the property, Damien's partner came running at him with a bag in one hand.

'Here,' she said, handing the calico shopping bag over. 'Since you and your friends took a liking to my homemade bread, I thought you might like some more,' Nikki stated drolly.

She was up as early as the lads were, baking up some more bread so Danny wouldn't leave hungry. She didn't really know Danny that well but took on board what Damien had said about him in the past and knew him to be a good-hearted person. Although she wanted him off her land, she also wanted him to leave with no hard feelings.

Danny peered into the bag to see it contained at least a dozen bread rolls, all with different spreads, much to his delight, and thanked her that they wouldn't go to waste. As Danny proceeded to leave with a nod of gratitude on his newly acquired horse, he heard Nikki's voice from behind.

'Good luck, Danny Pruitt, you're going to need it.'

Danny didn't respond, he didn't even turn around; he just mumbled to himself that he needed more than luck to get him out of this mess, nothing short of a miracle he whispered under his breath. He moved away at a slow canter before extending into a steady gallop as he disappeared through the adjacent paddocks leading into the forest.

He was heading into Kensington National Park, a group of mountain ranges that he knew well and visited often. To the North of Graceville, the ranges took in over 50,000 hectares of native forests with the Kensington National Park being in the middle of them with the Tangiloo state forest to the West and the Black Forest further to the North and East. The mountains still gave employment to locals through limestone mining and commercial logging; however, it wasn't done the way they grew up with.

The workers weren't left with anything in the way of machinery to make their jobs easier. They compromised as best they could with what was left over, but most of the work was performed the old fashion way, with shovel or pick, or using the strength of bullocks or horsepower on newly laid snig tracks. It was hard labour for little reward, but the workers dare not complain if they wanted to feed their families. They had to find work somewhere and the small mining and logging companies were some of the few industries left in the area.

Danny loved the area, especially where he was heading to hold up for a day or two until he heard from Greta. He took the gravel and dirt road of Syrian creek, which log trucks, 4-wheel drive enthusiasts, trail bike riders and tourists used years before. It was a wide road that was surrounded by tall native eucalypt forests mingling in with all the wattles and giant tree ferns. It was going to take him a few hours riding at a steady pace to reach his destination near the Cascades, maybe even longer if the annoying characteristics of his new ride was anything to go by.

The Cascades was a collection of waterfalls that came down the Kensington River deep in the heart of the National Park. The waterfalls fell over 35 meters in height from the top of the falls to the bottom, cascading its way over smooth bluestone and granite rocks, which displayed a spectacular view from any point you wished to see it from.

Any spare time Danny had while in the area would always be spent at the waterfalls edge. He loved the tranquil sound of the rushing water and in times gone by would often sit and stare into nature for hours at a time. Across the old walking bridge, which crossed the river midway down the falls, a walking track commenced to take you along a 15 km walk through the forest running parallel to the river down to designated camping sites which used to be heavily populated in the good old days. Tourists and campers would pack the area in its heyday, but as it was with a lot of things these days, people from the city found it hard to find the time or transport to get away and observe the beauty this area had to offer.

Not far off the now overgrown walking track lay two caves embedded into the mountain side where Danny was planning to hold up. It offered plenty of shelter, but more importantly it offered a whole lot of privacy. Hardly anyone knew they existed, even the bush walkers who traipsed through these parts knew nothing of its existence. Danny had only found out about them through pure luck when he decided to go for a stroll through the virgin bush. It was on one of his lone winters visits a year before the world degenerated and as there was no logging allowed in the National Park, private places like this were a lot harder to find than in other areas. Danny surmised it would be the perfect hide out to gather his thoughts and try and decide what his next move would be.

Nearly two hours had passed since he had left from his overnight stay as the morning sun rose above. It was the first time he was alone since the shootings and the reality of the situation began to weigh heavily. He had no one to talk too; no one else to think about. For the first time, the stress had sunk in of what he had done, especially towards Greta and his sons. He had let her down tragically and was beginning to think she would never forgive him for what had happened. There was no way he would get her back; his life was ruined he was cursing to himself. The torrent of emotions was drenching as the pace on his horse began to decrease.

He soon arrived at Tambourine Bridge to check the old hollow log he had told Damien about; it was still there the way he visualised. He decided to give his tired and sore body a rest, particularly his backside. It was the most time ever he had spent horseback riding in consecutive days without a decent break and the constant rigorous riding was taking its toll.

He sat upstream of the little creek that flowed under the bridge to have one of the rolls that Nikki had given him. Looking around at the peaceful forest surroundings, he took his jacket off and splashed some pristine fresh water over his face and head and took a couple of deep breaths to gather his composure. An echidna waddled past nearby on its daily routines, clawing and rummaging at the forest floor as it went. He could hear the native bird life darting in out of the tree canopy above, from the pinging of the bellbirds to the squawking and chirps of the rosellas and King Parrots.

Each time Danny breathed in, he could smell the aromas of the forest. The smell of the abundance of eucalypts was dominant, the damp, mossy and earthy smell of the forest floor would not go unnoticed to his senses also. He exhaled a large breath and noticed his new equine partner had ventured to the water's edge.

'What are you doing, did I say you could have a drink,' he mused angrily as it lowered its neck to the shallow stream.

He wasn't in a good mood towards the big black gelding. He stood a tad under 17 hands and Damien warned him the night before that he had a bit of an attitude problem. He loved to thrash his head from side to side and would always try to outthink his rider, and Danny, not being the most experience rider was slowly but surely losing his temper with him. His arms were sore from fighting the reins from the moment he had left Damien's; however, his friend did assure him that this was the strongest, fastest and most durable horse he had ever put a saddle over.

Danny didn't even know the horse's name, much to his disgust, and for the next ten minutes was trying to make up one to call it.

Asshole, pig head and mucus were examples of a host of not so flattering titles he was trying to label him with. Scarface was another one, referring to an old sewn up gash the horse had received to his head from a previous paddock accident.

Danny's mood was beginning to change. He was getting a lot of amusement from the suggestive names the horse was receiving. A smile was back on his face, he shared a bread roll with the strong-willed beast and though he didn't know it then, the big black gelding was to become one of his greatest assets in times ahead. He never did name it properly; he called it a myriad of things, mostly derogatory, but in the end, it didn't matter.

As the days rolled on Danny would on many occasions lose his temper with him, but when it came to ask the horse to do the extraordinary, the big black gelding would always respond in full, and for the first time in his life, Danny would eventually, somewhat, become attached to an animal that was bigger than him.

Rest time was over; he had spent more than enough time taking in all the serene sounds of the bush and acquainting himself with his new partner and decided to move on towards the Cascades, at least another hour away, but just as he jumped aboard big black, who thrashed to the side to unbalance him, Danny had to dismount him in a hurry.

The tranquillity by was broken by the sound of thundering hooves echoing down the dirt road, closing at every second.

Danny was about twenty meters off the road nestled away in the bush. He grabbed one of his handguns in fear and back pedalled behind one of the massive Mountain Ash trees. He poked his head around to see if he could get a closer look at the riders. They rumbled past at full tilt, four men on a mission. He looked sternly again, his heart rate steadied, it was no enemy or unknown persons, it was the four men he left behind this morning.

To his surprise and pleasure, Barny, Ricky, Harry and Tom were rapidly making their way along the road. Danny was curious to say the least, *what are they doing here?* What made them come back? but the thought that crossed Danny's mind that worried him the most was what were they riding from.

He remounted big black, falling off at the first attempt as the horse swung to the left. A few swear words later and he was atop. He began to ride hard to try and catch up with his buddies, only then realising the power he had underneath him. It was the first time he had asked his newfound horse the question as to how fast can you go. He rode low in the saddle and before he knew it, he was right up the behind of his stampeding friends. It was the fastest he had ever travelled on horseback. It was exhilarating *and* scary, in fact, he was going that hard he was struggling to pull the damn horse up. He went straight past the men before the four could get a handle on who was coming at them from the rear.

The men were stopped in their tracks, they swung their horses around and watched with open mouths as Danny went whizzing by them. They were glad to see him; after all, they had come to find him. But they couldn't tell him why they were there because Danny couldn't control his horse. He was yelling at big black to stop, but the vivacious steed was in a mind of his own, reefing and pulling, ignoring all of Danny's orders as he swung around in circles and tried to sprint even further down the forest road.

'Whoa boy, whoa boy,' Danny coaxed him.

He grabbed the reins tight and tried to pull the horse up, but still big black wanted to continue.

'Stop, you fuckin mongrel or I'll shoot ya!' he yelled.

He tried everything he thought would work, ripping tightly at the reins, turning them side to side, grabbing and pulling the horse by its mane, he even punched the horse on the top of his head. The boys were looking at each other in amazement as they steadily rode behind, not knowing whether to sit there and laugh, or get over and give their friend a much-needed hand. However, before they made up their minds what to do, on its own accord, big black finally came to a halt, much to the angst of the scared rider on top. Again, Danny's lack of horsemanship was exposed.

He immediately leapt from the horse and gave it a tirade of abuse as the lads rode closer, astonished and mystified as to what was going on in the private love-hate relationship that Danny had just formed.

The men were trying to calm Danny down; They wanted to explain to him what they were doing there. Danny on the other hand, was too busy telling them about this wild nutcase of an animal that Damien had given him.

Minutes went by until Ricky screamed at Danny to shut up so they could get his attention.

They finally calmed their friend down and began to explain that they were only an hour into their journey and had reached behind the old mill when they noticed a group of men on horseback coming at them from the opposite direction. They weren't too sure as to whether they were policemen or not, they couldn't get a positive on them. The group consisted of about a dozen men, and for the boys to get to where they were going, they would have to pass straight by them through the clearing. They hit the panic button; they couldn't risk a confrontation no matter who they were, so decided to retreat to where they came from. They remembered where Danny said he was going and with the help of Tom's directions they decided to find him and hook up with him again.

Ricky, Barny and Harry's knowledge of the area was almost nil and, in their wisdom, thought if they had any chance of getting out of the region safely, Danny could show them the way, and without him they would either get lost in the mountains or ride directly into the waiting hands of the law. The lads were sure they hadn't been seen and told Danny so after he inquired about the possibility of them being followed.

Danny told his three buddies where he was going, but concerned for Tom's wellbeing, asked what he was going to do. 'You don't belong here,' he stated 'I would only make your life a lot worse if you stayed,' he continued to counsel.

Tom didn't know what he wanted to do, he had nothing to go back to in Graceville, his family had left him, he had no close friend to call on other than Damien, and so after some tough deliberation decided to stay and ride with them for the time being. He loved the area almost as much as Danny did and assumed he could leave anytime he wanted to, but curiosity was getting the better of him, and he wanted to be with the boys a bit longer yet. Danny was surprised, he thought Tom would have parted the first chance he had, being a man who liked to keep his tail clean. But he couldn't make him leave, other than to physically kick him out, so the boys reluctantly accepted him into their midst.

As the lads' trials and tribulations were occurring throughout the morning, unbeknown to them, the net was tightening around them. Within a couple of hours of Danny leaving Damien's, Dane and his posse had ascended on his property. With Karl's expertise, they had followed the boy's tracks down from the hut all the way to the entrance of the gates. Dane knew that Danny and Damien were mates; he knew whose property it was and continued through the gates to see if they could find some answers to Danny's whereabouts.

Damien was saddling his horse up to make the trip to down to Graceville and try and find Greta to hand over Danny's letter as Dane and his men approached.

The sergeant dismounted off his horse with the other men. Damien politely asked if he could help them with anything, as Nikki watched on from the front porch of her house. They knew Dane was a cop, Damien had met him a few times through Danny and he and his partner also knew what he was doing there.

'Damien, isn't it?' Dane asked as he shook his hand.

'That's right, and you're Dane Grainger, aren't you?'

'Yeah, and these are my friends,' Dane said. The handshakes did a full circle as introductions were made. Making a point that Ryan was Danny's brother-in-law.

'We're looking for Danny,' Dane announced. 'I don't know if you've heard anything, but he's gotten himself in a bit of trouble and we need to find him, have you seen him at all recently?'

'I was down in Graceville yesterday and heard the Minister's statement. I know what's going on with him,' Damien said, covering his nerves.

Dane and Damien were continuing with their conversation about the circumstances surrounding Danny's involvement in the shootings when Damien noticed both Karl and Ryan had drifted away, then peering into his stables.

'Hey, what are you doing?' he objected, knowing they might catch a glimpse of Danny's horse still in his stable.

'Sorry mate. Just having a look around. You've got a great setup here,' they admired.

Dane was positive that Danny was there at some time and stressed to Damien that they must find him for his own safety, but Damien wouldn't concede that he was there. Nikki joined her partner by his side and told the men that she and Damien had a busy day ahead of them and if it was alright by them, they would like get on with their day.

Dane was getting more frustrated by the second; he wasn't getting the answers he wanted and was about to lay down the law to the now edgy couple when he noticed a nod from Ryan. Dane wanted to grill Damien more, but relented to his mate's gesture and remounted his horse after Ryan had a whisper into his ear. They abruptly parted company but not before Dane warned him if they knew anything at all to report it to Inspector Vaccaro for their own sake.

'Danny's horse is in the stables,' Ryan informed Dane when they exited the gates of the property.

'It's got fresh bandages around one of its legs. It's gotta be the one that's badly injured,' Karl added.

'Are you sure it's Danny's?' Dane questioned.

'It's got his rego numbers on it,' Kane said.

Both Ryan and Karl had ridden with Danny many a time and knew his horse distinctly, and its registration number that was branded on its hindquarters.

The men had the proof that Danny was there, and with the short time that Ryan and Karl had to look around they saw no sign that he or his buddies were still at the property hiding away. There was no gear or saddles lying around the barn or stables and with some empty horse boxes, along with the mare that Damien was saddling up, it was obvious to them that the lads had already moved on, and in Danny's case, on a different horse altogether.

Dane and the men stopped outside the gates of to reassess their game plan. They had no idea which direction Danny or his buddies had gone. It was difficult for Karl to pick up any tracks. There were a multitude of fresh hoof marks heading in and out of the property on the dirt driveway, also making it difficult was the bitumen road that led into it. Anyone could ride along it for miles without being detected other than the manure the horse would leave behind. They would only be guessing if they were to try follow what they thought was a lead, after all, they didn't even know what type of horse Danny was riding now.

As the men were trying to get into the mind of Danny, attempting to guess his whereabouts or his next move, Damien casually rode past on his way to Graceville. Dane decided to give it one last shot in trying to get some information from him.

'Stop!' he yelled as he moved his horse closer.

'Listen! Danny and his friend's lives are in real danger. I can't tell you why but it's the way it is. If you were a real friend, you better tell me what you know,' Dane stressed.

Damien was sceptical at first, but as Dane pressed, he could see that he was genuinely concerned for Danny. He also knew that the three were solid friends of his. He gave it deep thought; he was caught between a rock and a hard place. Do I give up a friend who entrusted me or do take the word of another ally of him and help try and save his hide. He turned his horse around and with a nervous sigh, not knowing if he was doing the right thing subtly said.

'You might want to try the old scenic reserve inside Kensington.'

It was the only information that he gave as he rode off, but it was more than enough for the hunt to go on.

Dane's posse immediately made their way to the dust and gravel of Syrian Creek Road; about a steady 10-minute ride from Damien's property off Mason creeks road. Dane knew exactly where the scenic reserve was situated and began to ride at a solid pace along the road hoping Karl would pick up his tracks along the way. They estimated they would be only a couple of hours behind him and if they moved quickly, they might be able to catch up with him by mid-afternoon if luck was on their side.

Meanwhile, deep in the forest, Danny was leading the way as the now gang of five were nearing their destination. He blabbered away about the Cascades beauty and how they would love it there, not knowing that Dane and his crew were making inroads into the gap between them.

Danny's thoughts of Greta had waned as he tried to impress his mates with the picturesque scene he had set for them, however, if Greta was feeling she was already living through a nightmare, it was about to take another turn for the worse.

It was mid-morning, the children were playing outside, Greta enjoyed a quiet cup of tea with Sarah, trying to relax her mind. The worry for Danny was almost at a level where she could cope no more. The women were trying to put a smile on each other's face, trying to distract their thoughts away when they heard a loud knock on the door, a panicked voice followed.

'Greta, Greta, are you there?' the voice yelled.

Both Sarah and Greta raced to the door to see Kate with a distraught look upon her face. Kate was Ryan's wife, but also the much-cherished younger sister of Danny and loved sister-in-law of Greta. Kate already knew about the events that had taken place from what Ryan had told her before he left and was devasted on hearing the news on her older brother. She held Danny up on a giant pedestal and loved him dearly. She adored and admired him and would always ask his advice on just about everything she did.

She was three years Danny's junior with similar coloured light brown hair, which she would often dye dark red tints through, as it was today. She had a lightly framed body and soft blue eyes and was one of the few who transitioned from automobile to horseback with ease as she was a keen rider beforehand. Kate thought she would do the right thing by Greta and offer her some comfort and reassuring. Thinking she was still at her home, she decided to pay her a visit. On arriving at the top of Danny and Greta's property, all she could see was total anarchy.

On the order of Minister Johnston, the re-po squad had paid an early morning visit to the Pruitt's household. Danny was still in front on his payments, albeit by a small margin, but enough to cover him through the next month or so; however, the Minister still gave the go-ahead to trash the place, and trash it they did.

Johnston was adamant that the whole saga would be over sooner than later, it was the reasoning behind yesterday's statement. It made Danny out as a cold-blooded murderer, trying to get the sympathy vote of the public, knowing that Danny would never have the opportunity to defend himself, and since he still had received no news on the newly dubbed outlaw, he decided to act. His expectations on the whole issue regarding Pruitt was that the matter should have been dead and buried by now, literally, and no one would care if a murderer's house was re-possessed.

He had never met Danny Pruitt, never knew of his existence, but he was already becoming the Minister's nemesis in more ways than one and in his frustration ordered the re-possession of Pruitt's property knowing full well it was illegal to do so.

Kate couldn't believe her eyes; just about everything Danny and Greta owned had either been destroyed or left to blow around in the wind. Clothes, photographs, linen, anything and everything they owned, strewn across the property as far as the eye could see.

Kate raced down the steps towards the front door. 'Greta, Greta!' she yelled in search of her.

'She's not here. No one's home,' she was told by a woman looking on at the chaos.

The Pruitts' belongings were still being looted by the desperate and greedy onlookers who had made their way up on hearing the news. But not before members of the balaclava clad Re-po squad had already claimed their own booty.

Kate was alone, she was angered and shocked with what she was witnessing. She was yelling at the mob to stop, to show some compassion. No one would listen. It was like a frenzy, people grabbing anything they could find and running off with it, completely ignoring her angry pleas, while police stood back and laughed with conniving comments. Being outnumbered and alone, Kate despairingly decided it was a futile exercise in trying to stop the looting. She asked the lady stranger if she knew where Greta was and upon being told, charged down to Sarah's house to alert Greta before she would lose everything she owned.

'Oh Greta, thank god you're here,' Kate gasped, 'You've got to get back home, the Re-po squad's been.'

Kate tried to catch her breath.

Greta didn't understand what she was saying. Kate forced herself to calmness and explained the situation clearer. Sarah immediately raced through the house looking for her husband.

'Corey, Corey!' she yelled.

He had just arrived in the backyard through a gate that backed onto a little alley way behind their property. 'Greta needs help,' she wailed. 'The re-po squad's been at her house.'

'Harness up the cart in the driveway. I'll ride up and meet you there,' he yelled at Greta and Sarah. 'Look after the children,' he politely yelled at his elderly neighbours who were overhearing the commotion.

Before he had a chance to unsaddle his horse, he was back atop of it and furiously riding to the Pruitts' property with Kate beside him, passing the policemen that were trying to be inconspicuous in the stakeout of his home, looking for any signs if Danny were brazen enough to try and contact his wife.

It was the first time Greta had ventured outside since she began her stay at Sarah's, and it was feeling like the longest twenty-minute journey of her life. She had no idea what to expect and on arriving she was totally mortified. Sarah halted her horse then Greta quickly jumped out from the seat of the cart. She stood silently looking down on her property in disbelief.

People were still rifling through their belongings, Corey grabbing and chasing down those who were trying to ride or run off with possessions, ripping them from their grasp. Piece by piece he tried to get back what he could—clothing, tools, children's toys. One overzealous couple were even trying to load a bed onto their own run-down rickety cart.

Two police had remained at the carnage. With eyes of rage, Greta approached them.

'How could you let this happen!' she roared.

She knew the face of one of them. She had seen him before with Danny on the odd occasion.

'You wouldn't be standing there if Danny were here,' she scolded. 'You're just a coward, that's all you are.'

There was no response from the embarrassed and deadpanned officer, he looked away with his cowering partner, unwilling to look Greta in the eyes.

She slowly made her way towards the house, step by step down the pebbled pathway. She pushed her door open; books were laying across the entrance floor, randomly dislodged from their shelves. A glass framed picture of her late parents lay cracked, she picked it up and held it to her heart. She walked through her loungeroom, furniture broken and missing.

Out onto the rear decking, she ambled in numbness, her pot plants smashed to pieces and deck chairs gone. She rushed to her bedroom, to see only the frame of her bed remaining. Her wardrobe had been pillaged, her bedside drawers open and removed, her personal belongings stolen. Tears of shock began to fall from her trembling body. She walked outside, stunned with a look of blankness.

Greta stopped then knelt, picking up a shredded piece of clothing. With shaking hands, she recognised it as the remains of her beautiful black fleecy laced up blouse that Danny had bought her. It had been torn apart in the wild rummage as the remnants melted into her clasping fingers. Everywhere she looked, just about everything she owned had either been stolen or tampered with. A jewellery box lay open, its contents gone, including family heirlooms that had meant so much to her.

Family photographs had been trampled over; clothes that weren't stolen lay around the property in all directions, Danny's favourite recliner chair lay in ruins in the yard where the Devlin Brothers took their last breath, smashed to pieces by the Re-po squad.

Greta fell to her knees again, holding the ripped clothing to her face, the sobbing began uncontrollably, she was at breaking point, and she could take no more.

She was horrified and humiliated, never before had anyone came close to treating her in this manner. Her soul had been shattered.

If ever she needed her husband by her side, to tell her everything would be all right and give her that dependable embrace she always got, the time was now. But no hug would come this time, no reassuring, no words of strength or wisdom, not today, not tonight, maybe not ever again she wept inside her heart.

She looked up into the heavens and begged silently.

'Where are you, Danny, come back to me, please, please come back, I need you,' she repeated as the tears rolled down her cheeks and onto the dress she had showed to Danny in all her glory that fateful Sunday morning.

She looked around to see several strangers staring at her raw emotional display.

'Go away!' she screamed. 'Leave me alone!' She wanted to suffer privately.

Seeing she was close to almost fainting in distress, Sarah and Kate wrapped their arms around her and started to lead her to the cart and take her away from the nightmare. She could hardly gather the strength to walk; not only had this destroyed her dignity, it had destroyed any faith she had left in society itself.

All she ever did in her life was give, whether it be as a school teacher, in the church where she was loved so much, or to family and friends, and to have this bestowed upon her was to cut deeply into the optimistic outlook she always had on life. She had never seen first-hand what the Re-po was capable of. Of course, she had heard about them and their ruthful tactics. Danny hated them immensely; heartbreakingly for Greta, never in her worst nightmare did she think the first time she would come across them would be at the expense of her own virtues.

Chapter 9

'Anybody home?' he shouted.

Corey walked to the front door of the Pruitts' house. He was inside trying to decide what to take back to Greta. He had a fair idea what meant the most to her and slowly packed those together, photographs, paintings and any clothing that remained. It had been almost an hour since the women had left when he heard a raised voice from outside.

Damien was standing there with a staggered look upon his face. He too thought that Greta would still be at home.

'Can I help you?' Corey asked.

'I'm Damien, Danny's mate. You're Corey, aren't you?'

'Yeah, it's been a while, good to see you again.'

'What the hell went on here?' Damien asked, stunned as he peered over the property.

Corey emotionally explained what had transpired through the morning. After taking in the entire horror story that Corey had divulged, Damien asked where Greta was as he had something important to give to her.

'It's going to have to wait, mate, Greta's not here,' Corey said as he began to load her possessions into bags.

'I think she would want what I've got,' Damien reiterated.

'And what's that,' Corey replied.

'Just take me to where Greta is, and I'll hand it over to her,' Damien politely said.

'I'm not taking you anywhere until you tell me what it is that's so important,' said Corey who was getting agitated at Damien's stance.

Damien looked around to see if anyone was close by and seeing the coast was clear quietly admitted that he had a letter from Danny. Corey was confused.

'What do ya mean?' he asked.

'Danny and his friends were at my place last night. He gave me a letter to hand over to Greta,' Damien confided.

Corey couldn't believe it; it was the first sign of anything about Danny since Sunday. He excitedly inquired more before demanding that Damien give him the letter.

'Sorry mate, but Danny specifically told me hang around and get a reply from her,' he argued.

Corey accepted his standpoint. He invited him to follow back to his house.

Corey passed friends who were helping with gathering and loading the Pruitts' possessions.

'I'm going to have to leave it with you. Something important has come up. Can you bring everything down to my place and I'll meet you there later?' he told the helpers who replied with support.

Corey and Damien hurried down along the highway riding at near full pace. They turned left before the main street, across the parklands, then up side streets and before too long arrived at Corey's home in the neighbourly cul-de-sac.

'If the coppers ask what you're doing here, just say you're visiting, okay?' Corey warned as he nodded to where the two policemen were watching over the premises.

On dismounting from their horses in the front yard, Corey burst inside the front door with Damien following.

'Where's Greta?' he asked Sarah who was taking time out alone relaxing on the sofa.

'Out on the back veranda.'

Greta was staring into space as the children innocently played below her. She was still in a state of shock, trying to comprehend what was happening to her life when Corey excitedly confronted her. He sat next to her and calmly gained her attention.

'I've got some good news for you.'

'What, what are you talking about?' Greta enquired.

'Damien's got a letter for you. It's from Danny, he was up at Damien's last night,' he softly told her with a smile on his face, glad he was the messenger of good news.

Greta was immediately awoken from her self-imposed living coma. She stood, her body shaking with anticipation of what was in the letter.

She looked at Damien and rapidly started to fire questions at him. How is he? Where is he? Is he hurt? Damien pulled the letter from his pants pocket and handed it to Greta. He told her that Danny was a little scared and tired but otherwise, he seemed to be himself and advised that the letter will probably tell her all she needs to know.

Greta hastily made her way into the kitchen, sat down and opened the letter. Corey, Sarah and Kate, who had now joined Greta in the kitchen continued to ask Damien what he knew on Danny. Damien had to keep up a veil of secrecy concerning what he knew on him; he had been requested to do so by him and asked his stunned audience to respect the instruction given . He did however give them some information regarding Danny's health and the truth of what had happened in the shootings.

The conversation continued outside on the veranda while Greta was left alone to read the note.

Her hands were shaking, she struggled to keep the piece of paper steady and after a couple of nervous deep breaths, started to read as she sat at the kitchen table.

To my beautiful Greta,

I guess you probably heard what happened at home and I am so sorry to put you through this. You know I love you very much and would never do anything to harm you or the kids in any way. I am all right and hope you are too, I have no injuries, but I am very tired. I don't know what to do. If I come home, I will go to jail and lose you forever, I would rather die than let that happen, but I know in my heart we will be together again. I don't know how long it will take, but you must believe that we will be together again. I just need time to think things through. I will get myself out of this madness somehow, trust me.

You are the most beautiful and bravest woman I have ever met so I need you to be strong for Daniel and Darcy's sake. I don't know what will come of this, so I need you to reply to me and let me know how you are and what you're feeling. If you want me to give myself up, I will. I am heading into Kensington for the time being. I know I will be safe there until I hear from you next. Damien will drop off your reply.

About the shootings, don't listen to what they're saying, I know about the statement and it's all lies. You know I couldn't shoot anyone like they're saying.

The Devlin brothers kept at me, they shot our lamb, made remarks about you and threatened our home. I tried to stop Rosco shooting and the gun went off accidentally, then the little asshole Billy was going to shoot me, so I shot him. It was pure self-defence, I didn't know what to do, I tried to find you at the market, but the coppers already had you.

I blame them for what I have done and still have my conscience, but as you know, the law won't have a bar of my side of the story. Anything else I have done was simply to stay alive. I know I have done the wrong thing and left you and the kids alone, but you must keep the faith and believe that we will be together soon. I hope you are safe and being looked after. Stay strong, babe, and give my boys a big hug. Thinking of and loving you always. Danny.

Greta laid the letter down on the table, tears rolled down her cheeks. She was delighted and satisfied that Danny was safe but felt helpless and frightened for him.

'Is everything alright?' asked Sarah when she entered the kitchen. Greta handed the letter to her. She too was anxious and desperate to know what Danny had written. Greta nervously pranced around the kitchen looking for a pen and paper she could borrow to write a reply and yelled for Corey where he kept them as Sarah delved her eyes into the letter.

'In the second drawer down from the left,' he answered, pointing at the pine-lined drawers adjacent the sink.

'Thank you,' she softly replied through the window, this time with virtually the first smile upon her face since her nightmare began.

She was feeling better inside; at least she had some peace of mind of what happened to her husband and of his well-being. All she was pining for was some information, anything would do. To receive the letter was a godsend and couldn't have come at a better time.

With Greta's approval, Corey and Kate also read the letter after Sarah had finished. Greta didn't mind them reading it, they were all close friends and saw no harm in it, at least they could understand more of the wild predicament her family was in.

Damien had made his way to the front yard to give them some privacy and waited patiently until Greta had finished her letter. As she busily wrote away, Kate, with a determined look and folded arms, said she couldn't wait for Danny to get his hands on the people who did this to their property.

'Oh, they're gonna pay,' she warned,

Greta looked up from the table and turned to Kate immediately.

'There's no way I would tell Danny about what the Re-po squad has done to us. Danny will go off the deep end if he hears any of this. He's got enough to worry about; this would just make him angrier and more resentful than he already is. It would be like throwing petrol on a fire,' she roared at them. 'He can never find out,' she argued loudly.

'Danny should have the right to know,' Kate insisted.

She argued her point strongly, but no matter what she said, couldn't convince Greta to change her mind. All Greta wanted was a peaceful ending, to get her husband back in one piece. Not to make matters worse by seeking revenge that she argued would only intimidate those responsible even more.

Kate was disillusioned with Greta; she wanted her brother to know how the Re-po squad had reached a new low, how the coppers sat back and did nothing. The same blood that pumped through Danny's veins pumped through hers, and she would be damned if she was going to let these people get away with what they did. She wanted justice, and she was sure her older brother would sternly agree.

When Kate was helping Greta back at their property, a young teenage girl had approached her as they were about to leave. Greta knew nothing of it, and neither did Sarah. At the time Greta was so devastated and consumed with sorrow, she didn't notice anything around her. She was crying into Kate's lap and never raised her head to see what was happening around her, she was too ashamed to let people see her face.

The overweight girl was a nearby resident who was next to Greta's place as the Re-po squad and police arrived. She loved Greta dearly, she thought of her as a princess. Greta helped her with her schoolwork and would always give time to her whether she was busy or not and would always stop to ask how her life was going. Janice would sit next to her in church and would envy her every move and just like her own mother, made it her business to know about everything and everyone in Graceville. Greta was her idol, and it was like her own heart had been ripped out to see her princess the way she was.

She introduced herself to Kate and discretely handed over a piece of paper.

'What's this?' asked Kate.

'It's the names of the men I recognised,' the girl quietly replied.

'What men?' Kate then paused. 'You mean the men who did this?'

Young Janice nodded her head.

'Don't tell anyone about this, it's our little secret, okay?' said Kate quietly as she touched her on the shoulders while sticking the piece of paper in her jeans pocket.

Janice had seen the men arrive and stop nearly two hundred meters away from Danny and Greta's property in the vacant adjacent parklands. They hid themselves under their balaclavas behind the fence where the pine trees lined the property. Janice was below them picking some stems off the wild rose bushes that were in full bloom, trying to get a sticky beak at where the shootings took place when upon hearing the men arrive, ducked out of sight.

Janice ripped out a page of her diary she carried and jotted down the names of the men she knew. There were twelve men in the group, but she could only manage to identify seven of them. She had never seen the other five men before as several had their balaclavas already on. When everything had died down, she waited for her opportunity and handed the list over to Kate who was now passing the information onto Damien without the knowledge of Greta.

It was hurtful for Kate to deceive Greta. They were as close as sister in laws could be, but her stance was solid, and in her belief, Danny had every right to know what happened to his family despite what Greta thought best for her husband and children.

Kate made her way to the front deck; she took a quick minute and also wrote a short letter to her brother. She confronted Damien with it and imposed on him that Danny must receive the important missive at the same time as Greta's.

As Greta was struggling to put her feelings on paper, appealing to Sarah to help find the words she so desperately wanted Danny to hear, Damien, not knowing of the contents inside the envelope, promised Kate that he would do his best to get it to him, he knew he wasn't about to win any debate with his friend's demanding sister.

An hour was almost up for Greta and Damien couldn't wait any longer. He was getting more nervous and apprehensive as every minute ticked by. He had spent the last 10 or so minutes outside alone after Kate had left him to say goodbye to Greta, and all he wanted to do was to get back home to his own partner.

He walked inside and asked politely if Greta had finished. She stood up from the table she was behind and walked towards him, still wiping the tears from her cheeks. She folded the letter into an envelope and handed it to him.

Greta took his hand in a grateful gesture. 'Thank you for doing this,' she kindly said.

'I just hope everything turns out for the best,' Damien replied.

He nodded his head in respect and left for the trek back up Mason's Creek Road, nervously looking back over his shoulder on his travels to see if someone was following. It would be the longest trip he had ever made back up the winding mountain road.

Greta was as tired as she had ever been, and on the strong suggestions of her friends, she would lay down for the afternoon catching up on some very much needed sleep. It had been almost three days since she last got more than two hours kip at the one time. Greta would need all the sleep she could as the worry and torment that gripped her was not going to subside for a long while yet.

As she heavily slept away, not immersing from her slumber until mid-evening, Corey and Sarah helped off loading the carts that would sporadically arrive with the Pruitt's belongings throughout the late afternoon. In between, the couple would at times have heated arguments. Corey felt it was his duty to go and find Danny, to let him know personally what had happened to his wife, but Sarah wouldn't have a bar of it. She argued strongly that he was needed here. It would be foolish and irresponsible to leave her and Greta alone, not to mention the children, they both needed a man around them and to go into the mountains searching for Danny would only give them more worry and heartache.

Sarah would have her way and reaffirmed to him that if she knew Danny the way she did, there was no doubt that he would never allow Corey to leave them alone, he was doing the best thing for him by staying and looking after Greta and his sons.

As the sun began to lower in the evening, producing another dazzling sunset, Danny and the boys had already made themselves comfortable in the hidden caves. The entrance was big enough to allow their horses in, protecting them from being noticed on the outside.

Tom and Harry had already caught some fish out of the Kensington River below the cascades using their hand lines.

The river was teaming with native blackfish and brown trout and on an average day now and it would not take long to catch a decent haul. Most of the catch was the perfect pan size for the lads to cook. It was safe enough to start a fire and cook inside as the roofs of the caves were up to 15 metres from floor to ceiling in some parts with smooth limestone texture. It made an awesome but spooky sight when night fell when the little fire flicked reflections off it. The smoke would waft out through different sized ceiling holes that had formed above over the years of erosion, in turn bringing clean air into its confines.

The men were devouring their catch with great delight, joking and sharing conversation about their lives, throwing kudos at Tom, who had little canisters of salt and pepper packed away to give the fish some extra taste when Danny joined them down below in the sanctuary of the caves. He had been atop of them scouring an ever-cautious eye over the area looking for anyone coming their way. He was always vigilant, no matter where he was. Even when he was talking to any of the lads, he would always be looking side to side or casting an attentive ear to the surrounds. It was getting dark and Danny reasoned to himself that the coast was clear enough for them to feel safe for another night at least.

But if he felt he was a long way from anyone for the time being, he didn't count on the resilience and perseverance of Sgt Dane Grainger and the tracking skills of Karl Turner. Danny knew both men had those exact traits, but it never occurred to him that they would be anywhere near him, after all, he had no idea that they were part of the groups that were searching for him. Danny knew that the police would be hunting for him, that he had no doubts, but what he didn't know, was that his good mates were closing in on him at every step.

Dane and his men had set up camp by an old car park to the side of the road only a couple of kilometres up stream. Although they had made substantial inroads, it was not as much as they would have liked. Their horses needed a rest and feeling hungry themselves decided it was no point carrying on in the darkness that was about to set, but unbeknown to them, they would quietly camp only a stone's throw away from the caves that shielded Danny and the boys.

Dane was also unaware that John Pringle and his vengeful partners were again back in the hunt. They had stumbled and staggered their way over Mt St Lucia and across to Tangiloo feeling the worse for wear. Pringle was not in good spirits, he had done all his work in the confines and shelter of the big city, shielded by the surrounds of the concrete jungle and his few days in the bush were already driving him over the edge. He was far from coping with the mosquitos, the ants, the flies, the cobwebs, and he was looking for a good wash and bed for the night in Tangiloo.

After they had booked rooms for the night and washed up, they decided to have a quiet drink in the local tavern. The bar inside was in a small-roomed area as the tavern also doubled as a grocery store and if you listened carefully, you could hear every conversation that took place within its walls.

Three men were sitting on stools close by having a beer at the bar. Pringle and his men kept to themselves in a corner overlooking a glass enclosed balcony. The hunting group listened as one of the strangers engrossed his friends on how he saw a group of riders enter Syrian Creek Road in the morning, the local sergeant from Graceville being one of them. After listening in more on what the stranger was relaying, Pringle didn't have to be Einstein to work out that he was talking about Dane and his partners.

Pringle approached him, making up a story that they were looking for partners in the search that were similar to the ones he had described and coaxed more information out of him. He was left with no doubt as to who the stranger was describing.

It was the break Pringle was looking for, the stroke of luck that he needed. He had never quit on any assignment before and was looking forward to getting this one out of the way as soon as possible, to take his money and head back to the comforts of his own home back in the city.

Pringle and his men quietly left the bar and made their way to the cabin they had booked for the night just down the road from the tavern and planned their hunt for the runaways. They retrieved maps that were laying around the cabin and studied them intensely, from the main entry road into the forest, right down to old fire tracks. Pringle called on the advice of the older Devlin brothers who had insight to the area.

Pringle's confidence grew as he studied more of the maps and although he knew it wasn't going to be easy tracking Danny down in his own familiar territory, nevertheless, he was back in the game. Wanting to finish it as early as he could, he talked and laughed privately with his two colleagues on how Danny Pruitt's days were coming to an end.

Matt and Eddie Devlin had adjourned outside the cabin to share a bottle a whiskey, totally oblivious to Pringle's plan to kill their hunted prey. They were only there to help in the apprehension of the slayer of their brothers they were told, and although the thought had crossed their minds in taking justice the old fashion way, they both knew they could never bring themselves to do it. However, like it or not, they were going to find out the real intentions of the men they had ridden with, sooner rather than later.

Chapter 10

'What a bloody ripper,' Tom bragged. He had just caught the biggest trout he ever had out of the Kensington River. 'The boys are going to love me for this!' he congratulated himself.

He strung the fish onto a large stick with the rest of his catch. It was going to make a magnificent breakfast, Tom was thinking.

He didn't need the sleep the other four men desperately required and was up at the crack of dawn. He thought best not to disturb them and let them wake on their own accord. He fathomed the boys would be hungry as soon as they awoke and decided to impress them with a nice booty of fresh fish for breakfast.

Tom had been at water's edge for nearly an hour, enjoying the morning chirps and caws of the lyrebirds, rosellas and king parrots. He would raise his face to the sun piercing through the tall thick forest as it was dawning into another beautiful warm day and proceeded to make his way back through the bush towards the caves when he stopped to adjust the load he was carrying. He laid the fish down on the ground amongst the native grasses that swarmed the riverbanks and slung his little canvas tackle bag over his shoulders. He stood upright to continue the walk when he noticed the peaceful noises of the surrounding bush and river being disturbed by the sound of muffled human voices.

Tom quickly hid behind the nearest tree and listened intently to where the voices were coming from. He ducked down below some of the taller grasses and ferns and before too long could see a group of men on horseback in the distance. They were on the topside of the gully across the other side of the river and slowly making their way down Syrian Creek Road.

He couldn't get a positive identification through the forest on who they were, or what they were doing there for that matter. He concluded that he'd better get back to the caves as soon as possible to alert Danny and the boys.

Tom ran as quickly as he could, keeping as low as possible, stumbling and tripping on his way back to their hide out, all the time keeping an eagle eye above and left, watching the strangers appearing sporadically from behind the tall trees.

Tom lost sight of them as the road wound itself away from him. He raced up a slight hill, densely populated with tree fern and low thick shrubs nestled below the tall trees, then down and across to the entrance of the caves, all the time holding grimly onto his catch making sure he wouldn't lose it in his panic.

He rushed into the caves and threw his bag and fish down on the sandy floor.

'Danny! Wake up, wake up.' He forcefully nudged him.

'Shit Tom, what the hell's wrong?' Danny asked, not happy at being woken from his slumber.

'I've just spotted a group of blokes coming down the road.'

Danny didn't need to hear the details; he was up in a flash and raced past Tom, almost knocking him to the ground as the other boys hastily followed, being woken up by Tom's animated warning.

Danny dashed through the exit of the caves, around to the side and up the embankment until he reached the outside top and took cover behind some shrubs with his trusty sawn off .22 rifle.

'Go down and get my binoculars,' he calmly asked Harry who had followed him up.

Danny made himself more comfortable by leaning his back up against a granite boulder as Harry raced back down into the caves.

'Who is it?' Ricky asked, as he Barny and Tom took their positions behind other rocks and shrubs, trying to get a look at who might be coming their way.

'I will tell you in a minute,' Danny replied confidently as he waited for Harry to return with his binoculars.

Harry scrambled his way back to the top. The men had weapons drawn and pointed in the direction of the oncoming threat. Dane and his men were still on the other side of the cascades, atop on the road, not knowing which direction they should take when Ryan remembered that they were directly on the spot that Danny used to rave about. Ryan could now see the majestic fall of the river down over the rocks through the silhouetted light of the forest. He had been to that very location with Kate and Danny a long time ago and never forgot how Danny would tell him how much of a fantastic place it was for him. It was all coming back to him as he convincingly told Dane what he was thinking.

Dane absorbed Ryan's case in point and after a brief chat amongst the group decided that it wouldn't hurt their cause if they were to venture down the old worn walking track to have a closer inspection of what lay near the river.

As the men slowly and carefully made their way down the steep incline of the path, negotiating the protruding tree roots and boulders at the horses' feet then making their way to the foot bridge that crossed the river in two sections, unbeknown to them, their every step was being watched.

Several minutes of silence had elapsed since Danny had the aid of the binoculars.

'Come on, Danny, do you know who it fuckin is or not?' Ricky asked impatiently.

The boys could see that the group of riders were coming down the path but couldn't see clear enough through the trees as to whom it was, they were still too far away, and they were getting more edgy by the second.

'Well, I'll be stuffed,' Danny mused.

'For Christ's sake, Danny, what do ya fuckin see!' Ricky blasted under his breath.

The other men shook their heads, not amused at the way Danny was keeping them in the dark. He dropped the binoculars from his eyes and turned to look at his buddies and with a somewhat bewildering look on his face, engaged his frantic pals.

'It's Dane, and he's got my bloody brother-in-law with him, and Karl as well.'

'The copper who was with us the other night?' Barny asked, surprised.

'Yeah,' replied Danny.

'He's a good mate of yours though, isn't he?'

Danny nodded, lifted his binoculars to his eyes once more and commented that he didn't have a clue who the other two riders were. He watched his searching friends slowly make their way down towards the first of the old foot bridges that crossed the river when Ricky, taken by surprise, asked as to whom this other person called Karl was.

Danny looked at Ricky as the others listened in. 'He mixes with the same group as us,' he said. 'I've known him for about four years or so. He's a really nice guy. We go around his place for parties and barbecues and stuff. All his better mates reckon he's the best tracker around these parts so no wonder they found us so quick,' Danny informed with pride.

In times gone by, Danny and Ricky knew everything and everyone that came across each other's lives. From whom they drank with the night before to the girls they went out with. They were partners in crime as teenagers, literally. The two had their adolescence rebellious days, stealing cars, fighting and minor burglaries until the partnership came to an end when Ricky was caught, charged and then sentenced to a three-month stint in juvenile detention when he was 15 years of age.

Another six months of incarceration followed before he turned 18, all the while as Danny stayed free to go about his life, guilty on all accounts as his best friend, but never caught or charged. A situation that Danny often joked about, but one Ricky secretly held a deep resentment of.

They had kept many secrets from the past between themselves, but from the time the short war started, and the world's crisis set in, their reliance on one another dwindled as communication between the two was getting increasingly less frequent as time rolled on and it pissed each other off that they had another life without each other, Ricky more so. He was always wary of the new friends Danny would introduce him to over the years and hearing of Karl in the situation they were in, made him even more sceptical and somewhat jealous that Danny had gone on with his life and made good friendships away from him.

The way Ricky saw it over the past few days was that Danny had the answer to everything, and those answers were proven right on each occasion. What irked Ricky most of all was that Danny was making those calls without any consultation with him.

His own insecurities were coming to the fore over his own life. A life that had never been fulfilled by his own standards and every time he looked at Danny, with the lovely wife, the good job, the wise investments and the happy stable family, it ate away at him.

But when the world went into its downward spiral, Ricky thought that everyone around him, including Danny, would feel the same mental hardship that he had endured over the years. The broken hearts and the drug abuse, the loneliness and resentment, he had experienced it all. So, when his long-time friend shot those two police and had nowhere to go but call on him, Ricky was somewhat gratified that Danny for once in his life had to rely on him for some solitude and guidance.

But from the time Ricky and the lads had to make an about face to re-join Danny, from what did turn out to be members of the police force back on the other side of the timber mill behind Tangiloo, he knew then that the man he was trying to either compete with, impress or get away from, had influenced his life again.

Dane and his men had crossed the second foot bridge. It was made from hardwood sleepers, chicken wire spread across the floor for grip, with metal pole handrails on either side protected by strong gauge wire to stop little ones falling through the sides into the cascading river below. They huddled together to discuss what direction they should take next, whether they should continue up the walking track or head back up to the road. To them, there didn't seem to be any sign of recent movement around the area. Karl dismounted his horse to take better look of the surroundings. It didn't take him long to find something they could go on. A pile of horse dung lay further up the track, just to the side of the path which gave the men the confidence to continue their search a little longer.

The old walking track was no place for the faint hearted to ride on, particularly on the eastern side across the river bridge on which they travelled. It was terribly uneven, and you could only take your horse at a slow pace because of the protruding tree roots, fallen logs and rocks that lifted out of the surface. Along with the overhanging branches in which some stretched the entire width of the path, it made for difficult and slow progress.

The boys above them were getting nervous. They were now in earshot and were hoping like hell that the posse would retreat across the river. Danny and his friends were laying low behind large rocks on the grassy top of the caves about nine meters above and around thirty meters in distance with their weapons drawn. They weren't about to take any chances, they didn't know Sgt Dane and the rest of the men as Danny did and, in their mindset, he was a copper, and he was coming to arrest them.

Danny crept closer to the ledge overlooking where the men were gathered and saw that they were about to continue up the track. He wasn't about to let anyone come close to their hide out, especially Karl. To the normal eye it was nigh on impossible to get any hint that the caves existed from where the walking track laid, nevertheless, Danny knew if anyone could find them, it would be Karl. He could find a needle in a haystack if given half a sniff and Danny wasn't going to give him an opportunity. His hideout was important to him. He may need the sanctuary of the caves a lot more if things didn't take a turn for the better, and no one was going to find out about them.

The boys were sweating in anticipation, their breathing heavy, keeping in sync with the pounding of their hearts as they saw the men slowly make their way single file up the track with Karl leading.

Harry was about to lose control. Rampant shaking buzzed through his body as beads of nervous sweat dripped off his forehead and into his eyes.

'Shit, what are we gonna do, what are we gonna do?' he babbled. 'They're gonna get us, shit, shit,' he kept repeating.

Danny looked at him with a steely glare.

'Calm down. I'll take care of things,' he said with control.

Danny had to do something, and now. A further fifty meters around the next bend and the searching party would be out of sight and close to the entrance of the caves. Within seconds, they were passing almost directly underneath them. Danny positioned himself between two large boulders and lifted himself onto one knee, raised his rifle and took aim.

'What the hell ya doing?' Barny anxiously asked with bated breath. Harry and Tom looked on in disbelief.

'Just going to give them a scare,' came the calm reply from Danny.

He took aim ten feet ahead of the leading rider. He had been itching to shoot a bullet out of his rifle since he left Graceville, and this was as good as time as any, he thought.

The early morning serenity of the surrounding bush was awoken by the piercing sound of a bullet ricocheting off a small boulder that was targeted. All five riders below were shaken to the core in the tranquil setting. Ryan was the first to react. He was off his startled horse instantly. The other men quickly followed, taking cover behind anything they could see. The next minute seemed to take an eternity. The men below fearfully whispered to each other if they knew where the shot had come from as they looked up and around the surrounding ridges. None of them had any idea who had just put the fear of God into them.

Everything had returned to silence except for the rumbling of the cascading river when a voice echoed from behind the elevated ridge giving the pursuing party some stern advice.

'That's as far as you go, boys,' Danny warned with a raised tone.

The three senior members of the party immediately recognised the voice. They had a startled but relieved look upon their faces. They had finally found him! But their friend wasn't going to be in an accommodating mood as they had hoped for.

'Is that you, Danny?' Dane yelled in return.

'Yeah, it's me.'

'You stupid bastard, you could have killed one of us,' Dane forcefully said.

'Get over it; you're all still standing, aren't ya!' Danny replied with a grin on his face, amused and sniggering at the way they had scampered to safety.

The men below shook their heads in relief. The situation was calming down by the tone of Danny's voice they perceived, but Dane was there to get him back to Graceville and a lot of negotiation had to be debated yet. Dane, along with Ryan had to be as tactful as they could as they knew Danny was under extreme duress. For all they knew, he might have lost his mind completely since the shootings and had to tread warily for all concerned.

'Are you okay, Danny. Do you have any injuries? How's your head space, mate? Been a big couple of days, hey!' Dane coerced, trying to get a gauge to what frame of mind his friend was in.

Although he could sense that Danny was a little agitated and being short in his answers, Dane and Ryan were convinced that he was himself and reacting in the manner they were accustomed to.

A moment of silence passed as the men lingered over whether it was safe enough to walk back into the open. Dane decided to throw caution to the wind and yelled to Danny that they were coming out of their hiding places.

'Are your friends from down the river still with you?' he asked as he opened himself from the tree he was hiding behind.

'Yeah, they're all here with me, Dane,' he replied. 'I see you got me brother-in-law with ya; how are you, Ryan?' Danny yelled, switching his attention.

'I would be a lot better if you came back to Graceville with us, Danny, everyone's worried sick about you, mate,' Ryan appealed.

Danny remained silent as he watched the men below pack their rifles back into their sheaths overhanging their saddles, confident that any danger had now passed. They knew that Danny had a history of crazy stunts but were adamant that he would never shoot with intent; after all, if he really wanted to put a hole in them, he would have done it already as Danny explained to them after Dane berated him for taking the pot shot.

'Took your time finding me, Karl, slipping in your old age, are ya?' Danny badgered as he reacquainted himself with his friend.

'Still trying to get over how you climbed that cliff face back at St Lucia, Danny, it took me mind off things a bit, you know,' Karl replied, doing his bit to try an ease the tenseness.

'Desperate times call for desperate measures, Karl,' Danny laughed.

The men below made their way to the middle of the walking track. They still couldn't make out where Danny was situated. They knew he was above them but didn't precisely know where. 'Can you come out and show yourself? We need to talk, Danny,' Dane cajoled.

'Sorry Dane but the answer is no. You should just continue on your merry way and leave us alone,' responded Danny.

'We're here to help you, mate, I'm not leaving without you, Danny,' Dane confided.

'Go, or I will take another shot at you.'

'You won't shoot us, Danny.'

'Maybe not you three, but I don't give a shit about the other young blokes you've got with you.'

Danny was upping the ante, hoping to call their bluff with threats so they would take his advice and move on. Unfortunately for Danny's sake, Dane, Karl and Ryan knew him too well. However, the young constables were taking his threats very seriously. Both Brad McNamara and Johnny Hayes had never met

Danny. They had heard of him through conversation with their Sergeant and other people around the valley but never had the so-called pleasure of meeting with him.

Although they had still yet to lay eyes on him, through discussion and inquisitive questioning over the last few days they thought they knew Danny as good as anybody. Warily, they followed Dane's lead and kept their mouths shut and obeyed every gesture from their senior officer.

'Maybe you don't give a shit, Danny, but I do, they're my friends and you will not harm them, okay?' Dane demanded.

The Sergeant introduced the two lads to him. He was putting a name to the face, hoping Danny would get any irrational thoughts out of his mind. The whole situation had reached a stalemate. Dane wanted Danny and his partners to come down from where they were, but the boys weren't about to budge for the Sergeant under any circumstances. The only way Dane would get them down from off the ridge was to go up with force which out of the question for him, knowing it would only inflame the situation.

'I know the shootings weren't your fault, Danny,' Dane sympathised, changing tact. 'The Devlins probably got what they deserved. If you come back to town with us, you can tell your side of the story. I'm sure everything will work itself out.'

Dane knew just about every detail of the shootings. He had talked to Inspector Vaccaro over the radio on their first night out. The Inspector, in his professional opinion, gave Dane all the information about the shootings so he could pass onto to Danny that all would not be a lost cause, that he would help him if he surrendered now.

Danny scoffed. 'I know what the Minister said in his press release. You can't fool me, Dane. I know what they branded me.'

'How does he fuckin know about that?' Dane whispered to his partners in frustration.

Dane was running out of options; Time was ticking on when Ryan decided to tug at the heartstrings.

'Surrender to us, Danny. Do it for Greta's sake if no one else. She's distraught, mate. She needs you home. What about your kids?' he pleaded.

The men were trying every trick in the book to try and coax Danny down, nothing was working. All they were greeted with was an eerie silence, it was if he wasn't listening anymore.

Dane's patience was running thin; a half hour had already passed since they were greeted the with the stray bullet and his only option left was to try and get up onto the ridge himself.

He started at him once more, hoping that the plain old truth would be enough to change his mind.

'Your only hope of getting out of here in one piece is with us, Danny,' he yelled back up the ridge. 'This is how it is, mate. There are hordes of coppers just over the next range, all converging on Tangiloo, and sooner or later they will be coming your way and they won't be as friendly as us.'

The men were greeted with silence again. They were starting to wonder if he had done a runner and were speaking to thin air. But Danny hadn't moved, neither had any of his buddies, in fact they were all quite comfortable up there, sitting back enjoying the morning sun that was spearing through the tree line. Danny was the using ploy to make them think exactly that, that they in fact had disappeared, and the boys were doing a good job of it, soaking in their child like prank, however, their mood was about to change swiftly. Dane looked back up in the direction where he thought Danny to be and again pleaded with him to come down.

'Three men are dead already, Danny, don't you think that's enough?' he said.

By Danny's calculations, the only men to die were the Devlin brothers and was intrigued to know who the third one was and broke the silence to ask Dane that question.

'The copper you shot down at the river, he's dead, Danny, he died of his wounds that night,' Dane disclosed with a tempered voice, softly bowing his head, knowing they would be upset on hearing the news. 'He was a good man, Danny. Robbie Dukes was his name, don't know if you heard of him or not. Had a wife and a little 3yo daughter, you know,' Dane continued.

The Sergeant, along with the rest of his partners and everyone else for that matter, had no idea that it was Ricky who had pulled the trigger on the officer. They were only going on the word of the dead officer's partner and Danny wasn't about to enlighten them with the truth.

On hearing the news, all the boys atop of the caves turned and looked at Ricky, he bowed his head between his knees. The mood among the boys had changed in an instant, their nightmare was only getting worse every time they received information that concerned them and were now at a dead end.

Danny looked to Ricky, apologised, and then to rest of the lads for what had happened so far and promised that he would get them out of this if was the last thing he does. He sat with his back against the rock facing his mates and called back down the ridge, 'Ya still there, Dane?'

'Yeah, we are all still here, as I said, we're not going without you, mate.'

'Here's the deal,' Danny ordered, 'I'll give myself up on one condition.'

'And what's that?'

'My friends here walk free. They've done nothing wrong except ride with me.'

Ricky looked at Danny, shocked; He knew he was trying to protect him along with Barny and Harry. Ricky shook his head at him. 'Don't do it,' he said.

Danny moved to him and put his hand on his shoulder. 'This was the only way to put this whole shit behind us. For you guys to walk away and get back a normal life.'

'Are you sure you know what you're doing?' Barny moved in closer and asked, concerned for Danny.

'It's time I faced up to it, Barny, and I'll be damned if I'm going to let you guys pay for it as well.'

Danny looked around at the rest of the men with a conceding look upon his face. They rose to their feet.

'I killed him, Danny, I'll go down for it,' Ricky said with a determined frown.

'It's my fault, I'll cop the blame,' said Danny.

'No way, man. I fuckin did it, I'll go down for it,' Ricky rebutted.

'I'm not taking no for an answer, Rick, I'm going down for it,' Danny argued.

The two men were about to erupt into another altercation, disagreeing on Danny's motives, when Dane took their attention away from each other.

'Speak to me, Danny, what's happening, mate!'

Danny ignored his request, angered that he was interrupted; however, Dane continued, 'I'll have to speak to the Inspector before I can promise anything, Danny. He's a reasonable man, I'm sure he'll work out something.'

'You go speak to the Inspector then, Dane, then you can come back to me with the answer, alright?' instructed Danny hastily.

That scenario was not an option for Dane. He wasn't about to leave Danny alone for one second and told him so. It's not that he didn't trust him, they had worked so hard to find him and he wasn't about to lose him. But the main reason Dane wasn't about to leave them alone was because of all the other police search parties on the march and one in particular stood out above the rest. He never wanted to tell Danny about Pringle or his vicious sidekicks but in the circumstances, he assessed he had no other alternative.

Danny wasn't coming down unless it was under his terms, which Dane could never agree to. He wanted to keep him alive and couldn't risk another hour out in the bush where they knew they were vulnerable.

'Listen Danny, what I'm about to tell you is no bullshit,' Dane assured. 'We think Johnston's hired a gunman to hunt you down and kill you, Danny, and probably your mates as well, he doesn't want you back alive. I don't know why, maybe it's to cover his ass over something, I don't know. But what I do know is that you're coming with me, so I can keep you breathing; you want to see your family again, don't you?'

Dane couldn't have been more direct. Although Danny was taking it seriously, he still couldn't quite comprehend what Dane was on about. A hitman hired to kill him? Danny couldn't get his mind around that thought at all and began to laugh it off.

'Oh yeah, this hitman got a name?' Danny asked. 'Josie Wales? Billy the kid? John Wick, Jason Bourne maybe,' he facetiously continued quoting names from history and cinema. 'Which one is it?' Danny sniggered.

'Goes by the name of John Pringle, and he's not alone, Danny,' Dane warned.

'Never heard of him,' Danny quickly scoffed. 'So why me, why us? Why are we so special to have this dude after us? What's going on, Dane?'

'As I said to you, mate. I don't know the reasoning. Wrong time, wrong place I guess,' Dane contritely replied.

Danny turned and looked at his mates, snorting to himself, but the look on their faces told him that this was no joke, especially Harry, he was turning white with fear.

'What's wrong?' Danny asked, seeing how frightened they had become.

'This is serious shit, Danny,' Barny told him.

He began to tell Danny what he knew of Pringle. Barny knew of what the papers had written about Pringle's exploits, that both sides of the law never had a good word to say about him. He, along with a quivering Harry informed Danny what he had allegedly done. They both approached and sat opposite him, returned their weapons to their holsters and began to let their feelings known.

'He's bad news, Danny, he's killed a lot of men. His name was all over the media a while back,' Barny warned.

'He can't be that bad, can he?' Danny brushed away.

'As I said, he's killed a lot of people, Danny. He's not to be fucked with,' Barny warned again.

'What! More men than the Cambodian Flu I suppose you're going to tell me,' Danny mocked.

He was referring to the spate of deaths that started in parts of the city ghettos and swept throughout the state and nation the previous year before killing over 6,000 people before health officials could contain the outbreak.

Seamen on a ship, which had sailed in from Cambodia delivering timber, bought in the strain of flu. Before the ship had even arrived from its point of departure it had already lost a quarter of its crew to the virus. Before the health department knew what was going on, workers from aboard the ship made their way to land as it was docked, spreading the virus at a rapid rate, starting inside the ghettos that had formed in the city where some of the crew had relatives.

It was a strain of influenza that had never been seen before. It was a sudden and painful death. Medicines and antibiotics were not as easy to come by for the average person anymore. The demand for important things such as medicines, antibiotics and penicillin for instance, were on a parallel never seen before. Authorities couldn't get it out quick enough to the people nowadays and because demand was so big, the price of such a thing that one took for granted five years ago was unattainable for most people. Even the simplest of pain relief such as paracetamol was hard to get your hands on. In some cases, you had to get a prescription through the local doctor as it was impossible to buy it over the counter in some stores.

Waiting for an appointment with your local doctor was becoming a class contest. Doctors, trying to make as much money as they could for their services would see the person with the most up-front money. If you had an appointment at a certain time, you prayed that no one came in just before you were due. If the next customer had more cash than you, he or she would be fast tracked ahead. Doctors were sick and tired of offering their services and not being paid for it after being promised otherwise from the needy people who had to see them.

In some cases, people would have to wait up to five hours after their original appointment and they didn't care if you were the elderly or the new-born, if you didn't have the cash, you had to wait your turn. Just like other essential services, the health system had become a giant sham. The only people relishing this were the people running the black market, selling basic medicines for absorbent prices.

Danny knew everything about the virus. Although it was indiscriminate in whom it attacked, it mainly struck the very young or the ageing and he had seen first-hand how it killed.

His mother had succumbed to the killer bug. There wasn't a thing he could about it. Within three short weeks, he saw his dear mum go from a healthy and vibrant person to a withering shade of her former self, looking more like a frail 90-year-old than the energetic 66-year-old she was. He had lost his father to cancer only 18 months prior. He loved and respected his parents very much and had gained much wisdom and faith from them and when they passed away in the circumstances they did, it was just another reason for Danny to direct his hate and disdain towards the world he now lived in.

Barny was a man of few words. So, when he spoke with such worry upon his face, Danny had no option but to take seriously what was being relayed about Pringle. Danny panned his eyes across his friends. He could see the hopelessness in them, not knowing what to do, especially Harry. Pringle's reputation preceded him, and the lads wanted nothing to do with him if they could help it.

'I'm scared, Danny,' Harry confided.

He wanted Danny to make the decision for him. He was the leader according to Harry's mind and would not try to argue against him, but he wanted his feelings to be known and as silence once again gripped the men. Harry continued with a pleading look in his eyes.

'I would rather do jail time than meet Pringle, Danny.'

'He's right, Danny, it's time we gave ourselves up and faced the consequences,' Barny added.

Danny looked across at Ricky to see if he agreed, and with a simple nod of the head, he could also see he wanted the nightmare to end, and to be escorted back to Graceville under police protection was as good as they could hope for while Pringle was still roaming the surrounding hills. They were desperate, they were scared, and it was the only option they had in front of them.

The time had come for Danny to listen to his mates and to adhere and respect their wishes but warned they must promise that there would be no argument over who was going to take the heat for everything that had transpired.

The boys smiled and patted their hands on Danny's shoulders with a thank you gesture and said that they would worry about that when the time came. They were extremely grateful for what Danny was proposing, but for the time being, the men just wanted to get out of mountains and into safety.

'Okay boys,' Danny sighed at them. 'Let's go home, if we're lucky, we might get a New Year's Eve drink in, what do ya reckon!' He proposed, lightening the moment. The men began to pick up what they had beside them and make their way down to the caves; Danny told the boys that he would handle Dane and to follow his lead.

The hunting partners were waiting patiently down on the walking track. They were going to stay there all day if they had to, but to their relief, Danny yelled that they were on their way down.

He suggested to meet them back at the old car park sitting up on the road above the cascades. He still didn't want anyone to find out about their hiding place inside the caves. At first, Dane was hesitant to leave them, but Danny persisted and strongly advised that they wouldn't come down unless they did what he requested.

Enforcing Dane that he had or trust him, or nothing was going to proceed, to his satisfaction, Danny would get his way.

After watching the men ride back across the foot bridges and up the steep track until they were out of sight, Danny and the lads hurried back inside the caves to gather their belongings and horses. They were all somewhat excited that their three terrifying days on the run was ending, however, Danny was still greatly apprehensive inside and was not as animated as the others. He was happy and contented at the prospect of seeing his wife and children again but terrified at what lay ahead for him personally.

He knew if he played his cards right his buddies would walk away free men, to get on with their lives and try and put this ugly mess behind them. He owed it to them for what they had done, but Danny knew he was never going to walk away a free man. His deepest fears were coming to the fore and he was going to have to confront them. The way it stood now, there was no doubt in his mind that he was going to have to serve jail time and probably a long stint at that. He was now willing to face his demons and take his punishment for the sake of his friend's freedom, however, that was a scenario that was a long way off from being finalised yet.

It was just after 8.30 am as Dane and his colleagues waited for the lads to arrive at the carpark. It was cut into the side of the mountain on the high side of the road. The cleared area was about forty meters square that also had picnic benches, toilet block and wood-heated barbeques for tourists to enjoy lunch on day trips in the tranquil setting. It was a popular destination in years gone by, but it had been a long time since anyone had enjoyed a chop or a sausage on the old barbecues as they were overgrown with weeds and grasses poking through the plates.

After a wait of about 20 minutes, Danny had joined the Sergeant. With help from the boys, he bought some time to make sure that any sign to entrance of the caves were well and truly covered. The so-called two leaders started the introductions to the ones that had never met before and when they were over, Danny was straight to the point with Dane.

'Well, what's the verdict with the Inspector?' he asked, assuming Dane had already spoken to him.

'Haven't spoken to him yet,' Dane replied.

'Why the hell not, Dane?'

'I can't get any reception,' he hollered back, unhappy at Danny's tone. 'We're too deep in. We're three mountain peaks away from Graceville, if you didn't know already.'

The Sergeant had been in contact with the Inspector on a regular basis since they had left, keeping him up to date on proceedings at least three or four times a day. The only time they hadn't been able to communicate was from about three hours in from the time they entered Kensington National Park. The Inspector had instructed Dane to use a different channel than the other police search parties were given to report back on. All police issue radios had twelve channels on them. UHF Channel four was given to the search parties to communicate back to headquarters in Graceville and Tangiloo on their positions.

Inspector Vaccaro and Sergeant Grainger were liaising over channel eight and a different frequency band on their radios. They needed to keep their conversations as private as possible, away from Minister Johnston's ears and the men who were coordinating the search. The plan was working except for one major hitch.

John Pringle had the technology with him that the others weren't privileged to. He had the latest in communications that could be afforded. Radios that were compacter, lighter, and had frequency range a lot more powerful than the police issue. If any comms were going over the airways, he would pick them up. The radios Pringle had could pick up over one hundred frequencies.

If someone were trying to communicate, a digital display would appear on the face showing which frequency to tune into, it allowed them to tune in on any conversation they chose to. It had a far greater radius of what was being used by the Graceville police and they had listened into the communications between all the parties involved, and in particular, the Inspector's and Dane's since the manhunt had begun.

Unfortunately for John Pringle, Dane and the Inspector never gave away their location, communicating only what was necessary without giving detail on information they had. Their conversations were short and gave away nothing that Pringle and his men could use to their advantage, however, it was all about to change in Pringle's favour.

After hearing and believing Dane about the poor radio reception, Danny suggested that he try an old fire track not far away from where they were. He explained that when he was in the area in the past, his mobile phone would cut in and out all the time; however, there was one location where he could get at least one bar. It was about a thirty-minute return ride up an old dirt track to the west called Willem Creek Road. It was a steep incline that led to a flat clearing and once there, the reception, reason's unbeknown to Danny was sometimes almost perfect. He had used the position a few times when visiting the area and was confident it would also work with radio reception.

Dane took along his two young constables up to the spot where Danny suggested. A narrow-overgrown road with plenty of ditches and wheel ruts to negotiate left from four-wheel drive expeditions from years before. Ryan and Karl stayed behind with the boys and were told by Dane that if the lads decided to make a premature exit that they were allowed and sanctioned by him to use any means possible to keep them there, an order that highly amused Danny.

However, the order was never going to be necessary as the lads had yet to have breakfast and thought it a good idea to cook up that large trout Tom had caught for them. They cleaned up the old barbeque and gathered firewood and before too long they were all helping themselves to a tasty and delicious breakfast with cans of soup provided by Ryan and Karl, much to the delight and satisfaction of the lads.

The mood was joyous between the men. Particularly for Barny, Harry and Ricky, they hadn't spoken to another person for days and were enjoying hearing someone else's voice besides their own. Tom was the quietest of the bunch. He knew he didn't belong there and had nothing to do with what had gone on but the last day and morning had been an eye opener for him. He was full of admiration and envy for the mate-ship that the men shared with each other. To do the things they had done for one another had never been seen by Tom before. He thought he had what he called mates, but none of them would ever contemplate sacrificing the things that these guys had done for each other, and Tom was feeling a better man for seeing it.

It was creeping on towards 9.30 am when Dane once again joined them at the car park, minus one of his constables. The boys had enjoyed a good breakfast as Danny lit up his last cigarette and threw the remains of the crunched-up packet into the smouldering fire of the barbeque as he saw Dane approach.

'How did you go?' he asked.

All the men looked at Dane with anticipation, hoping he had only good news with him. Dane dismounted his horse and puffed his chest.

'Mission successful,' he said. 'I relayed your terms to him, and he's agreed.'

The quartet smiled and patted each other, relieved of the news.

'On one condition though!' Dane interrupted. 'We've all got to meet him in Tangiloo to answer questions he wants answered.'

Danny wanted more information. He demanded exactly what was said, word for word. Dane expected the questioning, he knew his friend well.

'Calm down,' he said. 'It will work itself out. Just trust what I'm doing!'

'So, where's your young mate gone then?' Danny enquired with suspicion.

'Constable Johnny Hayes has ridden forward to Tangiloo to meet with the Inspector. He's going to contact him again at the Twist Top picnic grounds before he gets there with more info. Vaccaro wants an end to this as quickly as possible, the same as we do. He said to tell you that the other three would walk if you were willing to face all the charges laid against you. He knows what went down with the Devlin brothers and said that he would do everything in his power to get the truth out. He said that he would even testify on your behalf if needed. He said he would take care of things at his end and the only thing we needed to do was to get all of us back to Tangiloo in one piece,' explained Dane.

Danny's cautious curiosities were somewhat satisfied and after a quick conversation between him and his three pals, the decision was made to endure the ride back to Tangiloo. It was going to take them a good three hours to reach their destination at a solid rate and then another trip down the mountain if they were going to get to Graceville for New Year's Eve celebrations, a promise all the men riding with Dane had made to their partners before they left.

The mood was as good as it could have been amongst the now nine men. Dane was proud of his achievements in finding Danny and negotiating him back to his senses. Although he was sad and fearful of what may lay ahead for him, he was pleased that the promise he had made to Greta was going to be fulfilled as he explained to Danny, who replied to him pragmatically that he had always been a man of his word. Secretly, Dane knew the job was only half done and a long nervous day still lay ahead of them.

Getting to Tangiloo was going to be the easy job according to Dane. He knew that half of the search parties assigned to find Danny and his gang would have already made it across the Mt St Lucia range and back into Tangiloo by now. It was now his job to enter the small township unnoticed and into the designated point in which he had assigned Constable Johnny Hayes to relay to Inspector Vaccaro.

The location was going to be the sight of an old disused reception centre. It had a long and twisting dirt entrance off the main road, but the men were going to enter it from behind through an old single vehicle fire track which snaked its way into Tangiloo from just inside the start of Syrian Ck road. The Sergeant decided it was the only way to get to Vaccaro without anyone else trying to lay claim to Danny before the Inspector could process anything. It was a huge risk Dane was taking, second guessing the Inspector's thoughts on how he might react to the situation, but it was a risk he had to take; otherwise, he might lose Danny for good.

The morning hours went along. Johnny Hayes had made it to his destination at the Twist Top car park to communicate his orders to the Inspector in full. He was gasping for air from the hastened ride and had to wait a few minutes before he could get his breath back. He knew the importance of what he was about to say and wanted to be sure that he was to be fully understood.

The reception was surprisingly clear compared to the last communication they had from that position and after hearing through the Constable what Dane had planned, the Inspector relayed he would sort out the issues concerning Pruitt when he met with them and the Sergeant at the agreed rendezvous point in Tangiloo.

He signed off with a warning to the young Constable to tread warily. He knew that Pringle and his men were still out there, and no one knew better than him, that if someone or something hindered Pringle's assignment, he would stop at nothing to get whatever or whoever it was out of the way by any means necessary.

Inspector Vaccaro was immediately on his way from his private office from inside the Graceville police station, he would make the hour-ride trip up Mason's creek road to Tangiloo by horse. It was best not to take the police cruiser, he wanted to be as inconspicuous as he could to try and put an end to the manhunt before any harm came to Danny and those who rode with him. It wasn't only Pringle who the Inspector was worried about.

There were other elements in his own police force who would take the fugitive down at first sight and claim a piece of the reward that had been offered by the Minister. He desperately wanted Danny at the meeting point in Tangiloo, to process things his way, however, it was going to be a mission and undertaking that neither he nor Dane could sustain.

The peaceful and amicable ending to the three-day saga they thought they were about to achieve by night fall, was in a matter of hours about to take a turn for the worse that would forever destroy any hope of an acceptable and peaceful conclusion.

Only a few miles up the road from where Constable Hayes was communicating with the Inspector lay Pringle and his entourage. They had stopped by a little stream coming down off the mountains to have a short rest. As fate would have it, it was only a few hundred meters from where Danny had asked Damien to hide Greta's letter in the log at Tambourine Bridge. Greta's reply was already in its place, also in the envelope on a separate piece of paper were the names of the men who trashed Danny's house, with a few short paragraphs from Kate.

Damien, on the stern advice of his partner Nicki, had ridden out there with her the previous night to drop it off. After informing Nicki what he had agreed to do for him, his partner, not wanting anymore to do with the men's situation, suggested they get it over and done with that night and not have to worry about it tomorrow in daylight hours. She was paranoid that someone from the law might see what they were up to and with the new moon shining brightly in the night sky, it gave them enough light to show them the way.

The couple rode nervously to where Danny wanted the letter to be dropped off. She despised being out there but knew Damien had made a promise and his mate relied on it being followed through. Nicki begrudgingly helped him out on the proviso it would be the last favour they would do for him.

'Hey Boss!' Stewie Morris said to Pringle. 'Check this out.'

His partner pointed at the red light flashing on their comms radio.

'Tune it in,' Pringle ordered.

'Already happening, boss,' replied Stewie.

The hunting trio couldn't believe their luck when they tuned into the frequency. Their comms started broadcasting loud and clear the conversation that Hayes and the Inspector were having and Pringle's killer-like smile was broadening by the second.

Constable Hayes had made the mistake of telling the Inspector not only his exact location but that of the Sergeant's proximity, along with the names of each and everybody that was coming in with him. It was a huge error of judgment, one which would give Pringle and his men the scope to set up a planned assault, knowing exactly how much time they had and how many they were up against.

With the help of the Devlin brothers riding with them, picking their brains on the locations and time proximities of the said places, Pringle set his plan in motion and once all his men understood what was to be done, all they would do now was to wait in hiding for their opportunity to pounce on the unsuspecting targets.

Chapter 11

The New Year's Eve celebrations were already in full swing in Graceville as the Inspector jumped on his mare to hastily head to his rendezvous point with the men. But the celebrations were not just confined for New Year's Eve. It was the news that everybody throughout the state and the country had been yearning and dreaming of for the last five years. Although people were slowly but exasperatingly compromising and adjusting to the world that had been thrust upon them, they're deepest hopes and wishes for the good old fast paced electronic computerised world to return were somewhat about to be realised.

It wasn't even mid-morning as people from all over the valley found the same headlines in their morning papers as were being told in the big city:

LIGHTS, CAMERA, ACTION.
FULL POWER AHEAD.
SWITCH IT ON.

They were just some of the headlines the editors of the leading newspapers went with on their front page in big bold letters to explain the announcing of both the Federal and State governments press release.

Rumours had been sweeping throughout the cities and lands for the past year, just as they did in the sleepy hollow of the Hexagon Valley, and just as Ricky and Barny tried to explain to Danny in the hotel a few days ago, however, no one, except for those high up in Governments and the business world knew exactly how much of a scale it would be. Governments waited until major refineries were up and running sufficiently enough so they could ensure infrastructure could manage it before they made a public press release. Whatever machinery existed before the crisis remained, and it was only a matter of patience and timing before it could be restored to how it was.

Around the big city and beyond, technicians and engineering crews had been working discretely to restore power lines, phone lines, oil and gas pipelines to ensure that when the time came to flick the switch, everything would go off competently. The State Premier announced that electricity would be the first energy source to return on a large scale. Starting tonight on New Year's Eve, allocated power grid stations that almost came to be non-existent around the city would be turned on to accommodate the planned celebrations of the Government.

The Premier used his documented press releases through the print media and government-owned radio airwaves to outline job schemes that would be offered to the mass unemployed, to give them hope of a bright future and that the days of hardship could slowly be put behind them.

The information technology and plug-in push-button age that so many people relied on, taken away from them almost overnight years before, was going to make a comeback a lot sooner than people predicted. Satellite technology would soon become available once more to the populous, not just reserved for military and government as it was today, and the social media frenzy which people submerged themselves into previously would again take over their lives as soon it as it was available.

The Premier had been in office for the last three years, the toughest era of any leader had to endure in the state's history. He was a strong and assertive leader, but also a kind-hearted person along with being a visionary and genuinely put the people's needs first. Unlike many of his colleagues who saw the hard times as an opportunity to exert their influence and exploit the vulnerable. Minister Colin Johnston being one that the Premier would have expelled and charged immediately if he had any inkling as to what his under study was getting up to in his allotted shire.

But influential people, such as the likes of Johnston, often worked together to keep the Premier out of the loop. They knew he was popular with the people and needed him to stay in power if they were to continue to hold their own office. The Premier did have a task force in operation to try and eradicate these factions, but it was a tough job, considering nearly half of the task force was as corrupt as the people they were employed to flush out.

They didn't have the technology and instant information at their disposal as they did in the past to fight organised crime. The backlog of paperwork made solving crimes difficult, and as money was hard to come by earning it the honest and proper way, those people in a position to receive money under the table illegally did so without blinking an eyelid.

The Premier was hoping all the corruption that was rampant within the halls of power and other establishments was about to get its first nail in the coffin with the methods that were used in the pre-crisis days about to be reintroduced.

The streets of Graceville were abuzz with excitement and joy as just about every adult had a copy of a newspaper in hand, pushing the front-page headlines into the faces of those who didn't, cheering with excitement of the prospect of regaining their previous easier fast-moving lives, however, despite all the press releases, they knew they would have to be patient before it would all come to fruition.

With all the excitement about the news, it was the first time Greta had laid eyes on a newspaper since the morning she had left Danny at home to visit the market three long days ago.

Corey and Sarah sat around the kitchen table perusing through all the outlined schemes and prospective planning that the government had released in the media, while Greta sat next to them with her own copy. She too was happy and relieved on hearing the news, but she was not looking at the main headlines in the paper. Greta had only one thing on her mind as she flicked through the pages, to try and find anything that related to Danny and the ongoing search for him.

The main newspaper in the valley had only written what information the Ministers office had released in previous days since the shootings, with only a four-paragraph story several pages in from the front. It wasn't the first police shooting in the region, far from it, it didn't even rate a mention in the main scribes down in the city because they hadn't even got a whisper of what had gone down, even if they did, it wouldn't have been important enough to rate a serious story, as that type of tragedy was occurring every day in the overcrowded and crime riddled streets of suburbia.

There was no mention about Danny in today's newspapers. All its pages had been taken up with the announcement, much to the smug satisfaction of Johnston who had done his bit to make sure that it was the case. The quicker the people would forget about what had happened and asking less questions, the better for his cause, and through his henchmen, had already subtly warned the editors of the surrounding minor newspapers that they not make a mountain out of a mole hill on this story. The editors took heed of the Minister's advice as they did not want to cross him because of the fear of reprisal.

The only thing in today's papers relating to the shootings was the time and place of Rosco and Billy Devlin's funeral that had been printed in the classifieds a couple of pages in from the back. The double funeral was to happen tomorrow, New Year's Day at 3.00pm at the church Greta had been attending nearly every Sunday morning for the past twenty years, a prospect that she sneered upon coming across it in the paper. She had never once saw any of the Devlin family inside her church and commented to Corey and Sarah on how inappropriate and double standard it was.

Greta read as much as she could about the news that everyone had embraced but was wishing to Corey and Sarah that if only it came a week earlier, then maybe, just maybe, Danny would be by her side at this very moment. Thinking if he knew officially that the world was going to change for the better, his outlook on life, along with the overzealous and spiteful Devlin brothers, would change from having vindictive attitudes to one of tolerance and understanding.

It had passed mid-morning when Greta suggested that she make the trip into the main street to the bank. They had done enough reading of the papers for now and Greta also wanted some money to repay Corey and Sarah for their kindness and hospitality. She wanted to give something back for the help and compassion they had given and wouldn't take no for an answer when her two good friends insisted that there was no need for her to do so.

Other than the wild trip up to her property to see the carnage that greeted her, Greta had hardly stepped outside.

'Are you sure you want to do this?' Sarah asked, concerned.

'I've got to face the music sooner or later,' replied Greta. 'I'm not going to hide.'

She was a proud and dignified woman, and nothing was going to stop her from leading a normal life around the town she had spent most of her life in.

They decided to leave the horse and carriage behind and make the small journey on foot with the children by their side. As the three adults and four children slowly made their way closer to the main street they would soon be overwhelmed at the sympathy and support Greta would receive from those who knew her, especially from those associated with the church.

Danny hardly knew anyone from the congregation that Greta called her second family, he was not that way inclined, but his wife was popular amongst them. No doubt rumours had swept across town on what the re-po squad had inflicted on her and she was amazed and humbled at the good willed offers being put forward to her. Every person whom she knew and came across on her way to the bank would offer help, from accommodation, clothes, even money, but she politely say that she was coping alright, being looked after as well as she could be, thanks to Corey and Sarah.

Most people she met were genuinely concerned for her wellbeing. But for all those who would embrace her and give moral support, there was the small element who would stare and make unfounded sniggering comments that on occasions could be overheard concerning her husband and the shootings.

Nevertheless, Greta wouldn't give these people the satisfaction of letting them know she was hearing them, although a fired-up Sarah thought differently. She would've loved to plant a right cross on their jaw, only to be halted by Greta and Corey who quietly asked her to ignore them and move on, much to the disgust of the protesting Sarah.

The thirty-minute walk to the bank from their house took nearly an hour and a quarter due to the stoppages enforced upon them. Gestures that Greta was grateful for at first but was quickly becoming a burden as every word that was being said about Danny continued to build on her already fearful and worried mind, not to mention the inept attempt by police to cover themselves as they followed every move she made.

'The bank looks busy,' Sarah said as they arrived at its doors.

'I suppose people have more to celebrate than New Year's Eve tonight, don't they!' Greta responded.

'I'll take your boys,' Sarah offered.

'Are you sure?' Greta asked gratefully.

'Yeah, you don't want them running around inside. I'll take them with mine, not a problem.'

'It's these times I wish we still had electronic banking. I hate the waiting.' Greta sighed.

'Look on the bright side,' Sarah smiled. 'At least we know what's coming and going with our money and not getting pilfered by the cybercrime bandits.'

'Good point!' Greta nodded in agreement.

As Sarah and the children browsed through nearby shops with a close eye being kept upon them by Corey, the time had come for Greta to advance to the nearest vacant teller after queuing for a short time.

'Good morning, ma'am, how can I help you?' the young clean-shaven male teller greeted Greta through the steel bars that separated them.

'Just withdrawing some money,' smiled Greta as she handed over her banking details under the bars.

'Just a moment, ma'am,' he politely responded.

Greta watched as the young teller sifted through the files that lay on the desk next to him, trying to ignore the whispering behind from people in the queues about the plight of her husband.

She was getting more agitated by the second, she just wanted her money as quickly as possible and get out of there, away from the cameras for eyes that had focused on her.

The teller had left his seat and was talking to a man at the rear of the bank outside an office door as they looked over in her direction, she knew something wasn't right. A transaction that would normally take a couple of minutes was already dragging over the five-minute mark and Greta's heartbeat started to gain momentum. A further two minutes would pass before the now nervous teller would emerge from his conversation with the man in the stylish suit.

Who is he? Greta was thinking to herself. *Is he the bank manager, if so, what's so important to be discussing my finances, and why the veil of secrecy?* Her fingernails started to tap at the counter at a vigorous rate as the teller approached her.

'I'm sorry ma'am, but your account seems to have been closed,' he said apprehensively.

'What are you talking about?' Greta asked, confused.

'You have no money,' was the broken reply.

'No, something's wrong here,' she argued. 'I want to see the Manager.'

'I'm sorry ma'am, but he's not in,' the teller informed her.

'Then who was that man you were talking to?' Greta enquired calmly, trying not to cause a scene, knowing customers were waiting anxiously for their turn at the counter.

'He's the assistant manager, ma'am.'

'Well, can I see him then?'

'I will go and see, if you would like to take a seat over there, I will see if he will talk to you,' he said, pointing at a section in the bank just inside the entrance in a small alcove where people would sit and discuss any problems with banking. It was far from being private. There were four seats around a table and was in earshot of everyone inside, and after keeping Greta waiting for more than enough time, the assistant manager finally arrived to talk to her.

Greta stood to her feet when seeing the man approach her.

'What's going on, why can't I access my money?'

'You have forfeited on your mortgage, Mrs Pruitt,' he quietly said.

He was trying to avoid a scene as much as Greta was and was doing his best to avoid such a confrontation as he sheepishly explained the situation.

Greta was confused, she didn't understand what was going on. The last time she looked at her finances almost a week to the day, a task she oversaw with the blessing and trust of her husband, there was almost $1,500 in their accounts, a fair amount compared to the plight of some of the less fortunate families in the valley. Some of them were lucky to have five dollars to their name and lived each day as it came.

The bank, in cohorts with Minister Johnston, had closed the Pruitts' account, sighting unpaid mortgages and acquired all monies owed out of their savings account with interest. It was the catalyst to engage the re-po squad at the Pruitts' property.

Greta argued her case, only to see her words were falling on deaf ears. It wasn't the assistant manager's fault what had happened, she understood that, he knew nothing of what was going on behind the scenes and sympathised with her plight, he was only going on the stamped and signed paperwork he had in front of him.

Just about all the customers in the bank were ears dropping in on the conversation; the murmurs and insinuations had already begun as people watched on at Greta's embarrassing state of affairs. Her whole private financial matters had just become public for all to see. Greta was getting nowhere with the gentlemen she was talking to; no answers were coming from him. She grabbed her handbag off the table and began to leave the bank and it was becoming clearer to her with every step she took, why her home was paid a visit by the re-po squad.

She was still getting over the humiliation and despair of seeing her home destroyed, and to be subjected to this in front of the peering eyes of the townsfolk could have been the final straw. But there would be no tears of ridicule this time, no giving satisfaction to those who took joy in other people's misfortunes.

Greta would hold her head high as she exited the bank, knowing what they had done was totally wrong and unjustifiable. She walked defiantly, eyeing off people with her angry beautiful brown eyes who dared to look at her. It was a gesture to all around that she was not going to be walked over by anyone, especially corrupt bureaucrats, and she was preparing herself for a fight.

The things that Danny had told her over recent times, about the nastier elements of life in the world they now lived in, were racing through her mind. It was all making sense now, the way that Danny had been feeling, and it was giving her a feeling of determination she had never felt before. The law wanted her husband and he was being hunted down like an animal, and now, for the first time, she was starting to feel the waves of rebellion and resentment that had engulfed her husband for so many years.

She finally understood where he had been coming from and wasn't about to surrender like so many of her friends had done in recent times. It was happening to her this time, and with her husband now a fugitive, she would have to change and adjust to a lot of things in her life, a change that she was already steeling herself for.

She threw her carry bag back over her shoulders and flicked her long flowing dark hair away from her maddening eyes as she exited the bank and walked up to her sons nearby and grabbed them by their hands.

'Take me home,' she ranted to Corey and Sarah.

'Why, what's going on?' Sarah asked, disturbed.

'Not now. When we get home,' she seethed.

Greta was angry as ever inside, if she started to tell her friends what was happening, she was afraid she would yell and curse in front of everybody in the street.

She quietly walked with her friends back to their home as rapidly as she could. She hardly spoke a word as so-called well-wishers continued to try and confront her. She was in no mood for sweet conversation and would deliberately try and avoid people by taking alternative routes back to the sanctuary of the house.

She entered through the front door ahead of her friends and threw her bag across the loungeroom floor and let off an almighty scream of frustration. However, there were no tears of self-pity this time, only anger and outrage. It was a tantrum that both Corey and Sarah had never seen from her as she let them know what the bank had done while the children looked on frightened before Sarah led them outside.

It would take Greta a good ten minutes to vent her frustrations at the powers that be and after she calmed down her thoughts once again turned back to her husband. As Corey left the two women to check on the children outside, Sarah joined Greta on the couch to give her a reassuring embrace.

'All I want is Danny home. I don't care about the money. I don't care what's all over the newspapers. Nothing else matters, Sarah, I just need him by my side,' Greta grieved.

Her stomach started to churn inside again as the tears start to well in her eyes, however, this time she refused to let them out. Danny asked her to be strong in his letter, and that was what she was going to be. She stood up from the couch and took a deep breath, looked at Sarah, and defiantly announced that none of this was going to beat her.

'Danny will be back soon,' she said with a determined look. 'He will come back to me, he could never spend more than a few days away from me, no matter what,' she reaffirmed.

The power of positive thinking was what Greta was adhering to. To allay her fears, ignoring what was deep inside her heart and relying on her faith. Greta was confident in the belief that her nightmare would soon be over, and her family could get back to how it was.

It was the only way to cope, to stay focused and not to go insane with worry and anxiety she preached to herself. As support and encouragement came from Sarah, Greta made her way outside to give her two young sons a hug of reinforcement, to let them know that mummy still loved them and that everything will be alright, while an ever-increasing concerned Corey and Sarah watched on. They admired the brave front Greta was displaying yet shuddered to think how they would be coping if they were in her shoes.

But whatever way Greta thought best to manage her plight, the plight her husband was about to venture into would test every ounce of courage, nerve and wit that was left in his already teetering and troubled body.

Chapter 12

It was almost pushing midday, the sun rising high in the clear skies above. It was going to be another warm to hot day and the men were all down to either their T-shirts or singlets.

They all had some type of cap or hat with them to prevent the harsh summer rays from burning at their cheeks and noses and with some spare sunglasses that Karl had supplied to Barny and Harry, they were all now looking the part as they rode through the twisting and winding dirt road of the forest.

As the men talked about anything that arose, they continued to ride, passing cigarettes around, getting to know their new acquaintances a little more. But the one conversation that was bought up that Danny couldn't get his head around was the one about this mysterious man that was supposedly hired to kill him.

He regarded himself to be a well-read person. He would always read the daily newspapers from front to back and fathomed that he knew everything that was going on in the world, especially in his own backyard and if Pringle was so well known, why hadn't he heard of him.

He would always read about politics in his state and what was happening on the crime front. It intrigued him immensely and couldn't for the life of him understand how he hadn't come across Pringle's name the way his buddies had.

He prided himself on his gifted memory and trivia knowledge. When he would sit himself down to watch television, which seemed a lifetime ago to him now, if nothing took his fancy on the sports channels, the first programming he would switch to would be the History or Documentaries. He would watch it any chance he could, engrossing himself in the people and events that shaped the world before him.

Anyone or anything that had made its mark on history fascinated him. From legend warriors and leaders to visionaries and businessmen and to all the great wars in the history of the world. He admired it all and often joked to his friends that all he wanted to do in life was to make the history channel, and then, and only then, would he be contented that he achieved something in his life.

But whatever the suspicions he held on John Pringle, he and all the men that were with him on this day were about to find out first hand on who John Pringle really was, and unbeknown to Danny, he was going to get his wish, whether he liked it not. He was about to mark his own niche in the state's history, especially in and around the Hexagon Valley and for all the wrong reasons.

'Here they come,' whispered Stewie Morris.

He was lying on his stomach, peering through his binoculars as the men slowly rode towards them. They sat above oncoming group and were camouflaged behind the thick bush and tall forest trees.

'How far?' Pringle asked.

'About 400 metres,' replied Morris.

Pringle ordered his men into position. They were situated atop an S bend in the road which swung around to the left from the direction the group was coming from. Pringle, Morris and his other partner in crime Max Miller sat approximately four and half meters atop a cutting in the road. Eddie and Matt Devlin were ordered down to road level just beyond where it straightened out, with Matt on one side and Eddie on the other. The Devlin's were there just in case any of the fugitive four slipped through their ambush and should that happen, they were to stop and arrest them.

Pringle and Morris watched with excited breath as Max Miller loaded and aimed his high-powered semi-automatic rifle at the oncoming group of men.

The plan for Pringle and his men was to take Danny out with a single shot and then make a hasty exit from the area before anyone could lay eyes upon them. They figured all the men would duck for cover, including the Devlin brothers as soon as they heard the bullet, the ensuing confusion should give them time and opportunity to get out of there unseen and back to Graceville to collect the rest of their money from Minister Johnston.

Max Miller had graduated top of his year at the police academy in marksmanship. Some say he could have made it to the Olympics if he so desired but as it was, men like Pringle for reasons other than good used his talents. He had worked with Pringle for some time now and was getting well paid in these times for doing so. He had cropped blond hair, shaved at the sides, pale skin with dull blue eyes and he would show no remorse once he pulled that trigger to end someone's life, a task he had done over a dozen times in the past two years. His psychotic mind gave him great enjoyment in what he did and the task of taking down Danny Pruitt was going to be a walk in the park for a man of his ilk.

Excited and nervous, the Devlin brothers waited for things to happen behind the cover of large trees by nodding and winking at each other from across the road. They weren't sure how the hired men were going to go about their business, they didn't really care, they only wanted revenge on the killer of their brothers. But any feeling of excitement they had inside them was about to quickly turn to terror.

Miller concentrated his aim as the men slowly neared with Pringle and Morris waiting anxiously behind him, rifles and pistols at the ready, and behind them lay Constable Johnny Hayes, bound and gagged, struggling to make a sound to warn his colleagues on the road below.

Pringle's posse had ambushed him earlier as he made his way up Syrian creek road. They knew he was coming and when it was time, dragged him off his horse at gunpoint and tied him up with duct tape around his wrists and ankles.

Constable Hayes could not do a thing to avoid it. The men moved swiftly and threatened to kill him on the spot if he refused or struggled against their demands and before he knew it, he was bound and gagged lying helplessly on the forest floor.

It was hard for Miller to get a clear shot at Danny. He was huddled in the middle of the ten riders. Karl was out in front of the pack, only fifty meters away from the aimed weapon with the rest of the men tightly bunched behind him, but as the men stopped, Miller was going to get the break he needed.

'Hold up, everyone, I need to take a leak,' Harry announced.

'Yeah, good idea, so do I,' Tom agreed.

The men dismounted from their horses and made their way to nearest tree on the lower left-hand side of the road.

Dane thought it a good idea to take a break as well, they hadn't stopped since they left the cascades an hour before and joined them in having a stretch as they all began to dismount, except for Karl.

'What's the matter?' Dane asked, concerned at the look on his face.

'Don't know,' Karl wondered. He looked at the densely populated forests around him. He could sense something wasn't right. The first hint was the silence of the abundance of bird life that rung out of these mountains, there was none to be heard or seen, the forest wasn't talking to him. There was something amiss. He couldn't put a finger on what it was in the short time that they were there. The men had only pulled up tracks for a minute or so, but he had a deep feeling of apprehension as he eyes panned around.

Not hearing the conversation that Dane and Karl were having, Danny and Ricky decided to join Harry and Tom in relieving themselves and walked in the direction of their buddy's newfound toilet. It was all Miller needed to finish their assignment.

As Danny walked away from the protection of his mates and horses, Miller now had him firmly in his telescopic sights. With his finger slowly edging down on the trigger aimed at the back of his targets head, Miller breathed out and slowly squeezed his finger.

The shot echoed like a thunderbolt throughout the surrounding mountains and gullies, immediately followed by the harrowing holler of immense pain, however, it was not the sound of human suffering, the high velocity bullet had entered through the neck of Karl's horse, with him still aboard. The bullet made an almighty entrance wound as blood spewed out at fountain like speed. The horse reared in its last ever action before rolling and tumbling to the ground as it took its last breath, with Karl underneath the 500kg equine beast.

Constable Johnny Hayes had squirmed and edged as quietly as he could to where Max Miller was taking aim on one knee. Pringle and Morris were so intent on watching proceedings over Miller's shoulders, they momentarily forgot they had a hostage with them.

Hayes, while lying on his back, had thrust out his right leg at the elbow of Miller's trigger arm as he took the intended lethal shot at Danny. Johnny Hayes, showing tremendous courage in trying to save the life of a man he had only met for a moment, would inadvertently cause the death of a man he knew better.

Karl Turner lay helplessly underneath his horse. The weight had instantly crushed numerous internal organs in his upper torso as his horse of eight years came toppling down upon him. He tried in vain to gather some air into his mashed lungs as those around him ran for their lives. Karl gasped and gurgled, blood oozed and spattered out of his mouth and nostrils from deep inside, but no air could be sucked into his crying lungs, 30 seconds is all it would take for him to breathe his last.

In the ensuing mad minute, Danny and Ricky dived for cover down an embankment where Harry and Tom had already taken cover from the gunfire. Barny and Ryan immediately scrambled to safety behind a boulder on the high side of the road as Dane rushed to help his friend stuck underneath the motionless horse. He had only taken a couple of quick steps looking up in the direction from where the shot had come from when Constable Brad McNamara opened fire. McNamara couldn't see any target and randomly let go a volley of bullets out of his handgun; he was usually a calm and collected young man under pressure, but in the instant panic, he had lost his cool.

'Brad, Brad, get the hell out of the way, stop firing!' Dane yelled.

McNamara turned at the bellowing Sergeant when another high-powered shot came from out of the forest.

'Shoot him, shoot him,' Pringle had ordered Miller as themselves ducked and dodged bullets from McNamara's gun. Pringle had already taken care of Johnny Hayes by rendering him semi-conscious by striking him on the head with the butt of his rifle.

Miller turned and quickly took aim again, he would get no interference this time around and from behind the protection of the giant log that lay in front of him on the ridge, pulled the trigger at the open target.

The men at road level looked on in terror as McNamara went down with his chest blown apart only meters from where Dane was crouching.

'Brad!' Dane yelled again. The Constable hit the ground as Dane gasped at the sight of his young partner's bloodied upper body.

The Sergeant looked on in despair. He knew McNamara had been killed instantly. He thought he would be next and swiftly crawled on his hands and knees over the dusty gravel road to safety where Ryan and Barny had taken sanctuary.

The siege was only a minute old when Eddie Devlin, in fright at seeing the mayhem from his position, wanted to get to his brother.

'Stay the hell where you are!' Matt yelled.

He didn't want Eddie exposing himself until the gunfire had ceased but his younger brother ignored his pleas. Eddie pointed his pistol up the road where the lads had taken cover. He couldn't see them; he only wanted to cover himself to make it across the road and started to run. Hunched over with his head low, he began to shoot repeatedly out of his pistol, never looking in the direction where the bullets were going as he tried to make the panicked 20 meters to his brother.

Matt Devlin watched as his brother try to scramble towards him. In protection of his sibling, he pointed his rifle up the road from behind the tree he was hiding and let go three successive shots to help with cover for his brother.

Danny and Ricky had their handguns already drawn. Stray bullets were flying and pinging all around them, tearing bark off the trees above them, ricocheting off the road in front of them, flicking shards of gravel into their faces and heads. The four men were trapped as they took cover any way they could; however, recklessly, or not, Danny was fighting back.

Eddie Devlin was almost in a straight line from where he and the other three men lay. Danny raised his head over the embankment to his left and saw Eddie stumbling to the ground in his haste to get across the road, continuing to shoot in their direction. Danny frightfully returned fire. Ricky planted himself next to him and followed suit. Tom and Harry buried their heads between their arms as both Danny and Ricky shot down Eddie before he could get two-thirds of the way.

Eddie Devlin took four bullets. The first one striking him in the leg above the kneecap. He tried to regain his feet as he continued to fire down the road. He took the next two in the upper body, and then the fatal shot followed, entering through his temple as older brother Matt looked on in horror only meters away.

Both Danny and Ricky almost emptied their chambers firing at him in their own terror-stricken panic; they didn't know whose gun the fatal shot had come from. They feared for their lives and Eddie Devlin had to be stopped and neither cared who did it, as long as it was done before a stray bullet had their name on it.

It was two minutes of absolute insanity and after the dust had settled, silence again gripped the surrounding forests as all the men involved tried to get their bearings back and comprehend what had just transpired.

Pringle and his men saw proceedings from their vantage point above and weren't distracted at what had happened to Eddie Devlin. He and his brother were only there for the knowledge of the area and nothing else, and since they had found their intended target, they were now both dispensable.

As the shootout was occurring, Max Miller had his eye looking down his telescopic sights waiting to get a shot on Danny. He knew where he was, but his target wasn't lifting his head from beyond the embankment. From where Danny and Ricky were shooting at Eddie Devlin they couldn't be seen from where Miller was, all he, Pringle and Morris could do was watch and listen to what was happening as the boys laid low and out of sight.

Pringle cast a vigilant eye over the hushed proceedings. He knew exactly where everybody was situated but unless they made a massive error in judgment, he was going to be there for a little time yet, a scenario that was out of the question for him.

He was there to do a job, and the quicker he got out of these uninhabitable mountains without being identified, the better for him and his partners.

'What do we do now, boss?' asked Morris.

Pringle ran his forefinger and thumb over his thick black moustache.

'We negotiate, Stewie,' he smugly replied.

Another minute passed before Pringle would break the silence overlooking the two dead bodies with a third further down the road.

'Can you hear me down there?' he yelled.

Dane was the first to answer. 'What do you want from us?' the Sergeant angrily responded.

'I've been hired by the government to arrest Danny Pruitt and bring him back to Graceville, I know you're down there, Pruitt, so give yourself up and no one else will get hurt,' Pringle demanded.

The two separated groups down at road level remained in scared silence.

Dane leaned to one side to see if he could get a look at them. He knew who it was up on the ridge, who else could it be, Dane insisted to himself.

'I'm Sergeant Dane Grainger, and I fuckin know who you are and what you've been hired to do, so don't give me any shit about taking anyone back to Graceville,' he roared back. 'Pruitt's staying with me and that's it, so you can forget about it and piss off out of here.'

'Afraid not,' came the stern reply.

Another nervous minute ensued until Pringle raised his voice again.

'I have one of your men up here with me, Sgt Grainger, a Constable Hayes I think his name is,' he calmly revealed.

Dane looked at Ryan with overflowing worry.

'So, here's the deal,' Pringle announced as his voice took on a more serious tone. 'You hand over Pruitt and I'll give you back your man; you've got two minutes otherwise the young cop dies,' he instructed.

Morris pushed Constable Hayes out onto the ledge of the sharp cliff for all to see. He was bloodied and dazed from the forceful blow he took from Pringle. Dane leant to his side again to peer up in the direction where his enemies were, wiping the dried dust from his whiskers and mouth. His young friend had a rope tightly wrapped around his neck with Morris firmly gripping the other end out of sight behind the thick bush.

Dane looked to a stunned Ryan. 'He couldn't be serious, could he? He's got to be calling our bluff,' Dane whispered.

'Where's Vaccaro, can't he help us? Radio him again!' Ryan quickly asked.

'I never contacted him, there was no reception, we're on our own. My radios on my horse anyway,' Dane said as the beads of sweat ran down his forehead into his whiskers as Barny listened in next to them.

'What!' Ryan said in disbelief.

'I didn't speak to him.'

'You mean all that shit you told Danny was all lies?'

'I had no choice. I had to get him back with us. He would've pissed off otherwise.'

'Jesus Christ,' Ryan mumbled. 'You better make sure Danny doesn't find out you lied to him.'

'We've got other things to worry about right now, Ryan,' dismissed Dane.

The men were frighteningly confused. They asked each other for ideas on how to get themselves out of the life-threatening crisis. On the other side of the road down the embankment, Danny and his friends sat silent, petrified, and stumped on what to do. The men looked at Danny waiting for him to either say or do something, but nothing was coming from him.

His body language and facial expressions were zero. He carefully tilted his head sideways to look where Constable Hayes stood. He wasn't about to give himself up, Pringle had already made his intentions clear, this was no time be a martyr, Danny wanted to live. They sat and waited helplessly, hoping that Pringle wouldn't carry through his threat.

'One minute!' Pringle yelled.

There was no movement from below and the clock was ticking. Dane started to plead with Pringle.

'Let him go, we'll work something out, no one else has to die here.'

'Not negotiable, 30 seconds left,' Pringle warned.

The men sat with fearful anticipation as the seconds ticked down. There was not a thing they could do, they were hamstrung, the sweat was pouring out of everyone, and then came the sound that shocked them all.

A single shot went off out of Pringle's revolver through the back of Constable Johnny Hayes' head. He was killed execution style. His lifeless body bounced off the protruding rocks and shrubs like a rag doll from the five-metre ledge until he came to rest at the bottom, his body lying in a twisted mess, rope still attached to his neck.

It was the most shocking and unbelievable incident the men had seen in their lives, their stomachs churned as they gasped at each other in fright. They couldn't believe their eyes, if three dead bodies weren't enough already, to see someone cold bloodily executed in front of their eyes was terrifying for them.

Another minute passed as the panic-stricken men tried to get a grip on themselves and the situation.

Behind the large granite rock, Dane and Ryan were in shock, they couldn't talk, they sat bewildered and open jawed. Barny looked around to see if he could somehow escape, but everywhere he looked there was too much open space to get to his horse who had taken fright and settled among each other a further 200 metres back down the road.

The men looked around with startled faces, too scared to move as Pringle began to bark threatening instructions once more.

'Give yourself up, Pruitt, or we'll take you and your mates down one by one, you can't sit there all day.'

Another five minutes ensued as Pringle continued to tell Danny that he was all out of options. 'Do the right thing and surrender, save the lives of your pals,' he directed.

Pringle was getting deathly silence from Danny. Dane and Ryan were starting to think that he had somehow escaped the net. Barny knew better though, he knew that Danny would never leave him in the lurch and was confident he was still around somewhere.

Pringle was running out of patience and motioned to Morris to start scouring the flank to the left of them. Slowly he walked through the bush to see if he could come across an opening to get a shot at anyone while Miller stayed with his boss aiming his rifle in the direction they thought Danny to be. Morris stealthily started his search, rifle raised at the shoulder, trying not to make a sound on the forest floor as Pringle continued to invite Danny out, promising him wouldn't shoot him and that his friends would walk free. Pringle had just proved to everyone around that he was taking no prisoners and Danny knew it. He lay back against the embankment to check his handgun only to see he had only one round left. He reloaded the magazine with bullets that sat deep in his pockets.

Tom sat silently next to Harry, the look on his face was numb. It was as if he was in his worst nightmare and hoping he would wake up and everything around him would disappear, but this was real, the bullets were real and the gunned down bodies in front of him were real. There was no escape from the reality and terrifying happenings that were before his very eyes.

'What the hell's happening to us, Danny?' Harry softly pleaded.

Danny could see his friends were at their wits end, they were trembling with fear, and they weren't alone in doing so. He felt for them tremendously, after all, it was he that again put them in a position of danger. Danny remained calm, assertive, he had to give them the confidence they were yearning for, he needed them as much as they needed him and had to instil some resolve into them, no matter if he was just as scared.

Danny looked at both Harry and Tom, crouching next to each other only meters below from where he sat.

'I'll get you out of here. You've gotta trust me, okay. Right Ricky!' Danny leered at his best man.

Harry and Tom looked at Ricky. They could see he was just as determined as Danny in trying to fight their way out of what was an ever-increasing losing battle.

'What are we going to do then?' Harry asked.

'Give me your gun,' replied Danny.

Harry grabbed his revolver from out of his waist belt and asked nervously what he was going to do.

Danny turned to Ricky.

'How many rounds have you got left?'

'Plenty,' he gritted.

'What the fuck ya doing, you don't think you're going to shoot your way out of here, for Christ's sake, look at the weapons they've got!' Harry pleaded.

'Harry,' Danny stated calmly, 'we have to do something. If we sit here and do nothing we will die, this psychopath will kill us. It's either us or them, Harry, and I'm not ready to die yet, are you?'

Harry and Tom looked at Danny and Ricky and conceded it was the only option left to them. This wasn't the time to complain or look for excuses and scapegoats. No divine intervention was going to help them, they were fighting for their lives and whatever Danny was planning they had no option but to follow.

Approximately five meters below and to the right of them lay an exit from a large concrete drain, 1.5 meters in diameter. The drain carried the storm water runoff underneath the road from the large gully on the higher side of the mountains. It was laid there many years ago to prevent flooding over the low spots that swept around the S-bend in the road. It was big enough for them to crawl through and try and get to Dane, Ryan and Barny without being noticed by Pringle and his men.

'We're going to make our way up the pipe and try and bring the other three back with us,' Danny explained. 'They shouldn't be too far from the ditch where the drain comes out. If we can't get away, at least we'll all be together. We'll work something out after that.' Danny's pulsating mind theorised.

Tom and Harry looked on as Danny gave them one last piece of advice.

'If you get a chance, shoot the bastards.'

Harry's and Tom's hearts dropped to their stomachs. They could tell by the look in Danny's eyes he meant what he said, but most of all, they knew if they had any chance of getting out of there, the sinking reality was that he was probably right.

He handed Harry back his fully loaded revolver as Ricky threw his spare to Tom who never carried a weapon with him. He caught it nervously in both hands.

'Above all, fellas,' Danny softly advised. 'If you get a chance to get to the horses, take it; just run as fast as you can.'

With a determined nod of the head between the men, Danny and Ricky commenced the scramble towards the open drain with handguns at the ready. They fell to their hands and knees, scampered down the dusty scaly embankment. The entrance to the pipe was now in front of them. The 20-meter slow crawl underneath the road began.

Embedded on the floor of the drain were hardened twigs and debris. The soft muddy soil and silt that had settled at the bottom of the pipe from the rain that came through a week earlier acted as a gluepot, the heat and humidity adding to the discomfort. The boys wiped the heavy beads of nervous perspiration from their brow, getting their fingers entwined with cobwebs. They slowly crawled and crawled, reaching a few meters short of the exit underneath the high side of the road.

Breathing heavily, the two rested momentarily with their backs against the wall of the pipe facing each other.

'Well, I guess this is it, if we go down, we go down fighting, hey, nice knowing ya, buddy,' Danny pronounced with a wry smile.

'Don't talk shit, let's just get the others down here with us,' grumbled Ricky.

This was not the time for Danny's nervous humour.

Danny poked his head out of the end of the drain. Ricky lay on his stomach aiming his gun through the debris that collected at the entrance in the direction of where he thought Pringle to be. They could hear the muffled voices of Dane and Ryan to the left of them.

'Dane, can you hear me?' Danny whispered aloud. 'Dane, Dane,' he repeated several times.

Barny was the first to hear. Dane and Ryan were still trying to find solution's on how to get themselves out of there.

'Shut up,' Barny chastised silently whilst raising his hand. 'Is that you, Danny?' he faintly asked.

'Yeah, is everyone okay?'

'No-one's hurt but we are shitting ourselves, mate, where are you?' Barny asked, keeping low as he peered down where he thought he could hear Danny's voice.

'Down here in the drain.'

'What the hell ya doing, Danny?' Dane interjected.

'Come to get you maggots out of here, but if you don't want any help, we'll just be on our way then,' belittled Danny.

Now it was Dane and Ryan who gave each other a look of disdain. They had neither the humour nor patience to listen to Danny's strung-out ramblings.

'What do you want us to do?' Barny asked.

'We're only ten meters away down in the ditch. If you all make a dive, you can make it to where we are. They can't see us from here. We'll figure out what to do next when you get here,' said Danny.

Barny had no hesitation. He trusted Danny, and if he had an idea, he was going to go with it. He turned to Dane and Ryan and said that he was going with or without them. There was no reaction from them. They thought it too risky, Pringle was still up there and being behind a bulletproof boulder was good enough for them for the time being. Seeing no response from the two, Barny quickly rose to his feet, took five or six running steps and took a desperate leap towards the ditch, landing on his side then quickly rolling himself over and over towards Danny and Ricky until he made it into the confines of the drain.

'Glad you could make it,' Danny said as Barny finally came to a halt.

'Fuck Danny, what's going on?' he asked, shaking his head in disbelief.

'What're the other two doing, are they coming or what?' Danny replied, ignoring Barny's comments.

Before he could give an answer, Ricky kicked at Danny's legs. He had spotted Morris up through the camouflage of the forest taking aim with his rifle. The hurried movement by Barny had grabbed the eye of the stalking sniper and it was only a matter of time before he would get a visible on Dane and Ryan.

Danny lifted his revolver and took aim. This was completely different to the shots he had fired previously. When he shot Billy and Rosco Devlin, it was pure reflex and self-defence, so it was with Eddie Devlin, but this was going to be pre-meditated murder if he were to pull the trigger.

Danny's heartbeat was thumping as he held the gun in both hands; he was following every move that the ex-tactical response member was making as he slowly traipsed his way through the forest above them.

Morris came to a standstill, he began to raise the rifle to his eyes, looking through the scope, he panned around. Danny knew exactly where Dane and Ryan were situated in relation to Morris. He was about to shoot at them, until the hired killer's upper body started to move leftwards, straight in his own direction and then stop. Danny knew he had just become the gunman's target.

Without hesitation, he let go two shots in quick succession, Ricky joining in with a volley out of his. Morris fell to the forest floor, his body disappearing into the thick undergrowth, paying the ultimate price for the decision both he and Miller made on not donning their protective vests when they left their horses to take up their positions. Danny was unsure he inflicted fatal wounds upon his adversary. He lifted his head to try and get a closer look at his victim to make sure the threat had passed when a volley of high-powered shots started to rage around him. He immediately ducked his body back down into the confines and safety of the drain.

Bullets were flying everywhere as Pringle and Miller took retribution on what they saw through their binoculars as they followed their partner traipsing through the bush.

As the sound of ricocheting bullets pounded the area and off the boulder that Dane and Ryan had taken cover behind, Ricky and Danny returned fire, receiving much needed back up from a source which neither expected.

Harry and Tom had positioned themselves just below the embankment and seeing Pringle and Miller standing up and exposing themselves for the first time in their quest to mow down the shooters of their partner, with frightful tears, both opened fire at the two exposed gunmen.

For the first time since the siege began, Pringle had lost the upper hand and was being fired upon from three different directions as Dane, realising the opportunity, drew his weapon and began to shoot in Pringle's direction as well.

Pringle and Miller were under full attack, the intensity of the bombardment was ferocious. They couldn't take aim at anyone, they were confused and rattled, and suddenly, in one spontaneous moment they went from being the hunters to be the hunted.

Pringle took a shot to his right hand, almost severing his thumb; he released his revolver in pain. It was a futile exercise to fire back, his experience told him that, although they had far more superior weapons at their disposal, it had become impossible for him to use, he could no longer hold his weapon and the potency of the assault was stunningly fierce.

He raced to take cover, pulling out a cloth from the front pocket of his trousers to wrap around his hand. He had totally miscalculated the fortitude and tenacity of his prey, and the firepower they had. Pringle knew they had weapons, most men did these days, but he grossly underestimated how many of them would use them.

His experience saw that most men would avoid a confrontation if cornered, to lay down their arms if it meant staying alive and take their chances surrendering to his manipulative and bloodthirsty ways. It was an ever-increasing violent world they all now lived in and John Pringle excelled in it. He had made a living out of people's vulnerability and saw first-hand that most men would give up almost anything, including their freedom to stay alive, however, he had underestimated this group of men whose commitment to each other would far and away exceed their own individual needs.

'Get to the horses!' he yelled at Miller.

The horses were tethered to a group of trees by the roadside, further up behind where the Devlin brothers were situated. They were positioned to make a clean and fast exit downhill from where they were located on the ridge. It was supposed to take one shot and they were out of there before anyone realised what was happening, but Pringle's horse seemed a long mile away to him now.

Pringle yelled again, 'C'mon Max, we've gotta get out of here.'

There was no answer from his partner.

'Max, where the hell are ya?' he bellowed.

Pringle stepped back to where he had come from and saw Miller laying in the scrub, gasping for his last breath. Pringle dropped to the ground and crawled to his friend's side. The barrage of bullets had ceased from the desperate men below, but it was all too late for Max Miller. He had taken a deluge of hits to the body from head to toe. His boss leant across him. Miller took one last look out of his devilish blue eyes and then relinquished his life in the same manner he had personally inflicted to many before.

John Pringle entered the Syrian creek road with four men by his side, thinking he would exit it the same way that afternoon, but now he would leave alone. His two best right-hand men had given their lives to the ways of his occupation and wasn't going to hang around to join them. He snatched the strap of Miller's rifle off the ground and scampered down the ridge towards his horse, running past Matt Devlin on the way.

He stopped for a brief second to see the oldest of the Devlin brothers hunched up behind a tree still in shock; a deadened look gripped his face. Pringle didn't utter a word to him, not even an apology or sympathetic word towards his slayed brother, who still lay on the road in a dusty pool of blood.

Pringle raced to his horse, with every step the pain in his hand worsened as the jolting of his running action pulsated through his wound. As he scrambled atop his horse, he took one last look back towards the mayhem and carnage that he had left behind and took off as fast as he could. He needed immediate aid to his wound before he would lose too much blood and needed to get back to Tangiloo for help, but if Danny thought that was going to be the last he would see of John Pringle, he could think again.

Pringle had just lost two of his closest allies. He was no longer working for the Minister anymore; this was a not a job anymore. It had just become personal, and as soon as his hand was half usable, he would come after Danny again. Wiser and more determined to finish what he had started, with or without payment.

Pringle struggled his way back to the cabin. It was a tortuous ride handling the reins in one hand and trying to keep his balance in the saddle only extenuated his pain. He finally arrived at the cabin where his partners had spent the previous night. By the time he had arrived he had no more strength to go on. He had lost a lot of blood and proceeded to do his best to sew his mangled thumb back to his hand. He had a lot of experience when it came to first aid, he had too to survive the job he was in, they were the risks. All he could was take as many painkillers as he could and get some sleep so he could muster the strength to move on when morning came.

'He's gone, he's pissed off!' Harry yelled across to his buddies after he had seen Pringle hurriedly ride off.

Harry yelled again to his partners as to what he had seen, and on his assurance, Danny, Ricky and Barny emerged from the protection of the drain and made a quick dash across the road back to Harry and Tom. They still had their guns at the ready. They kept as low as they could, looking attentively up and around the surrounding bush as they ran. They still didn't know whether the other two were dead and weren't about to take any chances as they jumped and slid over the embankment to safety.

'Everyone alright?' Barny asked.

He looked around to each of his buddies to get a reassurance that they had survived without injury. The only scar they would carry away from this twenty-minute nightmare would be the ones they couldn't see.

'It's a miracle, what a bloody miracle, thank you, Lord,' Barny sighed.

'What do we do now?' asked Harry.

'We get to our bloody horses and get the hell out of here,' Danny hurriedly instructed.

The men ran towards their now settled horses mingling together about 400 meters down the road.

'Go back to the caves. I'll meet you there later,' Danny ordered as he climbed aboard his horse. He turned his horse around in the opposite direction ready to take off.

'What are you doing?' Ricky blasted.

'There's something I have to do; it won't take long.'

'What do ya mean? You're not fuckin going after him?' Ricky insinuated, thinking Danny had completely lost his mind and wanted to get to Pringle.

'What! Do you think I'm that stupid?' Danny forcefully retorted. 'I just need to get something, no time to explain, I'll meet you back at the cascades.'

Danny didn't hang around for any more conversation and left his buddies abruptly. They too took off towards their destination.

Danny wanted to get to Tambourine Bridge. It was his only chance to see if Damien had delivered Greta's letter. He was going to make up an excuse to stop there beforehand and wasn't going to let the opportunity slip without trying to hear from his wife.

He flew straight by Dane and Ryan, ignoring their requests to stop, then quickly disappeared out of sight around the S-bend, leaping his horse over the dead body of Eddie Devlin. Within a few minutes of hard riding, he came to the bridge and hurriedly dismounted from his horse, falling on his hands and knees in his haste. He ran through the bush, swiping away low-lying branches until he reached the log. With pleading anticipation, he reached his arm into the hollow log and felt around until he could feel the sensation of paper on his nervous fingers.

'Bingo, oh, you're a good man, Damien,' he excitedly said as he dragged two envelopes from out of the hollow.

He sat against the log and feverishly started to rip open one of the letters, screwing up the envelope it came in and throwing it away. He firstly opened the letter from Greta and anxiously began to read, forgetting about the madness and danger around him.

Dear Danny,

I can't begin to imagine what you are going through now. I know you must be frightened at what has happened. I am safe and being looked after at Corey and Sarah's for the time being until the police allow me back to our house. Corey and Sarah have been wonderful looking after our kids as well. I still don't understand what went on but believe you when you say that it was self-defence. I know you could not shoot anyone in the way they are saying.

I can't give you an answer on whether you should give yourself up or not, that has to be your decision, I don't want you in jail, but I don't want to lose you either. I will stand by you in whatever decision you make, as I too know in my heart that we will be together again soon. I'm going to try my best to get the truth out and help clear your name as I can't sit back and do nothing. I will fight as best I can for you, Danny.

Darcy and Daniel are okay. I don't think they realise what has happened to their daddy yet, but I fear it's only a matter of time before they do. I am coping the best I can but not getting much sleep as I miss and worry about you terribly. I love you more than anything in the world and only want you back in my arms as soon as possible. You know I will wait for you; I don't care how long it takes, so whatever you decide to do, just make sure you stay out of trouble for a while until everything can be sorted out.

Try not to worry about me too much, I will be fine. You just look after yourself and no matter what happens or no matter what you do, never forget that I will always love you and will be thinking about you every second until you are safely back with us.

Love you forever.
Greta.

Danny started to wipe away the tears that had formed in his eyes, sniffling back hard, still looking at the letter wanting to read it again. He was so engrossed in hearing from Greta his awareness of what was around had slipped dramatically.

He lifted his eyes and saw a rifle pointing directly at him. Matt Devlin had had him in his sights as Danny had lost himself in the letter. The eldest of the brothers had watched Danny ride past from behind the safety of the large tree, awakening him from the shock that had set in over the death of his brother. He made sure he couldn't be seen and then followed Danny to Tambourine Bridge.

Danny froze upon seeing him there. All he could do was look down the barrel that was aimed squarely between his eyes from only a couple of meters away. He slowly drew his eyes to Matt Devlin's and thought this was going to be it. He was finally going to meet his maker. He resigned himself to the fact that he was going to die and as he sat there helplessly, a strange feeling came over him. There was no begging for his life, no trying to make excuses for what he had done to Matt's brothers. Danny didn't want to die, no one does, but at least he was going to die knowing that his beautiful wife understood and still loved him dearly.

It was a thought Danny could die peacefully and contented with. Going to the grave with Greta close to his heart, but as the eternal seconds ticked on, he was starting to realise that Devlin wasn't about to shoot at all.

As Danny was busily reading away, Matt had crept through the bush until he came across him only meters away from the log and began to raise his rifle, slowly squeezing at the trigger. He wanted to kill him; he had him where he wanted him, Pruitt wouldn't know what was coming, an easy open shot. No one would ever know that he did it. It was the best chance he had of avenging the murders of his brothers but the longer he waited, the more he couldn't execute that fatal blow. He was not a killer like the men he rode with into Kensington, no matter how hard he willed himself to pull the trigger; he couldn't bring himself to do it.

'What are ya waiting for?' Danny calmly asked.

Devlin looked at him in silence. His hands were trembling as the nervous sweat poured from his forehead. He began to slowly lower his rifle.

'C'mon, I haven't got all day,' Danny continued, gaining confidence as every second passed.

'Throw your gun away,' Matt Devlin nervously ordered. 'I'm taking you back to Graceville.'

Danny tossed his revolver to the ground. Devlin slowly made the uneasy short walk and picked it up. He then backpedalled to his horse which had slowly followed him with the big black gelding and shoved the gun in his saddlebag, whilst never taking his eyes of Danny.

Devlin silently gave off a sigh of relief; his heart rate dropped a couple of notches.

'Good or bad news,' Devlin asked as he nodded his head, referring to the letter Danny still had firmly grasped in his hand.

'It's from my wife,' Danny confided. 'I was halfway through it before I was rudely interrupted. There's another page I haven't read yet, so with your permission I would like to finish it and then I'm yours, what do ya reckon?' he asked, hoping Devlin would show some compassion. 'Listen, I don't want any more killing than you do, let me read the rest of the letter and I will come with you, I swear. I've had enough, I just want to go home. It's from my wife, let me read it.'

'Alright, but hurry up,' Devlin replied.

Danny ripped open the second envelope, thinking it was another page from Greta as Matt Devlin searched through Danny's baggage on his horse, relieving it from any weapons that he had attached. He confiscated his sawn off .22 rifle, three more handguns, all ammunition and his trusted hunting knife and packed them onto his own horse, still with his rifle at the ready in his right hand.

Devlin was busily preparing to take Danny back to Graceville, wanting to get moving as soon as he could. Dane was still in the area and he surmised that he was a friend of Danny's and wouldn't take very kindly to him riding with the likes of Pringle, and mourning the loss of his brother, Matt Devlin was in no state of mind to confront anyone else at the present time.

Within a few short minutes, Devlin was pressuring Danny to get up on his horse and leave with him. Danny didn't budge; he sat like a statue against the log, his whole demeanour had changed. It wasn't a continuation of the letter from his wife as he had thought. He had just read that his house had been pillaged by the Re-Po squad. His sister had described as best she could on what had happened in the short letter with the names of those involved beneath her description.

The calm and solitude that Danny had felt minutes ago had all but disappeared into a growing rage that was building inside his now muscle tensed body.

Devlin immediately sensed the change in Danny's persona.

'What's wrong, the missus leaving ya?' he quipped.

Danny didn't answer. He rose to his feet and strode towards his horse, shoving both letters into his front pocket, refusing to give Devlin a second look.

'Before we go, you're going to help me get my brother and bring him back with us,' Devlin ordered.

Again, Danny refused to acknowledge. He jumped aboard his horse, ignoring requests to dismount. Devlin no longer existed to him. He turned big black in the opposite direction and began to ride away from his captor deeper into the bush. Danny was full of fury; his mind was racing; he didn't know where to turn. He desperately wanted to see his wife, but revenge on the re-po squad soaked his mind. He had to get out of there, and nothing was going to stop him, not even a bullet in the back.

'Get back here!' Devlin yelled.

Danny kept riding; he ignored the gun pointed at him. If Devlin had the courage to shoot him, he would have done it before when he had had the chance.

Devlin rode furiously after him, yelling orders to stop, threatening to shoot if he didn't come to a halt. Danny rode his horse like a man possessed, charging through the virgin bush, ducking at low branches, storming through clusters of shrubbery and undergrowth, disregarding any safety measures for himself and the big black gelding underneath him.

Devlin pursued, he knew he was the better rider out of the two and strived to keep up, hoping Danny would be his own worst enemy. Devlin had had enough, he was the law, and he was well within his rights to shoot a prisoner on the run, and now he had drawn the courage to fire. Danny was ducking and weaving in all directions as Devlin tried his hardest to get a clear shot away, but the tall forest trees were making it difficult. He stopped his horse and fired a warning shot, hoping Danny would come to his senses and give himself up, but he aggressively kept on.

Devlin again urged his horse forward then halted meters before a shallow dip; Danny had quickly disappeared from his sights. He noticed the big black horse appear out of the dip where Danny went in at suicidal pace. Devlin then dismounted and look around cautiously. Unbeknown to him, Danny had taken a nasty fall trying to negotiate a second dip in the terrain that fell sharply away into a shallow mossy flat bed.

Silence again gripped the surroundings as he crept through the bush in the direction where he thought Danny to be. With rifle to his eyes and not hearing a sound except for the refuse beneath his feet, he slowly moved forward towards the dip. The upbeat pounding of his heart was thumping through his body as he came to a slight ridge whilst looking down across the moss-covered rocks and fallen rotten timber that lay below him.

Was Pruitt injured? Was he still there? Had he gotten away on foot? *Do I turn around, get my brother and get out of here?* The agitated thoughts rushed through Devlin's mind.

Five slow steps down the little ravine he took, looking to see if he could get a glance of where Danny may be. Nothing but untouched forest was in front of him. He encroached further down the angled embankment, keeping his balance, rifle at the ready in both hands. The sweat was profusely dripping down his face as he steadily made his way to where the forest floor flattened out. He was almost at the bottom, about to pass the last tall mountain ash where the terrain levelled to a section of low-lying native grasses and shrubs.

Devlin relaxed; his target had escaped him, his senses told him. He lowered his rifle to his waist to figure out what direction Danny would have taken by foot, when suddenly, an almighty blow descended on his face, instantly knocking him to the ground, releasing the grip on his rifle from the impact of the savage strike.

Devlin lay on his back in an instance. He looked up through the blurred vision of his eyes from the forest floor and raised his shaking right hand. Blood was streaming from his face; the severe hit had opened a gash across his forehead and nose.

Wet and dripping from his fall into the small shallow wetland, Danny had concealed himself behind a large tree and bided his time until his pursuer came to him. The fall from big black gave him no injuries. A solid branch lay beneath the giant tree he hid behind, around a meter in length and as thick as his arm. He clasped in both hands and when his senses told him that Devlin was within striking range, he unleashed the most powerful swing he could produce.

Danny leapt towards the now isolated rifle as Devlin lay on the ground. He grabbed it in both hands, rolled several times over on his side until he was out of reach from his adversary. He regained his balance, lifting himself to one knee.

Laying on his back, Devlin's right hand was reaching underneath his vest. Danny fired a single shot from the already cocked rifle into the side below his ribcage. The already wounded Devlin let out an almighty howl of pain from the impact. Danny jumped atop of him, opening his vest in a hasty panic.

'Where's the gun, you bastard? Where's the fuckin gun?' he raged as he rummaged through his clothes.

Danny almost stripped the vest off Devlin's upper body in search of the alleged weapon. There was no gun to be found, only a handkerchief in one of the inline pockets that Devlin needed to wipe away the blood that had instantly dripped into his eyes.

It was a gross misjudgement from Danny; he had put a bullet into someone who was unarmed and defenceless. It was a split-second call and, in his mind, it was an unavoidable incident. He was sure that Devlin was reaching for a weapon and with all the carnage that had happened around him in the previous hour, he had no hesitation in thinking as such and held no sympathy towards the wounded Devlin.

Danny grabbed the handkerchief in his hand and shoved it into his side.

'Why did you shoot me, you didn't need to shoot me,' he mumbled in pain.

'Shut up, just shut up!' said an anguished Danny.

He grabbed a towel from Devlin's horse then pilfered through his saddlebags until he came across his first aid kit. He raced back to Devlin and filled the entrance wound with packing to try and stop the bleeding. Danny went back to grab Devlin's swag off his horse. He laid it underneath his head to give him some comfort and gave him a drink from his water bottle. Not a word was spoken between the two for the next five frantic minutes as Danny did his best to ease his pain.

Danny sat himself up against a tree metres away from where he lay when Devlin turned his head at him.

'You've got to get me back to Tangiloo, you've gotta get me help,' he pleaded.

'In a minute; first, you're going to answer some questions,' Danny snapped back.

He had read Kate's letter again and the anger was building inside once more. He envisaged his wife being dragged away as his sons watched on, helpless and afraid. It was unbearable to him and the comment that young Billy Devlin had made about touching up his wife was eating away at him at unstoppable speed. She may as well have been gangraped, was Danny's mindset, and as every second ticked by, he became more enraged.

Kate had forgotten to mention in her short letter that Greta was nowhere near her home at the time. Although Danny was pleased and relieved that Greta was safe at Corey and Sarah's house, he also knew that Greta would never tell him if anything of the sort had taken place. He knew his wife wouldn't give any bad news. Knowing how the Re-po squad worked, he envisaged the worst, and he was going to take it all out on the now wounded and eldest Devlin.

Danny opened the piece of paper which listed the names of the men who were with the Re-Po squad. Kate had written that twelve were involved, seven of which she had written down and four that Danny recognised. One he knew the address of, a man named Kenny Jamieson, a local man with good reputation, it surprised him when he saw it written down. Danny wanted the addresses of the other men on the list and determined that Matt Devlin would be able to help him. After all, he was a copper and Danny knew for a fact that all the brothers had boasted that they knew associates who had participated in the low life acts of the Re-Po squad.

Danny started with finding out the addresses of the men he knew.

'Mark Cox, do you know where he lives?' Danny asked.

'Yeah, why?'

'Just give me the address.'

'I'm not telling you shit!' Devlin replied.

'Listen here, if you want help, answer the questions or I'm gonna walk away and let the bugs finish you off, do you understand me?' Danny warned.

'Hillside road, 23, I think,' Devlin spluttered.

'That's better, now we're getting somewhere,' Danny said as he took his seat back up against the tree. 'Victor Slacek, who is he and where does he live?' Danny continued.

'He's a copper, he lives up on Mt Rickshaw Road, on the corner of Denham.'

'He's a big blond-headed bloke, isn't he?' Danny asked.

'Yeah.'

'What about Malcolm Dewhurst, you know him, don't ya?'

'Yeah.'

'Dark-haired bloke with tats, is that the one?' Danny hurriedly asked.

Devlin nodded his head in agreement as he sighed in pain. Every breath he took was now feeling like someone was driving a red-hot knife deep into his body.

The interrogation continued. 'Where does he live?'

Devlin didn't answer as Danny busily wrote down the information he was receiving on the envelope.

'Where does he fuckin live?' he bellowed.

'Three houses down from Cox,' Devlin answered. 'Why do you want these names for, just get me some bloody help, I'm dying here, for Christ's sake!'

Danny ignored his plea; he was only intent on getting the identities and addresses of the remaining men and again warned Devlin that he would leave him if he didn't cooperate.

'Terry Bishop, Steve Carrington and Tony Docherty, do you know any of these men?' Danny interrogated again.

'I should have killed you when I had the chance,' Devlin retorted, whose moans of pain were getting more intense and longer by the second as he gasped for air that was quickly disappearing from his blood-filled lungs.

Danny leant over him again, grabbed him by the hair, pulled his head backwards and whispered into his face, 'There's an old saying in this world my boy.'

'Yeah, and what's that?' Devlin strained.

'Don't hunt what you can't kill.'

Devlin knew exactly what the comment meant and not only regretted his earlier decision not to shoot, but most of all, ever meeting up with Pringle and his men and entering this damn forest. Danny roughly released the grip he had on him and once again vigorously asked if he knew any of the men he had just mentioned.

'I'm not telling you anymore until you tell me why you want these names,' Devlin spluttered.

'You want to know why; I'll tell you fuckin why!' Danny angrily yelled. He waved the piece of paper in Delvin's face. 'These men destroyed my house and stole from me. My wife and sons have nowhere to live anymore and I'll get every fuckin one who did this us.'

'You won't get nowhere near them; you wouldn't even get within five miles of town,' Devlin sniggered, coughing away his blood. 'And you can forget about ever seeing your pretty wife again. We're watching her like a hawk; I know that for a fact. You go near her and you're dog meat, cop killer.'

Danny was shaking in anger; he needed more information on the men he didn't know. He ignored Devlin's comments and sat back against the tree and continued to grill him on the names. 'Bishop, Carrington, Docherty, who are they and where do they live?'

For the next few minutes, Danny continued as calmly as he could, trying to coax the information he desperately needed but only now quiet moans and groans of pain and the sporadic coughing up of blood was coming from the hapless Devlin.

He was losing blood quickly. The bullet had pierced internal organs and if he wasn't going to die losing the blood out of his wound, he was going to drown in it. He couldn't muster the strength to talk any longer and Danny's frustration was exploding. Fire was running through his veins; he blindingly needed the information and sanity was leaving him. He snared the branch off the ground and began to poke it into the wound on Devlin's side.

Jab, jab, he poked, while his teeth grinded. Jab, jab, jab, again he forced the branch into the bleeding hole in Devlin's side, twisting and pushing as he went.

'Talk to me, you bastard!' he yelled.

Push, jab, jab again.

But the only noises coming from Devlin were splutters of pain. There was no strength left in his body to muster anything else other than a stare of death whilst gargling for air.

Danny straddled himself atop of him and grabbed at his bloodied vest.

'Don't you die on me yet!' he shouted.

Devlin shook and inhaled his last breath, his eyes frozen still.

Danny stood up next to the lifeless body. 'You haven't told me who the others are, tell me who the others are!' he screamed over and over.

He started kicking into him in violent frustration, one thrust after another, but Devlin's body lay motionless on the ground, only moving from the vigorous blows of Danny's boots.

Danny was incensed. He threw the branch as far as his strength could muster then walked up to the nearest tree and with tears of angst bursting out of his weary eyes, began to punch the trunk as hard as he could, drawing blood on his knuckles within the first few strikes. He pounded the bark off the tree with every bruising blow until he could muster no more strength then slumped to the ground, howling to the skies.

Danny was at the lowest point he had ever been in his life. The anger, the frustration, the remorsefulness he now felt, the extreme loneliness around him, and along with the enormous fear and uncertainty he had held within was all coming out in one massive explosion. He had a pain inside he had never come close to feeling before, the gigantic knot twisted and turned inside his stomach with every breath he took, which in turn made him physically ill from the torment within.

This was not the man he was, the killing of other human beings, the threats, the vengeance he felt. His life had changed forever in only a few short days and he now knew that there was no turning back. The life and peace he once treasured had all but gone.

He held his head between his bleeding hands, spitting away the saliva and internal muck from his mouth. For the first time since he had left Rosco and Billy Devlin in his yard, he began to ask himself, 'Why, why has all this happened?'

He whispered Greta's name aloud, hoping she would appear out of nowhere and give him the guidance he so badly needed. Finally, leaning up against the tree which now displayed the blood stains from his outburst, and with only the peaceful sound of the native bird life that had re-emerged, he started to regain his composure. Slowly immersing himself out of his self-pity, he rose to his feet and took a deep breath.

The realisation of never setting foot back in Graceville engulfed him. After the last hour, the law would want him more than ever. He decided to head back to the sanctuary of the caves where the support of his buddies lay in wait, but before he could do that, he would have to pass straight back through Dane and Ryan.

With the help of Tom, they had spent the time gathering the dead bodies from the positions they laid after Dane took photographs for evidence. It was as gruesome a job as it could be for them, particularly trying to remove Karl's horse off his crushed and listless body. Failing to remove it by themselves they had to attach a rope to Ryan's horse and dragged the 500kg animal off the body of their close friend, leaving copious amounts of blood on the dirt road as they dragged the horse away.

Everywhere they looked, the area was blood-soaked from the dead as they laid the bodies next to one another across the road, six in all. Dane couldn't leave the bodies behind, especially his friends, and although he had no ounce of sorrow whatsoever for Morris and Miller's corpses, he knew it was his duty to get them back to Tangiloo to the right authorities. The photographs would insure and back up his statements of the shootout.

With blankets they had attached to their horses, the men wrapped the bodies up and secured them. It was the hardest and worst task the men had ever undertaken. Although Dane had seen dead and bloodied bodies before in his time in the force, nothing could prepare him for something of this magnitude. To see it unfold before his very eyes and to see his friends die the way they did was almost unbearable. Holding their emotions in check to get the job done, hardly a word was spoken between them as they went about their tasks, only looks of despair and disbelief passed among the grieving men. The three were in the middle of hoisting the bodies over each of the dead men's horses when they heard hooves nearing them from around the bend.

Still on tenterhooks and believing it could be Pringle returning to finish his assignment, they rushed for cover with Dane and Ryan drawing their revolvers and took aim at whatever was coming their way. With great nervous relief, their weapons were soon back in their holsters when eyes were laid on the oncoming rider. Danny appeared on his horse while leading another behind him, Devlin's horse with his lifeless body across it, minus its saddle and gear.

Danny stopped his horse as the group ousted themselves, still adjusting his weapons and belongings he retrieved off Matt Devlin. He surveyed the area with a sorrowful look upon his face then turned to Dane and Ryan. There was an eerie silence between the men, none of them knew exactly what to say to one another, until Danny broke the icy stare off.

'Got another body for you.'

'Yeah, we heard the shot,' Ryan replied in disapproval.

'It was either him or me, just like the others,' Danny said with a sense of apology as he looked across to the men hoping for sympathy. It would not be forthcoming.

'How does it feel, Danny?' Dane angrily retorted.

'How does what feel?'

'Single-handedly almost killing off a whole fucking family!'

'You can't put that on me,' Danny replied shaking his head.

'What do you want to do next, find young Mickey, then their mother and make it complete?'

Danny was in disbelief of what Dane was saying. Surely, he would understand that he had no choice. He continued to cast blame on everything that had happened towards Danny, accusing him being responsible for all the dead, including Karl. Now ignoring Dane's bellowing, Danny dismounted and walked towards the horse of Eddie Devlin. He couldn't come back with a reply to what Dane was accusing him of, even if he could, no one would be able to hear over Dane's ever-increasing shouting.

Rightly or wrongly, the Sergeant was taking it all out on Danny, he was giving it to him with a verbal tirade and Danny only added to his anger by not looking at him as his volatile words gathered momentum.

Danny reached into the tightly packed saddlebag draped over Eddie Devlin's horse as Dane's tirade continued, thinking that if Matty was partial to a drink, maybe his brother would be as well after raiding his belongings. Three bottles of the finest bourbon were to be found. He pulled them out of the saddlebag and squeezed two into what room he had left in his, the other bottle went into one of the side pockets of his worn and dusty khaki jacket he had just donned and then climbed aboard his horse.

'Where the hell do you think you're going?' Dane blasted.

'I can't fuckin go home, can I?' Danny answered calmly. 'I'm sorry for all this, Dane.' He continued, 'I'm sorry for Karl, he was my friend too, don't forget that. I'm sorry for ya two mates, but none of this is my doing. You didn't have to come looking for me, that was your choice, not mine. And as for the others, they can go to hell; they wanted to kill me, so I don't give a shit about them. They all pushed me too far, Dane, and now my life is over, so don't you dare try and blame me for any of this or tell me what to fuckin do.'

Dane finished strapping up the body of Johnny Hayes to his horse, spitting away the dryness in his mouth.

'You're coming back with us,' he firmly said.

'What, so you can lead me into another ambush? I don't think so,' Danny argued.

'We'll take the back tracks; you're coming back with us,' Dane reiterated.

'I'm not going to jail, Dane, no way, you can't make me,' said Danny.

Ryan interrupted. 'C'mon Danny,' he pleaded. 'We'll work things out. If we tell the truth, you shouldn't do much time,' he confidently predicted. 'Nothing is worth throwing away your life like this. If you ride away, you're showing your guilt and it will make things a hell of a lot tougher on ya, come with us back to Tangiloo.'

'Sorry Ryan, I can't do that,' came the stern reply. 'There's probably more like Pringle out there waiting, so if I were you, I would be worried about yourselves and forgetting about me.'

Ryan looked at Danny with a look of desperation on his face, he didn't want his brother-in-law to ride off; if he did, there would be no turning back for him.

'Come home with us, Danny. Go home to Greta, she's probably going out of her mind, don't leave her like this.'

'I have no home anymore,'

He produced the letters out of his pocket that he had received and waved them in front of Ryan. 'Greta's alright, mate, I've already heard from her, she understands,' he said.

'Where did you get them from?' Dane forcefully interrupted.

'That's none of your fuckin business,' Danny promptly replied.

He turned to Ryan again whilst shrugging off his persistent pleas. 'Oh yeah, say thanks to Kate for me.'

'What for?' he asked, bewildered that his wife could in anyway be involved with this moment.

'She will know what for,' Danny said as he turned his horse around.

He wanted to tell them all about the Re-po squad and what they had done to him, it would justify his stance even further, but couldn't do so. If he did that, it would mean divulging his sister's involvement with him. She had written in her letter that it was against the wishes of all around and knew that Ryan and Dane would have the same opinions. He knew Ryan would drag Kate over the coals for letting him know, so if they were going to find out, it was not going to come from him.

He was extremely grateful towards Kate for going out on a limb for him. He also agreed that she was damn right in saying that he had a right to know, so for the time being he would keep the snowballing anger of the re-po squad happenings to himself.

Danny looked at Tom and asked him what he was doing.

'I'm going back home, Danny. This is all too much for me mate, I want see my family again.'

'Good luck, it's the right thing to do.'

He reached into his coat pocket and pulled out the bourbon bottle and threw it towards Ryan who caught it in his right hand.

'Happy New Year, boys, I hope it starts better than this one has finished,' Danny said as he began to slowly ride off, however, Dane wasn't about to let Danny off that easy, he was a policeman and had a job to do.

He pulled his revolver from his holster once again and pointed it at Danny as he slowly cantered off with his back to the Sergeant.

'Danny!' he yelled. 'I order you to stop as a police officer of the Hexagon Valley.'

There was no response. Danny increased his speed on his horse as again, Dane yelled at him to stop.

'Danny, pull your fuckin horse up,' he loudly demanded.

'I couldn't if I tried,' he snapped back.

Dane's repeated requests were falling on deaf ears, he was desperate and didn't want him out of his grasp again. He took aim with his revolver, as an astonished Ryan and Tom looked on.

'Don't do it, Dane,' Ryan nervously pleaded.

The tension was palpable; with all that had happened to the men, no one was sure who was thinking straight and who wasn't, and for a brief second or two it looked as if Senior Sergeant Dane Grainger was going to put his work before friendship. Moments after, he lowered his gun as Danny rode out of sight with the sound of the Sergeant's frustrated obscenities echoing through the mountains.

Danny was free again to ride through the familiar surroundings of the bush he knew well. The helplessness had left him, slowly being replaced by a feeling of invincibility as he thought what might have been. From the time Rosco and Billy Devlin paid that visit at his house he had had a hostile gun pointed at him no less than a dozen occasions from a dozen different individuals and never once had a bullet even come close to nicking him.

He had walked away without a mark, and by his own hands had inflicted fatal wounds upon so called more experienced men. He was six-nil up, his distorted brain was telling him, and the game had just begun. If you include the officer that Ricky shot, which he was getting the rap for, that made it seven-nil.

The more he delved into his reckless conscience, the more he was smugly laughing to himself. He was arrogantly losing perspective on what had happened to his life, his thoughts for Greta and his sons had all but disappeared. There was only one thing that was going through his mind as he confidently rode the big black gelding through the winding road back to the cascades, the payback and revenge on all those in the re-po squad who took part in the trashing of his beloved home.

It was a highly dangerous mulling from a now desperate, lonely and vengeful man, whose mental demons and single-mindedness would infiltrate all those who would come across him in the times ahead.

Chapter 13

'Good evening, boys,' Danny announced with a broad smile.

'Danny! Shit mate, we were beginning to think you weren't coming,' Barny said, relieved that he had once again joined them.

Danny had just arrived back at the caves where Barny, Ricky and Harry had spent the last few nerve-wracking hours discussing what they should do next.

'Couldn't leave you boys behind, you'll all get lost out here without me,' Danny gibed.

'What's happening, Danny, what are we going to do?' fretted Harry.

'Well, we can't hang around these parts anymore, get your stuff together and let's get the hell out of here.'

Danny shared his fears that the Kensington Forest would soon be crawling with police after what had happened. However, the frightened group of four were unaware that nearly eighty percent of the police search party assigned by the Minister were already heading back down to Graceville. The news from town about the government announcement had filtered through to the troops in the Mt Lucia range and to the anger and frustration of those in charge, the ones who had already made it through to Tangiloo were descending back to Graceville.

After hearing the great news, the only concern to the officers was getting back to their family and friends so they didn't miss out on what was going to be the best New Year's Eve party Graceville had seen in a decade. They had left their posts almost immediately and didn't want to waste their time stuck in the bush going after a man most of them thought they had no chance of catching anyway. A large percentage in the search parties already knew Danny and respected him well, and any excuse to forfeit the manhunt was good enough for them.

Hardly any of them had a good word to say about the Devlin brothers in the first place and if they had a choice of spending another night in the bush or partying with friends, the latter won hands down. By the time Dane and Ryan arrived in Tangiloo later that evening, on the thin hope of meeting Inspector Vaccaro to give him the gruesome news about the shootout and slayings, the makeshift police headquarters set up in Tangiloo where the search parties were all supposed to meet had only a handful of members left. The Minister's need for a quick fix to law enforcement in his Shire was biting back at him and the usual lack of discipline was showing its head when he least needed it. So, for the moment, not enough officers were available to send out any kind search party and it was looking like the boys were going to put some valuable time between them and their pursuers whether they knew it or not.

Barny and Harry were quickly gathering their belongings as Danny spoke of his plans.

'We'll head up to Domino Falls, it's only a couple of hours away up an old walking track I know. We'll camp there the night and start heading over the Midnight Range in the morning. In a couple of days, we'll hook on to an old fire track on the ridge that will take us right back to the Northeast tip of Graceville. From there I'll show you how to get back to the city without too much hassle, at least we'll be out of here until things blow over,' Danny ended.

Barny and Harry were excited about the prospect of finding a way home, however remote it may have sounded, but Ricky was going to take a lot more convincing than some bizarre story about traipsing through virgin forest he knew nothing about with the law on their backs.

'What's wrong, you're not packing?' Danny asked.

Ricky stood defiantly as the other two gathered what they had and jumped aboard their horses.

'C'mon Rick, let's go,' Harry insisted.

Ricky looked up at Harry, shaking his head in bewilderment on how easily they had both succumbed to Danny's suggestions without so much as blinking an eyelid. He then turned his attention towards Danny and with ever increasing anger began to display his objections.

'Blow over, blow over, you think all this will just blow over. You're going fuckin mad, Danny!' he blasted.

'Just a figure of speech, Ricky.'

'I don't fuckin care. How many people have died because of us?' he said, exasperated. 'Eight, nine?'

'Make that ten, I killed Matty Devlin,' Danny almost joyfully said.

'Is that why you left? To hunt him down and take him out as well, you've completely lost it, Danny!' Ricky thundered.

'It wasn't like that,' Danny replied, trying to calm his friend down by moving towards him and laying his hand on his back.

Ricky picked his swag up off the cave floor in haste. He was in no mood to hear any details of what had happened and forcibly pushed at Danny when he stood.

'If you think I'm following you up into those mountains, you've got rocks in ya head, mate,' Ricky bluntly announced. 'People are dying around you, Danny, and it's only a matter of time before it's one of us. You can go wherever you want, but I'm out of here as of now.'

Ricky was about to jump aboard his horse, ignoring the pleas from Barny and Harry to reconsider his stance when Danny walked over to the exit of the caves and stood in its pathway.

'Get out of my way,' gritted Ricky.

'Where ya gonna go, mate?' Danny asked as his frown deepened. 'You don't know ya way around these parts. Besides, it will be dark in a few hours and the joint will be teaming with coppers and if they find you, which they will, they'll probably shoot ya as quick as look at ya. You already know what they're like, especially now,' Danny pleaded, using all his persuasive powers as he held Ricky's reins tightly.

Ricky's frustration was at overload; he dismounted off his horse and charged towards Danny, knocking him to the ground. 'Get out of my way!' he yelled. The men wrestled vigorously on the sandy floor of the caves. Barny and Harry quickly separated the feuding buddies before they could inflict damage on one another. The two then dusted themselves down as the verbal stoush continued.

'I'm not letting you go out there alone,' Danny insisted.

'You don't rule my fuckin life, Danny, not you, not anyone,' Ricky responded, almost shoving his finger down Danny's throat.

'You won't have a life to live if you try and make a run for it,' said Danny. 'But if you want to run, that's your choice, doesn't surprise me anyway, it's always what you've done.'

'What's that supposed to fucking mean?' Ricky argued.

'You've always ran when the going's got tough, every time something's gone wrong, or you've had to show some responsibility, or you have to commit to something, or show some leadership of some kind, you take off like a scalded cat.'

Danny wasn't holding back about his deep-down thoughts of his buddy and wasn't about to stop there and began to give Ricky examples from the past.

'That's why you could never hold down a job for a long time. Every time they would try and promote you, you would piss off to another job, so you wouldn't have any responsibilities, you've done it all your life, Rick, in everything you do, not to mention Jacquie.'

'What about Jacquie?' Ricky angrily retorted.

Danny knew he had touched a raw nerve. Jacquie was Ricky's one and only true love. Their relationship was a rocky one to say the least because of Ricky's inability to commit to her. She was a beautiful woman who loved Ricky just as much, but every time Jacquie would ask for a little more in their relationship, he would make some excuse to distance himself.

He couldn't handle the pressure of being tied down, whether it was because of his deep-down lack of confidence or the free spirit that manifested inside of him. Whatever it was, in the end, it cost him any chance of true love as Jacquie couldn't wait around for him anymore to maybe someday commit to her. It was the one thing that Ricky really regretted in his life above all else.

Danny continued to hound his mate over it. Ricky had no answers to Danny's comments, he knew he was right in a lot of the things he was saying, but that didn't make it any easier to accept. He knew where he had gone wrong in his life and didn't need to be reminded of it by someone else, especially in this situation. He wasn't as quick tongued as Danny was. He could never find the right words to come out of his mouth in tense situations, probably because he only knew half the vocabulary as a man like Danny did.

Although he was brilliant with his hands, Ricky wasn't overly blessed when it came down to the academic side of things and often struggled to keep up in that category. So, when it came down to a verbal argument, Ricky would never last long and would try to end them with his fists if things weren't panning out his way.

Barny could see that Ricky was building up to punch Danny's lights out and he knew Danny well enough that he too would come back fighting just as hard. It was the last thing the group needed.

'Shut up! Shut the hell up!' he yelled. 'I'm sick of you two at each other's throats all the time, what the hell's wrong with you both?' he demanded as his voice lowered. 'You'll end up killing yourselves before anyone else does; listen to yourselves,' he pleaded, 'you're supposed to be mates, best mates. For Christ's sake, you've got to be on each other's side otherwise none of us will survive this.'

Barny looked at both, begging for them to end the hostilities now and forever. 'We're all in this together, whether we like it or not, so for everybody's sake, cut this shit out and let's move on, *please*.'

The argument ceased as both the men made their way to the horses. All Danny wanted to do was keep his buddy close to him. He knew he wouldn't last more than a few days without being either shot or apprehended. If it took a few home truths then so be it, and he was beginning to think that he had won the mind game. He pulled out one of the whiskey bottles he had stashed away and threw it at Ricky.

'Happy New Year,' he said.

Ricky clasped it tightly in both hands, looking the bottle up and down in silence.

'Shit Danny, where did you get that from?' Harry excitedly asked.

'I've got another five here, along with half a carton of smokes I got from Matty Devlin, but we can only drink them on one condition,' he said.

'What's that?' Harry said.

'If we all get up to Domino falls where we can enjoy them.'

All the men's eyes turned to Ricky to see if he would agree to the terms that Danny had so gracefully put to them.

'What do ya reckon, Rick, want to get pissed, it is New Year's Eve, mate, c'mon.'

Danny threw him the radio he stole out of Matt Devlin's bag. He knew it would make Ricky happy considering the way he had carried on back at St Lucia after he had lost the first one.

'I thought you might need it,' Danny joked.

'Alright, let's go,' Ricky breathed out quietly while nodding his head at his buddies.

It was the response the lads were looking for and within a couple of short breaths, Danny led the way out of the caves for the two-hour journey on the old walking track that took them up to Domino falls. The track was relatively easy progress for them and their horses. The climb was gradual but long, not like the steep terrain they had endured climbing Mt St Lucia. In parts it was wide open as the forest thinned out but as they neared the falls, the track got steeper, and the forest would once again close in on them. Danny would point out landmarks to the lads as they rode on the soft dirt path, dodging the rocks and boulders that laid in their way.

He would also show them the letters he had received. As the boys took turn to read them whilst they rode, they expressed their sorrow and sympathy towards Danny and his family for what had happened, commenting that the people responsible in the re-po squad should get what's coming their way as Danny determinedly spoke about revenge. Time passed quickly for the lads as they engrossed themselves with ideas on how to extract that revenge and before too long, they had arrived at the top of Domino Falls just before nightfall.

Domino Falls was a rugged expanse of smooth granite rock where the water had made its path over centuries, stretching over 50 meters in width in some parts only interrupted by the crevices in its foundations. It was a huge drop over the falls of nearly 150 meters, but at this time of year it was only flowing at half capacity compared to late winter and early spring when it made an awesome sight for those who were privileged enough to see them. The boys were immediately impressed by all its rugged beauty and quickly set up camp upstream from the falls and after successfully trying their hand at catching some native trout, they settled in for a well-earned meal after the sun had set for another day.

As darkness settled in, the glowing embers of the small fire gave them enough light to make sure the small fish and cans of soup were cooked to perfection with Harry doing most of the waitering, much to the delight of the other three lads.

As the whiskey started to disappear into the gullets of the thirsty men, they spoke openly to each other about their feelings on how they felt about the shootout with Pringle and his men. They discussed how scared they were, how they thought they were going to die and the more they talked, the more confidence they were inadvertently supplying to one another. They recalled in detail, at times with a little exaggeration, on the brave deeds each of them did, however, one thing that they bought up amongst themselves as they sat together which got them solemnly thinking to themselves, particularly Harry, was that of the actions they took, actions they thought they were never capable of.

It was deep reflection and led to a belief that they were going to find a way out of this terrible mess, no matter who or what stood in their way and as Danny pointed out to them, that if it doesn't kill you, it can only make you stronger.

It had seemed an eternity since the boys laid their heads down the previous night. It was the longest day any of the men had endured throughout their lifetime; a day in which never in their wildest dreams they could have imagined. A day that had turned a devoted father, a loyal husband, ordinary everyday honest men trying to eke out a living in these hard times into wanted murderers and thieves who were now desperate and reckless enough to make sure the killing wouldn't stop unless they were left alone.

As the alcohol started to take effect, they were becoming more determined as ever on not getting caught. A pact was made that they were never going to spend one second in jail. They assured themselves that what had happened was not their fault and they would be damned if they going to accept blame for any of the killings.

Danny put the blame solely and squarely on anyone and everything from the highest official in government to the lowest appointee of the local Shire and insisted it was them who now taken away what life they had.

As they sat and spoke, drinking away the whiskey and bourbon, Danny preached and drilled his theories into his pals. The more Danny would use his domineering traits, the more and more his buddies were starting to believe and agree, enthusiastically conforming to Danny's passionate hatred of the powers that be, smacking their bottles together in forceful agreement. They all concurred that no one was going to rule their lives anymore. No more obeying the rules of corrupt politicians, no more instructions from corrupt police officers. From now on, they would only answer to each other. It was a desperate single-mindedness that could only lead to more bloodshed if they kept up their newfound treaty. The men already shared a tight bond before, but now the bond between them had strengthened considerably and they would need to call on it continuously if they were to get through the troubled times that lay ahead.

The private party for the four lads became more boisterous as the night went on and the party was also in full swing on the streets of Graceville as the hour closed in on midnight. Everywhere you looked, people were celebrating hard. Greta sat alone quietly on the veranda at Corey and Sarah's house overhearing the festivities from a distance. She was feeling terribly lonely and the more she thought about things, the more the fear of losing her husband forever would engulf her.

She was doing her best to stay strong; the tears would come and go as the night went on. Corey and Sarah did their best to comfort her, even welcoming friends who would come and go during the evening. They would try and coax Greta into joining the festivities, she would politely refuse their requests. All she wanted to do was wait on the thin hope of hearing any news on her husband.

At Tangiloo, Dane and Ryan had arrived late that evening, minus Tom, who had escaped their grasp as soon as he had the chance, much to the angry amusement of them both. They finally met up with Inspector Vaccaro behind the old reception centre where they had planned. The Inspector knew that something had gone terribly wrong, as the lads were long overdue on the estimated time that Constable Hayes had given to him.

Dane still had no idea whether his young partner had ever got in contact with Vaccaro, he didn't even know if he was even in Tangiloo, the radios had either been lost or broken during the shootout. The Inspector was the only one in officialdom that Dane could trust and if he couldn't find him, he had no idea on what move he would make next and was relieved to see the Inspector in waiting.

The Inspector's suspicions that something was amiss was confirmed when he saw nine horses approaching with only two upright riders in the saddle. As

Dane and Ryan neared him, he was horrified at what lay in front of him, seven wrapped up dead and bloodied bodies. From the time he had laid eyes on John Pringle back at the Minister's office, he knew that trouble would not be far way, but even he couldn't comprehend the scale it would be on. Inspector Vaccaro helped untie and lay the bodies on the ground and listened in shock as Dane filled him in on all the appalling details of what had transpired earlier in the day.

Vaccaro was greatly saddened and angry that two young constables had lost their lives at the indirect hands of Minister Johnston and immediately laid blame on him. He promised Dane and Ryan that he would make sure that the Minister would take full responsibility for what had happened and would pay for his ways. It was a promise that he meant, and a promise he would try to the best of his abilities to see through.

Dane and Ryan were too exhausted to travel the extra hour or two down to Graceville, their horses were spent and so were they. They knew they had a duty to inform Karl's wife and the mothers of the two Constables of their deaths but were in no emotional state to do so. They were still trying to make sense of what had happened themselves, so the idea of facing grieving wives and mothers was too much to bare right now. The thought that John Pringle may still be in the vicinity was also in the back of their mind.

Unbeknown to them, he was only a ten-minute ride down the southbound road, resting up in his cabin; however, according to their thinking, he was still out there, and they knew if they came across him in the dark, he would have no hesitation in eliminating the witnesses to his crimes. Both elected to stay in Tangiloo with the Inspector until morning while a Constable was sent back down to Graceville to inform their own families that they will be home tomorrow.

It would be a New Year's Eve that none of the men who came out of Kensington National Park that day would ever forget. They had put their lives on the line and were glad it was all over for the time being at least. Dane and Ryan had a home to go back to in the morning and were feeling grateful and downright lucky that they were able to do so, unlike Karl and the two young Constables, who had seen their home for the last time.

Up at Domino Falls, the liquor bottles had all but been drunk by the time the first hour of the New Year had passed as Danny held the last few sips between his legs. He sat alone against a tree looking over his sleeping friends. They had crawled into their swags before they dropped where they stood after almost drinking themselves into oblivion with Barny slurring his prayers before crashing for the night.

The boys had let their hair down after days of non-stop angst and misery and Danny was pleased with himself for making it possible for them to forget about things, even if it was for only a few drunken hours. But the silence, broken only by the peaceful sound of falling water in the near distance, quickly turned his thoughts back to Greta and his family as he gazed out into the lonely darkness.

The fireworks back in Graceville had been in full swing as the night sky above lit up with explosive colours as the clock struck midnight. The general townsfolk could finally see some light at the end of the tunnel after years of poverty and hardship, but the only light Danny could see out of his eyes was a tiny little star far off in a distant galaxy that would take a miracle to reach.

Chapter 14

'This bloody well better be important, it's 5.30 in the morning,' Minister Johnston bellowed through his security phone from his bedside.

'Sorry to disturb you, sir, but there's a man here at the gates that says he needs to see you and won't take no for an answer,' the security guard relayed.

'Who is he? What's he want?' the Minister angrily replied.

'He says he is working for you, looking for Pruitt he reckons.'

Immediately, Johnston knew it was John Pringle who had arrived unexpectedly at the front gates of his luxurious abode, who else could it be arriving discreetly and unannounced, he pondered.

'Let him through, send him up to the west stables, tell him I shall meet him there in around ten minutes,' ordered Johnston.

Minister Johnston leapt from his bed and threw his dressing gown across himself as he told his wife; awoken by the phone call, not to worry about anything after she had asked what was going on. He hurriedly made his way downstairs and exited the front door and began to make his way across the grounds to the stables.

Minister Johnston had one of the most prestigious properties in the Hexagon Valley. It was a short way out of Graceville to the east, deep in the heart of the wine-growing district. His two-storey mansion sat on the western boundary of the 1000-acre property that used to be one of the most popular and successful cellar door restaurants in the valley. Johnston secured the property after the previous owners went to the wall and had to sell. He ensured he was going to be the one who would lay claim to it by using his position of power in any way he could. Any other prospective buyer of the property would be scared off into purchasing it, and finally it came to the point where the previous owners had no choice but to sell at a price that was nearly half of what they thought to be a reasonable figure for the times. It was just another case where the Minister would use and abuse his power to the maximum to satisfy his own greed by standing over and taking advantage of the vulnerable.

Pringle slowly made his way up the Poplar tree lined crushed rock driveway until he reached the stables, a 200-meter walk from the roundabout that stood underneath the steps that led to the front door. With the first hint of morning light starting to take over the night sky he dismounted and entered through the stable doors.

The stables were huge and could box over thirty horses if filled but as it was now, only a dozen horses were in its enclosures. The other stalls were being used to house carriages and coaches, all professionally made by craftsmen within the last couple of years with pristine paint jobs and polished chrome trims. It was a collection that the Minister was proud of. He had them made to match his fleet of prestige automobiles he kept in an adjoining shed under wraps and would often show off his accumulation of coaches and cars by flaunting them on well-protected day trips around the valley.

Pringle patiently waited for the Minister to arrive, still holding and twitching his mangled thumb where the blood was now clearly visible as it soaked through the bandages when his attention was grabbed by a flashlight directed into his eyes.

'Mission successfully accomplished, I gather,' Johnston said adjusting his revolver back underneath his dressing gown. He confidently brushed past Pringle and began to unlock a safe that lay behind an elevated toolbox on some shelving when his hired assassin began to talk.

'No, afraid not.'

'What do you mean?' the Minister asked curiously.

'Pruitt's still alive.'

The Minister took a couple of steps towards Pringle until he was face to face. He switched the flashlight off and calmly laid it on the bench and with his hands now firmly entrenched in the deep pockets of his dressing gown began to impatiently ask why the hell is his target still breathing.

As the Minister listened to Pringle's version of events of what transpired, he was becoming more and more livid by the second. He relayed to Johnston how he had lost his two partners while raising his wounded hand to the face of the Minister, adding he too was lucky to escape with his life. The details he was giving centred on the truth except for one giant fabrication.

He alleged that they were the ones who were ambushed, and the other deaths were a result of Dane Grainger and his partners being in the wrong place at the wrong time, stating that most of the gunfire had come from Danny Pruitt and his gang. Pringle vowed revenge as soon as he could get his hand operable again, but Minister Johnston was having nothing to do with that scenario.

'Do you know what this could do to me? If anyone found out I hired you, I would be finished, do you realise that?' he shouted. 'I want you out of here, out of my town, out of my Shire. You are to never come back, you hear me?' ordered the furious Minister.

He grabbed a satchel from inside a toolbox lying on the bench that contained the rest of the blood money and hurled it at Pringle.

'That's for services rendered. The first train leaves here at 6.30, be on it. Leave your horse here, one of my men will take you to the station, I'll take care of things up here, you just keep your mouth shut, not a word to anyone, goodbye,' Johnston ended.

The annoyance in Pringle was building as Johnston forcibly brushed past him heading back to his home. He was the one used to giving orders, sure, he took his assignments from people in higher places, but never have they questioned him on how to do his job. Pringle would have loved to put Minister Johnston back in his place right there and then, but the pain in his hand continually reminded him that he needed urgent treatment.

He begrudgingly accepted the Minister's demands and was soon taking the lift to the Graceville station to wait for the first train back to the city. He took his money, but he wasn't about to take his advice, and before Pringle left the property, he was muttering to himself that he will be back to finish Pruitt off, and maybe you as well, as he turned and gave the Minister one last look as Johnston disappeared back into his mansion.

A 30-minute wait greeted John Pringle on the platform where he passed the time changing the bandage around his hand in the men's toilets, hiding the wound under his coat whenever a few early bird commuters would enter. He was growing weaker from the amount of blood he was losing and knew he would be in serious trouble if he were not to get on that train as soon as possible.

As the train halted at the platform at the end of the suburban and semi-rural rail line, John Pringle discreetly made his way to the last passenger carriage to get a seat to himself for the 90-minute trip to his destination. He was relieved that it was early New Year's Day and patronage was only a sprinkle, unlike the overcrowding that would normally cram the carriages of suburban train system.

Services had been reduced beyond 50% of its previous scheduling and being a public holiday, it would be another two hours before the next would arrive. He struggled to carry the overpacked bag he had with him and let off an exhausted sigh of relief and spread his body across the carriage seats, knowing for the time being at least, he would be safe, and treatment was not far away for his mangled hand.

The same time he boarded, another man from the front passenger carriage was disembarking. A well attired man wearing a black suit with leather shoes to match, tall with broad shoulders, clean shaven with neatly cut short brown hair. The two brief cases he carried by his side suggested that he never cared about the New Year's Eve celebrations the night before. He was fresh as a daisy, not like the sparingly grouped men still sleeping off hangovers on the platform that he had to step over to get through the station offices. He was a man both Minister Johnston and John Pringle were soon going to wish had never stepped foot in Graceville.

Martin Conroy was one of a dozen assistants to the police commissioner in Marlboro, but more importantly, a senior figure on the taskforce that tackled corruption among politicians and the police force. He was as untouchable as they could be, a rare commodity in senior officialdom these days and worked tirelessly and desperately to clean up the reputation of the force.

Conroy was a long-standing friend of Inspector Vaccaro who had informed him of the happenings in Graceville days before. The Inspector needed help from a man he could trust and there was none better trusted than Martin Conroy. Inspector Vaccaro had given Conroy a short rundown on the Minister's actions by mail and wrote that it was urgent that he comes to Graceville for a face-to-face meeting to discuss in detail his concerns.

Conroy had heard of rumours and accusations coming out of Minister Johnston's region in recent times but never had the proof or firm enough reasoning to lead an investigation. They had enough on their plate to look after in the city. As soon as he opened the letter from his good friend, he knew it serious enough to at least come to Graceville to have a look, and besides, he would love nothing better than to put away a crooked politician, let alone a corrupt member of the force. Conroy made his way out of the Graceville station and set about the walk to Inspector Vaccaro's home where they agreed to meet, a good 10 km journey from where he was.

Although there were rickshaws, trishaws and others with horse and carriage trying to earn a dollar waiting to act as a taxi service, Conroy was a man who preferred to go on foot.

As he made his way through the streets of Graceville, Inspector Vaccaro, along with Sgt Dane Grainger and Ryan, were starting the journey down from Tangiloo. Vaccaro commandeered a large cart with a canvas tarpaulin from the makeshift police camp to transport the dead bodies back to Graceville. They wrapped up the seven bodies in official police body bags and hid them under the tarpaulin in the cart. Vaccaro wanted to get them to Dr Carlisle at the hospital so he could perform proper autopsies and try to piece together the events, so the evidence could back up the eyewitness accounts of Dane and Ryan without any interference from outside sources.

Dr Carlisle was present when the autopsies of Rosco and Billy Devlin were performed and was one of the men threatened and sworn to secrecy by the Minister, but his conscience and his long-standing friendship with the Inspector would see that he would not remain silent for long. Vaccaro knew he would get the right help from the doctor and the sooner he got the bodies to the safety of the hospital the better for his and Dane's cause. He knew he was going outside the guidelines. In situations like this, the protocol was to inform your direct superior and in Vaccaro's case, that was Minister Johnston, but there was no way he was going to inform the Minister of anything until the bodies had been processed and the evidence was laid out to Martin Conroy.

But if the Inspector thought he was getting one up on the Minister, he could think again. Johnston was about to set the wheels in motion to try and cover his tracks. After an hour sitting in his private study pondering his situation, he hurriedly picked up his phone and punched in the direct line to the police station.

'Graceville police. Snr constable Symonds speaking,' the voice said.

'This is Minister Johnston, get me Detective Cribbs.'

'He's on annual leave sir, he's off for the next month,' the snr constable tentatively replied.

'I don't give a shit,' Johnston yelled down through the line. 'This is an emergency, you either call him or get someone to ride out there and tell him to get his ass over to my place now, do you hear me, snr constable! Take one of the vehicles if you must.'

'Yes sir,' was the prompt reply.

The Senior Constable quickly hung up the phone and tried to get a line through to the detective's home. After several failed attempts and listening to the phone ring out, he summoned one of the constables drive out to Detective Cribbs' property. Cribbs was on his morning run when the constable arrived at his front gates 20 minutes later. After receiving the message and still in his sporting attire, he quickly jumped behind the wheel of the police vehicle, dropped the Constable off back at the station and headed towards the Minister's luxurious abode.

Lucas Cribbs was the new breed of detective. He didn't have the morals or ethics of former detectives such as Vaccaro and Conroy. He came through the ranks in a corrupt environment and hardly knew anything different, so he was the perfect right-hand man for the unscrupulous Minister.

Detective Lucas Cribbs wasn't the only one who Minister Johnston had summoned to his house. A second phone call was placed to another man on his payroll.

Adrian Mance was the owner and chief editor of the Valley News, the biggest selling newspaper in the Shire. Over the last twelve months his paper was out selling the major city tabloids in the valley which was delivered to Graceville every morning by train. Mance was a big, fat, chain smoking slob with a thick drooping moustache who exhumed total arrogance. He knew all the right people with any title or influence throughout the region and always let people know about it the first chance he had.

Mance would never have anything detrimental printed in his paper against the Minister or his office. His paper was totally bias in its journalism towards the powers that be and would always support any press release that the Minister's office needed to get out, even if he did know it to be untrue. His paper turned a blind eye to anything that would either question or bring any suspicion on the Minister's office.

Johnston did everything in his power to ensure that the only news be written up about his tenure in the region was positive only, and what better way to make sure that happened was by having the owner and chief editor of the largest selling paper on your team.

Although most of the staff at the Valley News quietly despised their boss, journalists and others were attracted to the paper because Mance paid the best wages. In these difficult times, people found it easy to sacrifice integrity and honesty for the very hard to come by almighty dollar.

Detective Cribbs soon arrived at the property and was greeted by a nervous and anxious Minister Johnston.

'Welcome Lucas, glad you could make it at such short notice.'

'No worries, you know I'm always on call for you,' Cribbs firmly replied.

Johnston led him down the hallway to a small study room where he had the privacy to do most of his business and dealings.

'This sounds important, sir, being New Year's Day and all, thought you would have been resting up,' Cribbs enquired as he sat and leant forward onto the table opposite the Minister.

'I'll get straight to the point, Lucas,' Johnston said. 'You know about this man called Danny Pruitt and his sidekicks?'

'Only what I've read in the press release; other than that, not much,' Cribbs answered.

'Well, up to now, he's been responsible for the death of six of your fellow officers, and another one is missing, probably dead as well.'

Minister Johnston deliberately left out the deaths of Pringle's men. Even though Cribbs was a trusted employee, it was a time when your closest ally could turn on you the next day if the price were right, and the Minister was taking no chances.

'This Pruitt guy probably did us a favour in getting rid of Billy and Rosco Devlin, from what I hear anyway,' said Cribbs.

'Doesn't matter, they were police officers and that's that,' The Minister snapped back.

Detective Cribbs, now seeing that Johnston was in no mood to be amused by remarks, abruptly straightened up his posture as a serious tone now took over the room.

'What do you want me to do, sir?' he asked.

'I want you to find Pruitt and his sidekicks. I want him taken down, and anyone else who decides to ride with him before he kills again. I want you to harass anyone who knows him, anyone who might know where he might be or where he is going. I don't care how you do it, but I want him finished. Do you understand me!'

'Yes sir,' Cribbs answered.

Detective Cribbs sat silently nodding his head up and down, taking in every word the Minister was forcing upon him as he continued.

'You can have unlimited resources, take the vehicles if you want, any manpower you need, weapons, money, you name it. You can have anything you think you need. I want you in charge of this. But above all, I want this kept in house as much as possible, no one is to know what's happening, not even Inspector Vaccaro. He still thinks you are on annual leave, doesn't he?'

'Yeah, I guess so.'

'Good, keep it that way. Only tell the men you and I can trust. Do I make myself clear, Lucas?'

'Very clear, sir,' Cribbs confidently replied as he stood from out of his seat.

The Minister gave him maps of the surrounding area where Pringle relayed the last sighting and explained what had transpired the previous day. He gave him photo kits and names of each of the men who were involved and a brief rundown of their background.

Minister Johnston also warned Cribbs that Sgt Dane Grainger was not to be trusted any longer. The Minister was going on the lies that John Pringle had told him and accused the Sergeant of being an accessory, helping Pruitt and his colleagues out in the gunfight when he should have been arresting them.

Johnston knew that Pringle was lying about the true events. His own skin was on the line and if lies and deceit, along with murder, was going to save it, then so be it. It was nothing new to him, he had been playing the political game for a long time and confidently getting away with it, despite the sour feelings that now consumed him. He knew that he had bypassed the official protocol.

When it came to a police search of any kind, the proper authorities had to be notified before anything was to be put in motion, that was the law, a directive that he had totally ignored, and with his plan to make his story public through Mance's newspaper, it was only a matter of time before the big wigs in the city got a hold of what was happening in the Minister's territory.

He needed Pruitt and his gang mowed down before any story came from the other side of the fence. He had already put the word out to any of the renegade bounty hunters around the district that Danny Pruitt and his entourage were fair game, and no questions would be asked on how it was done. Time was now the enemy for him, he wanted things put to bed yesterday, and this was just another back up scheme put into action to cover any mistakes from his hired help.

Detective Cribbs leant across the table and shook the Minister's hand.

'You leave it to me, sir; I'll get the bastard. I'll get some men together straight away. I'll keep you informed as we go,' he assured.

As Detective Cribbs exited, the Minister slumped back into his chair and let off a nervous breath. He needed Cribbs to get the job done as soon as possible. Pringle had failed, a man whom he thought would never do so, and Cribbs was his last source. Any other man on the force from now on would have to go through Inspector Vaccaro, and he already knew through John Pringle that the Inspector already had a good grasp on what had happened near Tambourine Bridge. The Minister was already putting the feelers out on Vaccaro's whereabouts. It had almost been 36 hours since Johnston had last heard from him with updates on the search as requested, and the paranoia and suspicion was building by the hour.

As Detective Cribbs left the property, he passed the ample figure of Adrian Mance slowly making his way up the steps to the front door. Huffing and puffing with a cigarette at the side of his mouth, he offered a nod of acknowledgement to the Detective as they made eye contact.

'Good morning, Detective, must be something big on offer if your presence is required, can you give me a headline?' he quipped.

'No comment,' Cribbs replied.

'Still the same old comeback, hey, one day you might get a personality, Detective,' Mance badgered as he stopped to take another puff from his cigarette.

Cribbs kept walking until he reached the bottom of the steps where the police cruiser was parked without giving the newspaperman another look. He didn't have much time for Mance, or any other journalist for that matter.

Cribbs was a private man who on a whole kept to himself. He had solved many a crime and made many arrests without the fanfare that most policemen in these times hungered for. It didn't matter to him who got the accolades if mister bad guy got his just deserts, but he was loyal to Minister Johnston and if his boss told him to keep things on the hush, then that is what he would do.

'Good morning, Adrian,' the Minister greeted him at the front door. 'I hope you're looking for a headline story tomorrow?' He put his arm around his shoulder and led him into the entrance of his house.

'Well, that depends on what you've got for me, Minister!' Mance chuckled, trying to restrain his lung-infected cough. 'There's still plenty of headlines about the power resurgence, sir. Hell, I might even tell the people about how I'm going to get my old Porsche back on the road, it's been sitting in my garage wrapped up in cotton wool for a while now,' boasted Mance.

'Never mind that, Adrian, I have got a story for you, my friend, oh, have I got a story for you,' Johnston sniggered back.

The Minister led him to the same room where he chatted with the detective and began to give the chief editor all the misguided trumped-up information that his imaginative and conniving mind could conger up. Through Adrian Mance and his paper, Johnston was going to make sure that Danny Pruitt and his buddies were going to be portrayed as soul mates to the devil himself. Mance sat in his seat, notepad in hand, scribbling away with delight as he took down everything that the Minister had to say whilst wiping away the ash from another cigarette that fell onto his lap. At the same time Mance was taking notes, the very man who was the subject of their plotting had already awoken high up in the mountains at Domino falls.

Danny had risen earlier than his friends. He could never get a decent sleep in and was one who could never have an unbroken sleep during the night. Even when his mind was at peace with the world, he would always wake up several times during the night and with all his present troubles planted deeply in his mind, there was no hope of an adequate and generous sleep for some time yet.

Danny had taken what clothes he had with him out of his saddlebag, including the clothing he had on and had given them a decent wash to rid the stink, sweat and dust that had gathered. He sat there naked under one of the many little waterfalls that eked out from atop of the rocks to the side of the main falls and gave his body a decent wash down. He sat there, silently watching his clothes dry on overhanging branches when Barny approached.

'Good morning.'

'How ya doin?' Danny responded sombrely.

'Not bad, a little seedy but all right I guess,' said Barny.

'How's the other two?' Danny inquired.

'Harry's feeling the worse for wear. He's still lying down, not used to the whiskey I reckon. Ricky's playing with the radio trying get it to talk back to him.'

Danny nodded his head in acknowledgement and peered back out into the distance as Barny asked if he could join him next to the mini waterfall.

'Go ahead, don't need tickets here, mate, but I warn you, it's not all that bloody warm,' he replied.

'Yeah, I can see you shaking a bit.'

'It's not because of the cold, trust me,' said Danny.

Barny stripped off his clothes and began to give them a light wash in the running water while getting a little soaking himself. He asked Danny how he was, concerned about the worried look upon his face.

'I'm scared, Barny,' he confessed.

'We're all scared, Danny. There would be something wrong with us if we weren't,' Barny confided as he put his hand on Danny's shoulder.

'I think I'm more scared of what I did than what could happen, do you know what I mean?' Danny stated.

Barny wasn't exactly sure what Danny meant and asked him more about his feelings.

'About last night, what we were talking about.'

'Which conversation, there was a lot of whiskey talk last night,' Barny mused.

'About all the gung-ho big talk, taking shit from no one anymore. I'm not so sure if it's the right thing you guys should be doing, ya know. I don't want you have to fight my battles. You shouldn't follow me. I don't want to drag you guys into it even further.'

'This isn't just about you anymore, Danny. As Ricky said last night, our names were on that statement too, and those bullets flying around us yesterday didn't just have your name on them. From the moment we saw you down at the market, we knew what we were getting ourselves into. So, it is our battle just as much as it's yours now, it was our decision, not yours.'

'Fair enough,' said Danny. 'No point in arguing that'

Danny thought he could talk to Barny without being judged or maligned. Although he had known Ricky a lot longer, he could never talk openly with him about his true emotions. They shared all and sundry except one thing, their real inner feelings, and Harry, well, he just didn't want to let Harry down. To let him think that he was vulnerable like any other human being was not on, it would destroy the humorous myth that he had over him, and so it was Barny who was going to get the earful.

'Did you see Pringle shoot Dane's young copper, mate?' he asked.

'No, I missed it, thank God,' Barny replied.

'I never seen nothing like it. Half his head got blown away, and the other guy's chest being torn apart, it was like it exploded or something. Shit, not to mention Karl, he was a real decent bloke you know. All I can picture in my head is blood all over them. Dane blames me for Karl, I know he does.'

'It wasn't your fault, Danny, if Pringle wasn't there, every one of them would still be alive today,' Barny forcefully said.

A few moments of silence aired between the talking buddies as they stared into the wilderness before Danny continued with his thoughts.

'I scared shit out of myself yesterday, Barny, shooting those people. It's not me, none of this is me. I know I had a lot of anger in me, but I had no idea what I was capable of when pushed like that, and now I know, I hate myself for it,' Danny admitted, as the tears started to well in his eyes. 'I miss Greta so much,

I'm worried out of my brain about her, Christ, what have I done to her, Barny, what have I done to her.'

Barny listened intently as his close friend continued to pour out his emotions. Danny wiped the small tear drops away and stood from out of the little waterfall. He tried to regain his emotions and made his way across the flat bedrock to where his clothes were hanging and began to dress himself continuing his talk.

'You know, I thought I had my life all planned out. Working hard, doing the right things by everyone. I said to myself by the time I reached the age I am now, I would be on easy street, you know what I mean, and all my life turned out to be is one of struggle and hardship, butting my head up against the wall every fucking day for the last five years.'

Barny was sympathetic, but also told him that he wasn't the only one to fall on hard times.

'There are a million others in the same boat, Danny,' he stated.

'I know, I know,' he agreed. 'But that doesn't make anything easier, does it? All the stuff I've held inside. It all came out yesterday. Shit, I stole off a dead man, Barny, how low does that get? It's amazing how one incident can change a man, a fucking stupid lamb, for crying out loud. I should feel some kind of remorse for those dead bastards, but I don't, not one ounce, and as for those mongrels who trashed my house! They're all dead men walking,' Danny threatened, shaking his head angrily.

Barny stood upright from where he was washing his clothes and looked Danny directly in his eyes. He was concerned the way his mate was talking. He gave him a quote from his trusty pocket-sized Bible he carried around with him, trying to let Danny know that he understood him completely.

'Your joy is your own, and your bitterness is your own, no one can share them with you.'

Danny looked back at Barny and was somewhat impressed by his quote. He was not one for profound statements, Danny thought.

'Geez, where did ya get that one from?' Danny asked.

'It's all in here, my friend,' Barny replied.

He leant over and dipped into the top pocket of his shirt and pulled out his Bible, lifting it towards Danny's face.

Danny grabbed the Bible off him and clasped it tightly in his hands and with a serious look reeled off a quote of his own. 'Doesn't it also say that wicked people bring about their own downfall by their own evil deeds, but good people are protected by their integrity.'

'Yes, that's right, it does,' Barny said, raising his eyebrows in surprise that Danny would know any of the contents in the good book.

'I'm a good man, Barny, honest and true to myself, honest and true to my wife and friends, so the people who did this to my home are getting what's coming to them. They're the worst kind of men, Barny. Faceless cowards who I despise more than anyone in this world, and if it's the last thing I do, I'm gonna get them, each and every one,' Danny determinedly promised. 'I just can't get this vision out of my head of Greta being hauled out of the house, pushed around, the bastards groping her all over.'

'They wouldn't do that,' said Barny.

'Bullshit,' came the stern reply. 'That little bastard Billy Devlin was already threatening they would do exactly that, and there are worse pricks than him amongst them, believe me. An eye for an eye, isn't that what the bible also says?' Danny continued to say, returning the Bible into Barny's hand.

'I know how you're feeling, Danny; I can feel your hurt and frustration. I will fight this battle with you, we all will. We'll see it to the end no matter what the outcome, but I pray that no more lives must be taken. It doesn't have to go that far,' Barny pleaded. 'Let's take one day at a time. It's not a lost cause yet,' he reassured. 'We're still alive, so let's make the most of it while we can. You will see Greta again, that's what you promised her, didn't you?'

'The only way I reckon I'll ever see her again is if I storm back into Graceville, kidnap her and the boys, shoot my way out of town and then take off interstate or something,' Danny meekly argued.

Barny gave off a little chuckle at hearing Danny's suggestion.

'Don't be too hard on yourself, mate. You've done what any proper man would do in the same situation. Well, probably not, but nevertheless, just don't rack ya brains over it.'

Barny's comments reminded Danny of one of the millions of sayings he had stashed away in his brain. It was a line he used often and let his buddy hear it for the first time. Slumping his shoulders forward, he timidly looked towards him and quoted, 'You can look back, but never stare. For what's done is done, so don't go back there.'

'Exactly,' Barny said, nodding in agreement. 'You're an intelligent and resilient man, Danny, you'll think of a way to get Greta back when the time's right.'

'I hope you're right, Barny, I hope you're right!' Danny sighed.

He took a deep breath and puffed his chest out. A small weight had been lifted off his shoulders. He was still deeply troubled, but his thoughts changed quickly towards his friends.

'But first things first, I've got to get you guys over the ranges and on the other side of Graceville, haven't I?' he informed his now smiling friend.

Barny had succeeded in snapping Danny out of his mini depression and with a load off his chest, thanked Barny for lending him his ears.

'You're a good man, David Barnard, I'm gonna need your help to get me out of this,' Danny said sincerely.

'Consider it done,' Barny replied as he moved closer towards Danny.

'Hey, no hugs, that's going a bit too far, just put it here,' Danny jokingly said thrusting out his right hand. He then turned away from his friend and with all his washed clothes in hand, started to make his way back to their makeshift campsite. Barny followed in tow and couldn't let Danny slip by without knowing how he knew about the quote out of the bible.

'How did you know that?' he asked, walking up behind him.

'Know what?' Danny replied, fully knowing what Barny was asking.

'That quote from the Bible. I thought you said it was a load of trollop,' Barny insinuated.

'Greta leaves it hanging around the house sometimes; I sneak a preview at it every now and then. Life can get boring these days; it fills the time in every now and then,' Danny said facetiously. 'Don't you tell anyone though; I got a reputation to protect,' he joked.

'Your secret is safe with me,' Barny smiled.

The men knew they couldn't stay around in the one spot for too long. Ricky and Harry had already eaten when Danny and Barny were in conversation and gave themselves a quick wash and change of clothes at the waterfalls edge as Danny and Barny helped themselves to some satchels of soup for breakfast.

As the men slurped down every bit of chicken noodle soup out of their cups, Danny decided it was a good idea to lay out all the belongings they had with them. He advised that they had at least thirty-six hours tough travel ahead of them and the lighter they travelled, the better for them and their horses.

They perused over what they had, from personal trinkets to the assorted array of guns and knives they had accumulated, to cooking utensils and fishing gear, but the thing they were most perturbed about was the limited food supply. The only food they had in front of them was a 500-gram bag of rice, three satchels of soup, three cans of baked beans, a can of fruit salad, three apples, a rotten banana, a canister of salt and a stale bag of potato chips that Harry didn't even know he had. The boys voiced their concerned to each other about the lack of nourishment before them.

'Don't worry about it,' Danny insisted. 'We'll pick up food along the way. There's plenty of wildlife out there when we get hungry,' he assured them.

The men stood around lightly arguing on what should be taken and what should be left behind and buried. They were all strongly guarded of their own belongings when it was suggested to get rid of a personal item or two, arguments erupted. For the next ten minutes, they were all banging their heads against a brick wall. No one could agree on anything, so as it stood, they were all going to pick up their goods and repack them away.

'Well, that achieved a lot, what a fuckin waste of time that was,' Danny sarcastically commented.

'Yeah well, it was your idea in the first place, Danny,' Ricky retorted.

Ricky was about to give Danny another earful, but before he could open his mouth, Barny sounded a warning. He had turned his head in disgust, shrieking at the thought of Danny and Ricky arguing again when he glanced down over the high ridge and looked down the track they had travelled up the night before.

'Shut up, there's someone coming,' he warned.

The mood had changed in an instant as panic and paranoia gripped the four. They all quickly grabbed the closest weapon they could find, picking up their choice of gun that was lying on the ground and dived for cover.

'Can you see who it is?' Danny asked, keeping low, scrambling on all fours across to Barny.

'Not yet, he's too far away.'

'Is it a cop?'

'I don't think so, he's alone whoever it is,' Barny confirmed.

Danny raised his head above the mound they were behind to see if he could get a look at the lone rider as Ricky and Harry hurriedly joined them.

The visitor was in no hurry as he painstakingly made his way up the track to where the lads had taken sanctuary. The boys sat there silently until they could get a positive visual on the oncoming threat. As horse and rider slowly approached, the boy's heart rate was dropping accordingly. They didn't need to tell each other who it was coming their way. They waited until they were positive through the aid of the binoculars and Harry's keen eyes that the oncoming rider was alone.

Harry panned around the mountainous terrain several times as the boys waited for the all clear.

'I can't see anyone else,' Harry said assertively.

Danny stood up from behind their camouflage and made his way over to the edge of the waterfalls to make himself seen to the rider.

'What's he fuckin doing here?' Ricky grumbled as Danny walked away.

'We're about to find out, I think,' said Barny. Rightly second-guessing what Danny was about to do.

Danny could see the oncoming rider down below. He positioned himself in the open on one of the flat rock edges. He waved his arms above trying to catch the eye of the unsuspecting rider. The lone traveller was unaware of Danny's overtures. Danny wanted to grab his attention but stopped short of echoing his voice all over the mountainside. He turned to his buddies.

'Can one of you whistle?' he asked, knowing his inability to give off a high-pitched blow.

Ricky rolled his eyes, sat back against the dirt mound then stuck the little fingers of both hands into the side of his mouth and let go a short sharp blast. Straight away, the rider's attention was caught. He stopped his horse and looked up and around to see if he could recollect where the strong whistle came from.

The rider finally laid eyes on Danny above, standing and waving his arms. Danny motioned to make his way further up the track and within a few short minutes, he had arrived.

'How the hell are ya, Tom?' Danny greeted, throwing out his hand as he dismounted. 'What are you doing up here?' he asked.

The men gathered around as Tom explained how he had escaped from Dane the previous evening when they were heading back to Tangiloo. Tom was petrified that he was going to be arrested for his role in the shootout. Dane threatened that he was going to take him into custody when they reached Tangiloo. Sgt Grainger was so distressed that he was venting all his anger and frustrations out on Tom with wild threats and intimidation. Tom was scared out of his wits, and the more Dane bullied him on his possible impending arrest, the more Tom panicked.

At the first opportunity, he raced his horse into the forest with the loud threats of the Sergeant echoing behind him. He risked that Dane and Ryan wouldn't chase him as they had a heap of dead bodies tagging behind. He hid in the bush until nightfall and then made his way to the seclusion of the caves at the cascades and held up for the night. He told Danny that he took a calculated guess and headed for Domino falls, trying to find him.

Danny was astounded to hear Tom's story. 'Dane wouldn't do that,' he said. There's no way that Dane would threaten Tom in this manner. Tom was adamant and pleaded to Danny that he was telling the truth.

'He said he was going to lock me away. He didn't care what I had to say,' Tom said distressed.

Danny walked away. He didn't know whether to believe him or not. He had no reason to doubt his word, but no reason to think that Dane would act in the way he was saying. He was the fairest and decent of all blokes, even as a copper. Danny scoffed at what Tom was saying.

'You probably misunderstood him; he was probably just hanging shit on ya.'

'No, he wasn't. He was dead serious,' Tom assured.

But Danny was about to hear more news on Sgt Dane Grainger that was going to be hard to take.

'He lied to us, Danny,' Barny interrupted.

'Who did?' he bellowed back.

'Dane did.'

'What do ya mean?'

'I was with Dane and Ryan behind the rock when the shootout with Pringle occurred. He said to Ryan that he never contacted Vaccaro. He didn't even speak to him. He was bullshitting you all the way,' Barny divulged to his now agitated mate.

Barny described word for word as best he could about the conversation as Danny became more infuriated by the second. He lowered his hands from his face in frustration and looked Barny in the eyes.

'Is this true?' he calmly asked.

'I wouldn't lie to you, Danny. I have no reason to. I know he's your mate, but he was screwing with you,' Barny firmly said.

The men looked at Danny with bated breath. They didn't know what his reaction would be. They anticipated a tirade of obscenities to be unleashed from his mouth; a tantrum of hurricane proportions, but neither was forth coming. He coolly walked towards his horse and finished saddling up.

'What are we doing?' Harry asked everyone.

'We're getting the hell out of here, Harry,' Danny said.

Barny and Ricky had no argument and immediately began to saddle up their horses with Harry hastily following. They packed away what they had as they listened to the quiet obscenities towards Dane muttering through the air from Danny's mouth.

'Let's go,' he ordered.

Danny had an empty feeling inside of him, an unfamiliar feeling of betrayal. He had never been let down from a friend like that before. Inside his mind he couldn't justify what Dane had done to him. His head was shaking from side to side in utter disappointment as he slowly rode off with the other four men.

Tom asked the men where they were heading as he rode up behind them. Danny explained what their plans were as he pointed in the direction of the Midnight Ranges.

They could see the mountain range from where they were. They were high enough at present to get a good look in what direction to take, but first they would have to pass over several smaller ranges and gullies before they would reach the dirt road of Kelsey's track, which in turn would take them up to the top of the Midnight range. There they would follow the Summit Road that would lead them back to the eastern tip of Graceville, and beyond that, the men would take their own separate ways. There were no walking or fire tracks to help them on their way this time.

Danny surmised that Kelsey's track was still a good day's ride from where they were. Any tracks leading up to Domino falls ended right there and then, so they were going to have to get to their destination the hard way. He assumed that they would be able to ride in a straight line to the first destination of Kelsey's track, however, that was an assertion that was going to prove totally wrong. Although he had the direction right, getting there was going to be another thing completely.

Danny had never trekked through these parts of the mountains, no one ever did. In fact, Danny was totally naïve and ignorant about the reasons why no tracks went through it. Although he knew the Midnight Ranges area well, he had only stuck to the designated roads and tracks. He had no idea what he was about to lead his friends into as they slowly tried to move Southward. The ensuing part of the mountains were as inhospitable as you could get.

The Midnight range forest was nearly 40,000 hectares in area. It was named so because of the dark tinge it gave out from a distance. It was a densely populated semi rain forest in parts, dominated by the native eucalypt with every different species of wattle and blackwood imaginable. Intertwined amongst it were huge dangling vines, giant tree ferns and large native grasses that grew from the steep slippery ravines and gullies and with no controlled burn or forest fire in these parts for a very long time, it was as dense as it could be.

The undergrowth was as thick as anyone could imagine in certain parts making it impassable and not much sunlight forced its way through to the forest floor because of the thick canopy above. Even in summer, it could lead to a sometimes damp, dangerous and uncomfortable expedition if someone was foolish enough to take this part on without the right preparation, and along with the native predators that lurked deep inside its interior, it added to a not so pleasant excursion.

If Danny thought he had already gotten through the toughest of tests yesterday, he was about to get a rude awakening. He and the lads were about to endure another that would again test their minds and bodies to the limit. But this battle could not be fought with fists or guns. It was going to be a battle against man's worst enemy, and Mother Nature was not too finicky in who she chose as her next unsuspecting victim.

Chapter 15

The men had trekked off into the shadows of the forest. The first few hours were forgiving. They encountered enough open areas to progress through without too much difficulty but by mid-afternoon, the forest was turning on them quickly. They were met with pockets that were impassable, the vegetation too thick to push through. Cliff faces, gullies and ravines, too dangerous to climb or descend, had dangerous vines hanging over them with numerous bracken fern protruding out. They were continually forced backwards and sideways as they looked for a passage to lead them in the right direction.

One obstacle after another confronted them. Before they knew it, nightfall was upon them and they had lost all sense of direction. At times during the day, they had no idea what direction they were heading and turning back from whence they came was not an option. The boys had regularly passed quiet comments that Danny was getting disorientated the longer the day went on.

Danny would ask Tom, who was riding up front with him, if he had any suggestion on how to advance through the forest, hoping his experience in the area would be of help, but Tom had no more idea than Danny did. Tom tried to make out that he did, merely to have the forest make a mockery of his directions and only succeeded in leading the men into dead end after dead end. The only thing Tom was successful at was making the riders behind angrier and more frustrated, and by the time nightfall was upon them, the riders thought they had just spent a day in hell. What they didn't know yet, was that only just entered through its gates.

The ensuing 72 hours was one misery after another. As each hour passed, they were becoming prisoners of the untouched mountains. They were completely lost, constantly going around in circles, encountering the same steep cliff faces and riding to the edge of sharp descending ravines covered in the slippery growth from the forest. They travelled at snail's pace and had made no inroads in the direction they needed to go; the ruthless forest wouldn't allow it.

Another night passed with the never-ending buzzing and biting of mosquito's, some as big as your thumb nail. The insect repellent was rendered useless. Bush spiders of all descriptions decided to make the men's makeshift beds home, leaving vicious bites behind if you happened to lay in the wrong direction. Bull ants, sugar ants, leeches and every conceivable insect that hid underneath the thick canopy of the forest at one time or another said hello to them. The only intermission Danny got from his angst-ridden journey was when he came across a scorpion on one of his smoke breaks.

He was leaning up against a tree and noticed the 40mm creature wiggling out from below some bark that laid on the ground. He captured it in an empty tin can he was fiddling with and explored the arachnid family member from top to toe. Danny got a brainwave and remembered that they had passed a bull ants' nest not far back. He took himself on a stroll and as the boys watched, wondering what he was up to, he collected a bull ant and re-joined them a short time later.

He dug a deep hole the size of a large dinner plate with his spade and threw both the scorpion and bull ant into their new fighting pit. He watched in awe as the two little bush warriors battled it out, twisting and weaving, stinging with their barbs and biting at one other. Danny thought the scorpion would win the conflict, going by the misinformed legends that the scorpion held; however, he was somewhat shocked at the result. Within minutes of the conflict, the bull ant triumphed.

Danny looked on captivated by the way it clutched the scorpion in its mandibles, curled itself around its victim and delivered multiple stings into the now defenceless scorpion. He lifted the bull ant out from the mini fighting arena with a stick and watched it angrily point its nippers at him, defiant and courageous, a trait that Danny instantly admired in the little bush gladiator. He then laid the stick down on the ground, releasing the bull ant back into its habitat—to the victor go the spoils.

It would not be the last time that Danny would pit the two creatures up against each other.

Snakes were always a constant danger, some of them the most venomous in the country. Not only to their already tired and aching bodies, but to their horses as well. They knew if one of their horses became a victim of a snake bite there would be no way out other than by foot, a scenario that none of them were prepared for. The sweat from their overheated exhausted bodies was reeling off an odour that they had never smelt on themselves before. They only changed their t-shirts or singlets when they came across tiny creeks of water that if you didn't look or listen for, you could easily ride right over.

They ringed the sweat out of their tops in what little water was available, then hung them over their tired horses to dry. Most of the time they went bare chested to save their clothes becoming stink bombs. It was a constant fight against nature and their own mental state, and on the third morn after breakfast, a harrowing realisation engulfed them all. They were out of food.

There was nothing left. Not even the old chewing gum they had stashed away, everything had been eaten. They rationed as best they could with two light meals each over the last 72 hours, that's if you could call a handful of rice and half a can of baked beans a meal, but they always held onto the thought that they would be out of the forest within hours of each one passing. Danny had promised them! They believed him! Why wouldn't they! He hadn't let them down so far, however, he was grossly wrong on his assumptions this time.

Danny said to them before they trekked off that there would be plenty of wildlife to prey on if things got tough. They were to never worry about running out of food if things went wrong on their journey, but the only source of food that was seen or edible along their travels were the numerous snakes they would encounter, and none of the men had the skill nor the courage to capture them. They were too afraid to use their guns, that would give away their position to anyone who may hear, but unbeknown to them, not a living soul was within range to hear a bomb go off, let alone a firearm.

They desperately needed a break soon, a gigantic change of luck, and with the temperature soon to rise around the 40-degree Celsius range and with the humidity rising, the one thing they did get right was stocking up on small water supplies they gathered from the little creeks they negotiated through the deep ravines and gullies. With the rise in temperature also came a rise in tempers and the boys were becoming more and more agitated at each other the more sleep deprived they became.

Tom suggested they get moving. 'We're not far from an old track I reckon, I think I know roughly where we are,' he said with newfound enthusiasm.

'Good, you go. It's one less mouth to feed. And when you get lost, which you will, going on your other stuffed up efforts to get out of here, don't expect us to come looking for you.' A frustrated Ricky swore.

Tom looked at him in surprise. Ricky deadpanned him. It was another taste of Ricky's contempt towards him and his annoyance and frustration at Tom was at boiling point. All the frustrations from the previous days that he held within was about to burst, so why not take it out on the man he knows the least.

'You don't belong with us anyway,' scathed Ricky.

He was never sure of Tom from day one. Along with Harry, they both felt that they couldn't trust him. Sure, they felt sorry for him over what the Re-po squad had done, as well as his wife leaving him, but there was something about Tom Potter that annoyed them both. They couldn't put a finger on what annoyed them. Whether it was the way he talked, the way he walked or the way he ate! They didn't know, they just put it down to an old-fashioned personality clash. They had always cut Tom some slack when he said or did something that raised their ire, particularly when Tom would tell somewhat exaggerated stories about his past conquests in life.

From the time they left Domino falls, both Ricky and Harry, and to a lesser extent Barny, thought him to be acting strange. They commented amongst themselves, away from Danny's ears, that he seemed to be half drunk all the time, or that he had a few loose screws in his head but couldn't quite put their fingers on it. If it was the former, they had no idea where the alcohol was coming from.

The three finally confronted Danny over their concerns, but Danny assured them that it was just him, that's his personality, he said. 'Don't worry about it,' he would reiterate. It was enough assurance for the trio to leave it alone and the boys always bit their tongue about Tom's little antics, however, this morning was going to be different.

They assumed Tom was out of the picture and when Barny spotted him approaching back at Domino Falls, it was not going to take long before Ricky gave Tom a taste of what he really thought.

Tom turned and looked at Danny for some solace, a backup, someone to stoke up what confidence he had left in him, but his friend wasn't concerned at all with what Ricky had to say. It was in one ear and out the other to Danny when it came to Ricky blasting off.

'Well, go on, piss off! You've done nothing but lead us on wild goose chases. Well, what are ya waiting for, piss off.! We're better off without you; you're not one of us. You've been full of shit since the day we met,' Ricky's tirade continued at Tom.

Tom had been feeling the most scared and lonely out of all the men, and to see he had no support from any of his so-called new buddies was enough to sap any confidence he held. He again looked around; no eye contact would meet him. It was a clear message that none of them cared for what was said.

He turned his horse around and started to head off into the bush.

'Hey, where ya going?' Danny yelled.

'No one wants me here!' Tom screeched.

'Geez mate, you're a bit sensitive, aren't you?' suggested Danny with mirth surprise.

Tom stopped, coaxed his horse closer to Danny then shook his head in quiet disgust at the attitude towards him.

'I'm going, Danny, you can't stop me.'

'I wouldn't want to stop you, Tom. You're a grown man. Although you could have fooled me the way you're carrying on, mate,' replied Danny.

'I'm not the one going around abusing people.'

'Oh, come on, Tom, if you can't take a bit of stick now and then, you'll never get ahead with anything, grow a second skin, will ya!' Danny advised.

'I'm not taking that abuse from anyone. No one has ever talked to me like that before, Danny. I don't have to take that, and I won't take that. They don't want me here so I'm off, I'll catch ya later,' Tom stuttered through his angst.

He gave his horse a dig in the ribs and began to take off through the only clear part of the bush around when Harry noticed he had left a small leather satchel behind with his water canteen and black overcoat.

'Hey,' he yelled at Tom, 'you forgot something.'

Harry hurled the satchel and canteen in Tom's direction, happy to see him moving on. Both fell short of him and hit the ground beside where Danny was standing. He bent over and picked them up then straightened his over-stressed back and peered inside.

'What's this?' Danny asked inquisitively.

'Give it to me,' Tom quickly responded, throwing out his right arm in haste.

Danny stepped away from Tom's horse as he neared him and pulled the contents out of the satchel, a crumpled up black plastic bag was now firmly in his clasp.

Tom leapt off his horse to retrieve his belongings as Danny untwisted the bag to see what was in it.

'What the hell is this?' Danny roared.

'It's mine, give it back.'

Danny threw the bag over to Ricky's waiting hands before Tom had the chance to snatch it off him. He peered inside the bag as Danny asked if it was what he thought it was.

Ricky pulled some of the contents out of the bag, rolled it between his fingers and put it to his nose.

'Bloody oath it is,' he thundered.

'Where did you get that shit from?' Danny asked, astounded that Tom would have such contents with him.

'It's my marijuana, give it back,' demanded Tom.

'Not until you tell us where you got it from.'

Before Tom could reply, the insinuations started to fly.

'That explains everything,' said Harry.

'Yeah,' bellowed Ricky.

'Why you've been pissing off into the bush all the time. Why you've been acting like a friggin idiot. You've been stoned out of your brain most of the time. Shit, I knew it, I knew something was going on, we could smell the damn thing. I knew it was dope, I told you guys, shit, why didn't I pick this up?' Ricky chastised himself.

'Where did you get it from?' Danny asked again.

'I found it in the bush when I was hiding from Dane. There was a little plantation with some already bagged,' Tom sheepishly replied.

Danny shook his head in disappointment and continued to berate Tom.

'One, you kept it from us.' He pointed. 'Two, I gave you the benefit of the doubt. The boys have been at me since we left, telling me there's something going on with you. But I said nah, nah, don't be stupid, he s alright, leave him alone I said, how foolish was I. What if we came across someone, Tom, or coppers for that matter and we had to protect each other, you would have put us all in danger,' Danny furiously argued. 'God, no wonder you didn't know where you were going half the time, you've been stoned off your head. You probably cost us two fuckin days in this hellhole.'

Danny shook his head in anger and spat at the ground. He turned away from Tom and apologised to his buddies for letting them down.

'Not your fault, Danny, he fooled us as well,' Barny said.

'He didn't fool you guys, only me,' Danny reluctantly replied.

He made his way towards his makeshift bed from the previous night as Tom walked behind, trying to justify himself to deaf ears while Harry's fingers delved into each sleeve of Tom's saddlebag.

'Look at all this stuff!' Harry yelled.

The boys looked to see what Harry had in his hands. He threw some of the contents towards Ricky and Barny. Food satchels, nearly a dozen of them, from soups to noodles to assorted jam spreads. Three empty hipflasks that reeked of bourbon that Tom had consumed over the past few days. Maps of surrounding districts with gradients, latitude and longitude and kilometre points, everything the boys needed long ago. *What was going through his mind to keep this stuff from them?* Danny mystifyingly thought.

Ricky was about to explode; this was the last straw. He hurriedly moved towards Tom. Fire was blazing from his nostrils and saliva spraying as the abuse steamed out from his mouth.

'You fuckin dog!' he yelled.' I'm gonna kill you.' He lunged with a wild left hook, grazing the top of Tom's forehead as he tried to sway out of the way of the incoming assault. Tom hurriedly backed off to avoid the next onslaught from an out-of-control Ricky, losing his balance and falling to ground. Tom was about to get the beating of his life, deservedly so, according to the thoughts of all there. He had completely lost the boys' trust by withholding the things he had, but before Ricky could launch another attack, Danny took the initiative and jumped atop of a quivering Tom before Ricky could pounce.

With a handful of dirt in his clenched fist, he forced it down his besieged friend's throat so he could only listen and not talk. Tom spat and gasped for air as the tirade of abuse rang through his ears as Danny let rip what he thought of him. It only took a minute, but it was enough to send a clear message on how things were. Danny dragged him to his feet, forced him towards his horse and told him get on it and ride off.

'You're on your own now, you're not with us anymore. Get back to town and go find your missus, maybe she can forgive you for whatever you've done because we can't forgive you for what you've done here,' Danny warned.

Tom perused the men once more, spitting and wiping away the dirt from his mouth with his forearm. He knew there was no sense asking for his stuff back. He grabbed a tight rein on his horse, gave it a jab and cantered off through the bush, a broken and dispirited man. The men looked on silently as Tom quickly disappeared and as soon as he was out of sight, Danny turned and made his way towards to his own horse. He caught sight of Barny's eyes along the way, who could see the disappointment in Danny as he acknowledged his actions.

Barny knew Danny had only intervened to stop one mate from smashing the living daylights out of another; he did what he had to do, to virtually save Tom's life. It wasn't like it used to be when tempers flared previously. The worst that usually happened between mates was a couple of nasty cuts and bruises. However, with the easy accessibility of guns today, people who lost their tempers as Ricky had, sometimes pulled the trigger without thinking, and with Ricky, that was a genuine possibility going on previous happenings in days gone. Barny perceived Danny's thoughts more than the other two.

If it were between two strangers, he knew Danny would happily sit back and take in the entertainment, but when it was between two friends, Danny would not have a bar of it. Nevertheless, as much as Danny hated doing it, he had to make an example of Tom, and if it was throwing dirt down his throat and sending him on his way then so be it. It was better than possibly digging his grave.

Barny could see Danny felt for Tom. If he were his mate, he must have had some good traits about him otherwise Danny wouldn't have given him the time of day. He also knew that Danny was a great judge of character and in tough times, and these were extremely tough times, a man can make many errors of judgment when extraordinary pressures are forced upon him, as it was with both Tom and Danny.

After a brief pause of silence, Danny asked the men to peruse over the maps they had confiscated off Tom. Within minutes, the boys' mood took a huge swing for the better. They rightly worked out that they were on the cusp of Kelso's track, a few kilometres south of where they believed to be. With new found enthusiasm the boys immediately saddled their horses up and were on their way, swapping maps between themselves as they trekked through the dense forest. They pushed and coerced their horses through the thick undergrowth, weaving in between the giant forest trees and assorted low spiny branches of wild wattles.

The temperature began to soar through the canopy of the forest with only thick shadows giving them some respite from the heat. By late afternoon, the men had reached their first destination when without warning, out of the thick forest and down an embankment appeared a gravel road. They panned up and down, and to left of them, engraved in an old fence post were the words Kelso's track. For the first time in days, the men were on target.

They studied the maps again and worked out that the Summit Road was within 5km eastbound and upwards of where they had come out. Although there were still 2-3 hours of daylight left to keep riding, they decided it was time to pull up stumps and rest when they reached the Summit Road. There was a nice trickle of water coming off the peaks of the mountain into the culverts of the road and since it had been a searing hot day and the horses were as tired as they were, including the big black gelding that had fought Danny's requests all day, they decided it would be a good spot to camp up for the night. The soups and noodles they took from Tom were enough to half fill their empty stomachs and what little running water was available was enough to have a wash and get some needed hydration into their horses.

Danny worked out it was probably only a day's ride, maybe two, to get to the North-East tip of Graceville where the towns reservoir stood, so a good night's sleep was well overdue and a fresh start in the morning was paramount. The men rested and joked in the remaining daylight hours whilst talking in circles on what they were going to do with the lives that had now been forced upon them. They were still alive and that's all that mattered, and although they still had no idea what they were going to do, or where they were going to go, they were just glad they had a road to guide them to wherever it may lead.

Another night in the untouched forest would have driven them to despair, but now, tomorrow gave them hope and expectation of finally making their way back to what civilisation they had left behind. But if the men believed the assumption they held of being out of the forest and on the back roads of Graceville by the same time tomorrow, it was going to prove totally false, and it was going to take a lot more pain and time before the surrounding mountains and its inhabitants would unleash the grip it had on the four fugitives.

Chapter 16

'What the hell is this?' Assistant Commissioner Conroy demanded.

'This is the result of our precious Minister Colin Johnston, Martin,' answered Vaccaro.

'What are you trying to insinuate here Noel?'

'If Johnston hadn't taken things into his own hands, these people would still be alive, Martin.'

'You're going to have to explain yourself a bit better, Noel, I'm not following you one bit, my friend. What have these men got to do with Minister Johnston?'

Inspector Vaccaro explained how the deaths of the men that lay before them came about, and once John Pringle's name was mentioned in the alleged shootout, the Inspector had the undivided attention of his trusted colleague.

Inspector Vaccaro and Sgt Dane Grainger had made sojourn down from Tangiloo on New Year's Day to the Graceville hospital to meet with Dr Carlisle. All the dead bodies from the Tambourine Bridge shootout had been removed from the tarpaulin covered cart then loaded onto trolleys and taken into the hospital morgue so the Doctor could perform his autopsies and confirm cause of death. Dr Carlisle met with the men at the rear of the hospital after communicating over radio before they arrived. They waited for the doctor's all clear before they transported the bodies into his care.

After all the bodies had been laid out in the cold depths of the morgue beneath the hospital, Inspector Vaccaro used one of the hospital's landlines to ring his own home on the chance that his comrade from the city had arrived. Martin Conroy obliged by answering the call. They talked for several minutes before the Inspector insisted that Conroy meet him at the hospital so he could fill him on proceedings with the terrible evidence sitting right in front of his face.

Doctor Carlisle was prepping himself to perform his autopsies when he was brought to a halt.

'Stop what you're doing,' Conroy roared.

'Why, what's the problem?' Vaccaro and the doctor asked.

'No offence, Doc, but I want my men to handle this one. I'm going to get the head of crime scene to get their main man up here to do the autopsies. If we're going to get Pringle, and the Minister for that matter, I better do this the right way, I'm not going to let them get away with anything this time, I've got to make this fool proof.'

'That could take a bit of time, Martin, time we might not have,' Vaccaro quietly protested.

'I know you want these bastards to pay for this, Noel, but we must do this right. If it takes more time than we bargain for, then so be it. The evidence cannot be compromised in any way until the crew from crime scene gets here.'

The Inspector agreed, knowing that Conroy was right. If the men who caused these deaths were ever to be convicted, the evidence and bodies had to remain untouched until the proper authorities arrived, and once he saw through his own haste the Inspector offered any help he could.

'Has next of kin been notified?' Conroy asked.

'Only the two young constables and Karl Turner,' Vaccaro said, pointing at their bodies.

Dane had the unenviable task of informing the families of Karl and the two young constables of their senseless and wasteful deaths. He had asked Ryan to accompany him, but he understandably refused. Ryan needed to get back home as he was already 48 hours overdue and knew that Kate would be overly worried by his absence.

It would take Dane the best part of the day going from family to family to relay the shocking news. He vowed to each of the families that the people responsible for the deaths of their loved ones would be brought to justice as he told of the events leading up to, and what had transpired during the shootout. It was equal to the worst day in Dane's life, seeing the grief and sorrow come from the people he genuinely cared for, not to mention the guilt he carried with him over their deaths. By the time he arrived back at his own home in the late evening he was a totally spent and exhausted man.

'When's official identification?' Conroy asked.

'I told Sgt Grainger to tell the families it would be tomorrow morning,' Vaccaro replied.

'I want you to hold it off for a few days until we're finished with them,' Conroy instructed. 'I assume these two are the Devlins,' he asked.

'Correct.'

'What about these other two?' he added, pointing at the bodies of Pringle's dead offsiders. 'Have you identified them?'

'No, not yet! There was no identification on them. The only thing we're definite on was that they were both with John Pringle and they were just as savage as their boss,' informed Vaccaro.

Conroy ordered fingerprints off the two dead bodies so he could run it through the Cops database down in Marlboro. The Inspector queried the time it was going to take as he knew from past experience that it could take up to a week on occasions to get use of the computers that stored the necessary information, access which needed permission from high authority. Conroy assured the Inspector that he knew the right people in the right places, and it would not take long before they had the identities of Pringle's colleagues. Identifying them was crucial, it would strengthen their case that the hired killer had been in town on the Minister's invitation.

Conroy and Vaccaro dispatched three of the Inspector's trusted officers down to the city by train with all the information regarding the alleged shootout and cover-ups. They sent off official letters of recommendation of what Conroy thought was needed in Graceville. Included were witness statements, photographs of the slain bodies, all they thought necessary for the insiders of the task force to take swift and prompt action, along with a phone call to Conroy's superior to let him know what to expect when the officers arrived at his office.

With the Premier's approval, the first of the Crime Scene Investigators would arrive in Graceville the following morning to start processing the bodies, while over the next few days, other members, including work mates of Martin Conroy who were with the State Government's corruption task force would sporadically arrive at the Graceville train station. Strict orders were given to keep the investigation as secret as possible.

They wanted their man and all measures were being taken to ensure secrecy was maintained. They went to the extent of having the men scattered to different accommodation outlets around town to keep a low profile, all for Minister Johnston's benefit. They were taking the allegations against Johnston deadly serious and as the days went on gathering information and the evidence continued to mount, it was becoming abundantly clear that Johnston's days in office were numbered.

Crime scene experts were sent to the scene of the shootings at the Pruitt house. They were sent down to the Watkins River and up in the mountains near Tambourine Bridge, accompanied by Sgt Dane Grainger to piece together evidence of the Pringle shootout. Taskforce investigators discreetly interviewed members of the Minister's staff, along with banking officials, police members, newspaper employees; anyone who they thought could assist them with their inquiries. But as it was with any member of parliament being investigated, not to mention one who ruled their region with an iron fist, it was going to take time to put together a watertight case.

Most people were reluctant to talk, however, there were others who were all too happy to spill the beans on what they knew and the more time investigators spent in Johnston's territory, the more likely it was for the Minister's cronies to get wind of what was going on around them. Within days of their arrival, Johnston knew who was in town and what they were doing there.

He immediately began the process of trying to destroy or silencing any evidence that would incriminate him, but above all, he wanted Danny Pruitt and his merry band of men silenced the most. If they were captured alive, the hiring of Pringle would be known, an option that could not be accepted by the now nervous politician despite any future statement from Sgt Dane Grainger and Inspector Vaccaro. Minister Johnston already had Detective Cribbs trying to gain information on their possible whereabouts. He had others already positioned up in the mountains, but the trail had been lost. No-one knew where they were.

Cribbs was upping the ante. His investigations had established no leads whatsoever on the outlaws and started to interrogate all known associates of Danny. He didn't have enough information on the other three men yet, they were out of towners who had no known fixed address, so Danny Pruitt was his main objective. Cribbs' men forcibly started to raid the houses of friends and families of Danny, hauling them in for questioning hoping someone would break under the pressure, but no one was giving up any information, not that they had any to give. He had Corey and Sarah in; Kate and Ryan were questioned heavily, so were Damien and Nikki, but like all others, they stood faithful.

Greta had just arrived home from church service when she was met by Detective Cribbs and a half dozen of his men that methodically tore apart Corey and Sarah's house looking for any evidence on her husband's whereabouts. The raid found nothing and with Cribbs' patience wearing thin, ordered Greta to the police station for more questioning.

Greta remained defiant and loyal to her husband for the entire two hours they had her locked away in the questioning room. She would never give up her husband under any circumstances despite threats of her being arrested for aiding and abetting. Separation from her two sons was another threat, but Greta replied to their menacing overtones with calmness and resoluteness, she was never going to concede to their demands.

Greta was left alone after Cribbs and a partner decided to talk privately when into the interview room walked Officer Steve Sandilands. He arrogantly strutted around the table that Greta was seated at, his eyes creepily zeroing in on Greta's cleavage. He commented on how much of a good-looking woman she was.

'You know, if you were mine, I wouldn't leave you in the lurch like your husband has. I wouldn't let you out of my sight,' he smugly sighed. 'There are all types of maniacs out there that would hurt a gorgeous woman like you. There's a lot of mental cases out there these days, you know! No, you would always be by my side,' Sandilands mused.

With both hands on the table, fingers spread in anger, Greta stared steadfastly across the room into the blank wall in front of her, refusing to give the overconfident officer the satisfaction of a reply. Sandilands moved across to stand directly behind her.

'No, I doubt if I could keep my hands off you if you were mine,' he smoothly said.

He placed his hands across each of her bare shoulders, flicking her black bra straps that were exposed from the thin strap of her sky-blue summer dress. Greta started to shake. His hands moved slowly down until he roughly cupped both her breasts. Greta gulped down a breath in fear. She instantaneously stood to her feet, the chair hitting Sandilands in the knees after she knocked it over in her haste.

'Get your filthy hands off me,' she demanded.

Sandilands immediately became aggressive. He grabbed at Greta again and violently turned her around. His strength was too much as he held her tightly against himself, then in a low bloodcurdling voice talked in her ear from behind.

'We're going to catch your husband; I assure you of that! And when we do, it's not gonna be pretty. After we put about twenty bullets into him, I'm going to cut his balls off for making a fool out of me.'

Greta mustered all her strength and managed to untangle herself from the hold the determined officer had on her. She pushed herself away, turned and faced him, and with raging fire emblazoned in her eyes, gritted her teeth and angrily responded.

'Even if you did cut off his balls, not that you would have the courage to get within 10 meters of him without a gun, you would still be half the man Danny was. But that's who you are isn't it, a poor excuse for what a real man is all about. Beating up on defenceless females, that's right. I know you raped those women on your re-po squad raids.

'At the back of the church, for God's sake, some as young as fifteen, who you knew had no way of fighting back, you filthy animal. But that's probably the only way you would a get a bit isn't it, no one would want you for who you really are, you ugly, despicable fuckin asshole of a human being.'

Words were coming out of Greta's mouth that never had. The anger and persecution she felt was over burdening and she was not about to fall victim to this corrupt predator.

Greta knew the man who was intimidating her. Sgt Dane had told her what had happened between him and her husband down at the river. She also knew all about the sexual abuse Sandilands had inflicted upon young women in her church congregation as many had confided in her what he had done to them, too scared to go to the police.

Sandilands grabbed Greta and threw her up against the wall of the interview room and made his next vulgar move. With his left arm over her throat, he forced his right hand up her dress and between her thighs. Greta kicked and punched to try and fight him off.

'Get away from me!' she screamed.

Sandilands muzzled her mouth with his left hand, trying to silence her screaming. Greta was trying her hardest to slip the hold that he had on her. She could feel Sandilands' hand marauding down the front of her underpants. She ducked and thrashed, up and down and side to side, lifting her left leg in absolute defiance, twisting and wrestling. She could feel his fingers about to enter inside of her.

Fearing she would be digitally raped, Greta bit as hard as she could at his hands, forcing Sandilands to release his grip then screamed as loud as she could, enough to rouse those outside of the room. Inspector Vaccaro was first to hear the stressing pleas for help and stormed into the room.

'Get your hands off her,' he rumbled. 'What the hell do you think you're doing?'

'Sorry sir, I was trying to get information out of her on Pruitt's whereabouts,' Sandilands said as he released his clutches.

'Get this rapist away from me!' Greta yelled.

Inspector Vaccaro was no fool, he knew what his nephew was like, and wasn't having a bar of his behaviour. He forcibly removed Sandilands from the room under a tirade of obscenities and told him that he would deal with him later.

'I'm terribly sorry, Mrs Pruitt,' the Inspector said. 'Do you want to file a complaint against him?'

'A complaint, a fuckin complaint, where's that going to get me?' yelled Greta. 'Nothing will get done about it, you know that. That bastard has raped at least five women I know of, and nothing has been done about that has it! So what hope have I got getting that asshole to answer to anyone. Just let me go home, I just want to go home.'

Greta slumped to the floor, kneeling, her arched back against the wall, cupping both hands to her face as uncontrollable sobbing overtook her. The brave exterior had waned. One minute she was courageous, the next weak and vulnerable. The Inspector knew she didn't deserve to be put in this position, no woman of her ilk did. He knew she was innocent in this entire calamity and felt enormous pity for her.

He gave her time to regain her composure, repeatedly apologising for what had occurred and after she was steady on her feet again and the tears had stopped, the Inspector helped lead her out of the police station to be with her children again. They directly passed Detective Cribbs who was standing at the front desk perusing over some files.

'Do not harass this woman ever again, detective,' was the stern order coming from the Inspector's mouth. 'She has no information that would help you in any way, I know that for sure, so your business with Mrs Pruitt is over, do you understand me?' he demanded as he led Greta out the front doors of the police station.

Cribbs looked on in silence, sighed to himself in his arrogant smug manner and turned back to delve back into the files he was perusing through, blowing off the Inspector's order as if it meant nothing to him. Inspector Vaccaro was his superior, but that didn't matter to Cribbs, he was his own man, and only Minister Johnston he would take orders from.

Up in the mountains, the four men were up at the crack of dawn. They had made their beds atop of the thick native kikuyu grass that spread over a little clearing and had their best sleep for what seemed an eternity to them. It was a godsend to them to be able to rest their weary bodies on top of a nice cushioned surface and not be invaded by the ruthless insects that had been biting and buzzing at them relentlessly throughout the days, always making sure they would not get more than an hour of continuous slumber.

The men saddled their horses up and headed southwards along the Summit Road. No breakfast was taken due to the lack of provisions. They were quickly into a light canter when almost immediately the men notice rock formations on the right side of the road. The first formation their eyes came across was a little statue like impression of a man. It was made up from clay quarry rocks with assorted little pebbles, bark off different species of trees made up finishing the touches of the figure. The men didn't think much of it until another one appeared some 100 meters down the road, even more impressive than the first, and then another two after that.

The men dismounted and curiously walked slowly up the road. They looked side to side to see if there were any more figures, but now all they could see were arrows, pointing in the direction they were traveling, again, made up of little rocks, the biggest the size of a man's fist, each arrow around a metre in length. They came across five of them, then six, then seven, approximately 20-30 meters apart as they walked. They came to an old track off to the side and saw another arrow formation pointing down it.

Just past the rock arrow on the ground was a sentence laid out with the same sort of rocks that had been used with the arrows.

THIS WAY DANNY! It read. The boys' attention was now at feverish levels. They looked at each other with amazement and intrigue, and a touch of danger in their eyes.

'What the hell's going on here?' Harry enquired.

'No idea, but we're gonna find out, what do ya reckon?' replied Danny.

Barny was nervous, he didn't like that idea one bit.

'Curiosity killed the cat, Danny,' he softly quoted.

'I know that, Barny,' Danny responded. 'But doesn't a cat also have nine lives, and I reckon we've only used up around 4 or 5 so far, am I right?'

The boys didn't argue with his statement as a collective smirk crossed their faces when Danny raised his eyebrows. Without a word, they started to walk their horses down the slight incline of the track. Crusty signs of old wheel ruts were visible to let them know that vehicles once frequented it.

Minutes down the track, Ricky, who was to the front and left of Danny, stopped, then nodded forward and left. The boys could see smoke drifting up in the air as their senses went into overdrive. The smell of cooking meat engulfed their nostrils as the threat of an ambush began to wane.

They bunched as tightly as they could, putting their horses between them and where the now obvious campsite was.

'It's alright, Danny, come in and grab yourself a feed, I've been waiting for ya,' a voice rang out.

All three looked at Danny to see if he had any inclination of who the relaxed tone of voice belonged too, all they got was a wide-eyed shrug of the shoulders. Danny drew his revolver and gave his reins to Ricky then gently moved forward, pushing aside the baby native wattles, tall grasses and shrubs. He peered into an opening where a single man was sitting next to a fire pit. Another four old deck chairs were sitting in a circle around the fire where it looked like a nice big hunk of deer was being cooked.

The man was unflappable, he turned his head to his left as Danny came into the open five meters away.

'G'day mate, long time no see,' he said, as giggles tremored under his breath.

'I'll be buggered, is that you, Benny? Shit mate, how the hell are ya?' Danny replied, relieved.

He walked over to Benny who stood from his chair, and both gave each other a strong welcome embrace.

'Thought you and your mates might want some breakfast,' Benny said, pointing down at the ready to eat venison.

Danny excitedly called the others in and introduced them to his long-lost friend and before they knew it, they were soon chomping away at hunks of venison.

Ben Stevens was a descendant and full-blooded member of one of the local indigenous clans that had made the Hexagon Valley home since time could remember. Benny, as he was known to everyone, was six years Danny's junior. The two worked together briefly when Benny got an apprenticeship with a landscaping company. Their paths often crossed when projects were underway and hit it off with each other immediately. At times, Danny would use him for weekend work when he got busy. Benny had a sense of humour that Danny loved—dry, quick-witted and always with a cheeky grin across his face.

He was a well-built young man, standing around 180cm tall with cropped dark hair and muscular arms to add to his athletic physique. He was a hard-working young man who left school early but soon after reaching his twentieth birthday things started to go astray for Benny. He liked his drink, he liked to party, he liked to go on benders and soon enough his employers would lose patience and move him on his way.

When the world started to nosedive, Benny soon got addicted the scourge of all drugs, ice! In a short time, young Benny, as Danny affectionately called him, hit the low points of his life. Continual usage and dependence on ice and other drugs saw him distance himself from his family and friends and in time homeless and without hope in his deepest depressions.

When Benny lost his way, Danny lost contact with him. But the times when they met each other, which was seldom these days, Danny would always ask about his welfare as he was genuinely concerned and sorry to see him the way he was. Danny and Greta gave him a roof over his head when he needed it, loaned him money to get him out of a jam and always told him that if he needed help, not to hesitate in coming to see them. Benny never forgot the kindness and sometimes hard advice that Danny and Greta gave him, and Benny always had a place in his soul for them.

But as the world crises deepened, with no work, a family which he thought no longer cared, and no real place he could call home, Benny saw the light. He weaned himself off the dreaded methamphetamine habit, stopped the alcohol intake, packed as much of his belongings as he could and headed into the mountains.

It was easy for him compared to people like Danny and his friends, he had it in his blood. His elders taught him from a young child how to survive in the bush. All the traits and wisdom he learnt off them were lost in the modern society where they were no longer required, but once he went into the mountains, it all came back to him. Not only has he survived these last couple years living off the land, but he also thrived in it.

The boys were as intrigued on how Benny knew it was them coming up the road and asked accordingly.

'I've been keeping an eye on you for days,' Benny said.

'What, while we've been half dying in the bush?' scorned Danny.

'Yep.'

'You prick! You knew we were struggling and did nothing to help us?'

'Yep.'

'Why the hell not?'

Benny's giggle was vibrating through his body by now.

'You guys seemed to be going okay, it wasn't that bad, was it? Although I did wonder why you came through that way. It's the worst possible way you can go through these mountains, I don't think anyone has gone that way,' he pondered.

'Because we didn't want to be seen, you idiot,' Danny retorted.

'That's right, you guys are in deep shit, aren't you!' Benny laughed as he wiped and sucked the venison out of his teeth.

'You obviously know what's happened then!' Barny asked.

'Yeah, I do,' Benny said. 'I was in town for New Year's Eve celebrations and heard everything that was going on. Talk of the town, you boys are. Most people think you're a bit of hero, Danny,' he giggled.

'How did you find us anyway?' Danny asked, shrugging off the hero label.

'I was heading up Kelso's track on my way back here a couple of days ago, something caught my ears. It was no animal, so I rode off into the bush and about a kilometre in, I spotted you guys. I thought it would be fun to sit back and observe unskilled bushmen traipsing their way through the thick forest. You guys were turning everywhere, north, south, west, doubling back on yourselves,' he laughed.

'We don't think it's real funny, Benny!' Danny scowled, as Barny, Ricky and Harry's smiles toughened.

'Don't worry, you were in good hands,' Benny assured with his infectious smile. 'If you took a turn that would have led to disaster, I would've been there to guide you out.'

Although Danny and the boys were far from happy with being Benny's private amusement show, they grudgingly accepted the funny side of his comedic stunt as the hunger they felt over seeded any sought of humorous payback on their part.

Benny cut away slices from his roasting deer then listened as Danny had his say on what the truth of the situation was from their standpoint. Ricky, Barny and Harry sat on the rickety old deck chairs that were provided, scoffing down their long-awaited meat serving from out of their now greasy fingers and added bits and pieces from their perspective as they listened intently to the conversation.

After the boys had finished off their meals, with a dessert of bananas and apples that Benny had provided, he asked them to follow him on foot.

The boys walked behind him until the forest started thin out dramatically within 300 metres from his camp. The tall eucalypt and mountain ash quickly disappeared to reveal a massive clearing. The boys couldn't believe their eyes as they scanned the area. What they saw was an old logging coup from days gone by, about fifteen acres square, they surmised.

There were about a dozen piles of wood rows scattered around the disused coup, some raised up over 20 feet tall surrounded by dirt tracks in all directions, but what really raised the boy's attention was all the machinery that was left behind. Large excavators, bulldozers, D9's, log trucks, 4wd wagons, twin cab utilities. The place gave the look of a graveyard for prehistoric metal creatures. To the side of the coup where they had entered were shipping containers that held all types of tools and other little machinery along with three large portables where the long-gone workers had their offices and lunchrooms.

'I came across it about twelve months ago,' Benny explained, after seeing the amazement on the boys' faces. 'I've never seen a soul return to the coup since. I've been using what I need from it.'

'Like what?' Danny asked.

'You know! Chainsaws to cut firewood, rotary hoes to cultivate my veggie patch. The hand tools have come in handy. I used the fuel out of the vehicles to help start fires during winter, not to mention taking a few of the big machinery and vehicles for a quick spin around the coup,' he giggled. 'No fuel left now though, but I've still got a few 44-gallon drums left of diesel in reserve for the Toyotas if I need one in an emergency. I power my little fridge with the generators left behind. It keeps my food preserved.'

'What food? Do you bring it back from town?' Harry asked.

'Nah, the animals I kill,' Benny said. 'I'm a wizard with my bow and arrow!' He laughed.

The boys were amazed and excited as they looked over the old coup. They couldn't work out why millions of dollars' worth of machinery would be left behind, but that was the way it was. People just packed up their worksite and left. Maybe they just couldn't get the machinery back home the boys guessed, but whatever the reason, Benny used it to his advantage.

'There's another abandoned coup five kilometres to the southwest of here,' Benny divulged. 'Not as big as this one and with less machinery, but still very handy. I've got another four little campsites scattered around as well. It's good for cover and privacy.'

'Sounds like you've made yourself at home up here,' Danny congratulated.

'It's easy. You just gotta know what you're doing. Not like you guys,' chortled Benny.

The boys enjoyed themselves for best part of day, forgetting about the peril they were in. They had fun jumping into the driver's seats of the big machines, climbing up and down the huge hydraulic booms, perusing over and testing all the tools. They found a football in the portable lunchroom, conveniently pumped up to right compression. They filled in hours playing kick to kick and having goalkicking competitions, aiming through the posts set up from logs laying around.

Danny found himself another scorpion in amongst the timber stacks and went hunting for bull ants, excited to have another rematch between the little bush warriors. It didn't take him long to find a nest and perused the candidates until he settled on the largest, he could see.

'This one's got muscles on his muscles,' Danny boasted as his mates gathered around to watch the entertainment. The bull ant came out victor once more.

They drank water from plastic bottles that Benny had amassed in one of the containers as the heat and humidity climbed steadily throughout the afternoon. Copious amounts of bourbon and whiskey straight out of the bottle went down their throats that Benny had provided. Not that he drank anymore, life itself was a great high for him now, but he would never begrudge anyone else who would partake. He knew the boys had gone through hell lately and it was giving him joy to see the now fugitives letting down their hair as they joked and bantered between themselves.

By around six o'clock in the evening, the boys were getting mighty hungry, and a little bit worse for wear alcohol wise, so Benny cooked up a mighty stew. Ingredients included a great arrange of vegetables. Potatoes, broccoli, peas, corn and spinach, all from his well tendered vegie patch and to the boy's delight, a tasty French onion-based sauce to go with chunks of kangaroo meat that rounded off the meal.

The boys were grateful to Benny as they washed down their last spoonful of dinner with the remaining whiskey and bourbon, and as dusk fell upon them the conversation turned to the serious.

Danny asked whether he'd seen any sign of Greta while he was in town on New Year's Eve.

'No mate didn't see her,' came a soft reply.

'I miss her so much; I'm worried out of my mind for her and my kids! I wished this never happened,' Danny confided.

'Yeah bro, I'm feeling for ya,' Benny said, as he laid a friendly hand on his shoulder.

'You know what they did to my house, don't ya?' Danny said, as the grip around his bottle tightened.

'Yep, I rode past it when I went into town, had a look. Assholes!' replied Benny.

'I've got a list with names of who done it, not all, but I'll get the rest, and when I do, I'm going after them, all of them,' Danny sternly promised.

He produced the piece of paper given to him by Kate and asked Benny if he knew the remaining names on the list that he wasn't familiar with.

Benny couldn't help him, He knew a couple of them, Kenny Jameson and Mick Cox, but Danny already knew who they were.

As the sun quietly gave in for another day on this hot and humid evening, Ricky, Barny and Harry dozed off to sleep after chatting quietly amongst themselves, but not before Barny produced his bible and said his prayers. Danny and Benny passed the next hour catching up on all that had happened in their lives. With a small flickering smoky fire to look at, only alight to keep the mosquitos at bay, they pondered what lay ahead for Danny. There were no plans made on Danny's side, no strategy, no methods, no sympathy, but only one desire, to have this whole nightmare go away so he could have Greta and his sons in his arms again.

As he slowly drifted off to sleep, feeling the never-ending ache in his stomach, and at times wiping away the sadden tears that would drip from his eyes caused by the guilt he now felt, all his thoughts were with his family and how they were coping without him.

Chapter 17

'For as much as it hath pleased almighty God to call hence the soul of our dear brother here departed, we therefore commit Karl's body to the ground, earth to earth, ashes to ashes, dust to dust,' Reverend Samuels finished.

Family and friends of Karl Turner slowly and tearfully passed the hole in the ground where he now lay, dropping roses and fists full of dirt on his draped coffin. A life taken to soon. He's only crime being in the wrong place at the wrong time where the now infamous shoot out at Tambourine bridge on Syrian Creek Road occurred a week before.

It was a huge turnout at the Graceville cemetery. The day was hot and humid, and amongst the mourners stood Greta, wearing her large squared dark sunglasses, dressed in a light black cotton dress, cut just above the knee with her hair tied back in a ponytail.

She had her misgivings about attending the funeral, she knew Karl well, was even closer to his now mournful wife Jade. She knew some were blaming Danny and his friends for Karl's death but had reassurance from Dane after a visit in the morning that the family and close friends knew the truth of what happened and held no grudges towards her husband.

By her side throughout the funeral service and burial was her sister-in-law Kate and husband Ryan. Kate would hardly leave Greta's side, she was getting protective of her brother's wife, shielding her from any busybodies from asking the wrong questions, but as the funeral crowd inside the cemetery gardens mingled amongst each other in separated groups, Kate received a tap on the shoulder.

'Excuse me Kate, can I have a minute?'

'Oh, hi Val, sure!' Kate replied. 'Excuse me, Greta, I'll only be a tick,' she continued, grabbing Greta's hand in both of hers in reassurance.

Val moved Kate away from the crowd to a spot where they could not be overheard.

'What's up, Val?' asked Kate. 'You look like you've—'

Val interrupted, her eyes darting from right to left to make sure no one was in listening distance, 'You asked me if I could find out anything on the Re-po squad regarding Danny and Greta's, well, I think I hit the jackpot, I've got the names of all who were there,' Val excitedly said in a soft voice.

'You're joking,' was Kate's surprised reply.

'I kid you not, I wouldn't say it if I wasn't absolutely sure,' Val confidently said.

Valerie Corbett had been a long-time friend of Kate's. They met at university in their studying days, Kate studying Teaching, Valerie journalism. Kate formed a strong bond with her, admiring her drive and intellect and respected her greatly.

Valerie was fast tracked to become a crime journalist with one of the city's major newspapers through her hard work and intuition before the hard times hit. She was one of many who were let go from her employment and so moved to the Hexagon Valley and Graceville to start up her own little newspaper. Her publication was called *The Mountain Scene*, which produced an issue which came out every Tuesday morning. She had her run-ins with Minister Johnston on what she could and couldn't print.

Her paper survived because she bowed to the Minister's requests and threats and only reported on the minor issues, such as life interest stories, sports from around the Valley, along with personal ads in which she would charge a small fee. Valerie hated the major newspaper in the district, the lies and misquotes they printed, yellow journalism she would rant about them, turning the truth into myths and vice versa, and never associated privately with their scribes. But through her experience she could smell a rat from a mile.

She loathed the Minister, and all the sycophants around him and wouldn't need much encouragement to gather any information that could possibly bring them down. She had a file cabinet of papers at her home, full of documents and statements ready to be produced when the time was right.

Valerie pulled an envelope from her handbag and furtively passed it to Kate. Inside the envelope was a printed A4 sheet of paper with all the names involved in the trashing of the Pruitt's property.

'How did you get it?' asked Kate.

'I was following up a stupid story on one of Johnston's employee's dogs, never mind, that's not important,' she said, waving her hands as if she was swatting away some pestering flies.

Valerie continued, words quickening in excitement, wanting to get the news to Kate as fast as she could.

'I was in this waiting room in the shire offices when I saw this door ajar to one of the offices down the hall, you know me, I couldn't resist. I snooped around the room and found a whole lot of manila folders behind one of the desks. I don't know whose office it was but the shit load of information in there would blow your mind. I came across a folder with Repossessions on it. I open it up and flicked through and there it was.

All the names of those involved, not just Danny and Greta's, but all the properties that had been repossessed in the last month. It had who was in charge, who was with them, pay rates, addresses, the whole kit and kaboodle. There was a photo copier in there, so I tried it, and blow me, it worked!' Valerie finished with a wide cheeky grin.

'My god!' came Kate's astonished reply. 'Thank you, thank you, thank you!'

Kate opened the envelope immediately as they turned their backs to funeral gathering and slowly wandered further away towards the large Cyprus pines that stood by the fence line of the cemetery.

Kate was perusing down the information on the sheet, looking at the details that were before her eyes. The names of those involved were on the left-hand side. On it were the same names that young Janice, the Pruitt's neighbour gave her, the very same ones she passed onto Danny. This gave her the confidence that what she was looking at was the real deal.

'Have you had a look at the names?' Kate inquired of Valerie.

'Yeah, I have, didn't recognise any of them, some of them ring a bell but couldn't put faces to them,' Val assured her.

Kate continued down the page.

'Oh my god!' she whispered under her breath.

Kate's heart almost stopped beating, her knees buckled, her left hand went to her mouth. She checked the home address associated to the final name.

'I don't believe it,' she said, nodding her head from side to side in shocked repulsion.

'What is it, do you know one of them?' Val asked impatiently.

'Yeah, I do,' came the solemn reply.

'Who?'

'Corey Porter!'

The very same Corey Porter who reached out with his heart to give Greta and her kids a bed and roof over their heads.

Kate gave Valerie a tight hug and thanked her for everything. She knew it was a highly risky thing to do and was ever so grateful. She walked back and joined Ryan and Greta as the mourners were starting to disperse away from the cemetery burial site. Most mourners were heading to the Depot hotel to toast and celebrate the life of Karl. Kate's mind was spinning at a hundred miles per hour as they walked the 20 minutes towards the hotel.

She was poring over everything. Could Corey really have been with them? Does Sarah know? If so, how could they react the way they have towards Greta? Do I tell Greta? How would she react? It would tear her apart, it would be last thing she could take. Do I approach Corey? How do I bring it up with him?

Arriving at the hotel a short time after, Kate looked at people mixing with each other in the bistro lounge in between small talk with passing acquaintances, drinks in hand, hers a glass of bourbon and coke with a straw to sip out of. No matter what her overwhelming thoughts were, she knew deep down that there was no doubt that Corey was involved, the proof was there, although she was finding it hard to accept.

For the time being, she would keep the information to herself. She won't tell her husband Ryan. He had already berated her for giving Danny the letter after he asked her what Danny was talking about when Ryan saw him after the Tambourine bridge shootout. Kate finally confessed to her husband that she gave her brother the names of some of the members of the re-po squad. Ryan was livid, he wanted nothing more to do with the situation. He was scared that he would be implicated in it all somehow.

Their marriage was already on a downward spiral, and this just added fuel onto an already raging fire. But, as she did with the first list, she was going get this one to Danny as well. She didn't know how yet, but she was going to find a way.

The hunt for the four fugitives was back on again in earnest, minus the members of the shire force who decided that New Year's Eve celebrations far outweighed the importance of obeying orders and continuing the search. They were all called into the police station late New Year's Day and were immediately sacked from their posts, 18 in all now unemployed. Although a skeleton team were still in Kensington state forest, no inroads had been made on the whereabouts of Danny and his crew.

They were soon to be joined by another three groups of police in the next 24 hours consisting of four men in each, on the orders of Inspector Vaccaro with consent from Martin Conroy. Their orders were only to locate the fugitives then report back, not to engage them under any circumstances. The Inspector was not going to risk another massacre, too many lives had been needlessly wasted already he sadly stated to his search parties before they embarked.

The assistant commissioner was already in the process of organising his own elite search squad to arrive in Graceville if no arrest was made within the next week. The representatives of the anti-corruption unit in town were making steady progress in gathering evidence against the Minster, despite his efforts to cover up or destroy anything linked to him. The unit took advantage of Johnston's short absence due to parliamentary duties in the city, continuing to interview employees of the shire, including police officers, some who were just given their marching orders and all too pleased to tell what they knew.

Both Vaccaro and Conroy needed to apprehend the fugitives as soon as possible. The feel on the streets was that Danny was becoming some type of martyr, the people's hero. He already had a lot of respect from his peers and associates and was getting a wave of sympathy and support from the ordinary person in the valley as truth swept around of the events that led up to all the shootings, starting with what triggered it all in Danny's yard. Most ordinary folk were dismissing all the mistruths and fabrications about the men that were written in Mance's paper.

In protest, some were burning issues of his print in front of the newspaper's head office in Graceville. Everything the Minister wanted to achieve through his accomplice's bestselling newspaper was starting to take a dramatic twist against him, and Adrian Mance's ample frame was sweating in anxiety. However, the one thing the Minister did have in his favour was the loyalty and perseverance of Detective Cribbs. He and his team were still putting the pressure on friends and family of all four men, with allies of the Pruitt's their main target.

Infuriatingly for Cribbs, all he was getting for his efforts was a frustrating wall of silence and ignorance. Cribbs had been granted access to the police vehicles to start a search by road but was not going to waste any unnecessary fuel on wild goose chases through the back roads of the forest until he had what he believed to a be strong lead to act on, and within the next 48 hours his patience would be rewarded.

Tom Potter would soon scrape and scramble his way back into Graceville. With no decision made on where he would go and in a total state of depression, he thought the best place to mull it over would be at the Graceville hotel on the corner of the main intersection in town. He didn't know why he kept things from the boys, maybe it was his warped way of staying around them, the longer they were lost, the longer he had company. He had no other pals, the ones he did had given up on him, a fact that Danny was totally ignorant to.

His alcoholism was well entrenched before the re-po squad came visiting, it was the sole reason his wife had left him. He had lost his job because of it, however, he continued to pretend that he was still employed, rising every morning to leave the house and go to a job he never had, too embarrassed and frightened to admit his well-covered failings. All he succeeded in doing was spending day after day alone, trying to drink away his accelerating depression, wandering around aimlessly and hiding, another fact that Danny had no idea about.

When Tom's wife found out about his ruse after continually questioning him where his supposed wages had gone, it was the final straw for her. With all his internal private battles and along with the sickening images of Constable Johnny Hayes being executed still embedded and replaying in his mind, together with the trauma of the shootout and the bodies left behind, Tom would soon find himself in a drunken stupor and high as a kite, mumbling away and causing a minor scene as he sat alone at the bar and within a couple of hours, he would find himself in handcuffs and on the way to the police station.

Both Inspector Vaccaro and Detective Cribbs were there to greet him and had him in an interview room immediately. Both knew that he could possibly be the last one to see the men and grilled him accordingly using their well experienced techniques of getting to the truth and it didn't take to long for Tom to start singing like a bird. He hadn't eaten in two days; the alcohol intake was severely affecting his judgement, and the consequences of what he was saying didn't even dawn on him in his inebriated state. He was still angry at Danny and the boys for throwing him out of their midst. Tom gave up everything on them, what their mindset was, what their plans were, the last place he saw them and in what direction they were probably heading—he babbled and babbled.

The two senior police offices believed the information they got out of him was credible enough to act upon. With the interview room needed for another investigation and the eight prison cells already full, the decision was made to move Tom to a storeroom at the rear of the station. They provided him with a table and chair, sandwiches and a bottle of water and instructed him not to move. They left him alone and adjourned to Vaccaro's office to discuss their options on how to move forward with the search.

Vaccaro was wary of Cribbs' plans, he knew all too well his allegiances with Johnston and wanted assurances from the detective that he wouldn't act alone, that they could put their animosity aside and work together from now on to produce a quick and safe resolution. Twenty minutes later after their talk, Cribbs decided to resume his questioning of their now informant; however, not another word would be coming out of the mouth of Tom Potter.

As Cribbs swung the door open to the storeroom, his attention was grabbed to the rear left corner. He saw Tom's lifeless body slowly swinging from the ceiling. He had assembled some ropes and cords that were bundled away in the corner of the room, affixed a noose around his neck, stepped onto the table, tied it to an exposed metal beam above himself, then jumped.

Chapter 18

The fugitive four had a good old-fashioned sleep-in at Benny's home away from home, making the most of his comfortable surroundings. It was almost midday by the time they were truly awake from their slumber, bodies still aching from their arduous days in the saddle. The visible reminders of the insect bites, Harry being the worst victim with minor infections scattered around his body from the constant scratching of the irritations, continually distracted them. Delightedly, Harry was about to get some much-needed relief.

The boys watched curiously from their deck chairs as Benny grabbed a metal rake that was leaning up against a tree then continue over to where his tent was pitched and began to scrape away with the teeth of the rake, removing the forest foulage that lay on the ground. He then got down on his hands and knees, brushed away the excess, leant over, and with both hands pulled a metal locker out of the hole in the ground.

'What have you got in there?' Danny asked, after Benny produced a key to open the lock.

'You name it, I got it,' giggled Benny.

Benny delved into the locker and picked up a tube and threw it in Harry's direction.

'Oh, you're joking, you bloody beauty,' elated Harry. He quickly unscrewed the lid of the antiseptic tube and began to smooth the cream over his infested bites.

'What else ya got in there?' Ricky inquired, anticipating a look inside.

'Have a look,' Benny happily said. 'Got everything, dude, Panadol, bandages, pain relievers, brushes, toothpaste, shaving gear, creams for all sorts of shit,' Benny went on as he proudly displayed his mobile bathroom cabinet.

'I'm interested in that,' Barny gleefully stated.

'What's that?' Benny asked.

'The shaving gear,' replied Barny as he picked up the disposable razors, still wrapped in their plastic resealable bag.

'Go for it, I got a couple of hair clippers here as well, with all the combs that go with them.'

'Christ mate, where did you get all this stuff?' Danny joined in.

'I got most of it out of the first aid kits left behind in containers at the logging coupe. I also make a trip into Graceville at least once a fortnight, sometimes weekly. Every time I'm there, I take whatever I can get my hands on. You never know when you might need something. I'm not completely a bush Neanderthal,'

Benny laughingly mused, receiving double the laughs in return from the grateful men.

With broken pieces of mirror that Benny gave them, the men soaped up, and with scissors and razors, immediately began to give themselves a handsome grooming. It had been well over a week since they put a razor to their face and Barny was particularly annoyed at the growth which now engulfed his. He went for the absolute clean shave, after all, it almost matched what was on top his skull the boys reminded him.

Ricky decided he too would go for a clean shave, taking off his now extenuated goatee he wore, while Danny decided that he would leave his newfound goatee beard for the time being. He went the extra yard and produced the battery-operated clippers and with the number four comb attached, proceeded to give his head a nice buzz over. Harry decided he wasn't going touch the way he looked. He liked the full beard look that he now donned. It was the first time he ever grew one, however, Harry had other motives. He was paranoid that someone might recognise him after the photo's went out and was taking no chances.

After the grooming had finished, the five men sat around enjoying a lunch that Benny had at the ready for them. Kangaroo fillets with sides of boiled vegies, washed down with more slurps of Jack Daniels and Jim Beam while Benny stuck to his water. As the boys chewed away pondering about their next move, an old used exercise book landed on Danny's lap.

'What's this?' he asked, looking across at Benny after he tossed it at him.

'Maps, my friend, you might need them.'

For the first time since they came across each other, their new ally had a serious demeanour about him. He started to strongly advise the four not to go the way that Danny was suggesting. Danny was going off the maps he attained from Tom, also by his jaded memory of the surroundings. The maps were over twenty years old, and things had changed Benny warned them. Some tracks didn't exist anymore while new ones have appeared, mountain bike trails were everywhere throughout now.

It had been a long time since Danny had travelled anywhere near these parts, years before his twins were born. He wanted to head southward on the Summit Road, get to the T-intersection where it ended, turn right down Molloy's track, then left up and over a track called Satan's elevator. From there he was planning to take one of the fire tracks down through the old pine plantation that led down behind the town reservoir.

From there, he was going to trek around through the catchment area and into the parklands near his property before entering Graceville. Once he arrived in Graceville, he didn't know what he was going to do, but at least he had a chance of somehow seeing Greta. Danny said that they should be there by lunch tomorrow if everything went okay.

'You don't wanna go that way,' Benny advised.

'Why not?' Ricky interrupted.

'You're walking straight into Sultan territory,' Benny warned.

'They're further east, aren't they? Over near the pass, that's what I was told,' Danny said.

'Nah bro, they're right above Satan's elevator. They've got the whole fucking land up there; the whole plateau is theirs now. They border the pine plantation along the catchment area as well. All the way east over to the pass and up to the summit of Black Mountain, it's all theirs. The boundaries are all fenced with little pine plantations as an extra barrier for them. They own the lot now, and you don't wanna go anywhere near the joint,' explained Benny.

'Hang on, who the hell are the Sultans, not that biker gang? Do they still exist?' Ricky bluntly asked.

'And what the friggin hell is Satan's elevator?' Harry added perplexed.

The boys listened on as Benny began to tell them what he knew, from the location and boundaries of the club and the huge dope crops that grew and warned that some without an invite who had encroached on their land were never seen or heard of again. Unbeknown to Benny however, he only knew the tip of the iceberg.

The fact of the matter was that the Sultans were a notorious outlaw motorcycle club with over a 50-year history in and around the state of Venturia. Police taskforces had been relatively successful in disbanding a lot of outlaw clubs over the years but not when it came to the Sultans. They had over 200 members in various clubhouses around the city and more interstate, and although the world crisis reduced their numbers they were still as powerful as they had ever been while other clubs went by the wayside. They were right at the heart of the drug and guns trade, and along with other ventures they were high up when it came to the kingpins of the organised crime syndicates.

They had swapped their Harleys for horses, and their new leader was looking for greener pastures as the crisis deepened, away from the overcrowded and hostile city. With links to the Hexagon Valley, he made a play for land so he could re-establish the Sultan brand and reputation and continue with what the club did best. With shoddy dealings between the club and Shire government, they somehow acquired over 2,000 hectares of forest land northeast of Graceville and would build a clubhouse and facilities that more resembled a fortress.

The soil content was perfect for marijuana plantations, and they grew it in massive amounts. The boundaries of their land were protected right around the perimeter by cyclone wire fences or wooden barriers cemented into the ground. Signs warned intruders against unauthorised entry every hundred meters and were attached to either trees or guard rails. Just inside the west and north boundary lines laid a 500-meter buffer zone of pine plantation of all species and maturity which adjoined the 4,000-hectare government owned catchment area.

It was there to remind trespassers who missed the signs or got through a fence, the pine plantation would be their last warning to turn around or suffer the consequences of trespassing on their now sacred land.

As for Satan's elevator! With the help of Danny's input, Benny described to the other three that it was a short sharp steep rise of almost a kilometre of dirt track where only the best, and craziest, four-wheel drive enthusiasts would take on. The track had boulders of all shapes and sizes to negotiate, along with the massive wheel ruts, some as deep as your knee if you stood in them. Young men would take on the challenge of driving their vehicles up and down the notorious strip of road, risking damage to both them and vehicle, which was more often than not.

The quicker it was accomplished, the more accolades one would get from their colleagues. As wear and tear and help from mother nature eroded the stretch of road it became more dangerous than ever, and Satan's Elevator would eventually take the life of a young man and his girlfriend who grossly overestimated their ability when it came to hard core four-wheel driving when they lost control, flipped their vehicle and rolled several times off down the steep graded embankment.

Forest authorities decided enough was enough and blocked the entrance to the track with concrete bollards at the base to prevent any more needless accidents. But if they thought it was tough then, through lack of maintenance of any kind, unbeknown to the lads, it was almost impassable by any means now.

Barny, Ricky and Harry had a quiet look to each other once the boys finished their history lesson on the legend of Satan's Elevator when, finally, Ricky broke the silence.

'And you are going to take us up there are you Danny,' he scoffed.

'It's not as bad as it sounds, we've got horses, mate, not vehicles, it's the quickest way back to Graceville,' Danny reminded him.

'You can't even get a quad bike up there now, Danny, even tough for horses, bro,' Benny warned.

He sat down next to Danny as the other boys gathered around and started to open pages of the exercise book that he had given them. Benny had drawn little mud maps of all the tracks he now used to get in and out of the forest. It was a labyrinth of roads, trails and mountain bike tracks, some established, some he had discovered, and a few that he had made himself to cut the distance between points.

He was no cartographer, but after lengthy, frustrating, and at times amusing arguments, the men got their heads around what lay in front of them. Some tracks were big enough for vehicles, some only small enough for horses two abreast, while others were only tight enough for mountain bikes, or of the motorised kind. He gave alternative routes back to Graceville, including short cuts back to the caves at the cascades and Tambourine Bridge, but in Danny's mind, that was not an option. Any track that would lead them back towards Tangiloo via Syrian Creek Road was a no go. The boys agreed strongly that it was too much of a risk with all the active police presence in the area.

Danny perused his finger up and down pages looking at the road and track maps in front of him until he came to a stop and tapped his finger on a certain section.

'What about this track?' he questioned Benny.

'That's a walking trail, Copperhead it's called.'

'Is that what it says? Geez, your writing is crap,' Harry chimed in facetiously.

Ignoring Harry's attempt at humour, the boys refocused their eyes back on the maps.

'Can we use that? That should take us down to the back of the reservoir, shouldn't it?' Danny surmised.

'Yeah, you probably can, it's a bit tight, but if you go single file, it should be okay. It runs on the edge of the pine plantation that's on Sultans' land. Stay clear of that and you might be okay,' Benny said.

Copperhead walking trail was a tourist track sparingly used by bushwalkers of today. When tourism was at its peak, nature enthusiasts would park their vehicles in the reservoir car park, a short 5km drive northeast from the heart of Graceville off the main highway that took you over the mountain range. Walkers would take the 15km round trip to a lookout located on a cliffs edge which incorporated hiking up a fire track for the first 6km until the copperhead trail would branch off to a tight walking track. Hikers then followed a minor track, enduring a steep climb for the remaining distance.

It was the way Danny decided he wanted to go, but from the high side in reverse. After some studying, he concluded that they could take the exit path of the trail off Molloy's track, another few kilometres down from the base of Satan's elevator and continue down to the lookout. From there it would be easy sailing he guaranteed, by shadowing the side of the pine plantation and then through it, all the way down to the banks of the 26,000 megalitre reservoir, avoiding any trespassing of Sultan land. It would add an extra 4-5 hours to their journey, but discretion is the better part of valour they agreed, so Danny reluctantly had to stall his entry into Graceville for 24 hours at least, however, on the bright side, he mused it would give him more time to formulate a plan before he arrived.

It was late afternoon by the time the boys were saddled up and ready to move again, stomachs full and little intoxicated from the emptying of what whiskey bottles remained. They were extremely grateful for the friendship and hospitality that Benny afforded them and let him know accordingly. In a gesture of good will, they left behind some items they thought he could use, including their cooking utensils, and in return, Benny supplied them with some venison and kangaroo jerky strips along with several bottles of water each.

'So, what are your plans for tonight, mate,' Danny asked.

'I'm gonna head into Tangiloo to get some supplies I need. I should be back here an hour after dark, I reckon,' Benny informed him.

'What! You ride through the bush after dark?' Barny marvelled, not knowing the extent of Benny's bush skills.

'Dark skin, bro, no one ever sees me,' joked Benny.

As the boys had a collective complementary chuckle over Benny's reply, Danny had a thought that immediately crossed his mind.

'You know Damien Lewis, don't you?'

'Yeah, he's a good dude, why?' Benny inquired.

'If you can, I want you drop into his place and thank him for delivering Greta's letter. Tell him I'll never forget what he did and what it meant to me, okay, can you do that?' Danny asked.

'Not a problem, I'll drop in before I get my supplies,' Benny vowed.

'Good one, young Benny, appreciate it big time, bro. And tell him that his fuckin horse is still giving me grief,' Danny finished with a growl under his breath.

The humidity was increasing by the hour as the boys mounted their steeds and said their goodbyes to Benny, who gave them an ominous warning about approaching storms that were well overdue. It had been unusually oppressive over the last couple of days and today was at an extreme. It wasn't long after the boys were on their way that the sweat was causing duress to their already chaffed bodies. The saddles were becoming a lathering soapy mess for both horse and rider, slipping and squelching with every step they would take, and after a half hour of riding, the boys decided to dismount and walk, keeping themselves in the shadows of the surrounding canopy of the trees to try get some relief from the searing sun.

For the first few hours there was not a breath of wind coming out of the gullies or ravines to help cool the excessive sweat that their bodies were exuding and before too long the blue skies were giving way to an eerie overcast look that extenuated the humidity. They could feel the electricity in the air as the native fauna gave them the first hint of what was about to be unleashed by mother nature.

On the traverse on the Summit Road there was a total absence of any local wildlife, a fact that Ricky bought to the others attention, along the with the brief ballistic behaviour of their feathered friends above. It was if the forest had gone to sleep, taking cover from an unknown beast that was about to enter its domain.

They were making slow progress, unaware about the magnitude of the incoming threat. It was impossible for them to get any kind of visual on what was about to hit them, the encasing of the forest was too high, and by the time they made it to the turn at the end of the road, the rumblings above were starting to increase in sound and momentum. It was early evening when the boys remounted and turned their fractious horses into a circle to face each other.

'I think we need to find some cover ASAP,' Barny fretted.

The boys didn't need convincing as Danny looked around frantically for a place to get some protection. The stillness that had surrounded them throughout the day had given way to an increasing wind which was strengthening by the second as the canopy of the forest began to sway in anger. Within minutes, the noise that went with it forced the boys to communicate in raised tones and soon they were lowering their heads into the driving rain that was now pelting down on them, forcing the donning of their jackets.

'We gotta keep going down here,' Ricky demanded. Keeping course with their plan.

The boys turned their horses to start the ride down Molloy's track looking for some cover, increasing their speed in their haste. They looked left as they rode, but the 30-foot-high cliff's edge would give them no shelter. There was no cut out at the base, no cover from the young saplings and bracken fern that protruded out of the steep embankments, while to the right was thinned out flat eucalypt forest. They kept riding when the first clap of thunder exploded above their heads, unleashing a deafening sound. The rain increased its intensity from what seemed a heavy shower to a blinding deluge of rain drops as big as a thumb nail. They kept persisting down the track, yelling at each other for suggestions on where to go as the storm gathered momentum.

Visibility was becoming almost impossible with the amount of rain that was falling from above. Daylight turned to twilight as lightning strikes began to pound the area, quickly followed by the blasting thunder as the eerie grey green heavens engulfed them. The horses were becoming incredibly hard to control, taking fright form every flash and thunderclap as the surrounding trees started to bend from the increasing howling winds.

The men were hoping like hell that the storm would be brief and pass over them as quickly as it ensnared them, however, it was only the beginning of what would be an unprecedented tempest that would be unleashed on the mountains.

The men kept goading their horses forward, at the rear of the four, Danny fought to bring his big black gelding to a halt.

'This way, we gotta go this way,' he shouted.

The boys could only just hear his raised shouts and stopped their rides.

Barny was closest to him and shouted back, 'What are you doing?'

'This way,' Danny repeated. 'If we can get up the top, we can get cover in amongst the pines,' he continued.

'How do you know that?' Ricky angrily questioned, as the voices between them rose to another level.

'That's Satan's Elevator, that's how I know. The pine plantation is up top of the ridge, fuck this, we need to get out of here, we're going nowhere, it's getting worse,' Danny roared.

The notorious stretch of road was not how he remembered. The concrete bollards gave away its location, but his memory told him that it headed straight up the ridge, not on the 45-degree angle that was before his eyes. It also had a dog leg to the right which had also slipped his memory, but nevertheless it *was* Satan's elevator, that he was sure of.

'We're not going up there, didn't you take any notice of what Benny told us?' Ricky blasted.

'That's right, Danny, we can't go that way,' added Barny.

'We need to get some shelter, look at us, look around you, it's getting fucking dangerous,' Danny hollered.

The boys had no answer. They didn't know what to do. Barny and Harry looked at Ricky to see if he were going to counter act Danny words, but only worried looks of dismay would they see from him.

'We'll be up the top on the plateau within five minutes, the pines are not far off,' Danny reassured them.

He turned his horse and cajoled it around the bollards, turned at his friends and yelled for them to follow.

'What about the Sultans?' Harry cautioned.

'Don't worry about it. Do you think anyone in their right mind would be out in this?' Danny defended, panning his head around the rage that swarmed. 'We'll be gone off their land before they know it, now let's friggin go,' he added, losing his patience.

The boys were already drenched to the bone as they began the climb. Danny led them, followed by Barny, then Ricky with Harry at the rear. About 5-10 meters separated each rider but it was becoming almost impossible to see what was ahead. The biting driving rain forced their heads down behind the neck of their horses and soon the distance between them would increase.

The timing of the climb could not have been worse, they were not even a third of the way up, just turning through the dog leg when the storm's fury would gather in cyclonic proportions. Of all the storm cells in the system that was now pounding half the state, the biggest and most dangerous was about to explode straight above them.

The track was getting increasingly unsafe with every rising step they would take. To the left, an undulating embankment that rose over 10 foot into the forest, to the right, pockets of steep ravines that fell over 100 feet into the abyss. Parts of the road had given way and was only wide enough to get one horse past at a time. It was as treacherous as it could be, and with visibility lessoning by the second, their next step could be their last.

The noise around them was increasing as the howling of the wind started to sound more like a Boeing 747 jet engine coming their way. Trees started to uproot and snap like toothpicks before their eyes. Torrents of water started to gush down from above at an alarming speed through the crevices in the road. Danny kept pushing his horse forward as the torrents of water accelerated off the high side, crossing the track like raging rapids, then a giant *swoosh* gripped the immediate area. A large tree was uprooted and came tumbling down only metres ahead of him, blocking anyway forward.

There was no turning back for him, no time to think things through. He gave the big black gelding a forceful dig in the ribs and took off towards the fallen tree. He focused his attention onto the lower trunk end of the fallen mountain ash, and with an almighty leap, his steed cleared the confronting obstacle. The landing was disastrous, the horse slipped and jerked, both its forelegs buckled at the knees on the perilous surface. Danny lost his balance from the soaking saddle and fell shoulder first onto the moving rocky ground. Ignoring his horse, he quickly stood up and looked downwards back over the fallen tree to see if he could see his partners following.

More trees were falling around, the road was giving way to the torrents of water cascading down the track as Barny and Ricky stopped to see if Harry was still in sight.

They could just make out the silhouetted figure of their terrified friend though the torrential rain, he was still beyond the dog leg of the track. They looked on in despair as an enormous fork of lightning struck an 80-foot-high gum tree right above where Harry was situated. The top half exploded, lighting the vicinity up like a giant light bulb, splitting the mature tree in half. Harry looked up in petrified amazement as the blown off top of the tree started to fall upon him.

His mare took fright and with evasive action, reared and reefed itself to the right, dislodging Harry from the saddle. The mare lost its balance in a water filled deep crevice, snapping its near front foreleg instantly. Harry's grip on the wet reins gave way as he watched his panic-stricken equine companion tumble and turn in pain, until it awkwardly fell off the edge of the track, down the ravine, then disappear into the unknown below.

Danny climbed atop the fallen tree trunk. Darkness had set upon the area, only lit up by continuous strikes of lightning. He tried in vain to contact his buddies, yelling and screaming to get their attention, but the unrelenting noise of the storm was drowning out his hollers of distress. Large branches were snapping off trees and flying around like balsa twigs, sending life threatening missiles in all directions.

A row of established trees on his high side fell like dominos. He dived for cover under the already fallen tree as another huge Blackwood tree came tumbling down from the west side, the resting canopy now blocking any possible way of getting to his endangered mates. The storm cell was now at its dangerous peak and Danny knew he had to find cover before it claimed him.

He rushed up the track, guided by his left hand feeling up against the embankment, knee deep raging water continued to cascade into him when he would step into the crevices, at times the force knocking him over. He looked for his horse, it was nowhere to be seen. He repeatedly wiped away the driving rain drops from his eyes, trying to get a location on it, but the big black gelding had taken off.

Danny was now on his own, the storm relentlessly pounded. He staggered and reeled himself up, his quad muscles burning from the lactic acid build up as he dug his legs into the unstable ground for more power. After 10 minutes of unrelenting urging from within, he could finally feel the steep grade underneath him level out. He stood upright and stared back down Satan's Elevator between the brilliance of the lightning strikes. It was if he was looking into an apocalyptic landscape. The intensity of the rain eased up a fraction, he raised his hands to protect the water from his eyes and continued to peer down, hoping for some sign of his buddies, but all he was able to see was total carnage. It was as if in petulant anger, God had given a back hander to his tiny little toy forest.

Danny dipped into a feel of suspended animation, unable to comprehend what was before him, until another deafening sound of a thunderclap awoke him from his nightmarish illusion. He yelled once more down the track.

'Ricky!'
'Barny!'
'Harry!' He roared in intervals between virile curses.

No answer was forthcoming as the driving rain increased in its intensity again. He turned and desperately ran in the direction of where he could make out the pine plantation, a 400-metre dash across open rain-soaked native grasses that was turning to slush with every pounding rain drop. He scrambled his way into the plantation, kept running deeper and deeper into it, until he could run no more. He slumped his body up against one of the trees as tight as he could.

The canopy of the pine trees gave him some relief from the downpour. He rummaged through the undergrowth until he could piece together some branches and thick bracken fern for a makeshift shelter then huddled underneath it. He would sit under it with his back to the barrel of the huge pine for the whole night. The storms would come and go in short bursts throughout the night as the rain continued to poor. They would not be as intense as the first hit, nothing could be that bad again, but the lightning strikes and thunder would be constant throughout, never giving any peace to his rain-soaked body.

Danny was as lonely as he had ever felt. He was disorientated, he didn't even know where he was or what had happened to his buddies. Where are they? He stressed. Did they even survive? The guilt he was feeling for leading them up Satan's elevator was consuming him. He was feeling like the powers that be were punishing him for all the sinful deeds that had taken place. Everything was his fault, from start to finish, leading his buddies through this nightmare, abandoning his wife and family…

'What the hell was I thinking?' he cried. He brought his knees to his chest, buried his head, and seesawed back and forth, whimpering in moans, while his water-logged clothes penetrated his skin. It would take until the wee hours of the following morning for his shivering body to succumb to the much-needed sleep it craved, as the reflection of ever seeing Greta and his sons again seemed so impossible to him now, they may as well be on the other side of the universe.

Chapter 19

Graceville dawned with grey overcast skies as residents were up at first light to assess the damage from the overnight wild storms. The humidity had left them, and the morning temperature was gratefully cooler. There was extensive damage throughout town, trees down, roofs ripped away. Flash flooding from the torrential downpour was the main cause of destruction throughout properties and streets, and as people and shire workers started work on the clean-up operation, one resident had other important matters on her mind.

Kate was up at the crack of dawn with her mare saddled, donning her thick scarf and jacket with a blue woolly beanie over her skullcap. She was on her way up Mason's Creek Road. Tangiloo her destination, Damien Lewis' property. She had already quietly dropped in to see a weary-eyed Greta to let her know of her plans. Kate desperately needed to try and see Damien and get the remaining names of the re-po squad to her brother, with one name standing out above all others. If Damien were able to deliver the first letters to Danny, Kate reasoned that maybe he could get this one to him as well.

Kate and a dressing gown cladded Greta stood on the front porch while Corey and Sarah still slept in the rear bedroom of their house. With the first hint of daylight coming through the grey-coloured sky, they conversed with muffled voices.

She informed Greta where she was going, that she would try and get any information on her husband but warned her not tell a soul of her plans, Corey and Sarah included she discreetly argued. Greta didn't understand the secrecy. Corey and Sarah are our friends she said, perplexed at Kate's stance, but her sister-in-law wouldn't budge on her demands and promised Greta she would try and explain everything when she returned from Damien's, hopefully with some news on Danny. It had been seven long nights since she had heard anything of her runaway husband and Greta was distressed to the point of exhaustion.

They parted with a short tight hug with Greta's promise that all would be kept quiet until her return. Kate remounted her horse and trotted off quietly, panning the area for any police watchers, but she had nothing to fear. The wild storms and its aftermath had put a temporary cease to any law enforcement prying eyes, and Kate's short presence at Greta's new abode would go undetected.

Kate's journey up the rising winding road that connected Graceville and Tangiloo was not an easy one. She would have to dismount several times and move large branches off the bitumen road and negotiate around the larger ones which had fallen overnight due to the storms, adding an extra 30 minutes to her ride. By the time she arrived at the gated driveway to Damien's house, he and another man were already outside assessing the damage to his own residence, the stripped off plastic to his nursery igloos noticeably strewn across his yards. With cups of tea in hand they looked up and saw the lone rider at his gates about 200 meters away from they stood.

'Who's that, this time of morning?' quizzed Benny.

'It's Danny's sister,' was Damien's curious reply.

'What's she doing here?'

'Don't know, but I suspect we're going to find out. You ever met her?' Damien asked as he waved her through the gates.

'No, never had the pleasure.'

'Well, there will be no surprises, she's fuckin just like him,' Damien hinted with a roll of the eyes. Benny wasn't sure on how to take his comment.

While the overnight storms were unfortunate for most, it was going to be completely opposite for Kate. She needed a masterful stroke of luck, and she was about to get the break she so frantically needed regarding her lost brother. She was about to meet the only soul who could give her what she yearned for.

Kate trotted her horse up to where they stood, dismounted, and politely thanked Damien for allowing her onto his property. He introduced Benny to her and explained that he was trapped by the storms last night and accepted his and Nikki's invitation to play it safe and stay the night.

Kate had never met Benny, but vaguely knew of who he was and courteously said that Danny had spoken of him. They chatted small talk for a few minutes, with the storm being the main subject, but soon Kate was to the point of her visit.

'I want to thank you for dropping Greta's and my letter to Danny, I know he received them,' she said.

'How do you know that?' Damien quizzed.

'My husband! As you probably know, he was there, at the shootout. He put two and two together after Danny spoke to him. Plus, I told Ryan that it was me who gave him the information,' Kate confessed.

'And what did he think of that?' Damien asked.

'He wasn't happy. He reckons Danny would have come home with them if he didn't know about the re-po squad, but that's bullshit. They tried to kill him; he would have taken off anyway. But it doesn't matter what Ryan says anymore, he left me the other night, gone to the city to be with his parents,' Kate stated.

'Sorry to hear that,' replied Damien.

'Don't be, it's been a long time coming,' she confided.

'Fair enough!' was Damien's contrite reply. 'My friend here told me what was in your letter. You know, I would never have given it to him if I knew what was inside. You knew he would go off the deep end, you know what he's like!'

'That's exactly why I gave it to him. Those lowlifes need to get what's coming to them for what they did, they need to be stopped. He had a right to know, at least he will do something about it if he gets the chance, not like the other cowards around town who just take it without standing up for their rights,' Kate strongly enforced.

She pulled an envelope out of the front pocket of her dark-coloured moleskin trousers and handed it to Damien.

'What's this?'

'It's the names of the others who raided their place, along with how Greta and his kids are faring. I was hoping you might have an idea on how to get it to him, you're my only chance. I thought you might know something, where he is, or what he's doing,' she said.

The men could see the look on Kate's face; her worry consumed it, as she pleaded if they knew of any information. An overwhelmed Kate was about to receive more than she ever expected.

The men looked at each other and after a short moment of deep thought, Damien gave Benny a nod of approval.

Kate excitedly listened as Benny divulged all to her. From the time they met at his home-made bush retreat, to the days that ensued, and to the time he and his friends had left him, adding she was right about how he would react concerning the members of the re-po squad. She impatiently quizzed him on every detail, and expressed that Greta needed to know everything she could, to put her heart and mind at ease somewhat.

Benny obliged as much as he could, including how much Danny loved and missed his wife and the extreme gratitude he had for his sister for going out on a limb for him, and also, the guilt he was feeling. The only thing he couldn't say for sure is how they survived last night's storm, saying if they didn't make it to the rotunda at the lookout, he would hate to think what might have happened to them.

'I'll take the letter,' Benny said, relieving it from Damien's grip. 'I'll head into Kensington and cut across one of the minor trails I know, from there I'll be able to get to the bottom end of Molloy's and see if I can track them down. Should only take me a couple of hours. If I find them, and that's a long shot, and if the coppers haven't got to him first, I'll give him the letter and come back to Graceville and let you know what's happening,' Benny promised.

Kate was over the moon with elated emotions to hear that her brother was still pressing on, still surviving, and couldn't wait to get back down to Graceville and announce the long-awaited news to Greta. At least she would know that he was still alive and that his thoughts had always been with her. Kate vowed to keep their meeting secret and parted with the news that Corey Porter was to be trusted no more. Both men were not sure what she meant by her undertone order, but it was enough for them to heed her advice. She graciously thanked them for all they have done for her and Danny and affirmed to both that it will never be forgotten.

As Kate left for the ride back down to Graceville, her brother's trials and tribulations were about to take another unexpected twist.

The raindrops were slowly dropping from the overhead pine canopy as Danny was awoken from his mild slumber. He was still in a crouched position with his back up against the base of the large pine when he could feel the right side of his upper arm and shoulder being forcibly nudged. It would take him a few moments before he realised that he was silently being asked to wake up. He opened his overtired eyes as his senses returned. He panned his head to the right to see what was almost knocking him over and was taken aback to see the lowered head of his scarred face big black gelding eyeballing him, impatiently trying to awake his new-found master.

'Bloody hell, ya right there!' mused Danny.

He tried to give the steed a pat above his nostrils, but he shied away and took a couple of backward steps. Danny knew he didn't like to be touched anywhere around his head but thought it worth the try once more. Danny was pleased to see him, and proudly asked how he had survived the night. He owed big black a great deal, chiefly when he jumped the fallen tree during last night's storm. Who knows what might have been if he refused to take that risky leap of faith!

Other than aching bruises to his left hip and shoulder from when he was dislodged by the jump, Danny was relatively unscathed, thanks to his equine buddy. He pushed aside what was left of his makeshift shelter and stood to his feet, released his boots off one at a time and started to wring out his socks, watching the water flow out of them as he squeezed and twisted. He unzipped his water-logged khaki jacket and hung it over a low branch. Now only in his black T-shirt he wrapped his arms tightly around his biceps and rubbed to get some warmth back into his body.

He looked back at his horse and gave a curse of frustration when he noticed that all his saddlebags were missing off his back, including the saddle itself. The big black gelding was totally bare back with only his mouth bit and reins still attached. It was not what Danny needed, all his gear, his spare set of clothes, his limited food, his water, all the little goodies he had in his bags gone, but most importantly, all his weapons, including his favourite sawn off .22 rifle.

The only weapon he now possessed was his Bowie knife, still strapped to his left lower leg in its sheath, hidden underneath his dampened denim jeans, along with the map book and a water-soaked pack of cigarettes and matches. Folded tightly in an envelope in his jeans front pocket were the letters from Greta and Kate.

He could see an opening just past the remaining row of pines and strode slowly towards it. He found himself slightly elevated to what seemed to him an old, disbanded logging coup. There were some fresh piles of sawdust around from recently felled trees which Danny couldn't work out. There hasn't been any logging in these mountains for years he confidently said to himself. He calculated the area was about 10 acres squared with lots of tree stumps of all sizes scattered about, some old, some new amongst the low vegetation.

Mature gum trees of different species still stood scattered throughout amongst some immature wattles and blackwood. It looked like the storm had made its mark here as well for a lot of trees had been uprooted, some hanging precariously against each other. A dirt track was just below him, it seemed freshly made, within the last few years or so he gathered. No wheel ruts or signs of thick tread that he could distinguish. He could see the track stretched in a straight line around the square perimeter.

The sun was starting to poke through the overcast skies when Danny decided to go back and get his jacket. He walked back out to where the sun was shining and tried to light a cigarette. His entire packet was waterlogged. He pulled what he thought was the driest smoke out of the packet and tried to light it without success. In frustration, he screwed the pack up and tossed it way, then spat out the one in his mouth.

Danny had no idea where he was, nothing seemed familiar to him. There were dense mountain ranges to the east and left of him with more elevated forest in front on the other side of the clearing. About 500 meters down to the west and right of him was a pine plantation. Maybe he was on Sultan land, as Benny warned him about, but there was no sign of life other than the birds above, however, that was all about to change.

As he continued to look around the area, not concentrating on anything specific, his attention was grabbed by a large cracking sound. Big black was behind his right shoulder and quickly threw his head back and gave off a nervous whinny. Another cracking sound pierced the air and Danny's full scrutiny was now focused on five large gums standing close together about 150 meters slightly to the right of him down on the clearing. Three of them had been uprooted, leaning on each other, with the excessive weight of them pushing up against the fourth in line.

With the help of a slight breeze which had now arose, the large gums were in danger of falling and taking the other two with them. Not that it worried Danny, he enjoyed watching trees come down. He always liked the sound and graceful movements of large trees taking their dive to terra firma, but as he examined the position more closely, something grabbed his now alerted attention.

'What the hell is that?' he asked himself, noticing a bright orange form appear between the two trunks of the still standing gums. He squinted his eyes against the reflection of the sun from the low-lying clouds, the shimmering of raindrops off the dampened leaves and foliage added to the difficulty. The figure took a couple of steps forward,

'Is that a person?' It looked like it to Danny. He negotiated his way down off the elevation and once on level ground took a closer look.

'Christ! That looks like a little girl,' he spoke aloud to big black. 'What's she doing there?'

He was positive, maybe 7 or 8 years old he guessed, going by the age of his own twin boys. She was wearing a Fluoro orange waterproof jumpsuit, a large orange and white woollen beanie with pom poms.

Their eyes met, staring blankly for 30 seconds, then the little girl raised her right arm, and from the front of her fist, she slowly opened her fingers and with a friendly smile, gave Danny the cutest wave he had ever seen. He returned the favour with a smile and similar wave from his own fingers. He looked around to see where Mum was, maybe Dad, someone must be with her? He looked across, behind her, to the side, but not a soul could be seen. Another loud crack came from the distorted trees, but this time there was movement with them. Danny could see that it wouldn't be long before they all came crashing down, right where the little girl was standing. He started to move towards her, slowly at first, but with every crack of the trees his speed gathered.

'Move away!' he yelled. 'Get out of there!' he raised his voice louder.

The girl stood there, smiling, until she saw the alarmed look on the approaching stranger. Danny was within 50 meters of her when he pointed up at the trees, again, yelling at her to move away. The little girl looked up to where Danny was pointing then stared back at him, the smile on her face had turned to instant shock. A thunderous crack, bigger than any before sent a billowing sound throughout the surroundings, all three trees were coming down.

The girl froze in fear underneath them. She again turned to Danny with eyes agape. He was now at maximum speed on the undulating ground, crashing through the puddles that had formed overnight, when only meters away, he took an almighty dive at the frightened child. Wrapping his arms around her, he lifted her off the ground and with his momentum turned away from the falling trees as they came tumbling down with an almighty thud.

The thick barrel of the largest tree had missed them by only meters, the thickest branches by inches. Danny hunched under the crown of the fallen tree with the little girl safely underneath him. He pushed the branches and foliage away and got onto his knees to see if the girl was okay as silence again gripped the area.

'Are you alright, you're not hurt?' he frantically asked.

He turned her around, gently looking for any sign of injury or torn clothing, she seemed to come through it unscathed. He grabbed her by the shoulders with both arms and asked again if she was ok, however, nothing would come out of her mouth, instead, what he got in return was a tight loving grateful embrace around his neck.

Danny stood to his feet, held his hand out to the little girl, which was happily accepted by her, then pushed his way out of the fallen crown until they cleared the debris. Danny sat back down, looked at her again and gave off a big sigh of relief.

'How close was that?' he boasted.

There was no reaction from her, except a cute appreciative smile, but just when Danny thought the danger was over, the expression on his little friend's face would once again get the look of terror upon it. She looked over Danny's left shoulder and pointed past it, her eyes were ballooning from her sockets as she gulped in fear. He turned to look, and only 15 metres away stood an angry, ugly and wild hungry dog.

Where did he come from? Did the commotion of the falling trees bring him to their attention, did he already have his prowling eyes locked in on them? Danny didn't know, but he had no time to ponder.

He gently rose to his feet, not wanting to startle the wild hound anymore. He lightly pushed the girl behind him then slowly unleashed the bowie knife from his leg sheath. His attention was solely on the hound in front of him, a cross short-haired German Shepherd it looked to him, already licking his jowls while deeply growling in short bursts. To Danny's dismay, he was not alone.

Slight movement grabbed his attention to the right of the snarling shepherd where he saw two more dogs, and then another three when he counted and looked further around. One of them a half healthy looking Staffordshire cross Danny was sure, the rest were an assortment of ugly cross breeds with mangy coats and off-white unhealthy gums when they bared their gnarling teeth.

Danny regained his focus on the Shepherd cross. He was the largest, meanest looking of the pack, probably the leader Danny decided. The grip on his right leg got tighter as the little girl clung to him in fear. The packs growling became louder as the leader started to approach, putting one paw in front of the other as his ears pinned and head stooped.

'Go on, get out of here!' Danny bellowed.

The wild dog never flinched as the rest of the pack took closer order.

'Get the fuck out of here. Yah! Yah!' He raged at the dogs again.

The large Shepherd cross was now only meters away from where Danny stood. He now knew the dogs were not retreating from his animated orders. He pushed his left arm back to protect the girl in case the wild canine took a lunge. And lunge it did. With mouth wide open and teeth exposed, the big Shepherd took a leap at Danny.

Once again, he was in mortal danger, not with flying bullets, but with one mean-tempered hungry wild dog. He had heard the stories of these wild packs of dogs in the mountains, although he had never come across them, he believed the stories, and he was taking no chances. He pushed the girl aside, knocking her backwards to the ground, then thrusted his knife forward in his right hand while protecting himself with his raised left. The dog latched on to his left forearm, forcing him to the ground with its strength from the leap.

Losing his jacket from the grip the dog had on his sleeve, he and the wild dog rolled over with the latter waiting eagerly for another chance to dig his teeth into his human prey. Danny lashed out with his knife, stabbing with repeating forceful blows. The six-inch blade penetrated more than once, the dog retreating briefly with high pitched yelps.

The rest of the now agitated pack hunched together, and it looked like they were going to attack as one. Danny scrambled towards the young girl; it was if she was hyperventilating in fear. He wrapped his body around her, if they were going to attack, he was her only protection from the onslaught. He pointed his knife at the oncoming pack, ready to slash and hit as much as he could.

The cross-Shepherd leader was wounded and at its unpredictable worst. He started to come at them both again, backed up by his understudies to the left and right. Danny raised his knife while the little girl hid underneath him trembling. The wild dog sprung himself into mid-air with his open mouth ready for the death bite around Danny's throat. As Danny reeled back from the incoming attack, a thunderous blast echoed across the clearing. He watched stunned as the wild cross German Shepherd was sent airborne from the power of the impact, killing it instantly while the other wild dogs scattered in fright on impact.

The cracking sound of the shotgun discharge shook Danny, the girl beneath him did not flinch a muscle. He looked to his left to see where it had come from when another blast was sent off in the direction of the fleeing canines, hitting one and scattering the others even faster away from the area.

Two men, one with a double barrel shotgun, still raised to his shoulder were only fifteen meters away. They were dressed in black T-shirts and sleeveless vests with dark green camouflage pants that sported sidearms attached to their thighs. White insignias that Danny couldn't make out were emblazoned on their shirts. They were quickly joined by two more men on horseback in similar attire.

He returned his focus back at the lifeless body of the pack's leader as the little girl rushed out from underneath him. He was astonished at the damage the blast did to the wild canine. Not much was left above the dog's shoulders except for a mix of blood, mush and bone fragments. Danny casually rose to his feet, knife still in his right hand. He turned back towards the men, then the last thing he saw was the butt of the double-barrel shotgun about to engulf the side of his head, and that's when the lights went out.

Chapter 20

'Oh, hi Kate, how are you?' Sarah asked, when she answered the knock on her door.

'Where's Greta, I need to see her,' was the direct reply.

'She's in the kitchen.'

Kate hastily brushed past and walked up through the hallway, family photos and landscape paintings hung from both sides. She found Greta busily cooking up some French toast for her sons over the wood-fired stove when she arrived in the adjoining kitchen.

Greta was dressed in casual clothes, denim jeans with brown sandals and a loose-fitting white T-shirt with her long dark hair plaited and tied together in pigtails.

'Greta, Greta, I have some news, big news,' Kate excitedly said.

Greta threw down the tea towel and butter knife on the bench after seeing Kate's animated postures. The look on her sister-in-law's face indicated that she had news of her husband.

'What, what?' Greta grinned hesitantly.

'I can't tell you here,' enforced Kate.

She grabbed Greta by the hand and led her out of the kitchen through the laundry door and out to the enclosed garage, passing Corey on the way who was re-entering the house.

'What's going on?' he questioned.

Kate gave him a look of disdain as they hurriedly passed him, slamming the garage door behind her as Greta gave her an anguished look of curiosity.

She leant Greta up against the metal work bench that circled the outer wall of the twin car garage and asked her to brace herself. Greta listened intently as Kate began to talk.

'I was up at Damien's, as you know, and guess who else was there?' she boasted.

'Who?'

Do you know a guy called Benny, an indigenous guy, he reckons he's mates with Danny?' Kate inquired.

'Yeah, young Benny. It's been a while, but we know him well,' Greta assured.

Once Kate got the acknowledgment that Benny were friends of both, she began to inform her on everything that was bestowed upon her from the lads up at Tangiloo. Greta's excited smile was widening by the second as she listened to what Kate was telling her. She explained everything, from the time Benny came across them, until the time they had left, and everything in between. Kate's sparkle was bursting when she highlighted that he was safe, still healthy and was desperately trying to come up with a plan to make it home to her.

Greta was almost in tears of joy, she couldn't believe it, it's what she wanted so desperately to hear over the last week. Any information would have been enough, but what she was grasping was more than her wildest thoughts could ever endear, despite the fearful uncertainty that was beginning to churn in her stomach.

Both ladies were bouncing with energy, grabbing and hugging at each other when loud knocks started to bang up against the garage door from inside the house.

'What's going on in there?' Corey yelled.

'C'mon ladies, lets us in. Do you have news on Danny?' Sarah joined in.

Greta moved to open the locked door.

'Don't tell them anything,' Kate warned as she grabbed Greta by the arm.

Greta shrugged off the warning. 'They'll be excited to know,' she said. 'They deserve to know.' Greta unleashed Kate's arm and quickly opened the door to the garage before Kate could say anymore.

'We have some great news, Danny is safe, we know where they've been,' Greta boomed out.

Their friends' mouths were agape. Where? How? they thrust at Greta.

'Stop!' Kate blasted. 'Don't tell them anything,' she repeated.

'What is wrong with you, Kate, what's going on, why won't you let me tell them?' Greta objected, as both Corey and Sarah looked on in bewilderment.

Kate stared Greta straight in the eyes from only inches away. Her mind was rattling over and over. Do I tell her what I know about Corey? Do I just walk out of here? Her heart was pounding, she didn't want to upset Greta in any way, but her instincts and her seek for justice was taking precedence when it came to her brother. This was about Danny to her, and she knew that he would demand that Corey be called out for what he did, regardless how Greta would react. The air around was as tense as could be. Corey and Sarah had no idea what was coming but deep inside their core they hoped it wouldn't be what they knew.

'I'm sorry, Greta, you deserve to know,' said Kate after a brief pause.

She turned her attention at Corey, pointed her finger at him and challenged him to tell Greta where he was when the re-po squad raided their house. Corey remained silent; no words were coming out of his stunned mouth. Kate pushed the question at him again, this time louder and more animated.

'I don't know what you're talking about, I was here, you know that' came the nervous reply. Greta looked at both her friends then turned to Kate.

'What's this all about, Kate, what are you saying?' she asked.

'If you don't tell her, I will. I know you were there; I have the proof,' Kate angrily said. 'Tell her, tell her!' she continued to roar at Corey.

Corey and Sarah could sense she was determined to bring things out into the open. She was angry, and they knew what she was like when she got on a mission, but they were not going to confess their sins yet. They couldn't, not like this. They knew there would be no turning back if Greta found out, their friendship would be destroyed forever, there would be no forgiveness. They were hanging onto their guilt-ridden secret, but Kate was about to bring it all out into the open, she could see that no confession was coming out of Corey.

'The re-po Squad, Corey was with them when they trashed your house, Greta, he's a fuckin traitor, he betrayed you, Greta, all of us,' Kate scorned.

Greta couldn't believe it. 'No, you're wrong, impossible,' she said.

'I've seen the list, all who participated, you were with those scumbags, I know you were,' Kate furiously said to Corey.

Corey's head bowed in shame, Sarah's heart was crushed, she nervously moved closer to Greta and grabbed her hands in hers.

'We are so sorry, Greta, Corey didn't know,' she quivered.

'Know what? What are you talking about?' Greta asked confused.

'We needed the money, Greta. We had no idea it was going to be your house. They switched plans at the last minute, it was supposed be somebody else's home,' Corey interjected, pleading his reasons.

Greta was in shock. She couldn't grasp what they were saying. 'What are you talking about?' she asked.

'It's the only time I did it. I had no idea it was going to be your house. I'm so sorry, Greta, I'm so very sorry, you've got to forgive me,' Corey pleaded, as the welling tears of guilt ravished his face.

'It was you? You were with them? My clothes, my jewellery, my furniture, that was you, you helped them?' Greta asked in shock.

Corey had no reply. He sat down on a wooden chair next to the bench and clasped his hands to his head in disgrace and repeatedly uttered apologies.

'And you? You knew this all along?' Greta calmly asked Sarah.

'I knew Corey was going with them. It was only going to be a one-off. Our friend, Brad Neilson, he's been on raids before and told us it was easy money,' Sarah said with shaking tears.

Brad Neilson! That name was on the new list, Kate thought to herself as Sarah continued.

'We needed the money so desperately, Greta. Both of us have hardly slept knowing we betrayed you like this. We've been sick in the stomach, the guilt we have is unimaginable, Greta. We didn't know, we didn't know that they were going to your house,' she frantically relayed.

Sarah continued to ask Greta for her forgiveness as repeated venomous comments from Kate gathered momentum towards them. Corey raised his head from his arms and angrily ask Kate how she knew that he was there. 'It was all supposed to be secret who participated,' he guiltily expressed. 'How did you know who was there? What fuckin list have you got? How did you get it?'

'Never you mind. I'm not telling you how. The fact is I know that your name was on it, along with your friend, this Brad Neilson. Danny knows everything now. I know he got the first list, and I'm positive he will get the second one as well, the one with your name on it,' Kate seethed.

Corey's heart sank. What will Danny think of him now? Years and years of mate-ship down the drain over one error of judgment, a huge one at that, but he knew Danny as well as anyone, and he knew he would never be forgiven for what he had done. He was shaking at the thought what Danny would do if he knew that he was part of any re-po squad, let alone the one that ravished his own property.

Greta was trying to comprehend everything she was hearing. She had her hands cupped over her nose and mouth looking backwards and forth at her three friends when she turned her disbelief at her sister-in-law.

'You gave Danny a letter? With the names? I told you not to!' Greta incensed. 'I can't believe you would do that. Oh my god, Kate, do you know what you've done. You don't understand,' she anguished. 'There was a reason I didn't want him to know. He was already about to explode before all of this, and now he's with Ricky! Ricky and him together! You've got no idea what he's like, he holds more hate than Danny does. When they're apart, they can function rationally under pressure, but if they're together like this, they'll become one. They will feed off one another, oh my god! They will never back down now.'

Greta's seriousness gathered momentum as she spoke.

'You have no idea what they got up to before we married. I can reason with Danny, calm his ways. I've been doing it for years. He's a different person when he gets with Ricky for a time, they both are!'

Greta's voice took a darker threatening tone.

'you say he's coming back to me, but I tell you, if anything happens to him, if he goes after this re-po squad, if he gets hurt, or something worse. I'm holding you fuckin responsible,' Greta promised with her voice raising after every short breath.

Greta's knees weakened. The emotional outburst had every nerve in her body shaking as she almost fainted to the floor. She looked at all three in the garage, slowly shaking her head from side to side and with sorrowful resignation confided, 'He will not rest until he gets them. Oh my god. Oh Danny, oh Danny!' She wept.

She knew how Danny would react. She knew the anger that he held within. She knew the anger Ricky held within, and if both had vengeance on their desperate minds with all that had taken place, she feared the rage had already been released. She could foresee it could be the end for him if he sought his revenge, an action she knew that he would most probably confront.

'Leave me alone!' Greta shouted as Kate tried to console her. Corey and Sarah tried their best to comfort her as well, but Greta pushed passed them and made her way back to the kitchen and grabbed the now cold French toast for her twin boys. She yelled through the kitchen window out to the backyard where the boys were playing with the other children and calmly asked them to grab their pushbikes and meet her over at the nearby park.

Greta would never let her darling sons know that she was angry or upset. Her mind was numb by the time she met Darcy and Daniel at the park and was feeling that her world was falling apart. She had no control over anything anymore. No control over Danny, no control over decisions to be made in her now mayhem of a life. She relied on family and friends to help her through this nightmare, but the rock she thought she had had just crumbled. As she sat on the park bench surrounded by the overgrown grass and playgrounds, she hollowly watched her sons ride around and began to wish she had her late parents with her. Someone to cry into, someone to hug, someone who she could trust with no fear of prejudice towards her situation.

She thought about her elder sister that she hadn't seen in over three years. Zara had moved interstate over a decade ago. She probably wouldn't even know what was going on, she mused to herself. She sat quietly as people would come and go through the park. She saw Kate on horseback across the road looking at her in sadness. Greta gave her sister-in-law a wave and gestured that she would be alright.

She saw the not too subtle figures of the police watchers keeping an eye on every outdoor move she made as she wished upon wish that her husband would show from out of nowhere. Greta's state of mind was as fragile as could be. Where can my children and I go? Who would take us? Her beautiful friends from the church she gave deep thought to, they would help no doubt. She went over a plethora of names and places in her mind between talking to and hugging her sons around the playground; however, she eventually came to only one conclusion. She somehow understood Corey's situation.

She knew that they were deeply anguished and ashamed of what they had done, so Greta, as always, put her children first. Her boys loved it at Corey and Sarah's house, they had playmates, and to upheave them again would be too much, so by mid-afternoon she returned with her sons to her friend's house, much to the silent relief of Corey and Sarah. She was going to keep only positive thoughts in her distraught mind, rely on her deep faith and pray that her husband will be safe and unharmed. She believed in Danny, she believed in his capabilities, she believed in his resilience, his honour, but most of all, she believed in his undying love for her.

If he said he would come to her, then that's what would happen. Greta would keep her head high; she would hold onto her dwindling dignity, she would hold on to her faith, and would keep to herself for the time being until she would work out her next move.

Chapter 21

It was 8.00 am Tuesday morning and the weekly issue of Valerie Corbett's *The Mountain Scene* had landed on Minister Johnston's desk. He had only sat down for a brief minute, only arriving back in town the previous night, when one of his aides walked in with a humbled look upon his face and softly put the paper down in front of him.

'I think you better read this, sir,' the aide nervously said.

'What's the irrelevant little bitch writing about this time?' Johnston ridiculed as he grabbed the paper and leant back into his plush leather chair.

Johnston's face contorted; his blood pressure started to rise as he laid his eyes on the local publication's headlines.

CORRUPT TO THE CORE, the headline read, with smaller sub headlines underneath, with his name to the fore. The whole paper was dedicated to all the alleged dirty dealings that had taken place under his regime. From illegal land grabs to extortion, from the undertakings of the repossession office to the far-reaching allegations of involvements of unsolved murders.

Valerie Corbett had taken a huge gamble, not only on her career, but maybe on her life. She resisted making public the names on the re-po squad lists that she had discovered, she was too smart to do that. Valerie would keep them secret for the time being for she knew what the repercussions would be if she hadn't published her expose without an intense plan of action. The ex-crime journalist had been sitting on a plethora of incriminating evidence against the Minister for some time, statements, copies of illegal documents, signatures, secret recordings.

She had investigated money trails of property sales, goods sold from illegal repossession raids with signed statements from buyers and sellers, along with her own documented questioning of interested parties, all of which she duly handed over to one official she trusted – Sgt Dane Grainger, 48 hours before she went public with her edition. The information was quickly pushed up the chain. Sgt Grainger passed it onto Inspector Vaccaro to whom he trusted, who passed it onto Martin Conroy and his anti-corruption team who then forwarded it to the Police Commissioner. Finally, the damning information landed in the Premier's office.

Valerie didn't want to take any risk to her safety and skipped town before the sun would rise, but not before she made sure her edition was on the doorstep of all the outlets which sold her paper, along with a crateful of them outside her office in the main street of town which gave easy access to the public as they passed by. She had heard reliable whispers that an investigation was underway concerning Minister Johnston, and she was hoping her paper might give those investigating a little bit of encouragement to quicken up the process. Her longshot wish was going to come to fruition more than she could have possibly hoped for.

'Get me Cribbs,' Johnston roared to his aide. 'And get that bitch to my office.'

The Minister angrily snatched the receiver off his desk phone and pushed the number two on his dial which gave him a direct line to the local police station, but before the call could be answered, his office door was stormed by armed members of the anti-corruption squad, pushing aside his aide before he could relay his orders.

'Do not move, sir, put down the phone.' The order came from the first of the eight members who entered the room.

'Who the fuck are you? What is this?' the Minister angrily demanded.

Johnston was going to get a quick answer to his desperate animated questions once the room was secured by the uniformed taskforce members when in walked a tall male figure, dressed in a dark suit with an awe of purpose with every step he took inside the room.

'Minister Colin Johnston, I am Assistant Commissioner Martin Conroy, Chief Investigator for the Anti-Corruption Squad and on the order of Premier Kendall, you are under arrest for conspiracy to murder, fraud, embezzlement and misappropriation of public funds. And that's just for starters, my friend,' Conroy calmly stated.

'Conspiracy to murder!' Johnston mocked. 'That's a fucking joke, and who am I have supposed to have killed, you idiots?'

'Danny Pruitt is one that comes to mind,' Conroy affirmed.

'He's a fucking cop killer, and you're arresting me! God damn it, you've got it all fucking wrong, you morons!' Johnston hollered.

'Don't you worry, sir; Pruitt will be dealt with soon—the legal way,' Conroy assured.

Johnston was defiant. His beady blue eyes squinted as he stood up and unleashed a tirade of obscenities, repeating that they would not get away with what they were doing and snidely remarked that he would be released by dinner time.

'I'm the fucking Minister and you got no idea what you're doing. You got nothing on me!' he blurted as the saliva spat out of his ever-increasing dry mouth.

The verbal onslaught continued from Johnston as he was led out the door then down the stairs and past his office workers desks which were being ransacked by taskforce agents. He was then loaded into the back seat handcuffed of one of the SUV's parked outside, destined to return to Marlboro.

The powers that be did not want the investigation made public before they made any type of arrest but knowing that it would be there for all to see the following morning, they decided to respond. They had enough evidence to warrant an arrest as it was but were going to withhold for a few more days while they gathered more watertight evidence, however, after viewing the information provided by Valerie Corbett's documents the Premier gave the green light to act.

The taskforce was commissioned with a convoy of dark coloured SUV's and set off pre-dawn from police headquarters in Marlboro. They travelled up the deserted freeways to the eastern suburbs then onto the highway that took them through to the outer lying outskirts of the city before the final 20-minute drive up the rural highway and into Graceville itself. There they parked in the industrial precinct of town among the graffiti clad disbanded warehouses and businesses as the sun rose waiting for the order to proceed with the raids. When the orders came, each team headed to their designated targets around the valley making arrests and gathering evidence from the searches that were held.

By the end of the day the taskforce had made over 60 apprehensions around the Hexagon Valley and Graceville, with police officers, including Detective Lucas Cribbs, shire workers and senior banking staff among them. Adrian Mance, the editor and owner of the Valley news could not escape the net and by the end of processing, a combined total of 287 charges were laid against 39 individuals with Minster Colin Johnston topping the list. A state-wide warrant was also issued for the arrest of John Pringle on three counts of murder.

The Minister's tenure was up. He knew Conroy's squad was coming but he thought he had his bases covered. Nothing would be proved he blindly assured himself, however, his corrupt reign of greed, power, fear and intimidation was what led to his downfall as some closest to him gave up all they knew to protect their own self interests.

Over the next few days, the town of Graceville was abuzz with news of the Minister's arrest and all that went with it. The city's main newspapers ran with Valerie Corbett's story two days later, along with the unfinished saga of the fugitives on the run in the mountains. While an interim Minister would be appointed by the end of the week, Inspector Vaccaro was given full power to oversee policing matters across the shire as government would hurry through legislation to take back full control of the States police forces.

Vaccaro only had one pressing assignment on his mind, find and arrest the Graceville four, the title the city newspapers had auspiciously dubbed the fugitives. The Inspector didn't care too much if justice was not to served when it came to the Devlin brothers, and definitely not to Pringle's men, but he wanted justice for the family of Robbie Dukes, the constable shot dead down at the river when the boys were making their escape out of town.

In the ensuing days, the Inspector briefed all search parties on their new objectives. There weren't many leads to go on other than what the late Tom Potter had drunkenly confessed despite unsubstantiated stories and rumours that the four fugitives had absconded interstate or had a made a run for the city. They were leads that he couldn't dismiss totally, but until he had proof to the contrary, he was only going to concentrate on Graceville and the surrounding mountains.

He would tactfully re-interview associates and family, including Greta, Kate, Corey and Sarah, but would get nothing useful from them, they would all stand loyal to Danny and his friends and keep silent on what they knew. Knowing now the mental state and capabilities of the men, Vaccaro was going to use diplomacy and negotiation towards them. Locate, but do not engage, unless in extreme fear of life was the new protocol.

Violence begets violence he implored to his officers, and he did not want a repeat of what happened near Tambourine bridge, however, before he could put any of that to fruition, he had to find them first. Two Police four-wheel drives would be used daily throughout the mountain roads and backtracks where the boys were last seen, but one reluctant member would stick to horseback. Sgt Dane Grainger, against his wishes, was given the orders to head back into the mountains and try and track his friend down once more.

He had done it before successfully and the Inspector was hoping that he could do it again before Martin Conroy would engage the elite special operations group, men who were experienced, armed and ready for a manhunt. Sgt Dane Grainger wanted to be on horseback, it gave him more accessibility to the forest. It would be a lot quieter, and he wouldn't have to return to town every night like the vehicles were required to do. Dane would travel back into the mountains with four other men, two who he would meet for the first time. Senior Constables Mike Whitehall and Jeff Hill, both bought up from another station from the eastern suburbs.

Dane was not prepared to take any of the young officers he knew after what had happened at the bridge. He would forever carry the burden of guilt after losing his two young friends to Pringle. The other two members accompanying him he knew, but the one with the least experience in policing made him the most nervous and was not a great fan of to say the least, his name, Steve Sandilands. Dane knew his history, he knew that he accosted Greta, and he knew that Sandilands was embarrassed and angry at what Danny had done to him down at the river.

The Sergeant vigorously protested to Inspector Vaccaro about travelling with him; however, he was told to suck it up and he and Sandilands had to get along. His nephew's experience in the bush would be an asset for him the Inspector enforced. The other member of the party was Senior Constable Victor Slacek. He had no problems with him, the tall well-built blond-haired officer had handled himself respectably when Dane had worked with him previously.

Dane knew most things about Sandilands, which put him on edge, however, what he what didn't know about Victor Slacek was that he was one of the men that raided Danny's property, and his fugitive friend already had his name locked in for revenge.

The other problem Inspector Vaccaro had was sorting out the rest of the search parties. He needed dedicated officers from now on, not the reckless types that Minister Johnston and Detective Cribbs turned a blind eye to. The officers he could rely on were sent on the search in separate groups of four, while others were restricted to duties in town or across other parts of the valley. It was a headache he didn't need but was necessary for him to try and get a quick resolution before Conroy could implement his own forces. But he wasn't the only one with a headache to ponder, up in the surrounding mountain ranges of

Graceville someone else was regaining consciousness with a giant headache of their own, literally!

Where the hell am I? Danny asked himself as his faculties began to return.

He looked around from his canvas stretcher that he lay upon and pushed away his thin blanket and pillow. He could see that he was in a wooden shack about six by three meters. A barred window on his right gave light into the room. The interior walls were made up of half rounds of pine with full rounds making up the beams that stretched across the ceiling. The floor was covered in soft pieces of chipped bark and sawdust with a single canvas deck chair sitting up against the wall adjacent to his stretcher. He noticed his clothes and boots were atop of a table, it seemed his jeans and T-shirt had been washed and folded and sat atop his jacket.

As he tried to lift his head, a sharp pain shot through it. He raised his right hand to the side of his head and could feel an almighty lump bulging inside the bandage that was strapped around it as his memory slowly started to return. Danny swung his legs around to sit upright when his eyes caught sight of the company he had within the shack. He recognised the cute wave of the fingers straight away, but there was no beanie on the little girl this time, her snowy blond hair was glistening off the natural light that was coming into the shack. It was cut just above the shoulders in a bob style with a straight fringe across her forehead which enhanced her already beautiful innocent smile.

'Hello, I remember you, can you tell me where I am?' Danny asked.

The little girl walked up to Danny and quickly gave him a hug before she made a hasty exit out the door, locking it from the outside as she left.

Danny unsteadily rose to his feet, feeling the throbbing from his head. He gingerly retrieved his clothing and dressed himself before slipping his favourite tan boots back on. He slowly walked around the confines peering out of the barred-up window trying to get a guide on where he might be. The window was encased with multiple strands of chicken wire on the outside covering the metal bars. He couldn't get a good look at the surroundings.

He could make out some other shacks and huts set out in spacious surroundings in amongst the towering gum trees while silhouetted figures passed by, but his vision was limited from the angle he was on. He tried unsuccessfully to open the locked door and for the next fifteen minutes he nervously paced around as wild thoughts ran around in his brain.

'Shit, am I a prisoner?' Are they going to hand me over to the cops? What the hell's going to happen to me? Are they going to *kill* me?' Danny's mind was racing. His memory was back to full capacity. He had a pretty good idea where he was. The last thing he saw before the butt of the shotgun were men who were dressed like they belonged to the Sultans, and he rightly gathered that he *was* on Sultan land.

He was trying to get a better view through the window when he heard the jingling of keys unlocking the padlock outside of his door. Danny moved back to sit on the canvas stretcher and tried to act as coolly as he could when in walked the little girl with two companions.

If Danny had any doubts of where he was, they were put to rest instantly. The male stranger with the little girl had Sultan patches all over his sleeveless vest. He was a burly-looking man around forty years of age Danny guessed. He stood around 194cm tall with broad shoulders, tattoos on both upper and lower muscular arms. He was clean-shaven with short dark hair and a full rounded face with studded earrings in his left ear lobe.

With him was a woman around the same age, a petite little blonde with a diamond stud through her nostril and dressed in jeans and a tight white T-shirt.

She produced a little torch out of the satchel she had and asked Danny to lean back on the makeshift bed. She flashed the torchlight into his pupils then began to change the dressing above his temple.

'How are you feeling?' she asked.

'Hungry.'

'That's good,' she grinned.

Danny added that he was feeling okay, he had a bit of a headache, but his legs felt a bit jelly-like.

'Yeah well, that's the after-effect of the Rohypnol and tranquiliser my husband gave you, not my doing, I assure you,' she feistily said. 'He thinks it's funny injecting strangers. That's after he smashes their heads in with the butt of a gun.' She turned her head towards the burly man in the room and gave him a sarcastic look of marital bliss.

'Yeah, sorry about that. Protocol, you know how it is. We like to keep our privacy around here,' the male stranger smugly told Danny with a forgiving smile.

'Where am I?' Danny asked, knowing what the answer might be.

'You're in the compound of the Sultans MC,' the woman answered with a wry smile, expecting a look of fear from his face.

Danny coolly paused for a moment then asked how long he had been here.

'Nearly 24 hours,' the woman said.

'Shit, another wasted day. Oh well, guess I needed the sleep, haven't been getting much lately,' Danny quipped.

The large, tattooed man sniggered at his comment which put him at ease a little. *At least he's got a sense of humour*, he thought.

As the woman started to leave, she told the big man that their visitor would be alright and handed him some painkillers if his headache continued.

'Thanks Mia, I'll see you soon,' he quietly replied.

Danny's anxieties were dropping. *At least they're looking after my health*, he surmised. He was still fearful inside; however, he was going to play it cool on the outside to see where it would get him. Best to show a tough exterior around these types he concluded. He sat up on the stretcher once more and decided to make the first step in conversation.

'So, Mia's your wife,' he asked.

'Yeah, so I gather your hearing has taken no effect,' he said, impressed by Danny's alertness.

'Nurse?' Danny inquired.

'You *are* on the ball,' he said.

'I've got a wife! Two twin boys as well. Haven't seen them for nearly two weeks,' Danny confessed.

'Yeah, so we've heard. We know your story, Danny Pruitt,' the man commented.

Danny immediately pondered anxiously if it was a good or bad thing if they knew who he was. He quickly confided what they probably heard was none of his doing and that he never asked for what had happened.

'Well, since you know my name, do you have one?' Danny cautiously asked.

'Drake,' was the reply, as he thrust out his hand for an official greeting.

As Danny reciprocated with a firm handshake of his own, the confidence was growing inside of him. The longer they talked, the more he thought that no harm was coming his way and pressed the issue of how he ended up in this shack.

Drake took off his patched vest, laid it across the deck chair and pulled it in closer to Danny. He sat with the backrest afront while the little girl joined them on the floor with her legs crossed, keeping her smiling face entranced on Danny as he listened to Drake.

'We were out checking for damaged perimeter fences caused by the storm when we noticed you running across the clearing.'

'I didn't realise I was on your land. I got lost in the storm,' Danny interrupted justifying why he was there.

'We thought it the most plausible reason why you were there going on all the breaches in the boundary fences,' Drake calmed him. 'You're lucky I had my bino's with me. One of the brothers with me was going to put a bullet in you until I saw what you were running at,' Drake said as he ruffled the hair of the little girl. 'We didn't even know little Maddy here was missing out of the compound. She does get the wanders every now and then.'

Drake stopped to communicate with sign language to little Maddy then turned back to Danny and told him that she was asking if he was alright, adding that she thought that he was a bit of a hero. Her knight in shining armour, he quoted from her.

Danny gave her a smile and then commented to Drake that anybody would have done the same thing if they were in his shoes.

'I don't think so, mate. We saw what happened. It took a lot of courage to do what you did. She wouldn't be here now if it wasn't for you. If the trees didn't get her, the dogs would have. It was too far away for us to do anything about it, but you! You done good,' Drake praised.

Danny accepted the accolade and put the dying question to rest.

'She's deaf, right?' he asked.

'Geez, your wisdom astounds me, you *are* on a roll,' Drake drolly said. 'Yes, she is, totally,' he added, smiling at Maddy.

'Well, that explains a lot, and I thought she was just shy,' Danny joked.

'She's become quite attached to you. She hardly ever left your side since you've been here. She had company, of course, no offence,' Drake expressed.

'None taken,' Danny happily forgave.

'Things could've been different for you if it wasn't for her,' he warned. 'She's been worried about you. She has great ability to read people. We use her instincts often when we meet people for the first time, but I must confess, Danny Pruitt, we've never seen her act like this around strangers before, particularly ugly bastards like you,' Drake jibed.

'Well, you haven't enhanced my looks, have you,' Danny quipped, pointing to his head wound.

Drake gave off a contented smirk from the side of his mouth as he stood up from the deck chair. He turned to Maddy once more and started to communicate with her again as he grabbed a bottle of water that Mia had left behind and took a big swig out of it. There was a minute of quiet in the room as Danny watched the animated silent conversation that was taking place and was wondering what was going to happen next. He decided to make a brave move to see what would come of it.

'Well, I guess I'll be on my way then, hey!' he announced confidently.

'Don't think so, mate,' Drake firmly chortled, as he and Maddy were about to exit through the door. 'Now that you're conscious, I think the president of the Sultans MC would like to meet the man who saved his daughter's life.'

After hearing the keys lock the padlock outside of the shack, Danny sat back down on the stretcher, comprehending the last comment he heard. Wow, he thought to himself, saving the life of the President's daughter, that's got to work in my favour, doesn't it? He shook his head in amusement the longer he pondered it. '

Oh Danny boy, you've done it again,' he chuckled to himself as he grasped his good fortune. Of all the places he could've ended up, of all the roads and tracks he could've taken, the perfect timing of seeing little Maddy in danger! Maybe the storm sent him to that clearing for a reason, maybe it was the wish of the powers that be, Barny would agree that it was God's plan all along. If it was, he's got a warped way of doing things Danny happily theorised to himself.

The thought of Barny jolted him back to reality. Where is he? Where's Ricky and Harry? I wonder what's happened to them he fretted. Worse case scenarios started to race through his mind. It had been over 36 hours since he had seen them last, a lot can happen in that time he chastised, but as it was, there was nothing he could do about it being locked up the way he was.

He started to pace around, going over thoughts in his head when Drake's leather vest caught his eye. Did he leave it here on purpose? Did he do it to remind me where I was and not do anything stupid? Did he remove it to show off the handgun he had strapped under his left armpit? Or was it just an honest mistake, Danny questioned himself.

He scanned the patches on the front of the vest. The 1% patch was there with the words Vice President and years of membership. Sultans was written down the right side in white with red outline, along with a side rocker of the state's chapter down the left. A small club ensign and a few other personalised mottos were embroidered onto it finished it off. Danny turned the vest around to get a better look at the larger patch that crossed the entire back of the vest.

He was immediately entranced by the workmanship that went into it as he ran his finger across. He had never been this close to an outlaw club's patch before. He had only seen them from afar as they rode by, or from a discreet distance away at a rare party or drinking at a pub or from the confines of his loungeroom when he used to watch documentaries on his television.

The top rocker read **SULTANS**, once again in red with white outline as the state's name of Venturia made up the bottom rocker, but it was what was in between that he was intrigued with.

The head of a ferocious bear in attack mode made up the top ensign. On the bottom was the body of a scorpion, to the left side a wolf's head, and to the right, a hawk in full flight with talons showing, all morphing out of three strands of intertwined chain mesh that encircled what was on the inner. Inside displayed two crossed scimitars, the chosen weapon of the ancient middle eastern warrior, with the Latin words *credere nemo* circled around above, and *negare omnia* below, with the year of the club's formation between the scimitar's blades. Although Danny had some knowledge of Latin terminology, he had no idea what it meant, but he would find out in the coming days what the words would mean, TRUST NO ONE, DENY ALL.

He would also find out soon enough what the animals would represent to the members of the Sultans. The Bear represented power, strength and adaptability. The Scorpion represented the affirmation of self-protection and defence. The Wolf represented loyalty and perseverance while the Hawk represented cunning and spirituality. Motto's Sultan members would take an oath to and strongly uphold all four creeds after they received their patch. If any member were to in any way disparage or detract from these values or not conduct themselves accordingly which would affect their business or otherwise, they would be bought to the club's judiciary.

The judiciary was made up of the three Vice Presidents, the Sergeant at Arms, secretary and treasurer, along with two nominated senior members. In the event of a tied vote the outcome would fall to the President to decide, and if found guilty they would be most likely treated to the three B's, beaten, blackmarked and banished, or if in an extreme case, such as disloyalty, the fourth B would be invoked, buried!

As Danny worked his eyes over the vest, taking in everything that was on it, the sound of keys opening the door once more alerted his senses. He laid the vest back down on the chair and resumed his spot on the canvas stretcher when in walked the President of the Sultans. If first impressions counted for anything, Danny's was one of awe and surprise. He would introduce himself as Solomon, but as soon as Danny saw his face, his memory knew it was the man who put fear into people on both sides of the law.

Solomon Pike had just recently celebrated his 50th birthday, but his physique and demeanour would belie his age. He was an ex-military special forces member who had done numerous tours of duty throughout middle eastern hotspots and Africa. After his discharge from the army, he worked as a private security contractor in some of the most dangerous war zones on the planet. He had seen it all when it came to mankind's brutal leftovers of hatred inflicted upon each other, and he had been responsible for some of it himself. In between contract work overseas he would spend his time with the Sultans, riding and conspiring with his only family member at that time.

His younger brother by two years was the then Sultans' president, until his only sibling met his untimely death in a rival gang war nearly seven years ago. Solomon Pike never got the chance to fight in the recent energy war because he was still cleaning up the mess that had been left behind from a private war of his own. After the shooting death of his brother, the gang war deepened between rival clubs in all capital cities over revenge, territory and drugs.

In the ensuing years, the Sultans would come out on top in all categories and Solomon would be voted in as President not long after. His face was all over television news bulletins and newspapers when the gang war was at its peak, however, when the energy crisis began, he and his club enforced a low profile, a move that was deliberate and necessary for the club to remain viable, united and strong. Danny would find out over the ensuing days through conversation that he was an ultra-intelligent man. He received a reading of 141 in an intelligence quotient test, bordering on genius the military experts would gloat. He was adept in six different languages and was as articulate and precise as they came when he spoke his native English.

The first thing Danny would notice was his deep raspy voice, followed by the Māori symbol tattoo that snaked up the left side of his neck to his clean-shaven face and scalp. Solomon had the build of a champion athlete. Muscle definition on all parts of his body, even his chest and abdominal muscles were visible from underneath the tight black singlet he was wearing with his green camouflage pants and brown boots. He was of olive skin, Polynesian like, with deep set brown eyes that made Danny uncomfortable when his laser like stare dived into his sole. He was a figure of a man who drew instant respect and Danny would show it to him in spades.

Solomon drew the deck chair close to him, picked up Drake's vest and laid it on his lap when he sat.

'So, you know who I am?' he asked.

'Yes, I do,' Danny confirmed. 'Although it's been a while since I've seen your face in the media, hey! I had no idea you were around these parts,' he added, as Solomon gave a little snort out of his nostrils in jest.

'Good, I would like to keep it that way,' he warned.

He leant forward in the chair and concentrated his dark piercing eyes into Danny's and started to talk.

'First of all, we understand why you were on our land, but I make no apologies under the circumstances that got you here to this hut. You were trespassing on my land uninvited, which can very dangerous for some.'

Danny nodded his head and replied that he understood completely. Solomon took a deep breath and exhaled; his gravelly voice took a sincerer tone.

'Secondly, I want to thank you personally for saving my daughter's life. She's the only family I have. Her mother died at birth you see, so I've had to raise her myself. As you probably know by now, she's deaf. She contracted a rare case of the mumps a few years back which affected her inner ears. We tried get a cochlear implant but as you know, in these days it's hard to get things done, even for a man like myself. Or more to the point, probably *because* of a man like myself.' He winked.

Solomon paused for a second, took another deep breath and continued.

'She's the only bright light in this fucked up world to me, but thanks to you, I don't have to worry about losing her just yet,' he confided, keeping his steely gaze fixed. 'So, I am in your debt. Besides, you unwittingly did this club a favour.' Solomon grinned as he folded his arms.

'Yeah, what was that?'

'Stewie Morris! The bloke you killed in the shootout with Pringle. He was an asshole. He's given this club a lot of grief over the years. We had him marked, but you've saved us time and worry about that haven't you, so, we thank you for that as well,' Solomon expressed.

Danny had no idea who he was talking about. He didn't know the names of the men who were with John Pringle that day and knew nothing of the names that had been made public from the Tambourine bridge shootout. He still didn't even know what the infamous John Pringle looked like; he had only heard his raised voice. Over the last week he was still going on that he couldn't work out how he never knew of him. The only man he could describe was the one that both he and Ricky shot in the bush and after some descriptive chat about the incident, both him and Solomon were convinced that he was the Stewie Morris the Pres was talking about.

Danny was bewildered that Solomon knew so much about their escapades. Solomon assured him that it was his business to know everything that concerned him and his club, and now that he was inside the walls of his compound, it was his duty to know every detail about him and the reasons why he ended up where he was.

Solomon Pike took a liking to Danny the further they spoke on the events of the previous two weeks. He declared to him that it took a lot of balls to do what he and his mates did, especially when it came to a man such as John Pringle. Solomon knew of Pringle's exploits well, their paths had crossed numerous times in the violent circles they both lived in and warned Danny that there would be no doubt that he would come after him, a thought that sent shivers up Danny's spine. Danny had impressed Solomon with his wit, his courage, his intelligence, and the loyalty and mate-ship that the boys had shown to each other.

Solomon stood from his chair and continued to give firm directives.

'If there's anything you think I can help you with, come see me. In the meantime, the compound is yours to do what you like until you sort your shit out. Show us respect, mind your own business and you'll be alright. While you're in here, you have the protection of the Sultans. No police or any other wannabe can touch you. But I do warn you. If you go outside our gates, you are on your own.

'We will not compromise our club under any circumstances. The gates are manned 24/7. The members will be informed that you are welcome to come and go as you please. Do not tell anybody where you are. Your firearms will be locked up inside the turret at the gates, pick them up and drop them off as you exit and enter. I've banned you from having any type of weapons inside the compound until you earn them back. If you travel with any of our members, again, no weapons. But, if anything happens on the outside, if you put any unnecessary heat on us, if the law gets gist of where you are, we will not protect or help you. So don't come running back to our compound if you get yourself in the shit because we will disown you, hell, we might even shoot you,' Solomon finished with total authority.

Danny stood from his stretcher and posted his hand out to shake Solomon's, which was accepted strongly. Danny thanked him for his generosity and added he hoped he wouldn't be around for long, but before Solomon made an exit out of the hut, the President had some last information that Danny would want to hear.

'Oh, by the way. Your horse is down at the stables, along with all your gear. Feisty bastard, isn't he!' Solomon commented.

'Tell me about it. He's a pain in the ass. I've been fighting him for the last two weeks,' Danny scowled.

'One more thing...' the President added, still amused at Danny's reaction about his horse. 'There's three blokes out here that would like to see you.'

Solomon stood and pushed the door as wide open as he could. His proud muscular body stood upright, his eyes looked kind for the first time as his head nodded in approval as he watched Barny, Ricky and Harry pass him and enter the hut.

Chapter 22

LA FORTALEZA the sign read atop of the entrance. It was carved and burnt into a giant slab of redgum measuring almost five meters long and a meter in depth. Centralised above, affixed by a cast iron tripod was another slab of redgum, this one rounded and measuring two meters in diameter. Sculptured and burnt into it was the patch of the Sultans MC, including the four animal ensigns, the bear, the scorpion, the wolf and the hawk.

The magnificent work of craftmanship sat 3.6 meters from ground level and 1.5 meters above the solar powered rolling electronic iron gates that allowed entrance into the Sultans inner sanctum. On both sides of the gates sat enclosed turrets built out of metal and hardwood timber. They rose 2.7 meters into the air where the gatekeepers watched vigilantly. Adjacent to them was a reinforced metal and wire caged run which stretched over 100 metres in each direction occupied by Rottweiler guard dogs. If the on-duty members or security cameras could not see or hear any unwarranted disturbance on the outside, the dogs would give them an early warning. It was an intimidating and awesome sight for those who would visit the first time.

The name *la Fortaleza* (Spanish for forest fortress) was bestowed upon the property the day after Solomon Pike took control of the former bush retreat and surrounding lands. He named it after a little place that he had spent several weeks at during one of his time outs when he was working as a military contractor in the war-torn Middle East. His working partner at the time was of Spanish heritage and had a little cottage in the south of Spain which he invited Solomon to on several occasions. It was a modest two-bedroom wooden house in the middle of open olive farmlands which made Solomon laugh when he found out his friend called it la Fortaleza (the fortress). But Solomon enjoyed the peace and serenity of the house and farmlands. It was a place he could chill out, gather his thoughts and not rely on the clock, a memory he never forgot and in respect to his colleague, who was fatally shot in a fire fight during a mission together in Syria, named the clubs new piece of land after his war buddy's home. If la Fortaleza in the southern Spanish farmlands was only just a place to relax and gather some peace time, la Fortaleza in the mountains north east of Graceville was completely the opposite, it lived up to the name it was given, a fortress.

The former bush retreat and spa was a 9km drive off the main road that leads through the Graceville pass. It was a twisting dirt road that climbed and wound its way to a plateau in which the two story, 10-bedroom rendered stone slab Victorian style manor stood. The dirt road was called track 24 and was the only way into the front gates wide enough to fit two vehicles abreast. There were other single vehicle tracks that led to the property, all with their own designated numbers abundantly marked throughout the forest to help with the location of old fire tracks. There were also several self-made signs of the club surrounding the area, chiefly on track 24, warning off people from coming any closer, but nevertheless, the members were always on guard.

Of the 2500 hectares the Sultans now owned, the jewel in the crown was the 15-acre property in which *la Fortaleza* was situated. The manor was originally built in the 1930's and had many restorations over the years as ownership was passed on. It had survived three deadly wildfires over the last century with the last one being 25 years ago which almost destroyed the majestic house altogether. It was caused by falling and faulty power lines bought down by extreme winds, but that was not there worry these days as it had been over three years since electricity ran through the lines of the Hexagon Valley power poles, so the biggest danger when it came to wildfire were lightning strikes, and of course, arson.

Wildfire was always at the back of the club's mind. It was their biggest threat and experienced locals warned that they were long overdue for a big one. They did their best to prepare for such an event. They cut and maintained clearings atop of the plateau surrounding the manor and had several 10,000 litre water tanks situated around the compound with a sprinkler system installed to the main buildings along with a six-by-six metre concrete underground bunker that sat two meters under the surface. A filtered stoke pipe protruded out from the ground to give occupants air to breath when and if the emergency would ever arrive.

It was located southwest of the manor within a short walking distance from its front door. The club converted and renovated the manor to their specifications, including converting the large dining room into their church, the meeting place to make decisions and share intel regarding club matters. Inside, they had kept up appearances, but the outside walls and roof were well overdue for a paint. But that was how Solomon wanted it.

He liked the colour of the rendered walls had become through years of weather beatings. It was originally a brilliant white but was now looking an off-coloured pale green and tan in large patches, with creeping ivy growing up the walls and around the window recesses. Some of it had reached to the roof, crawling across it, then up the two large rendered chimney stacks that sat atop of the building, while the dark tiled roof had lichen and moss growing on it with overhanging vines creeping over the eaves.

As Danny and the boys would soon find out, the energy and fuel crisis seemed another world away compared to what they would discover inside the compound. La Fortaleza was as self-sufficient as could be. Amongst their members were high grade engineers, A-grade industrial electricians, mechanics, IT experts, carpenters, builders, plumbers, boilermakers, all highly trained and extremely good at what they did and were soon put to work. Inside the first twelve months of operating out of la Fortaleza, the club would have all the mod-cons from days gone by up and working that the normal person now only dreamed of in the present.

They cleared 2 acres of land on top of a rise and installed solar panels to maximise the sun. The energy stored was transferred to a large battery powered grid, then dispersed to the latest in generator technology, quiet and reliable, to individual buildings and structures around the compound, including operating the gates at the main entrance.

The system generated more than enough power for their needs and was used in a range of services such as switching on lights, heating hot water services, and powering whatever appliance the compound thought necessary. The Kensington River flowed at the back of the property. An abundance of natural springs across the apex of the range ensured the river was always flowing. Water was pumped from the river as needed and a state-of-the-art filtration system was also built to ensure the water was safe to drink. There was 2.5km of electrified fencing around the compound with three strands of wire each carrying 2500 volts and attached to the cyclone fencing that would stop any intruders in their tracks, human or animal. A 2.4-meter-tall Cyprus hedge sat three feet inside the fence to stop any snooping eyes peering at the grounds inside.

When you entered through the gates, a 100-meter elm tree lined gravel driveway led you to the front door of the manor, then continued around in a loop to exit. Inside the loop, the rock edging from the driveway encased a manicured lawn surrounded with more elm trees that had park benches underneath them. On the south side of the manor, across from the emergency bunker, the club had built several accommodation housings for members, most made from quarry bricks and rocks with timber trimmings and or Colourbond iron sheeting for roofs. For those who didn't have a roof over their head, they would make do with tents situated around the compound.

To the north side of the manor, they had built their own under cover operational mini timber mill and welding bay along with more open undercover working sheds. A row of lock up roller door garages backed onto a strip of young sapling eucalypts and shrubs. Inside the garages were stored fuel drums and oils, in another were their stored guns for trading and next to that sat their transport vans and much-loved idle Harley Davidson motorcycles, dormant, but ready to rev into action at a second's notice.

They had assembled a communication tower above a hut with dishes and receivers attached to help with radio comms when they travelled throughout the mountain ranges. They had a flushing toilet block, shower block, large chemical induced septic tanks and two separate undercover eating quarters where members would cook their meals along with several refrigerating units close by. Eight fixed 10,000 litre water tanks were strategically placed around the compound under main structures to gather rainwater. The 60 stall horse stables were kept immaculately clean as they knew the horses were just as important as the Harley's they once rode and treated them accordingly.

The Sultans tentatively cultivated a large scale arrange of vegetables for themselves. They planted and took care of fruit tree orchards. They had over 200 free range chickens on the property, over 100 head of sheep on cleared paddocks, but the largest, the most cared for, and most important plant they cultivated was marijuana.

They had over five acres dedicated to the exclusive use for cultivating the green weed, producing nearly 10,000 plants per acre at various degrees of maturity. To the northeast where the main road came down from the compound to the plantation, there were six large hot houses. Power was connected to the structures to quicken up the growing process with heat and lighting when needed. Water was pumped across from the river 500 meters away on the edge of the south east side of the plantation. It was the club's largest income and was guarded fiercely. Towers were installed in around the plantation with members deployed in shifts to oversee any problems. Drones with cameras attached were flown daily over the plantation and surrounding areas for added security along with regular sorties over the accessible parts of the 2500 hectares, with vision being scanned by members back in the communications hut in the compound, backed up by security patrols on horseback scouring the boundaries.

There were no less than 25 members at *La Fortaleza* at any one time to run operations, not including wives and girlfriends who were sanctioned by club leaders. Sometimes the numbers would grow in excess of 100 when club requirements insisted. Other than patched members or prospects, the only people that would step foot on Sultans sacred land would either be trusted associates or like-minded business partners, along with the vetted family relation of a member. The whole operation was run with military precision under the leadership of Solomon Pike; if you were there, you were put to work.

Everyone there had duties and it was carried through without complaint or prejudice. All Sultan members were well rewarded financially through their businesses compared to the masses that were entrapped by the poverty and hardship inflicted by the energy crisis.

Although the marijuana trade was their bread and butter it was complimented with other ventures. They had their own meth lab and were in the top echelon of the pill and ice trade. From crystal meth, crack cocaine or ecstasy tablets, their so-called duo of cooks were up amongst the best, and the Sultans MC were no small fish when it came to dealings in the lucrative illegal gun trade. It was a black-market business that in these days was as rife as it could be. From handguns, automatic pump action shotguns, to AK47 assault rifles, Uzi machine guns and M4 Carbines, through criminal associates, Solomon, with the help of Drake, could get his hands on almost anything that came across his order desk.

They transported their consignments in and out of the compound using a fleet of former 10-ton Armaguard vans. The trucks had their wheelbases lifted, appropriate tyres were fitted, along with modified heavy-duty suspension to allow smooth driving when they had to take them off road. The occupants always travelled in fours, two up front, two in the rear. They hid their consignments in a recess under the rear floor and in coffin like crates on shelves against the interior walls of the van. The trucks would drive to and from the city along the near deserted roads and highways, hardly ever raising a suspicious eyebrow, to several warehouse's that adjoined the Sultans city clubhouse down on the wharves.

Of course, it helped that Minister Johnston, along with a small group of corrupt officials, including Detective Cribbs, were on their payroll and would take a little percentage of profits in return for turning a blind eye and giving intel. The Armaguards went under the guise of government or shire owned vehicles with the appropriate decal stickers attached over them. The vans would come and go from *La Fortaleza* at least twice a week depending on the demand of their products.

It was a corrupt system that had worked for both parties for several years without repercussions, although, there had been occasions when a single van or a small convoy was stopped and searched by law enforcement who were not on the payroll, only to be sucked in by false papers and subterfuge.

The club was run on the traditional ways of an outlaw motorcycle club, but Solomon tweaked the chain of command to his liking. Instead of having the one Vice President, he installed three of them, each to oversee the three main tasks that were paramount. Drugs, guns and logistics.

The drugs line of business was controlled by a man who went by the name of Crow. He was a tall, wiry, tattooed fellow who stood nearly 200cm in height. He was older than the rest, maybe in his mid-fifties with a long black beard that reached down to his chest with strands of grey noticeable through both beard and whispery hair on top. He had a thin looking face with larger than normal straight-lined nose.

Crow had been with the club for over a quarter of a century. He was a paranoid and distrustful man who kept to himself and never once did Danny and the boys see him smile. Crow was unimpressed that Solomon gave these interlopers access to *La Fortaleza*. So what if one of them saved the President's daughter, it wasn't enough for him to be anywhere near accepting.

It took years of trust and approval before anyone became a member of the Sultans and for these men to walk in here overnight was totally unjustifiable to Crow, however, the respect he held towards his President would override his displeasure, but that didn't mean he had to hold a conversation with any of the fugitives and he would hold true to that.

The guns and weapons line of business was controlled by Drake. He knew his guns like no other. His was introduced to them from an early age when hunting with family members and took the next step when he enlisted in the army at 18 years of age. Not long after, he found himself working overseas overseeing peace keeping missions for the defence force. By the time he reached his late twenties, through disenchantment and lack of promotion possibilities, he resigned from the force and took up work in the security business and before he knew it, through associates and his love of Harley Davidson's, he found himself inside the Sultans MC. He was an affable and likable person but beneath his exterior laid a ruthless and sometimes cruel lethal persona, a skill set that Solomon took an instant liking to.

The third Vice President oversaw all things logistical. If the club needed anything transported, stored, or delivered, Razor was the go-to man. He had connections everywhere and could acquire anything that was needed to be used. From vehicles to train carriages, to warehouses or tools, he was a genius at getting things accomplished no matter how difficult it seemed. His expertise was second to none and his solutions would always succeed, covert or otherwise. Razor was in his early thirties and of athletic medium build, tattooed down both arms and calves with a fit looking stature thanks to his rigorous weights program. He had short dark hair and blue eyes with a scruffy looking goatee beard. He spoke with an assured deep voice and had a habit of puffing his chest out when it came to serious conversing. He was confident in his abilities and was as loyal to his friends as anyone could be, but first you had to get through the hard exterior he displayed.

In the ensuing days, the boys would become friends and rely heavily on both Drake and Razor. They didn't ask how they got their names, it was none of their business, although they did have light-hearted discussions on the subject. Maybe Crow was named because he resembled a giant human version of the bird variety, they cackled amongst themselves. Maybe Razor was named because he was always using the array of knives he carried with him.

He would use them to peel his fruit, cut and eat his food, to undo screws and whittle away at timber or just to pick away food from between his teeth. Whatever the reason for the names, the boys thought it best not to push the subject. As for Drake, well, they just concluded that Drake was his real name but didn't have the courage to ask otherwise.

The four fugitives would respectfully call *La Fortaleza* home for the time being. They set up camp under a cluster of trees inside the compound, each with a two-man tent for sleeping quarters under an open annex behind the working sheds. They would slowly earn a little respect from the members as they were put to work in between the times they made their sorties out of the compound. They were four fit men, so digging a hole, wielding an axe, or swinging a hammer would be no discomfort to them. They did what was asked of them and slowly would gain some trust from those within, even if it was a little nod of the head, it was good enough for Danny, Ricky, Barny and Harry to feel a little at ease.

Ricky would pass the time between chores mixing with a few like-minded members when it came to electronics and furniture-making. He was good with his hands and enjoyed putting his talents to use. Barny found a few members who had strong beliefs in Christianity and took pleasure in discussing issues out of the bible with them, along with flaunting his talent with the guitar, while Harry would spend most of his time fretting around in awe and bewilderment, asking himself how the hell he had ended up in a place like this.

As for Danny, in between strengthening his bond with Drake and Razor, discussing past war battles from history with the elusive Solomon and learning sign language with an enthusiastic little Maddy, he would spend a lot of his downtime chasing and digging up bull ants and scorpions. Although the scorpion was a lot harder to find, Danny would persist for hours looking under logs and fallen bark until he was successful in his search.

Some days he would go unrewarded but looked forward to the hunt the following day. It was a fascination that he had become obsessed with. He enjoyed the combativeness of the fight, especially from the bull ant, and would continue to pit them against each other hoping that the scorpion's time would come, however, the bull ant's reign of supremacy always mesmerised him. At given times after the bull ant would prevail, Danny would challenge it himself by prodding sticks at it, allowing it to crawl up then flicking it back off into the confines of his makeshift fighting pit. He would torment the mini beast for over an hour, admiring its fearlessness and tenacity, it's never give up attitude, and took self-counselling from its bravery, learning that he must react and persevere as it did, if he himself were to survive and prosper.

However, of all the time he would spend watching and playing with his little bush warriors, it was nothing compared to the time he put into trying to come up with a plan to see Greta. He needed to get his way out of the horrible predicament he had found himself in, but the greatest enraging thought he couldn't get out of his mind was plotting his revenge on each of the men who were on that re-po squad list.

Chapter 23

'Excuse me, boys, but I know how I can make your job easier,' Danny cautiously stated.

Contemptuous looks from the dozen or so men digging out an 800-meter trench with shovels was all he received. They were preparing a line in which they could lay more power down to the sheds of the marijuana plantation.

'I can get my hands on a backhoe for you! Be a hell of a lot less back-breaking. With a bit of help, I could have it here by tomorrow,' Danny confidently added.

Suddenly, he had the men's attention. Within ten minutes, Drake and Razor were summoned to the impromptu meeting as Danny set about explaining the location and contents that sat idle in the old logging coup the boys were introduced to by Benny. It was the morning of the third day that the boys had been inside the compound. They had been well fed, lamb chops, kangaroo, venison, sausages, bacon and eggs and home-grown fruit and vegetables was their diet.

They had been showered, given new clothing to replace the worn and torn pants and jackets. They now donned fleecy hoodies, Danny and Ricky in black, Barny and Harry in dark army green. The four had fully recovered from their bruises and irritations that were bestowed upon them from the previous week in the forest and by lunchtime, they were about to get their first journey out of the compound since they had been temporary captives.

After receiving the go-ahead from Solomon, Drake, Razor, three other members and the four boys made up a posse of nine men on horseback that set out for the 50-minute ride at cantering speed to the logging coup. Another two members on horseback ten minutes ahead of them acted as point scouts. The mood between Danny and Ricky was still a little cold as Ricky was not over Danny's decision to lead them up Satan's Elevator. Ricky had met him with a double-fisted shove to the chest when they finally caught up in Danny's prison hut, blaming him for the death of Harry's beloved mare and then being forced by gunpoint to *la Fortaleza* not knowing their fate, or the whereabouts of Danny himself.

The night of the storm, Ricky, Barny and Harry eventually found each other in the chaos and took refuge in a giant hollow at the base of a mountain ash tree and huddled together throughout the night. The following morning, they tracked down where Harry's horse lay, still hanging for life unable to move. They then had the sad and unenviable task of putting the mare out of its misery through Harry's tears and gun barrel.

The ensuing single gunshot out of his pistol alerted the patrolling Sultans members and knowing that there were three more fugitives out there after they identified the unconscious Danny Pruitt, and also aware that the gunshot did not come from the confines of their boundaries; under the orders of the President, the scouting Sultans members pushed out quickly and surrounded the outnumbered and petrified men. With silence and stone faces, the leather-clad members escorted them back to *la Fortaleza* and placed them in a hut of their own.

Danny was excited to get out of the compound; it gave him a chance to get a few credits up concerning the Sultans MC. He was always thinking ahead, he had to in the life that was now forced upon him. If he done them a favour that they considered beneficial, maybe they would repay him when the time was right. Better to have more allies than enemies he quoted to his three buddies before they left, however, the one thing he was less excited about was being reunited with the big black gelding.

The love-hate relationship had resumed and the reefing and pulling started as soon as he jumped on his back. The swearwords and cursing were coming out of Danny's mouth quicker than his company could tell him to button his lips as they approached the marijuana plantation on their way out.

They were exiting out of the rear of *la Fortaleza,* down a dirt trail only wide enough for two abreast on horseback on the northern side of the plantation traversing across a slight ridge overlooking the astonishing amounts of plants. The boys were in total amazement of its scale and gave looks of wonderment to each other. They thought best not to discuss Sultan business with their new comrades.

With the watchful eyes of Crow peering up from a distance as his workers went about their detail, the group continued to lead Danny and the boys along the track until they came to the electrified gate and fence. Razor dismounted, then punched a combination of numbers into a camouflaged panel hidden in a metal box. He pulled out a remote control attached to his key set, pointed it at the gate and watched it slowly close after they pushed through, re-electrifying the fence once completed.

The forest started to thicken as they rode. They soon made a steep decline down a cutting until they came to a 2.7-metre-high cyclone wire gate that was covered with corrugated iron for added security. Another wire fence either side morphed into a wall of monstrous cliff faces alive with forest vegetation. Razor dismounted again and pulled out his set of keys and opened the gates then waited until all had passed through before locking up behind them.

The boys realised they were now off Sultan territory when they saw a post sign that read Molloy's track. Not long after, the Sultans turned their horses right and led them up a single file dirt trail. Tree ferns and adolescent wattles overhung the track in between the well-established eucalypts that grew out of the thick undergrowth of wild native grasses. The track took them up and over a small ridge until it flattened before descending and coming out onto Summit Road, not too far away from the logging coup. It was a short cut Danny put in his memory bank for future use, if and when he would ever require it.

The conversation was amicable between the group as they discussed present day affairs along the journey, skipping and avoiding the storm damage left behind and all agreeing to the hatred and contempt they possessed towards the re-po squad. Drake put a halt to the trek and radioed the men ahead wanting to know if it was clear to proceed. The reply was what they wanted to hear, no sign of man or beast except for the presence of wallaby's and the odd wombat wobbling in and out of the forest while the rosellas and lorikeets darted majestically overhead. Drake and his fellow members listened in and corresponded with the lead duo as Ricky quietly reminded Danny that they weren't too far off the entrance and suggested they not give away Benny's camp, a conveyance that Danny wholly agreed to.

'Hang on, guys,' Ricky barked. 'The entrance is just up the road here.'

The boys remembered another entrance to the coup about half a kilometre up from Benny's camp which they had passed after they had left him. The dirt entrance was overgrown with a cluster of trees and regenerated Wattle and shrubs, blocking the view to the coup, however, the start of the entrance was still visible on the side of Summit Road and that was the way they would lead Drake and Razor into it, avoiding the risk of giving away Benny's abode.

The men dismounted and gave their bodies a stretch as they waited to be joined by the lead scouts. They passed around cigarettes and helped themselves to water and whiskey out of their cannisters and flasks when Drake quizzed Danny on what his plans were. Over recent conversing, the Vice President deduced they had a lot in common and it was the reasoning behind his question, to broaden the talk and get more of a feel of his outlaw guest.

'Well Drake! In life, we all get dealt hands, don't we?' prophesised Danny. 'Every year, every month, every day. And I've been dealt a hand that is forcing me to play, and this time I'm refusing to fold. So, I'm going to play this hand my way until I can no longer.'

Drake gave him a hardened smile of approval, one that reinforced Danny's inner opinion of him. Drake enjoyed Danny's company and Danny knew it.

A moment of silence followed from the present company at Danny's prognosis of life, and with added confidence on the Vice President's reaction, he continued calmly and resolutely, 'I've got no house to go back to. I can't go back to Graceville, so all I want to do is try and get some money somehow. Grab my wife and kids and get the hell out of here,' he finished bluntly.

'Any place in particular?' Razor scoffed.

'Yeah! Heaven,' Danny confided with a wry smirk.

'That place is reserved for nice law-abiding citizens, isn't it?' Razor snarled.

'I'm talking about a different heaven, my *heaven*,' Danny said.

Barny noticed the look of bewilderment on the Sultans faces, also knowing they probably didn't care too much on what Danny was talking about, nevertheless, he thought best to explain what his friend meant by *his* heaven.

With input from Ricky, he tried his best to describe Danny's dream home up in the northern state.

'Impressive,' came Drake's reply. 'But I don't like your chances of getting their any day soon.'

'We'll see!' Danny replied as the men remounted their horses when the lead duo approached.

'I already own nearly half of it,' he continued to Drake.' I sent a letter to Steve just before Christmas before all this shit went down. He's my mate who owns the other bit of it. I told him that I'll be arriving by the end of the month. I was going to sell my house, whatever I could get for it anyway, then move north and take that job offer helping on the horse stud. I hadn't told my missus yet; it was going to be a surprise hey! But I'll get there, whatever it takes, all I need is some money,' Danny confidently explained.

The men looked on in silence admiring his determination, no matter how delusional they thought him to be.

'Shit, you can all come to Heaven with me if you want, you're all invited,' Danny said with excitement as he waved his arms around. 'There's a sign above the gate as you drive in that actually says Heaven, no bullshit,' he boasted. 'That's where I'm going and fuck anybody who gets in my way. What do you reckon, Barny, coming to heaven with me or what?' Danny brazenly asked.

I've already given my soul to the lord, Danny, so, I *hope* I'll be going to heaven, yours *or* Gods. What will be will be, my friend.' Barny beamed.

Danny liked his answer.

'Harry! Coming to heaven with me?'

'Uuhhmmm, yeah sure, why not?' was Harry's nervous reply.

'Ricky?'

'Yep, I'll follow you up. Why the fuck not! But first, we have a job to do!' Ricky strongly conveyed.

'Oh yeah, what's that?' smiled Danny.

'Before we go to heaven, we gotta send those Re-po squad bastards to hell.'

Danny instantly felt delight through his body. *That's the Ricky I know*, he said to himself. *Strong, pestilent, full of fortitude and ready for a fight at any given notice, that's the man I grew up with!* He was pleased to have his best man back on the same line of thought. Danny nodded his head at his buddy in resolute determination as both produced a noxious look in their eyes that went with the muffled chortle and defiant grin.

Even for tough men such as Drake and Razor, the steely display almost sent a chill up their spines. It was the first outward glimpse that they had seen from Danny regarding the anger and vengeance he held within, and from now on, the members of the Sultans would show a little more warier respect towards the Graceville four, whether earnt or otherwise.

Razor was listening intently when he abruptly turned his horse at Danny as the lead scouts descended upon them. He moved the reins around his hands as his horse jostled and gave a strong word of advice.

'Sounds more like you'll be going to hell with all the other misfits if that's your attitude!' he grimly predicted.

Danny's response was immediate. 'Well, that's got a bit of a ring to it, hasn't it?' he happily suggested.

'What has?' Razor snarled.

'To heaven or to hell? I like that!' Danny smugly countered with a look of endorsement to himself, much to the dismissive bafflement of the company around.

The men entered the track towards the logging coup and once they negotiated through the thickness of the camouflage, the machines and vehicles were there for all to see, much to the delight of the Sultans who gave a look of surprise and satisfaction.

Drake and Razor quickly put the other members to work, starting with the front-end loader with backhoe attached that Danny had suggested. It was an LA 534 Kubota, the perfect size for them to use back at la Fortaleza, not to large but possessing enough grunt to accomplish their tasks. The head mechanic was one of the lead scouts, Rusty was his name, presumably because of his whispery ginger hair and whiskers. The boys didn't have much dialogue with the other members while they were trekking, they hardly spoke unless Drake or Razor raised an issue with them. Most of the time they sat atop their horses expressionless, other than the stern rugged looks they would portray across their faces.

Rusty got the others to work around him, checking fuel lines, battery charge, oil levels, etc, whilst Danny and the boys took time to laze about in the sun smoking cigarettes and chatting amongst themselves about the two wedge tailed eagles magnificently soaring above. They had been idling about for half an hour, about 100 metres from where the Sultans had gathered near some machinery to discuss plans of action, when *whoosh*, an arrow flew straight over Harry's left shoulder and into the large tree stump that Danny was sitting next to.

The boys were startled, all four bodies jerked at the sudden fright. Ricky was first to react. He bounced off the log he was sitting on and investigated the forest edge, 50 metres rising towards the east to see if he could get a guide on where the shooting arrow had come from. There was nothing the boys could see. He tugged and pulled the arrow from the stump until he could prise it loose. Danny looked towards where the Sultans were situated, they didn't see or hear the arrow come in.

'There's something on it,' Ricky informed them. 'It looks like a note or something.'

Looks of apprehension engulfed the boys.

'Open it,' said Barny.

Ricky ripped the adhesive tape from the arrow and unfolded the piece of A4 paper and began to read.

ARE THOSE SULTANS WITH YOU?
IS IT SAFE TO COME OUT?
THUMBS UP OR THUMBS DOWN?
BENNY.

Danny immediately turned in the direction the arrow came in from, raised his arm and gave the thumbs up. The boys looked on sternly waiting for some movement to appear from the forest and within the minute, leading his horse with bow slung over his shoulder and quiver attached to his back, Benny emerged.

His movements had caught the eye of the Sultans and in turn his appearance was met with drawn revolvers and rifles. Danny rushed over and stood between the line of fire that the members had on Benny. Waving his arms, he focused on Drake who was slightly ahead of the others with his rifle locked into his shoulder.

'He's with us!' he yelled. 'It's Benny, the guy I told you about, Drake! It's all cool. No need for any shooting here,' Danny pleaded in calmer tones.

Drake and Razor warily asked their comrades to lower their weapons then started to walk towards where the boys were congregated, keeping their guns at the ready, Drake with his rifle, Razor with his revolver. The uneasy minute had passed, especially for Benny. For a second, he thought Danny had completely miscalculated the faith he had in his new associates. His heart rate was through the roof when he saw a plethora of guns pointed at him; however, once Danny's quick introductions began and then weapons lowered and holstered, Benny's thumping had dropped back to a normal rate.

After handshakes and greetings had been done, Danny explained to Benny the reasons why they were at the logging coup. He thought Benny may have been a little peeved that they were encroaching on his hidden haven in the bush, but his ally was quick to put any misgivings to rest.

'It's all no use to me anymore, they can go for their lives' He said. 'If you can get any of the machinery going, good luck to ya.'

Drake and Razor signalled to their crew to continue working on the Kubota as Danny and the boys started to push Benny on any news that might concern them. Benny chortled to himself as he took his arrow from Ricky's hand and replaced it back into his quiver.

'News! I got plenty. Where do I start! Take a seat, grab some popcorn and I'll tell you all about it. But I'm gonna have to start with some bad news.'

'I doubt if there's any fuckin good news,' Ricky expressed as he lit up a cigarette.

Drake and Razor remained standing as the other boys sat around on stumps and logs as Danny asked him what it was.

'Tom Potter hung himself at the police station,' Benny said.

'Really?' was Danny's shocked response.

'Yep. From what I hear, he was pretty plastered when he did it,' said Benny.

Not that the other boys' heartstrings were tugged, but Danny felt deep sadness and a large sense of guilt. It was him that had sent him packing.

'If we'd kept him around, he'd still be alive,' he mumbled aloud.

His friends abruptly dismissed his thoughts and insisted not to hold any blame. Just another example of how these tough times can push a man to the brink, a common occurrence nowadays they discussed.

'I met up with your sister. She asked me to give you this,' Benny continued as he passed the envelope.

Danny proceeded to open the contents as Benny continued to inform the boys on what had been written in the newspapers about them. The city's scribes now dubbing them the Graceville four was one subject that the men found interestingly funny, if not scary.

Benny convinced the men to be extra vigilant. His demeanour changed to the serious when he explained that the police search parties were not the only ones in the area. The mountains were starting to crawl with vigilante groups looking to cash in on the bounty that was still on their heads. The money was still on offer if it led to the arrest and conviction of the fugitives, but some, as with the cousins and friends of the Devlin brothers, had other things on their mind.

They had privately formed a vigilante group and were hell bent on getting retribution for the death of their family members. They were ten strong on horseback trying pick up any sign on the boy's whereabouts and they were not taking any prisoners if they came across them, and as such, Benny warned they were not to be ignored or underestimated.

However, for every man with vengeance or money on their minds, equally, there were allies of Danny that were congregating throughout the ranges. They held a lot of sympathy towards his plight. A lot of men had no jobs, marriages had broken down, income was hard to find. Many had been victims of the re-po squad, mixed with the police corruption and brutality. They were bored and angry and were waiting for a reason to rebel against the hard times and it was becoming clear that Danny's cause was the trigger to start the process of venting their anger and resentment against the rule makers. If they could assist or help the Graceville four in any way that the boys requested, they were happy to oblige.

Benny had come across a few pockets of the so-called allies and mentioned some names to Danny to see if they were genuine or not. Danny would give nods of acknowledgement, but they could see his mind was beginning to change direction as he read deeper into Kate's letters.

'What's up, Danny, what's in the letter,' Ricky inquired.

'The rest of the Re-po Squad who trashed my house. Kate's given me the remaining names,' Danny quietly said.

He passed the list to Ricky.

'Look at the name on the bottom,' he spat.

'It's gotta be a mistake,' Ricky objected.

Kate had written Corey Porter in capital letters with the proof on how she came across the rest of the names. Ricky knew Corey well; he too was shocked to see his name.

'It's all there, mate, no mistake, Kate doesn't lie, you know that,' Danny replied.

They were both were stunned. How can a mate do this! No one can be trusted in this fucked up world anymore they growled to each other, as Benny advised them that Kate's parting words were to that effect about Corey Porter.

'And Greta's still living with them, according to this,' Danny lamented, swishing the other letters that were in his hands around in the air.

'Why would she do that, I would burn his house down and get the hell out of there,' Harry anguished.

'Because that's who she is, Harry. She forgives too easily. She'd be devastated, no doubt, but she always sees the good in people, not the bad. Ricky will back me up on that,' Danny bemoaned.

Harry continued to quiz him on the remaining four names on the list, if he knew them at all, and got a chilly sensation up the back of his neck when Danny told him that he knew them all.

' Brad Neilson, he's a mate of Corey's from down the suburbs, a fuckin' dickhead. I'm gonna take pleasure in nailing him!' Danny quietly boasted.

'As for the rest? They're all locals. Didn't have much to do with them but thought they were good blokes! Had beers with them all. Oh well, their mistake, hey! Dead men walking, that's what they are, fuckin dead men walking,' he calmly cursed.

Harry shook his head in disbelief. 'How can people turn on their mates like this,' he raged.

'Sometimes the people you'd take a bullet for are the ones with the hands on the trigger, Harry!' Danny brooded.

He persevered through the letters as the boys spoke around him. With each paragraph he finished, his anger, impatience and guilt started to rise. He was doing his best to control it all. He didn't want to let go with an outburst in front of the Sultans, he needed to keep a cool persona, however, it was almost getting to the stage of an eruption when he came across Kate's writings regarding Sandilands attempted rape of Greta inside the police station.

Drake and Razor were intently taking in the conversation between the men as Danny kept silent, trying to keep the bubbling volcano inside. The more the Sultans knew about Danny and the boys, the better for them if they were going to keep them around. Intel can come from many different angles was their truism and they were getting a good insight through the emotion that the boys were displaying, but the one thing that pricked their ears was the information that they had on the Re-po squad members.

Razor's cousins had been victims of the vitriol tactics, he confided to the gathering, and he and Drake had the same disdain towards them and hearing that Danny had the names of some of the perpetrators, they were all too keen to hear more. For the last twelve months, members of the Sultans MC had been trying to get information on who were joining the ranks of the repossession squads. They wanted to do their part on trying to put a halt to it.

They knew they couldn't stop the powers that be from continuing with the practice; however, if they could find out who was involved, maybe then they could send a message to others that it would be dangerously unsafe to sign up then be found out and the fear of repercussions would be enough to dissuade potential recruits from joining. It was their way to help the vulnerable. Contradictory or not, it gave them an excuse to irritate the establishment that they were also in cohorts with, a way of justifying to themselves that no one controls the Sultans and having a list with proof of names involved in any raid was going to be like gold to the Sultans.

Drake interrupted the conversation and grilled Danny on the information he had on the re-po squad members and once hearing that he had the rest of the names hidden away safely back in his tent at *la Fortaleza*, Drake strongly suggested that he hand them over.

'We'll take care of any retaliation. It will be our fuckin pleasure,' Drake enforced.

Before Danny could give an answer, Benny had more information he needed to relay to his friend.

'You asked me a few days ago if I knew any of the names you showed me. There was one I now know.'

'Who?'

'Victor Slacek, the copper. I saw him this morning,' Benny stated. 'He's with your Sergeant mate, Dane Grainger. There are three others with them. A local cop called Sandilands and two other coppers I've never seen before,' Benny recalled.

'He's a persistent bugger, isn't he?' Barny stated regarding Dane.

Danny stood to his feet immediately.

'Yeah, he's like a dog with a bone. He hates leaving jobs unfinished,' he said with respect; however, it wasn't Dane that was attracting Danny's attention. It was who was with him that made his blood curdle.

'Sandilands? He's with Dane? Up here in the mountains?' he hungrily quizzed.

The men looked at Danny curiously. What was he thinking? They had seen this look before and it made them nervous every time.

'You're not thinking of going after him, are you, mate? We're done with him. There's no reason to confront him anymore. What happened down the river is finished.' Barny was exasperated.

'Yeah Danny, it'll be wise to stay away. You don't want to hurt another cop, mate,' Harry pleaded.

'Oh, I got a reason to see him now. At least say hello.' Danny angrily winked.

He thrust a portion of the letter into the chest of Barny and told him to read the middle paragraphs out aloud, then looked him the eye and asked him to give him a reason why he *shouldn't* go after him.

Barny slowly read the events about the attempted rape so everyone had no doubt what was being translated and by the time he was finished, Barny, Ricky and Harry had a look of resignation on their faces. They knew their friend wouldn't accept anything less than retribution when it came avenging any wrongs inflicted on Greta. A sunken feeling of despair and anxiety raced through their stomachs. They now knew if they were going to stay with their besieged friend, they were going to have to face more violence and danger, a conclusion that sent a harrowing tremble throughout their already withering and fretful constitutions.

The boys had formed an unconditional bond between each other. If it wasn't already there before, it was surely their now and they were in it for the long haul, no matter what the outcome, particularly Ricky as he had nothing to go home to. Both his parents had passed, he had no woman in his life, and his siblings, who he hadn't seen in years other than his elder sister Janelle, were strewn all over the country, and anyways, he was beginning to like the lifestyle, waking up each day not knowing what it will bring. It was becoming exciting for him. It gave him a rush of adrenalin that he was thriving on, with or without the whiskey, dope, and cocaine.

'Alright boys!' Danny said as he turned his attention to Drake and Razor. 'I'll make you a deal. I'll give you the names of the re-po squad members, but I have a few conditions.'

'Go on,' Drake replied.

'Along with the names, I also want my family's belongings back, the stuff that those scumbags stole during and after the raid, whatever you can find anyway. Then I want them returned to Greta. You also leave me Slacek, Corey and Neilson, I want them to myself. And you give us back our guns,' he firmly lobbied.

The vice presidents quickly agreed to his proposal and affirmed to Danny that they would talk to Solomon when they arrived back at the compound regarding the guns. And as for Sandilands? They had no qualms if Danny went after him. The Sultans knew Sandilands and what type of person he was. Members had given feedback to the Vice Presidents on the occasions their paths had crossed in Graceville and it was all bad in Sandilands' case.

But that wasn't the only issue that they thought they had to deal with. The Sultan President wouldn't be happy if hordes of people started to make their way into the surrounding forest as Benny had suggested. Their privacy was sacred and they would be damned if they were going to let people encroach near their protected lands.

Razor asked Benny for the exact locations of the groups he had talked about. He wasn't sure how the club was going react to the intrusions, that would be determined with Solomon before any action, if any, would be taken, however, he needed all the intel he could gather to give to their President.

'Most of them are either near Syrian creek road or south of Tangiloo and east of St Lucia. There's a few up near the cascades so they're a fair way off now. But it's the crew Dane is leading I reckon that might be the worry,' Benny advised.

'Why?' came the unified response.

'I saw them trekking up at Kelso's track, probably heading onto Summit Road here. There searching every side-track and path they come across. It's as if they're taking the same path as you guys did before you caught up with me. I don't know if it's a coincidence or not, but it's like they know which direction you travelled. They're the only ones in that area and by my calculations they should be coming up near where we stand at any time,' he cautioned.

The boys couldn't work out how they would know. Animated discussions began on how it could be. There's no way they could have followed where they had been was the confident prediction. They concluded the storm would have washed any clues they may have left behind, until Ricky raised the name of Tom Potter. He had never liked him. He had no trust in him and put it to the group that he probably hung himself in shame by blabbing to the cops on their location, a suggestion that Danny scoffed at; however, he didn't know that Ricky was closer to the truth than he ever imagined. Nevertheless, it really didn't matter if Dane and his group knew their tracks or not, it's what they were going to do about it that mattered, the very point that Danny firmly expressed to them.

The six men were about to part company. The continuous cranking over of the Kubota front end loader was grabbing their attention. Drake looked at his wristwatch and saw that time was passing. They had other pressing issues back at La Fortaleza to contend with and before they left, they were going to get one more surprise that would concern them, more so than the four fugitives.

Benny walked over to his horse and grabbed a couple of newspapers out of his saddle bags. He gave one copy to Drake. Razor sidled next to him while Benny gave the other copy to Danny. The newspapers were editions of Valerie Corbett's expose on the Minister and the somewhat truthful version of what had happened with Danny and the boys. The men started to read as Benny added that Minister Johnston and a whole lot of his cronies had all been arrested. The two Sultan leaders were totally taken aback, surely, they would have heard something if that were to be the case. It was club's duty to know all regarding the ventures of Johnston, it was their business *to* know.

'How do you know he's been fuckin arrested; you've been up here in the mountains, haven't you, going on what you've told us so far,' Razor vigorously questioned.

Benny picked up his quiver and slung it back over his shoulders, picked up his bow and mounted his horse. He didn't like his integrity being questioned and gave Razor an emphatic reply as pleasantly as he could.

'With respect, dude. I'm not the only creature who lives off the land in these parts. And I can assure you that our bush telegraph works just as fast as what Facebook, Instagram or Twitter ever did. The only difference is, ours holds more truths.'

A stare-down followed between Benny and Razor before Danny light-heartedly suggested that the Sultans should put Benny on their payroll.

'You could do a lot worse. No one knows these mountains better than Benny. A possum could fart 500 metres away and he would know about it. He would be a great asset to you guys,' Danny said with zest.

He was proud of Benny. The way he didn't back down, the quick response to Razor's short grilling. He gave him an appreciative wink to let him know that he was with him all the way as the cogs ticked over in Drake's mind. Maybe

Danny had a point, the club might be able use a man of Benny's talents to our advantage his ever-alert mind idled.

It was time the group had to depart from their Indigenous mountain confidante. They lined up and shook hands with him, including Drake and Razor, which Danny thought a big positive step. He knew that the Sultans didn't take to outsiders at a whim, and to him, Benny's character just received a big tick, another foothold that strengthened his position he envisaged. There was one last request from Danny before they parted ways and that, he needed the blessing of the Vice Presidents to make it come to fruition.

His desire to contact Greta was overwhelming more than ever, he had to let her know that he was alright. He knew his wife would be tormented. It had been agonisingly too long since they last corresponded and needed to let her know what his true feelings were, and above all, he needed forgiveness for all that he has put her through. With the approval of the senior patched members who assured Benny that the gatekeepers would be expecting him, they arranged a meet outside the front entrance of la Fortaleza at 10.00am the next morning so Danny could hand over the impassioned letters for Benny to deliver.

'Stay safe,' were Benny's parting words as he cantered off into the distance and into the sanctuary of his mountains. Whilst the boys took time to read more of Valerie's article, waiting as the Sultans organised the machinery, they now had a little peace of mind knowing the truth was somewhat out to the public and the reasons that bought them to be standing in this abandoned logging coup on this brilliant summer day.

The mechanics had been successful in their endeavours and by mid-morning tomorrow, thanks to a couple of tandem trailers that laid idle in the logging coup, the club would have their new Kubota and backhoe hard at work digging out the remaining trench they had left behind at La Fortaleza. Adding to the Sultans booty was the bonus of another mini excavator and the two Toyota Land Cruiser 4WDs.

The group were vigilant on the return trip to the compound now knowing they could have company at any time. They were constantly looking and listening for any movement other than the animal kind, favourably for the travellers, it was to be a non-eventful ride. By the time they entered back through the main gates of *la Fortaleza* late afternoon, Danny, still in awe of the overhead sculptured club ensign, their stomachs were crying out for some sustenance and feast of kangaroo fillets, chicken pieces cooked with onions and bacon rashers over the open-brick BBQ would await them.

Chapter 24

The lengthening late afternoon shadows began to overtake the grounds of the compound.

Danny had taken up his position on one of the park benches that sat underneath one of the majestic Elm trees that was encircled by the looping driveway. Little Maddy kept him company under the secretive scrutinising eyes of Solomon from inside the manor. She was looking cute as a button with her rainbow sunglasses on, dressed in cut off denim jeans at the knees and leather sandals with an open black leather jacket that covered her white T-shirt.

They didn't communicate much, she knew Danny was busy, but that didn't worry her, she just liked to be near him. She passed the time seated by his side with her deck of cards playing patience. With the warm late afternoon sun poking through upon him, sunglasses donned and unthinkingly taking in the tranquil bush surrounds that encased him when he lifted his head, Danny got to work expressing his feelings to his cherished wife. He stopped and pondered every minute or two, wondering how to put his thoughts down on paper for his wife to understand when in through the gates came the rumbling sound of three converted Sultan-owned Armaguard vans.

It was an opportune time as the very thing Danny was procrastinating over was the issue of money. How much did Greta have? How can I get some to her? But more importantly, where do I get some? All he needed was money, it was his only ticket out of this nightmare he racked to himself and then, and only then, he would somehow plan his escape out of the mountains and northwards interstate to his heaven, and seeing the vehicles that normally carried such a thing enter the compound, it immediately switched on a large light bulb in his head.

Danny laid his pen down on the park bench and closed the notepad. He leant back on his seat, folded his arms, and articulated his thoughts. The more he thought about the Armaguards, the broader his smile and glint in his eyes became, much to the amusement of little Maddy who took self-satisfied delight imitating his movements.

He was getting flashbacks of how the Armaguard would always arrive at 10.00 am on Monday morning at the Country Club in Graceville. The Country Club was one of the big jewels in the Hexagon Valley. It was grandeur in its architecture and was one of the very few establishments that had kept up appearances. It was owned and ran by the nation's largest insurance company and also had establishments in Marlboro and coastal locations.

The company's board was stacked with politicians and rich businessmen which in turn had the elite and well connected on its high-end membership list which enabled the Graceville Country Club to bypass laws that affected lower scale businesses. It was one of the very few companies that had survived in the current busted economy. In fact, it had thrived, thanks to the corrupt influences of their scrupulous and influential board. They had a similar solar powered set up the Sultan MC ran at la Fortaleza, which gave them power 24/7, a sight for all to see around Graceville as it stuck out like a lone beacon after the sun would set.

The club also had concessions allocated to them through rations of diesel fuel, not only for their emergency generator, but to keep their mowers at work on the pristine fairways and greens of the golf course so they could keep up the standards that their fickle golfing members demanded.

It adorned its more fortunate members with luxury accommodation, conference Centre's, five-star dining, indoor swimming pool, gyms, saunas, tennis courts and more state-of-the-art facilities inside its privileged walls and was on the to do list for the elite club members all over the country.

For the last three years at least, Danny, thanks to his good friendship with a golfing budding who could afford the membership fees through his past employment with the company, had made Monday morning their time for swinging the clubs over 18 holes. He couldn't get there every Monday, however, there was always a spot reserved for him when he could find the time away from his commitments and family. There was no better way for him to forget the hardships that had been forced upon him by taking in a round of golf, forgetting his troubles by following the little white ball around for four hours enjoying the peace, serenity, laughter *and* frustration that the game provided.

10.30 am was tee off time for his group but Danny would always get there an hour early, honing his game on the practice green and in the nets, and it was doing the latter which would catch his attentive eye of a certain Armaguard van. He always wondered how much cash the van would be holding within its steel cocoon and always took mental notes of how and when the men employed by Armaguard went about their deliveries and pick up. He would secretly watch from a distance as he practiced his swing on the open lawns not far away from the practice nets.

The van would reverse down the end of a slanting concrete driveway as Danny stood incognito behind the camouflage of some tall trees and shrubs. The sloping laneway was left of another rising wide concrete driveway entrance that led to the delivery area of the establishment's kitchen. The sloping laneway which the truck reversed down was enclosed by large brick walls on either side which deepened upwards to 25 feet at the bottom.

There, the van would come to a stop adjacent a large roller door which led to the underneath corridors of the building. There he would see two of the guards disappear into the corridors with their trolley while the third guard would lean up against the wall to light up his long-awaited cigarette. On one particular morning, he spoke to a waitress he was on good terms with, a lady who had worked there for years, before and after the crisis, and facetiously said to her how easy it would be robbing the Armaguard as she crossed the lawn on her way home after her breakfast shift.

Danny was shocked when she humorously agreed that it actually would be, particularly as they always left the van running with the keys in its ignition. A fact she knew when she would pass by it after her shift was over. Danny went fishing about how much knowledge the waitress had and one important piece of information she passed on was that the security cameras positioned above the roller door and laneway never worked, they were only there for show and deterrence, laughing off the lack of surveillance measures the Country Club had employed due to their budgets when it came to saving valuable power.

It was information that Danny would install into his memory bank, but never in his wildest dreams thought the day would ever come to put the information to use. He had always kept it to himself. No use telling anyone, they would all laugh it off Danny mused, as he did himself. The only person he mentioned it to was Greta, and they both joked over it every time the Armaguard subject was bought up. She liked it when Danny played golf. He always returned home in a jovial mood no matter how well or bad he played, and she always admired the way Danny's mischievous mind would work sometimes, no matter how farfetched his brainstorms seemed.

Up until a month ago, he never had a reason, he never had the courage, nor the audacity, and plainly never the motivation to even contemplate such an idea of an armed robbery; however, today is different. Today, he is in a totally different life to the one he lived in a long month ago, and now he unquestionably had all four necessities by the bucketful. But the burning question was, did his three desperate mates have the same impulse and disposition?

Chapter 25

'Good morning, Miss Valetta, in town to defend the guilty again, are we?' a wry voice echoed across the foyer of the Graceville courthouse.

'Innocent until proven guilty, Martin, you know that,' came the confident reply.

'How are you, still looking as lovely as ever, I see.'

'Thank you! And the best suits still look good on you, I might add,' she complimented as they softly shook hands.

Assistant Commissioner Martin Conroy was back in Graceville, aiding Inspector Vaccaro process the paperwork on the charges involving the raids on Minister Johnston. He and the Inspector had just finished their duties and were having a private conversation near the large wooden framed glass exit/entrance doors of the courthouse when the stunning figure of Zoe Valetta appeared out of an adjoining office inside the foyer.

Zoe Valetta's striking looks would turn every man's head. She oozed grace and elegance whenever she walked or talked. She was lean and slim with eyes of distinctive jade green that seemed to naturally blend with her red mahogany coloured hair. Her style cut was similar to a long bob that bounced around the back of her slender lengthy neck as she walked. She was known for her boutique dress sense and collection of drooping earrings that dangled from her lobes.

Today, she was dressed in a loose cream-coloured blouse, sleeves folded above her wrists and tight black business slacks that flared just above the ankles showing off the intertwined black leather strapping of her stiletto heels. A beautiful silver-chained cross pendant sat tight around her neck along with the silver-plated bangles that ringed her wrists. It was not the look that people in the legal fraternity first expected when they met the experienced and determined criminal defence lawyer, and she would use it to her advantage whenever possible.

She had arrived in Graceville by train early morning and was greeted with a ride in a plush enclosed dual horse drawn carriage, courtesy of the Sultans MC, which was driven by two young prospects from the club's stronghold.

Zoe was 33 years of age, born to wealth and privilege. Her mother was a successful businesswoman who built and owned a national advertising company while her father was a retired county court judge, which in turn encouraged the path to her own career, but Zoe's youthful looks and young age belied the knowledge, proficiency and exposure that she had gained in a 15-year career in the legal profession.

She had started out as a teenager putting herself through university until she gained an internship at one of the prestigious legal firms in Marlboro. She worked as hard, long, and diligently as anyone possibly could and soon found herself a senior barrister at her firm, earning a great reputation in her own right. However, when the world's crisis hit, the firm she worked for soon had to let go employees soon after, herself being one of them, the reasoning in her mind? Simply because she was a woman.

Not to accept the doom and gloom of unemployment she decided to set up her own firm and one particular case would open up a whole new world for her. Although she had defended criminals successfully in the past, her big break came when she exonerated the son of a notorious organised crime figure of murder and drug charges. Her notoriety exploded through the criminal ranks and as a result, she has been kept busy and well paid ever since. She had an incredible success rate and knew all the loopholes that the legal textbooks could offer.

She had read them backwards and again, and studied just about every precedent set in the criminal court, leaving some of the most senior prosecution lawyers astounded, bewildered, and in awe, when the not guilty verdict or early dismissal of charges would come her way for clients. Her success would soon capture the attention of the Sultans MC and they used her talents regularly to help their members in the courtroom. She may have had the looks that could easily have been at home on the catwalk, nonetheless, she had a rigid hard edge to her gained from the exposure and elements to the unforgiving and violent criminal underworld that she was now embedded in.

The pleasantries between the two senior law officers and Zoe lasted a few minutes before Conroy asked Zoe if she was in the loop of the happenings in and around Graceville recently, regarding one Danny Pruitt and his partners.

'Yes, a little bit,' she said. 'I read what the papers had to say, that's all I know. Put this so-called sleepy hollow on the map, hasn't it?' She smiled.

'Maybe, but it's getting to crisis stage now, and that's why you might be able to help me,' Conroy admitted.

'I don't see how I can help, but I'll do my best, Assistant Commissioner,' Zoe replied with a smiling cynical downturn of her head.

'We're at a loose end concerning the search for the missing fugitives. All our search parties had come up with zilch. We've got men on the roads in and out of Graceville, including all the tracks and roads leading out of the mountains and still we've got nothing. It's like they've disappeared into thin air and we're getting a little desperate. The last thing I want to do is waste resources in getting the big boys up from Marlboro to take over the search then still come up empty handed, not to mention the vigilante groups and sympathisers congregating in the forest causing headaches for us,' Conroy explained.

'We are still waiting on reports from one of our Sergeants and his team from their latest trip, but if he's going to come up with no solid leads, we're at a dead end again,' Inspector Vaccaro added.

'So, what's this got to do with me?' Zoe shrugged.

'Well...' Inspector Vaccaro paused, working on a hunch. 'We think you may be able to help us.'

Zoe's eyes raised and motioned for him to continue.

'You're heading up to La Fortaleza, yes?' Vaccaro asked. Assuming there would be no other reason for her to be in town.

'That would be right. I have some clients there to brief, yes,' Zoe guardedly confirmed.

'We have suspicions that Pruitt may be there. We think it might be possible that that's the only way he's avoiding the net,' Vaccaro stated.

Zoe was shocked at the accusation. She laughed it off, explaining that the Sultans never allow outsiders into their realm.

'It's hard enough for people like me to get in, let alone four scared men on the run from the law, impossible! If they came across them, they would have warned them off, if not worse. They like to be left alone, you both know that, no, I like your imagination Inspector, but I doubt it very much,' argued Zoe.

'We just want to eliminate it from our investigation. Rumours say they may have escaped through to the city but nothing's substantiated. We just need any information that might help us move forward,' Conroy interrupted.

Zoe nodded her head. 'Okay, if I hear anything, I'll let you know. I have a carriage waiting for me. Their meeting me again soon to take me up there. I'll be back in town to catch the last train out tomorrow, so if I've got anything, you'll be the first to know, but don't hold your breath,' she light-heartedly warned.

The two thanked her for her cooperation but there were more things they needed to inform her about before she picked up her briefcase and left.

'We've spoken to the DPP (department of public prosecution) as well,' Conroy added.

'Oh yeah, about what?' Zoe asked, intrigued.

'They're willing to drop all charges against Pruitt relating to the shootings of the Devlin brothers, and anything to do with the shootout at Tambourine bridge if he hands himself in, but only if he hands himself in. The evidence is overwhelming, so he will only be cleared if he comes in and tells his side of the story to match our theories. He and his partners will have to face the manslaughter charge of officer Dukes down at the river on their escape, along with other minor charges of resisting arrest, assault and so forth, the same as his partners who are with him. In return, we will want a statement and possible testimony against Minister Johnston regarding Pringle, it will help his cause, and ours.'

'Pringle, there's one man I would gladly be on the other side to help get off the streets,' Zoe cursed with agreement from Conroy and Vaccaro.

'We are only going on a hunch here, Zoe, but if he's up there, or if someone knows where he is, be sure to relay the message. I'm sure Pruitt would like to see his family again before it's too late,' Conroy said.

'As I said, I'll see what I can do, *if*, he's up there,' Zoe promised.

Conroy and Vaccaro were counting on Zoe Valetta to see through their request as they parted company out of the courthouse. They passed a manila folder to her with the lists of charges he may face from the DPP, along with statements from the coroner. Also contained within was Inspector Vaccaro's statement regarding Minister Johnston's hand in all proceedings and signed accounts from witnesses to the shootout at Tambourine Bridge, all of which would clear Danny's name. She had come through with information that had been asked of law enforcement previously and the senior officers were hoping their instincts were correct regarding the whereabouts of Danny Pruitt and his friends.

Zoe tied up some loose ends regarding her work and with her overnight suitcase being tugged behind was soon entering the carriage for her ride up to La Fortaleza. The four-horse driven carriage arrived on time to greet her on the curb outside the courthouse. The door was opened by one of the two club members of the Sultan owned carriage. Zoe thanked him as he took her arm and helped her aboard. The interior of the carriage matched the shining timber craftsmanship of the exterior, including the two leather and sheepskin-lined bucket-style seats that sat atop for the driver and his jockey.

Inside, two bench seats sat opposite each other which could seat three adults either side. The seats had red velvet cushion for sitting and the backrest surrounded by polished oakwood timber from floor to ceiling with gleaming studded metal strips added for extra binding. Two four-foot dark stained pine sash style windows that slid open vertically adorned either side of the bench seats for passengers to open and shut at their whim.

Zoe would have hers down today for the ride up the mountain to soak up the glorious sunshine and gentle warm breeze that would waft over her face. The four inched diameter rimmed spoked wheels were of polished chrome that sat inside the bus sized pneumatic tyre's, emblazoned with the manufacturers name. Heavy duty suspension was attached to give passengers a smooth and comfortable ride wherever they travelled. It was one of only three that the Sultans handy workers had built, and they took smug joy in parading them to show off what they could do, joining the past with the present in design.

Zoe would sift through her paperwork on the one-hour journey up the bitumen highway of the Graceville pass in between taking in the view of the giant tree ferns that morphed out of the forest. She would then stretch her legs for a short time when they arrived at the Fernbank picnic ground. A beautiful little stream passed by that she always strode to the banks of to breathe in the crisp fresh air and take in the peaceful sounds of the little rapids cascading as the parakeets and rosellas sang and chirped around her. The only time she ever got to Fernbank was when she had business with the Sultans MC, and it was a stop she always made. After she felt satisfied with her short break, Zoe resumed her seat in the carriage.

They would turn left up track 24 to *La Fortaleza*, the entrance being only a short distance upwards from the picnic ground for the remaining hours travel along the gravelly dirt road before arriving at the notorious gates of the Sultan compound. Her eyes caught the manila folder that had been given to her when she left Fernbank, it laid on the far-right seat opposite her. She gently tossed it there when she hopped aboard, ignoring it, *it has nothing to do with me*, she thought.

But curiosity got the best of her and as the carriage started to make the winding incline up track 24, she opened its contents and began to read about this man called Danny Pruitt and the events that surrounded him. She was almost at the gates before she had finished perusing through all the statements when she put them away inside her carry bag which held her own files. She never thought much of it. She will never meet the accused, she will be in and out of here within 24 hours, just another tragic story to emerge from these dark days, heard it all before she sighed inside.

However, as the carriage came to a halt outside the gates of *La Fortaleza*, Zoe Valetta had no idea that it would a be a hell of lot longer than 24 hours until she escaped the whirlwind that is Danny Pruitt. Not only would she lose her heart to the man she had just read about, she would risk her whole career for him, and also her life.

Chapter 26

'Are you out of your fuckin mind? You've lost it, Danny; you've completely lost it!' Ricky blasted.

Danny had slept on his idea. He mulled and mulled over it in between his broken sleeps, and the more he planned his assault on the Armaguard, the more confident he was growing on pulling off such a daring undertaking.

The four had gathered around the wooden table that sat in the middle of the small hut that Danny had awoken when he arrived at the compound. They had all met Benny 30 minutes previously outside the gates to hand their letters over for delivery. Solomon would read through them first before he gave the okay. Security and privacy were paramount to him, he didn't want to see any words or sentences that would mention his club, let alone give away their businesses or fugitives location.

Danny had an extra envelope to pass onto Benny for Greta to receive. He sheepishly called on Solomon for a favour. He didn't know where it would get him, but he was going to try. With what Kate had written in the letters, it was obvious that Greta needed money. He knew what the bank had done, he was concerned out of his mind for her, so went to Solomon and reminded him what he said when they first met. Quote—if there is anything I can do for you, let me know—unquote.

To Danny's surprise, Solomon silently listened about the worry he had for his wife. The President told him to wait and returned with an envelope containing $1,000 in cash, a lot more than Danny had expected and needed. This would be a godsend for Greta, a $1,000 went a long way these days, it would give her some of the security she desperately needed, not that Danny was going to tell her where it came from. He was greatly appreciative and promised Solomon that he would pay him back the first chance he had, a notion that the President silently mused would never come to fruition, but the pressure was on Benny to deliver it.

In his own intimidating way, standing underneath the iconic carved out animals and insignias of the Sultan MC patch that sat above the gates, and with the peering eyes of the encaged prowling Rottweiler guard dogs looking on ready for an overdue feed, Solomon cautioned Benny that if he ever found out that the money did not get to its proper destination, he would personally come looking for him. It was a message Benny heeded, without his customary giggle and quick-witted retorts that the boys had become endeared to.

Danny had laid down his roughly drawn sketches on the table regarding his plans for the robbery. He told his three buddies to bear with him, hear him out and let him finish what he had to say, outlining all his methods and intentions. They listened to his enthusiasm for over ten minutes, relaying his fool proof plans until he completed his pitch. He looked around at his three mates, a stunned bewilderment had engulfed their faces, the following half a minute of silence was finally broken by Ricky's hostile assessment of Danny's plan.

'No, I'm not out of my fuckin mind, Ricky. In fact, I see things clearer than I ever have before, my friend,' Danny coolly said.

Barny took a deep breath.

'Danny, Danny, Danny!' he noddingly sighed.

'What?' came Danny's reply as he shrugged his shoulders with open palms.

'I don't think you want to add armed robbery to your resume, mate!'

Danny pushed; in his mind, the plan will work. 'Look around you,' he said. 'Look where we are. We need money, it the only way out of this. We can't stay here forever. It's time to make a move, it's all or nothing,' he enforced. 'These guys won't protect us forever. We're all on borrowed time, you know that as well as I do,' he said, exasperated. 'I know this will work.'

The four stood around the table, Danny replying to the cynical 'what if' and 'how' questions that the boys were bombarding him with. Some he had answers to, others he didn't. They were going back and forth until Danny decided to take a break and walk out of the hut and let the boys talk amongst themselves. He leant his back up against the pine cladding of the exterior wall, bent his right knee and rested the back of his foot up against it as he lit up a cigarette.

He took his first draw when his attention was grabbed by the entrance of a magnificent looking horse-drawn carriage entering through the gates of *La Fortaleza*. He watched curiously from a distance as it gracefully passed him, around the compacted gravel looped drive until it came to a halt further along outside the two-story manor. He then watched as one of the members disembarked from his driver's perch and opened the carriage door. Danny pulled down his sunglasses from their resting spot on his head, the midday sun was glaring, he wanted a better look at who the visitor was.

Zoe Valetta slowly hopped down off the step plate with a helping hand from the member. She was always uncomfortable arriving at the club's fortress. She didn't like the business they were in; she didn't like the way they treated people, particularly their ladies, and there wasn't many she had met that she liked on a personal level; however, her job was her job, and they always paid handsomely.

She took a second to stretch her back a little as the members laid her overnight case at her feet. She too lowered her sunglasses over her eyes then casually turned to her left and quickly noticed a lone man dressed in a black T-shirt, denim jeans and dull tan boots, leaning up against a hut looking directly back at her. The distance was too far to get a distinctive look at who it was, but she intuitively knew he wasn't a member of the Sultans MC.

A nervy flutter passed through her stomach. Her heart palpitated for moment, she couldn't restrain the sensations, she didn't know why. The only time she had felt similar nervous twinges was before she walked into the courtroom to face her adversaries on big cases.

'*Is that who I think it is. Oh my god! It can't be. No way!*' She quickly dismissed to herself, however, the photo she saw in the folders given to her sure did resemble him. Her engrossed attention at the stranger was short-lived when Maddy came bursting out of the front doors of the manor and straight into the arms of her well-loved friend. Maddy was excited to see her again, she adored her. She thought Zoe to be the most beautiful women she had ever seen, and Zoe would give her the love back that created a wonderful bond between the two that had nourished over the three short years they had known each other.

Danny banged on the door of the hut with his knuckles.

'Hey boys, come out here. I think you wanna see this,' he said.

His three buddies made their way out and stood next to him.

'Check this out,' Danny whispered as he nodded his head in the direction of where Zoe and Maddy stood.

'Holy shit! Who's she?' Harry drooled.

'Don't know. But she knows Maddy well. See, they're doing sign language and stuff,' Danny commented.

The boys were fixated on her. It had been a while since they had laid their eyes on such a gorgeous and elegant woman. The teenage schoolboy barbs began to bounce off each other at a rapid rate as they commented on her looks and anatomy, but the thing that intrigued them the most was whom she was, and what she was doing here!

Zoe held the hand of little Maddy as they walked the bluestone path to the eight-foot double doors of the Manor. She gave one last peer over her shoulder towards the hut, wondering if it *was* the Danny Pruitt that had occupied her mind since she had left the courthouse back in Graceville. Two hours after discussing club business with Solomon and his underlings around the church table, Maddy was allowed to re-join her, and with information provided by the senior members and the little one, Zoe's now anxious curiosity on who, how, why and when, the man leaning up against the hut had made La Fortaleza his temporary home, and by late-afternoon, the four fugitives were going to get their own answer about the mysterious woman also.

The boys were munching away on apples and oranges from the orchard inside the hut, still going over Danny's plan. Ricky was warming to the idea, Barny and Harry not so. They wanted no part in an armed robbery, too many things didn't make sense they were reiterating, when they were taken by surprise by the abrupt entrance of Vice President Drake.

'Stop what you're doing, boys, you have been summoned,' he announced.

'Aahhh, can you give us a few minutes?' Barny politely responded.

Danny's papers were still strewn across the table. Barny looked down at them and then to Danny.

'No I can't. Remember where you are, boys. If we say move, you move, now get your asses going,' Drake powerfully asserted.

The boys silently gazed at each other, not knowing if they should remove the papers or not, but before anyone could make a grab for them, Drake, this time louder and more impatiently, thrust the door wide open and told them to start moving.

Drake ordered two members waiting outside the hut to escort the men.

'Tell Solomon I'll be there in a minute,' he added.

He watched as the boys were marched off, waited, then re-entered the hut.

'Shit, he's going to find your plans, Danny,' Harry quietly fretted.

'No big deal, Harry. Hell, he might even be able to help us. Maybe he can take your place, since you're not interested in helping me,' Danny disparagingly replied.

Just another taste of his hurtful sarcasm. The boy's half scoffed at it before the friendly wink came from Danny's eye.

The boys were not in a position to argue the point though, the escorting members were only a meter ahead. Danny *was* worried about the outcome if Drake sussed out their plan, however, it was too late to do anything about it, and they sure weren't going to let another set of ears get any idea on what they were planning. They closed in on the entrance of the manor over the bluestone path to its front doors. Either side stood two 12-foot spartan conifers potted in large ceramic tubs.

Danny childishly played with the hanging seed nuts on the left one as they waited for the doors to open after the members gave two knocks on it. They had been there almost a week and had never been inside. It was the Presidents abode, and more importantly, doubled as the inner sanctum of the Sultans and never dared to ask for an impromptu invite. They had seen associates come and go, mainly senior patched members, but today, whether it be good or bad news for them, they were about to get a first-hand look of what lay inside.

The large cast iron latch was lifted from the inside, it matched the large ringed handles that were attached to the front. The two-inch-thick doors opened, made from the toughest oak. The four were greeted by the unfriendly face of Crow, who dismissed the two members that ushered the boys. The four of them warily traipsed onto the slated tile floor entrance of the foyer. They still had no idea what they were there for, their nerves were bouncing as they panned their eyes around. The first thing that grab their attention was the giant chandeliers that hung from the high ceiling. They were faded and dusty, just as the ceiling fans were, but they could see how brilliant and majestic it would have looked in its prime.

Ahead of them hung another set of chandeliers and fans which oversaw a large sitting room. Couches, tables and chairs were sporadically laid out in various areas, some new, some antique, and some that needed to be put in the hard rubbish. Opposite were grand old open fireplaces that were embedded into the walls, large mirrors stood resplendently above them. Floor to ceiling windows sat beyond that led out to the gardens. A balustrade arched staircase wound its way up to the second floor hugging the wall on the far-right side, it too could do with a coat of paint, along with the cornices and skirtings. The walls had framed paintings and pictures of leather clad gatherings hanging from them, mixed with portraits of people which Danny had no idea of who they were, except that they all belonged to the Sultans MC at some past point in history.

To their immediate right they could see another set of large oak double doors. Behind it laid the dining area and kitchens, but the boys would not get a look at it. Crow pointed the boys in the opposite direction, 'This way,' he grunted. Another set of oak double doors greeted them, Crow turned the ringed handle on the right one and pushed it open.

The boys walked through and were immediately taken aback. More chandeliers and fans hung from the ceiling, Harley Davidson motorcycles graced the perimeter of the large room, polished, gleaming, looking immaculate, including Solomon's much beloved customised soft tail fat boy. More pictures of anything Sultan adorned the walls. Pool tables sat near the rear of the large room, along with gaming tables.

To the right of them as they looked, a dark stained palatial looking bar made of hardwood stretched most the distance of the room with barstools lined underneath. Four sets of bay windows lined the left side that took in the view of the compound, however, at this point, the blinds had been pulled down. But what seized the boy's attention most was the grandiose table that was central to the room.

It was at least six metres in length, two metres in width, made of pristine oak, again, stained and lacquered in what seemed to be the go-to colour for the Sultans when it came to timber, dark reddish brown. Its legs were thick and intertwined with skilfully lined chiselling and etchings. Meticulously carved atop were the four animals representing the club's patch. The bear was engraved at the top end of the table where Solomon sat, to his right in the middle was the wolf, opposite the hawk, and at the near side end of the table was engraved the scorpion.

The scimitars were sleekly carved out up the middle. *CREDERE NEMO, NEGARE OMNIA* was encrypted on the edges of each side in smaller scale. Four by four-inch clear glass squares were fitted atop in front where people sat. Cup and bottle holders were shallowed out to safely rest their choice of drink. It was equal to the most amazing piece of craftsmanship the boys had seen.

'At ease boys, come take a seat,' Solomon said. He could see the look of anxiety on their faces as he gestured towards the chairs that were on offer.

The four moved around and took their seats tightly together at the scorpion end of the table, the seats were of dark wooden frame with high back rests. They began to sit when Danny, with tongue in cheek, whispered to his buddies that the Bull ant was much tougher than the scorpion from what he had seen, and *it* should be showcased their instead. Barny suggested that maybe the club was channelling the death stalker scorpion from the Middle Eastern deserts. 'I'm sure that would take care of your bull ants, Danny,' he quietly argued.

'Yeah!' Danny said surprised. 'I would like to meet that scorpion, Barny.'

Danny twirled his wedding ring with his right fingers after they had sat. It was a nervous trait he subconsciously did when he wasn't sure of his surroundings. His ring was gold with fig leaves interwoven. The underneath read, *Love Greta*. Two other rings sat on his right ring and index fingers, both gifts from his wife.

With apprehension, the boys said their hellos to the rest of the congregation. The members had their patched sleeveless vests on with assorted T-shirt's underneath. Razor was to the right and side of Solomon as they looked, Crow to his left. Next to him were two other members. Teeto was one, a clean-shaven guy with similar looks and stature to Danny with the same-coloured hazel eyes and brown hair, but longer and thicker. The boys had met him several times since they had been there, they thought him to be a nice guy. He was cleaned skinned, no visible tattoos, very odd compared to the rest of the members the boys had focused on previously.

Sitting next to Teeto was the Sergeant at Arms. They had only met him once before; he was in and out of La Fortaleza on a regular basis and never had much to do with him. Lars was his name. He was an intimidating figure, 6ft 5in in the old and the weight to go with it. He had a large mop of dangling sandy blond hair which looked to be unwashed most times that matched his scruffy full faced beard. He reminded the boys of an old Viking warrior. Also, at the table to their left sat another person, a figure which already had the attention of the visitors.

Solomon leant back in his chair and motioned towards their female guest.

'Boys, I would like you to meet Zoe Valetta. We think she might have some information that you should hear,' he disclosed.

Zoe stood from her chair with the manila folder in hand and started to sort through the papers as she began to speak. She started from the far left where the four were seated and panned across as she spoke.

'First of all, let's get this right. You're Harry Mitchell, yes?'

A quiet affirmative came from Harry.

'You're Ricky De Graaf?' she continued. Ricky nodded his head. 'And you're David Barnard?'

'Yes I am. People call me Barny,' came the friendly reply.

'And you must be Danny Pruitt,' she finished.

'At your service,' he replied.

'You look a bit different from the photos I've seen,' Zoe smiled.

Danny scraped his hand over his head. 'Must be the haircut! And the goatee beard,' he happily responded as he played with his new thickened chin whiskers.

'I prefer you clean-shaven. You look a lot more handsome,' came Zoe's quick smirking retort.

She laid her documents on the table in front of the boys and began to explain what her occupation was and the circumstances that have led to the gathering that they now found themselves in. She verbally repeated what was in the documents as the boys took turns in reading the contents after each had finished their page. Danny was first to read; they now had her undivided attention as she continued to outlay the terms that the DPP had offered in return for their surrender.

The men were reading intensely as Zoe continued to speak. She reiterated that she was only the messenger, nothing else, and that she told Inspector

Vaccaro and Assistant Commissioner Conroy that it was a long shot that she would even come across them, however, as she could see, that had all changed now and thought it her professional duty to inform them of the offer. Zoe pressed that it was entirely up to them what they did with it.

'I'm leaving back to Graceville in the morning. I can meet with the Inspector and Assistant Commissioner, so, if you agree to their terms, I can tell them on your behalf, and we will go from there. If you disagree or won't accept their offer, I can just go tell them that I never saw you and pretend that this meeting never took place,' she stated with approval from the Sultan hierarchy seated around.

The boys were mulling over the paperwork, looking at each other in between, quiet smiles crossing their faces. They could each see that Barny, Ricky and Harry were facing much lesser charges, and with a decent lawyer, their chances of not doing any time behind bars was encouraging. If they did, it would be minimal, Zoe assured them; however, Danny was a different matter, and that's when he started to question his most serious charge.

'This is all good news, and we thank you for it. It gives us peace of mind. We know the truth is out there now, but the charge of manslaughter against officer Dukes! One problem! I didn't shoot him, Ricky did,' Danny steadfastly said.

'Good onya, Danny, fuck you!' Ricky blasted as he leant forward from his chair and faced his buddy.

'Settle down, Rick, it's all good. I'm not going to lie to her. She's here to help us, mate,' Danny responded.

Ricky was almost out of his chair in anger, Danny likewise. Ricky was none too pleased that his mate would put his name in as quickly as he did. The insults continued.

Barny sighed towards Zoe, 'It's alright, you'll get used to it if you hang around long enough.'

The short outburst was halted when Solomon ordered them back into their chairs. At the same time Drake entered through the doors. He immediately headed behind the bar and grabbed several bottles of their home-made beer brew. He distributed glasses around the table. A bottle and glass each for the members, two bottles to share among their four visitors. Zoe asked for her Vodka and orange with ice. As the men poured their beers and the calm resettled, Drake took his chair to the side of Danny.

'Can I have a pen and paper, please?' Danny politely asked. 'I want to write down a few counter offers that the DPP might consider on my behalf.'

'I don't think you're in a position to negotiate, but sure, there you go,' Zoe said.

She was curious what counters Danny could possibly up come with. A flippant smile illuminated across her face as she passed the stationary over.

As Barny, Ricky and Harry took their turns asking Zoe about their concerns and possible outcomes, for the next ten minutes, Danny continued to ponder and write in between sips of his beer.

Solomon was advising the boys to take up the offer. It was better than what they could ever hope for, he urged. Danny wasn't listening, he was pretending to, but he was only listening to himself. The other members were offering their smirking advice on the do's and don'ts of prison life. Much to the amusement of themselves, however, their laughs were going to be elevated to another level once Danny had finished with his counter offers.

'There you go, Barny. Read my counter offers out,' he smugly said.

Other than Zoe, she stood as she sipped on the cool drink that Drake had just given her, the rest of the room leant back in their chairs as Danny passed his paper onto Barny and waited for what he had to say.

Barny hesitated as he perused down the page.

'Come on, read them out,' Danny impatiently asked.

Barny raised his eyebrows and took a deep breath and began to read. Danny leant back in his chair and took a longer sip out of his beer and poured another as Barny spoke.

'1...I, along with my friends, want to be cleared and pardoned of all crimes against us dating from 29 December until the present day (including the death of officer Dukes).

2...I want the titles of my property at 999 Graceville Hwy reinstated in my name.

3...I want to be compensated by the State Bank by clearing my mortgage of any debt due to illegal process of which they took it off me.

4...$10,000 compensation for all the furniture and personal items that were damaged or stolen from the illegal re-po squad raid at the above-mentioned address.

5...$10,000 compensation for pain and suffering caused to my wife by the constant harassment enforced on her by police and being forced to leave her home.

6...$10,000 compensation for the sexual assault on my wife by one Constable Steve Sandilands.

Danny interrupted, 'Forget about that one. I'll take care of that concern myself.'

Everyone turned their eyes at him. He never lifted his head, deadpanned, he took another swig out of his beer and asked his friend to continue.

Barny cleared his throat, flicked the paper straight again and persisted with his reading.

7...$1,000 compensation for loss of income while I have been forced to live like an animal in the bush.

8...$5,000 compensation for defamation of character.

The frowns and grins of the Sultans members started to rebound off one another as they continued to listen to Barny's crackled voice.

9...My children's future education to be paid for by the government for putting them through undue torment for not having their father around.

Barny's voice slowed, in broken tones, he read the last counter offer.

10...Billy and Roscoe Devlin to be charged with attempted murder, assault and trespassing, and for their family to replace our dead lamb with two new ones, one for each of my sons.'

Zoe interjected; her long earrings jangled as she shook her head in subtle disbelief. She spread her arms across the table, and along with everybody else's eyes, beamed her own magnetic pair towards Danny's.

'Excuse me if I'm wrong, but given an account of what I've read about your events. Aren't those two mentioned people dead?'

With an eerie calm, Danny responded, 'Yes, they are! But I want them to be held accountable for what they've done to me and my family. I'll be fucked if I'm going to let them rest in peace for what they did to me. I'm here because of them, and I want the world to know how much of a piece of shit they are, them and the rest of their hopeless family. Now, do you want me to sign that?' he finished as he leant back and folded his arms.

A moment of silence gripped the room. *Is this guy for real? He can't be serious*; the Sultans were thinking. They were admiring his fortitude, if not his misguided intentions. Raucous laughter started to fill the room, it echoed off the ceilings and walls. Solomon started the spontaneous laugh fest; his deep laugh was in raptures. It was the first time anyone had seen Crow smile in years. You could hear Lars grunting from ten miles away.

Razor and Drake's chest were pounding in chuckles as they shook their heads at Danny's demands. Teeto was just laughing because his superiors were. He didn't quite understand what the hell was going on as he slurped on his beer, and Zoe? Whilst she greatly admired Danny's understanding of the law, she was also silently disgusted that the men couldn't see the seriousness of the matter. As for Barny, Ricky and Harry, they were looking at each other, again questioning the mental stability of their trusted friend.

The men refilled their drinks as the laughs and mockery settled. 'Cheers,' Solomon said as he raised his glass towards Danny.

Danny knew the intelligence of the men around him and that he wouldn't be taken seriously with his demands. They hadn't survived for so long in the business they were in through pure luck. He loved the reaction though, especially the astounded look upon the experienced lawyer's face. It showed him a vulnerable side to her, and once everyone had regained their composure, he stood up from his chair and addressed her with vim and purpose.

'With all due respect, I appreciate what you're trying to do here, I really do. As you say, you're just the messenger, and I understand that. I don't speak for my friends here; they can make up their own minds on what they want to do. But I will *not* surrender to any corrupt police force or government. It says here they want me to give my side of the story before they clear me.

'You and I know that not to be true. They will throw me behind bars before I open my mouth. They're the ones who have destroyed my life, not the Devlin Brothers. They were just pawns in this game of misery we now live in, and everybody else for that that matter who does not live a privileged life. I know the system, and I do not trust it one iota. It will be at least two years before I will be even be stamped to go to trial and I will tell you now, I will not spend one second in jail. I will die before I do, and God help anyone who tries to put me there.

'I will not leave my family alone to be preyed on by vultures and become destitute. I hope you understand this. You can go back to them and say that you never saw me, and this conversation never took place, or you can give them my terms, either way, I don't give a shit. All I want to do is grab my family and head up North. If I'm to lead a life on the run, looking over my shoulders every day, then so be it, and that's where I ask you, Solomon.'

Danny turned his focus to the President, he already had his undivided attention as Solomon lifted his head a little, intrigued to know how he could help his visitor.

Danny's voice was drying as he spoke, his emotions were getting the better of him. He was trying to stay as calm as he continued.

'You and your club have been a lifesaver to me, to all of us! We don't know where we would be if you didn't take us in. We are in your debt for life. We can never repay the generosity you've given us, but all I ask of you is to give me two more weeks of shelter. Two more weeks to sort my shit out and then I will be out of your hair. We will lay low as we possibly can and once we leave, your name, and anything else Sultans will never be spoken out of our mouths, that is my word. Two more weeks, that's all I ask.'

Danny resumed his seat. Silence gripped the room as stares crossed amongst the Sultans, waiting for a response from their President. Harry bowed his head into his lap, Ricky and Barny stared up at the ceiling not knowing what would come next while Danny kept his unbroken watch on Solomon, hoping he would respect the conviction and frankness in his words.

'Alright,' Solomon paused. 'Two weeks, then we'll take it from there. All those in favour!'

A collective 'aye' echoed around the table, Crow being the last. Solomon's gavel came crunching down.

The boys remained in their seats, unsure of the protocol when it came to the inner sanctum meetings of the MC, they didn't want to show any disrespect so waited. Solomon would dismiss them within a few minutes to continue with their meeting, without the company of the Graceville four.

The four made their way out of the manor and were making tracks towards the hut, hoping that Drake didn't pay to close attention to the papers left behind. Not much was said between them until Barny flippantly told Danny how impressed he was with his speech. He cited that he had missed his calling, and would not be out of place inside parliament, or the pulpit of a church congregation, a suggestion that sent light chuckles amongst them.

They approached the hut, Ricky opened the door and was first to enter, the other three rushed in behind him. The chairs and table seemed to be untouched, however, Danny's drawings and plans were missing. A collective sigh of fretting expletives filled the small room.

'Shit! What do we do now?' Harry gulped.

A gap of silence ensued until Barny spoke, 'Nothing, we wait.'

'Barny's right. We do nothing. We wait until he comes to us. When and if that happens, I'll explain it. As I said, he might want to join us,' quipped Danny.

Once again, the boys thought him to be delusional.

It had been a long day already for the four. They would again bounce off their thoughts amongst each other over Danny's plan, sometimes heated, other times rational, however, being around each other for a time was getting on their nerves once more. They had been living out of each other's pockets since their experience began. They knew the smell of each other's sweat, the smell of the not too pleasant aroma that was released from each other's bowels. Their annoying little habits and the smell of their feet were entrenched in their memory, so if they had a chance of getting a break from one another while they were inside the compound, they would take it.

They agreed to talk again tomorrow and spent the rest of the evening alone. They ate dinner at different times at the open BBQ, keeping to themselves afterwards. Harry lying in his tent pondering and lamenting. He was missing his family terribly and wondering how he could get out of this mess. The talk of armed robbery, the violence he had seen, and now being entrenched in the bosom of an outlaw MC was becoming way too overwhelming for him.

Barny passed the time reading away at his bible, surmising and answering the many the questions that the good book threw at him, while Ricky made his way to the work sheds to blow some more cocaine and feverishly get to work helping two of the prospect members with their furniture making. As for Danny, he was about to get an unexpected enchanting twist to the evening, one he never saw coming.

There was still a good hour of sunlight left in the day as he sat on a deck chair underneath one of the gumtrees that towered over the compound near where his tent lies. He had already devoured his hot can of chunky beef soup and was wiping his lips clean from his desert, a platter of assorted fruits. He was about to grab his hand line and try a bit of fishing down at the river when in the distance, he noticed Zoe and Maddy having what looked like to be fun catch up with each other underneath one of the majestic elm trees.

There was lots of laughter and animation from both as he watched from afar until the alert of eyes of little Maddy observed him sitting alone. She left Zoe at the park bench and raced over to him. She grabbed him by the arm. Danny was hesitant, but Maddy was joyfully incessant and won the little tug of war. She then led her life saver towards the park bench where Zoe was freely watching on, and before the two adults knew it, they were uncomfortably sitting opposite each other as an awkward moment ensued.

They both concentrated their attentions at Maddy, playfully going along with her fun-loving antics until Zoe broke the uneasy lull by thanking him for saving Maddy's life. She explained that both her little friend and Solomon had filled her in on the near tragedy and expressed that she too was grateful for his heroics, adding she now knew what a misplaced fugitive was doing inside *La Fortaleza*.

Danny watched on admirably as the two communicated. Some sign language he understood from the learnings Maddy had taught him in the short time he was there, but most of it was beyond him. He just went by the smiles and expressions that radiated off their beautiful faces. It wasn't long before Maddy was on her little pushbike and riding off around them. It was Zoe's cue to make sure Danny was clear on all his options, legally.

Her charm and confidence were to the fore as she explained that a lawyer of her ilk and experience would have no trouble in putting enough doubt into a jury that he never pulled the trigger on Officer Dukes. She pointed out that it would be far better waiting two years behind bars than enduring a lifetime on the run, adding that the two years he adamantly thought he would have to spend in remand could be a lot less, as she would do everything in her power to fast track him through the courts.

Danny put a halt to the discussion by raising his hand. He then leant forward and flirtatiously asked, 'Are you saying you want to represent me, Miss Valetta? We only just met, I *am* humbled and honoured.'

Zoe could feel herself blushing. *What is it about this man?* she was silently asking herself. Even when Maddy was leading him to the bench they were sitting on, flutters were trembling in her stomach. The more she eyed and conversed with him, the more she was feeling nervy and skittish.

Zoe was a single woman, married to her job, no time for serious relationships. She'd had a few meaningful ones before, engaged at a young age with one, but they never ended pleasant for her.

Danny relieved the awkward moment; he could see he had caught her off guard. 'I could never afford you anyway,' he said.

'Don't worry, I'll do it pro-bono,' Zoe revealed in her own flirtatious tone.

Danny thanked her for the generosity and politely said that she would never have to worry about it. Zoe was persistent though. She spoke for next 20 minutes on all things legal that could help his cause, but Danny's paranoid and distrustful brain was telling him not to trust her. He had been let down too much in recent times, why should she be any different. The Sultans motto of trust no one, deny all (credere nemo, negare omnia) was at the forefront of his mind and couldn't understand the care and interest she was showing in him.

It was getting towards dusk when Teeto joined them at the outdoor table to say that Solomon wanted his daughter inside the Manor. Zoe liked Teeto, as the boys did. She helped him out with literacy skills when she could, teaching him to read and write and found him a genuine nice man. He was different to the rest she would explain to Danny when he left them shortly afterwards.

He was a loner, no next of kin, except for a four-year-old son that resulted from a one-night stand. The mother refused to give Teeto any access to him, fearing the company he kept would have a bad influence on the rearing of the child. She lived somewhere in Graceville, but Teeto accepted that he was never going to be a proper father so never hassled her and had no contact with the child whatsoever.

Teeto didn't even know his own real name. He never had a proper home, no identification cards, no license, no birth certificate, and drifted through life like so many did these days. The electronic way of tracking people's business and history had all but been diminished and for a person such as Teeto, who had been shunted from foster home to foster home until he found the streets in his early teenage years, he became one of the many that lived today, invisible and unknown.

Solomon took him in as a favour to one of his ex-lady friends and after a while, took a liking to him and invited him into the inner sanctum of the Sultans. He worked hard, did what he was told, kept his mouth closed and was loyal to the club and would become a faithful ally of Drake, who kept a big brother eye over him.

Danny kept their conversation on Solomon. He was intrigued to know more about this leader of men, and Zoe seemed to be in the know, but what she was about to say would make him think twice about the man he was respecting.

'He seems a decent bloke deep down,' he commented.

She panned her eyes around the surroundings, not wanting any hidden ears to hear what she had to say. No one was around. Most of the men had left on horseback for a gathering down in Graceville. Solomon had a lady friend who had arrived not long before to keep him company. The Vice Presidents had left to be with their wives back in Graceville and the others that were left were keeping to themselves in their assorted tents and huts. Other than the men who manned the gates, *La Fortaleza* was as quiet it had been for some time.

'Don't let him deceive you,' she cautioned.

'What's that supposed to mean?' Danny asked.

'I know what he is, believe me. He's probably looking at us right now from inside the manor. You're only here because you saved his daughter. She's the only thing he loves in this world, he fuckin hates everything else. But he likes and respects you, Danny Pruitt, I heard him say so when you left the meeting. But let me tell you this…' she sternly said, 'you don't want to double-cross him or piss him off in any way. He will turn on you in an instant. I know what he and his club have done to people and it's not nice. He scares the shit out of me, and so does this place, there's nothing I like about it.'

'So why are you here then, why do you help them?' Danny inquired.

'It's not as easy as that,' she mocked.

Her tone and demeanour changed. Her eyes deepened and fixed on Danny's. She paused as her voice took a quieter tone.

'Make no mistake, this club is a ruthless criminal organisation. They have connections everywhere. You see, I know too much! Their guns, their drugs, their buyers and sellers, and everything else they have their fingers in. I never wanted to know, I never asked, but I'm caught up in their web now and wouldn't dare risk opting out on them. If I did, I would become a threat, and then they would do what they do best, nullify it. I would disappear like all the rest before me,' she confided. 'So be careful what you wish for.'

Her jade green eyes were intensifying as she stood from her bench seat.

'Sometimes it's a case of better the devil you know, and you don't want to get involved with this one. I don't know why you want two more weeks here, that's none of my business, but if I were you and your friends, I would seriously consider taking up the DPP'S offer, because if you stay here any longer, it's only a matter of time before the club will turn on you. You're an outsider, remember that, and trust me when I say, it's only a matter of time before the authorities come storming through those gates.'

Danny listened with intent. He could see that her fears were genuine and thanked her for her openness and honesty. The hard conversation halted as Maddy again approached them at the table to say her goodnights. Danny reciprocated her engaging hug then watched as Zoe led her away towards the Manor.

Danny thought their little liaison was over but before he stood, Zoe turned and hesitantly asked if they wanted to continue their conversation after she had tied up things inside.

'Sure, why not?' agreed Danny.

He wanted to know everything he could that might concern him. Information is power, maybe he could use some of it down the track. If she wanted to vent her sentiments to him, then so be it. Anyways, he couldn't think of a better way to spend the evening than with a gorgeous-looking woman, even it was for conversation only.

'Great. I'll meet you down near the stables at the rotunda. I'll be about half an hour, see you then.' She smiled.

Danny slowly wandered down towards the rotunda. He lit up a cigarette as he strolled, taking in everything that Zoe had confided in him. He walked down the gravel track adjacent to the Manor and then beyond, passing the open work sheds and storage garages to his left.

Looking beyond them was where his own tent lay underneath assorted gum trees and protected by the long metal poled iron covered annex. The road came to a fork, to the left it would take him down towards the plantation. He would veer to the right, passing the stables then onto the rotunda. By the time Zoe joined him again, the sun had set and the last of the twilight was dying.

The filtered lights of the compound gave enough light to show her the way where Danny was waiting. The first thing he noticed was she had changed out of her business attire. She was now in casual washed denim pants, strapped just below the knee and wore a tight-fitting maroon coloured cotton top, almost matching the colour of her hair. It was dual strapped over her shoulders which showed off a little butterfly tattoo above her right breast.

As she lit the glass covered candles inside the rotunda, her mini crystal chandelier earrings dangled as she moved. Her dark leather sandals gave her protection from the rough gravel underneath her feet when she approached.

She lifted the lid of the ice cooler that she had bought with her and presented Danny with three bottles of home brew beer and a bottle of Jack Daniels whiskey, along with a bottle of wine for herself. She then pulled out two bags of flavoured potato chips and laid them on the wooden bench.

Danny was silently impressed and gestured so. He did the gentlemanly thing and poured her wine before he filled his own beer mug.

'Are we on a date, stranger?' he cheekily questioned.

'Call it what you want. It's Friday night and I need a drink,' Zoe jested.

'Here's to life and sanity while we still have it,' she pessimistically said as they charged their glasses.

The unplanned encounter would start off a little timid. She apologised for her brash comments earlier. She didn't even know why she would tell him such things she exasperated. Danny brushed off her concerns, telling her that it was probably what he needed to hear as it was his deep-down feelings regarding the club anyhow. The small talk gained momentum as the alcohol slowly settled in and under the warm rising moonlight, they would gradually let their guards down and learn more about one another as they happily conversed.

They would discuss all things life, sometimes with laughs, sometimes holding back sorrowful tears, from their fears and dreams, their failures and triumphs, to their faults and loves. Zoe had never opened to anyone the way she had tonight, and to do it to a man she had only met earlier in day was hard for her to fathom. It was also an unexpected counselling and venting session for Danny. He listened as she spoke wisely and passionately. He thanked her for it, which in turn was reciprocated. Even at times when his concentration would wane, just to take in her stunning looks and the musky exotic scent of her perfume that would waft under his nostrils on the warm mountain breeze, it was enough therapy for him to put his mind and body at rest for a while.

It was 1.00 am by the time they emptied the bottles and gave each other a tentative thank-you embrace to end the night. Their eyes locked as they separated, the amorous stare and near kiss only broken by the screeching cry of a wild animal close by. They left the rotunda together and parted ways at the top of the drive. Zoe made her way inside the manor, tip toeing her way upstairs to her bedroom, trying not to disturb Maddy who was in the bedroom opposite. She pulled the drapes back on her window, switched her lamp off and laid her head down on the pillow and stared into the clear starry night, restlessly engrossed in her belief that she may have just finally met her long-lost soul mate, married or not!

Danny entered his tent to lay his own head down, naively thinking that Zoe was just a great chick, who in her own ways had just as many problems and conflicts as he did. He was certain that he had gained an ally in the mysterious attractive lawyer and was happy that he had met her. His mind once again turned to Greta and his sons, but he would quickly nod off and get his first deep unbroken sleep since his torment began.

Chapter 27

'Knock knock,' Kate's knuckles brushed on the door.

'Oh, hi Kate. Come in,' Greta said.

'Are you alone?' Kate asked.

'Yeah, just me and the boys. Just having breakfast. What's up?' Greta asked, concerned at Kate's reception.

'Good! Grab your boys. You need to come to my place,' Kate forcefully pleaded.

'What's going on?

'I've got important news on Danny. I don't want to explain it here. Follow me home,' she said with haste.

With a tidal wave of apprehension, Greta excitedly saddled up her horse. Daniel and Darcy would keep up on their pushbikes for the twenty-minute journey though the side streets of Graceville until they arrived at Kate's modest three-bedroom weatherboard abode on the town's eastern fringe. Kate was lucky, through hard work and wise money handling, Ryan and she owned their house outright before the crisis hit at its hardest.

Kate was doing her best while she was alone as Ryan had yet to return from their abrupt separation and with the double concern of her brother's circumstances was feeling the loneliness the previous night. However, her mini depression was to be interrupted by an unexpected visitor with information that would put her marital issues to the back of her mind.

Greta arrived ten minutes after Kate, tethering her horse to the railings in the front yard, she was duly rushed inside the house by her sister-in-law. Kate laid some toys out for the children to play with in the loungeroom then led Greta though her kitchen then onto the enclosed veranda to meet her guest. As soon as she saw who was standing there, she felt certain it could only be good news.

Benny had arrived at Kate's late last night. He expected to meet Greta at Corey and Sarah's or wait for Greta to exit the house after he had posted the letters for Ricky, Barny and Harry. He kept a secretive eye on proceedings from a distance and as night fell was almost ready to knock on the door when Inspector Vaccaro randomly arrived with two uniformed constables to update Greta on the investigations concerning her husband.

Benny covertly waited, but as time passed, he knew his opportunity was lapsing and after marking time for almost two hours decided best to postpone his surprise rendezvous with Greta. Despite only having met Kate on the one occasion at Damien's property, on the counsel of Danny, Benny took the chance that she would take him in without any rebellion. Kate would stay up to the wee hours as she listened to Benny entrust her with the adventures of her escapee brother and couldn't wait to deliver the news to his distraught wife.

Greta immediately embraced Benny with an expressive squeeze, already knowing what he had done for her husband and expressed her gratitude instantly. Benny laughed it off. 'Ah, no big deal,' he smiled.

Greta demonstrated her usual calm and eloquence, traits that Benny was accustomed to as she led him to the pair of old cane chairs that sat against the exterior wall underneath the kitchen windowsill. She expressed how wonderful it was to see him again and although she was bursting inside, she would slowly and patiently ask him what he knows.

Benny handed over the envelope that contained Danny's letter as he spoke of how her husband was faring. Greta sat quietly, intense, as she read through the missives. Kate re-joined them with a fresh brew of coffee heated over the briquette fired stove.

Greta read, and read, all four pages, then again, and by the time she had folded the last page and bundled them back into the envelope she was feeling uncertain by its contents. She needed more. More information to satisfy her worry and distress that was not forthcoming in Danny's writings. In the previous letters she felt the emotion, the pain and burden in his words, but not these missives. These words were more calculated, assured, no mention of regret or responsibility on the lives that had been lost, no mention of how he has survived over the missing weeks, and it gave her a feeling of disquiet.

Danny had assured his wife that his health was fine. He once again expressed his love for her, along with the sorrow that he had caused her, but kept reiterating that he will find a way out for them both. You must keep the faith he sternly cited in the best way he could in writing, to hold strong and never give up on him. He wrote about a plan he had in motion and everything would be ok, that he would let her know when the time was right to act upon his instructions.

However, there was not a word of where he was, who he was with or what he had been doing to survive in the mountains, a concern that grasped Greta immediately. The words of Inspector Vaccaro were replaying on her mind from the previous night about how desperate men change for the worse the longer they remain on the run.

Greta sat quietly, pondering, looking around at both Benny and Kate when Benny handed her another envelope with the $1,000 cash inside.

'Where did you get this?' Greta gasped as she flicked through the money.

'Danny asked me to give it to you. He knows what the bank did. It's to hold you over for a while, he told me to tell you,' Benny informed.

'How does he know what the bank did?' Greta snapped back.

'I'm pretty sure he knows everything that's happening with you and the boys,' Benny smiled smugly, expecting an appreciative acceptance from Greta, but her reaction was the opposite.

'How?' she chastised.

Benny went silent, his shoulders slumped. 'Bush telegraph?' he quirked. The last thing he wanted to do was upset Greta in any way. He respected her greatly, he didn't know what to say as his eyes inadvertently cornered towards Kate.

'Anything you might want to fill me in on?' Greta asked her.

'He has to know what's going on, Greta,' Kate said firmly, explaining what she wrote in the letters that Benny delivered.

Greta shook her head and sighed in disgust. She repeated her feelings about Danny receiving any information that would upset him, however, she would quickly resign herself to the fact that it was all too late now for her to make a stand. The damage has already been done she contritely said, as Kate offered hollowed apologies.

Greta sat still in her seat, leant forward with the cash envelope and waved it in front of Benny. 'So, tell me where he got this from?' she asked.

Before Benny could come up with a convincing story, Greta interrupted, 'Don't worry, I got a pretty fair idea. He got it from that biker gang hidden up in the mountains, didn't he? That's why he hasn't been caught yet, isn't it? They're hiding him, aren't they?

Benny was expressionless. How does she know?

'What are you talking about, Greta?' Kate chimed in, needing clarification on what Greta was insinuating. Kate had no idea where Danny *was*, Benny had kept it secret from her at his request, only saying to Kate that he was hopping from campsite to campsite to stay a step ahead of his pursuers. Greta was thinking the worst. All the warnings from the meeting with the Inspector were racing through her mind. Vaccaro did not lie when asked the question about jail time. What happened from now on depended greatly on how much time it would be, but nevertheless, he would be doing time he regretfully informed.

'Oh my god,' she lamented quietly. One thing being a wanted criminal on the run, but to associate with an outlaw MC while evading them! There is no turning back for him now Greta mourned inside. She prayed on her pillow last night that he would receive the DPP offer and take it before it was too late. She knew jail time would kill her husband inside, but at least they would be together again, whether it be 5 years, 10 years or 20 years, she didn't care, she would wait.

In her vulnerable moments, she almost confessed to Vaccaro everything she knew about her husband, including the letters that she had received. She was at a loss, unable to fathom how to help her husband and what was right or wrong regarding his welfare.

She inhaled some deep breaths, gathered herself again and stood from her chair. She took a sip out of her hot tea and calmly explained to Kate and Benny about the visit by the Inspector last night. He revealed that they were running out of time and patience and warned it may be taken out of his hands if her husband was not bought into custody soon. The Inspector confided his suspicions on where her husband may be located, including the offer from the DPP that Zoe Valetta had been asked to forward onto to him if his hunch was proved to be correct.

Greta flicked her wind-swept hair back to the side of her forehead, her dark eyeliner intensified her deep brown eyes, she focused, then calmly challenged, 'Is that where he is Benny, with these Sultans, is that where he is?'

Benny couldn't speak. He started to bite on his lips. He looked in all directions except into Greta's. He didn't want to lie to her. He held her in the highest esteem, but he didn't want to betray Danny, however, his silence was enough to convince Greta thoroughly. She gently laid her right hand on his shoulder and looked him the eye. 'You don't have answer me, Benny, it's okay, I'll take that as a yes.'

Now Kate was worried. If it were true that Danny was with the Sultans MC, he could be in a world of trouble she nervously conveyed. Kate had small links to outlaw motorcycle gangs from her early adult life. She knew partners of existing members; she had dated one herself before she had met Ryan and knew first-hand the lifestyle and how ruthless they could be to outsiders.

She bared her concerns, but before Kate could put anymore dreaded thoughts into Greta's already fearful mind, Benny recounted in detail the time when he met both Drake and Razor at the logging coup and made it be known that Danny was in no way out of his comfort zone. He confidently expressed that according to his judgement, the alliance and dual respect he had with the two Vice Presidents seemed to be already set in stone, not to mention the free rein he had been given inside the compound by the President himself.

'The President! What do you mean, free rein?' Kate loudly quizzed.

'He saved his little daughter, twice,' Benny said.

Greta listened, astounded and proud, as Benny described Danny's heroics in every detail that had been passed onto him by the men. She softly took her seat again in the cane chair and bowed her head between her hands and perused over Danny's letter again. Kate persisted at Benny, trying to coax more information out of him; however, Benny could only give so much. He was not allowed inside the gates of la Fortaleza and duly stated that he didn't know what went on inside.

They were bouncing off each other, Kate forthright and aggressive, Benny polite and respectful, when Greta absorbed their attention. She gave off a muffled chortle and nodded her head with a wry smile as she finished reading over Danny's writings again, focusing on the part about his secretive plan. His words keep the faith were glaring back at her. Her demeanour was changing. She had to keep her hopes up, and was truly asking herself who is my husband? The man they say he would become or already is, or the man that she knows. The one that she has loved with, lived with, and shared with.

She thought about it more. If he's got protection, that's only good news, isn't it? Greta knew how Danny can win over anyone, in any circumstances, whether it be through his courage, his intelligence, his humour, or through his protective personality. That's why she loved him, that's how he protected her, that's how he made her feel safe always, and that's what she craved for most right now. Although angry, frustrated, and fearful, the undying admiration she had for her husband was now giving hope to her belief that maybe, just maybe, his writings had justification.

As his words sank deeper and deeper into her mind, she now knew that Danny was not going to walk away from his ideals and intentions, and if that was the case, Greta soberly grasped she had one choice only, and that was to walk with him.

Her resilience was stiffening. She stood once more and asked Benny if he or Danny knew anything about the DPP offer and the woman lawyer.

'I know nothing of that,' he said. 'If Danny knew, I'm sure he would have mentioned it when he passed the letters onto me.'

Greta believed him. She reassured that her reply won't divulge where she got the information from, clearing Benny's obvious conscious of any feelings of disloyalty towards Danny. She asked how much time he had before he left.

'I wanna be back up there before dark. I need time to get supplies from town before I leave. So, I'll give you time to write your reply. I'll hang around and have another cup of Kate's delicious tea,' a smiling Benny said.

Greta busily borrowed pen and paper from Kate, sat at her kitchen table and began to write. Moments in, she sarcastically turned to Kate who was standing at her shoulder and asked if there was anything she would like to add.

'No, it's all yours,' was her humbled response.

It was tough for Greta to put her feelings down on paper, so many questions, so many emotions. She decided it best to only express how she and his boys were coping, concentrating on what he would want to hear, to give him assurance and remind him that she is stoic girl, and only worry about himself. Within the hour, Greta had finished her reply, the last page giving her husband her unconditional love and that she will stand by whatever decisions he had to make.

It was late morning by the time Benny left the ladies, Greta's letter safely hidden in a leather pouch inside his saddle bag. He looked around furtively to see if Greta's police watch had been abandoned as promised by the Inspector and was confident that he had kept his word. Benny stealthily made his way into the main street of Graceville, tethering his horse to a covered stable bay below the main street at the disused car park. He walked up the alley way between shops to the hustle and bustle of the main street. With a dark baseball cap and sunglasses and wearing a soft brown shirt and denim jeans, he lost himself amongst the peoples, trying to be incognito, but noticeably seeing the main hub of town was busier than usual for a Saturday morning.

In between stocking up on some needed supplies from various shops that he discreetly confiscated, he panned his attentive eyes over the works which were being attended to by shire employed workers. There were Crane trucks attending power poles and electricity lines through the main section of town. Workers receiving animated accolades by pedestrians walking by, finally seeing progress being made on Government promises. Vans and other smaller trucks were sporadically making their way through the main street, dodging, weaving, hooting, and beeping as they passed rickshaw, horse and pushbike riders going about their Saturday morning business.

The traffic lights at the main intersection were operational, townsfolk joyfully discussing seeing the green, amber and red lights for the first time in years. He was seeing first-hand how the government's pledge to get infrastructure up and running as soon as possible was coming to fruition. People were excited as civil works started to gain momentum. Benny did his best to keep to himself, taking in everything around him, from what he could see, to what he could hear, and was soon off out of town to make his way back into the surrounding mountains.

A few kilometres out, he could see a mounted police presence with two patrol vehicles as he trekked his way out of town further East. A roadblock was in place in the distance before the openness of the highway would give way to the winding and bending forest engulfing Graceville pass, ironically, only 500 meters past the former Pruitt's property. He could see Sultan MC members were to the fore, huddled together at the edge of the roadblock on a wayside stop, club patches distinctly noticeable. Horses, wagons, carts, and men were grouped together as police executed a search and seize operation for illegal guns and drugs, the first sign that law enforcement was taking a different approach without Minister Johnston in charge of business.

Benny didn't know exactly what was going on at the roadblock, it didn't concern him, he was not going to pass through it anyway and so did what he does best, disappear unnoticed. He turned down a side street, through vacant properties, across some parklands, moving like a ghost until he would find a suitable track down on the other side of the Watkins River that would take him high up into the ranges. If the tracks situated throughout the base of the rising mountains were occupied by police on horseback, or just civilians out for the day, it didn't worry him. He would take his horse bush until he came across another.

No one knew these parts like Benny, no search party was going to bother him. He was on a mission, he enjoyed it. It gave him some excitement in his life. He loved his skills being tested and what better way to exert them than helping his fugitive friend and by nightfall he would be arriving at the gates of *La Fortaleza* to hand over Greta's missive to his mate.

As Greta and her sons casually made their way back to their temporary home, she pondered over the letter she had written and mulled over thoughts in her mind. Sometimes smiling that her husband was ok, and all would work out for them both, other times feeling gloom and sorrow on what may lie ahead. *Did I miss something he should know? Did I express my feelings well enough? Did I do the right thing supporting him? Maybe I should have made him take the offer*, her confused mind battled. But one thing she took great solace from was that she had proof that her husband was alive and well, not lying in the bush somewhere, alone, maimed or dead, thoughts that had more than once infiltrated her vulnerable mind over the previous week. She willed herself for only positive thoughts as she entered through the door with her sons to take a seat in the lounge next to Sarah who had arrived back home. She asked where Greta had been.

'Nowhere, just out to get some fresh air,' she lied. Her trust had been lost. No one would know any more news on her husband.

Danny ensured his letter portrayed confidence and assurance in what he was doing, but as the hours past during this day, he was going to have to face knew battles that would again test his inner being on more than one front, and one of them would come from his closest ally.

Chapter 28

The warm early morning sun silhouetted over the compound as Danny met up with Zoe for breakfast. They returned to the rotunda enjoying their bacon and eggs which Danny had cooked on the nearby BBQ plate. Zoe supplied the fruit, sliced apples and a punnet of strawberries washed down with freshly squeezed orange juice. The conversation flowed easily between them, smiling and laughing on topics of no real relevance. Danny was completely ignorant of the fact that he was pushing buttons within Zoe.

He was not looking for female company, far from it. He reckoned he was married to the most beautiful and intelligent women on the planet, no reason for infidelity or harmless hanky panky. He was just being who he was, completely oblivious to the feelings that were building in Zoe from the first time they met the previous day. He didn't even notice he was bringing out the inner teenager from the hardened professional and the emotions that Zoe was feeling last night as she fell asleep were only increasing as she spent more time with him.

The moment had come for Zoe to leave *La Fortaleza*, her work was done and the carriage was waiting for the trip back down to Graceville so she could board the train to the city. Before departing the compound however, she could not leave without posing the question again to Danny about the DPP offer. Zoe stressed that it was a good deal to take and pleaded again for him to change his mind.

'Thanks, but no thanks,' Danny respectfully said. 'Can't do it. As I've said to you, I will not spend a day in jail. Anyway, I have a plan. I'll be alright.'

'So you've said. Well, it better be a good plan, Danny Pruitt, because if you spend any more time with these people, there's only one path you'll head down,' Zoe strongly advised.

Her demeanour changed, she stepped in closer and lowered her voice, her crystal-studded earrings dangled whenever her head made the slightest move. 'I know you think Solomon is a good bloke, but he doesn't give a fuck about you or your friends. He will turn on you in an instant if it suits him. Don't trust him. Get out of here as soon as you can, or you will be caught up in their whirlwind of madness, and believe me, it's coming, and that's a warning, not an assumption.'

Zoe was forthright. She wanted the best outcome for both Danny and his partners, and to her, the legal way was the only light at the end of the tunnel for them. She tried her hardest, and although Danny could see genuine concern in those lucent green eyes of hers, which seemed to intensify the more serious she became, his mind was made up, which in turn disturbed her immensely.

'I will advise the Inspector and Assistant Commissioner that I never laid eyes on you, or you were anywhere near Sultan territory, for that matter,' Zoe said as she began to depart.

'Thank you,' said Danny gratefully.

She gave him a quick embrace, turning her head so she wouldn't make eye contact, stepped up and entered the carriage and in an instant was on her way out of the compound. Although it had been less than 24 hours, the connection she felt inside towards Danny seemed like a lifetime, and she was sadly wondering if it would be the last she would ever see of him.

Danny watched as the dual horse carriage exited the gates. He lit up a cigarette, not thinking too much of the time he had just spent with her, except surmising that she would make a good friend for Greta, they would get on famously he thought. Both intelligent, both professionals, similar interests, yeah, they would make great friends he was sure, and although he was grateful for Zoe's advice and company, he acknowledged it was probably the one and only time they would ever cross paths.

Danny made himself comfortable on a deck chair underneath the large gum tree near where his tent lay. He adjusted a log to relax his feet upon and started to read a borrowed newspaper which had arrived with members who had been coming through the gates at regular intervals as the morning grew. For the next half hour, in between perusing over the paper and exercising his brain with the crosswords and puzzles, he watched as the compound became more populated.

Some he knew the names and faces of, Drake and Razor being two of them, others he had never seen before as they sporadically arrived. Some would give a respectful nod when they passed, others would stare blankly at their temporary boarder. Danny didn't think much of it, it's their property, none of his business really, but before he could ponder deeper why all of a sudden the previous peace of *La Fortaleza* was being disturbed, Barny appeared by his side.

He dragged an adjacent chair and sidled up next to Danny. 'What do you think is going on?' he asked.

Danny lit up another cigarette, inhaled deeply, then blew the smoke out above his head. 'No idea, mate,' he responded.

A quiet minute passed as both looked out across the compound until Danny noticed that Barny was too silent by his reckoning. He looked him up and down, trying humorously to get his attention and could clearly see that Barny had things on his mind.

'What's going on, mate, something up?' he asked.

'I need to talk to you,' came the serious reply.

Danny shuffled his chair around to face him as Barny leant forward on his.

'Well, what's going on?' urged Danny.

'It's Harry. He wants to leave,' Barny nervously confided.

'Yeah. Shit! Okay! Whatever he wants to do,' Danny shrugged.

'He's over it, mate. He's a nervous wreck. All this stuff, it's not him. He's depressed, not sleeping, me and Ricky think he's about to go over the edge,' Barny added.

'All good. As I said, he can go anytime he wants.'

Barny was surprised at Danny's flippant reaction. To him, it seemed he didn't care about how Harry was feeling. He was at his insensitive best. Danny had no time when it came to the talk of men's mental health. These were tough times for all concerned, deal with it was his motto. Depression and suicide were almost epidemic amongst young to middle aged men in these times, his friend Tom being an example, however, Danny had no time to listen to other men's problems. It wasn't his greatest forte, to have men crying on his shoulders and avoided any conversation to the like.

Danny could see the bewilderment on his friend's face.

'What!' He gestured vigorously. 'I am no one's master, Barny. As I am no one's slave. He doesn't need my permission if he wants to go. He's a big boy, if he wants to go, go. No skin off my nose,' he growled.

'You've got no idea, have you?' Barny frustratingly questioned.

Danny leant back in his deck chair, not sure where Barny was heading with the previous comment. 'Enlighten me,' he said.

'He looks up to you, Danny,' Barny stressed. 'He holds you up on a pedestal. He needs your blessing, to make him feel that he's not abandoning you. He doesn't want you to think he's a coward. He won't go unless you tell him it's okay to go, you need to put him at ease.'

Danny was a little taken aback. Sure, it was a boost to his ego to think that Harry would have that much respect for him, but still, he was surprised that he had that much influence on those around him. Barny decided to push the situation further, and with his calm candidness started to explain his own theories as to why his friend held him in high regard.

'I'm going to be honest with you, Danny. Because deep down, I know you believe you have it over people, not just Harry. You do have an energy about you, dude, you always have,' Barny stated.

Danny laughed. Then mocked, 'Yep, I'm some sort of champion patron, aren't I, Barny?'

'Well, I wouldn't go as far as that, my friend, but I must say, divine intervention has been bestowed on you on more than one occasion, Danny.'

Barny paused for a moment. He wanted Danny to take him seriously, to take in what he was saying so he could understand more of how he saw things. He continued.

'Nothing ever seems to happen to you compared to others in the same circumstances. Look what's happened over the last few weeks. People have died, mate, but you! and us! not a scratch, we've all survived. It seems that anyone or anything that comes after you is cursed. You have allies everywhere, Damien, Benny, those two Vice Presidents. You enter the territory of the most feared outlaw club in the country, so what happens? You save the life of the President's daughter and get immediate respect and a haven so no one can touch you.'

Barny was getting more animated as he continued, his hands gesturing as he ousted his inner thoughts. Danny sat back taking it all in, smugly smiling on how interesting Barny's descriptive thesis on him was transpiring.

'Look at Zoe, that lawyer lady.'

'What about her?' Danny asked.

'I know you were with her last night. I'm not saying anything happened, I know how much you love Greta, but this morning! I saw the way she looks at you, she's fallen in love with you within 24 hours,' he declared.

'I don't think so,' Danny scoffed.

'She just another example of how people are drawn to you, mate,' Barny continued 'You see! There's something about you, Danny, you're like a disease. Once people let you in, they can't escape you. Something from above likes to protect you, mate, I could go on with other examples if you want,' he boasted cheekily.

'I don't see myself as someone who the lord looks over Barny. I think you're taking your faith a little too far,' Danny smirkingly replied.' If that were the case, I wouldn't be in the almighty pile of shit that I'm in, hey!'

He thanked him for his honesty but suggested it was folly to think it was anything else but pure luck, not some kind of divine intervention that have helped them survive so far and further added they were going to have to rely on a lot more luck if they were get out of their situation.

They both stood to their feet, Danny lit another cigarette and asked if he and Ricky wanted the same as Harry.

'Ricky loves you, mate. He would never leave your side, despite calling you every name under the sun.' Barny laughed. 'Me, I'm staying with you as well. I believe I'll stay safe if I keep around you. I think the lord has something in store for you my friend, and I'm not leaving until I see for myself what that is. No, I want to be there at the end of this journey you've taken us on. Besides, where else can I go, and, I want to see what your heaven looks like,' he jested, referring to Danny's northern property.

Danny was happy to hear that Barny was staying by his side. He needed him; he was his confidante. Their friendship had strengthened over the last few tumultuous weeks and Danny knew that his friend would give his life for him, it had already been proven.

Danny thought he had heard the last from Barny concerning his beliefs for a little while, but his friend was about to give another analogy as they walked. Danny was quickly back on his spiel regarding his revenge on Slacek and Sandilands.

'They're out there, Barny. Close by, I can feel it. I'll get them for what they've done if it's the only thing I do up here.' Adding he was looking forward to his help when the time would come.

'Wait right there,' Barny said.

He tightly grabbed at Danny's arm. His face contorted. Barny was looking for the right words as his head shook in anguish. His voice churned in angst as he looked through Danny's eyes.

'This anger! This talk of revenge! It must stop, Danny. It will consume you. This talk of vengeance, of armed robbery, it's not good my friend. Focus on Greta, your boys. Focus on what you need to do to get your life back. You've done a lot a good in this world so far, Danny, I've seen that myself. The good has always outweighed the bad. That's why the lord has cut you some slack on recent events. But I fear if you pursue this path, *this rage*, sooner or later, the scales will tip the other way, and when it does, everything you hold dear will come crashing down,' Barny implored.

Danny's teeth were grinding, his lips almost drawing blood as his friend's words drove a nail into his core.

'We're all closer to the tomb than the womb right now, Barny, so I need to make the most of life before I'm there,' Danny replied with vigour, however, he also knew that Barny spoke with substance and truth, nonetheless, it was an entirely a different matter if Danny would comply to his wisdom. Danny nodded his head in acknowledgement of his friend's advice then turned and proceeded to walk towards the entrance of the hut whilst Barny hoped his words would change Danny's reckless objectives.

Danny was first into the hut, banging the door open abruptly, hoping to give his friends a scare which was successfully achieved, much to his amusement and anger from both Ricky and Harry. Barny quietly entered behind him. Harry was sitting behind a table, playing cards solo, Ricky was on a wooden chair, sharpening his favourite knife on his wet stone.

'So, Harry, you want to leave us, do ya?' Danny boomed.

Harry looked stunned. Ricky stopped his sharpening. Danny looked at both, detecting that Ricky was obviously high again, eyes glazed, fidgeting with everything in front of him. Harry didn't know if Danny was angry or opposite, but his apprehension was soon put at ease as Danny smiled and expressed that it was alright if he wanted out. He sat next to him engaging in conversation, listening as Harry conveyed his fears and concerns, reassuring him that he didn't have to justify his decision. 'I'm surprised you hung around this long,' Danny laughed.

He apologised for ever getting him into this situation in the first place. Harry was not a fighter, nor a troublemaker, he was just in the wrong place at the wrong time, which the boys had already acknowledged.

The four of them banded together, taking up seats around the small retractable wooden table and for the next ten minutes supported the sometimes-teary Harry on his decision to leave. They thanked him for his loyalty and courage as Barny and Ricky brainstormed plans with him what would be the safest way back to his family.

It was a massive burden off Harry's shoulders to have Danny's blessing and he was extremely relieved that he could try and put this nightmare behind him with no animosity coming from the men who had suffered through it with him. The mood was good between the four companions; however, all was about to change. Danny rose from his chair and wished him well, warning him he was going to need all the luck in the world to reach his goal.

Ricky could see that Danny was changing tack. It was obvious to him that he never gave any input with trying to help Harry with a way out.

'What do ya mean by that?' he snapped.

'I just don't know how he's going to get back,' shrugged Danny.

Angry silence gripped the room.

Danny looked at Harry, whose confidence had just taken an arrow.

'You can try your best, Harry, but you will *not* make it,' he succinctly said. 'How are you going to get past all the police search parties? You don't know the mountains. You know no one in Graceville. You can't do it alone; you'll need help, Harry. They're looking for you too, ya know, not just me, it's all of us. We have a bounty on our heads mate, and there's pricks out there who want to cash in on it,' Danny flatly ended.

'What about Benny? He can find a way out for me, can't he?' Harry asked.

'Ah nah! You're not using Benny. I need him more than you do. I'm not risking him becoming involved in an arrest because of some stupid dash for freedom.'

Barny was flabbergasted at Danny's comment. He could see that Harry's morale was quickly dipping and as Ricky's face screwed up in anger, Danny continued, 'If you reckon you've tested yourself over the last couple of weeks, you've got no idea what will lay ahead for you if you go alone. That's the only reason why we are still on our feet, still free and not locked up, it's because we've been together, strength in numbers, Harry. You'll be on your own, mate, no one to back you up.'

'I don't care if I get arrested,' Harry affirmed. 'That lawyer lady said we'll be alright, that I probably wouldn't go to jail.'

'You'll go to jail, Harry, you can bet on it, but if that's what you believe, good onya. Just don't give away our location when you're in cuffs being questioned,' Danny softly demanded.

Danny put his hand on the door to exit the hut, paused for a moment as the boys looked around at each other. It wasn't what they were expecting to come out of Danny's mouth and before he left, he added one more thing that would get under the skin of his pals.

'My advice! Just give it another few weeks, Harry, I'll get you out of this mess, I promise. But if you want to go, go. I won't stop you. Solomon might! But I won't,' he said while giving a scurrilous wink. 'Give us a yell when you're going, I'll say goodbye then.' Danny smiled as he closed the door behind him.

He started to make his way back towards where Barny had met him, pondering how Harry would react to his critique of the situation but he wouldn't make it back to the comfort of his deck chair. Ricky was furious with what Danny had done. He was close to Harry, he was his best mate away from Danny, and he wasn't going to let him get away demeaning him the way he did.

He was supposed to be there to help and encourage, not escalate his already fragile mind. Danny planted the seeds of doubt in Harry's head which grew immediately and when Harry fretted he wasn't going to leave anymore, Ricky blew up.

'Fuck him!' he blasted.

He jumped from his seat, knife still in hand. Barny knew it was a dangerous situation if he left with it to chase Danny. He stopped him before he could exit and demanded he hand it over. Ricky threw it across the sawdust covered floor of the hut and angrily warned he was not going to need it. His eyes were emblazoned with rage, every vein was bulging out of his body, muscles hardening and strengthening out of his tight-fitting blue singlet. He stormed towards Danny and roared.

'You bastard. He's fuckin staying now.'

Danny stopped and turned.

'Great, it's for his own good.'

'Bullshit!' Ricky yelled back. 'You only want to use him for whatever you got planned in your fucked-up mind. You don't give a rat's arse about him.'

'I'm trying to protect him, you idiot!' Danny yelled back.

The boys were bringing attention to themselves from around the compound. Their raised voices were pricking the ears of the members who were stopping what they were doing and transfixing their eyes on the feuding pair.

Ricky was frothing at the mouth, deep grumbling emerging through his throat as his face snarled and teeth gritted.

'You're a fuckin asshole, Danny!' he hollered.

'And you're a fuckin coke addict, it's fucking up your thinking,' Danny replied as he waved his arms aloft. He turned his back and started to walk; he could see Sultan members starting to gather close by. It was the last thing he needed. He and the lads were under instruction from the President to keep a low profile, a directive which they had adhered to so far and Ricky's outburst was not helping, however, it was only going to get worse for both.

Danny's comment sent a shudder through Ricky, it couldn't sting any worse. He clasped a rock which laid amongst the gravel and dust at his feet, and with his accurate left arm threw the fist-sized missile at his retreating target.

An enormous thud hit Danny between the shoulder blades, he fell like a house of cards and wondered if he had just been shot. He grimaced in shock then swung around on his knees to try and gather what had happened. Before he could muster any sense, Ricky was charging towards him. He had no time to react as Ricky's swinging right boot connected to the side of his head. Danny was reeled over a metre from the force of the impact.

Disorientated from the blow, he tried to roll further away from the conflict. Ricky pounced on him, throwing wild punches as he straddled atop, yelling and screaming incoherently. Danny deflected the tirade of punches, but some were passing through his defence., He wrapped his arms around and wrestled the enraged Ricky from side to side until his advantage was controlled. They separated and stood to their feet. They had forgotten who they were, it was all survival now, best mates had turned to fierce enemies and both had switched to fight mode.

The momentary lull gave enough time for Danny to get his bearings back as the crowd now closely gathered around, shouting barbs at the two fighting men while encircling them. Barny and Harry's attempts to stop the fight were thwarted as members grabbed at them and warned not to intervene. Danny had the strength, height and weight advantage but knew the capabilities of his friend. He had seen him fight many times and being milked up on cocaine made him extra dangerous.

Ricky came at him again, connecting a punch to Danny's mouth and chin area, drawing blood immediately. They traded blows to head and body, some landing with force, cutting, bleeding, and bruising both. Danny forced Ricky into a headlock when he neared. Ricky counter acted the tightening squeeze by landing a forceful blow with his right forearm to Danny's groin. They separated once more but Ricky attacked instantly. Danny evaded and blocked the volley of wild punches; he waited for an opening and landed a heavy hit to the side of Ricky's cheekbone. He reeled from the hammer-like blow, Danny followed up a powerful right knee to the head as his friend turned enemy stumbled backwards and fall to the ground.

Ricky tried to regain his feet but staggered awkwardly then lost his balance and kissed the dirt again. Danny was hoping the five-minute war was over. He backed off and fell to the ground, exhausted. Ricky lay 15 meters from him in a semi-conscious state, huffing and gasping for breath also. The members were shouting at them to get up. They wanted more carnage between the outsiders, but the fighting pair could only hear muffled voices in the background as the ringing in their ears and concussion took hold, until one voiced boomed over the top.

'Finish him off,' it yelled.

Solomon's deep gravel voice had just echoed over the compound. He had heard the commotion from where he was standing outside the entrance to the manor and made his way towards the disturbance. No one fought without his permission. The Club's protocol had saved many lives to stop fighters drawing guns and knives during combat and the President's permission was paramount, or repercussions would follow, a code of behaviour that the feasting mob were well aware of.

'Finish him off,' he repeated. His raised voice gathered intensity. 'He's just a fucking coke addict as you said. He's no good to you. He'll be the death of you, Pruitt. Nullify your threat!' he boomed.

Danny was still on the ground sitting on his backside, legs apart, spitting the blood and dust away from his mouth when Solomon drew his revolver from the back of his pants and threw it in front of Danny. It was a Ruger 9mm. The handgun was an old one, but his favourite amongst his vast collection amassed over the years and he always kept it on his person somewhere.

'Now finish him off,' he said, this time more coolly and direct.

Danny looked at the handgun lying in the dust. He turned back up at Solomon and shook his head to say no.

Solomon picked the gun up and forced it into Danny's right hand. 'Pull the trigger,' he yelled. 'Just treat the subject as an object, Pruitt,' he advised in lower tones.

Danny threw the gun away. 'No.'

Eternal seconds passed as Solomon snorted, 'Just as I thought. Weak as piss,' he scorned. 'You disappoint me Pruitt. I had these silly thoughts that you had the same nucleus as us. You're just a fuckin coward civilian.'

The feuding pair were hoping it was all over, that Solomon had said his piece, that everyone would walk away, but what would happen next would even stun some of his own members.

Solomon leant over and retrieved the handgun off the ground, wiped the dust off and casually cocked it with his thumb and looked down on Danny. 'Well, if you won't finish this insubordinate rebel off, I fuckin will.'

He strode towards Ricky who was now on his knees. Danny rose to his feet. The warnings from Zoe raced through his battered mind. Was this the Solomon that she spoke about? The Solomon that those in the know spoke about? How foolish was I to even think that he would accept me!

Danny shouted for him not to do it. A heavy backhand smashed into his face. Crow was looking for any excuse to inflict pain on the trespasser and delivered it with satisfaction. 'Shut your mouth, know your place, civilian!' he warned, as two other members restrained Danny from behind.

Silence gripped the surrounding mob as they watched Solomon stand next to Ricky and raise the gun to his temple. Barny and Harry looked on in horror, there was not a thing they could do to help.

Murder was in the club's DNA, all members knew it, and they also knew that their President could be dangerously unpredictable, but a public execution would be a first for the outlaw club, particularly inside *La Fortaleza* where the tension built to extraordinary levels. Barny lowered his head to silently pray as they listened to Ricky wail in fear. He was sounding a like a wounded animal; howls of fear and anger were releasing from the depths of his stomach. He knew he couldn't fight or defend himself; he was sure it would only inspire more pain or a certain bullet.

'He's bluffing, Ricky!' Danny yelled.

Ricky stared back soulless, moaning, snarling. 'Don't worry, he won't do it, he's fucking bluffing,' Danny reiterated.

'Solomon don't bluff,' Crow whispered into Danny's ears.

Is this it! Ricky rued inside. *Is this how it ends? At the hands of some ex-military madman dressed in leather. On top of a mountain range where no one would ever know of it.*

The President stretched his arm to full length, a stare of darkness entranced his eyes, beads of sweat ran over his shaven head under the warming sun as his finger slowly squeezed back on the trigger.

Click the barrel rotated. Empty! He squeezed again, click. Empty. Again. Empty! Three more clicks and rotations of the barrel would quickly follow, all empty.

Solomon was expressionless. He placed the revolver back into the rear of his pants, turned and walked away, not a look or gesture to anyone would come from him as the crowd parted to let him through.

'Get back to what you were doing,' he ordered to his underlings.

Crow gave the nod for the men to release the grip they had on Danny who immediately slumped to the ground, never taking his eyes off the tormented Ricky. The crowd slowly dispersed, glancing and glaring at the two humiliated and forlorn intruders as Harry and Barny made their way to Ricky's side. He was panting and puffing, trying to get air back into his lungs to calm his shaking and aching body.

Only moments ago, he was convinced he had taken his last breath ever and was sucking in the oxygen as quick as his body would allow. A few minutes passed before his breathing was almost back to normal and the realisation that he had just dodged a bullet, literally, started to sink in.

Danny rose to his feet again. He nodded at Ricky in a gesture to see if he was okay. A nod of similar overtones came back as Barny and Harry helped Ricky to his feet.

Danny turned away and made his way to the shower block, took off his stripped and torn black T-shirt and started to wash his swollen bloodied face over the basin, cusping hands of water and gently rinsing away the blood and dust, grimacing from the pain in the process. He raised his head to look at himself in the old stained and cracked mirror which sat above the basin and tried to comprehend what had just happened. It wasn't what Solomon had done so much that churned him, but his mate-ship with Ricky. Had he just severed the kinship that they had shared for almost a lifetime, did he just destroy a bond that he had with no one else. He couldn't fathom a life without Ricky by his side, somewhere!

He dipped his head under the running water of the tap, keeping it there, still spitting away the blood from the cuts to his lips and forehead when he heard shuffling feet enter the shower block to his right. Ricky stood there, bruised and bloodied, the same as Danny. Their eyes locked, and one look at his face told him he wasn't there to continue the fight, he knew him as well as himself. Silence gripped as they sombrely stared at one another until Danny drolly commented, 'Shit! What the hell happened to you?'

Ricky shrugged his shoulders, grinned and quietly chuckled.

Danny looked back at himself in the mirror.

A wry smile came to Ricky's face. 'You should see the other guy; he looks like he hit a truck.'

It was Danny's turn to grin and snigger.

'I'm sorry, man,' he heard Ricky sigh.

'Me too,' replied Danny.

The two best mates embraced; thankful they were still together.

Danny carefully dried his face with some paper towels hanging off a dispenser on the wall, screwed it up after use and threw it in the wastebasket that sat in the corner and started to leave the shower block, but not without a friendly suggestion to his buddy, 'Get some rest. We're gonna need it.'

Chapter 29

The party was in full swing. Music blared from the speakers from the tattooed live band. They played covers from past rock and heavy metal greats. La Fortaleza's serenity from the previous night had been broken by hordes of members from the Sultan MC. Horses were tethered to any available tree around the compound as the late comers were unable to find a booth in the now packed stables. More members had arrived from the city and states minor chapters throughout the day and evening. They stood around large rotisserie spits that sat above wood and briquette fire pits spaced around the compound.

Large legs of beef, whole lambs and pigs slowly turned, readying themselves to be feasted upon while the alcohol, cocaine and marijuana was freely absorbed. The population had grown to over one hundred as wives and lady friends joined in the revelry.

The only people Danny saw exiting the premises during the afternoon was little Maddy. With her were two adults in the seat of the dual horse open buggy, she sat in between them. In charge of the reins under the warm clear blue skies was an older looking male member, tall and skinny with a long grey streaky beard and withered face. He was in the company of Solomon's lady friend Danny saw from the previous night. Carla, he thought her name to be. A middle-aged woman with a pale complexion who wore knee high black boots and denim jeans with a Sultan labelled T-shirt, she showed the tell-tale signs of drug abuse according to Danny's assumptions. Maddy looked sad as she gave Danny her now accustomed little wave from afar as she left. He wondered why she was leaving. He wondered even more if she saw the fight hours before, he hoped not!

Solomon sat like a king on his favourite outdoor couch, raised above the ground by short steel scaffolding on the now drying grassed area outside the Manor. Danny watched as members would come and go from the President, asking for advice or permission on subjects that he could only guess about. The music was heard afar by nearby campers as the soundwaves travelled on the wind through the ranges and valleys off the plateau.

One group of campers took more interest than others as they set up for the night. Sgt Dane Grainger and his party were down wind of La Fortaleza and had no doubt where the music was coming from. Dane wondered silently if Danny was there, dancing and drinking and having a fantastic time of it all while he had struggled through the mountains trying to locate him. He knew it would be impossible and foolish to find out for sure.

It was Dane's last night on the manhunt for his friend. Their allotted time was up, and all involved wanted to get back to Graceville by Sunday night, and the Sergeant couldn't wait to see the last of at least two of his colleagues. He was at boiling point listening to Sandilands boast about his forced conquests with the fairer sex. He listened contemptuously how Slacek would laugh at the frivolous excuses he would use to repeatedly beat up on his wife, getting unabated support from Sandilands.

Dane was repulsed by them both but had held his tongue. He tried to ignore the conversations, vowing to himself that they would be somehow held accountable for what they had done when they returned. The search party had exhausted all trails and leads and had come up with nothing and when Inspector Vaccaro radioed and gave permission for them to head home on the morn, they all had to accept their mission was unsuccessful, gladly or otherwise.

The Sergeant had informed Vaccaro on all areas and tracks that they had passed through. They questioned all riders and campers they came across. They even rode to the gates of La Fortaleza and asked the question of Danny Pruitt, which was either met with utter silence or forceful denials from the gatekeepers. Every road, horse trail, bike and walking track known to them had been patrolled relentlessly from inside and out of the ranges. Along with Dane's party, other search units had scoured by horseback, by foot and by vehicle, and not a trace could be found of the fugitive four. The fruitless searching and the time he briefly caught up with Zoe Valetta in Graceville left no doubt in the Inspector's mind that Pruitt and his crew were entrenched inside the Sultan MC.

It had just passed noon earlier in the day and the Inspector stood at the steps of the police station, discussing matters with three uniformed police members when he noticed the distinct carriage of the Sultans MC passing on the way to the train station. He peered intently towards it, trying to get an espy on who was inside and sure enough, Miss Valetta was the sole occupant. He dismissed the officers and retrieved his horse from the stables at the rear of the police station and hastily followed before she could disembark and board the train.

He arrived beside the carriage before Zoe could retrieve her bags and dismounted to offer a hand with her luggage while the Prospects looked on from the driver's seat with despise. Zoe thanked the Inspector and allowed him to unload her luggage and when her bags were grounded, thanked the carriage drivers for their help and protection and advised it was okay for them to leave.

'Miss Valetta! You're early. I thought you weren't leaving until the last train. You weren't about to leave town without seeing me on certain matters now, were you?' the Inspector asked as he watched the carriage slowly exit the busy railway station carpark.

'There was nothing to tell. The man you're looking for is not with the club. I didn't want to waste your time. I know how busy you are, Inspector,' Zoe tried confidently to convey.

Vaccaro diligently tried to press for more information, however, nothing could be gained from her short and direct answers.

'You're wasting your time with this line of investigation. He is not there. The club has never seen him or his friends,' she advised.

Vaccaro was having none of it. He knew she was lying. Although Zoe Valetta was quite adept at telling untruths, as her job demanded at times, it would take the smartest femme fatale to get past the Inspector's intuition and he was adamant the Sultans MC were hiding Danny Pruitt and his band of merry men. He cordially said his goodbyes to Zoe, who was alert to the Inspectors doubts and suspicions herself. Her acquired shrewdness was too good to let that slip as he allowed her to continue her journey on the crowded train back to the city and as soon as Noel Vaccaro was back in his office, he was on the phone to Assistant Commissioner Martin Conroy.

Danny had spent most of the late afternoon laying and sitting around his tent, recovering from his injuries inflicted upon him by the nasty confrontation with Ricky, only moving away to grab some water and ice from gathered portable drink coolers to soothe the swelling and soreness.

He was soon joined by Ricky, Barny and Harry as he moved into his comfortable deck chair under the cluster of gum trees that towered over the work sheds. Danny and Ricky saw each other's war wounds for the first time since they parted. The swelling and blackening around their eyes and cheekbones were noticeable to both, along with the dried blood seeping through the Elastoplast strips on their cuts. The four sat and spoke miscellaneously about the proceedings in the distance. The fight was not mentioned.

The night sky was slowly taking over when they saw three men approaching, hands full with long neck bottles of home brew beer. Drake, Razor and Teeto crossed the compound and decided to pay their guests a visit and offer them a round of beer which was gladly accepted. Drake tossed a newspaper onto Danny's lap.

'Congratulations,' he chuffed.

'What for?' Danny quietly asked.

'You've made the top 20,' Drake proudly advised.

'What are you talking about?' shrugged Danny.

'The state's most wanted. You've made the top 20. Well done!' Drake said, as his smile broadened.

Danny was shocked. He opened the pages and perused over its content underneath the spotlights hanging from the sheds nearby when the realism started to sink in. It wasn't what he wanted to hear. He had been reading through the Hexagon Valley papers throughout the day and there was no mention of him or the events that had taken place. '

'You thought you were just a blip on the radar, didn't ya?' said Drake.

The Vice President knew that Danny had read an article that over 400 criminals were wanted by Venturian law and that he also had mused to himself that no one would care about any incidents from a rural town like Graceville. He flippantly told Drake when their paths crossed earlier that all their focus would be on the murderers and high-end criminals from the city, however, Danny was naively and sorely mistaken.

On the back of all the media frenzy concerning the alleged charges and pending trial against Minister Johnston and his cohorts, the publicity from the larger newspapers in the city was gathering momentum with every front-page edition, and one of the side story's which journalists were delving deeper into was the one on the so-called Graceville four, and inside the eight page spread for all the boys to see was all the recent happenings in Graceville. They took turns in passing related articles amongst themselves and Danny was astounded and frightened to see his name to the forefront.

'Six counts of murder!' he blasted with shock. 'This is bullshit. Who the hell are the six?' he asked aloud as he perused the articles.

The boys casually started to count the toll. The four Devlin brothers were the first quickly marked off. Then came the officer that Ricky had shot, Danny taking the blame for him as all knew. They couldn't make out the sixth victim until Barny suggested that one of Pringle's men would probably be the next.

'The guy in the bush you and Ricky mowed down. That would be it,' Barny affirmed.

The men talked and spun the candidates. They couldn't work out how they could ever connect Danny with the killing of any of Pringle's men, until Danny shook his head in anger, looked around at his audience then suggested that Dane and Ryan must have disclosed it to authorities in their statements.

'Six fuckin murders,' he brooded.

Ricky chuckled at his animated reaction. 'Serial killer *Danny Pruitt*,' he joked.

'Not funny!' Danny pushed his head forward and gave a sharp reply. 'You helped with at least three of them,' he reminded.

Ricky just smiled and took a larger swig out of his beer bottle, seemingly proud to have played a part.

Danny stood to his feet. He was still in denial and refused to take blame for what he had done. To him, he didn't kill any of these people, they killed themselves. Everything he did was in self-defence, so to him, it was all justified. 'I'm not a murderer,' he announced. 'This is bullshit,' he repeated.

Harry saw his name with Ricky's and Barny's in the small paragraph below Danny's charges and with naïve frustration commented about the DPP offer.

'How can they make an offer like they did and then write our names up like this?' he asked.

Harry got a volley of expletives on how the powers that be cannot be trusted. They're all liars Danny and Ricky reminded him, as Ricky apologised to Danny, admitting he was correct in not taking the offer.

Drake butted in on the boy's conversation and humorously suggested that the reason they withdrew the offer was because they looked at the demands Danny had written, a comment which was met with laughter from Razor and Teeto, along with wry smiles from the lads, other than Harry.

'You reckon?' he asked, disappointed.

Barny tactfully reminded Harry that the paper they were looking at was today's edition, and it would've been impossible for Zoe to pass on his demands even if she wanted to. She hadn't left the compound until this morning Barny calmly said. Harry embarrassingly accepted his explanation.

But as it was, Inspector Vaccaro had already read the morning edition of the city newspaper before he stopped Zoe Valetta at the station. He frustratingly recognised that any discreet and peaceful resolution had all but disappeared now that the city journalists had got their claws around the story that is Danny Pruitt. He angrily lamented that the web Minister Johnston had cast was going to be now nigh on impossible for any of the Graceville four to accept any offer of faith from this time on.

Danny immediately thought of Greta. It sent a shiver down his spine to think that she would see these headlines. To see her husband branded a murderer for all the public to see. It was adding to the already volcanic anger inside of him as he envisaged her pain and embarrassment.

Drake and Razor filled the boys in on the missing links that were published, knowing two of the six large photos would interest them. Detective Lucas Cribbs was one of the said photos, who was asked after by Barny as soon as he saw his face and inquired what he had to do with their exploits. The boy's eyebrows raised when told that he was the detective that Minister Johnston had assigned to bring them in, and more surprised that he had made bail and suspended with pay after reading what charges were laid against him. However, it was the photo of the second man that had Danny's undivided attention. He could finally put a face to the name. His top lip curdled as he spat out the sugary content from the home brew.

JOHN PRINGLE, it read underneath the photo. He studied the face, nothing grabbed him. Just another face in the crowd he thought, other than the dark bushy eyebrows and moustache along with the closeness of his eyes. Nothing sinister, nothing abnormal about this so-called hired killer. Danny had never laid eyes on him before. He had only heard his voice back at Tambourine bridge when all hell broke loose, and as he read, was pleased to know that he too was on the most wanted list and commented that justice may come after all for the death of his friend Karl Turner.

He passed the page around to get confirmation from his friends that it *was the* infamous John Pringle and once satisfied, tore the photo out of the page, folded it, then placed into the back of his wallet and caustically commented that he may need it one day.

The boys leered at each other with expressions of desperation. The whole state now knew who they were and what they had done, and they were resigning themselves to the fact that any door still left ajar for salvation had now been firmly slammed shut. They didn't have to explain it to each other as their looks portrayed everything that they were thinking. Drake, Razor and Teeto could see the look of gloom engulfing their guests.

However, the three members were not there to deliver a newspaper to the boys. They didn't really care what was happening in the outside world. Although they had hidden respect and a building camaraderie with their guests, especially towards Danny, throwing the newspaper was just a conversation opener to them.

They had two matters on their mind to converse. The first was information regarding a deal that they had struck with Danny days earlier, the second far more serious. After a quick whispered conversation between the two Vice Presidents, Razor broke the atmosphere of pessimism that surrounded Danny and the boys.

'Cheer up, boys,' he said. 'We've got news for you that isn't in the paper which will make you a bit happier.'

Razor's chest puffed out and was pleased that he was the giver of information that Danny would be chuffed to hear. The live music continued in the background as he proudly announced that the men on the Re-Po squad list that Danny gave to them were all about to get a well-deserved surprise. Danny knew that Razor had the same disdain towards the re-po squad as he did. It was probably the only subject that both would have a meaningful and animated conversation about, and Danny's undivided attention was Razor's when he began to explain what the club had set in motion.

While Danny was being enchanted by Zoe the previous night and wondering why the compound was almost empty, his leather-clad allies were at an affiliated club meeting at a property on the outskirts of Graceville, planning revenge on the men he hated so much.

The boys sipped on their beers and puffed on their cigarettes, Ricky inhaling something stronger as Drake and Razor took turns in supplying details to the eager ears on how the systematic revenge was starting as they spoke.

The Young Bloods were a teenage street gang who were gaining a feared reputation as every month passed. They formed on the streets of Graceville around three years ago and had now spread to outer eastern suburbs and surrounding districts of the Hexagon Valley. The gang was growing in numbers as every self-destructing month passed. Authorities estimated they were over 200 strong and had members aligned from ages as young as 12 years old. They wore red caps and bandanas or red rags and handkerchiefs that hung out of their pants pockets to identify their allegiance to the gang.

Most thought they got their name from the infamous street gangs that formed in Los Angeles in the 1980's, taking a leaf out of their insignia red paraphernalia, but if you spoke to the founding members of the Graceville Young Bloods, the name simply came from the local football club's nickname, the Bloods. Youth unemployment was at epidemic proportions and schooling was a low priority for the poor and fractured family. Boredom, bitterness, domestic violence, detached parenting, poverty, and the need for acceptance and inclusion lured the vulnerable adolescent to the streets and to the life of crime and substance abuse that followed.

The gang were high on the agenda of law enforcement with taskforces assembled to try and subdue and extinguish them from the streets and although most of the crimes they committed were of minor offences, it was not uncommon for them to be involved in larger crimes that resulted in detention or jail. The Sultans MC saw an opportunity and quickly moved in with incentives for the youth gang if they completed some dirty work for them, and it took no time for the Young Bloods to become an ally of MC, receiving money and drugs for services rendered that wouldn't tie the club with any crime committed.

The Vice Presidents met with leaders of the Young Bloods after checking and certifying the addresses of the intended targets, and with a down payment, outlined to the Young Bloods the new task the club had set for them.

With the names of the men who took part in the repossession raid on Danny's property, the gang were targeting their first victim on the list as the Vice Presidents spoke at La Fortaleza and within the next three days finished off the orders that were given by the Sultans MC and hit the remaining targets.

The Young Bloods showed no mercy. They didn't care if some of the names on the list were police officers or not, it just gave them more incentive, and with excited boldness and disregard, went about fire bombing, alighting, ram raiding and destroying all the dwellings and homes on the list. If they weren't burnt to the ground, the houses were vandalised to such an extent that they were left uninhabitable from the destruction left behind.

They always struck after dark and disguised themselves with masks or balaclavas and didn't care if the occupants were home or not. If they were, they received a vicious beating at gun point while wives, partners and children fled to safety. They were violent, they were numerous, and they moved with cohesive speed with the element of surprise which left any effort to repel the attacks futile. When morning came around, painted graffiti signs on roads and placards were glaringly prominent that left all surveying the damage in no doubt that the house occupiers were members of the despised and hated repossession squad.

With help from other members of the Sultan MC, the Young Bloods also tracked down the miscreant poachers who had ravished the Pruitt's belongings after the Re-po squad had disappeared. Once they had a name, they used threats and violence to gather more names on who were present. After a week of terrorising and intimidation they had retrieved a large portion of what was taken, from Greta's jewellery and clothing to her son's toys and bicycles along with personal possessions that belonged to both Danny and Greta.

Not all was returned, however, when Sarah answered a knock on her door to see garbage bags and carboard boxes at her doorstep along with six members of the teenage gang, she quickly summoned Greta to her side after the crew's spokesman relayed that he had a message for her. Greta sifted through the boxes and bags and with smiles and delight, instantly deciphering what were in its contents.

'What's the message and who is it from?' she asked.

'It's from your husband,' the spokesman said. 'No one steals from us!'

Danny was delirious on what the club had launched and undertaken. He was out of his chair fist pumping and hi-fiving all around, much to the bewilderment of his friends. They had heard all the threats and anger from him and now knew how much the payback burned inside going by his reaction. The retribution he was promised had come to the fore and he approved glowingly on how they were going about it.

'I hope they all burn,' he grimaced in delight. 'I hope they all fuckin burn. I hope they're all going to be fuckin homeless just as I am.'

The Vice Presidents offered more beers to the lads now that the woes they had felt minutes ago had disappeared. Barny, Ricky and Harry were happy for Danny, maybe now, the load of anger he had inside would be released knowing he wouldn't have to deal with it anymore, nevertheless, it still didn't halt the deep misgivings the three had on their own future.

'Just four to go,' Danny said as he took his position back in his chair.

'What do you mean, what four?' Harry asked.

'Slacek, Sandilands, Neilson and Corey,' replied Danny.

'Just leave it,' Barny advised. 'Let it go, mate. Don't you think that's enough? The main instigators are going to get what's coming, so let it go.'

'I said they're *all* going to pay, and they all will,' Danny bit back.

Barny lowered his head and bit his tongue. He mistakenly thought the revenge that Danny carried may have been subdued by the news, however, going by the venom in his reply, he knew the fury was still within, and soon Danny was about to get the whereabouts on two of the remaining said people.

Conversation ensued before a now serious Drake produced some papers out of his pants pocket as Teeto passed around a fresh batch of beer. Danny immediately recognised what they were. His three buddies were also aware as the looks of trepidation crossed their faces.

Danny wondered when Drake was going to come to him about the missing plans to his robbery, and it looked if this was going to be that time. The tempo of their heartbeat gathered momentum as Drake asserted that they needed to talk. The boys had no idea what was about to come from the Vice Presidents. Drake began to fire questions at Danny who nervously tried to laugh the subject off. 'It's nothing,' he said. 'Just our imagination running wild,' he scoffed, but Drake was having none of it. The plans were detailed enough to show him that careful planning had transpired.

'Don't bullshit us,' Drake firmly ordered. 'Tell us what you know.'

Danny didn't want to argue, Drake was not a man to play games with. His bulging tattooed biceps expanded as he folded his arms when he once again demanded information. Danny decided to throw caution to the wind. He had nothing to lose and began to tell what the plans all meant, much to the worried surprise of his three buddies.

Danny outlined all his thoughts and plans and when he had finished, tried to satisfy his own curiosity by asking why they wanted to know. Surprise, shock and, for Danny, delight started to engulf the boys as Razor interrupted and abruptly announced that they wanted in. Although for the time being, the reasons were going to be kept to themselves and Danny didn't push why.

The men made their way to the rotunda away from peering eyes and ears as the live music blared inside the compound and used the table inside to lay out the papers. Danny did his best to answer the questions about his plan that were fired at him by Drake and Razor. Some he answered confidently, but as the men delved deeper into his plan, errors and flaws rippled to the surface that Danny had no answer to, and that's where Drake and Razor advised that they could use their own skill and resources to help make it work.

The secretive group was brainstorming the if's and but's regarding the armed robbery when Teeto gave Drake a nudge to his side. He saw a member approaching from the direction of where the communications hut stood. The club had no idea what their two Vice Presidents were planning, or the deals and arrangements they were working on with Danny. They needed to keep it secret, if Solomon ever found out, it would not be good for the respected VPs, so the conversation had to be halted.

'Marco. What's up, bro?' Drake asked as he neared.

Marco oversaw all comms in and out of *La Fortaleza*. He was of light build and stature, long brown hair and goatee beard, tattooed body and face with light framed spectacles. The boys had never met him officially but had seen him crossing the compound on numerous occasions.

'I have a message from the gatekeepers,' he said.

'Go on,' Drake said, as he and Razor moved him away from where the boys were congregated.

Danny and the boys watched on. They tried to listen inconspicuously to the lowered voices but to no avail. One thing for sure was that Danny could sense the conversation surrounded him going by the looks in his direction.

A few minutes later, the conversation broke up. Marco made his way back to the communications hut while Drake and Razor confronted Danny once more.

'Looks like you have a visitor,' Drake announced.

Danny gave a look of surprise and trepidation. Who the hell knows I'm here, and who the hell would want to talk to me, and why are they so calm about it?

'It's your bush buddy. The dark fella. He's got some news for you apparently,' Drake informed.

'Of course, Benny!' Danny responded.

They had organised a meeting at the gates with the blessing of the club the last they met. Straight away he thought of Greta. He was busting to get any news of her and was quickly asking if he could see him. Drake and Razor agreed, saying they'll pick up their conversation later, then escorted him to the exit of the compound, all under the distant and curious eye of their President.

The large steel gates drew back, operated by the gatekeepers who sat perched in their elevated turrets as the Rottweiler dogs grumbled and roared from their cage runs. Danny could see Benny ahead of him as he passed through the now closing gates. He was atop of the road before it dipped away down to the T-intersection of track 24 and was sitting on a rock holding the rein of his grazing horse.

Danny looked back over his shoulders and then upwards. He could never get enough of the empowerment that the Sultans MC entrance gave off. The large carved out wooden features of the four animal ensigns were always a sight to see, he was in awe of the workmanship and meaning that looked down on him, especially now with the turret spotlights beaming down on the entrance.

'Benny! Good to see ya, bro.'

Benny rose to his feet as Danny neared him. He thrusted out his right hand and received a light embrace from him. Handshake greetings followed with Drake and Razor. Benny retrieved an envelope from his saddlebag and passed it to Danny.

'From Greta,' he happily announced.

'You bloody beauty!' Danny thanked him. 'Is she okay? How's my boys? What's happening with her?' He feverishly asked.

'It will all be in her letter,' Benny assured, telling him that she was doing fine.

As Drake and Razor watched on, Benny did his best to fill Danny in on what was happening around his family. They spoke quickly for about five minutes; Danny knew his friend couldn't stay for long. It was after dark and Benny needed to move on and set up camp for the night. With an approval nod from the Vice Presidents, they both agreed to meet tomorrow morning so he could gather Danny's reply to his wife.

But just as Benny was leaving, he decided to give Danny some information that he would be greatly interested in. Benny had chewed it over in his mind whether to pass on what he had seen and heard. He knew what repercussions may lay ahead if he did, however, he knew his friend wanted revenge on a certain person for accosting his wife and if Danny only had one opportunity to have it, Benny was going to give it to him.

'I was making my way up here when I heard voices. I poked my head through the bush and saw some campers,' Benny explained. 'I was above them off the track and looked in. Your mate Sgt Dane Grainger and his posse were setting up camp for the night. They're only an hour away from here.'

Danny's heart raced a little quicker. 'Is Sandilands and Slacek with them?'

'Yep. Guarantee it.' Benny nodded. 'Sgt Dane went to take a piss and I overheard him talking on the radio to the Inspector. They were talking about abandoning the search and returning home in the morning so if you want payback, you're going to have to move quick,' Benny relayed.

It was a window of opportunity for Danny to have his retribution if he desired, but as Benny advised him, it would take some careful planning.

They quickly put their heads together on a plan but whatever fast ideas they were coming up with, they agreed on one thing, they lacked the manpower to achieve anything that wouldn't either get them arrested or shot. Danny was beating his head against the wall. He knew Dane was a smart man. Walking in guns ablaze was not an option. Negotiating with his policeman friend was out of the question.

Dane would never agree to any delusional terms that Danny would come up with, he was on the job and the Sergeant wanted an end. Danny badly wanted his chance to confront Sandilands and Slacek but time was against him. Everything he suggested, Benny shot down with logic or safety concerns, until Danny's eyes smiled devilishly at his bush companion.

'I've got an idea,' he said.

It was ambitious, a wild long shot gamble. He knew it could backfire before it could even be discussed, but Barny was right, the stars aligned when Danny needed help and his ultimate grand plan was going to come to fruition, and what better way to get the manpower he needed than from the men who had taken him in.

Chapter 30

'Get up, get up. It's time to go,' Danny aggressively whispered.

Barny wrestled from his sleep as Danny nudged and pushed. He sat up from his mattress inside his tent as Danny exited to give the same message to Harry whose tent was a further ten metres away. Harry was already awake, sleep was hard for him, even at 5.00 am when most people were at their deepest. Danny made his way to Ricky's tent and when he pushed his head through the front flaps, he was pleasantly surprised that his partner had company.

Ricky befriended a single lady as the previous night's party was at its crescendo and duly escorted her back to his makeshift abode. They shared a common like for the white powder and soon found themselves wrapped together in their naked bodies. It had been a while since Ricky had enjoyed some female company and with only one hour's sleep, he was a tad slow to adhere to Danny's demand.

As for Danny, he had received no sleep at all. After sharing drinks and brainstorming plans in between life stories with the Vice Presidents, it was 2.30 am by the time he got back to his tent. He read through Greta's letter more than once before he penned his reply, and with the adrenalin, excitement, and trepidation of what lay ahead, any ounce of sleep was impossible.

The rising sun was still an hour away as the four hideaways met up with Drake and Razor at the rotunda. They traversed as quietly as they could to the stables where Teeto already had the horses saddled and ready to go. They did not want to be seen or heard. This was not club business. Drake and Razor had their own motives and incentives to join up with Danny and help him on his morning crusade. They knew Danny was desperate, not only for revenge, but money as well, and it was the latter that the Vice Presidents were also in desperate need of for reasons of their own, so as it stood, if they wanted an input and a cut from the robbery, they would have to agree and help Danny on his early morning conquest.

Importantly for Drake and Razor, it had to be kept secret from any members of the club, other than their trusted sidekick Teeto. The group of seven stealthily made their way out through the back lands of La Fortaleza until they set upon Molloy's track where they turned left and met up with Benny at the base of Satan's elevator. Under the cover of the morning darkness, the now group of eight were heading for the campsite where Dane Grainger and his group were still in the land of slumber.

Benny led the way towards the campsite through tight undulating tracks that not even the Sultans knew about. They travelled in single file until they came across a wider fire track where they turned left for 200 meters and dismounted from their horses in a cut away. Everything from now would be by foot as the group separated.

Danny and Benny made their way through the bush in an easterly direction for about 20 minutes then moved across until they came to the same spot where Benny overheard Dane radioing the Inspector. It was elevated, secluded, and it had a clear shot into camp. A declining twenty-minute careful silent walk took Drake, Razor, Teeto, Barny and Ricky to the west side of the camp. This was more open with sporadic tall trees and low grass shrubs and bracken fern at their feet, the ground was soft with thick undergrowth which allowed their steps to be almost undetectable. Harry stayed with the horses. Now in position, the two groups would wait for first light and stand by until Danny's plan was put into action.

The first inkling of light peered from the morning skies above, synchronising with the early squawks and chirps of the wild bird life. Both groups had been in position for nearly 20 minutes. Another 15 minutes would pass before any movement came from the search party's encampment. The portable binoculars were raised to the eyes of both waiting groups as the first sign of movement came.

Senior constable Mike Whitehall exited his small tent. It was on a flat part of the ground closest to the little stream that flowed by their camp, a kilometre down, the shallow stream would connect into the larger Kensington River. He exercised his morning stretches before he grabbed a thermos and poured himself a cold brew of tea before checking on their horses tethered to a cluster of trees close by. Over a 30-minute period, one by one the members of the search party would awaken, keen and eager to make their way down the mountain and back onto the streets of Graceville for a well-cooked meal and the comforts of home.

Over an hour passed since the stalking groups had taken up their positions. Their impatience was building as every minute ticked by. Danny had to wait until his target was where he needed him to be, and as he knelt with his binoculars behind the shoulders of Benny, he leant close to his right ear and quietly declared, 'It's showtime.'

Benny raised his weapon and pulled back the arrow from his bow, his left eye shut while his right zeroed in, fingers and hands steady as a ship in a calm harbour. His breath slowly exhaled and then, release. The arrow sped like a torpedo through the air, pinpointed through the tight openings of the forest until it embedded into the large eucalypt 50 meters away, right next to the head of Dane Grainger. The Sergeant could feel the wind on his thick whiskers as the arrow zoomed past before he jumped back in fright.

The heads of the other four men in the camp snapped around to see what had happened. Other than the sporadic early morning sounds of wildlife and the trickling of the stream, nothing else could be heard on this windless morning and the sound of the arrow piercing into the tree grabbed their attention immediately.

Dane looked around to see where the arrow may have come from but only saw stillness from the surrounding bushland. He snapped the arrow from the tree as the others gathered around. He tore away the adhesive tape that was attached to the shaft to hold the large piece of paper attached. He unravelled the note and drew it close to his face as his colleagues impatiently asked what was held within its contents. He looked closer and couldn't believe what he was reading to himself.

HELLO DANE,

WE'VE BEEN FOLLOWING YOU FOR THE LAST COUPLE OF DAYS WAITING TO CATCH YOU ALONE. THE OTHERS DON'T SEEM TO LEAVE YOUR SIDE. WE WANT TO GIVE OURSELVES UP. WE ARE TIRED OF LIVING LIKE ANIMALS AND ARE STARVING HUNGRY.

I DO NOT WANT TO SEE SANDILANDS OR SLACEK. THIS WILL ONLY MAKE ME ANGRY AND THEY'LL PROBABLY SHOOT ME ANYHOW. MAKE YOUR WAY SOUTH UNTIL YOU GET TO TRACK 19 THEN TURN EAST. THERE'S A CLEARING UP ON THE RIGHT NOT FAR UP, 10 MINUTES ON HORSEBACK. MEET ME THERE WITH YOUR OTHER TWO MATES WHO ARE WITH YOU IN 30 MINUTES AND ME AND THE BOYS WILL GIVE OURSELVES UP TO YOU. PLEASE DO AS I SAY. NO GAMES, NO BULLSHIT AND I'M ALL YOURS.

DANNY.

P.S. BRING SOME FOOD!

Danny saw the search party congregate. He could see animated gestures coming from the men, particularly from Dane. Danny waited for their next move and soon he would be smiling smugly as he watched Dane and his two partners from the suburbs take the bait and straddle their horses. Danny's arrogant theory had paid dividends, Dane would always heed the cries from a friend in need.

Danny packed his binoculars into his backpack and moved away from his position. He had to be at the clearing before Dane arrived. With Benny leading the way, he quickly manoeuvred his way up through the bush, then crossed fire track 19 to the high side, climbing the embankment then hiding and moving themselves low until they reached refuge near the clearing.

The wait was not long. Dane and his partners had arrived before the suggested 30 minutes. The Sergeant wasted no time, the urgency within was overwhelming and the prospect of finally putting this epic saga to rest was the only thing on his mind. He wanted Danny in custody, not only for his own self-interests but also for the safety of his long-time friend. Dane's motives were all well intended, but as he was about to find out, Danny did not consider a man who had twice hunted him down a friend anymore!

Dane turned his horse into the clearing and was followed by his partners. The grass clearing was approximately 200m x 150m in area surrounded by knee high treated pine pole barriers at its entrance to the South and its boundaries to the East and West. It was formally used as a turnaround for log trucks and doubled as a quiet bush picnic area for weekend travellers.

The three dismounted and waited, Dane looking at his wristwatch several times as the minute hand ticked over. Danny nervously spied them through the thick forest camouflage, earnestly hoping that *his* partners were succeeding in *their* roles.

The set time for the ambush was nigh and as the 30 minutes ticked over from when Dane and his two partners had ridden off from their camp, the team lead by Drake donned their balaclavas, produced their newly acquired revolvers and shotguns and burst into the camp with an aggressive violence akin to a military unit. Hearts were pumping through their chests. Barny was reluctant to participate when they discussed Danny's plan the previous night. He was not an aggressive or hostile man, and this type of action was not in his DNA, but loyalty to his friends won over through tough convincing from Danny.

As for Ricky, he was high on a cocktail of alcohol and cocaine, and still was this morning, so was all too willing to join in anything that would give him a buzz. Finally, all agreed that Harry be kept away from the action, someone had to stay with the horses.

As for Drake and Razor, this was nothing new. They had experience when it came to smash and grab raids and as for Teeto, he just followed orders no matter how terrified he felt inside. Maximum terror in minimum time Razor commanded to the first-time raiders. They waited for when Sandilands and Slacek were within meters of each other before they struck. It was a rush that Barny and Ricky had never felt.

They had given each other a look of teenage fear the moment before Drake gave the signal to raid. It was too late to pull out now, that they understood clearly, and with nervous laden legs ran into camp listening to Razor and Drake order Sandilands and Slacek to their knees with thunderous intent and revolvers aimed at their bodies. Both men were unarmed, Sandilands weapons still inside his tent hanging off his trouser belt, Slacek's rifle and handgun already secured to his saddlebags.

The raiding party hit with such surprise, authority and precision; the two stranded victims found themselves surrounded before they realised what was happening. The two startled officers had no hope of defending themselves and before they could comprehend what was going on, they had been belted across the heads with the butts of the assailants' guns, Razor exercising his right to excessive force when it came to the rapist Steve Sandilands. Within a minute, their hands were quickly cable tied behind their back.

They were gagged, eyes blindfolded with dark pieces of cloth and had hessian sacks draped over their heads and tied with rope around their necks. They were hustled to their feet then marched through the bush until they came to where Harry stood waiting with the horses. Their two victims were thrown like ragdolls sideways aboard Danny's horse then tied down to the saddle. They knew the big black gelding would not be happy, a perfect objective to give their now prisoners the roughest ride possible.

They rode northbound until they hooked up to the Bullock Road extension. The roads origin started 16km away at a T-intersection down on Syrian creek road. It started off as a wide gentle winding road, enough for two vehicles to pass with room. It continued to climb to where the lads were situated, across several crossroads and bridges where small creeks would flow underneath, then tighten dramatically with overhanging branches and encroaching shrubs from the shoulder with deep wheel ruts on the disappearing road before it would eventually come to a dead end.

The destination Danny had organised had a four-wheel drive track that came off the rough extension that led to an old logger and miner's shack. He had visited the site years ago by chance and always thought it the perfect place to get away from everything and everyone as not many campers would ever go there due to the lack of nearby running water and accessibility, however, this time, only sinister thoughts made him recall the location.

The early morning sun was still not visible as the mountains started to wake from its slumber. Thin sunrays poked through the low miniature gaps of the forest as Danny ousted himself from his camouflage while Benny kept himself hidden. With a nudge and the drawing of his weapon, Senior Constable Mike Whitehall drew Dane's attention to a sole figure walking towards them across the grassed clearing. Dane gestured towards his partners to lower their handguns after he accepted Danny's response that he was unarmed.

'Good to see you, Danny,' Dane greeted with authority. 'People reckon you might have slipped through the net, but I knew you'd be around here somewhere. As you can see, I got your note. Didn't know you could fire an arrow so good,' he remarked.

'Been practicing, had to find food somehow,' Danny shrugged in return.

'You look alright. Except for your face. What happened, run into a tree, did ya?' Dane mockingly asked, noticing Danny's cuts and bruises from his fight with Ricky, which were still very visible.

'Wrestling wombats, Dane. You know how wild they are up in these parts,' smiled Danny.

Dane laughed off his reply knowing that he had received a beating somewhere, but now was not the time to delve and kept the conversation as light as he could.

'Gone with the goatee beard, I see. I was expecting to see a skinny and shrunken man!' Dane replied.

In the Sergeant's eyes, Danny certainly didn't look like a man who had been roughing it in the bush on limited rations for nearly 20 days, he looked fit and healthy in his mind, and the perception he was giving off alerted Danny to the fact. But nevertheless, Dane was inches away from taking him in, and he would put his questions on the back burner for the time being.

'Don't let the looks fool you, Dane, I'm fucking spent, mate. All we want to do is go home and face what's coming,' Danny said calmly. 'Good to see you did what I asked and not bring the other two. That bastard Sandilands touched up Greta, you know!' he angrily added.

'Took some convincing, but they did what they were told,' Dane replied with a wry smile. 'I understand Sandilands, but why Slacek? Why has he pissed you off?' he asked.

'He raided my house with the re-po squad,' Danny bluntly said.

'Oh,' was Dane's one-word reply.

Dane immediately wondered how Danny knew about the incident with Greta, and how he also knew about the re-po squad. Someone was getting information to him he quickly concluded, but he would keep that conversation short.

He reached into his side bag and grabbed an apple and aged banana, brown in skin and soft as pulp inside. 'Sorry, it's all I got,' he said. He tossed them at Danny who offered thanks and asked if he had any more for his friends.

'Just another couple of apples. Speaking of which, where are they? 'Dane queried.

Dane knew that Danny couldn't have possibly darted that arrow at them. He knew he had some raw talents that others didn't, but archery was not one. His trust in Danny was thin to say the least. He understood what pressure his friend was under and was worried another arrow could be coming at them as he panned his eyes around the surrounds knowing that Danny's boys were around somewhere.

'They're close by. Just needed to see if you came without the other two parasites first,' Danny answered.

'Fair enough,' was Dane's contrite reply.

Danny walked closer to the men as he peeled the banana skin away and tossed it to the ground. He gulped it down and turned towards Dane's partners and extended his right arm for a greeting handshake and introduced himself. Mike Whitehall and Jeff Hill reciprocated and assured Danny that they knew all too well who he *was*. Dane had told them all about his fugitive friend but even they were surprised how friendly an alleged cop killer could be at first encounter.

He turned his attention back to Dane. He took his first bite out of the gifted apple and casually spoke, 'This is how things are going to proceed, Dane.'

Dane interrupted, chortling at Danny's arrogance, 'I'm in charge here, Danny, and I will say how things will proceed.'

Danny responded quickly, 'Well, can you guarantee that there will no ambush this time? No phantom hitman ready to put a hole in us like last time. No dudes out there that want to cash in on us. Can you guarantee us that?' he forcefully asked.

'You and your friends will be safe,' Dane assured. 'We're inside three hours from the outskirts of Graceville from here. I'll take you towards the Graceville pass. Then we'll cut down through the pines and through the catchment via the back of the reservoir. It will be steep and rough, but it will keep us away from the roadblocks, or anyone else that wants to make a name for themselves for that matter.'

Danny agreed to his terms, including having Sandilands and Slacek ride ahead of them after Danny requested that he didn't want to lay eyes on them. Satisfied with Dane's strategy he asked them to sit tight for ten minutes while he went and got his three buddies. He walked back into the camouflage of the bush and disappeared out of view. The three officers remounted their horses and pensively began the wait.

Dane was nervous. He knew Danny well, and in his mind, things weren't adding up the way he was acting and soon enough, his inner anxiety would be justified. The officers wait was only five minutes in when another whizzing arrow flew past them and embedded itself into one of the pine log barriers, only meters from where the men were atop of their horses.

Benny's job was done. It was all Danny had asked of him. There was no need for him to hang around if things went wrong. He didn't want him exposed or involved in what was to come. Danny patted him on the shoulder and thanked him, still in awe of his bushman friend's talents as Benny quietly gave him a giggling thumbs up and left the area.

Dane jumped from his horse and raced over to pull the arrow from the barrier. As soon as he saw it go in, he knew Danny's act of surrender was all a ruse. Once again, the arrow had a note attached. The Sergeant ripped the adhesive tape away and hurriedly began to read:

DANE,
    IF YOU THINK I WOULD TRUST YOU AGAIN, YOU WERE WRONG.
    I KNOW YOU LIED TO US ABOUT CONTACTING VACCARO. IF YOU WERE STRAIGHT WITH US, KANE AND YOUR TWO YOUNG COPPER MATES WOULD STILL BE ALIVE AND I WOULDN'T HAVE ANOTHER THREE MURDERS ATTACHED TO MY NAME. I TRUST NO ONE ANYMORE. DO NOT TRY AND PERSUE US AGAIN. IF YOU DO, I PROMISE THAT YOU AND WHOEVER RIDES WITH YOU WILL END UP THE SAME WAY AS THE TWO CAMP MATES YOU JUST LEFT BEHIND. IT SEEMS PEOPLE ARE DYING AROUND YOU ALSO, DANE. DO NOT INCREASE IT!

HAVE A NICE DAY. DANNY!

Dane screwed the letter up in frustration. It hit a raw nerve with him. He took it as a personal attack from his old friend. Everything he had worked for since the day Danny shot the first of the Devlin brothers had now been obliterated. He knew something was amiss with Danny and was cursing himself not to have acted. He ordered his partners back atop of their horses. They rode as hastily as they could back down to their campsite to see if Danny's threat was real, updating his partners on the way.

The campsite was empty when they arrived, no sign of Sandilands or Slacek. All their belongings were still laying where they had left them, horses still tethered nearby. Dane rushed to the openings of their tents, ripped the flaps back to see nothing. His anger was boiling. He started to kick and throw all that was around him, pots and pans, cups and clothing, rocks and branches. He was cursing as loudly as he could, saliva and spit spurting out of his mouth, his face reddening by the second as the realisation that two of his party under his command had just been kidnapped.

'Fuck you, Danny!' he roared. 'I'm just trying to do my job!' he hollered as he stared into the surrounding mountains as his colleagues looked on, taken aback by their Sergeant's tantrum.

'What shall we do?' Whitehall asked.

'We should go after them,' Hill said.

'No,' Dane ordered. He was taking Danny's threat seriously 'I'm not going to put any more lives at risk. They've already got a 30-minute break on us. We don't know what direction they've taken. They could be anywhere.' Dane cursed. 'There's nothing we can do except stick to our plan and ride home.'

He knew Danny had the help of more than his three buddies to pull off what he did, that he was sure of. He didn't know how or where he got it from but had a strong inclination inside, and if so, they were likely to be outnumbered. If by chance they caught up with them, they would probably come off second best he rumbled to his partners with anger and fluster when they questioned his order.

Dane sat down on a nearby log still cursing. He bought both hands to his head in despair. Danny had outsmarted him and with-it came dire consequences. All had gone bad, a waste of time he cringed to himself and he was already wondering how he was going to explain it to his superiors as he tossed the radio about in his hand, trying to draw on the courage to contact the Inspector.

Sergeant Dane Grainger was hoping like hell that Danny's threats to kill were hollow ones. Hopefully a severe beating at worst was to be given, then left behind to fend for themselves would be the outcome, however, his reliable gut feeling was that he may have just seen the last of Steve Sandilands and Victor Slacek.

Danny rushed and pushed his way through the bush as fast as he could on foot. He made it to where the Bullock Road extension had fizzled out then proceeded along its path. Puffing and panting atop of the loose and creviced surface, he finally reached the entrance point where the boys would be waiting. It was how he remembered, a little overgrown in parts since last he was there, but the shed was still standing and looked how he envisaged it other than the graffiti across its rusted corrugated iron walls.

The huge mountain ash tree stood majestically next to the old hut with the red spray-painted bullseye target still noticeable. Rusted and dirt ridden pots and pans and old BBQ plates lay around in parts, assuring that it had been a long time since they had been used. He was greeted with a familiar snort and wild look that came from his equine partner. The big black gelding was first to acknowledge the intruder as Danny entered the clearing that surrounded the hut. He was tethered with the rest which gave Danny nervous relief to see that the boys were where he wanted. Now all he needed to see was if they had two guests with them.

'Anybody home?' he called.

Barny was first to emerge from behind the hut. He walked towards Danny and gave him an embrace. 'I will never do that again,' he growled under his breath.

Danny nodded his head in sombre consent. Ricky and Harry appeared from behind the other side of the hut, while Drake and Teeto outed themselves from the inside. Razor remained with revolver in hand keeping an eye on the still gagged, blindfolded and cable-tied prisoners who were sat down inside the hut with their backs against the corrugated tin wall.

'They're inside where you wanted them,' Drake said as he faced Danny. 'Make it quick. We want to be back inside *La Fortaleza* before anyone notices we're missing.'

'Have you said anything to them?'

'No. Silence all the way,' assured Drake.

The Vice President turned back to the entrance of the hut and motioned to his equal to exit. Razor joined Teeto and the three Sultans legged themselves up onto their horses. They advised Danny that he had one hour to meet them at the back entrance of *La Fortaleza* off Molloy's track, otherwise they were on their own trying to find a way back into the security and sanctuary of the compound. Danny overheard Drake tell Teeto it was time for him to get moving. He asked where he was going. 'Let's just say he's got some homework to do on your Armaguard,' came the straightforward reply from the burly VP, Danny contented with the answer.

Danny accepted their advice and ensured that he would be there before time. He watched as the black cladded members rode off and within a few minutes the four fugitives were alone in the bush once more. They gathered around Harry and exchanged embraces and pats on the backs with him. It was time for him to leave.

Danny had organised for him to meet Benny at his camp and from there, the master of the mountains would show him the way out and a safe passage into the abyss of suburbia. It was Harry's utmost desire to rid himself of the mania around him. He could see the reckless change in Danny, he could see what he was becoming, and could also see it with his closer friend Ricky which scared him the most. He wanted no part of it, no part of Danny's revenge, no part of the robbery, no part of the Sultans and above all, no part of living in the mountains anymore.

He pleaded with Barny to join him, but his loyalty was too strong to break. Barny had no family to return to as Harry did, the boys were as close to one as he could get, however, he did go out of his way to help relay Harry's feelings with the group late last night and this time, he received no hostilities, only blessings, and Danny was only too happy to organise a way out for him. It was done without the knowledge of Drake and Razor.

Danny knew that they would veto the exodus of their friend. No supposed tenant left *La Fortaleza* without Solomon's consent and the Vice Presidents didn't want to jeopardise their seniority within the club by endorsing decisions without the compliance of their President. But the four fugitives considered themselves a single tribe now, and the wellbeing of each of them took precedent over everything else, and they would deal with the fallout afterwards, whatever it may be.

The farewell for Harry was over. The ride to the logging coup for Harry was the most fearful hour of his life. For the first time he was riding alone, always nervously looking side to side and over his shoulder. Every sound that came from the forest was the sound of encroaching police or bounty hunters ready to pounce he surely thought. He made it to the Summit Road and then into the logging coup and was over gladdened to see Benny waiting with his giggling welcome and by nightfall, Harry was exhausted and sore but safely on the outskirts of suburbia working on a way to reunite and have the comfort of his distressed and worried family by his side.

'The scales, Danny, the scales! Don't tip them,' Barny pleaded.

'I have to do this, Barny. There's no turning back,' he answered.

Barny could see the look in his friend's eye. It was all he had talked about since they had been on the run and the moment had arrived. He knew there was nothing he could say to prevent Danny from enacting his revenge. It was an obsession, and the point of no return had come. Barny lowered his head and conceded he could do no more to prevent what was about to come. He muttered that he would meet him on the extension road then turned his back and led his horse out of the area.

'You going with him?' Danny turned to Ricky and asked.

'Fuck no! I wanna see this,' was Ricky's energised reply.

The two childhood friends entered the shack and lifted their prisoners to their feet. The muffled panicked gargles stirred from the underneath their gags. The walk was slow as they pushed and prodded the still tied, blindfolded and sacked officers up a cleared slope until they reached another smaller shed that contained two drop boxes, the old-fashioned toilet of the bush, five metres deep that consumed human waste. The iron and timber walls and ceiling were infested with cobwebs, spiders and insects.

Danny unwrapped two lengths of rope he had carried on his shoulders and threw one to Ricky. They knotted the ropes into a noose then forced them over the heads of their prisoners. They tossed the excess rope over a large beam above and tied the loose end of the rope to a thick metal pipe protruding from the shed wall. They tightened the slack then manoeuvred the men close to the drop boxes, Sandilands on the left, Slacek to the right, there feet only just able to settle on the rotted deck beneath. Ricky produced a whiskey flask and took a huge swig, passed it to Danny who finished its contents.

Danny nodded to Ricky to lift the hessian sack off Slacek's head then release the blindfold, and in turn, he did the same with Sandilands. It had been an hour since the two prisoners had seen the first daylight. Their eyes flickered to adjust to their surroundings and when they did, their hearts dropped to an unsinkable low when they saw the face of Danny Pruitt staring back at them.

The two suspended prisoners, arms still cable tied behind their backs, started to gurgle and flay in panic. The look in their eyes was of unbridled frightened astonishment. After all this time, Danny had them at his mercy and he was not going to give them the freedom to plead for it. He kept the gags firmly entrenched in their mouths. He had no impulsions to listen to what they had to say, he was going to do all the talking.

'Hello boys. You finally caught up with me,' Danny ridiculed.

His anger started to surge inside as the reasons foreclosed on his mind why he had them there. Visions of his house being trashed and destroyed engulfed him as he looked at Slacek. Visions of his beautiful wife being groped and manhandled by Sandilands were generating a volcano inside. He looked at Slacek and calmly gave him the reasons why he was about to die.

'Victor Slacek! For the crimes of trespassing and illegally raiding the homes of innocent people, including mine, and dealing in stolen goods for financial gain, and also for beating up on your wife. Yeah, you thought no one knew about that, didn't you! I now sentence you to hang until you are dead.'

He turned his attention to his second prisoner.

'Steve Sandilands! For the crimes of raping innocent women and young girls, and also engaging in illegal re-po squad raids, I here now sentence *you* to hang for these crimes. But most of all, for touching up my wife, you fuckin dog! You should've never done that,' Danny angrily finished. 'And you said I was going to hang,' he added with laughing disgust.

Both hostages started to release panicked screams and hollers from behind their still tightened gags. Their heads jolting from side to side as they tried in vain to release themselves from the bounds around their wrists.

'Shut up and take your medicine,' Danny scorned. 'You bastards signed your death warrants the moment you agreed to hunt me down.'

Danny refused to release the gags. He didn't want to listen to the pleads for life or the begging of forgiveness. What they had done was unforgivable in his mercilessness mind and he gave them no recourse.

The ruthless stone hearted avengers stalked around like wolves, spitting and snarling, they had their prey where they wanted them. They slowly walked behind the men and grabbed the ropes from their tie downs and started to pull down with all their force. Wrapping the rope around the steel pipe with every strained pull, they lifted Sandilands and Slacek from the support of the deck below and into the air.

The noose immediately began to tighten around their necks, slowly crushing the larynx as it moved up and under their chin with every tug and pull down of the rope. Legs kicked out in terror as they desperately gasped for air. Danny and Ricky tied the ropes down again, satisfied that the 12 inches they had elevated them from the ground was enough for the nooses to complete what they were intended to do.

The thrashing of legs and hips was frenzied as the weight of their bodies started to contribute to the crushing of their throats, pressure mounting on the vertebra of their necks, ready to snap the bones at any moment. As the seconds passed, the blockage started to affect the brains of both men as it starved for oxygen. Their faces were turning blue, spit and drool leaking onto Sandilands beard. The panicked thrashing began to slowly decrease and within three minutes they started to lose consciousness, however, Danny wasn't finished just yet. His hate filled mind was over ceding any rational thought.

He unholstered his Glock 22, .40 calibre pistol, a gift from Drake from his array of illegal arsenal and pointed it at Slacek. He extended his arm, the short barrel only inches away from Slacek's chest. Numbness had consumed Danny, his chronic sleep deprived body fighting the last bit of moral conscious left inside his will as Ricky watched on in palpable anticipation. Snorts of rapid heavy breathing in and out of his nostrils filled the air as he gestured to Danny to finish what they came to do. The trigger was squeezed, CRACK!

The kickback was minimal through his wrist as the bullet entered the chest cavity of Constable Victor Slacek. Another shot quickly followed; Danny stunned as he watched Slacek's body sway from the impact. If his heart was still beating it had surely been extinguished now. Danny's momentary shock was broken by further cracks, this time from Ricky, who exploded two rounds from his exact weapon into the body of the already deceased victim.

Barny heard the shots from where he was waiting on the extension road. He motioned the sign of the cross as he bowed his head in respect for the victims. Danny then fixated on Sandilands whose eyes of terror were already rupturing out of their sockets. He squirmed and convulsed in frenzied hysteria knowing his life was about to end as he desperately held on from unconsciousness and suffocation.

'You should've never touched my wife,' Danny quietly tormented, and then with a soft squeeze of the trigger, watched emotionless as the bullet entered between the eyes of Constable Steve Sandilands, terminating his life instantly, blood and brain matter spattering against the wall behind. Danny panned to Ricky, waiting for a shot to come out of his pistol, he helped himself with Slacek so was expecting the same with Sandilands and was obliged when another two shots were fired by his pal into the chest of their second victim.

Both lifeless men swung from the rafters by their necks as the last beats of their hearts pumped blood out of the entrance and exit wounds. After a minute of morbid fascination at the swinging limp bodies, they helped each other guide them above the drop boxes, first Sandilands, then Slacek. They ripped away the wooden seat to gain more access to pit hole. They cut away the nooses from their necks, then the ties from their wrists and funnelled them down into the holes, Slacek the more difficult being the larger man. Feet first, they lowered them down into the cylindrical cavern, blood from their victims' wounds smearing on their own clothing as they descended them in. They held the dead men's arms above their bodies, ensuring they would not be snagged.

Their legs and torso disappeared, then their heads and arms followed into the depths of the drop boxes, coming to a halt a couple meters from the top before their bodies crumpled down in the confine space of the rounded pit. Danny grabbed some loose iron lying around, bent it around to his satisfaction and covered the entrance to the drop box while Ricky gathered some metal strands to tie and clamp the makeshift lids down. They set about destroying the remainder of the shed and laid the demolished timber and iron atop of the holes, then struggled and heaved a large log over the remainder, trusting it would forever become a permanent tomb.

They returned to their horses with maniacal looks of satisfaction and deranged expressions of achievement beaming across their faces as they garnered each other's reaction. Mounting their steeds, they absconded from the area without so much a look over their shoulder and within minutes had quickly met up with Barny. Not a word was spoken on what had transpired as the three continued onwards to the rendezvous point with Drake and Razor.

The Vice Presidents asked where Harry was when they arrived.

'No idea,' was the group reply. He could be anywhere; they countered the questions with short answers, insinuating that he had vanished in fear. Drake and Razor were livid. They warned for their own sake that he better stay mute regarding the inside running of the club. The boys laughed it off, advising he would never do anything to jeopardise them or the club. Drake and Razor pensively accepted what the boys had to say and strongly advised that they were the ones who would have to explain their missing friend to Solomon.

The now group of five re-entered the lands of *La Fortaleza* three hours after they had left under the cover of darkness. The morning sun was quickly rising from the east and would soon be beating down on the plateau, but not before the men would be back inside the compound and in their sleeping quarters, unnoticed and unseen, avoiding the security sensors and cameras inside *La Fortaleza* and breathing a whole lot easier.

Danny entered his tent and lay his sleep-deprived body down onto his thin mattress. He adjusted his pillow to his liking and chillingly comprehended that the real killer inside had well and truly emerged out of his soul. The line had been crossed, and it was going to take him a legion of adjusting.

Chapter 31

'Oh my god, they match!' she gasped. Valerie Corbett was in her office perusing over the addresses which had been hit by the Young Bloods. She was preparing an article on the failure to stop the escalating violence in and around Graceville and the Hexagon Valley. No arrests had been made concerning the destruction and havoc released upon the properties. Proving who was responsible was difficult for police as the investigation intensified. Another hot day was looming, it was only mid-morning and without the luxury of air conditioning it was already uncomfortable in her office.

Valerie was going over the names of the property owners whose houses had been destroyed and they all had a familiar ring to them. She couldn't put her finger on it, it was bothering her immensely. She racked her brains over and over until it finally dawned on her. She stood from her seat behind her desk and raced over to her filing cabinet in the corner of her office. She unlocked it and rummaged through its contents until her hands lifted papers from inside a manila folder.

She hurried back to her desk and compared the names on each of the documents. The names of those on the re-po squad list involved in the raid on the Pruitt property matched the names whose properties had been obliterated. It had been four days since Danny had his revenge at the extension road and five days since the Young Bloods started and finished their rampage.

'This cannot be a coincidence,' Valerie concluded. 'This has to be Danny's work.'

She gathered both documents together and put them in her shoulder bag, the draft for her impending article could wait. She stormed out of her office and mounted her horse which was tethered to a post rail on the street outside her office building in the heart Graceville. Frightened and shaken, she was off to see Kate. Valerie knew very well that it was her who divulged the names to his sister and never in her wildest dreams thought it would ever come to this, however, she was also awestruck in admiration of how Danny had orchestrated his payback, she didn't know how he did it, but was free from doubt that his fingerprints were all over it.

She rode hurriedly to Kate's and made it known what she had discovered. The two women were immediately off to see Greta. Kate was sure that her sister-in-law would be pleased to hear that the men who ravished her belongings had finally gotten what they deserved through the deeds of her husband.

Corey greeted them at the door. Kate burst past him, grumbling under her breath that he was lucky that Greta was still staying with them as Valerie followed her in.

Greta was taking in the warm sun, stretching out on a recliner lounge in the backyard wearing a loose sarong tied around her waist with sunglasses to go with her bikini top. She always loved the sun on her skin to keep up her tanned complexion. She had her long dark crinkled hair tied in a double bun as she kept half an eye on the children frolicking in the blow-up one-meter deep pool.

Kate rushed down the steps off the veranda to where Greta was relaxing on the lawn with Valerie in tow. Sarah heard the commotion from her bedroom and with Corey, stood atop the veranda and listened in to what their visitors so hastily wanted to inform Greta about.

Kate allowed Valerie to relay her findings and when she had finished, both women were surprised at Greta's nonchalant reaction. She sat up from her lounge chair and shrugged her shoulders as if she didn't care. Kate pushed and pushed a reaction from her, adding how fantastic it was to see that Danny still had the reach to inflict misery on their perpetrators despite being so far away, however, all they got in return was deadpan emotions from Greta.

Kate and Valerie were concerned at Greta's reaction, they expected smiles and relief. *Something's wrong here*, Kate thought, this was not what she expected.

'What's wrong, Greta. Is everything okay?' she asked.

Greta slowly raised her sunglasses to her forehead.

'If you think people's houses getting destroyed is good news, Kate, then that's all good. But I don't,' she calmly replied.' Innocent women and children have been left homeless and that does not sit well with me.'

She looked up at Corey and Sarah who she knew were listening.

'You two don't have to stress. Your house is safe,' she declared. 'He forgives you, Corey. He knows the circumstances on how you were involved, and he's okay with it. I told him in my letter. He said he has nothing but love for you guys. I just wished he would've forgiven the others,' she lamented. 'He also said to tell you that your friend Brad Neilson has dodged a bullet. His words, not mine, only because of your friendship with him,' Greta added.

It was a huge relief for Corey to hear. His conscious had been racked with guilt ever since. He had lost sleep and had stressed every day believing that his good friend despised and no longer trusted him, and Sarah was happy that any ill-conceived ideas Corey had of running into the mountains to find Danny could now be put to bed.

Greta conceded that she knew what was about to happen with the re-po squad members. She was expecting it, and it came as no surprise to her she confessed. She had recognised the victims' names from the list that Kate had shown her previously. Danny had promised retribution in his last letter and when she read about the destruction on the properties, it somehow gave her confused hope that the promises he made concerning other matters maybe, just maybe, will come to fruition as well, including making her way to a place called heaven.

He had revealed the long secret he had kept from her of his part ownership of the property in the northern state. Although Greta knew that the property existed through Danny's excited stories, she never realised that he owned a piece of it. Tears of happiness welled in her eyes as Danny explained in his letters how it was all going to be a big surprise for her when he had eventually paid it off. He knew how she loved the warmer climate and the beach, along with her dream of owning a ranch-style property one day. Danny again described it as best he could in his writings and informed her that he had already posted a letter to Steve Goulding, a man Greta remembered as a good friend of Danny's.

Danny wrote that he would soon have the money to pay him outright and take full ownership and promised all going well, that he would meet her there before her birthday, three more weeks away, but stressed not to mention a word to anyone. It all had to be under the veil of secrecy, not only for their own security, but for the safety and wellbeing of their loved ones, the less they knew, the better was his assumption.

Greta had no idea how her husband could achieve what he had promised. It all seemed delusional for her, to unrealistic and farfetched, but it was the only thing she could cling to, and cling to it she would. It gave her hope, and all she could do was play the agonising waiting game and wait for Danny's next correspondence, or of the news that she dreaded the most.

Greta excused herself and retired to her bedroom, fighting the vulnerabilities that churned inside. Refusing to answer questions fired at her by Kate, Sarah, and Corey regarding her contact with Danny.

'I just want to be left alone,' she graciously conveyed in her calm and stoic way, reminding them that everything will be okay. 'Danny and I will be together again. It will just take some time,' she said before closing the door to her bedroom.

There was a myriad of things that Greta deliberately failed to mention to her concerned friends, one being a meeting with Sgt Dane Grainger two days before, and that was the subject that laid on her mind the heaviest. Dane thought it his duty to confront her over his brief meeting with Danny and the events that led to the missing policeman under his care, and Greta was mortified to hear what he had to say.

She never asked questions as she listened to the detailed description of the events that took place, with Dane adding he had no choice but tell the truth in his statement to authorities. Greta courageously kept her emotions in check as the consequences of her husband's actions started to sink in, with Dane warning that Danny may have changed from the man he was.

He conveyed that he understood the tremendous stress that he was under and not even he could comprehend what he was going through, but he was making judgement calls that only made things worse for him Dane forewarned, with the ominous prediction that she may never see him again. Greta rued and grieved that she had no power over the decisions her husband was making. Greta knew that she was the only one in this unforgiving world that could subdue his anger and irrational emotions, Dane knew it and so too did Ricky and Barny, quoting many times, 'If only Greta were here.'

Not being there by his side to make him think clearly shattered her to the bone, and the repercussions were starting to take a deadly toll, and that's what terrified her the most, however, rightly or wrongly, Greta's faith would remain unbroken.

Dane advised her with tormented regret that the search was being ramped up in earnest. Every available officer was sent to the area where Sandilands and Slacek were last seen within hours of Dane's report, but days had passed and there was still no sign of either the outlaws or missing policemen. Police vehicles and motorbikes had been commissioned to join the numerous men on horseback. On the second day by chance, four police on trial bikes stumbled on the clearing that contained the remains of the shed which held the executions, but no signs or inklings gave them reasons to search deeper and left with the sight being ticked off and no need for a return.

They more than once stopped at the gates of the Sultans MC compound on the directive of senior management, only to be met with the baying roars of the rottweiler guard dogs in concurrence with the veil of silence and denial from the members. The threat of search warrants didn't deter them, Solomon laughing at the suggestions from behind the gates.

But if the President was giving the impression to his club that all was good and safe with the Sultans MC and *La Fortaleza*; inside, Solomon was gearing himself up for war.

Now that Minister Johnston was not in control of the Hexagon Valley, transporting their wares was becoming a lot more difficult. The rules of engagement had changed, and Solomon refused to change with it. His whole operation was now under threat without the aid of Johnston turning a blind eye and taking his percentage cut of the club's drug and arms profits.

Solomon had already been given a hint of things to come when one of his converted vans was intercepted before it had even left the roads of the Hexagon Valley shire. It was searched, stripped and then impounded by the new law enforcement led by the interim Minister with all drugs on board seized and members arrested.

Solomon was receiving intel he did not want to hear from his many informers that police headquarters in the city were already discussing plans to confront the Sultans MC and that a raid on La Fortaleza was imminent. The President had already put out feelers on a proposed meeting with the new Minister, to talk business which would benefit both parties. He even tried to seek out Inspector Vaccaro, but both times he was given a flat refusal, they didn't want to meet with the outlaw MC President under any circumstances.

He called a meeting between all senior members from the club. Drake and Razor were present and did not believe for one minute when their President guaranteed to his underlings that club business would run unhindered and progress would continue as normal, with or without Minister Johnston on their payroll. Solomon had built La Fortaleza from the ground up. Everything inside was of his doing.

It was his citadel, his castle, his land, his club, and he would be damned if he were going to let anyone or anything take it off him. He had seen a lot in his lifetime, more than the average person could ever comprehend. All he wanted was to be left alone, his club to be left alone by outsiders and get on with the life that was forced upon him by the incredulous and suffering times created by the very establishment that now wanted to take him and the club down.

Drake and Razor knew what was coming if their President did not back down. They knew that Solomon would not easily give up what he had built inside these mountains. They grasped that he would fight to the death if necessary and that's what had got the two Vice Presidents heads together to make a play and unite with Danny and maybe risk all for their cut of the robbery.

They loved their club dearly. It had given them a comfortable life compared to what may have been. The club had fed them, housed them, and kept the finances rolling in, and in return, they had given all to the patch. They had been loyal servants to the creed and done things that they had regretted for the good of the club, however, there was one thing they agreed they wouldn't do, and that was to die for it. Both men were married, Drake a son, four years of age, while Razor's wife Candice was pregnant, four months gone, and the two Vice Presidents were adamant they wanted to see their children grow up. After the meeting inside the Manor around the club table, the decision had been set, whatever the risk may be.

Heated words were exchanged over the table between Solomon and his two Vice Presidents. With Lars and Crow, two visiting senior members from the club's city stronghold were present, supporting their President, and any suggestion put to Solomon regarding the restriction of drugs and gun movements were instantly shot down. Razor was the logistics man and knew the conduit of their supplies was in serious jeopardy without the backing and aid of Minister Johnston. He mooted that they cease movement for a time, bag and store, until they had a better idea on what was happening with the law or until they could find another route. When Razor questioned Solomon's motives and decision making, he was met with a verbal onslaught that sent a clear message to all who were present.

'I will never abandon *La Fortaleza* under any circumstances. The club will not be halted, and if anyone dares to enter through them gates or stop one of my vans again, I'll meet them with all the force I have. No one stops club business, *no one*!' he thundered.

The President's tirade was backed up by the Sergeant of Arms. Lars was adamant that they should fight for what they had built. It would put a huge financial dent in their coffers if trade were to be ceased which could not be tolerated, and if a confrontation was imminent, he was in. The big Viking lookalike didn't care if it was the law or not. If there was a fight to have, he would happily smile while he engaged, and along with the angry haunting stares of Crow who had the same sentiments as Lars, gave the President their loyal support. '*La Fortaleza* cannot be compromised,' they agreed.

A vote was put around the table, to cease business and shut down *La Fortaleza* until the heat passed, or to continue club business as usual and fight and repel anything that may come their way. Sensing the mood, Drake and Razor subtly backed down from their original concerns and the unanimous decision was for the latter, 7-0, and the gavel came down.

Drake and Razor did not want war. They knew what the outcome would be if the police came visiting with all their might and both rued that their senior club members were too loyal to their President. They didn't know if the loyalty was through their own lack of foresight, or whether it was the deep fear they held towards Solomon. They gathered that all other members and prospects would follow Solomon through fear alone, no matter what he asked of them, so as it was, Drake and Razor would not even bother to determine if they could gain the numbers and support throughout the club.

They were playing a deadly game of Russian roulette with their decisions, the most dangerous being to unite with Danny and the planned armed robbery, they didn't know what the proceeds from it would be if it succeeded. Would it be enough to tie them over? Would it be enough to help them with their escape plan? Would it be enough to buy them safety?

Both had been banking money away under pseudonym names; however, it was well short of what they needed to abscond with surety. All their plans relied on three men who had never pulled off anything of the kind, but the worst scenario for the men would be if Solomon ever found out. Even if the two Vice Presidents successfully combined with Danny and the boys to pull the job off, the deadly game of survival would have only just started as both understood that it was a lot easier to join the Sultans MC than to leave it. They, more than any, were well aware of the rules and clearly understood the consequences that went with betrayal.

Chapter 32

It had been four days since the evil inside Danny was released on the two policemen. He had struggled to come to terms with it, constantly questioning himself, 'is this the real me?' He had kept to himself most of the time since, keeping busy as the club put him and his two buddies to work, pruning and picking throughout the orchards and helping with maintenance and building chores.

He had sought counselling off Barny, *he always listened to me*, Danny avowed to himself, but no matter what was discussed between the two, it would never change what he had done. Although Barny could sense a softening of Danny's rage and vengeance, it was still obvious that his friend still had a lot of combat left in him to complete his mission and reunite with his wife.

The boys had not left *La Fortaleza* since the slayings. It was a good idea to lay low for a while, they agreed. The outside mountains were flooded with angry police hell bent on trying to re locate their missing colleagues, a fact that was being repeatedly enforced by the Sultan members who came and went from the compound.

Danny had an inkling that all was not good inside *La Fortaleza*. He sensed the mood of the members on their daily routines had changed over the last few days, more reserved, more tense than usual. It was not his place to ask, so quietly went about his own business, watching, listening, until he could get a hint on the reasons why to satisfy his suspicions. He humorously raised the subject with Drake but with no luck, again with Razor, who shook it off and told Danny that he was imagining things, however, Danny knew something was going on and hoped whatever it was, it didn't interfere with his date with destiny regarding the time frame of his robbery.

Crow had vigorously raised the issue of the over police presence around the mountains with Solomon. 'It's too close for comfort,' he worried. 'We must sacrifice Pruitt and his mates to ease the pressure away from us,' he suggested. 'We're being choked, and it's all because of him,' Crow added earnestly.

Crow was referring to the tactics of police who were now stopping and questioning their members as they came and went from La Fortaleza. Surrounding roads and tracks were becoming a major thoroughfare for law enforcement, especially track 24, which made the Sultans more than nervous.

Assistant Commissioner Martin Conroy had been employed with the authority to take over the search for the fugitives and with Inspector Vaccaro as his 2nd in charge, they knew Pruitt was around the area somewhere, and inside

La Fortaleza they were 99% sure of, and harassing club members on his whereabouts was the number one directive.

All they needed was one mouth to confirm that the Graceville four were being harboured inside, which in turn would give them the legal go ahead for a full-scale, fully forced raid on Sultan territory, hopefully killing two birds with one stone, arresting wanted cop killers and shutting down the biggest supply of arms and drugs in the state in one fell swoop.

Solomon rejected Crow's strong suggestion. He liked Danny, after all, he did save his daughters life the President reminded his underling and would have nothing to do in setting up his demise. But Solomon's real motive to keep Danny around had nothing to do with the honour of repaying the debt of saving little Maddy's life, he had other plans installed for his guest. Danny had respectfully tackled him about the disappearance of Harry, he thought it a chance to gain some points with the President by being proactive.

Danny despised Solomon over what had taken place with him and Ricky, and at times wished he could have made it three at the extension road. Ricky's howling despair of fear on his face will forever be framed in his mind but he knew their whole survival depended on Solomon allowing them sanctuary, so for the time being, Danny would pander to the President's ego.

Two days had passed after Harry had absconded and Danny was nervous by the non-reaction and so approached the President. At the time, Danny wasn't sure if he had even noticed Harry wasn't around anymore but was soon reassured that nothing gets past Solomon when it came to the comings and goings of *La Fortaleza*. Danny was nervously surprised by the nonchalant reaction, considering the wave of concern shown by Drake and Razor, and spent little time on the subject.

Solomon thanked him for his honesty. He admired his courage in confronting him, but he knew better than the excuse Danny gave for his runaway friend. The President was no fool when it came to the bond the fugitives shared and knew better for one of them to up and leave without the consent or aide of the rest of the group, but for the time being, he would put it on the back burner and deal with it when the time was right, because for the moment, he wanted Danny for other purposes.

News of the missing policeman quickly made its way back to Solomon. Radio interceptions gave the club updates on all matters regarding the search for Sandilands and Slacek, and the name Danny Pruitt was blared to the fore over the initial transmissions when it came to a suspect. Solomon met Danny while he worked away in the apple orchard, his job discarding any rotten produce the local bird life had destroyed and asked if he had anything to do with the missing policemen. When Danny replied with a guilted half smile of denial, Solomon's suspicions were answered. He accepted the reasons why. They deserved what came to them he acknowledged after Danny spoke, saying that he would've had no hesitation in doing the same.

'Don't worry about it. You'll live with it,' Solomon assured him, then continued to offer his wisdom. 'Every man who's ever lived has had the craving to kill at some point, it's up to him whether he wants to fulfil that urge in that moment. For those who have, it's just like inhaling one of my finest plants, you always want to go back for more.' The President smirked while sniffing hard up his nostrils. 'What's done is done. No remorse!' He directed, 'I knew you weren't just a normal civilian, Pruitt. After all, we all eventually become who we really are!' he succinctly finished.

The words jolted Danny like an earthquake had hit him. He started to combat his emotions: *Is Solomon telling the truth? Am I really like what he says? Why don't I feel more guilt, more remorse? Who the hell am I anymore?* However, in the end, Danny would settle on what he believed. He trusted his own perception that he was still a good person.

All his adult life, he had been a law-abiding citizen, well, most of it, he tried to do the right things by people and authorities. He never harmed anyone without justification, when he did, it was only through absolute necessity, or for the protection of loved ones, and if he was now perceived as a bad person, then so be it, because none of it was his making, he reminded himself. It was the world who had turned him bad, nothing else. Governments and authorities were totally to blame, and any guilt would quickly be dismissed and directed straight back on those responsible.

The only guilt he would carry, and it was a heavy one, was that he had to abandon his wife and children. In every letter, he would convey it to Greta. She was the only one who mattered, the only one he would listen to. What she said, what she thought, and if she asked him to surrender, he would do it in a heartbeat. But Greta had never asked him of that.

In her letters, she would always remind him of her undying love and faith which gave him the strong-willed conviction to continue what he was doing, so any statements from Solomon he would ignore and convince himself that he knew exactly who he really was, no matter what the Sultan President insinuated.

Solomon conveyed that he respected that he was a man of his word. Danny had threatened and promised that he would have his revenge, and seeing it take place only heightened Solomon's esteem for their fugitive guest.

To him, Danny had displayed all the creeds of the club's ensign. He had proven that he had the strength and adaptability of the Bear by his survival through adversity. He could no doubt defend himself and had the self-preservation as the Scorpion portrayed. He had the loyalty of the Wolf, his bond with his fugitive friends had certified that, and he had just shown the cunning of the Hawk over the slayings of Sandilands and Slacek. All the same, the President would stop short of offering Danny the honour of being patched up, despite giving it serious consideration.

'You got rid of them in the right way, I presume?' Solomon questioned dubiously before exiting his company, knowing that any mistake could bring undue trouble back on the club.

'No need to worry. They'll never be found,' Danny quietly promised.

Solomon squinted and lowered his eyebrows then nodded with twisted lip acceptance. He never asked anymore questions on how it was done. He never asked who was with him, maybe he knew all the details anyway, he knows everything else Danny mused silently, but he did feel nervous for Drake, Razor and Teeto if he did.

Solomon's mind was ticking over. He saw Danny in a no-win situation. He had proven he would never give up his freedom and Solomon perceived that he would only fight on his side if things were to escalate which gave him the arrogant confidence that he would have three extra guns by his side, when and if his own private war were to come to his door step.

'Oh, by the way,' Solomon said as he turned to leave the orchard, 'it seems we have a common enemy now.'

'What do you mean?' Danny asked, confused.

'John Pringle! Apparently, he's turned crown witness against Johnston.'

Danny shrugged his shoulders; he didn't know what the comment had to do with him.

'Last I heard, he was wanted for murder, wasn't he?' Danny said.

Solomon turned the peak of his black cap around to shield his eyes from the sun. He had a determined and distorted smile on his face and calmly spoke in his raspy tones.

'Not anymore! His lawyers have cut a deal. He's turned star witness. He's going to testify all that he knows about Johnston and other politicians, not to mention all the crooked cops who have hired him, which in turn will put our club in a not too good outlook.' He drolly commented, 'He's going to spill the bucket on all of us. In return they're going to drop his charges down a few pegs, and that could give him bail. He might be walking the streets by the weekend. So, watch out, Pruitt. I know him well. He'll be coming after you for killing his mates, but not if I get to him first.' Solomon winked as he left.

Danny's testicles tightened in unison with the quick thumps from his heart. The thought of crossing paths with Pringle was not something he desired. He lowered his pruning saw contemplating the outcome, however, within minutes, he was soon chuffing to himself that as long as he stays inside La Fortaleza, the hands of John Pringle couldn't touch him. He relayed the news to Ricky and Barny. He humorously couldn't wait to see their reactions and his pals didn't let him down, they both strongly argued that anything to do with John Pringle was no laughing matter.

The legal fraternity was abuzz with the turnaround of John Pringle and once the news was leaked to the media, not only did it send a shockwave through the seats of parliament, it rattled like an earthquake through police ranks and organised crime alike. There were many who had hired Pringle on both sides of the law and those involved were either running for the hills or scramming for legal advice.

Pringle had run out of resources, there was no one left he could turn to. The reward for his apprehension was too much of a carat for those who collaborated with him, that was the world they lived in. He knew he wouldn't last one day in prison. Scorned inmates would make sure he never saw breakfast, so he took the only option left to him, turn on those who had paid his wages.

The Premier was keeping his word on the fight against corruption, no matter where it came from. He accepted the deal that was offered from Pringle's lawyers, better to dig out the roots than to trim the leaves he quoted. One hundred convictions far outweighed the imprisonment of one hired thug, and so stuck to his promise that he would come down on government dishonesty and criminality with an almighty sledgehammer.

The decision did not sit well with the likes of Martin Conroy and Inspector Vaccaro, and it certainly didn't sit well with Dane and the grieving families of the young constables who had lost their lives on Syrian Creek Road, but Premier Kendall was adamant that he had bigger fish to fry. He wanted the biggest heads he could possibly get, those of the politicians, crooked cops, and leaders of organised crime.

Public confidence was at its lowest ebb in the state's history and he was not using the struggling times as an excuse. He could see there was finally a silver lining at the end of the darkest cloud ever to hover above modern times, and he wanted to still be in power to utilise its benefits. However, protecting John Pringle was going to be a task within itself. The Government knew that people would be looking to silence him before the undated trial would begin. No charges or arrests had yet been laid, no names bandied around as authorities were still questioning and detailing Pringle's statements and until indictments were issued, the DPP's number one witness would be kept under state protection.

It had been five days since Danny sent his last letter to Greta via postman Benny and he was fretting for her reply. They had not left the compound since the morning of his vengeance and was sweating on seeing Benny. The nearby police presence had been too risky for them to venture outside, also for Benny to try and deliver at the gates. Benny knew better than to expose himself to anyone that might link him to the boys, Danny had advised him repeatedly, so he patiently bided his time, keeping his secretive eye on proceedings inside the mountains. Luckily for Danny, he was going to get the break he needed.

The last few days had been extremely hot, up to and over 40 degrees Celsius at its afternoon peak, and today was going to be even hotter. Temperatures were on the rise and reaching dangerous levels for people inside the mountains as the hot northerly winds started to gain momentum. Humidity was almost down to single figures and combined with the gusty oven like winds, it was a recipe for disaster if any spark were to be lit. Police protocol was safety first for their members.

There were only a few firefighting tankers with access to fuel, and no aerial support to help in emergencies in the present day. No bulldozers to cut fire breaks, not enough vehicles to form a mass evacuation, so in their wisdom, authorities started to withdraw all police members out of the ranges. With the day scaled at a code red, the highest possible on the scale chart when it came to the risk of forest fire, only a brave skeleton staff remained to continue their jobs as commanders concentrated more numbers on escape routes at the bases.

It was nearing midday when Danny decided to make an exit and try and find Benny. He had a letter for Greta in his back pocket, Ricky also with writings to his family but Barny had no such thing. He thought he had embarrassed his friends and distant family enough already as he reluctantly joined Danny on their sojourn out of the compound. With the withdrawal of police numbers came the withdrawal of club members out of *La Fortaleza*.

The pressure valve was released somewhat for a brief time, so members took advantage and retreated to catch up with friends and family. Drake and Razor being two of them who took to being husbands again at their own rental places back down in Graceville, but the number one absence the boys noticed immediately was the President himself. It was the first time the boys knew of Solomon departing his land and it put them on edge, because as it was, with the absence of other senior members, Crow was left in charge of *La Fortaleza*, and any excuse to get away from under his nose, they were going to take.

The boys waited on horseback on the track that overlooked the marijuana plantation, Danny's horse already giving him a hard time, swinging his head from side to side, and moving around at his will. The big black gelding was giving the obvious hint that he didn't want to go anywhere on this hot day after relaxing in his stable for a few days, only being walked for brief breaks at a time. They wanted to use the same route that Drake and Razor had guided them through when last they ventured to the logging coup, avoiding any potential eyes that maybe looking over the main gates of *La Fortaleza*.

They met a member named Pepper, Pep for short as most called him. He was of short stocky stature with solid arms and legs that displayed numerous tattoos. A thick dark beard rounded off his youthful face. The boys didn't have much to do with him but recognised him as ok fellow from previous short talks, but they also knew he was Crow's right-hand man when it came to the cultivation of their contraband.

If the boys wanted to leave *La Fortaleza*, they knew they needed Crow's permission to do so and waited for his confirmation. They had heard he wasn't in the best of moods, which was saying something as the boys had still yet to see a smile from him. The plantation was under duress because of the extreme heat. Shade cloth had been extended above the plants for protection, however, it could only cover half the crop, rendering the exposed plants vulnerable to the hot winds and heat, wilting and burning unprotected leaves and plants as the club pulled on all water supplies from the dwindling Kensington River nearby.

Pep radioed his Vice President who was in a shed down on the edge of the plantation and after a minute of silence his reply came through loud and clear for all to hear, letting the boys know that his opinion of them had not waned.

'Yeah, go ahead, let them through, hopefully the fuckers get shot or arrested. Or bitten by a fuckin snake, yeah, that would be nice,' was his terse response.

'Copy that,' Pep replied with a wry smile directed at their three guests.

'Gee! That's a bit harsh, isn't it?' Danny smirked.

'Yeah. Not a nice man that Crow person,' added Barny.

There were light-hearted smiles as the boys progressed through, Pep walking beside them until he opened the digital coded gate then giving them the keys to open the large gates further on and soon the boys were on the mountain roads making tracks to Benny's camp, crossing their fingers that he would be there.

All was quiet except for the sound of the swaying crowns of the tall forest trees as the hot northerly wind gained momentum as the day grew longer, along with the incessant buzz of cicada's echoing in their ears. The three made it to the Summit Road, sweating and drinking from their water flasks. They had only donned singlets and shirts, jeans, boots, and caps. Holsters hung by their hips old western style, loaded with their Glocks and semi-automatic rifles attached to their saddles. They slowly eked their way along until they neared the first entrance to the logging coup when the first of what would be many voices coming out of the coup grabbed their attention.

Startled at what they were hearing, they quickly dismounted and led their horses onto the high side of the road then climbed a two-metre-high embankment, camouflaging themselves on the rising terrain from the threat. They attempted to take refuge behind thick shrub and trees, but before Danny could join Barny and Ricky, the grip on his reins was jolted free by the strength of his steeds thrashing head. Big black bolted free and headed across the road and straight into the logging coup where the strangers were gathered.

'Get back here, you bastard,' Danny growled under his breath, knowing that any sound would give away their whereabouts.

'Shit, shit!' He cursed, as he watched his horse continue free and unabated.

'Forget about him,' Barny called.

'Fuck! My rifle's still on the saddle!' screeched Danny.

Big black galloped through the light shrubbery then entered the coup along the southern perimeter track that surrounded the vast area. He then swung right, reins dangling and bouncing with the stirrups, Danny's tying skills of his saddle straps being tested with every twist and turn of the liberated equine, and once in the open, it didn't take long for the group inside the coup to notice the lone horse coming at them.

Danny crossed the road and peered through the thick bush and watched his steed in full gallop as it approached the strangers while Ricky and Barny took cover on the high side of the road, Barny leading both their horses higher into the bush to shield them from any eyes, tethering them to a low branch as Ricky took cover behind a large eucalypt.

Big Black continued his lone rampage as the spooked strangers watched on. Danny watched his horse shy away from them, then continue through the logging coup at full tilt towards the sloping incline on the western perimeter where the forest would thicken back to its native growth. Three men mounted their horses and began to chase big black into the forest while the others congregated in astonishment.

Barny had joined Ricky and were signalling and grumbling to Danny to get out of sight. Danny wasn't budging as he continued to peer through the scrub looking at the group around 300 metres away. He counted eleven of them, including the trio who had given chase to big black. He watched nervously at the remaining group of eight mass together then mount their horses, with the front two taking off in a fast gallop towards where Danny was hiding. It was his cue to leave. He scrambled up the embankment and joined his two buddies, all drew their guns from their holsters as they waited. The heat of the day was forcing perspiration out of their bodies like a flowing river as they geared themselves for a confrontation.

Within minutes, the group on horseback had made their way out of the coup and onto Summit Road. The boys could hear their conversation clearly as the strangers enthusiastically guessed where the lost rider of the rogue horse had disappeared to.

'Do you know any of them?' Ricky whispered.

'No idea, never seen them before,' replied Danny. 'What the hell is anyone doing out here on a day like today anyway?' he added.

'Well, we're out here, aren't we?' Ricky snapped with sarcasm.

Danny ignored his reply. He too was starting think it was not such a great idea venturing away from the solitude of *La Fortaleza*.

The boys continued to watch and listen stealthily. They did not want a confrontation. There were too many of them. Although their Glock handguns could hold almost 40 rounds of ammunition in their magazines, the last thing they needed was another shootout. Danny knew that any spent shell casing could ignite a wildfire with the increasing hot winds. It would be like putting a cigarette lighter to paper from the heat of the shells if it landed on the tinder dry floor of the bush. The boys didn't know who they were, or what they were doing there, and nervily waited for the situation to unfold.

'They don't look like police,' Barny whispered.

'Yeah, too young for that. Not one of them look over twenty-one,' Ricky added.

'Yep! That puts bounty hunters out of the question too,' said Danny.

Five long minutes elapsed as the group in front of them rode and walked about, searching for any clues that may lead them to the missing rider and were soon joined by the trio who had given chase to big black, informing their partners that the wild horse had out ran them and disappeared into the forest, bringing a relieved smile to Danny's face.

The boys dared not move. The forest floor was baking underneath them, the undergrowth was crackling and snapping with any step or side movement, any sound could give away their location. They watched on as the group moved slowly away in a northerly direction, away from where Danny and the boys had come from. Their anxiety was slowly being relieved as they watched them move off.

Frightfully for the boys, it would not last long. They had waited ten minutes and were almost about to exit their hideaway when five riders returned to the logging coup. They watched through the gaps of the tree lined coup, and it seemed to them that they were doubling back to where they were situated before big black broke loose. The boys waited patiently to see what would happen next.

Danny's patience was wearing thin. The heat was almost unbearable, sunrays were beating down on their burning necks and shoulders and sitting still was only adding to the discomfort of it all.

'Fuck this! If they come anywhere near us, I'm going to shoot 'em,' he threatened.

'No way,' Barny broke in. 'I'm not shooting at an innocent man, Danny. I'm not shooting at random. If they fire at us first, then maybe I might shoot back, but not before, alright! They're just kids, for Christ's sake.'

'Ain't no rules of engagement here, Barny,' Danny bit back. 'Anyway! There's no such thing as an innocent man.'

The boys were on their stomachs, pistols ahead of them as they laid behind a slight mound, a thick fallen branch giving them extra protection. Barny was in the middle of his two friends and shook his head in frustration at Danny's comment.

'What do ya mean, no such thing as an innocent man?' he grilled.

'I don't know! We're all guilty of something, aren't we? Especially these days,' said Danny.

Barny rolled his eyes in flustered dismay as he listened to Danny's convoluted reasons to justify his statement.

'One of them may have killed his dog because it pissed on his couch,' he said. 'See the dude with the white T-shirt, he belted his younger sister for eating his biscuit. The other one on the white horse, he stole money off his bloody mother.'

'What a bastard! I would never do that,' said Ricky, angrily shaking his head, giving the impression that what Danny had said was gospel. He even chimed in with his own thoughts.

'See the one with the big cowboy hat.' He pointed. 'He probably molested a child last week,' Ricky alleged with scorn. 'And the other one! He probably knows everyone in the re-po squad and took some profits.'

'You reckon? I'll fucking have him. Guilt by association! I love that law,' Danny snarled.

'Yeah! You see, Barny! There's no such thing as an innocent man.'

Barny's bewilderment was met with soft pats on his shoulders by both his pals. Smiles and silent laughs came from them as Barny begrudgingly accepted their perplexing anecdotal reasons, giving off a light-hearted smile himself after Danny told him that not all men are as kind-hearted and caring as him. The serious mood was broken for a time as the inane rhetoric finished and they were feeling a lot more at ease when they saw the five men begin to ride off.

It looked as if the horsemen had forgotten something and had retrieved whatever they were looking for. Maybe they were there just to look at the large machinery left behind they commented. Some of them were probably too young to see most of it in operational mode. It would be like something out of Jurassic Park to them, Ricky gibed. The three waited again for a short time until they sensed the coast was clear. Danny and Ricky scaled down the embankment, peering their eyes down Summit Road to see if the group had moved on as Barny went to retrieve their horses, but if they thought they had just escaped a big problem, another would catch them totally by surprise.

Barny came down flailing through the bush, his face consumed in absolutely shock and fluster.

'The horses, the horses! They're bloody gone!' he blurted.

They raced back up to where they were tethered, not believing they had disappeared. They looked around in panic, looking for signs which might indicate the direction they headed but nothing was there. It was though they had vanished into thin air.

'No wonder they were quiet. They weren't even fucking here,' Ricky scowled.

It was a worst-case scenario for them. If anyone were to be out looking for them, they would be sitting ducks without the aid of their rides, not to mention the 8km undulating walk back to *La Fortaleza* in over 40-degree heat without any water. The boys were cursing, Ricky eyeing off Danny, off-loading profanities that they should never have left in the first place, readying himself for another argument, but Danny didn't reciprocate. He looked around, up and down, pushing his tongue against the inside of his cheek in deep thought.

'C'mon, let's go,' he said.

'Where?' Barny said, shrugging his shoulders and extending his arms.

'To Benny's camp. It's only 500 meters up the road. That's why we're here, aren't we?' Danny answered with authority.

He made his way back down to the road, Barny and Ricky followed, there was no option left for them. They couldn't afford to be separated, not now, so fell behind Danny with handguns by their side. They crossed from side to side as the road cornered and twisted, trying to keep camouflaged. Ten minutes later they entered the track that took them to Benny's camp.

They crept lightly though the bush, the same way they did when they first discovered it following Benny's rock formations, then shook their heads in disbelief to see Benny sitting alone in his favourite canvas deck chair, hand feeding the two mares that belonged to Ricky and Barny. A further noise grabbed their attention to the right, and from about 20 meters away they could see Big Black slurping away out of a large plastic trough, getting some much-needed water into his system, saddlebags and rifle still attached.

'What the hell, Benny!' Danny exasperated. 'You stole our horses?'

Benny's customary giggle greeted them as he rose from his chair. He grabbed a tin can at his feet and began spooning some pineapple rounds out of it, enjoying the taste immensely as the juice dripped down his chin.

'I never stole your horse, Danny. He showed up himself. He knows where he can get water and food. The big boy has got a great memory. Your big black is no dumb arse, mate,' Benny said in a matter-of-fact tone. 'In fact, he's probably the most intelligent beast I've ever come across, so that probably explains why he hates your guts.' He laughed.

'What about ours?' Barny asked suspiciously while Danny tried to come up with a reply to Benny's friendly taunt.

'Oh no! I took yours. Thought it would be fun to see your reaction when those other dudes left,' he joked.

Benny couldn't stop giggling. He thought it was his greatest prank. It took a little time for the boys to come around to his humour and finally accept that they had been a victim of his jocularity and were soon were laughing off his tomfoolery and comments, collectively joking to him that if he ever tried anything like that again, they would shoot him themselves.

Benny walked over to his hidden cache under the forest surface, brushed away the refuse that sat atop and open its lid. He threw each of them a can of assorted fruits so they too could enjoy some thirst quenching, Danny opening his with his bowie knife with ease, but it was the envelope he held in his left hand that drew Danny's anticipated attention. It was Greta's reply safely sealed for reading.

'Bet you been sweating on this. I thought you would be wanting to see it by now,' Benny smiled.

Danny fumbled excitedly as he tried to open the seal on the letter, more than once dropping it to the ground as he eagerly tried to read its contents. He took his position on a deck chair to concentrate on its writings as Barny and Ricky quizzed Benny on the safety of Harry.

'Did you see him off okay? How far did you get him? Which way did you take?' The questions were fired with haste as Benny tried his best to quell their anxieties over their friend by saying that Harry was safe. He relayed that he got him as far the western side of the Tangiloo state forest and that if Harry took the roads and tracks that he suggested, he would've made it to the city's suburbs without too many problems, news that relieved them. 'No news is good news,' they agreed.

As Danny read away with half an ear to what Benny was saying, he was getting chuffed by the minute as he finished each paragraph of Greta's writings. He read that his twin boys were fine and healthy. He read about the town's happenings and was gloating inside to read that his wife was so looking forward to moving up north and to a place called heaven. He couldn't believe the enthusiasm in her writing.

Tears of pride welled in his eyes as he read further, then was somewhat surprised when he read about the circumstances regarding her knowledge about the offer from the DPP and her meeting with Inspector Vaccaro. Danny could count on one hand the number of times that he had heard his wife swear, and to see the words in capital letters in front of him, FUCK THE OFFER, it made him feel prouder than ever of his beautiful wife. To read further that her faith and love in him had not waned and the promise that she would wait for the time when he would send for her, only gave him added strength to try and complete what he was planning.

Benny explained that he had only returned to the mountains early this morning. He had been down in Graceville avoiding the police and vigilantes that had swarmed the mountains previously to the hot weather setting in. He put the boys at ease when they questioned if he knew the group who was in the logging coup, saying they were just young travellers who had made their camp near Domino falls.

They were the only ones he had seen during his travels throughout the morning, jokingly saying that they had travelled the right way from Domino falls, 'not like you guys,' he smirked, referring to the lost days that Danny and the lads had to endure before Benny saved them.

'They meant no harm. They were only having a look around the coup. I know a couple of them,' Benny said.

'See Danny! Innocent men,' Barny chided.

Danny shrugged his shoulders and smiled at the comment and quickly returned to Benny wanting to know all what had happened around the mountains since they were last in touch. Their bushman friend confidently predicted that the young group were the only ones around now. 'People aren't stupid,' he said. 'Most know better than to be here on big fire danger days like today. Except for a four-wheel drive cop vehicle that's been hovering around; but you can hear them a mile off.'

Benny explained what the boys already knew about the flooding of police around *La Fortaleza*. He thought it a good idea to get back down to Graceville for a while to avoid any contact and confided to Danny again that he would be wanting to see him by now, knowing he was awaiting Greta's reply. Ricky asked Benny if he had a run-in with any of the police search parties. He replied with great humour on the sole incident when he did.

'I met a group of four on one of my hidden tracks when I was heading out. I had no idea how they stumbled across it, but I had nowhere to go. They were in front of me before I knew it. They started asking me all these questions. Who I was, where am I going? Have you seen this bloke called Danny Pruitt and his mates?'

'What did you say?' Barny asked.

'I just jabbered away back at them. They thought I was talking some ancient aboriginal dialect. Fuck, it was funny!' Benny laughed as the boys joined with him.

'They let me go after about five minutes. One of them called me a black c**t too,' Benny added.

'Did you get his name?' angered Danny. 'We'll track him down and teach the racist prick a lesson.'

Benny laughed at Danny's threat. It never worried what they called him and asked Danny to settle down, advising him that he would be a very busy man if he were to have his revenge on every redneck racist that lived in the Hexagon Valley. He reminded him that there have already been enough shootings in his life recently and that he probably had more important things to worry about than protecting the honour of an indigenous bushman.

Benny quickly changed the subject and asked the boys if they had heard about the confrontation at the swing bridge camping grounds down from the cascades. 'No,' came the collective reply.

'It happened last Monday morning,' Benny informed them. 'It got a write up in the papers.'

'We haven't read a paper all week,' Danny replied. Explaining that all was quiet at the compound.

The boys were curious to know what had happened and when Benny filled them in on the events, Danny would have more pride instilled inside of him.

A vigilante group, ten strong, which included cousins and friends of the Devlin brothers were out to make a name for themselves, wanting to be the first to track down the slayer of their family members, however, they didn't count on eight others that had formed a vigilante group of their own. Their purpose was to prevent that exact thing from happening by protecting and helping Danny and his friends any way they could. Their paths crossed at the base of a large swing bridge which crossed the Kensington River and what started out as swearing and badgering, soon erupted into an all-in brawl with bodies being slung everywhere across the campsite.

The fight was no more than three minutes in when one of the Devlin associated group fired his weapon in his panicked haste, narrowly missing its random target which set off a fire fight on both sides, resulting in two deaths and three severely wounded on the Devlin side, and two wounded on the other.

Police in the region who had their hands full investigating the whereabouts of the Graceville four were quickly notified by radio and swarmed onto the site convinced that the search for the fugitives was about to come to an end, wrongly believing that the four would have certainly been involved. Arrests were made and the injured and dead transported back to Graceville hospital, by the sole police vehicle for the wounded, and by horse and cart for the deceased.

It was soon obvious to those in charge that the Graceville four were nowhere in the vicinity at the time and had nothing to do with the shootout. They quickly enforced laws that nobody was to be in the area without a legitimate excuse. From now on, anyone who looked suspicious or couldn't validate their reason for being in the region were told to leave immediately, if they refused, they were arrested and transported back to the Graceville police cells.

It was the only way they could prevent another confrontation, to save lives, but more importantly, stopping reckless vigilantes interfering with their work, and it was a directive that played straight into the hands of Danny. The boys gleefully and arrogantly acknowledged the fact. The less people around, the less eyes would be around, and all the safer for them to travel about unnoticed if they dared.

Benny couldn't help the boys with any names that were involved. Danny took some guesses on who it may have been. Ex footy teammates he hazarded a guess, maybe the boys from the pub who he played pool with, they were a loyal and wild bunch. Nevertheless, he would never find out who was out there trying to help his cause, he just asked Barny to give them a prayer and hope no harm or jail would come to them.

Along with the gusty Nor Westerly winds, the temperature was rising quickly, and the boys decided that it would be a safe option if they parted ways with Benny and make a retreat to La Fortaleza. The boys looked at Danny in amusing disbelief when he told them that he had left his letter for Greta back in his tent with the change of pants before he left. He was angry at himself for doing such a thing and wasn't too pleasant in response to his friends badgering, and so organised another meeting with Benny in a couple of days, this time with the letter in his hands.

The three fugitives made it back to the compound unscathed and unseen, much to the gross disappointment of Crow. They were red faced from the heat on their return and along with their horses needed some much-needed hydration, big black giving Danny his most hassle-free ride to this point. After they took care of their horses and sucked in some water, Danny entered his tent to retrieve his letter to Greta from the back pocket of his other pants, this time putting it in a noticeable and safe location with his belongings so it would not be overlooked next time. He was adjusting his surroundings when he was taken by surprise as the flap of his tent was pulled back.

'Get Barny and Ricky. We need to talk,' Drake ordered. 'Meet me down at the stables in ten minutes.' He walked off with purpose.

Danny had no time to answer. He was surprised to see that the Vice President had returned; at least that got Crow off their backs, no walking around on eggshells anymore, Danny mused, but the way Drake had spoken, he knew it was serious, and a myriad of thoughts crossed his mind, all with negative overtones as he went to round up Barny and Ricky.

Drake was standing in front of a five-foot mezzanine which stored horse feed and accessories. A group of horses stood in front of him in their stalls, making it difficult for the boys to find him when they arrived. Drake needed to make sure that no eyes and ears were around. The boy's apprehension quickly turned to nervous tension when Drake earnestly panned his eyes around them and asked, 'Are you ready to take back what you've lost over the years?'

Danny knew exactly what he was talking about and questioned if he had some news on a certain Armaguard van, knowing that Teeto had been sent on a reconnaissance mission.

Drake confirmed his suspicions and the three waited eagerly to hear what he had to say regarding the information and planning that concerned them. Barny and Ricky were still apprehensive in their thoughts on the robbery, however, Danny's confidence in achieving his plan was about to get a huge boost.

The Vice President oozed confidence when he acknowledged to Danny that all he had told them had been proven, including the red-bearded man who took his cigarette break outside of the van. Drake and Razor had their insiders and associates working overtime throughout the week. They pulled in favours that were owed and secured a contact inside the Armaguard Company that allowed them clandestine access to the van which transported the money.

A GPS was attached underneath the vehicle which gave them data on all stops, time frames and route of the vans journey. They gained access to rosters, driver names and protocols that the company vans and employees followed and learned that the same three drivers had been on the roster of the Graceville run, which included their stop at the Country Club, for the last sixteen months. The same three men travelled every Monday as Danny had assured, which gave the planners confidence that the men would no doubt be victims of their own familiarity.

Drake couldn't estimate how much the Armaguard would be carrying after the boys had enquired, but did confirm that after the van left the country club, it made its way to the three banks in the heart of the Graceville Township before it returned to its base in the city's inner eastern suburb of Glenthorn. But Danny wasn't interested in the bank's fortunes, and Drake agreed, the only window of opportunity to make a hit on it was at the Country Club. He was, however, interested in the information that Drake and Razor had received with the Vice President going as far as guaranteeing that it would already be holding a vast amount, confirming Danny's suspicions previously, and it would be more than enough for them to attain their escape and buy them safety.

'So! Are you in or out?' Drake asked with authority. 'We need you! And you need us if we are to pull this off,' he affirmed.

'Of course, we're fucking in. Right, boys?' Danny said.

Barny and Ricky pensively looked at each other, shocked that Danny would agree without any consultation. They had never promised that they would participate. All along they thought him to be a tad delusional and it would never happen. They were certain that he would come to his senses and it would all blow over, but in one excited sentence, they now regretfully realised that they had grossly underestimated Danny's villainous ambitions.

Barny and Ricky nodded their heads in agreement that they were in. They didn't want a heated confrontation inside the stables, the temperature was hot enough without raising it further. They knew that Drake wanted to keep things quiet, so they would wait until they were alone with Danny again to voice their uneasy disquiet.

Drake extended his right arm and firmly shook the hand of each of them, acknowledging that this was a pact of the highest code. 'No turning back now, right!' he pledged, with accepting gestures from the boys.

'Alright! We hit it Monday morning,' Drake affirmed.

'Shit, why this Monday? Shouldn't we give it another week?' Barny asked.

He was looking for time, any time, time that would give him a chance to reason with Danny to take another course. It was going to be to no avail. The boys had given Drake nothing but respect since the time they had arrived, and it was the Vice Presidents time to give some back and come clean on their reasonings. Transparency and trust was the only way they could move forward.

'We *have* to go now. We might not have another week,' Drake confided. 'Solomon is adamant that the law will be banging down our gates at any moment. With Johnston out of the picture, our whole operation could come crumbling down. We've tried to talk to him but he's gearing himself up for war and we want no part of it. I have a wife and son. Razor has a child on the way, and we don't want them to grow up without us.'

'We're putting everything on the line the same as you are. Razor will be back at the compound Saturday morning. He's finalising some details. We'll go over plans then, and then we'll go over them again, and again and again, until we have got it down to the second because there is no plan B. If something goes wrong your end, you'll be the only ones that go down, understood!' Drake sternly said, switching the subject back to the job at hand.

The men accepted what Drake enforced and after another round of handshakes departed from the cover of the stables, the hot winds at least cooling the sweat off their bodies with Drake's warning ringing in their ears. Danny's stomach was churning in mix of excitement and fear. He couldn't wait for the meet with Razor to see what planning they had established at their end. He knew there were loose ends that he had not covered. He relied on Drake and Razor to take care of them. He knew he had to succeed and was under no illusion that he had the most dangerous part of the whole reckless exercise.

Never in his craziest drunken stupor had he ever thought of attempting such a thing, but these were unprecedented desperate times. It terrified him to the core knowing that the time had come to back up his words, and to Danny, his fate was sealed. If he had any chance of freedom and reuniting with his wife and children, it was the solitary way out, and he could not fail. The only thing left to make it a fait accompli was to have the knowledge that Ricky and Barny would be by his side.

Chapter 33

'I think we have gotten it all,' Sarah yelled from the Pruitts' veranda.

'Thanks Sarah. I'll be inside in a minute,' Greta replied.

Corey and Sarah had arrived with an open cart to help Greta retrieve any belongings that had been left behind from the re-po squad raid and post intruders. It was Sunday lunchtime; the heat of the previous week had subsided somewhat but was still hovering around 30C-degree mark. It was a pleasant change to the scorching week they had just endured; however, it was going to be a brief respite as the temperature was predicted to soar once more within the next 24 hours.

Greta didn't expect to find much to take back with her but needed to satisfy her anxieties on what may be left. It was the nation's birthday on the Friday and people enjoyed the public holiday and partied well into the Saturday with festivities taking place all around Graceville. The mood was uplifting for the people with the double celebrations of the country's birthday combined with the predicted end to the hard times and anticipated surge in the economy, paving the way to a return of their previous fast-paced lives.

Greta took advantage of the Sunday lull with most people recovering at home or resting up with family. Although she had ventured out into public domain sparingly, it was still hard for her to socialise so the quicker she was able to get to her property without having to be stopped or having gossiping eyes trained on her the better.

It had been nearly three weeks since she had last set foot into her home. Police tape still surrounded the properties perimeter, torn and flapping around on the gentle breeze. Greta had asked Dane to accompany her. She needed security and police permission to gain access and approached him the night before to ask for his help. He was the only one she could trust with any type of authority and the Sergeant had no hesitation in assisting in her wishes.

Greta knew there wouldn't be much left behind from the raids and the vultures, and with the help of friends, she had already recovered what was most dear to her on her previous visit along with the unexpected drop in by the Young Bloods. Returning this time to her property was more an excuse to have Dane by her side to find out what had really happened in her yard on that fateful morning when the two Devlin brothers lost their lives.

Greta needed some type of closure, to get a real time appreciation of what her husband had been through, the reason why he had to make the decisions that he did. She thought that she could get a better understanding by being there and seeing for herself and asked Dane to go through the events step by step as they walked around the yard.

Dane was clear and circumspect as the questions came from Greta, until silence gripped her as she panned her saddening eyes around her property.

'Are you okay? If it's too much for you, I'll stop,' Dane asked with sincerity.

'Everything's gone!' Greta sighed. 'I raised my children in this house, Dane. It's the only home they've ever known. It was my home. Danny and I worked so hard for it and now look. Look what they've done, everything's gone!' She motioned around.

'I know this sounds harsh, Greta, but you're not the only ones. It's happened to hundreds, thousands. It's the reality we've been living in,' Dane asserted softly.

'Not like this,' she grieved.

Greta didn't care about what anyone else had been through. A month ago, she had. She cared deeply about the less fortunate, but not now, not after her own world had been so ruthlessly dismantled.

Greta bent over and picked off the top of a Mr Lincoln rose from her garden as they walked. It was her favourite variety of rose, a perfectly shaped bud with a deep aroma, crimson coloured with a long thorny stem. She was surprised it was still untouched by the intruders as other plants were. Greta mused that the uneducated scum that trounced her garden wouldn't know a beautiful plant if they stood on it, it had to be the only reason that her treasured plant remained. She bought the flower to her nose and smelt its fragrance, she then turned to Dane and commented that she understood why Danny had done the things he had.

Dane let off a frustrated sigh. Greta could sense his vexation. She continued to bring the rose to her face in intervals as they walked around. In between short silent pauses, they continued to speak in soft tones.

'How did they get the picture of him in the paper? Was it you?' Greta asked.

'They scoured pictures from Facebook archives. The other three were easy, but Danny, as you would know, was a bit more difficult.'

'He always hated social media, didn't he? Never wanted his image on somebody's Facebook. And we thought he was silly,' Greta huffed. 'So, you gave them a picture?'

'Yes, I did.'

'I thought I recognised where it was taken. Caught between duty and friendship again, hey Dane?'

'You have no idea how hard it is, Greta,' the sergeant bemoaned.

'He told me not to trust you anymore, Dane. Why? What did you do to him?' Greta gently probed.

Dane explained the lie he had to tell regarding the Inspector on their travels before the shootout at Tambourine Bridge. He justified his stance and reasons on why he had to do it. Greta listened impassively, which in turn confirmed the burning question that had been alight in Dane's mind.

'You've kept in contact with him, haven't you? Right from the start, am I right?' he asked. 'That explains how he knows everything! You've been telling him, haven't you?'

'It's not just me. He gets the nasty stuff from others. I've never fuelled his fire, that I have never done. But do not ask who else because I will never divulge it. They're only trying to help him, we're all just trying to help him,' Greta said, this time in a determined tone.

'Well, you can help him by telling him to surrender,' Dane firmly said as he grabbed Greta by the arm and stopped her walk. 'Listen to me when I say this, Greta. His life is in real danger. This is no fucking game anymore. The big boys, the S.O.G and others are coming after him and they will not hesitate in shooting him dead if he puts up any resistance. They know he's with the Sultans, in their compound, and my information is that it's going to happen sooner rather than later,' Dane steadfastly expressed.

Greta stood silently. The thought of an *OK Corral* style shootout concerning her husband had already passed through her mind, but once again, she gave no emotion towards Dane.

'Are you hearing me, Greta?' Dane asked concerned at Greta's non-reaction.

She sniffed at her rose again, placed a dangling strand of her flowing hair behind her right ear, looked again at Dane and asked solemnly, 'Why did you hunt him down again?'

Dane explained that he had no choice. He enforced on Greta the reasons and all the good intentions that came with it and as he spoke, Greta was surprising him with her coldness. He had never seen her this way. The gentle, caring, compassionate Greta was nowhere to be seen or heard, and her newfound resistance was about go deeper.

'We all have choices in life, Dane,' she argued in passive tones. 'You, the Devlins, the banks, the Minister. Sandilands! You all had a choice on your actions, and you all chose the wrong one. Now my husband is making his, and I'll stand by him whatever he chooses to do. I will see him again. Danny will see it through. He always does, you know that, Dane,' Greta vowed with a smile.

'Not this time,' Dane warned with hopelessness.

Greta thanked the Sergeant for his presence after Corey and Sarah interrupted their private conversation, saying that all was packed and ready to go. She asked him to escort her back to Kate's house who was taking care of her children. Greta took one last look around her former house. She pragmatically resigned herself to the fact that it was no longer hers. It was now under the ownership of the banks with no possible way of reclaiming her castle.

As mid-afternoon approached and with thoughts of Danny occupying their minds, both Greta and Dane took their seats on the horse drawn carriage waiting atop of the property on the cut away from the main highway. Little did they know as they began their trip back, that only moments before, a woman and a child had passed them travelling the other way. Two people that were already forming a strong bond with their beloved husband and friend, and, had the answers to a lot of burgeoning questions that both Greta and Dane hungered the answers to.

Zoe Valetta was finishing up her work in her city office Saturday lunchtime when she was paid a visit by two women as she was exiting through the foyer of her office complex, and with them was Maddy, looking afraid and lonely. The two women introduced themselves and explained sheepishly that they were friends of Carla, the woman who Solomon entrusted as carer for his daughter.

Zoe was shocked and angered when the women explained that Carla was now lying in hospital in an induced coma after overdosing on a cocktail of heroin and amphetamines and were there looking for guidance and advice on what to do with the now frightened 8-year-old. They claimed that they couldn't take her in and banked on the female lawyer of the club to have the answer on what to do with the President's daughter.

Maddy was overjoyed to see Zoe again and communicated that she wanted to be with her. 'Don't let them take me away. I want to stay with you,' she pleaded in expressions and over animated sign language.

Zoe had no hesitation in acceding to Maddy's wishes. She told the ladies that she would take care of her and politely asked them to leave while she spoke with Maddy alone. Zoe had never met the two ladies and instantly acknowledged that they were associated with the club in some way or form, from not only the clothing they wore, but also the respect they showed towards her, how else would they know where to come for help.

Zoe took Maddy in her hand as she left the building. She flagged down a cycle powered rickshaw, the nowadays taxi inside the hustle and bustle of the city business blocks and being Saturday with all the festivities around, it was more than busy. With Maddy by her side, she hopped upon the seats and soon arrived at her plush ground level apartment by the docklands to ponder what to do with her loving little friend. It would not take long for her to make up her mind.

Danny Pruitt had been in her dreams and thoughts from the moment she had left him. She constantly thought about him wherever she was. Whether it be lying in bed alone at night, in meetings with clients or in the pressure cooker of a courtroom, she couldn't get him out of her mind. She hated it and didn't understand why. It was affecting her work and hindering her sleep with all the silent questioning and mulling racking over in her mind.

How was he doing? She would ask herself. *Is he safe? Who was he with? What is he doing? What would it be like to be with him?* All these self-examinations and more she couldn't let go.

She repeated in her mind that it was all professional. She wanted to help Danny with his cause. She believed her skills could possibly make him a free man, however, her heart kept telling her a different story, and Maddy was the perfect excuse to find the answers to the questions that she had been paining herself over.

Over another sleepless night wrestling with her insecurities, she had Maddy and herself packed and on a train to Graceville on the Sunday morning. Zoe knew what she was doing was inane. She felt like a foolish teenager, but something was drawing her to this married man. She also knew that the same man could also easily brush her off. A man who could easily be arrested at any moment, and also a man who could easily be killed at any moment, nevertheless, she couldn't fight the magnetism that drew her towards him.

Regrettably for Zoe, as soon as she arrived at *La Fortaleza* unannounced by a taxied dual horse-drawn carriage which she had boarded from the Graceville train station, the realisation of it all hit her like a brick, and within minutes knew that it *was a* huge mistake.

Solomon was furious. It was the last place he wanted his daughter to be. He was sitting in his chair around the inner sanctum of the club table discussing matters with his senior members when he got a call on his radio handset from the gatekeepers that his daughter had arrived. He stormed out of the manor, ordered one of his underlings to escort Maddy into the manor then confronted Zoe.

'Why are you here?' he bellowed. 'And what the fuck is my daughter doing with you? I don't want her anywhere near the club at the moment.'

Zoe cowered at the intimidating verbal onslaught. In front of club onlookers, he raised his voice vehemently and questioned her motives, with Danny Pruitt's name coming to the fore. Nothing got past Solomon. He knew that they had spent an evening together and could see the look in Zoe's demeanour when she had last departed.

Zoe blushed it off and explained the only reason she was there was to inform him of the circumstances surrounding Carla, but the President angrily lectured that she had other options than to bring his daughter back to *La Fortaleza*.

The offensive from Solomon continued and the sharpness and confidence that Zoe normally presented had disappeared. She was being belittled and embarrassed from the tirade as club members and associates looked on.

'You're wasting your time with Pruitt. He's no longer here. He's gone. You'll never seen him again,' Solomon mocked and derided.

Zoe's core shrunk.

'Get into the manor,' he ordered. 'You can stay in the spare room next to Maddy.'

Solomon stopped short on sending her back out through the gates right there and then. He would have to organise a horse, carriage and driver and it would be nightfall by the time she would arrive back in Graceville. Above all else at the forefront of his mind was that it would be far from safe if his daughter were to travel at night.

'I want you out of here at first light in the morning with Maddy. I'll let you know then where you can take her,' Solomon berated before Zoe could get through the doors.

Zoe made her way inside the Manor, exasperated. She charged upstairs towards her temporary bedroom then forcefully threw her overnight bag against the wall when she entered, slamming the door behind her. She felt humiliated, embarrassed, angry at Solomon and angry at herself. She had never felt so foolish.

'What a wasted trip, what a waste of my time. What was I thinking?' she cursed to herself. She couldn't wait until morning so she could forget about

Solomon Pike, forget about the Sultans MC, forget about her foolishness and get back to the comforts of her own home, but most of all, forget about Danny Pruitt. As night fell, she laid her angry head to rest, fighting back the frustrated tears, totally unaware that she had just landed herself into a life and death situation that only intervening fate would decide if she were to ever make it home again.

Under the command of Assistant Commissioner Martin Conroy, Special Operations Group (SOG) members had descended upon the area surrounding La Fortaleza and its compound with clear objectives. To shut down the Sultans drugs and arms empire, arrest key players within the club, gather evidence in the corruption case against former Minister Johnston and arrest the Graceville four, with Danny Pruitt and Solomon Pike at the top of their list.

The Special Operations Group had been disbanded over a decade ago, splitting into other units under various names, but with crime escalating to unprecedented levels as the energy and economic crash deepened, they were reformed. The new look SOG took no prisoners and enacted the full force of the law when activated. The whole unit was highly trained akin to a military unit and the success rate of their missions was the envy of all police command. They had moved into the area overnight, entering the mountains east of Tangiloo and then circling around to the northern end of the Graceville pass and encamping themselves at a place called the Apex, the highest point of the pass, only seven winding kilometres upwards of track 24.

It was a planned offensive not to bring their team through the township of Graceville. The element of surprise and secrecy was paramount and taking the long way into the mountains was only going to be of benefit they surmised. With back up from the Critical Incident Response Team (CIRT) encamped behind the picnic ground area of Fernbank at the base of track 24, all was in place for the SOG to make a move on the compound at the first hint of daylight the following morning.

They had planned thoroughly and meticulously and trusted that their intelligence was solid and hoped to have the whole operation concluded within two hours of incursion. They planned on the Sultans being at ease with themselves. It was Monday morning; and the intel gathered assured them that it was party time every weekend at the compound and were counting on members to be hungover and not to responsive to early morning surprises. Command had given the impression that they wouldn't plan a raid while the weather was hot and dangerous.

Police had withdrawn from the ranges on high fire danger days and the Sultans, believing their own intel, were satisfied that any imminent raid on their premises would come another day, so police command were confident that the outlaw MC were going to be overwhelmed before they could muster any form of defence.

They had six converted prison wagons, each powered by four horses waiting at Fernbank for the impending arrival of arrested Sultan members, in which they would be transported back to Graceville, then onto a prison bus that would make its way down the highways to holding centres in Marlboro. Members of the SOG planned to make their way up track 24 on foot before sunrise, all with handset radio comms and fully armed with semi-automatic weapons and military aids. Accompanying them would be an eight tonne BEARCAT armoured plated rescue vehicle. Attached to the front of it was a reinforced steel arrowhead bull bar ready to smash and bring down the iconic gates of La Fortaleza if the club did not adhere to their instant demands.

SOG numbers added up to 22, and along with senior officers closely behind and aside of them, the initial raiding party were made up of 32 men. A further six officers were embedded in the plated vehicle and the rest of the CIRT team in waiting if back up were required numbered a further 40 men including senior command. Police estimated that Sultan MC numbers would be around the 20 to 30 men inside the compound.

Their spying eyes had seen up to 25 members exit out of the compound sporadically through the weekend giving them more confidence that they could overpower those inside with ease and proficiency. They had plans on where all the sleeping quarters were situated and detailed maps of all the rooms inside the grand old manor, with Solomon's room and the camp sites of the Graceville four high on their agenda.

Mistakenly, it was the first of several major errors that police command had made. The first was underestimating the brotherhood of the MC, and what the creed to the patch meant to them. The Club believed that they were an army within itself, a band of militia men, above the law and untouchable, but most of all, police underestimated the fear and power that the President had over them. Solomon had them trained for such an occurrence when and if it arrived. They were highly motivated and reckless in their endeavours to accede to their President's demands.

Police command also got it terribly wrong when it came to the weaponry inside. They had been monitoring all consignments out of La Fortaleza for months and intelligence had wagons and vans full of arms leaving the compound last week with no returns. But what they didn't know was that the wagons and vans had left empty due to a breakdown in dealings between the club and an organised crime syndicate from the city, a standoff between the two outlaw operations that was already heading down a violent path. As it stood on this day, stored away in shipping containers and sheds inside the compound were enough weaponry to hold a mini war if required, they only needed the men to engage them.

Another major error was grossly underestimating the numbers of men inside the compound. There were still 53 patched members of the Sultans MC inside, and along with wives, girlfriends and associates, the population inside La Fortaleza stood at 74, a figure that grossly escaped the attention of police scouts hiding in the mountains, and it was going to be a standoff siege that only the feeding frenzy of the tinder dry forest could end.

Danny, Ricky and Barny had left *La Fortaleza* before lunch on the Sunday. At first, Danny was going to attempt to sneak out of the compound without confronting the President, however, his pride and arrogance could not be subdued and decided that a face-to-face meet with Solomon could only benefit him. He didn't want the President looking at him as a coward of any sought by exiting permanently without his recognition. Although he despised Solomon inside, he also had great veneration for him and thought he was probably the most admirable man he had ever met, and Danny needed his avowal so he himself could move on without any enmity left behind.

Danny was granted permission to meet Solomon at the club's table. He took in all the features that the table had to offer once more before he sat. Solomon with the carved-out bear at his lowering eyes, Danny the scorpion. He panned the awe-inspiring table they sat around, the majestic length of the bar, the mighty bay windows that gave the scenic look out through the compound to the gates in the distance, including the majestic elm tree that he and Zoe had sat under.

The snooker and gaming tables lay beyond the shoulder of the President, the Harley Davidson motorcycles, perched on stands, glistening and impressing at every glance with Solomon's own ride the focus of attention rested nobly, and Danny wondered with envy what lay above on the second floor.

'Have you something important to say to me?' Solomon opened.

'I'm going! Me and the boys are leaving,' Danny said forthrightly.

'Go on!'

'I asked you for two more weeks. You gave it to me. So now it is time for us to leave, Sol,' Danny said, hoping for a non-reaction addressing him by his short name. 'I know it's not exactly two weeks, but time waits for no man, as they say!' Danny finished with a nervous tongue waddling around his bottom lip.

He waited for the reply.

Solomon checked his vest. He twirled his fingers around the embraided patches that adhered to his convictions, palmed his right hand smoothly across his bald head and stood up from his entitled chair.

'I'm gonna miss our war-time stories, Pruitt.' Solomon laughed. 'In fact. I'm gonna miss you being around period! I was looking forward to you and your friends joining us, riding with us, sharing the battles and glories with us,' Solomon deadpanned.

He then paused, walked to the left of his table, above the hawk that was chiselled beneath him. He spread his arms across the table and focused his dark desensitised eyes upon Danny's and continued, catatonic, 'But I know you're not one of us. You're a loner, Pruitt. I could never control you. I'd end up having to banish you, wouldn't I?' Solomon smirked. 'So, tell me! Where and what the fuck are you gonna do?'

'I'm going north to heaven,' Danny declared.

'I've heard about your heaven,' Solomon said.

'It's the only place that Greta and I can be together again,' Danny said with blind assurance.

He saw the look of duplicity on Solomon's face. The President fathomed that his guest, the saviour of his daughter, was not being true to him, but it didn't matter to him. He knew that Danny's destiny lay elsewhere, and even though Danny continued to lie that he was putting the Sultans ahead of his own self-interests, stating that the more he hung around, the more the police pressure would come across his club, Solomon whispered that he needn't speak anymore.

They bantered small talk on how they would've made good partners in another lifetime. But this was now, not yesterday, not tomorrow, it was today, and both knew that they had their own private wars to fight.

Danny and the President of the Sultans MC left on good terms. Barny and Ricky gathered when the two exited the manor and shook the hand of Solomon before they mounted their horses and left beneath the gates of La Fortaleza. It was what Danny planned, and it was Danny forecasted, even though his best buddy Ricky wanted to slit the Presidents throat right there and then.

The three exited the gates and rode stealthily through Benny's secret trails until they arrived at the cascades, spending the afternoon and evening there. Danny wanted to see it one more time, just in case there were to be no other. He knew it may be dangerous but was banking on the hot weather and directives from police to keep riders and campers away from the area and his chancy punt came to fruition. They enjoyed their private time by the running water, sunning themselves by the falls and the solitude of the caves.

The boys made the most of their seclusion, Danny sitting on a big granite rock below the large fronds of the tree ferns that gave him shade, dangling his bare feet into the running water as it passed underneath him. He still hadn't engaged in conversation with his two buddies whether they were committed to the robbery or not. He didn't raise the issue for the fear that they would tell him they wanted no part of it, but Danny facetiously banked on the theory that if they had come this far with him, another day or two wouldn't hurt.

Time passed slowly for the boys as they waited for Benny to arrive at the caves to lead them through the darkness to their overnight destination. It was a long dark trail, they relied heavily on Benny showing them the way. Although they had no doubts on their bushman friends' abilities, it was still a nervous and apprehensive ride through the darkness of the forest. They passed through the cutting at Tambourine bridge on the Syrian Creek Road and although it was dark, the images of what had happened there were still embedded as they rode over where friends and foe had lost their lives.

Finally, they arrived at their destination and after three hours of riding they were glad to be out of the saddles. Danny and the boys thanked Benny for all that he had done, with Danny emotional in his goodbyes.

'No words can describe what you have done for me,' he confided. 'I thank you; we thank you, and Greta thanks you. We wouldn't have survived without you, mate,' he openly admitted.

Benny laughed it off as he did with most things. It would be the last time they would see and hear his affable and giggling character. Benny turned to leave but not before Danny decided to give the big black gelding a tearful pat and hug goodbye. The steed had been his friend and had been his foe. He had been his saviour and his nemesis, and when Danny sobbed and teared up while saying his goodbyes, Barny and Ricky looked on in amazement to think that after all he had been through, the first time they would see him cry would be over an animal he had nothing but abuse for.

Benny finally disappeared into the darkness, leading the three horses behind his own mount on his way to Damien's with a thank you note from Danny for lending him the big black beast. Benny became the only man outside the six who knew what they had planned. He enquired what their plans were on their night travels and when Danny explained what they were about to embark on and the reasons why, it would be the first time that Benny would remain speechless for a period.

He knew the boys were desperate, knew they needed money, he also knew that they were bold and brazen in their deeds, and probably did have the fortitude to carry out such a thing, but whether they would be successful or not was another matter Benny mulled inside. He kept his thoughts to himself, he just nodded his head and wished them luck and hoped that they would all survive the day.

Benny would stay the night at Damien's before heading down Mason's creek road in the morning to deliver Danny's last letter to Greta. The contents were short and sharp, with Danny writing that she would not hear from him for a while, and reiterated that he would send for her when the time was right, a promise that Danny himself was starting to have self-doubts over as time closed in on his daring plan.

But if Danny thought that Benny was now the only one outside of the planning six who knew what was to come, by mid-morning tomorrow, he was going to be educated otherwise as another two men in the know would be waiting with deadly bated breath on their arrival in Graceville.

Danny had underestimated the prying ears of *La Fortaleza*. Unbeknown to any of its hierarchy, an informant had been entrenched inside the club. Pep, right-hand man to Vice President Crow, had been a detective's mole for nearly a year and had been extorted and blackmailed against. He and his wife were continually threatened with imprisonment on past crimes, which if were to happen, would leave their young children destitute if he did not comply when asked for information. It was a threat that Pep took very seriously and saw no option but to agree to the detective's demands for the protection of his family, and when the now bailed Detective Lucas Cribbs wanted information, Pep had to oblige.

Cribbs' motives were clear. He was still loyal to Minister Johnston and his job of apprehending the Graceville four had not been fulfilled and after a meeting with the imprisoned politician on the Thursday, their elaborate plan was put in motion. With a wad full of cash, and information provided by Pep on the impending armed robbery, Cribbs went about bribing and paying his way to the whereabouts of one John Pringle, and once found, he had absconded the government's star witness out of protective custody in a heartbeat.

John Pringle had no hesitation in accepting the $50,000 in cash from the hidden coffers of Johnston and Cribbs to lure him out. It was a lump sum that in these impoverished days could set him up for a decade, and with Cribbs using the aid of more cash and the helping blind eye of corrupt lawmen that still hadn't been weeded out by the authority's moral purge, Pringle was out of his inner suburban safehouse in the wee hours of Saturday morning. He arrived in Graceville by a commandeered unmarked police vehicle with Cribbs at the wheel and was soon holding out inside the private abode of the Detective on the promise of more cash, revenge, and freedom.

Cribbs was playing a dangerous game of deception with a man who had more than equal capabilities when it came to survival the violent way. The plan was to eliminate two prime witnesses in the case against Minister Johnston at the one occurrence. If alleged cop killer Danny Pruitt were to be fatally shot in a standoff while committing an armed robbery, any potential future testimony by Pruitt would never make it to court, helping the Minister's cause when it came to one of his charges of conspiracy to murder.

Equally, it would also look good on his own resume if he were ever to be granted his badge back again. But the number one motive was to see that John Pringle would never see the inside of a courthouse himself. If Pruitt and his buddies didn't take him out at the anticipated standoff, then it was his job to enact it himself. It was a double cross that John Pringle's instincts was all too aware of. He was privy to the fact the Lucas Cribbs was Johnston's ally and heavily questioned his motives.

Pringle suspiciously listened as Cribbs lied that Minister Johnston had deserted him and hung him out to dry. He was no longer on Johnston's payroll and had no interest in whatever retribution the former Minister faced and emphasised that he was purely working out of his own interests, interests that both mutually desired. Cribbs convincingly pretended that he needed help, and what better way to have a man by his side that had bigger motives than himself to finish the saga that was Danny Pruitt, he cajoled.

Pringle's belief in Cribbs' story was minimal, but $50,000 cash was an almighty lure. The promise of revenge for his two dead comrades was a huge driving factor, but the money also bought a chance for him to escape the hole in which he had dug for himself, so for time being he would accept the company of Lucas Cribbs and play along until the expected rendezvous with their intended target.

Until then, it would become an unpredictable game of psychological cat and mouse between the two hardened professionals, both waiting for the precise moment to turn on one another.

Chapter 34

Pockets of warm breezes greeted their campsite at first light, it was an ominous pre-curser for what would lay ahead that afternoon. The forecast was for another extremely hot and windy day, a follow up from the scorching days that had descended on the state at the end of the previous week. The three fugitives had enjoyed benign weather over the weekend, slight breezes with sunny days around the 30-degree Celsius mark, but today, this date of January 29 was going to be the hottest of the summer in more ways the one, and it would also infamously etch itself in the annuls as one of the blackest days in the state's history.

Danny, Ricky and Barny had awoken at the place where it all began, at the top of Mt St Lucia, underneath the large communications tower where they spent their first tormented night on the run. It was Monday morning and the Armaguard would be arriving at the country club in four hours' time, Danny's make or break date with destiny had arrived.

He opened his can of assorted fruit and ate them down for breakfast, his mind fully occupied on what lay ahead, hoping that all plans had been finalised. Barny and Ricky awoke shortly afterward, quiet, pensive, they too ate fruit for breakfast washed down with water, refilling their cannisters from the nearby pump from the water well.

There were no horses to attend. Their mode of transport down the mountain would now be on mountain bikes, stealthily hidden nearby under tree branches the previous day by members of the Young Bloods on the direction of Razor.

The trio searched around for their rides. They had been well hidden and after ten minutes of frustrated sleuthing they came across them. Helmets, gloves, and protective pads were attached to the 18 speed geared bikes which Danny thought to be highly amusing.

'Look at this shit!' He laughed. 'I've been shot at a hundred times. I've been thrown from horses, dodged lightning bolts and falling trees, attacked by wild dogs. I've been punched and kicked. I've fought off tiger snakes, brown snakes, scorpions, bull ants and every friggin biting insect known to man, and these fools think I'm gonna meet my maker if I don't wear a fuckin helmet! Good one, idiots!' he chided.

'They'll be good to hide our identities if anything. We're still wanted, you know,' said Barny, easing Danny's angry sarcasm.

Ricky agreed and convincingly coerced Danny, much to his reluctance, that it might be a good idea for them *all* to wear the protective gear. They retrieved the bikes from out of their camouflage and replaced it with their camping gear, they wouldn't be needing it anymore. They gave the bikes a test ride around the campsite, laughing and mocking each other as they wheeled around in circles, testing the suspension and gearing, before they were satisfied with what they had. The boys took the chance to rest up some more, it was still too early to make the dash down the mountain. Everything had to be time perfect. If they were to be in the one place for too long, it would only bring sets of eyes upon them, a risk that could not be taken.

They sat around on tree stumps, quietly keeping to themselves when Danny and Barny noticed Ricky laying out a line of cocaine on a piece of foil prepping for a snort.

'Is this what we have become?' Barny lamented inside as he watched Ricky loudly inhale the powder up his nostril. Danny saw Barny's reaction and gave off a wry smile. He knew he hated Ricky's newfound addiction. He also knew it upset him; however, Danny wouldn't say a thing to Ricky. He knew that it only made him bolder and angrier, and it was exactly what he needed from him when the time came to confront the Armaguard, so Danny wouldn't interfere with his habit, it only worked in his favour.

The conversation was sporadic and light as the boys sat around smoking cigarettes, nervously peering at their wrist watches, waiting for the time to get moving when Danny approached a worried looking Barny.

'Having second thoughts?' Danny lightly questioned.

Barny had the bible in his right hand. He looked at the dirt that laid beneath his fidgeting feet and thought about how to answer Danny's question.

Before Barny could reply, Danny interrupted his thoughts. 'There was a wise old horse trainer I read about once. He said the future belongs to those who plan for it, and I believe he is right,' he said with bluntness.

Barny held up the good book as he looked up at Danny and began to give some quotes of his own.

'*Riches will do you no good on the day you face death*,' he quoted.

'Aahhh! Proverbs, hey Barny, my favourite part of the book,' Danny noted. 'Doesn't it also say that a lazy man will never have money, but an aggressive man will get rich?' adding his own quote.

'Wealth you get from dishonesty will do you no good. Honesty is the only way to a fruitful life,' said Barny.

'A sensible man gathers the crops when they are ready. It is a disgrace to sleep through the harvest,' Danny fired back with a concentrated smile.

Barny had forgotten Danny's ability of memory retention. If he had read it, it was in his mind somewhere, and Danny had told him that he had perused the bible during the days of his boredom, particularly proverbs, but nonetheless, Barny kept persisting.

'The riches you get through dishonesty soon disappear, but not before they lead you into the jaws of death.'

Danny looked at Ricky who wasn't quite understanding what was going on. Ricky wondered what all this biblical rhetoric was all about and was intrigued to hear some more. He listened to the counter acting between them, however,

Danny had nothing left to quote. He just looked down on Barny and frowned, deepened his glaring eyes and said, 'No answer to that one, my friend, but how about, are you fuckin with me or not?'

Barny turned his sights back to the earth beneath. Twirled his lips and cursed his reply. 'Of course, I am!'

The time had come for the lads to seat up on their mountain bikes to make the journey down Mt St Lucia to the outskirts of Graceville. The only baggage that they carried were their back packs. Inside was a cannister of water, a few personal items such as wallets and notepads along with their handguns, balaclavas, cable ties, a roll of duct tape and, of course, Barny's bible. They were totally reliant on the plans that Razor had put in place when they arrived at their first destination before they would traipse by foot to the Country Club, however, by this time, the Sultan MC and police command back at La Fortaleza were also finding out that nothing was going to go according to plan for all involved on this tumultuous day.

In the shadows of the early morning dawn, police command had descended on the compound. Solomon had already been alerted that unwelcomed visitors were approaching. He was always an early riser and was wrestling from his sleep when Marco had alerted him by radio from the communications hut. The club's laser senses and hidden security cameras had picked up movement on track 24 and again close to the T-intersection that led to the gates.

Marco couldn't make out the grainy images coming through on his screens. The pre-dawn darkness made it difficult to be certain, but knew it wasn't good news. The President asked if he had any idea on who it may be. 'No,' came the nervous reply. 'But whoever it is, they're coming in numbers.'

'Keep me posted on anything,' Solomon ordered through his handset.

The President immediately contacted the men in the turret and relayed to expect uninvited company.

' Do not to allow them through the gates under any circumstances. Do you understand!' Solomon rumbled.

'Affirmative,' came the instant reply.

Solomon was convinced that it could only be one of two adversaries—members of the Halabi family, the organised crime gang down in Marlboro that they had an impasse with over the gun trade, or the long arm of the law—he was hoping for the former. The President gave the order for Marco to set the warning alarm off from inside his comms hut. The piercing sound of the air raid style siren howled throughout the compound. It was only ever engaged for two emergencies, wildfire warnings the first and foremost, invading trespassers the second, and the Sultan brothers gathered quickly that there was no sign of smoke in the air.

The nesting birdlife across the surrounding ranges were abruptly awoken. Animals and poultry inside the boundaries roused in fright. All Sultans from inside their huts, tents and assorted lodgings knew exactly what it meant, and they quickly rose from their sleep and hastily donned their colours and armed themselves.

The alarm also alerted the SOG that their cover had been compromised ahead of time. Captain Dennis Grundy oversaw the SOG operation. He was an ex-Gunnery sergeant in the Navy and took up law enforcement when his time was up. The highly motivated crime fighter moved himself through the ranks until he was embedded in the police special forces where he had made a name for himself over the past five years. He was in his mid-forties and had a slender, muscly body frame. He had whispery short blond hair and a truck load of experience. But he also had a reputation of going it alone without the consent of command which had landed him in trouble with authorities in the past, and his actions were going to be heavily scrutinised once more in the weeks ahead once the dust settled on this quickly deteriorating operation.

The incursion team approached above the rise to the flatness of the plateau and halted before the gates.

'This is the Venturian police. We command you to open the gates,' Captain Grundy hollered through the loudspeakers over the warning siren. No mentions of warrants were communicated.

Ignoring the order, the Sultan guards in the turret snatched their shotguns and directed them at the assemblage below. The dangling interior light in the gatekeeper's perch gave the trained intruders a clear view inside and the split-second decision to use deadly force was applied. SOG members let off a volley of shots from their SIG MCX semi-automatic rifles at the danger, shattering the glass windows of enclosed turret, striking down the Sultans members in an instant, eliminating the threat to themselves and their colleagues gathering behind.

The rapid fire of the shots and breaking glass sent the Sultan members into overdrive as the noise echoed over the warm morning breezes and siren. The Rottweiler guard dogs on either side started to whip into a furious frenzy, leaping up onto the fences of their caged runs, their deep baritone roars resonated around. Grundy immediately ordered the BEARCAT through the gates of *La Fortaleza*.

The large 4x4, 6.7 litre, V10 turbo diesel engine rumbled as it accelerated at fast pace until the steel arrowhead bull bar smashed thunderously into the iron gates, moving it forward with each thrust of the powerful engine. SOG members followed up behind on foot, guns raised to their shoulders. The plan was to arrive at the front door of the manor, disembark from the vehicle, then storm the manor, seizing the President inside.

Disastrously for the raiders, the cover vehicle came to a premature halt. The twisted large gauge cable wires, corrugated iron and pieces of metal frame from the ruined gates had entangled itself around the wheels and driveshaft of the vehicle, lifting the front axle from the ground. The rear wheels spun furiously from the revs of escape, stirring up burnt rubber. Dirt and shales from the gravel driveway spat out in fury underneath. The large reinforced vehicle had become stuck only meters inside the entrance and couldn't move from its position.

In her bedroom on the second floor of the manor, Zoe was awoken by the abrupt commotion. First the shrilling sound of the alarm aroused her, followed by gunfire then the tumultuous sound of smashing metal. She couldn't gather what was happening as her frantic senses heightened. She quickly clipped her bra on, threw her singlet back over her then hurriedly stepped into her cargo pants and raced barefooted over to Maddy's room, knowing she was unable to hear the danger.

Zoe pushed and shrugged her awake and signed that she needed to come with her. Maddy tried to communicate back as to what was happening but Zoe had no time; however, the look and demeanour on Zoe quickly convinced little Maddy that she had to go with her. Zoe scooped her up from the bed and raced back across the hallway holding Maddy as tightly as she could. She re-entered her bedroom, placed Maddy on the floor, then peered out the second story window.

Zoe was frightened to the bone at what she could see and hear. Sultan members were running across the compound, some dressing themselves in the process while aiming and firing at the unknown and unseen targets. The warning alarm had ceased and was now overtaken by the sound of more erupting gunfire. Cradling Maddy, Zoe cowered into the corner of her bedroom for protection, terrified and stunned at what was happening.

SOG members began penetrating through the entrance, jumping and climbing over the vehicle that had now been stopped in its tracks by the damaged cables and iron. The invading force spread out into their allotted groups. Smoke emissions were pouring out of the vehicle as the driver tried to free it from its giant metal spider web. The brief hesitance from the raiding party enabled fierce resistance to form from the Sultans.

Over the last month, Solomon had his men build a 1.2-meter wall around the circular driveway with walk through gaps every four to five meters. He said to the club that it gave a great ascetic look to the area, enclosing the majestic elm trees inside of it along with the lawn and gardens, but those in the know knew that it was his protective barrier between him and any intruders that dare enter uninvited.

Solomon's military background and his own paranoia were completely behind his motivation to erect the quarry rock and bluestone cemented wall, and those who were taking cover behind it as the invading enemy approached, were now grateful for their President's forethought and their own hard work. A group of six SOG's made a beeline towards the front door of the Manor, covertly nearing in single file crossing over the lawn and past the park benches. They slipped by the last Elm tree and entered into the open, fifteen meters from the newly formed wall when they were ambushed from the dozen Sultans members who had already converged behind it.

For two of the intruders, the protective vests were made redundant as bullets sprayed their legs and penetrated the Perspex covers of their face and head helmets. They took fatal shots to the head and neck and fell instantly while the others took cover behind the Elm trees and bench seats with gunshot wounds to body, legs and arms. The club still didn't know who was invading their fortress in the morning silhouetted light, the assault was moving at lightning speed. The only thing on their mind was defending it. They continued to fire upon the enemy who were returning fire at will, and as Sultan numbers grew around the compound, their weapons intensified. Crow had unlocked the roller door to one of the sheds that stockpiled the high calibre weapons.

As the men hurriedly convened at the door, Crow locked and loaded the magazines and passed the weapons to the drilled eager members, and within seconds, had his brothers armed as well as the raiding party. Those who were too far way used their own assorted handguns and rifles to repel the attack, and now out numbering the SOG forces, the MC were beginning to take back the upper hand.

Another group of six SOG's were heading towards the tent and bark hut site where the Graceville four were believed to be hunkering. They quickly moved down the left flank of the compound when they were met by Sultan members who had just received their weapons from Crow. The first of the men appeared around the corner from the work sheds to see SOG's directly in their sight. They paused briefly, a move which would be fatal for three of them as the SOG's opened fire, with Pep, Detective Cribbs' informant, being one of the first casualties. Sultan members behind the front group raced for cover behind trees and sheds.

Others found protection inside the rotunda and horse stables, returning fire with venom as they ran, striking two of the officers down, forcing the other SOG's to the positions they came from. Remaining team members of the SOG were under a sustained barrage of gunfire around the entrance as they tried to push forward into the compound, running and ducking for cover after being thwarted in their attempts. Sultans were converging from all angles and corners of the compound, firing their weapons indiscriminately towards the incursion point. It was now all out war.

Outside the compound, command was listening to the startled events and communications through their headsets. The overbearing sound of high calibre bullets and panicked voices engulfed the radio waves. In an instant, all their well laid plans had dissipated. Grundy made the decision to abort the raid. 'Retreat, retreat out of the compound,' he blasted over of his comms.

Solomon, who had raced down out of his bedroom to the confines of the clubs meeting room, opened his private cabinet behind the bar and clasped his right hand around his SKS semi-automatic rifle. He aimed his weapon through a wooden slit above one of the bay windows and started to fire. He knew at first sight who had stormed his fortress, however, there was no hesitation from him, it only enraged him. He saw what had happened to his gatekeepers in the turret, he could see other members screaming in pain, he could see more of his brothers lying motionless across the grounds.

With calmed fury, the President fired off shots towards the stranded SOG members, instantly bringing both down. The driver of the BEARCAT had loosened the grip that the wires and metal had on his vehicle and hurriedly reversed out. The men inside shot out of their side gun ports to cover teammates as the armour-plated vehicle backed away from the pinging and darting bullets that were puncturing and ricocheting off it. As the vehicle reversed, more damage to the gates occurred. The edge of the main frame was hanging by a strand at its large metal hinges and eventually snapped under the strain. The hinged post connected was attached to the caged dog run and when the post came snapping down, it took the double wired fence with it, releasing the frenzied rottweilers from their enclosure.

Two of the rottweilers attacked a SOG member as he retreated over the twisted metal and wires that covered the ground. The combined weight and ferociousness of the dogs brought him to earth in the savage attack, the dogs reefed and gored at his legs and throat, the attack only halted by the quick thinking of his team mate who unleashed a volley of shots into dogs, killing them instantly. Tragically for the raiding party, the wounds inflicted by the dogs would eventually become fatal for the SOG victim. Under fire, the last of the SOG members exited the compound, dragging their dead and wounded teammates with them. As the swift halt in gunfire descended across the compound, the Sergeant at Arms jumped aboard the front-end loader that was parked behind the working sheds.

Bravely and fearlessly, Lars shoved it into gear then drove it hurriedly towards the mangled gates. He lowered the two-metre-wide bucket of the loader, and with all the power that the hydraulics could muster, lifted and pushed what remained of the twisted metal frame back into its original position. He reversed it again and lowered the bucket once more, pushing and scraping all the iron sheets and debris that laid about and bull dozed it up against the gates, blocking access back into the compound.

It was ten minutes of utter violence and mayhem with deadly consequences. Within that time, five SOG members had lost their lives, another seven were wounded. Tragically for the Sultans, it was devastating. Fourteen Sultan members were shot during the bungled raid, four of which were killed instantly, another three would die from their wounds within the next half hour.

Lars jumped from the front-end loader and rushed towards the manor, crouching, leering back towards the entrance, waiting for the bullet that had his name on it. He frantically dashed through the front door, carrying his large frame with speed he never thought he had and finally found refuge inside the protection of the meeting room. Crow had also joined them as they looked out through the windows to survey the surroundings. The gunfire had ceased as they surveyed the bodies of their brothers lying about the compound as others raced to the aid of the wounded and scurried them out of the danger zone.

'Fuck me. What the hell just happened?' Lars raged in anger. 'They were fuckin' coppers! Shit! What the fuck happens to us now?'

'We had the right to defend ourselves,' Solomon justified with vigour. 'Did you hear any of them announce who they were? Did you hear any of them say they had a warrant? Did you hear any of them ask for demands? No! The fuckers just stormed us. They deserved what they got. We were totally justified to defend our land,' he affirmed resolutely.

Solomon exited the manor. He kept his weapon trained at the mangled entrance as he scampered to be with his men who were lowered behind the wall. He ordered them to remain in position as he bellowed to those in the distance to keep cover, unsure if another sortie would come. Everyone was in a sweat of nerves and fear as the situation started to sink into their confused and disorientated bodies, except for Solomon. His military history had him put in worse situations than what had just occurred and the adrenalin inside of him was only just beginning to rise. An eerie silence had descended on the scene as an acrid smell of spent cartridges hinted in the air. Solomon snorted his nostrils; it was a familiar scent.

He sent scouts in all directions around the perimeter of the compound, some on horseback, some on foot, some on their garaged Harley Davidsons to see if another point of entrance had been breached and to repel any attacks that could be underway. They combed down the southside of the thick hedged electrified fence and to the north. He sent them to the marijuana plantation and to the solar panel paddock to see if their power grid had been compromised, but no attack had been forthcoming. The information he was receiving over radio made him breathe a little easier but there was one piece of news that disturbed him greatly—where were his other two Vice Presidents?

He sent two prospects to bring them to the meeting room but when they relayed that they were nowhere to be seen, saying that both their lodgings were empty. Solomon was ropeable. He thought about it deeply and concluded he hadn't seen either of them since they spoke at dinner last night.

He made his way back into the meeting room. He asked Lars if he had seen them. 'No,' he answered. He got the same response from Crow.

'Where the fuck are they?' he angrily boomed.

Solomon needed them by his side. He needed all hands-on deck. He needed their leadership, he needed their experience, they were the backbone of the club he knew, and for the first time he had no idea where his to right hand men were. They had always communicated with their President no matter what the circumstances and Solomon's stomach was wrenching inside. Did they have something to do with the raid? Were they the ones that gave information to the law? *Credere nemo, Negare omnia* (TRUST NO ONE, DENY ALL). Solomon tried to dispel his thoughts, but in the business they were, nothing could be discounted.

Drake and Razor were waking up next to their wives in the comforts of their home beds in Graceville. The two of them had left after dark from *La Fortaleza* the previous night driving their vehicles which were commandeered from the logging coup. They had them parked across the river, camouflaged down a slight gully behind the marijuana plantation, far enough away so the starting engines would not be heard inside the yards of the compound. Teeto was on duty on the eastern side of the plantation, making sure their plan was not foiled.

Razor used his carpentry background to modify the rear of the vehicles with cabinets and drawers, ready to load from the expected loot from the robbery. Hexagon Valley Shire decals and stickers were attached to ruse anyone from the public when it was time to hit the roads. The Vice Presidents took the vehicles across the uninhabited forests and bushlands of La Fortaleza until they hit a thin trail which eventually led them out to the bitumen of the Graceville pass.

They riskily drove with headlights off to avoid any detection until they arrived at a five-acre vacant property near where Drake lived on the outskirts of Graceville. They parked the vehicles inside a lock up garage and from there walked to their respective rental homes. They spent the night with their wives, informing their partners on their bold plan to exit the hold and tenure that the Sultan MC had on them.

Drake and Razor were oblivious to what was transpiring at the compound. Within the hour of waking and saying their goodbyes to their wives, they had retrieved the vehicles from the hidden garage and were making their way unnoticed up into the ranges through the disused fire tracks of the catchment area. They eventually hooked onto Molloy's track and onto the rendezvous point where Danny and the boys were to meet them, if, and only if the robbery would go to plan.

As Solomon assessed his situation, re enforcements were gathering outside his compound. The CIRT team waiting at Fernbank had been mobilised and were already on their way up track 24. Every police vehicle and available officer from around the Hexagon Valley had been summoned to the siege and within 2 to 3 hours, with the temperature ominously peaking over the 35-degree Celsius mark already, over 200 law enforcement officers had congregated in the area of Fernbank and *La Fortaleza*.

Solomon was aware of the gathering forces after they sent up a drone with cameras attached. He looked over Marco's shoulder with trepidation as the video images were relayed back into the comms hut as it hovered above. It was in reply to the police drone which buzzed over the compound earlier. Lars shot it out of the sky after only one minute of reconnaissance and the club was repaid the favour when their own was met with the same finale, but Solomon wasn't bothered, as long as the message got through to police command that they also had the same sustained technology.

It was almost 9.30 am and a tense standoff had ensued. It was into its fourth hour and anxious negotiations were already into its first hour between police command and the President of the Sultans MC as the hot northerly winds began to stir from overnight dormancy.

Chapter 35

'Where's the key? Where's the bloody key!' Danny frantically searched.

'I've found it,' said Barny.

He fumbled at the lock in his eagerness to open the little shack positioned off Rickards Road behind the golf course. Danny pushed back the door when it opened and saw that everything was in place as Razor had said. Golf bags with full sets of clubs. Polo shirts, pants, hats and the newest in sporting footwear, all waiting inside the shed for them to change into, courtesy of the Young Bloods again.

The boys had an uneventful mountain bike ride down the trail from Mt St Lucia. The 8.5km trip took less than an hour, briefly taking friendly hellos to a handful of walkers and riders as they passed, who were all oblivious to the fact that they were three of the fugitive Graceville four. The land flattened out at the base as they reached the end of the trail. Orchard and berry farms covered the landscape, some still active, others not.

Disused lands and fields were a sight that was all too common at the foothills of the mountains around Graceville, and the former strawberry farm that the boys were crossing still had the mounds and undulations underneath their wheels where the strawberries once grew. They diverted across another vacant field until they reached Mason's creek road, only 2km from the heart of Graceville. From there they pedalled towards the main township until they turned right before the highway and onto a backroad. Housing density increased as they continued.

They crossed the Watkins River over a two-lane bridge then rose to a roundabout. From there they travelled onto Rickards Road, a potholed undulating bitumen backroad that led them up behind the golf course of the Graceville Country Club. Houses and property lined both sides, some on small blocks, others spanned over an acre with the houses set back from the road. They passed maintenance workers high up on extension ladders trimming branches away with hand saws from the power lines which had grown unimpeded over the years.

The boys had heard and read about the dawning of the new era and it was their first glimpse of the promises that had been made by government; however, as they rode past, they wondered jovially if they would ever see the benefits, for what they had done could not be reversed.

It was on one of these one-acre properties not far from the rear of the Country Club that their golfing accessories were hidden, thanks again to a member of the

Young Bloods who happened to be renting a bungalow out front of the said property.

The three of them changed into their new attire. Danny wearing a black polo shirt with the Nike tick on its left breast with matching cap, black shorts, grey socks with his size ten athletic shoes. Barny wore similar, except his polo shirt was green with red collar and trims while Ricky donned a white shirt and cap. They replaced the golfing gear with their mountains bikes and riding gear and locked the shed behind them. All were fitted out perfectly, although Ricky's shirt was noticeably two sizes too large for his liking and didn't see the funny side when told by his two buddies with humorous derogatory remarks that he was the best they'd seen him dressed for a long while.

Lugging their clubs and buggies, they made their way up a steep rise on Rickards Road towards their entry point of the course. They were seen by a bystander from afar pottering about at the front of his property, but once again, the three fugitives never raised an eyebrow, just some silly over keen golfers on their way to get wasted in the hot conditions the stranger surmised.

The boys disappeared out of sight from the neighbour behind some thick shrubbery between the road and where a large hole was cut out of the protective cyclone fencing of the golf course boundary. Danny was first through, then helped Ricky and Barny gain access as they passed the clubs and buggies through. They covertly walked up a grassy embankment and found themselves situated behind the third tee of the course, a downhill par four heading in westerly direction. Danny stopped and panned his eyes beyond the fairways to see if any players were about and was happy that it looked noticeably quiet.

'What if your Monday golfing buddies are about? Have you ever thought of that?' Ricky questioned warily.

'They won't be there,' Danny asserted. 'They're a bunch of pussies. They never play when it gets too hot!'

Rick and Barny gave a look of hopeful trepidation at one another. If any one of them were about, they would recognise Danny in an instant and the whole plan would be blown. They crossed behind the second green adjacent to the third tee and linked onto a concrete golf cart path and walked casually down until they crossed to the bitumen road that ran along side of the dog legged first fairway. The bitumen continued past the work sheds of the greenkeepers who were conspicuous in their absence, maybe it was also going to be too hot for them to work the boys quietly deduced.

Danny checked the time on his wristwatch, it was 9.50 am, their timing was on schedule. They continued down the interior bitumen road of the members only Country Club. A group of three players were teeing off on the first hole. It was the only group they could see as their vista of the course increased the more they walked, and soon enough, they found themselves at the practice putting green. The green had two large Western Red Cedar trees at the surrounds casting a relieving morning shadow across the practice putting area. Another group of four were honing their skills on the carpet adjacent to the 19th hole, a small two-story building which housed the golf shop and little dining and bar area upstairs.

Danny didn't recognise any of them, he hoped they didn't recognise him. Other than that, there was no one in sight, the weather had worked in their favour. The boys kept their caps low and sunglasses taut. Beads of sweat gained momentum as they wriggled with the peaks of the cap. They casually moved to the left side of the road towards the practice nets situated on the lawns. Another ten meters beyond them was a row of hedges, 1.5 to 2.0 metres in height intertwined with young eucalypt saplings where the men could peer through the foliage and get their view of the sloping brick walled enclosed driveway that the Armaguard would soon be travelling down.

Danny led the way further across the lawn area. A large croquet lawn area sat empty 25 meters to their right, scorched and in need of a good soaking. The boys each grabbed an assorted club from their bags and practiced their swings, pretending to warm up for their impending game.

He looked at his wristwatch again, 10.02 am, he looked once more, 10.05 am, and again, 10.10 am, the van was late! 'Where the hell is it?' Danny stewed. 'It's always on time. 10.00 am on the dot, always!'

The boys were getting nervous. If the van was a no-show, they'll be stranded with no plan, no transport, no money and nowhere to go. But Danny was already thinking what he'd do if the van never showed. As he waited, he looked easterly into the distance towards the township where Corey and Sarah's house lay beyond, only four walking kilometres away from the Country Club.

He knew Greta was there. He felt that he could reach out and touch her. So close, yet so far away, he grieved. Right there and then, he vowed to himself that if he was going to risk all by robbing an armoured van, then he would have no hesitation trekking across town and risking all again, just to have a chance to hold his wife and sons in his arms again, even if it would be the last.

However, what Danny didn't know was that the Armaguard van had made a diversional stop on its way the Country Club. With all the public celebrations and festivities the town held over the weekend, more cash had been spent and bandied around and the money had to be housed somewhere, chiefly from the bookmakers who were standing the largest crowd gathering the Graceville picnic race meeting had seen for a long time. With prosperity on the horizon and talk of an abundance of new jobs about to be advertised throughout the Hexagon Valley by the civil works, power and manufacturing companies, all being subsidised by Government, people were now braver to part with their hard-earned money.

There were fetes and markets all over town during the weekend and the Saturday and Sunday race meetings was where the cash changed hands more than anywhere else by far. The bookmakers had two glorious days with longshots saluting the judge in all races bar one over the duel 18 race card meeting, and their winnings had to be kept somewhere as they didn't want to pay the exorbitant and inflated price to have the money transported to Marlboro on the Sunday night.

The Depot hotel was their chosen stronghold to safe keep the money as the cellar beneath its premises was more than suitable to house the money. Under 24 hour guarded surveillance, it had a large shelving area behind a row of iron bars, like an old jail cell that was under lock and key. All monies were boxed and bagged with each bookmaker's individual name and identification number attached, ready for easy distribution once the Armaguard van had returned to its drop off points in the city.

It was 10.25 am, Barny and Ricky's anxiety was at fever pitch.

'We need to get out of here,' Barny whispered in his ear, but before he could get a reaction, Danny was stirred from his fervent thoughts about Greta when the sound of a grumbling engine came into sight.

'Here it comes,' he gritted.

All three hearts of the waiting trio began to pound. The time of reckoning had come. The van neared quickly and closed to only fifteen meters from where they stood and watched it turn right opposite the practice green and stop. The driver engaged reverse and began to slowly edge the vehicle down to the pickup point at the base of the alley drive. They watched as two guards exited from the van after it had stopped.

The guards unchained two trolleys from the rear of the van then walked to the roller doors and opened them. From there they would make their way through the breezeway and ground floor passages, pass the maintenance shops and offices until they would climb some stairs and enter the plush carpeted area of the private smoker's den of the Country Club where the well to do would suck on their cigars. Continuing, they'd walk behind the bar, through another door, which then took them to the offices at the entrance foyer and pick up their consignment from the General Manager's office.

The whole journey for the two guards would take seven minutes. Danny's planned allowed two minutes grace either side of their departure from the van which meant they had a window of three minutes to overpower the remaining guard and complete their mission.

The trio focused on the parked van; its large V8 engine echoing sounds off the brick walls as it idled. They discreetly donned their thin black balaclavas, rolling them up to their foreheads, keeping their faces exposed and placed their caps atop. Danny retrieved the duct tape out of his golf bag and placed it in his back pocket. Ricky and Barny the same with the cable ties. A minute passed, and still no sign of the guard inside. The boy's nerves were palpitating.

'Where is he?' Danny silently grumbled.

Another 30 seconds ticked on, still no sign of him. Was it too hot for the guard to exit the van? Maybe he had given up his smoking since last eyes were on him, or was he just simply enjoying the comforts of the air conditioning inside, whatever it was, the boy's leers of anticipation at one another were becoming more agitated by the second. Suddenly, the side door of the van began to slowly open and out walked the tall lanky red bearded guard. He leant his back up against the brick wall, produced his cigarette packet out of his top pocket and lit one up.

'Showtime, boys! Let's do this!' Danny grated.

Barny and Ricky nodded with determination as they grabbed their buggies and walked through the camouflage of the hedges and onto the concrete driveway. They began their walk down the sloped laneway, keeping with the plan, heads low and idly chatting with each other. They chortled raucous fake laughs to convince the bearded guard that they were just guest golfers who had lost their way. As they neared with every step, the guard took a deep inhale out of his cigarette and looked up at the oncoming trio.

The guard raised his voice, 'Hey boys! This area is off limits.'

The approaching trio ignored him. 'Off limits, men. You're going to have to turn around,' the guard repeated louder.

The now unsettled guard looked to the ground as he stamped his cigarette out and was about to confront the three golfers; however, before he could lift his eyes, the boys pounced in unison with frenetic aggression. They were within ten meters of the van when they pulled down their balaclavas and drew their handguns from the front of their pants and raced at full speed towards the stunned guard.

'Get on the ground, get on the ground!' they roared in unison. The guard made a reflex move with his right arm towards his holstered revolver. Danny rushed with his handgun raised directly at the guard's head.

'Don't you fuckin' dare!' Danny yelled. 'Remember your company protocol, mate. Don't die for other people's money.'

The guard heeded Danny's stern advice immediately. He moved his hand away then raised both to his shoulders in startlement. The three men had descended on him with speed and aggression and before his arms reached full extension, Ricky had unclipped the sidearm from the guard's holster. Danny firmly pushed his gun against the guard's temple. 'On your knees and stay fuckin still,' he ordered.

He passed the duct tape to Barny who quickly ripped off a strand and covered the guard's mouth. Danny forcibly shoved his left palm into the back of the guard's head, ramming him to the ground. No resistance was forthcoming as the now frightened guard laid face down on the concrete driveway. Danny and Barny cable-tied his wrists and ankles and hogtied both limbs together then dragged him behind the open roller doors and out of sight, his back scraping on the concrete ground as the boys heaved at his tense and resisting body.

Danny thanked him for adhering to the company protocol, sarcastically adding that he should buy his employers a beer for saving his life. Ricky had taken his position behind the steering wheel of Armaguard van as Danny looked at his watch. They still had a minute's grace, another two before the other guards would reach the doors.

'Let's go. Let's go,' Danny calmly instructed.

But before Danny left the guard who was now lying on his side incapable of movement, he couldn't resist giving one more jibe of cynical advice. 'You should give up the smokes, bro! They could kill ya in more ways than one!'

He patted the guard's head and wished him luck in the future then watched as Barny hurried into the passenger seat then dive into the rear section of the van.

Danny entered behind him after locking in the outside strong bolts to the rear doors.

Ricky eased the van into drive, nudging away the golf buggies and bags that they had left in the laneway. The holdup took less than 90 seconds. Everything had gone to plan and not a shot was fired. They were in the van and making their getaway. Ricky slowly made a sharp right at the top of the laneway and then another sharp left to begin the escape journey down the interior road of the country club.

The group of golfers on the practice green never raised an eyebrow as Ricky kept the van at cruising speed, avoiding any attention coming their way. Danny urged Ricky on. 'Keep going, keep going. Turn left when you reach the bottom of the driveway,' he said.

No one was going to chase them. That was the plan all along. They had the horsepower under the bonnet, which was more than the four-legged kind could ever muster if a pursuit would follow. No attempt had been made on Armaguard vehicle in over three years. Simply put, no intended criminal had a getaway vehicle once the job was done, and they sure weren't going to blast their way in on horseback, and that was the genius of Danny's plan from the first conversation. They were never going to rob the van; they were going to take it.

The adrenalin was exploding, none of them could sit still as they exited the Country Club. Danny let off howls of satisfaction and achievement, bashing his hands against the dashboard of the van in maniacal excitement. Ricky kept repeating the 'f' word over and over with kinetic ferocity, while Barny repeatedly yelled to the Lord for forgiveness on what he had done. They were 25 minutes away from freedom.

The turn off at Syrian Creek Road at the top of Mason's was only 15 winding kilometres away. By the time the alarm was raised, the police cruiser and or 4wd at the Graceville police station would be at least 20 minutes behind them they calculated, more than enough time to disappear into the wilderness. However, as the day would unfold for all those involved around Danny Pruitt, nothing could be taken for granted and nothing ever appears to go seamlessly.

If the boys thought the most dangerous part of their daring plan had been completed, just around the corner lay two waiting hunters who were about to raise the danger to an unprecedented level, and the pursuers would not be on horseback, they would be in another vehicle. A lot lighter, a lot more manoeuvrable and a lot faster.

Chapter 36

John Pringle and Lucas Cribbs sat silently in a café opposite the main bank in heart of Graceville, sipping on their ice-blocked soft drinks. Cribbs was dressed in an open neck white collared shirt, cuffs rolled up around his forearms with black slacks and shoes. John Pringle wore a dark blue T-shirt with matching sleeveless vest, black denim jeans and faded white sneakers, handguns nestled firmly inside the belts of their pants.

Pringle's thumb was still noticeably bandaged from his wound received at Tambourine Bridge and now also sported a thick dark full beard that matched his original moustache. The information Cribbs had received from Pep, his informant inside the Sultans, was that they would hit the van at the bank, but as they were finding out, it was looking far less likely as the minutes rolled on. Pep had only overheard snippets of conversations between his Vice Presidents and concluded an armed robbery could only take place where the exchange was to be held, at the main State bank.

Where else would it be, he wrongly assumed. He never heard the Country Club mentioned at all when his attentive ears were dropping in. The two waiting men had been looking at their watches wondering where the van was. 10.15 am was due time and it had already ticked passed 10.30 am and as they panned their experienced eyes across the streets and surroundings, nothing seemed right to them. They knew something was adrift. Pringle asked Cribbs to again check the run sheet of the van they had acquired.

'Somethings wrong here,' said Cribbs.

'I know what's fucking wrong! Your friggin' informant is full of shit. That's what's friggin wrong!' Pringled angrily goaded.

They had a panoramic view of the intersection through the window of the café. Along with two female staff members, only a mother and her two children were seated inside. Directly opposite the cafe was the State bank, next to it on the corner was a tourist information building. On the other side of the intersection stood the historical Graceville Hotel, its balcony overshadowing the highway underneath it.

Opposite the iconic drinking hole was a building and hardware store. Tethered horses kept the wooden and metal bollards busy in between the cyclists as people went about their business. The streets were busier than usual for a Monday morning, those not fortunate enough to be employed were getting what shopping and chores could be done before the predicted roasting heat of the afternoon would set in.

Although John Pringle's face had been shown over recent press releases, the wanted man rested Cribbs' paranoia by ensuring the detective that his now neatly trimmed thick beard, cap and sunglasses, were more than enough for the general public not to recognise his profile. The two had been listening in on their police radios and were well aware of what was happening up in the mountains at *La Fortaleza*, but more importantly, also knew that the only police member left in town was Sgt Dane Grainger, who was desk bound at the station with no access to any police vehicle. The only vehicle in the vicinity was Cribbs commandeered unmarked police cruiser, silver coloured with black trims and interior, which was parked in front of the café amongst the tethered horses and waiting carriages and carts.

Pringle and Cribbs bounced their expertise and insight off each other as they watched the organised chaos negotiating the main crossroad in town. They watched without concern as the traffic lights once again failed to sustain more than thirty minutes of operation since power was partially allotted, and the more the anxious men talked, the more they knew nothing was adding up. All corners and off shoots of the intersection had been keenly perused. Everything was normal, nothing out of place, no sign of any misplaced horses, carts or carriages, no sign of suspicious activity.

Though it was before opening hours, they paid a passing teenage boy two dollars to enter the Graceville hotel to see if anyone was biding their time inside. Their investigative minds were satisfied when the lad came back and said all was empty. More conversation ensued as they sipped on their ice drinks and both agreed that the only way that an armed robbery could occur was if the culprits arrived on the run at the exact time the van would reach the bank in which was already proven to be late.

It didn't make sense to Pringle. He asked Cribbs the location of the previous stop before the bank. Cribbs flicked through the run sheet again and matched the times. He slowly raised his head and looked at Pringle.

'The Country Club.' He squinted in deep thought.

Pringle rose from his chair and gulped down the rest of his drink. 'Where's the quickest way there?' he said.

Both men hastily walked to their police cruiser. Cribbs took the wheel and turned left off the main road down towards Market Street, a short drive of 200 meters. Whilst the cruiser neared the lower t-intersection, negotiating the street crowds as they drove; Danny and the boys were making their way up the same Market Street in the opposite direction. To the left of them were tents and caravans strewn across the former fruit fields where the evicted made their abodes, the Watkins River flowed beyond it. To the right of them was the large security fences of train station and then further on was the half-filled bitumen car park of the marketplace.

It was where Danny had last laid his eyes on his beautiful Greta. He thought about her once more amidst all the chaos. Barny poked his head through the interior recess at the front of the van between Ricky and Danny.

'I think we've hit the jackpot, boys. You should see what's back here,' he said with excitement.

Danny raised from his seat and tried to have a look back at the cargo when Ricky grabbed him by the arm. 'Sit back down. There's a fuckin car there!' he yelled.

The two vehicles came within meters of each other as the police cruiser was turning left into Market Street. Pringle took off his cap and sunglasses to get a better look at the drivers inside the van and immediately gathered the drivers were not Armaguard employees. Ricky slowed the van down to a crawl. All five sets of eyes were now locked on each other, three from the van, two from the cruiser.

'It's bloody John Pringle,' Barny hollered.

'Bullshit!' Danny responded, astounded. 'He's in fucking jail.'

'Well, he's bloody well not now,' Barny fretted aloud.

Danny listened to Barny's animated worries. The look on his face told him the truth.

'Get out of here,' he urged Ricky.

'Are you sure it's him?' Danny questioned.

'One hundred percent,' Barny answered. 'And that's that Detective next to him. Lucas Cribbs, that's his name, isn't it? He was in the papers as well.'

The boys were instantly in panic mode as Ricky planted down on the accelerator. They thought they were home and hosed. Another half a kilometre and they would've been on Mason's Creek Road and heading away from town, but the one thing they fretted over most, was whether the occupants of the cruiser recognised them, and when Ricky, who was looking into the side mirrors announced that the cruiser was accelerating up behind them, their worst fears were answered.

Pringle and Cribbs had identified the fugitives immediately. Danny Pruitt's face had been indented into Pringles mind from the time his partners lives were taken at Tambourine Bridge. It was not easily forgotten to him and was licking his lips in anticipation that luck had given him the chance to extract his revenge. The two hunters raced up behind the van and tailgated them as the van negotiated a left turn that took them over a bridge that covered the Watkins River. Another quick right, then a left turn, put them onto Mason's Creek Road and the wild 15km winding and twisting chase had begun in frightening earnest.

Cribbs tried to make his move past the van at the first length of straight road they came to, but Ricky swayed the ten-ton van to his right and cut off the manoeuvre. The same was done on the next straight as they negotiated the bends at the foothills. Ricky pushed the weighty van to its limit. Danny and Barny held onto the metal handrails to keep their balance as the van lifted on two wheels when Ricky took a right-hand sweeping bend at high speed. The police cruiser was sticking to them like glue. It was lighter, more powerful, and it was a lot more adept around the bends. The boys could not throw them off as the pursuit up the mountain road gained perilous momentum.

With every twist and turn, Ricky did his best to cut off the cruiser as it attempted a pass. Halfway up the scenic bitumen road, a small loaded cart with a single horse was making its way down to Graceville. It was carrying furniture items tied down by rope. The rider looked forward in horror as the van appeared out of nowhere from a tight turning bend. The rider jumped for his life from his bench seat and down an embankment as the van ploughed into the back quarter of the horse, smashing its hind legs and the cart with it.

The furniture exploded like a bomb had hit it, debris flew across the road as the horse whinnied in agony. The boys were shell shocked as Ricky eased off the accelerator in fright. He direly investigated his mirrors to assess the carnage and instantly knew the damage was severe, maybe life taking. He would never know the outcome, there was no time to stop and assess because his foot was pushing down on the accelerator again when the cruiser came into his rear sights, closing with speed at every second. A kilometre on, and four more twisting bends, they swung around a tight left turn and scattered a group of five cyclist's, Ricky almost losing complete control of the van in his avoidance.

They had almost reached the top of the mountain and still had another two kilometres to the dirt road turn off onto Syrian Creek Road before the village of Tangiloo. Ricky's arms and shoulders were aching as he wrestled the steering left and right. The weight of the vehicle was making it near impossible to manoeuvre at the speeds they were reaching. With each bend, the van was teetering from side to side, threatening to roll over at any instant. The boys could hear ricocheting gun shots bouncing off the side of the van when the passenger side mirror shattered into fragments.

Danny was startled back into his seat as he gripped the stable bars inside. Cribbs and Pringle had fired upon the van from their open windows, first aiming at the van's tyres unsuccessfully, the lowered guard shields gave its wheels enough protection from the duo's wailing bullets. Pringle then focused on the side mirrors. If they could destroy them, it would cut off the driver's rear vision and give them a chance of slipping past before he could react.

Danny yelled to fire back. 'Open the rear window!' he roared to Barny.

'It's locked. It won't slide open,' he replied.

Barny searched frantically around the rear of the vehicle for keys, anything that could help him prise open the latch. He was being rocked from side to side, repeatedly losing his balance, falling over the boxes, sacks and metal casings that the money was being held but couldn't find anything that would help.

The boys could see no way of ending the pursuit. They couldn't outrun them, and now they couldn't outshoot them. The panicked profanities blasted throughout the cabin of the vehicle. The turn off to Syrian Creek Road was nearing as Cribbs tried another pass on the right-hand side as the road straightened atop of the range. The chasing duo rightly guessed they were heading into Kensington and deeper into the forest, but the attempt again failed as Ricky kept his van swerving from side to side.

The armoured van screeched right onto the dusty gravel road with the police cruiser following in hot pursuit. Cribbs blasted out the driver side mirrors of the armguard van with a volley of shots, now Ricky had lost his visual from what was behind. The same deadly game of cat and mouse continued along the forest road. The armoured van was not meant for off road and with every corrugation, bump, and pothole they crossed, the reverberations shook the occupant's bodies to the core. The dust and gravel were spitting out of both vehicles' undercarriage.

Four kilometres in, Cribbs took advantage of an open flat knoll that appeared on the right-hand side of the road. He planted his foot to the floor in an attempted pass. The shoulder of the road allowed his vehicle traction. The V8 police cruiser sped up to the side of the van and took Ricky completely by surprise. His eyes hooked onto Pringle as the cruiser drew even.

'Stop 'em! Stop 'em!' Danny yelled.

He knew if they got in front, it would all be over for them. He didn't want another face-to-face shootout; Danny knew he didn't have too many lives left. His luck had been ridden to the extreme and knew as such, and he was going to avoid another confrontation at all costs. The police cruiser was almost past. Gravel, rocks and dust hurtled and pinged in all directions off the speeding vehicles.

'Hit him,' Danny yelled. 'Fuckin hit him.'

Ricky reefed the steering wheel right hand down. The van sharply careered into the rear left quarter panel of the cruiser. Ricky kept the wheel hard down. The pace of the vehicles was equalising each other out as sparks flew and the scraping of metal shrilled. Ricky strengthened his force on the steering wheel and the weight of the ten-tonne van began to lift the rear left wheel of the cruiser off the ground.

The speedometer was at 95kph when Cribbs lost control of the cruiser. The impacting force turned the cruiser around to its side and lodged in front of the van. Its right wheels dug into the gravel as the Danny and Ricky looked down on the faces below. Within a moment, the velocity and weight of the short impact sent the cruiser into a violent spiralling roll over. Dust and the sound of thumping metal and plastics enveloped the air as the boys looked on in frightened amazement as the cruiser continued its roll over, bouncing and contorting off the hardened gravel road as Ricky eased off on his accelerator.

Over and over and over the cruiser went, finally coming to a twisted and smashed up crumpled halt. Ricky stopped the van and waited for the dust to settle and as it slowly disappeared on the wind, they saw the Cruiser lying on its roof a further 60 meters down the road.

A shocked silence took over the cabin of the van as the engine crabbily idled away, the smell of burning brakes drifted across them as they tried to get a better look at the wreckage of the cruiser.

'Shit. What do we do now? It's blocking the fuckin road,' Ricky agonised.

Tense seconds had passed when Danny smiled at both Ricky and Barny and with an eerie calm and eyes focused ahead advised them of his plan.

'We go straight through it.'

'What?' said an exasperated Ricky.

'We go straight fuckin through it,' Danny repeated, only this time louder and more determined.

Ricky tightened his gripped on the steering wheel and grunted with venom.

Danny and Barny gripped the interior stable bars once more as Ricky began to throttle down the van to its maximum. The van rumbled wildly towards the stricken vehicle and with the bull bar out front of the van, smashed violently into the front end of the cruiser. The impact pirouetted the cruiser around on its roof like a spinning top, twirling around in a dozen rotations, with John Pringle and Lucas Cribbs still inside.

'Stop the van,' Danny ordered, as the smoke and dust dissipated into the surrounding forest.

He turned the handle of the door to step out.

'Don't do it, Danny,' Barny advised in reserved tones.

'I want to meet this fucker face to face,' gritted Danny.

'They're probably dead already,' pleaded Barny.

'We'll see about that!' came his reply.

Danny stepped out of the vehicle. The first thing that hit him was the intensity of the heat that the wind was firing in. He wiped his brow as he drew his revolver from his pants. He took tentative aim at the mangled wreck as he neared with each nervous step.

'Fuckin hell! Is he ever going to stop?' Barny posed to Ricky.

Ricky nonchalantly shrugged his shoulders. 'I don't know.'

Ricky didn't care either way what his best mate was going to do. They were all at the point of no return. 'Just think of the money, Barny,' he said. 'All we have to do is make the exchange and we'll be free. It will all be over soon.'

'It will never be over,' chastised Barny. 'Don't you understand? It will never be over for as long as we live.'

Ricky ignored his friend's pleas. He unwrapped the foil from his front pocket and snorted, then turned at Barny and gave him the most demonic smirk and giggle that Barny had seen from him.

'Oh mother of Mary! You're just as mad as he is,' said Barny, shaking his head in disgust.

Danny walked around the smashed vehicle, carefully looking for any movement from inside the crumpled heap. The right rear wheel was still spinning, squeaking at every revolution. A little flame was noticeable from the overheated and smashed up engine block, no bigger than a flicked cigarette lighter. Petrol was slowly dripping at the rear from a hair line fracture of the fuel tank.

Danny walked to the left-hand side of the upturned vehicle. He knelt over with his gun pointed and saw that the passenger was still alive, eyes open and silently groaning. He panned his eyes across at the driver. He was dead. Lucas Cribbs' neck had been broken and skull severely fractured. The car roof had caved in from the repeated rollovers. There was only a gap of nine inches from the floor to ceiling on the driver's side and Cribbs' head laid on his shoulder blade at a contorted angle as his open lifeless eyes stared into oblivion.

Danny turned his attention back on the passenger. He had broken limbs and was bleeding profusely from a large gash to his head that had already swelled in a mix of blue and red. He was pinned into his mangled and dislodged seat by the caved in door, the safety belt squeezed at his torso with every painful movement. Danny surveyed the interior of the car, picking up the array of pistols and shotguns that had been strewn around by the rollovers. He grabbed them and gently then laid them out on the road, thanking his lucky stars that they didn't have to shoot it out with them.

Danny was sadistically sniggering inside; it was his golden opportunity to put an end to John Pringle. This was the man that was trying to kill him, the man who would hunt him down relentlessly and knew that his desperate planned reunion with Greta would never eventuate if Pringle was not stopped, one way or another, and Danny would be as morbidly belligerent as he could.

He grabbed his wallet out of his back pocket then knelt a meter from the smashed window and sorted out a torn-out paper clipping he had kept. He raised it to the face of the injured passenger and then brought it closer to his own eyes. He then wrestled a wallet out of the inside pocket of the passenger's vest and looked at the identification cards inside.

'Yep! That's you, isn't it?' he smugly stated. 'You've grown a beard since,' he said, showing him the picture that he had kept. 'So! John Pringle. I finally get to make your acquaintance. I hear you've been trying to find me. Well, here I am! In the flesh. It hasn't worked out too well for you though, has it?' Danny laughingly sneered. 'Both times!' he added after a pause.

'Fuck you!' came Pringle's muffled grunt. 'Get me out of here,' he moaned.

'Oh no! I can't do that. You would just come after me again and I can't have that now, can I?' Danny mused.

'So, what then? You're going to kill me?' Pringle asked between gasping and gathering breaths.

'Not me! I think you've done a good enough job on yourself.'

Danny had panned his eyes over Pringle's injuries. He had a compound fracture to his right lower leg, the bone protruding out of his leg as blood oozed out of its wound. His right ankle was drooping and sitting at side angles. Both shoulders looked like they had been dislocated or broken. The gash on his forehead was deep and bleeding out, but the most serious injuries were internal. Blood was oozing out of his mouth as he struggled with every breath and word. Danny pushed the Glock barrel into his rib area. Pringle almost fainted in pain. Shock was beginning to blanket his body.

'Broken ribs too! That's gotta hurt! I think your lungs are smashed by the way you're breathing. Geez, I would say you're pretty well fucked, hey!'

Danny was taking psychotic delight in deriding the man who had tried to assassinate him and was showing no mercy as he continued to torment the stricken ex lawman now gangster for hire.

'I would love to put a bullet in your head, but I won't do that. That would be too quick. Monsters like you deserve to die slowly for the misery you've inflicted on people, but you *will* die today, John Pringle.'

Danny took a deep breath as he again surveyed Pringle's injuries. He could sense that the smell of petrol was worsening as the fuel started to pool on the ground beneath the upturned rear of the cruiser as the engine bay smouldered away silently. Danny knew the danger was increasing and gauged that he couldn't hang around for long, nevertheless, he was enjoying his one-way conversation. Pringle could no longer muster the strength to speak but Danny savvied that he was listening to every word he was saying. Pringle's eyes and facial expressions proved his anger and disdain towards him.

'It's funny, you know,' Danny contemplated with smiles and sarcastic sighs. 'Everyone who comes after me dies! The Devlins! Your two mates when you ambushed us! The bloke lying next to you! The two innocent young cops that travelled with Dane, and that's just naming a few. And now it's your turn, Mr Pringle. My friend Barny thinks I'm protected in some way. And you know what, I'm starting to believe him. He says we all meet our maker on the seeds we've sewn, and I've only sewn good seeds, including my two boys. Everything I've done has been for good.

'Having said that, I'm glad I've finally met you, John Pringle, because assholes like you bring the bad out in me that's been festering for years. You see, I've been through hell in the last couple of weeks and I shall show no mercy to anyone until I'm in my Heaven. As for you! There ain't no fuckin' Eden for what you've done. You're going to die a lonely death, my friend.

'I've done my homework on you! They say it's wise to know your enemy, don't they? You haven't got many friends, have you? You've got no family, no loved ones, you got no one who cares about you, so the way I see it, your lonely insignificant existence is going to end in either one of three ways. You're going to suffocate to death, you're going to bleed to death, or you're going to burn to death with no one there to mourn. I wonder which one will get you first. Pity I won't be around to see it. I'll be long gone with my money, and soon I'll be back with my family enjoying the northern winter sun and palm trees in a place called heaven. So, I'll leave you to it, John Pringle.'

Danny rose to his feet and gathered the guns around him. He took one last look at his deadened adversary. 'See you downstairs,' he snarled in departure. The last thing Pringle saw was the dust raised from the boots that slowly walked away.

Danny re-entered the armoured van to see Ricky and Barny trying to comprehend what was gained in the rear of the van. And it was more than they ever bargained for.

Danny snapped to Ricky. 'Get back behind the wheel. We've got time to make up. All this shit has put us behind schedule.'

Barny and Ricky never asked what happened while he was away. They both had a fair idea that he wouldn't leave any loose ends behind. That was the man he had now become, and although they were uncomfortable with it, they also knew it was totally necessary if they were all to survive and break free from the brutal and savage web that had entangled them.

As the boys continued their journey through the back roads of the forest, Danny was unaware that it was not only Pringle's life he had put in grave jeopardy. By the day's end, thousands more would pay the price for his personal hellbent fury and single-mindedness. By forgetting the real danger and havoc that a day like this one could inflict and ignoring to extinguish the flickering flame in the engine bay of the demolished police cruiser, nature was about to unleash an inferno of its own.

Chapter 37

'Where the hell is he?' grumbled Razor.

His fingers were tapping aggressively on the dashboard, impatiently turning to his right, looking up through the vacant trail. He was seated behind the wheel of the Land Cruiser, Drake asking his partner to calm down.

'He'll be here, brother. Give it a few more minutes,' he said.

The two Vice Presidents had parked below the plateau on a bush track one kilometre east of the fenced boundaries of La Fortaleza, they were waiting for Teeto. A grassy siding off the rock ridden trail gave them room to park. Native wild grasses and tussocks plagued the small temporary car park that was surrounded by the tall forest. The grassed trail that led back in the direction of La Fortaleza had wheel indentations from previous usage, but now only patrons on horseback used the rarely occupied trail. Their self-adopted little brother was already thirty minutes overdue from their planned rendezvous and his nonappearance had the men worried.

Behind them waiting were also Danny, Ricky and Barny in their allotted Land Cruiser 4WD. The windows were down as the men turned their mouths away from the uncomfortable hot nor westerly winds gusting through the cabin. The air conditioning was the only thing that Razor could not mend on the long-idled vehicle they commandeered from the logging coup. The temperature was increasing with every passing hour and was now crossing over 40C, and with humidity levels down to almost single figures, the mountain ranges surrounding the Hexagon Valley was not the place to be.

The men had made an untroubled and successful transfer of the stolen money from the armoured van to the Land Cruisers. The counting would be done later, however, by the time they had transferred the loot, the realisation of how much they had was starting to sink in. Barny excitedly estimated to the men that there could be over half a million dollars from what he had quickly rummaged through, equivalent to over five million dollars a decade ago in the deflated busted economy of the present times.

There were boxes and metal cases still inside the armoured van which they could not fit into the 4WDs. They ransacked through all boxes, bags, sacks and containers, then disposed of any cheques and money orders, cash was only what they would keep, along with the metal strongboxes that the gold coins were stored in. They kept a few strongboxes that contained the silver coins but sacrificed most, and along with the discarded cheques and money orders, threw them back into the van.

They rolled the armguard further into the bush so it could not be seen from any passer-by who happened to venture down the road then covered it with lying branches and shrubbery. A thirty-minute drive through the channelling corrugated fire tracks got them to their rendezvous point where Teeto was supposed to be waiting. The undulating track was tight either side of the vehicles. Spreading branches and foliage from the overgrown bushland continued to brush and bang up against the front and sides of the vehicles as they pushed along as quickly as they could.

Once Teeto joined them, the six would drive east through another steep descending winding bush fire track which would take them to the bitumen highway of the Graceville pass on the other side of the apex. From there it was a four hour drive northbound to a designated property on the border of the central state of New Banksia, and then freedom, however, time was of the essence, and Teeto's absence was elevating the nerves of the waiting party.

The Vice Presidents were adorned in black T-shirts with black baseball caps atop their heads, their club patched vests rested on the seat between them. The boys had already changed out of their golfing attire into their T-shirts, denim jeans and boots at the changeover, along with some much-needed bottles of water for their parched mouths, thanks to their newly formed allies.

Drake and Razor exited the vehicle. Drake pulled his radio from the glove box. He walked to the front of the car and rested his right leg on the bull bar as Razor sidled next to him. It was not what he wanted to do. No radio communication was to be made except in absolute emergency and Drake was concerned enough to qualify Teeto's absence as a critical situation. Teeto was the most reliable and trustworthy person Drake had ever met, and if he wasn't there like they had planned, then something was terribly amiss. The boys exited their own vehicle and walked to the side of the road, apprehensively waiting for the Vice Presidents next move.

Danny and the boys peered their eyes to the skies. The winds were picking up by the second as the tall trees swayed from side to side. The surrounding bushland was different to the western side of the range. They had congregated at the base of Black Mountain, the highest and furthest southerly peak of the Midnight Ranges before the topography dropped and levelled out until it would rise again on the next range across the valley. Danny had seldom been to these parts of the mountains. He only ever caught glimpses of it when he travelled through cuttings of the pass.

It was slightly more arid than the semi rainforests of the Kensington National Park and western side of the range where they had spent most their time on the run. Gone were the giant tree ferns, replaced by the abundant growth of small bracken fern, poking its dried fronds above the fallen bark and limbs from the towering gums. The smell of eucalypt fanned in the air as the hot weather enhanced its oily aroma.

The boys listened impatiently as Drake tried to raise Teeto on the radio. They had their secretly chosen UHF band to make communication with assigned codenames to confuse unwanted listeners if they happened to tune in, chiefly

Marco inside the comms hut at the compound. If any conversation took place over the airwaves within radius, Marco would know about it, and that was the Vice Presidents greatest fear.

Frustration was gathering momentum in the men's over heated bodies as Drake tried in vain to raise him. 'Big brother to little scorpion, come in little scorpion,' he continued to repeat into the radio, but silence was only thing he was greeted with.

The agonising decision of leaving Teeto behind was almost going to be made until the muffled voice of Drake's self-adopted little brother came over the airwaves, but relief was to quickly turn to bedlam when his young confidante frenetically relayed the events of the morning and the anarchy that had now taken over the compound.

Drake pushed the initial shock and disbelief aside to ask why he was still inside and not at the rendezvous point as planned, and when Teeto explained that Solomon had all exit and entrance points guarded, the men's anxieties were reaching fever pitch. Teeto explained that the President had him running all sorts of errands inside the compound, from getting water to the men, to retrieving ammunition from the container sheds. He could not get away without being noticed and wasn't about to risk the wrath of Solomon if he were caught abandoning the club.

The siege was into its sixth hour. Police negotiators were brought to the standoff when command decided that another raid would lead to more needless victims on both sides. Their early morning experience left them in no doubt that the outlaw MC was armed for a mini war and clear instructions came from above to avoid another potential slaughter. They enticed Solomon to the radios and from the communications hut the President continued to refuse their demands of an unconditional surrender.

Solomon would not adhere to their instructions until all police presence was out of the area to guarantee his members a safe exodus. In response, police command issued a deal that if he and senior members of the club, along with the Graceville four yielded to their demands and give themselves up, they pledged that all other members would walk free and avoid arrest, however, Solomon was having nothing to do with ultimatums. It was his way or no way, and warned that more people would die if they did not evacuate the area or attempt another raid, adding with laughter that he had never heard of the Graceville four when pushed on the matter of the wanted cop killers.

Negotiations were painstakingly slow for all concerned. Police command at the siege were one too many mountain ranges away from Graceville to get clear signals off their radios. They had to relay messages to a makeshift command post at Fernbank, and from there, Fernbank passed on the critical information to the Graceville police station that had now been flooded with senior officers from the suburbs. It was then a matter of contacting headquarters in the city by a landline phone to Assistant Commissioner Conroy who had the final say on all decisions. Each message or demand was taking a frustrating 30 minutes to relay back and forth from the compound, which played into the hands of Solomon, giving him much needed time to assess and act.

After receiving the affirmative that *La Fortaleza*'s southern and eastern alternate exits were not shielded by police forces, Solomon had all wives, girlfriends and associates gathered and organised an evacuation. Crow was commissioned with the task and oversaw the secret exodus by horseback and carriages and by foot, down the trails and one-way gravel roads that exited below the apex of the Graceville pass.

After the exodus was completed, *La Fortaleza*'s numbers had dropped to 44, with 18 of them situated at designated entrance points to protect intrusions. 24 were left inside the confines of the compound, armed and waiting for their Presidents next commandment, but there were two more inside the Manor who were not armed or patched. Zoe Valetta and little Maddy waited alone and frightened in the confines of the second-storey bedroom.

Solomon refused Zoe's pleas for her and Maddy to exit with the evacuation to escape the mayhem that had surrounded them. She bravely questioned his motives and parenting skills and was left shell-shocked and brooding when Solomon verbally shot her down with his gravelly aggression, reminding her that it was she, not him, that had put his daughter in the danger that now encircled them.

Solomon left the room content that if Maddy had protective company for the time being, all the better for him to get on with business, however, the one important thing he never shared with their club lawyer was that he had already planned for Maddy. If police had not cleared the area an hour before the sun was due to go down, or if the siege became too perilous, he was going to snatch his daughter, seat her on the back of his beloved Harley Davidson and ride off through the bush into the sunset with no regard for anyone else.

Drake and Razor pondered the situation. In days gone by, they had discussed that the imminent D-Day for the club was more likely than not, but for it to fall on this day just added to their confusion and agitation.

Drake paused on the radio. His eyes squinted in deep thought whilst his tongue twirled inside his bottom lip.

He took Razor aside, looked at him, nodding his head in the affirmative, and quietly said, 'We gotta go in and get him.' Razor had no hesitation in agreeing.

Danny grasped that there was going to be a change of plan. The expressions and body language of the Vice Presidents exuded unease. He knew that they would never leave Teeto behind. He could understand the reasons why. He liked Teeto, and so too did Barny and Ricky who always compared his features to Danny.

Teeto always gave time to the boys and his affable ways was always popular amongst them, and as Barny and Ricky's attention was occupied by two wild wallabies madly darting through the nearby bushland, Danny approached Drake and Razor and involved himself in their plans on how to extricate their young buddy.

'What about the entrance points?' Danny asked. 'Didn't he say that they were guarded?'

'We're their fuckin Vice Presidents, they'll let us through,' Drake confidently predicted in frowning determination.

Drake again raised Teeto on the radio and informed him that they'll be coming to rescue him out of the crisis that he had been cemented in, but as his resolute voice deepened, Ricky and Barny were comprehending what was about to occur, and Ricky was in no mood to enter back into La Fortaleza. Solomon was the last person he wanted to see. He was continuously having nightmares over the sound of that empty barrel that was pushed against his head, clicking over and over and it was a sound that was always with him.

'No way, Danny! I'm not going back there. I'm bloody not going risk everything by being arrested or confronting Solomon. You heard Teeto, there's coppers everywhere in there,' Ricky pleaded aloud to Danny. 'Barny and I will stay here with one of the vehicles, and you should too. He's their mate, let them get him out!'

Danny had no time to answer Ricky's concerns. The quick-tempered Razor abruptly intervened in the boys' conversation, and with nostrils flaring, angrily confronted them, aiming his short tirade at the smaller of the three.

'Do you think we're stupid enough to leave the vehicles with you?' he bellowed.

It was all down to trust with Razor, and the boys had yet to gain it fully, particularly Ricky. He still considered them outsiders, even though they had worked and planned together, and the club's motto *credere nemo* (trust no one) was still front and centre in his mind.

Razor couldn't take to Ricky as others had inside the club, and in return, Ricky never cared if he did or not. Ignoring Razor's short rant, he contemptuously turned his back and started to walk away. Razor aggressively shoved him in the back, forcing Ricky to lightly stumble.

'Don't you turn your back on me,' he berated.

With lightning speed, Ricky drew his revolver from the back of his pants in his left hand and had his arm extended at the forehead of a stunned Razor.

Drake already had confirmation what the outlaws were capable of and the cold and unnerving look in Ricky's eyes suggested calm intervention was desperately needed, the situation was only one misplaced word away from becoming deadly. Drake had been around and seen all types of men in similar situations, and experience told him that the stare that Ricky possessed was real.

The trio had already amassed a list of police victims and Drake had the suspicion that the toll had risen in the last hour, and rightly assumed that a man in a leather vest wouldn't mean one iota to them if they were pushed too far. If he couldn't play the successful mediator quickly, the intimidating bluff could cost his fellow VP his life.

He looked to Danny for assistance. He glared at him and gestured to calm his friend down. Danny was unmoving. 'Nothing to do with me,' he nonchalantly replied with dark-humoured arrogance.

Drake responded in disgust. If looks could kill, he had just fired a cannon as he shook his head in anger. The men were all highly strung. The adrenalin was still rampant in their bodies and were all on edge. Barny looked on in grave anticipation. He knew Ricky couldn't be thinking reason, he was still high on the blow after taking another snort when they had left the money change over and was expecting the worse at any second.

He glanced at Danny and couldn't believe his unmoved and uncaring posture. There was no feeling of nerves within him, no anxieties, the buzzing knotting sensations he would get in his stomach had all but disappeared. He was looking to the skies, deep in concentration, peering through the forest rooftops towards the northwest horizon, watching the wind gusts swaying the canopies of the trees while sculling down his water placating his craving thirst.

It was if he was becoming desensitised to it all. All the panicked yelling, the gun pointing, the threats, the blood, the killings, it was if it meant nothing to him anymore, becoming oblivious to all the constant danger that surrounded him.

Razor wasn't backing off. The short barrel was only an inch away from his head. He was resilient in his bravado, but deep inside, he was praying to whatever god he had that the 9mm hole he was staring at was going to lower.

Drake asked his partner to move away. 'C'mon Razor, let it go, mate. We don't need this, brother. We're all in this together,' he calmly pleaded.

The pair's duelling eyes never left each other as Razor began to step backwards. Both Barny and Drake were silently breathing sighs of relief as Ricky slowly lowered his gun with every reversing step that was took, the palpable tension only dissipating when Teeto's voice re-emerged over the airwaves.

As the battle of rabid honour between Razor and Ricky simmered, Danny, still ignoring the men around, had his eyes to skies, focusing on the real danger above, and he had a sinking feeling in his stomach that he may have been the catalyst for all that was about to horrifically await them in the coming hour.

As Drake moved away from the group to converse with his younger comrade, relieved that Razor had literally dodged a bullet, he forcefully reminded them all to take a chill pill then re-commenced his communication with Teeto whilst Danny sidled up to Razor and softly advised him that they were over his belligerent attitude.

'Next time you mightn't be so lucky,' he expressed with his smug smile. 'Listen!' he said after a brief pause. 'You need us as much as we need you. So, let's work together, hey dude! We all have an end goal here, right? So, drop the attitude,' he ended with another cocksure grin.

Danny extended his hand for an agreement shake, Razor begrudgingly accepted while he snorted and grumbled under his breath before joining Drake at the front of their vehicle.

Drake was gaining much needed intel from Teeto, from where people were positioned to whom was still left inside the compound. In his controlled frantic tones, Teeto relayed all that he knew to his mentor.

As Drake and Razor communicated further with Teeto, the boys stood on the side of the rocky dirt track chewing over scenarios that came into their minds.

Indecision plagued them; Danny didn't want to go against their wishes. The hard work of their dangerous venture had already been completed and all three were hesitant to go to the well once more and agreed that they had to get out of the forest as quickly as they could, but loyalty to a friend and conscious was going to override the perceived sensible decision to leave.

Danny calmly argued to his best man that the police were on the outside of the compound, not in, so the chance of an arrest was minimal at best. 'We'll be in and out before you know it,' he predicted, and as for Solomon? Danny enforced to Ricky that he ignores his hatred towards the President. 'Just think of the money,' he encouraged. 'Don't let him make you do something stupid to jeopardise everything we've done.'

With expletives venerating out of his mouth, Ricky reluctantly accepted that it was the right thing to do by extricating Teeto. He deserved his cut, that they all agreed on with Barny being the most adamant. Danny turned to Drake and Razor and inquired why they were stalling for time.

'If we're going to do this, we better do it now, because I reckon we've only got about an hour to get in, and then get out of these mountains,' he warned, and as the men asked why, Danny pointed to the skies and alerted them of the first ominous signs of gathering smoke that was starting to waft over their heads. Fearful expressions of haste covered their faces as they hurriedly scampered into their vehicles. Drake continued his grainy communications with Teeto as Razor gave a respectful nod of the head and thumbs up to the boys before jumping behind the wheel; the new respect had come quickly.

Ignition point of the fire was exactly where Danny had dreaded. The fanning winds flared the simmering engine flame of the smashed police cruiser until a shard of a burning rubber oil hose was blown onto the shoulder of the road. Within seconds, the dried leaves and grasses were alight and within the minute had entered the undergrowth of the forest. The forceful winds gave the ground flames strength and impetus and was quickly licking up the trunks of the trees.

The fire was starting to fan out in a cone shape, heading in a south easterly direction. Its front had quickly extended out to over 500 meters wide as it pushed through the bush and was increasing rapidly with every wild wind gust. The flames were quickly climbing into the crowns of the trees, spotting ahead of the main ground front, and as it stood, only 11km away directly across the ranges, La Fortaleza was right in the bulls-eye's target of the now raging out of control wildfire.

The men drove ferociously through the abandoned trail. The grassed track was tighter than what they had to negotiate previously as once again, over hanging branches and vegetation from the young saplings smashed and bashed up against their vehicles as they weaved and dodged oncoming obstacles with reckless fear.

After ten minutes of worried determined bush bashing, the terrain opened out on both sides and began to elevate towards the boundaries of La Fortaleza. Drake and Razor were in the lead vehicle and soon could see Sultan members ahead as they quickly approached the guarded point. Razor abruptly slammed the brake pedal down and came to sliding halt only meters from his fellow club members who had their weapons raised at the perceived oncoming threat. Drake jumped out of the passenger door and showed himself to his constituents who were relieved to see their Vice Presidents coming to the aid of their Club.

'Where have you bastards been? Solomon's been looking for ya,' said Big Taz, a burly long-bearded seven year fully patched Sultan.

'We're here now, that's all that matters. We know what's going on. I've just talked to Sol,' lied Drake. 'You guys are to get the hell out of here. There's a fire coming straight at us. Get on your horses and get out of these mountains, *NOW!*' he yelled.

'We're going in to help who's left,' Razor hastily added.

The assembled Sultan guards were quickly in their saddles and heading in the direction that the boys had just came from as Drake and Razor re-entered the vehicle and pushed on with the boys following close behind. The track continued to elevate then dip until it levelled out at the single lane wooden bridge that crossed Kensington River. Cleared paddocks adorned the north side across the bridge where the club's sheep grazed, all the jumbucks were huddled in the far corner searching for shade near the water troughs, restless and panicked, as if they could sense the danger. Thinly spread eucalypt forest was to the left and south side.

Another five minutes further on, the forest thickened either side again until they drove to highest point of the elevation. They were now just outside the electrified fence and hedge lined compound. Razor stepped out of the vehicle and punched the code into the panel to open the mesh wire and corrugated iron gate. It sprung open to the let the vehicles through, they didn't bother to close it behind them.

The vehicles passed more open paddocks where the large solar panel instalments sat, gleaming in their perch atop of the cleared hill. To the right of them down in a slight valley, they could see down to the marijuana plantation, tingeing brown and wilting on the ever-increasing intense heat, but more importantly from their elevated point, they now could see first-hand the dangerous large plume of smoke quickly rising far above the forest tops.

From the position on the plateau they had now reached, Danny focused his intense awestruck eyes towards the north, watching the sky turn orange as the rising smoke plume began to block out the sun above them. They could see beyond the plantation that the fire was spotting ahead of itself on the fierce winds and as the boys fearfully commented on the imminent danger, Danny, silently and fatefully, concluded that his assumption that they had an hour to complete their mission was now looking like the deadliest of gross overestimations.

The men pushed on driving as fast as allowed until they stopped in the middle of the orchard plantations. If anything could give the vehicles cover to protect the money, then this was as good as they could hope for. At least the greenery and moisture inside the densely populated sloping fruit trees wouldn't feed the fire as savagely as the dried barks and exploding oils the eucalypts held within. They three point turned the vehicles around and faced them in direction they entered. The men hurriedly exited the 4WDs and began the 500m race on foot up the gravel path towards the stables where Teeto was to meet them.

The heat from the inner furnace of the fire was being shunted through the air as the men kept low, shielding the whirling smoke away from their faces as it thickened by the minute and was now starting to enclose around the compound from the spot fires being set alight ahead of the front. In the distance, the men could see flames rising 50 to 100 meters above the canopy of the forest as they ran.

Time was of the essence. Teeto had to be there, if he wasn't, they were all going to be put at the mercy of the approaching fire if they had to waste time locating him. There was no margin for error, they had to grab him, race back to their vehicles and charge back out of mountains before the front or the leaping canopy fire ignited further raging infernos ahead of them.

Razor was leading the way towards the stables when all the men dived behind the first of the protective stables, taking cover from what they thought to be gunshots. Another volley of shots pierced the air as they grouped together behind a closer stall, now with their own weapons drawn.

'Release the horses!' Razor yelled to Drake.

The agitated and frightened horses galloped as one, frenzied and wide-eyed, taking off from where the men had come.

'Teeto, Teeto!' they yelled, peering through the thickening smoke while ducking in and out of cover points inside the stable. They moved to the end stall shielding their faces and heads from the small embers starting to fill the hot whirling air when Teeto, panicked and frightened, emerged out of the billowing smoke.

Police command outside the compound were the first to be alerted to the forthcoming danger of the fire. Although Marco had heard all the warnings from inside the comms hut and relayed them to his President, Solomon remained calm. He was waiting for all police to move from the area before he decided on an evacuation himself, but if worst came to worst, the underground fire bunker was there to be used.

Command had been given the critical lifesaving information as the fire was in its infancy and duly reacted without hesitation, evacuating all members out of the vicinity with precision and trained teamwork. CIRT captains and other senior officers who had joined Grundy and his team organised an exodus to the western side of the ranges, away from the south easterly direction that the fire was taking.

The backup command post at Fernbank had already left the picturesque sight and were racing back towards Graceville through the pass. Teams outside the compound were escaping on foot, horseback and all that could fit into the police vehicles westward through the pine plantation and catchment area to the safe haven of the reservoir, travelling down range on any track, trail or road that allowed them, and hopefully out of the danger zone.

Their orders were to get out alive, reassess, and live to fight another day, however, one member was not going to adhere to the orders, and with his team of volunteers was making one last incursion into the compound, the same time Danny and his partners were creeping in from behind.

SOG Captain Dennis Grundy was doing things his own way once more. Since the aftermath of the first botched raid, he had seen twelve of his team taken away, five of them in body bags. He knew all of them personally. He knew their families and had overseen all their initiations into the tight knit fraternity of the Special Operations Group and was damned if he was going to let an outlaw motorcycle club get away with the murder of his colleagues. The Graceville four had been forgotten by the experienced Captain.

The only enemy he had seen all morning were Sultans and taking down their leader had become the only thing paramount in his steely focus. He had sat angry, frustrated and impatient as he listened into negotiations that had taken place throughout the morning and let his animated feelings be known to higher ranking officers that they were wasting their time trying to deal with a man such as Solomon Pike. He pleaded more than once to let him and his selected team make another incursion inside the compound, promising the job would be done without mistake a second time knowing what they knew now, but was rejected on all approaches.

When evacuations were being hastily organised and completed around him, Grundy gathered his team around with retribution for his lost comrades the sole subject on his mind. Of the original twenty-two under his command, ten remained, and all had no hesitation in joining their Captain when he informed them of his plans. Grundy knew that he was putting the loyalty of the badge above the men's own safety. He offered his team members who did not want to engage the chance to evacuate.

No questions would be asked as that was the orders from above, but neither was he shocked nor surprised when his surviving men stood to a man and overlapped their hands and vowed to avenge the death of their colleagues. They had the BEARCAT on standby for their escape when needed. When the time came to exodus the plateau, they confidently expected its steel plated shell and covers would give them protection if the oncoming flames loomed around them. Grundy determinedly explained to his team that they had the warrants, a clear mandate, and to him, enough clear and present danger was obvious to permit the use of deadly force until they had Solomon Pike either in custody or dead.

If anyone were to impede their mission, the threat will be neutralised without hesitation if the sole order of surrender was ignored. Solomon Pike was not to escape the compound under any circumstances and their mission was already underway with more deadly consequences erupting around their incursion. They breached an entrance point through the broken fences of the guard dog run. Another Rottweiler had been shot dead by Grundy himself at the point of entry, two more still roamed free throughout the compound, thirsty, disorientated, and dangerous to everyone around, including Sultan members who were familiar to them.

'What the hell is going on, Teeto? Who's doing the shooting?' Razor asked.

The men had joined him on the cobblestone path at the arbour entrance on the north side laundry door of the Manor 100 meters up from the stables. Its green ivy and wisteria leaves that dangled through the battens were wilting before their eyes as the oven like winds began to suck away at the moisture within. Sparks of fire began to spit through the air as the men looked in all directions for potential danger.

'It's the coppers! They've raided the compound again. They're shooting at anyone who moves. Fires are starting everywhere,' Teeto wailed. 'We've tried to get to the water tanks, but they think we're trying to attack them. We can't even get to the bunker. The bastards are sitting right above it behind the concrete wall. They don't understand we're trying to save them as well. They want Solomon, but he doesn't give a fuck what's happening to us,' Teeto frantically finished.

Drake grabbed him by the arm. 'C'mon. We gotta go. The vehicles are in the orchard. We've got the money. There's nothing we can do here,' Drake insisted.

'We can't,' Teeto argued.

'What do you mean? Do you wanna fuckin' die here? Look around you, we got to go, Teeto!' Drake blasted.

'It's Zoe! She's trapped upstairs. We need to get her,' Teeto pleaded.

Drake and Razor couldn't understand how Zoe could be inside the compound. Other than members, only closely vetted wives and lady friends were allowed access in recent days, and when Teeto explained that he overheard Solomon and Lars say that she was never to fall into the hands of police for fear of her turning on the club, his concerns for her life was overpowering. He loved Zoe for what she had done for him. He treated her as the big sister he never had and would do anything to protect her and when asked collectively by the Vice Presidents why she was at the compound, the answer he gave astounded them all.

Teeto's face was reddening by the second, from both the heat and fearful frustration as he pointed his finger at Danny. Dried saliva exuded from his lips when in his animated vexation announced that she had come to see him.

'Me!' Danny replied with surprise. 'Oh shit!' Danny said, exasperated. 'Don't tell me they accepted my terms of surrender!' *Why else would she be looking for me?* he instantly thought. He cockily turned to Barny and Ricky. 'You hear that, boys? They've accepted my terms. How about that!' he gloated; however, his brief delusional thought was struck down.

'*No*, you fuckin idiot!' Teeto roared. 'Don't you understand? She's fuckin' besotted by you. She confided in me last night, tears and all. I don't know what you did to her, but she feels like a fool now.'

Danny didn't believe him. He knew they had hit it off and instantly felt a bond with her, but to say Zoe was lovestruck was ludicrous; he said, 'I only spent one night with her, for Christ's sake.'

Razor accused him of sleeping with her and asked the question furiously, but Danny denied anything of the sort had happened as the flashback of their near goodnight kiss jumped into his mind.

Teeto interrupted Razor's grilling to focus back on what he had to say.

'She used Maddy as an excuse so she could see ya. She was going to leave this morning, but all this shit went down and now Solomon won't let her leave. You gotta help me get her out!' He gasped for breath directing his anger at Danny.

Without hesitation, Danny asked Teeto to lead him to where she was at.

He followed behind him as they raced to the laundry door. For the first time, Razor and Ricky were in agreement. They called for them to stop.

'This is madness!' yelled Razor.

He turned to Drake and commanded that they leave now. Razor didn't want to confront his President, and neither did Ricky. They pleaded with Danny and Teeto to turn back, but Danny's mind was made up. He couldn't leave her there, especially now, and knowing the bond that she and Teeto shared, he wouldn't be able to live with himself if the predictions Teeto was asserting came to bare.

Danny gritted his teeth and with his determined frown told his partners that he was going in, with or without them. Ricky yelled and cursed him with every name he could muster. Barny shook his head in another sigh of disbelief and whispered to himself 'Here we go again'

Drake and Razor fearfully pondered at each other. The fire danger was getting to the point of no return. Embers were sailing past in horizontal sheets, burning, biting, and searing at their clothes and skin. Side buildings inside the compound to the north were beginning to catch alight from the spearing embers that were shooting across the clearings. Shards of blazing bark, some as large as a man's arm were flying into the compound setting alight any building that had timber attached.

The fire front had now spread over a kilometre wide, crossing Summit Road and now passing over Molloy's track. The gathering roar of the inferno could be heard from inside the compound, its angry mouth getting louder and louder with every dangerous passing minute as the atmosphere turned a glowing orange. The crown fire was whipping up the ridges at the pine plantation boundaries to the north. The very spot where Danny had spent, cold, wet and shivering after the storm that led him to little Maddy on that fateful morning.

The cluster of pine trees sent licking flames hundreds of meters into the air. Hurling winds of fire crossed the clearings and were heading straight into the heart of la Fortaleza. The raging inferno had surged six kilometres through the forest in thirty minutes. The big machinery that had established fire breaks in the past were long gone and what breaks were there had overgrown and were virtually non-existent.

The firefighting trucks and tankers that would have attacked the fire were no longer a force. What trucks they did have in Graceville and nearby villages were instructed to remain and protect the towns and property as the fire was moving too fast to form any kind of defence. Strike team capabilities were gone, and most importantly, there was no aerial support anymore to contain and douse hotspots ahead of the fire.

The inferno was free to rampage at its will. It was unhindered and unchallenged as it razed everything in its path. The compound was under fierce combat siege once more, but this time it was facing two battles, and the second of the two was going to be the enemy that they could not fight, as no one could have predicted the staggering speed that the fire breathing monster was descending on all participants who were now entrapped on the plateau that was *La Fortaleza.*

Chapter 38

'We have to get her out, brother,' said Drake. 'It's the right thing to do. We can't forget what she has done for us.'

Razor looked at Ricky, they both hated the idea and cursed at their partners.

Barny tugged at Ricky as he passed, following Danny inside the Manor. They're protests were ignored and before they knew it, flustered and alienated, they found themselves scurrying behind the others, racing through the backrooms of the Manor.

'This way!' Drake yelled to Danny and Teeto, who were baulking with indecision on where to go. With Drake now leading the charge, they stormed through the door that stood behind the bar in the inner sanctum of the clubs meeting room. If Solomon was going to confront them, then it was his duty to handle what would come. He was bracing for confrontation, and with Razor by his side was ready to take what the President gave, as long it could produce enough stalling time for the boys to slip by and rescue Zoe from the upstairs bedroom.

Drake hurriedly worked his way around the bar, he looked on confused. The meeting room was empty. 'Where was everybody? He panned across the church table; the gavel sat alone on the head of the bear. He looked towards the billiard tables to his right, no one was in sight. Had they all made it to the bunker? Had they escaped somehow? Were they now the only ones left to face the danger? He looked beyond the grand table, his stomach began to knot when he saw the body count of his comrades, lined up and laying below the bay windows. Blood pooled on the floor around the tarpaulin covered lifeless bodies, the aftermath of the early morning gunfight.

Drake and Razor were stunned into silence. Despite the speechless distress of what they were grimly staring at, both were soon shocked back to the grave reality that ringed them. As Teeto and Danny ran towards the dual doors that opened to the foyer, a huge rumble sounded throughout the Manor. Its walls' shook in vibration as the revving sound extenuated with every thrust, and as Drake looked to where Solomon's Harley Davidson should have been and saw it missing, he knew that his President was making a desperate bid for freedom.

The boys pushed the large doors open and ran into the foyer and saw Solomon and Lars ready to exit the Manor. Semi-automatic rifles were strapped across their shoulders; protective fire blankets covered their bodies. They had both donned full faced black woollen balaclavas depicting skull and bones in white. Clear plastic goggles covered their eyes to protect them from the outside elements that they were about to encounter.

They throttled down their right hands as the bikes idled in neutral, steeling themselves for the escape. The President had seen his men mowed down by the SOG as they attempted to find safety at the bunker. Solomon mastered that he was their target and on top of all the drug trafficking and arms charges that he likely faced without the aid and abetting of Minister Johnston protecting his enterprise, he surely now had added multiple counts of murder to his resume after the events of the morning.

Solomon Pike undoubtably knew that a lifetime of prison would now await, and he was not going to risk becoming their prized victim.

He planned to commandeer one of the clubs' converted vans but had to abort it when the garage that housed them was set alight by the incoming firestorm. He refocused and calmed his mind and assessed he had only two options left, stay inside the Manor and burn to death, or get on his Harley Davidson and make a dangerous dash for freedom, southbound on the clubs well maintained internal track that led to the bottom of track 24 and the Graceville pass. Solomon was not going to go down with the ship.

Solomon's concentration was disturbed when Danny and Teeto ran past him to climb the stairs to the second floor. He watched as they scaled them, pushing their right hands off the bannisters for extra speed in the race against time to extricate Zoe. Solomon swung his head and looked behind to see his Vice Presidents standing with Barny.

He removed his goggles and rolled up his balaclava, sweat drained in torrents from his reddened naked head as he leered his notorious stare of death at his right-hand men through the increasing smoke that was filling the Manor. He knew they had betrayed his club, he didn't know how exactly, but seeing them with the fugitives, who he had given shelter to, only confirmed his suspicions. Both he and the Sergeant at Arms had no time to confront them. Solomon gave a gesture to Lars to open the front doors, he then turned to Drake and Razor and snarled, 'You're on your own.'

No help was coming from him, they had broken the club code, and the President expected them to die.

Danny and Teeto kicked and shouldered the door down to Zoe's bedroom. She was huddled in the corner of the room wrapped in a bed quilt. She had been trapped in her room all morning, unable to leave. She was frantically seeing what was happening out of her south side upstairs window, the fire skipping and igniting ahead of the front, smoke venting under her door. She had been hysterically banging and kicking at the locked bedroom door, screaming, crying for someone to release her from her bedroom prison, no one was listening.

She had almost given up her fight, shaking and quivering in fright when in stormed Danny and Teeto. She looked up at the intruders, not knowing what was to come, but her diminished resolve got a lifesaving upsurge when she saw who was coming towards her. Danny was the last person she expected to see, and probably the last person she wanted to see, but her heart thumped a different beat seeing his face again and compelled her to briefly ignore the peril that surrounded them.

No words were spoken between them as he lifted her from the floor. He gave her an earnest wink and smile as he locked his arm around her, keeping the quilt tightly wrapped around to protect her from the thickening smoke and increasing heat.

'Where is Maddy?' Teeto urgently asked.

'Solomon took her off me. I don't know where she is!' Zoe replied, frightened what may have happened to her.

They exited the bedroom and rushed back down the staircase until they abruptly came to a halt on the base of the landing. Solomon's eyes were glued to theirs, throttling down on his 1600cc engine, adding the stench of petrol fumes to the already toxic air. Drake, Razor, Barny and Ricky were to the right of the staircase landing, hovering at the entrance to the meeting room.

Drake willed the trio to run towards him and grasp their last opportunity to escape the maelstrom. Ricky yelled for them, 'C'mon Danny, c'mon, we gotta get out of here.' His howls of impatience were being joined by the others, but slight movement behind Solomon's back had grabbed Danny's scrutiny. The fire blanket had slipped slightly off him, exposing his patched leather jacket. Danny couldn't make out what it was.

Could it be supplies in a large bag, could it be a stash of weapons, it could've been anything bulging out from behind his back. The shocking truth was revealed when the face of little Maddy appeared from a slit in the blanket, strapped tightly to her desperate father, the horrifying answer of her whereabouts petrified them all.

Little Maddy stared at both Zoe and Danny. She expressed unbridled fear, her innocent child face shot an arrow of despair through their hearts. Although Maddy could not hear the devastation taking place, her eyes and smell told her a thousand stories.

'Stop!' Zoe screamed. 'You can't take Maddy with you, what are you thinking?' She howled helplessly.

Solomon ignored the wailing pleas, he revved down his throttle and nodded at Lars to exit. They were good to go and about to take their headlong charge at freedom when a huge explosion thundered through the foundations of the Manor. Chandeliers swayed and rattled; windows imploded on both floors as everyone hunched in a reflex action of self-protection. The clubs stored fuel and oil drums that were housed in a garage behind the working sheds had detonated from the intense heat and sent a shockwave through the compound.

The garage container adjacent which roomed the club's arsenal had the walls blown off it. Flames engulfed the inner contents, heating up stored magazines and boxes of ammunition and within moments sent bullets of all calibres wildly afar in a frenzied fireworks display. Bullets were ricocheting off everything around, firing up against the side of the manor and across the compound grounds, club members who had not found shelter were being mowed down from the stray bullets.

Grundy and his men had found refuge behind the concrete wall atop of the underground bunker. The howls of burnt and wounded surrendering Sultan members were finally being heeded when they alerted Grundy and his men to the fact that their objectives were to save the lives of all inside the compound, not to take them.

Four of the men including Marco held their arms up through the darkening chaos in one last chance of survival. Their skin and faces burning with the intense heat, the leather jackets they wore were contracting and melting into their arms and back. They pointed and shouted towards the bunker and with the help of the SOG's lifted the 60kg steel door at its grassed covered 45-degree embankment and scurried down the fourteen 1.2-metre-wide steel steps to safety.

The members huddled with the SOGs in the 6x6 meter concrete bunker, relieved and thankful that they had found safety from the approaching firestorm, confessing that their President was still inside the Manor when questioned forcibly.

Grundy scaled up the internal stairs to shut the door behind him. His head protruded above ground level whilst reaching out to bring the door down when the explosion from the fuel storage almost shook his grip off the insulated handrails. He regained his balance and looked towards the sound of the explosion as bullets from the stored magazines began to whiz around. The forest of eucalypts outside the compound were now ablaze, along with the row behind the outbuildings.

The boundary-lined hedges were releasing flames in the air being set alight from the burning winds. The iconic redgum insignia of the club's creed that sat atop the entrance was alight, the front-end loader that Lars abandoned had caught fire, its large rubber tyres adding to the black smoke of darkness quickly smothering the compound. The cracking and explosions from the forest was releasing a deafening sound that was hard to decipher from the real ammunition.

Solomon and Lars throttled down their Harleys and in an almighty rumble exited out through the grand old front doors of the Manor. Lars was first to exit, he rode up the front path and swung his bike left onto the gravel driveway, Solomon quickly followed. The noise from the mayhem around was horrendous as embers and flames seared horizontally across the landscape. Day had now become night; darkness had set upon the plateau as the now low-level smoke completely blocked out the sun's rays.

Lars reached for his rifle. He lifted it off his shoulder and extended his left arm across his lap, keeping the throttle down with his right as he rode. Believing they were still under attack from the exploding stray bullets, he squeezed his finger on the trigger and let go a quick volley of defensive shots to the right of him at no particular target.

He only needed a few seconds grace for both he and Solomon to be out of sight, however, Grundy saw the muzzle flashes out of Lars rifle through the smoke and embers. The SOG captain concentrated his eyes on the danger. He could see and hear the silhouetted figures of the two motorcycles. Grundy had his chance, he knew that it could only be Solomon, at least one of them for sure.

In his unabated desire for retributive justice for his slain teammates, he blazed away with his weapon from the top rung of the internal step ladder of the bunker at the two Harleys that were making a crazed bid for freedom.

The group inside the Manor watched on in horror as they saw the second bike come crashing down, its rider blown backwards off the seat and flung up against the concrete protective barrier that lined the driveway.

'Oh my god! Maddy!' Zoe screamed, clasping her hands to her face in terror.

Without hesitation, Danny raced to the sidewall of the foyer and grabbed a leather jacket that hung from a row of a hooks. With it were helmets, balaclavas and assorted paraphernalia that the club displayed at the entrance. He donned the full-sleeved patched jacket and a balaclava to protect himself from the firestorm and raced out through the doors to the crashed bike. Teeto, Barny and Ricky quickly followed to aid Danny in his rescue of Maddy, hoping, praying, that she was still alive.

Complete darkness had almost beset the grounds of the compound. The radiant heat had intensified almost to the point of no return. The fire front had arrived across the clearings from the north. Everything was ablaze, wild tongues of fire licked in rage across the compound. The rescuing men could hardly breathe. They had to work fast to save Maddy. Time was running out; more minutes out there would mean certain death. Oxygen was being sucked out of the air, the fire seizing it for its own benefit. If you were to inhale, the furnace like heat could possibly sear your throat and lungs in an instant.

Danny arrived where Solomon lay behind the concrete barrier. He pushed him to the side, he was a dead weight. He struggled to keep him there. Danny pushed his back up against him and peeled back the fire blanket. Maddy was alive, her eyes of terror stared back at his from underneath her helmet. Danny pulled back his balaclava to show his face to Maddy, he smiled to assure her that her guardian angel was there once more.

He retrieved his bowie knife from his lower leg and hurriedly cut away the belt that was attached to Solomon. He wrapped the fire blanket around himself and Maddy and from his knees was about to make his retreat to the Manor when his arm was grabbed from behind.

'You take care of her. You keep my baby girl alive. You fuckin hear me! Keep her alive!'

It would be Solomon's last command. He signed to his daughter that he loved her, she too signed back before she suddenly disappeared in Danny's arms through the smoke-filled darkness and embers. Solomon then gritted his last breath before collapsing back off his elbow, half his body still trapped under the weight of his Harley Davidson. He had taken several fatal upper body shots out of Grundy's rifle, his protective vest not being able to repel the large calibre bullets, he would depart this life within the minute.

However, the President of the Sultan MC would not be the last fatality out of the flaying weapon of Captain Grundy. Grundy's lieutenant joined him at the top of the ladder believing that they were still under assault when he heard his captain fire at the bikers. Grundy eyed his telescopic sight through the darkness with scrutiny. What his vision saw was likened to a cataclysmic picture, akin to a burning astrological meteor shower.

Searing hot embers and flaming debris swirled around as if it were inside a giant clothes dryer being powered on the devil's wind. It was literally raining fire. He caught a brief sense of light in the orange-tinged darkness that gave him sight towards the Manor. Both he and his lieutenant could see what looked like another three leather clad Sultans running at speed out of the Manor's entrance, and with the deadly mindset of vengeance entrenched in Grundy's mind, knowing it would be his last opportunity before he had to take refuge, unleashed another volley of shots.

However, the targets he had aimed at were no Sultan brothers that he trusted were taking one last stand against him. The men he could not identify in the chaos were only there to save the life of an innocent little girl, who Grundy never even knew was there.

Danny never noticed Barny, Ricky and Teeto had followed up behind him. After respectfully nodding at Solomon's last demand and clasping Maddy close to him, he ran the 30 meters back inside the Manor with the fire blanket entirely secured around them, he had completely missed the sight of his three comrades in the chaos. On his retreat, Drake and Razor had already dashed past him onto the grounds of the compound without his knowledge, and by the time he had found the presumed safety of the foyer, Zoe's hysterics alerted him that all was not over.

'What's wrong? What's wrong?' Danny yelled, releasing Maddy at her feet.

'Teeto, Teeto!' she screamed. 'He went down! Barny and Ricky too. They've disappeared. Oh my god, oh my god! They've shot them, they've shot them!' Zoe shouted in distress, waving her arms uncontrollably between her head and knees.

Danny turned and raced to the front doors. He could make out Drake and Razor dragging a body back towards him. They had also donned blankets and balaclavas. Danny again covered himself and ran to help. Drake and Razor each had an arm of Teeto, hauling his body to safety, keeping low, ignoring the cracking and roaring that seemed to be crushing at their eardrums. The threat of bullets did not deter them as they risked their lives to secure their younger partner.

Danny arrived at his two lifelong buddies shortly beyond, Barny on one knee, screeching in pain, Ricky motionless, lying on the scorching earth. As hell swirled around them, Barny raised the strength to help Danny pull Ricky back into the foyer trying desperately to keep the blankets secured around them.

Both groups of men crawled and dragged their mates through the adjoining doors of the foyer and into the clubs meeting room where the windows seemed to be the only ones not blown in from the explosion, they slammed the doors behind them. Power was lost inside the Manor; two battery powered lamps gave them the only light inside.

Drake and Razor sat Teeto on the floor up against the front edge of the bar, Danny doing the same with Ricky as Barny slumped next to his buddy's limp body. Terrified shouts of anguish echoed throughout the room as the maelstrom continued outside. Embers had blown in through the shattered windows of the north side top floor bedrooms, setting alight curtains and linens, the floorboards were lighting as if putting a match to paper.

Drake and Razor did all they could to stem the bleeding out of Teeto's wounds. Drake pushed rags and clothing against his buddies' stomach as Razor clasped his hands around Teeto's face, yelling at him to stay with them. Tragically, the wounds were too severe, arteries and vital organs had been penetrated by the three bullets that entered him and the Vice Presidents could only watch on in sorrowful rage as Teeto's terror filled eyes shut and head slump to the side.

Zoe stood away from the men at the end of the bar with Maddy at her side, trembling and whimpering in fear, trying to comprehend what was happening before her eyes, her hands covering her mouth in terror. Teeto was dead. She turned her horror-stricken eyes at Danny hovering above Ricky.

He had received a single shot. The bullet passed through his neck, rupturing his jugular and spinal cord, tearing away the side of his neck and severing nerves to his brain, he was dead within seconds of impact. Zoe listened heartbroken as Danny cradled his best man.

Danny knew his lifelong right-hand man was gone as soon as he pulled the fire blanket and balaclava away, exposing the horrific blood-soaked wound from the deep crevice in his neck. The pain Danny instantly felt was like no other. His body trembled in trauma, almost causing him to faint. His empty stomach knotted then regurgitated bile out of his mouth. He spat it away with the tears that rolled down his singed and blackened face as he hugged Ricky's limp and lifeless body, rocking it back and forth in unison.

The incredulous pain and sorrow only worsened by the guilt that his best mate had lost his life all because of him. There was no instant urge of revenge, he didn't even know how or who inflicted the shot, at this time he didn't even know if it was a bullet wound. The reasons didn't matter to him, all he wanted to do was turn back time as he lost all bearings of the danger around.

'No, no, no, no,' Danny wailed, as he held Ricky's head to his chest. 'I'm sorry, I'm so sorry!' he repeated softly. 'I'm sorry, Ricky, I am so sorry,'

The history and adventures they shared were like no other, through the good times and the bad, from before they were teenagers to the present. The mateship that connected them was envied by all who knew them. They were inseparable in their loyalties to one another and the last tumultuous month had only strengthened their already unbreakable bond, but now it was gone, gone in an instant, taken away in a frenzied cocktail of fire and bullets. He never had the chance to tell him how much he loved him, how much it meant to him to have him in his life and if Danny survived, he would never be able to forgive himself.

Barny gripped at Danny's shoulders. 'He's gone, Danny, he's gone. Leave him! Save yourselves, save yourselves!' Barny grimaced while his own left hand covered the wound across his stomach. Danny pulled back Barny's jacket to see blood oozing out of large hole below his ribcage, other gunshot wounds were exposed at his right shoulder and hip. They looked to see Drake covering Teeto's body with a fire blanket, an angry and wretched forlorn face had absorbed both he and Razor.

The day that everyone had predicted had come. From the weather experts to the local in the streets of Graceville, all knew it was only a matter of time. No one was supposed to be in the mountains on a day such as this one, no one should've been in the mountains on a day such as this one. All knew it was a code red day, the highest catastrophic danger point that was able to be listed, but through reckless decision making, unrivalled circumstances, misguided loyalties and foolish self-indulgent egos, the firestorm had entrapped all who ignored the warnings, and those still left breathing were at the mercy of the inferno and had resigned themselves to the fact their last breaths were maybe only minutes away.

Despite the look of resignation and the horror and madness that surrounded them, the remaining six left inside the Manor were to have a saviour amongst them however, and it was going to come from the one they least expected.

Danny was stirred from his grief-stricken stupor by Zoe, yelling at him to come and help push the club's church table aside. In all the life-threatening chaos that besieged her, little Maddy had the courage and nous to remember the secret entrance to the cellar that led below the floorboards of the meeting room. Zoe frantically communicated Maddy's knowledge that she had imparted to her.

'Where does it lead to?' Razor challenged.

Zoe communicated Razor's question to Maddy.

'She said the tunnel comes out below the orchard.'

'Are you sure?'

Zoe communicated again.

'Yes, she is absolutely sure.'

The look between Drake and Razor was palpable. Had they found a way out? It was the only decision that they could make, the risk had to be taken, to stay would ensure certain death, it felt like the grand old manor was about to cave in; if not, they would surely burn to death before it happened.

The underground cellar was Maddy's little hideaway. She played there often with her daddy on the quiet private days they had together. Only she and Solomon knew of its existence, not even the Vice Presidents knew about it, let alone any other senior members. Running 750 meters long and standing six-foot-high and one-meter wide, the tunnel was dug out many years ago, for what reason, Solomon never knew for sure, but it was always there if he needed it.

Solomon had thought long and seriously about escaping through it himself before he made his decision to exit. He aborted the notion as he predicted that if the Manor collapsed on top of them during the fire, he, and anyone with him would be likely be entombed in an oven and scalded to death. He couldn't run out through the exit as he would be running straight back out into the firestorm. There was no vehicle waiting as the boys had, no horse to try and carry him away to safety, so in his wisdom, made the fatal decision to exit atop of his Harley.

The cellar's light source was controlled by four 12-volt batteries attached to a handle at the base of the six-foot ladder where you could pull it down and light up the cellar room and tunnel. The tunnel passageway had redgum sleepers for support on the roof and side walls every 4.8 meters for bracing and stability. 60-watt globes hung at every 20-meter interval from wooden battens that were fixed to the roof.

Danny covered Ricky's body with a fire blanket and rose to his feet to help Drake and Razor push the half ton table across the floor. They heaved and pushed until Maddy crawled underneath them and flipped the carpet rug that sat atop the trap door. She grabbed the dual cast iron handles and lifted the door open. She then stood and let the chained door sit upright by itself. Maddy waved and pointed to the vertical wooden ladder. She was first to climb down, pulling the lever handle down to switch the lights on when she arrived at the base. Zoe quickly followed as Danny went to Barny and tried lifting him from his position.

'Leave me here!' Barny said.

Danny ignored his request 'Leave me here, Danny,' he repeated, this time louder with authority.

'Don't be stupid, Barny. You'll die if you don't come,' Danny warned.

'I'm dying anyway,' Barny solemnly replied as he again looked at his stomach wound. 'I'll only slow you down.'

Danny looked closer at Barny's wound. He had seen it before. It looked and reeked of the same damage that Matty Devlin encountered, and Danny knew what the outcome would be if his friend did not have immediate attention, attention which was impossible to obtain.

'C'mon Barny. I can't leave you behind. I've already lost Ricky; I'm not losing you,' Danny pleaded.

'Go,' Barny commanded. Danny could see he was weakening by the second, but he was not going to give up on his mate. He tried to manoeuvre him to his side and latch an arm underneath him, but all it did was heighten the pain that Barny already was fighting.

'For Christ's sake, Danny, leave me!' he roared. 'If I come, you will all die the same as me,' he implored as the choking smoke and heat added to the difficulty of his speech.

Barny moved himself inches away from Danny's face, the pain intensifying with every flinch of a muscle. He lowered his head and locked his sinking blue eyes into Danny's.

'Go,' he quietly spoke. 'Go to Greta, go to your boys! All that we've done! It will all be for nothing if you don't go now. Go north to your heaven, Danny. I will be content in mine; I know you will be in yours. Go, my friend!'

The tears of resignation welled and dripped from Danny's eyes. He knew Barny was justified in his stance. He knew that he was right, he always is, and gravely understood his friend would probably depart from him before they got down into the tunnel, and as it was, it would be impossible to get him down the ladder anyhow.

He grabbed Barny's head with both his hands and gave his head a kiss and with smiling spirit, looked back deep into his confidante's eyes and said, 'I pray your lord has the same faith in you as you do in him.'

Danny stood and looked down on him once more. 'I love ya, mate,' he grieved. Barny nodded back and shut his eyes, ready to let fate take its course.

Razor yelled at Danny to come, there was no more time to waste. The flames were licking at the doors of the meeting room. Cracking and collapsing timber could be heard above as smoke enshrouded the room, monstrous fire balls were roller coasting over the compound as if driven by a gigantic flame thrower.

Both he and Drake couldn't hear the exchange between Danny and Barny but could fathom what had been said. They both climbed down the ladder, giving Teeto one last goodbye with a fist across the heart before disappearing into the cellar. Danny followed and lowered his legs onto the cellar ladder. To leave his two best buddies behind was the hardest and cruellest thing he ever had to do, it was soul-crushing to him.

He would never get over it if he were to survive the next hour, but as he stopped his descent into the cellar, his ever-alert mind was ticking over once more as he looked at the blanket that covered Teeto.

He lifted himself out of the hole in the floor. His movement attracted Barny's attention. He watched as Danny rushed to the wall of the bar. He first went to Ricky and pulled the blanket down from his head. He hurriedly reached into the front pocket of Ricky's pants and rummaged around until he felt the keys to the vehicle. He pulled them out and shoved them into his own. Danny stretched his right palm across the forehead of his dead pal in one last act of goodbye before lifting the blanket back over his head.

He then concentrated on Teeto and lifted the blanket off him. He grabbed the deceased's left hand and tugged it towards himself. Danny twisted, pulled and reefed at Teeto's finger, trying to release the two rings off it.

He then had the same trouble trying to remove his wife's gifted rings from his own burnt and swollen fingers. He pocketed the extricated rings then pushed his own wedding ring onto Teeto's left finger, then slid his other two onto the right index and middle fingers of Teeto, pushing and twisting until they were in position.

Danny then raised Teeto's body to the side, pushing it up against the covered body of his best mate who was between Teeto and Barny. Danny took his own wallet out from his jeans back pocket. Only plastic identification cards and his old driving license were in it. Small photos of Greta and his children sat in one of the sleeves along with the folded-up letters from her. He placed it into the back pocket of Teeto's pants, then settled his lifeless body back as it were, leaving his upper torso exposed from the protective fire blanket.

Danny looked to Barny through the mayhem and saw that he was watching out of the corner of his eye. He gave a fatalistic nod to him, Barny nodded back in return then bowed his head and shut his eyes as Danny vanished out of sight down through the hole in the floor, slamming the trapdoor closed.

The citizens of Graceville were taking any advantage point they could as word spread of the fire and it didn't take long for them to see the danger engulfing the surrounding mountain range. They braved the oppressive heat to look at the distant firestorm, finding shade to ease the belting of the sun's rays and although hot the wind gusts that blew across town and the valley were extreme, they were nothing compared to the catastrophic winds surging across the top of the mountain ranges.

A giant pyro-cumulus cloud was starting to develop over the Black Range, the wildfire was beginning to create its own weather system. Graceville locals watched on with fearful apprehension as huge plumes of orange tinted smoke took over the north east horizon rising to the heavens, it was an incredible sight for the first timers' eye. The older generation who had lived through previous wildfires were nervous and were hoping like hell that the rare easterly wind change would not eventuate, otherwise the town of Graceville would be decimated.

For the time being, the fierce north-westerly winds were blowing the fire away from town and over the ranges of the Graceville pass, however, the locals were all on tenterhooks. Everyone was preparing for the worst-case scenario; some were already evacuating town as volunteer fire crews scrambled to generate fire breaks behind the reservoir with what was at their disposal, but one women's concern was out weighing the unease that the average local was experiencing, and it wasn't the safety of her treasured town that had her troubled and distressed.

Greta looked up to the mountain horizon. She had Corey and Sarah by her side and looked on from their vantage point from the nearby park, astounded how quick the fire was travelling. Kate joined them soon after and the four worriedly debated on the location of the wildfire. They tried to convince themselves that Danny was safe, after all, they didn't exactly know where he was, for all they knew, he could be miles away, but Greta could not shake the uneasy feeling she had within.

From what they could see from afar, it would be impossible to survive if anyone were to be caught up in it. Of all the worries and premonitions she had fought and conquered over the past month regarding her fugitive husband, the unsettling intuition that was banging in her soul like a sledgehammer at present was almost making her ill. It only worsened when some passers-by relayed their apparent reliable information that the fire had crossed the Summit Road and was catapulting itself through Black Mountain. Greta, now knowing that Sultan's territory was directly in its path, walked back inside the house fearing the absolute gut-wrenching worst.

'I reckon it's safe,' said Razor.

He had his hand up against the old wooden gated door to see if he could feel any heat against it. It felt normally cool.

They had arrived at the end of the cellar tunnel, exhausted and afraid. They had respite from the heat and smoke as they ran the length of the underground pathway, Razor and Drake led the way, Danny carrying Maddy in his right arm and holding the hand of Zoe in the other. Razor asked Drake for help when he couldn't break the padlock which was attached to the outside latch.

'I'm staying,' Zoe said. 'I'm not going out there.'

It was against all her instincts to leave the serene safety and coolness of the tunnel. It seemed madness to her to dare go back out into the elements.

'We must! We've got to get to the vehicles,' Danny replied in calm tones.

'Why, we'll be safe in here,' Zoe fussed and wailed.

'I can't explain yet, but we have to get to the vehicles,' he insisted.

Zoe couldn't understand the desperate need to exit the tunnel. She had no idea what the men had been up to during the morning. No idea about the money that awaited them and when she looked at both Drake and Razor to see that they had the same desperation as Danny, she fell to her knees hugging Maddy, crying that she couldn't leave the tunnel.

Danny had to decide. He could see that both Zoe and Maddy were frightened to the core, but he was not going to leave them, one way or the other. Either decision he made was fraught with danger. To stay in the confines of the tunnel and hope to ride out the firestorm and risk being cooked in an oven or make the dash for the money that waited. The money won, and he was going to risk all for it.

Not wanting to enhance the near hysterics that Zoe was teetering on, he gently coerced and convinced her to come.

'We will make it,' he promised. 'You have to trust us,' he implored, and when he motioned to the gathering smoke starting to waft through the tunnel from the cellar end, Zoe had no choice but put her life and all her faith into Danny's hands.

The three men pushed and shouldered then smashed the door until the outside padlock gave way, releasing the right gated door that swung out from its old hinges. They could feel the radiant heat in their faces immediately, forcing them to shield their breaths from the searing temperature.

The exit path was akin to a mine entrance that gave them temporary sanctuary from the embers being carried on the wind. The path snaked around in a horseshoe direction shielded by the two and half metre-high ridges on either side. It then petered out in height the more they travelled before it levelled out to the contours of the landscape above. All five donned their fire protective blankets and masks, Maddy still with her helmet on, and followed Razor out into the unknown.

'I know where we are!' Razor shouted when he arrived atop the path.

Maddy's insights were proven correct as Razor recognised the road that ringed the orchard. He couldn't understand that he never knew of tunnels existence, particularly at the end they were at. He thought he had scoured every inch of La Fortaleza; however, it would be something he had to ponder later because right now, every second counted. They were situated down on the furthest south side position of the orchards, downslope from the where it began an acre and a half above.

Despite the searing embers sailing through the darkness above, the thickness of the orchard was giving them protection from the killer flames they could see all around. The front of the fire had skipped across the top of the orchard and had set the forest ablaze to the south of them. Flames were climbing tree trunks being fed by the undergrowth and leaping to the crowns in fury.

Razor led the group through the bottom section of the orchard, grapefruit trees seemed to be boiling as they passed. The men had parked the vehicles in the orange orchard, they only had to get through the next section where the nectarine and pear trees stood to make it to them. The choking smoke was almost unbearable, they could see the leaves of the fruit trees disintegrating before their eyes as they ran hunched and stooped.

Razor stopped when he was certain he had made the orange orchard. For a moment he became disorientated, not knowing which direction to take. He knew he was close, but which row were the vehicles parked between? He had to decide quickly, being exposed to the heat was starting to make their feet and bodies burn through the protective blankets. He ran to the next the row and looked to his right and through the blazing murk could see the outline of the vehicles.

'There they are!' he yelled, pointing to his right.

The rest frantically followed and ran the 40 meters down the tractor width path. Razor pulled the keys from his front pocket. He pushed his thumb down on his key set, the central locking system worked as the orange flash from the indicators illuminated through the mayhem; Danny did the same behind him. The door handles were scalding, burning his already whelped hands and fingers as they attempted to open the doors. Danny pulled off his balaclava and wrapped it around his fingers, turning his head down on his neck for protection and successfully pulled the door open.

He rushed Zoe and Maddy into the vehicle and yelled for them to take refuge in the footwell of the passenger seat. He jumped into the driver's seat then turned the ignition on and throttled down hard. Reaching behind the seat, he snatched two water bottles, another four sat upright in the crate that Razor had supplied.

He passed one to Zoe then took an almighty scull out of his and poured the rest over his roasting head and advised Zoe to do the same to her and Maddy. He took his jacket off so his skin could breathe again, his body was drowning in perspiration.

Zoe removed the helmet off Maddy, poured water over her then slipped it back over her head and clasped her tightly as they hunched into the cramped space of the footwell, cowering for cover as Danny threw the protective blankets over the top of them.

The fire was raging either side of the orchard, however, the cleared paddocks on the north side were giving them a chance as rolling balls of flames whirl winded through the air high above, sucking in the precious oxygen that they desperately needed to breathe, and despite all that was happening around him, Danny was as grateful as ever on the lifesaving decision by Razor to park up inside the sloping gully of the thick lush orchard.

He slammed the vehicle into drive as his two partners drove off in front. Their high beam lights shone through the smoky darkness. Danny could just make out the tail lights of the front vehicle through the fiery dimness as he tried to keep up, pushing the accelerator down as hard as he could as the wild drive for survival began. Flying embers of all sizes raged horizontally above and through the gaps of the orchards as the vehicles jumped and bounced along the dirt track.

They sped out of the orchard's, cleared paddocks were soon either side of them. Danny looked to the elevated hill to his right. The silicon and silver embedded into the solar panels were igniting from the intense heat and the constant barrage of the flaming cinders. The temperature inside the cabin was getting to crisis point. Danny poured more water over himself and across the blanket that covered Zoe and Maddy, the vehicles side windows hissed and sizzled from the spray.

He charged through the open gate following Drake and Razor, ducking his head behind the steering wheel in reflex action to avoid the flames coming off the line of hedges. They were starting to descend off the plateau, downslope and nearing the bridge that crossed the Kensington River and by the time Danny arrived he had lost sight of the leading vehicle. He stopped the 4wd in hesitation and looked to see the wooden bridge afire.

His gut-wrenching mourning of Ricky and Barny had been temporarily forgotten. His heart was pumping with adrenalin, his life and those of his passengers depended on what he would do next. He contemplated hard, trying to keep himself calm. 'If Drake and Razor crossed it, then so can I,' he willed himself, there was no other option. Another minute idling would set his tyres alight and if that were to happen, they would all be incinerated.

'Hold on!' he yelled to Zoe; she in turn clasped tighter at Maddy. He put his foot hard down on the accelerator and began the daring dash across the weakened and burning single lane bridge. He gritted his teeth and put a stranglehold on the steering wheel then sped across the bridge expecting to crash the into the tiny river beneath, however, within seconds, his fearful adrenaline was pumping a different beat, one of exhilaration and relief as the 4WD negotiated the crossing triumphantly.

There was no time to sit and bask in the accomplishment, they were still in the heart of the roaring fire front and as he sped forward, he knew he had to negotiate the young saplings that overhung the track that they bashed and crashed against on their way into the compound and frightfully for Danny, this time they would be ablaze. He continued the deathly dash, pouring more water of his body and blanket, gulping it down in between, and if he thought his wits had already been scared to their limits, they were about to be rocked to the core.

He was forced to slam his brakes on when a flaming figure came out of the bush ahead of him to his left. It then straightened up and was galloping directly towards his vehicle at high speed. Danny looked through the ash-covered windscreen terrified, he couldn't believe what he was seeing.

A terror-struck horse had appeared out of the blackness from nowhere. Its main and tail were ablaze, its hooves kicking up shards of fire as it galloped. The stricken horse's coat was a glowing orange from neck to rump, it was burning alive. It looked like it was going to trample straight over his vehicle, before it bolted right and disappeared into the bush in its disorientated rush for survival, only to take its last panicked strides before it succumbed to the raging inferno.

Danny shook himself back out of the shock and stupor that had swamped him and kept pushing the overheating vehicle forward through the track. Flames started to leap and dance across his bonnet and roof, fireballs rolled and tumbled across the landscape behind him as he scanned his burnt and ashen mirrors. He knew he was passing through the tight young eucalypt cluster, burning branches and twigs snapped and bounced off the now cracked windscreen as he continued to rush forward.

The vehicle was being pushed to its limits and despite knowing they would have no chance of survival if the windscreen were to cave in, he pushed on with reckless fear. Harrowing minutes later he had found himself outside the boundary of La Fortaleza at the first rendezvous point where Teeto was supposed to be earlier.

Danny cursed that there was still no sign of Drake and Razor. He stopped the 4WD and gained back his bearings on the directions. The ferocious intensity of the fire seemed to have suddenly abated; the darkness had lifted a small degree as Danny tried to establish which direction to take. He turned his vehicle right, opposite to the entry point that they had taken an hour before and drove hastily down the incline, continuing down the gravel road that soon came to a fork. He didn't know which direction to take.

Drake or Razor hadn't discussed the exit route to him and was cursing again at the two Vice Presidents for abandoning them. Although the flames had suddenly disappeared, he knew that the danger was far from over. The fire front could again engulf them at any moment. He called for Zoe, informing that she and Maddy could release themselves from the safety of the footwell and take off the blanket.

Zoe was bruised and battered from the rough and terrifying drive. Her face was reddened, and hair saturated from perspiration. She desperately swallowed all the water she could to re hydrate herself while passing the bottles to Maddy in between, spilling it over her head and shoulders after she helped remove her helmet as they took comfort in the front seat.

'Are we safe? Are we safe?' Zoe repeated fearfully.

'I think so! We're out of the worst by the looks of it,' Danny said, still peering around the surroundings.

He looked down the fork that went to the right. It was not the right way to go, Danny said to Zoe.

'That would lead us down towards Fernbank. Straight back into the fire. We gotta go left,' he concluded.

He turned the 4WD down the rock ridden dirt track and navigated the Land Cruiser as quick as he could without losing control of the vehicle, nervously perusing the skies and forest for danger as he drove. With every descending kilometre they travelled, the flames, smoke and heat were dissipating and soon vision of the forest greenery could be seen, still swaying vigorously on the hot winds, but nevertheless, a godsend for the fleeing trio. Danny's sense of direction was coming back to him.

He knew he was on the northeast side of the Apex, moving away from the raging firestorm and in another ten minutes of robust driving, they took the last hairpin bend that led them out to the bitumen of the Graceville pass. There waiting for them were Drake and Razor. They could see that their vehicle was looking the same as Danny's, beaten, dinted, blackened and ash-riddled. Drake immediately waved at them to follow, the time for conversation and debriefing would have to wait.

Maddy leapt across the seat and embraced Danny; he knew what it meant as he wrestled back control of the steering wheel as Zoe smiled in admiration, thankful, blessed to survive unscathed. Danny drove hastily, scanning his rear mirrors, anxious to escape the danger zone and soon found themselves out of the forest confines and passing through the small village of Marbynong at the base of the mountain range.

The bitumen highway began to straighten, and the blistering heat and smoke-infested darkness had given way to expanding grassland pastures and clear blue skies.

Chapter 39

'We've found another, Sir.'

'Where's your location?'

'About a kilometre south from the Manor. If you take the track down the perimeter, we'll you meet there.'

'Okay! We'll start heading down there. Over and out!' Assistant Commissioner Martin Conroy signed off.

The forensic team had found the charred remains of the Sergeant at Arms. Lars never made it to freedom. He was trapped by the wild inferno. The fire had skipped ahead of him and was raging all around. He revved his bike in vain trying to cross the bush landscape in a desperate endeavour to find an escape route, however, the wall of flames that surrounded him were too great. The radiant heat of the fire burned and starved him of oxygen and Lars fell from his bike, walked a few meters and collapsed, within minutes the fire engulfed his body.

Forty-eight hours had passed since the Syrian Creek fire had ravished through the Midnight Ranges and La Fortaleza. The fire continued its rampage across the valley and adjoining ranges until a southerly change in the weather halted it in its track's late afternoon. The change pushed it in a north easterly direction on a massive front back over the forests of the Graceville pass and surrounding mountain bushland and valleys.

The rural town of Marbynong which Danny had passed through on his escape was no more, and along with numerous other villages and properties, lives were lost in the fires wake. By the time it relented, it had burnt out over 330,000 hectares, 2700 structures were razed to the ground, the death toll would be over 300. Countless livestock, private and commercial perished. The loss of wildlife throughout the ranges was insurmountable, burnt carcasses of kangaroos, koalas, wombats, and possums to name a few, would be seen across the clearings or floating down creeks and rivers.

It would be almost midnight before any relief would come when the heavens opened with rain, light at first, then increasing as the night progressed. The god sending rain would not ease up until early afternoon the following day, giving fire fighters and volunteers the opportunity to extinguish and control any danger that could potentially threaten Graceville.

The following morning on the Wednesday, after it was deemed safe enough to enter back into the mountains as smoke haze choked the town, forensics teams dressed in full body suits were joined by law enforcement officers headed by Assistant Commissioner Martin Conroy and descended upon La Fortaleza and its compound to assess the aftermath. Inspector Noel Vaccaro and Sgt Dane Grainger would be by his side.

The surroundings had an eerie presence about it. Light drizzle came in intermittent bursts, dampening and puddling the ashen grounds as low cloud and fog enshrouded the plateau. The area resembled a lunar landscape. Everything was black, white, or grey, other than the burnt-out stumps and hollowed trees that were still smouldering and flickering off colours of red and orange and filling the air with the already choking acrid smoke.

Only the elm trees and the pencil pines located at the entrance to the Manor were left with any type of foliage, everything else resembled giant smoking and blackened toothpicks. Every structure inside the compound had been razed to the ground as teams continued to douse hot spots, traipsing back and forth from the Kensington River gathering water into their pump handled knapsacks and along with the water tanker were making sure any small fires were never to re-ignite as forensic teams detailed, logged, tagged and bagged the victims.

'What's the count now? Conroy asked.

'Thirty-seven, Sir. Another team found four more this side of the river. They were huddled together. They never stood a chance,' lead forensic expert Jack Lopez sorrowed.

Solomon Pike's remains were found beneath his bike. His charred jacket that displayed President gave away his probable identity. So intense was the heat, it melted and fused the aluminium and chrome metal from his Harley Davidson into the skin and muscle of his upper legs and hips. His face was unrecognisable. His skin had almost been incinerated away to his skull while his ears had been burnt away and his teeth protruding out of his jawbone, a gruesome find for first responders.

More bodies were found around the compound grounds like Solomon's, but the many with congealed traces of blood still visible on their blackened and burnt corpses proved to investigators that the fire was not the only cause of death.

The grand old Manor lay in ruins. The northern wall had caved in with the roof, only the skeleton of the other three walls stood with the dual chimney stacks. Although it was a question that could never be answered, the Manor may have been defendable from the inferno if members were able to get to the water tanks and hose pumps from the river, however, they never had the chance to defend it through Captain Grundy's assaults. Now all eight 10,000 litre tanks lay destroyed and melted in twisted heaps.

They carefully sifted through the wreckage of the manor. Piece by piece they removed the dampened twisted debris and rubble, avoiding smouldering hotspots when they came across more bodies, however, two in particular found away from the others gained their attention. One body had moderately escaped the scalding and was still in relatively good condition thanks to the protective fire blanket that covered the body. The other was burnt beyond recognition from the waist up, extremities of the fingers almost burnt back to the front knuckles.

'I think we've found two of your fugitives, sir,' Lopez commented. 'Their bodies were discovered sitting upright, the blankets protected what was in their pants pockets.'

Conroy extended his hands to retrieve the wallets from Lopez and flicked through its contents.

'Ricky De Graaf!' he said.

He then passed it on to Vaccaro for inspection and opened the second wallet.

'Aaahhhh,' he exhaled. 'Danny Pruitt, hey! Well, that accounts for three of them,' Conroy said.

He passed on Danny's wallet to the Inspector, who then passed it on to Dane after inspecting the contents himself. 'Sorry Sergeant. I know he was a good friend,' Vaccaro consoled.

Dane sifted through the wallet's contents and confirmed that they belonged to Danny. The letters from Greta were still intact and his identity cards had been untouched. Dane lowered his head in sadness after he returned the wallet. He was hoping the day would never come, however, from the moment he had last seen Danny, his instincts told him that the whole wretched saga was only going to end in one way.

'One more thing, Sir,' Lopez said. 'Like many of the others, it was the gunshot wounds that killed them, not the fire,' he affirmed.

'Make sure those two bodies are separated from the rest,' Conroy ordered.

He then turned to Vaccaro and with suspicion warped on his face, commented, 'I think our Captain Grundy has got a lot of questions to answer, don't you think?'

He and Vaccaro wanted a finish to the saga that was the Graceville four. It had been an intense and deadly month with numerous victims left in its wake and if the Assistant Commissioner and the Inspector could bring a quick resolution to it all, the better for everyone concerned, so would place an urgent priority on the formal identification process to rid the case as soon as possible.

Teams would scour the compound and surrounding property for the rest of day and next. Three more bodies would be found outside of the compound that would bring the death count at La Fortaleza to 40, however, the remaining three were found with no gunshot wounds. As with a lot of others, they had tried to outrun the inferno but had left it too late, the heat and flames giving them only brief moments to howl in pain before they were burnt to death.

By late afternoon, the bodies were assembled onto numerous horse drawn wagons to be transported down to the Graceville hospital, curtains draped from their frames to keep the bodies private from the general public as they travelled. The morgue inside the hospital was nowhere near large enough to cater for them all so vehicles were summoned to Graceville. The victims would then be transported to the larger hospitals of the city.

The presumed bodies of Ricky De Graaf, Danny Pruitt and Solomon Pike were to stay in Graceville, close to the heart of the investigation. Sgt Dane Grainger did his best to identify the bodies of Ricky and Danny before they left the compound. While it was not his duty to confirm the identity of Ricky, as they unzipped the body bag for him to see, he confidently assured his superiors that it was him. As for the body presumed to be Danny's, the forensic chief said that it was unrecognisable and advised against the Sergeant identifying it; however, as it was definitely Ricky, then there was no other reason to suggest that it wouldn't be Danny lying next to his best mate, the found wallet told them so.

If any doubt lingered on to who they were, Conroy was going to put it to rest by fast-tracking DNA samples from the bodies to verify their identification beyond doubt. To achieve that, they needed the DNA samples of relatives to match up with, and this task was going to be left for Sgt Dane Grainger to accomplish when it came to Danny Pruitt, a task which would test Dane's fortitude once more as he would be the one who would inform Greta of the supposed tragic outcome of her husband, and if notifying the families of the demise of his two young constable friends and his pal Karl Turner was the hardest thing he had done, this was going to tear at his own heart like never before.

It was Thursday morning, four days after the fire had wreaked havoc and school was resuming for students around the Hexagon Valley and Graceville after the summer holiday period but Greta would not be resuming her duties. The Principal had no hesitation in granting her extra time away after she applied for indefinite leave. It was a touch after 9.00 am and Greta had seen her twin boys ride off to school on their pushbikes.

She had just made her way up the four steps of Corey and Sarah's front landing to re-enter the house after fiddling in the garden for a short time. She was still wildly fretting about whether Danny had been in the mountains on the Monday as any news of known casualties had yet to be made public. Tragically for Greta, her morning was about to be turned into the nightmare she had been denying in her soul from the time the saga had begun.

She was dressed in morning casual clothes, a loose fitting dark blue pullover, tight ankle fitting denim jeans and fawn-coloured heeled sandals. She had let her beautiful crinkled dark hair out to flow in the light breeze. The overcast skies of the last 48 hours had given way to bright sunshine once more, although it was still only mild, it was great relief to get away from the heatwave that had engulfed the state over the previous two weeks and Greta enjoyed the cool morning sun.

No news was good news was her mantra when it came to Danny. Sarah had already sought out Valerie Corbett, she had a good nose for information they surmised, however, not even Valerie could satisfy their worry regarding any news on La Fortaleza and what victims the fire had taken. All Valerie could tell them, despite her snooping and contacts, was that she knew that there were numerous casualties but had no confirmation of whom or how many, as no names or identities were being released as yet, and the few who had survived were under guard at the Graceville hospital.

Greta was about to pull the handle on the front door when she heard a horse sidle up to the wooden barrier tether hold that sat outside the front lawn of the house. She turned to see Sergeant Dane Grainger dismounting behind the small wire and hedged fence and his demeanour immediately told her that he was not there for pleasantries.

Dane tethered his horse and then slowly walked through the front gate as Greta looked at him approaching from her vantage point atop the landing. Dane's walk was slow, his eyes stooped from the ground to Greta's. Tears were already welling in his eyes as he stopped his walk towards her. He hadn't even said hello, no words were coming out of his mouth, he simply just didn't know what to say, but Greta's heart driven instincts were sending shivers through her as to why he was there.

She stood frozen, fearful, hoping he was there for other reasons than Danny, however, she had known Dane for a long time and everything about him assured her that he was there to give news she did not want to hear.

Their eyes locked in silence. A sorrowful tragic stare down seemed to take an eternity before Greta reluctantly raised the courage to speak.

'No!' she defiantly choked. 'Don't you say it. Don't you dare say anything, Dane,' she warned in deeper tones.

'I'm sorry, Greta,' he replied with sorrow.

'No!' she challenged. With pauses between her repeated denials, Greta's voice lowered and became more broken and louder. 'Don't you tell me he's gone. You say something else, Dane,' her voice shook.

'We have his body, Greta. I'm sorry. He's dead. He didn't survive,' Dane answered mournfully.

The cup of coffee she held in her hand smashed on the deck below. Greta fell to her knees. It was if she had been kicked in the stomach. She raised her hands to her face then shakily pulled them down and clenched her fists. Grumbling and howling started to emerge from the inner depths of her sole as she again looked back at Dane. Screams of denial and pain came from her as she shook her head wildly from side to side.

'No, no, no, no. No, no! He promised me he would come back to me, he promised, Dane. Danny doesn't break promises, he doesn't!' Greta rebelled.

Dane could only repeat how sorry he was as he tried to move closer to her.

Greta's body started to shake in despair. The truth of it all was now hitting her with irresistible force. The quivering and tears of heart break gathered intensity with every agonising second that would pass as Dane's words echoed in her sole. Dane could see that she was almost at the point of a breakdown. Her face was turning pale and he feared she was about to pass out as she continually shook her head in distress.

He moved closer repeating her name, trying to get her to acknowledge him to avoid her completely collapsing. He softly put his hand on her shoulder when out of the front door came Sarah. She was readying herself for her new job at the Graceville hotel working as a bar lady when the commotion on her doorstep alerted her. She saw Greta on her knees and knelt to embrace her as Dane took a backward step.

'What's going on?' she frantically asked. 'Is it Danny? What's happened?'

'We've found Danny's body,' Dane informed Sarah.

'Where? What are you talking about?' Sarah asked confused as Greta teetered in her arms.

'I'm sorry, Sarah, he's dead. We found his body up at the Sultans compound. Both he and Ricky De Graaf were found deceased together. As I said. We're all shocked and sorry.'

Sarah was agape in horror. 'I don't believe you,' she snapped; however, when Dane painfully reiterated what he had said, the comprehension of the tragic news quickly grasped her. She embraced Greta as tightly as she could only to be vigorously shrugged away.

'Leave me alone!' Greta screamed.

Sarah stood to her feet, frightened at Greta's reaction. She too was horrified and totally grief stricken. Danny was her friend, her closest friend outside of her marriage and family and her first reaction was one of outrage and anger and demanded to know how Dane knew about Danny whilst Greta continued to grieve clasping her hands over her face.

'Let's move inside,' Dane suggested.

The Sergeant wanted them to have a few moments to gather themselves before he would subtly disclose what he knew and as Sarah encouraged Greta to her feet, this time allowing the helping arms of her friend to surround her, Dane politely followed them inside.

Dane stood in the living room, not taking his seat until Sarah had returned from the kitchen with glasses of water for each. He felt so sorry for Greta. He knew that she was an innocent victim in all this tragedy as he watched her slowly regain her composure at her seat, dabbing and wiping away the teary hint of her dark eyeliner. Greta refused the water, she needed something stronger and demanded her favourite choice of spirit. Sarah responded quickly and soon had a large glass of Gin and tonic in Greta's trembling hand, and another for herself.

Dane then sat opposite the two ladies and informed them that they could ask any questions that they would like and if he had the answers to them, he would oblige with as much honesty as he could, however, before that, he had to get confirmation from Greta on Danny's belongings.

Dane pulled a zip-up evidence bag from underneath his police jacket and retrieved the contents then laid them out in front of Greta on the living room table.

'Do you recognise any of these?' he gently asked. 'They were retrieved off the body.'

Greta picked up the identification cards. She turned them around in her fingers as she looked, then gently laid them back on the table. She looked at the photos of herself and her boys that Danny kept in his wallet. She flicked through the letters that were saved, knowing that they were hers. She listened deadpan as Dane told her that they have a signed eyewitness account that was helping prove it was Danny and Ricky found together inside the Manor. Greta picked up the three rings that had been displayed and then slowly focused on his wedding ring.

She twirled it in her fingers and read the inscription: 'Love Greta.' The date of their wedding was inscribed next to it. She played with it in her fingers, staring blankly before clasping it in her fist then bowing her head. She acknowledged with a nod after Dane asked her to confirm if they belonged to Danny.

Dane gave a moment for her to process what was being said. Tears of heartbreak started to fall again as the awaited reality sunk into her destroyed soul.

'Can I see him?' Greta quietly sobbed.

'That's impossible, Greta,' replied Dane.

'Why?' she snapped back.

'He was burnt severely, Greta. Only the waist down was preserved somewhat, that's how we retrieved his wallet. It's for your own good, Greta, you wouldn't want to see him the way he is, we could never put you through that.'

Dane was feeling her pain and tried to reassure her. 'I know it's hard, Greta, but if it's any consolation, all the evidence says he was already dead before the fire hit.'

Greta raised her head. 'I don't understand. What do you mean? How did he die then?' she asked, confused.

'He was shot, Greta. He died from gunshot wounds.'

Greta looked at Dane with fright and confusion.

'What happened, Dane? What happened to him? What gunshot wounds, who shot him? What are you talking about?'

Dane leant forward over the table to move closer to Greta. He took a deep breath and started to explain what they believed happened.

'You remember we spoke in your garden about the big boys coming up from the city, the SOGs. Well, they raided the Sultans compound early Monday morning. You knew he was there, didn't you?' Dane probed.

'Yes. I only heard through others,' Greta confessed.

'They weren't only looking for Danny and the boys, they were there to arrest the President and his senior members as well. But things went terribly wrong, Greta. It ended in a massive siege throughout the morning. We don't know yet whether he was shot in the first raid or the next before the fire engulfed them. They are still investigating the circumstances, but we will get to the bottom of this, Greta. We will find out for sure; I promise you! The Assistant Commissioner and his team are piecing things together as we speak,' Dane assured.

'Ricky was found next to Danny,' he continued. 'They died together, Greta. They found them sitting next to each other inside the house. He died with his best mate, that we know for sure. We have a statement from David Barnard, Barny as you know him. He backed up what we thought. He said all of them were caught in the crossfire. They were in the wrong place at the wrong time and said that Danny and Ricky died together.'

'Barny survived the fire?' Greta asked, surprised and relieved.

'Yes! He's a very lucky man. He has gunshot wounds as well, but he's recovering in Graceville Hospital. SOG members saw him exiting the house with a blanket over him as it was going up in flames. Three of them risked their own lives to save him and took him to the fire bunker, they deserve a medal for what they did,' Dane said.

'And Harry?' Greta asked.

'We don't where he is. In Barny's statement, he said he was never there. Harry left them the day after the shootout at Tambourine Bridge. We have officers trying to track him down.'

Dane took his hand in Greta's and squeezed it tight for comfort and repeated how sorry he was.

'I know this is not the right time; however, we are going to have to ask if your sons could provide a DNA sample to prove it's Danny beyond doubt. I'm sure you would want to know absolutely as well. They're already tracking down Ricky's family for the same request. We'll send someone around to gather them in a couple of days, there's no rush, so whenever you're ready. I'll make sure I'm here with them.'

Greta didn't answer or acknowledge Dane's request. She sat silently, staring blankly, drinking away hurriedly at her second glass of gin and tonic as the slow grieving tears continued to fall. She was comprehending how it all could end like this. How could she not sense that he was gone, his spirit still felt so alive within her. Danny was her rock, her only ever love, he was her world and everything more. If it were anyone else but Dane who came visiting, she would've just brushed them off and said that they had it all wrong and graciously asked them to leave, however, right now, her bereaving bitterness was starting to bubble to the surface.

Dane rose from his seat. He respectfully said that he would leave them alone and give her the privacy to grieve and repeated how sorry he was and was about to exit. Unfortunately for Dane, he was not going to leave the house without Greta venting her heart broken anger.

'Damn you!' she muffled under her breath, looking and twirling at Danny's wedding ring in her fingers.

'Excuse me?' said Dane.

Greta raised her head, and with resolute spite repeated what she had said in louder tones.

'I said fuck you, Dane! You, and all those around you.'

Dane was confused and stunned at Greta's comment, particularly the way she swore at him. He had never seen the maliciousness that her eyes were now spearing.

'I'm sorry, Greta. I don't understand!'

'If you could've controlled those Devlin brothers, he would still be alive. None of this would have happened. He would still be with me. He would still be with his sons and we would still have our home.' Greta shrilled with forcefulness.

She turned away from Dane. It hurt her to speak to him that way, but she was looking for blame, her heart could not accept that her husband was dead. She then clasped her hands to her head once more and in quieter tones cried, 'He would still be next to me, my boys. Oh my god, what am I going to tell my boys!'

Sarah reiterated Greta's anger with vigour as she held an arm around her while Dane could only take the insults directed at him. He knew Greta's tirade wasn't personal and accepted, and expected, some type of hostile reaction, delayed or not, and already knew that all of them in positions of power were derelict in their duty from preventing these types of tragedies from occurring.

Dane respectfully nodded his head. He wanted no argument, no confrontation, he let her vent her devastation at him. All he did was repeat his condolences and told Greta he would be in touch regarding the DNA samples before he sombrely exited the house.

As Dane made his way out, Greta numbly sifted through Danny's possessions that were on the table in front of her while Sarah comforted her. She stared deeply into the photo of herself, Darcy and Daniel, then flicked it across the table. She grabbed Danny's license and looked at the photo of him in the right-hand corner of the plastic card and gave it the same deep stare for a short time.

Greta then took a deep breath and determinedly wiped away at her tearful eyes then hurriedly rose from her chair. Surprised at Greta's sudden movements, Sarah moved out of her way and watched her rush to exit the front door.

'What are you doing? Where are you going?' Sarah asked alarmed as she followed Greta out to the top of the landing.

'Dane!' Greta yelled.

The Sergeant turned his head as he was about to give his horse a flick of the reins.

'I apologise. I know you did everything to help. I should never have spoken to you like that, I'm sorry,' she said with sincerity.

Dane nodded his head in acceptance. 'It's okay, Greta, it's okay!'

'I want to see Barny,' she asked.

Greta needed to know what happened to her husband, what his last thoughts were, what was he doing, all the how, when's and why's and more. Barny would tell her the truth, that she was sure of. They shared the same faith and she believed that he would tell her what really happened. She trusted Barny would not distort the facts, after all, he was there. She desperately relayed her pleading wishes to Dane, relying on the good will of their friendship to give her the blessing to meet with him.

'He's going to be transferred to the city this afternoon. Meet me at the hospital at 2.00 pm. I'll pass it by the Inspector. We'll need his approval, but no promises, Greta. I'll do my best,' he said.

Barny was in a private room in Graceville hospital with a police guard standing outside his door. He was recovering from his gunshot wounds well. The bullet that entered his stomach missed his vital organs. He underwent emergency surgery to remove it along with the bullet that had lodged in his hip region. The bullet that entered his shoulder had exited out on impact, a classic through and through, however, it would be the searing burns that he sustained that would take him longer to recover from.

With the help of SOG members under the leadership of Captain Dennis Grundy, Barny was carried through the darkness six hours after the fire front raged over the top of the plateau. They laid him on a makeshift stretcher made from timber and blankets, assembled from items inside the confines of the bunker. Barny's life was in grave danger.

He had been in and out of consciousness from the time he made his walk of faith out into the fiery abyss and with the encouragement of Grundy's team members, the SOG captain made the decision to exit the bunker. The team's medical training kept Barny going as they stemmed the bleeding from his wounds with the help of first aid kits that were stored on the shelves of the bunker and kept him wrapped in blankets to prevent shock from setting into his wounded and burnt body. It was an hour before midnight when they made the call to traverse down track 24.

Although it was still dangerous to do so with fire still surrounding the area, the wind had dropped to a zephyr which gave them the opportunity to try and get Barny and others the desperate help they needed. By the time they had reached Fernbank, light rain had begun to fall and communication over the radio had been restored. Grundy contacted the Graceville police station at 12.14am and police dispatched an ambulance to the carpark of the Fernbank picnic grounds to retrieve Barny and rush him to the operating table of the hospital.

It was as close a call as you could get, another hour or two and Barny would have joined his friend Ricky as another casualty of the reckless mayhem that transpired. The remaining four survivors of the Sultan MC who also had severe burns were placed under arrest and escorted to the hospital. Crow had made it to safety, along with all the people he had led out of the bush. The surly Vice President eluded authorities in the chaos and confusion as the fire threatened down on them and he passed through Fernbank unnoticed to Graceville before the inferno swept across the pass.

Barny underwent four hours of surgery and regained his consciousness in the early hours on Wednesday morning and by that afternoon had made his statement and given his accounts to the Assistant Commissioner and Inspector of what had ensued on that fateful Monday. However, the conversation between numerous policemen who came and went from his room and nearby hallway as he faked his recovering coma beforehand, gave him a confident belief that Danny was still well and truly alive.

He had secretly listened from his hospital bed as conversations spread around him. From the nurses, to the over exuberant officers and investigators, who were all too keen to relay what they knew to anyone who would listen about the now infamous Graceville four and Sultans MC. Barny kept his eyes closed and his ears open as the medical tubes and machines ticked away monitoring his vital signs.

He eavesdropped discretely as they spoke about what was left at La Fortaleza, how they scoured every inch of the lands that the club owned and more. They spoke about the siege, the demolished buildings, the burnt-out vehicles, the number of bodies found and where. Not once did he hear of two four-wheel drive Land Cruisers being found, although, one Armaguard van was mentioned, burnt out and empty, with talk on how no leads had been established on who may have been involved in the heist, though he heard chatter that the authorities thought the Sultan MC were most likely behind it and that the perpetrators in all probability were deceased.

He heard no mention of Zoe Valetta, no mention of little Maddy, no mention of the two Vice Presidents, dead or alive. He had heard absolutely nothing that would give him a slightest clue that the fleeing group had been found one way or another. Barny was confident that the authorities had no idea that they were even there. After hours of covertly listening, he confidently surmised that all five of them had somehow made it to safety. The only worry Barny had was the possibility that they all succumbed to the fire deep inside the cellar and authorities hadn't discovered them yet. Maybe they were still buried beneath the rubble he distressfully thought. Regardless, Barny's convictions were steadfast and ultimately believed that Danny was safe, after all, he is who he is, and surely the scales had not tipped yet.

Barny truly believed that his life force *was* protected and had told him so personally. He had seen it first-hand, even before what had transpired over the last month, and the Lord that Barny had unending faith in would certainly see his friend through to his aims. When he was visited by a certain nurse 30 minutes before being questioned by the investigators, his convictions and intuitions were to be made absolute.

Mia was not on duty at the time but donned her uniform anyhow, it would be the only time she would be able communicate with Barny without others being present or within earshot. Mia and Razor's wife Candice knew exactly what the men were up to on the Monday morning. Both Drake and Razor had confided with their partners with the promise of a better life once they had the money.

They were supposed to meet their husbands in a few days' time up on the border, however, the fire danger had put a stop to any trains entering Graceville until it was deemed safe again and the damage on the now impassable road of the Graceville pass prevented them going by road. Mia waited until the room was empty and passed by the police guard under the guise of her occupation. Barny was awake when she entered the room. Mia fiddled with the medical tubes and clipboard that held the patient's observation sheets to hide her real purpose from the eyes looking into the room.

'Hi, I'm Mia. How do you feel? Has the pain steadied?' she quietly asked.

Barny replied that he was feeling okay and that he had no change.

Mia leant forward towards the bedhead, adjusting the patient's comforter then whispered, 'Don't know if you remember me. We met up at the compound. I'm Drake's wife.'

Barny looked at her again, this time with concentration. He remembered. The light blue nurse's uniform threw him at first, he had only seen her in a white T-shirt and denim jeans the times they had briefly met, however, the studded jewel in her nose piercing jolted his memory.

'Read this, then destroy it,' Mia whispered again, as she passed a note into his palm under the bedsheet that Barny had over him, Mia using the clipboard as a shield. She gave a nod of acknowledgement then left the room before anyone could ask what she was doing there. Although only a chosen few inside the hospital knew that she was married to one of the Vice Presidents of the infamous Sultan MC, she knew that police did, and it would be only a matter of time before they would approach her on the whereabouts of her husband; nonetheless, she was going to make them come to her, and she was going to make that as difficult as she could.

Barny acceptingly nodded in return as Mia left the room then exited the hospital through a staff door hidden from the public. As soon as Barny had the chance, he casually ducked his head under the bedsheet and read the note.

DRAKE, RAZOR AND DANNY SAFE. THEY MADE IT TO THE BORDER. CARGO INTACT. LAWYER AND MADDY WITH THEM. HAVE LET THEM KNOW YOU SURVIVED.

Barny smiled. His faith had been affirmed. They made it, he chortled proudly inside; this was absolute confirmation. He tore the little note up into tiny pieces and disposed the shards into his bedpan and then did his business, content in the knowledge that his Lord had looked after his close buddy. Shortly after when being questioned by Conroy and Vaccaro, he took great satisfaction within when he falsely, and sorrowfully, advised the interrogators that Danny Pruitt had been shot and died the same time that Ricky De Graaf had.

2.00 pm had arrived and Greta, with support from Corey and Sarah, was at the hospital to meet Dane. Kate had also arrived on horseback after hearing the devastating news from Dane who felt obliged to deliver the sad news to her after he had visited Greta, and the Sergeant received the same grieving anger from Danny's sister as he did from his wife. The devastation of losing her older brother was still visible as she met Greta in the foyer of the hospital as the sad condolent embraces prolonged with tears.

The Inspector granted permission for Greta to visit Barny but only on the proviso that he and Dane be present when she did so, a demand that Greta was not comfortable with. She wanted privacy and asked to see him alone, however, the Inspector was rigid in his stipulation, so if Greta wanted to see him, she had to do it with company.

She was escorted down the east ward of the hospital and at the end of the corridor wing was asked to wait by Dane as the Inspector communicated with the nurse and Doctor who were present in Barny's room. The Inspector waved them forward after the hospital employees left and as Greta entered the room past the guarding policeman, she was shocked to see Barny the way he was.

All other beds in the ward had been removed, no interaction was to be made with the arrested fugitive unless in the company of the right authorities. The curtains were drawn back on the overhead circular rods. Venetian blinds hung down over the two windows. The room felt stuffy and sterile, although the oscillating fan twirling on a nearby table gave some relief from the humid heat that the room held.

Greta could see the bandages tightly wrapped around Barny's stomach; his right shoulder also tightly wrapped as his arm rested in a sling. She could see that parts of his face and neck had been reddened from the burns he had received; his right hand was packed in burns gauzes. Plastic tubes protruded out of his nostrils as the intravenous drip helped him with pain relief and provided him with antibiotics to fight infection; however, the smile on his face that exuded when he saw Greta enter was enough to tell her that Barny was going to be okay.

Greta clasped his left hand as she sat bedside. Tears welled in her eyes once more as she tried to raise the courage to ask him her fervent questions.

'How are you?' she softly asked.

'I'm okay.'

'I'm so sorry, Barny,'

'Don't be! None of this is your doing, Greta,' he quietly enforced.

'What happened, Barny? I need to know what happened to Danny,' Greta gently pleaded.

Barny turned his eyes towards where Dane and Vaccaro were standing in the doorway. They were both staring in their direction. Barny sensed that they were hanging on every word he would say. He paused, then looked into Greta's eyes.

'What have they told you?' he whispered.

'They say that Danny is dead. With Ricky,' she replied with another broken breath. 'They tell me he was shot before the fire. Is this true? What happened, Barny? Were you with him?'

Barny panned his grimacing eyes at the doorway. The timing couldn't have been more perfect as two officers entered the room to talk to the Inspector. He could hear the officer say that they had identified a body that was found in the burnt-out wreck of the police cruiser that was found on Syrian Creek Road.

Barny knew what they were talking about as the officer's conversation switched to the investigation of the Country Club heist. The impromptu visit and dialogue also gained Dane's attention which gave Barny the opportunity to gesture to Greta to come closer to him.

Greta leant her left ear over Barny's mouth as they clasped hands.

'Shhhoooshhh,' he whispered as low as he could. 'Stay with me, don't react to what I say.'

Greta remained still and acted if she was softly embracing her friend.

'Do not listen to them,' Barny whispered. 'He will come for you, Greta; he will come for you. Keep your faith. It may take time, but he will come for you.'

Greta softly turned her head and locked her eyes on Barny's. Her stomach knotted in flurried ripples. *Is he telling me that Danny is still alive? Is this what he is saying to me?* she frantically thought.

'Shhooooshhh,' Barny reiterated silently again with an earnest nod. 'He's on his way to heaven, Greta, heaven!' he emphasised.

Greta's whole demeanour changed. Barny could see it, and he could also see that Greta understood what he had said. Heaven could only mean one thing when it came to Danny, it was the only one he ever spoke about. He clasped her hand tighter and gave it a forceful squeeze of assurance and repeated, 'Keep the faith. He loves you. When the time is right, he will call for you.'

Barny eased Greta away from him. She had a look of frozen euphoric shock; her eyes could not leave him. She drove a stare deeply into his eyes. Was he hallucinatory, not knowing what he was saying? Was he delirious on painkillers? Greta searched, however, Barny's eyes were clear, no glassiness, no dilated pupils, they were only full of sobriety and intent, and with rapid conclusion, Greta's body started to quiver again as the nerves pounded through her stomach. Only this time it was through pure exultance, not devastation. The heart that had been destroyed and torn apart five hours previously was now beating to a thump that was fast repairing the fragmented strings.

Barny quickly changed the tone, they both could sense that the company in the room had refocused their attention on them. He started to inform her of the events that had occurred, with Greta acknowledging his lies. He virtually repeated everything that he had told the authorities in his statement and with diversional serious mirth upon his face, relayed to Greta that they had got caught in the crossfire of the SOGs and Sultan weapons and were struck down in their endeavours to hide from the siege.

He never mentioned Solomon, Zoe or Maddy, or the Vice Presidents, the same he kept from his interrogators. He spoke loud enough so Inspector Vaccaro and Dane could hear all he was saying, detailing the fabricated events to her and for the next five minutes, Greta listened and quietly questioned. She kept the appearance of the grieving wife as Barny truthfully related how sorry Danny was that he had to put her through so much pain and suffering, also relaying how Danny spoke of his love for her and his boys every single day.

Greta held his hand with secret gratitude and thanked him after the Inspector politely instructed that her time was up with the patient as he and the Sergeant needed more words with him before the doctor would arrive for his allocated rounds.

'Thank you! Thank you!' Greta softly said to both Vaccaro and Dane as she exited out of the room, keeping her eyes and head low, paranoid that they might suspect what had been secretly said.

Greta hurriedly made her way down the hospital wing. Her dark-coloured long-strapped shoulder bag was wrapped over her shoulder. She rested her left arm atop of it by her hip, comprehending what Barny had told her. Greta's mind was racing one hundred miles an hour. Everything had happened so quickly. The emotions that had streamed through her body in such a short time had her feeling numb.

She had no idea how to react when she saw her friends, all she knew that the resurrection of her husband had to be concealed, no one could know, no one! As her steps decreased when she neared the waiting room, she didn't know whether to burst out in happiness or burst into tears, her emotions were as mixed as could be. On one hand she totally trusted what Barny had told her; on the other, she frantically hammered herself over how they could have Danny's rings and belongings, nothing made sense, so many questions and anxieties.

All she could do was rely on Barny's word, that she would enforce upon herself, and believe the resolute spirit she had inside that her husband was alive.

Greta made her way around the corner to the waiting room of hospital entrance where Corey, Sarah and Kate were sitting, with the latter still angry and silent at Greta's housemates. Greta kept the presence of the heart broken widow and left the hospital with her friends and would continue to do something that she was now accustomed too, and that was to wait, wait until her Danny contacted her somehow, however long that may be.

Chapter 40

Whilst Greta battled with the turbulent uncertainty that plagued her, Danny was bunkered up on a rural property close to the northern border of the central state, three Shires away from Graceville. He was grappling with his inner demons and trying to come to terms with his life, and of those that were lost. It had been three nights since they had escaped the inferno on the Midnight Ranges.

As the surrounding mountains continued to be scorched by the wildfire on the Monday afternoon, the two Land Cruisers were slipping unnoticed out of the Hexagon Valley Shire. Within 30 minutes of driving, they found themselves in the shire of the Midlands, a further three hours North and they would be in the shire of the Northern Rivers and where they were today, on a riverside homestead, seven kilometres west from the heart of the border town of Twin City.

Danny's drive to their destination was one of trepidation, and in the beginning, mostly silent as the overwhelming burden and self-blame of Ricky's death and the presumption of Barny's demise consumed him as he followed the lead vehicle. Although Zoe was terribly traumatised herself, she tried to ease Danny's mindset, talking with compassion and empathy for his lost buddies whilst Maddy sat quietly in the back seat, scared, not quite knowing where she was going.

Danny confided to Zoe of Solomon's last words, declaring that he was now obliged to protect and care for the little one after the dying President's demands, a promise that he pledged to Maddy after she asked what was to become of her.

They were 90 minutes into their drive away from the Graceville pass and an hour into the shire of the midlands. The roads were empty and lonely as they dodged and weaved around the potholes and obstacles that littered the roads when Drake and Razor decided to make their first stop. Danny was looking forward to the break, he was hot and dirty, he was sore and scarred, and he was mighty hungry, and gestured a sigh of relief when he followed behind Razor.

120km northeast of Graceville, the two vehicles pulled into a service road off the highway and parked them up at the former lakeside tourist town Bonnieview. Barren rolling hills baked from the early summer sun dominated the landscape to north and west of them whilst pine plantation scoured the large lake further to south of them. It was the first contact they had made with each other since they escaped the inferno and all of them were looking forward to a quick refresh and some food.

The small town was one of the main conduits between the Northern and Southern shires and had a row of shops adjacent to the now disused service station and it was in one of these stores that the group of five got some much-needed nourishment. Danny had not eaten since he had woken up at Mt St Lucia before he made his way down the mountain to the Country Club, a time that seemed an eternity away from him now, so much had happened, and the day was only half over.

He remained at the vehicles with Zoe and Maddy, the latter grateful to be out of the furnace of the back seat with the temperature still around the 40-degree Celsius mark. Drake entered the main shop, a general store of sorts, while Razor took solace under the front annex in the shade and rolled himself a cigarette. Danny thought it a big step from Razor to allow him to be near the vehicles, but more precisely the money, without having any glares or orders of mistrust. He imagined he had him in the rear-view mirrors all the way.

Danny waited for his food and panned the area as Zoe took Maddy to a free-standing water tank nearby and gave themselves a wash, freeing the sweat filled dirt away from their faces and arms. Horses, drays, and carriages were assembled in the shade under a large tree at the end of the row of shops to his left. Empty fuel bowsers stood lonely and destitute in front of him, a lone rider and a single horse driven cart were the only passers-by. A children's playground lay between the service road and highway, weeds overgrowing the swings and seesaws near the brick toilet block as Danny remembered Bonnieview the way it was in its prosperous days.

Drake ordered a mix of chicken, ham, and salad sandwiches with assorted homemade soda drinks from the proprietors. It was on his orders that he would do all the conversing with the shop owners. He was good with small talk and diverted any suspicion away by smiling and engaging with affable dialogue and answered the question of who they were by saying that they were delivering postal vehicles to the Northern Rivers Shire, a ruse that was wholeheartedly accepted by the proprietors who were surprised to see motor vehicles visiting their little town, despite them being dirtied and dented, and having an eight year old girl with them who they could see from a distance also helped with the deception, although reeking of smoke and being dirtied themselves.

The food was ready for serving and the group of five congregated together on bench seating away from the shops and enjoyed the much-needed replenishment in the shade. It was mid-afternoon and the heat was still pounding down on them. The locals at Bonnieview knew nothing of the raging wildfire and along with anyone north of the Hexagon Valley, had yet to receive any news of the tragedy occurring.

The days of instantaneous 24/7 news and information from electronic devices had all but disappeared. So, as it was for most rural people in today's society, more so than the city or suburban dweller, country folk only received news via word of mouth, the Government radio, or through the newspapers who would be at least 36 hours behind on events, and it would be some time before the locals in the North would hear about the disasters that were sweeping through the Midnight Ranges and surrounds.

With the trauma of the morning tragedies still cocooning their bereaving minds they sat away from the row of shops on bench seat in the shade. They kept their conversation quiet and the more they debriefed on the events back at la Fortaleza, the more it dawned on Danny that he wasn't the only one who was grieving.

He was so drenched in his own pain over the loss of his buddies, he was completely oblivious to the feelings of those around him. Zoe was witness to things that was totally abhorrent to her, horrible images of both Teeto and Ricky that would have a place in her mind forever she tearfully confided. Danny sat and ate quietly, listening to Razor angrily and painfully disclose how much he was going to miss Teeto, cursing everything that had happened and wondering how it all went tragically wrong, threatening revenge on whoever pulled the trigger on their adopted little brother.

Drake backed up his co Vice President's sentiments, not as animated, but enough to show that he was deeply upset at not only losing Teeto, but also other club brothers who he had close bonds with.

'The authorities probably won't even know who he is when they find him. He probably won't even get a funeral. We're the only real family he had, you and me!' Razor cursed to Drake.

'There'll be nothing left to remember him by will there,' Drake sorrowed.

He shook his head in pain and with contrition added that he would hate to think what all bodies would be like after the ashes had settled.

The conversation turned to the demise of Solomon, angrily cursing at his actions and only then was their attention drawn to little Maddy. Whatever grief and anger they were feeling, they knew that Maddy would probably be the one who was feeling the most scared and lonely, as she had now become an orphan.

Danny watched with a heavy heart as Drake and Zoe communicated through animated sign language. Tearful hugs and hand-holding took precedent with the three as the two adults delicately explained the circumstances surrounding her father's death after she bluntly asked if her daddy was dead. Drake was quick to take the initiative after Zoe was lost for words when she asked the forthright question.

He knew Maddy was an extra intelligent girl for her age, and he also understood that she was well and truly observant to the life that her father led, however, the loss of Solomon was felt by her the same as any other little girl who loved their daddy.

They would take another 30 minutes before they would make the decision to depart, talking and listening to each other's distresses and sorrows. The time spent at Bonnieview was as good a counselling and debriefing session as they could get. It was spontaneous, sincere and open, surprising all who were there internally, even Razor, whose sympathy gene was not often opened as willingly as others.

The trauma and miseries within were exercised somewhat and it was not what Zoe expected. She saw another side to the Sultan men, away from the demands and code of the club. She discovered that the Vice Presidents were men with the same emotions, the same frailties, and the same vulnerabilities the normal man in the street endures and she would walk away better for it.

The only question left for the three men before they hit the road again was what to do with her and Maddy as they were never part of their plans. Zoe cordially argued that she had no possible way of getting home from where they were. She asked what their plans were and after hearing of their arrangement at Twin City, Zoe used her coercive ways to convince the men to take her and Maddy with them. From there she would train it back to the Marlboro with Maddy by her side, vowing to keep her silence regarding their whereabouts and stratagems, arguing that if she told of anything, it would probably mean the end of her own career.

Danny was pleased that Drake and Razor agreed. He needed a friend; he needed an ally and his trust in Zoe was almost absolute. The animated words from Teeto about Zoe's supposed infatuation with him had not left him, and the more he was around her, listening and appreciating her impelling ways, his attachment towards the alluring and stylish lawyer was beginning to build.

His entrustment in her was far greater than he had in his new partners in crime as he was yet to be totally convinced of their amity. He had put his trust in men who he had only known for a matter of weeks and that made him feel troubled. All he planned for relied on them now, he couldn't achieve his goal without their help. The erratic and suspicious questions were still running through his exhausted and tormented mind from the time they escaped la Fortaleza.

Regardless of his deep paranoia, Danny knew he had to set it aside and play the waiting game until he was sure that the Vice Presidents were genuine in their allegiance. Nevertheless, he would keep a constant vigil on any signs of betrayal coming from his new partners and at the slightest hint of deception, he vowed to himself that he would be the first to react to ensure that his heaven still awaited him.

'We've got to fix that radiator hose before we leave,' Razor reminded Drake as they began to leave the shady bench after they consumed their meals.

'Got problems?' asked Danny, seeing a pool of coolant underneath the engine.

'We got a split. I packed a spare when I fuelled up before we the left the compound last night. I didn't think it would get us all the way,' Razor said. 'How's your vehicle going?'

'Fine. Temperature's steady, still got three quarters of a tank. It's running well,' replied Danny.

'How long will it take you?' Zoe asked.

'30 minutes tops,' Drake guessed. 'Get some rest in the shade. We'll call you when we've finished.'

Danny noticed Zoe peering over towards the row of shops as they walked towards their vehicle parked further down the road from where the men were getting to work on theirs. Clothes were hanging from hooks outside the adjoining shop to the eatery.

'Wanna go shopping, do you?' Danny mused.

'I wished I had grabbed my bag before we ran from the fire,' she frustratingly lamented.

'Why?' Danny enquired.

'I had everything in there. My IDs, my make-up, my money,' rued Zoe, turning towards Danny when she said the latter.

'Need something, do you?'

'A change of clothes would be nice.' She smiled with sarcasm.

'Wait here!' said Danny.

He walked behind the vehicle and opened the rear door while Zoe waited with Maddy to the side. He released the canvas covering and unhooked the latch that sealed a drawer then pulled it out on its rollers. Reaching into one of the bags, he pulled a wad of cash out form its hiding place, mostly in small denominations and ambled back to Zoe.

'Here! Knock yourself out,' he casually said as he handed her the money.

'Where did you get this?' Zoe asked, stunned.

'Aaaahhh! You probably don't want to know!' He smiled reluctantly.

'What do you mean? What have you been up to?' Zoe questioned as she poked him playfully.

'I'll tell you later maybe, but I can assure you, there's plenty more of it,' Danny proudly said.

Zoe tried to pry more information out of the now coy Danny; however, he changed the subject mirthfully and advised she didn't have much time before the boys had finished fixing the vehicle.

'Take Maddy, she could do with a change as well. If there's a T-shirt, get me one as well please,' he added.

Zoe stood silently, hesitantly, twirling and grasping the money in her fist. The look on Danny's face had her thinking for sure that it was from ill-gotten gains. Whether she was naïve or not, she felt she knew him well enough after their night at the rotunda to get vibes about his character. Zoe ceased the light-hearted probing and surmised she would probably find out soon enough where the cash came from if she hung around long enough.

In the meantime, her desire to rid herself of the dirty and sweaty attire she had on was too great to ignore and duly walked across the service road and into the shop with Maddy in tow.

The shop owner was delighted when Zoe had finished her quick mini spree. It was the largest buy they had received for a long time as Zoe relieved them of a pair of jeans that was closest to her size. She also bought a soft cotton off the shoulder blouse, a comfortable pair of leather boots and ankle socks and the most expensive summer dress that was on display, dark green in colour, with gold buckled straps on the shoulders and zip pockets on the side.

She wasn't finished there, several pair of knickers for both her and Maddy were thrown on the counter, a pair of sandals for each, and a beautiful floral dress that was selected by Maddy herself. She threw in some deodorant and jewellery for good measure and purchased a black T-shirt that Danny had requested before she exited the shop.

The grand total was nearly $300 worth, more takings than shop had taken in the previous two months. Not long ago, the value of the items would have been ten times that amount. Zoe knew a bargain when she was confronted with one.

Danny and Zoe had hardly spoken a sentence before they arrived at Bonnieview but now they were speaking freely and continually engaging, nurturing Maddy as they resumed their travel. They used one another for support as they spoke of the losses and the fear that consumed them during the mayhem of la Fortaleza, at times softly laying their hands on each other's knee or shoulder for consoling support when the tears would well, for what they went through, would now bond them for life.

They drove the Midland's highway for 45 minutes then turned northwest onto the freeway that linked the two main cities of the central and southern states. For the next two and half hours it was a nonstop drive on the two-lane divided freeway. The interstate railway line ran parallel to the left side of them for a great part of the way. Mountain ranges could be seen on either side in the far distance as they travelled.

Freeway thirteen was significantly used more than the outer highways and byways in the present times. As soon as they turned and traversed down its pockmarked and cracking bitumen, they immediately noticed the traffic that inhabited it, despite the heat that a day such as this could bring. At times they would ensure they kept to a safe and inattentive speed not to draw any interest towards them from other road users, along with being wary of the fallen overhead town and kilometre gantries that encumbered the road in sections.

Danny would overtake and see vehicles travelling in the opposite lanes that he had never seen before. Along with the array of single horse riders and the common carriage and cart that were used these days, the freeway was mainly occupied by cyclists or by pedal and solar powered vehicles. Danny and Zoe were excited and amused to see what designs the innovative people of the countryside had come up with to fast-track a convenient journey between towns, not to mention Maddy's amazement as she pushed her face out of the wound down windows, at times lunging herself ahead of Danny and Zoe to gain a better view as her snowy blond hair ravished in the wind.

The vehicles were something Danny had never seen around Graceville before. Zoe commented that she had seen them around the city, but never in the abundance of different shapes and sizes that they were looking at as they passed in intervals. There were multi range geared pedalled vehicles from the cylindrical rocket shape to the squared box shape and everything in between. Imagination was no barrier to the do-it-yourself backyard engineer, and with the same inventiveness applied to the solar powered vehicles, it looked like the country folk were well ahead of the city folk when it came to ingenuity, an important necessity when it was forced upon them to travel longer distances than their city counterparts.

They left the freeway on a diversional road before they would hit the outskirts of the border town. Danny followed Drake and Razor as they turned down several dirt roads until Razor stopped his vehicle and watched as Drake stepped out and opened a large farm gate. The sun was beginning to set, only a few hours of daylight remained as the early evening shadows started to lengthen across the landscape. The road twisted and turned across barren paddocks, large red and river gum trees stood majestically across the flat terrain in amongst the dead stags that were occupied by an abundance of Sulphur crested white cockatoos overlooking proceedings from above. Drake would exit the passenger seat several times to open gates on the private properties with Danny obliged to re shut them once they had passed through.

Further on, they came to an old three-bedroom weatherboard house with rusted corrugated iron roofing and downpipes looking like they could do with some urgent maintenance. Two large willow trees gave shade in the front yard. Razor bought his vehicle to a halt inside the last gate and parked under the large swaying branches of the front willow tree and switched the engine off; Danny did the same. He exited their 4WD with Zoe and Maddy for a long-awaited stretch and watched as the two Vice Presidents shook hands and embraced the owner as they met on the timber-decked front porch.

It looked as though some serious conversing was taking place between the re uniting trio when Drake and Razor grabbed their belongings and took them to spare bedrooms of the house fifteen minutes after. The stranger left their side and began to walk towards where Danny and Zoe were standing.

'My god! He's huge,' Zoe whispered.

'At least 6ft 4,' Danny guessed. 'He looks like Buzz Lightyear with that jawbone,' he added smirkingly.

'Who?'

'Buzz Lightyear!'

Zoe gave him a look of bewilderment.

'What! You've never heard of Buzz Lightyear?' he asked.

'No,' Zoe wondered.

'You know! From Toy Story?'

'I'm not with you.'

'Don't worry about it. Obviously, you had a deprived childhood!' Danny laughed before the conversation could go any further when their host approached.

'Hello. My name's Anton,' he greeted with large smiles. 'Welcome to my home, but I must admit, I never expected a beautiful lady and an adorable little girl. Come! Come with me and I'll show you where you'll be bunking.' He gestured.

As Anton led them across his property, Danny took in the surroundings. More large gums stood majestically close to the horse stables. Pine logged work sheds with iron roofs were further on from the house with assorted tools and machinery exposed. Old car bodies, motorbikes, farm machinery and piles of iron, wire and timber laid idle across the yards as chickens, geese, goats and sheep walked freely around with the owner's three dogs, all crossbred healers of some sort.

Anton opened the front door to a paint starved bungalow with a self-contained kitchenette. It had a single bed and another bunk next to it and a small table and chairs with a small standing wardrobe. It was where Zoe and Maddy would make their quarters.

'I hope this is to your satisfaction. It's nothing special but should be comfortable enough. If there's any problems, just come and see me.' Anton smiled.

'Thank you,' said Zoe as she stepped up the two rungs with Maddy.

'You're this way.' He pointed.

Danny followed him to the large barn that was situated 100 meters away from the house.

'So, good friend of Drake's, are you?' asked Danny as they walked.

'Lifelong!'

'You with the Sultans also?'

'Not me! Although the club used to stay here every now and then when they were able to ride.'

'So, you know a few of them?'

'I'm only loyal to Drake, not the club if that's what you're worried about. I was privy to his plan of exiting the club and know the dangers that go with it, so I was expecting you guys. The boys filled me in on the day. Sorry for the mates you lost,' Anton condoled.

'Yeah, one hell of day,' said a saddened Danny.

Anton opened the door of the barn and walked inside to show Danny where he would be sleeping.

The barn was 60 x 30 feet in size with a pitched roof, a single level mezzanine surrounded its enclosure four foot off the ground which stored the stock feed and fertilisers amongst other farm utilities. Large 12x2 inch rafters were exposed above the sawdust floor where machinery sat idle. Large windows allowed sunlight in at all four walls.

'You're in the corner here,' he pointed. 'I'll leave you with it. As I said to your lady friend, if you need anything, call me,' said Anton before he stepped out of door.

'Lady friend, hey! That's an interesting way of looking at it,' Danny mused to himself after he was left alone.

The next few days at Anton's property were at times long and laborious for Danny, the nights festered with broken sleep as his inner demons tormented his subconscious, awakening him in sweats. The distressful thoughts of his family and his deceased buddies never left him as he made his bed inside the barn amongst the piles of hay whilst Zoe and Maddy made themselves at home as best they could in the adjacent bungalow.

Drake and Razor used the spare bedrooms inside the house for their sleeping quarters. The weather had cooled off and was hovering a touch below the 30C mark with sunny skies, the nights having a crisp cool edge to them. The rain and clouds that swooped the Hexagon Valley after the fire had weakened and never made it far enough north to make any impact on the Northern Rivers shire, however, the hot northerly winds that seared in from the inland deserts that enveloped the state had given way to gentle cooler southerlies.

Danny mostly kept to himself. At times he was left alone on the property as Zoe and Maddy horse backed it too and from Twin City, taking in the sights, shopping for clothes and miscellaneous items that they took a liking to, all courtesy of the stolen money, and of course, make up and perfume. Zoe always needed to be looking and smelling her best.

Between walks around the property searching for bull ant nests so he could test the patience of his little respected gladiator friends, Danny would seclude himself inside the barn and use the time to pen numerous letters to his wife. He was hoping that Zoe may be able to pass them onto Greta when she arrived back in the city.

On the third afternoon, he spent a few hours with Anton. They shared a bottle of his distilled homemade whiskey on his veranda, no mix, just straight from the bottle as Drake and Razor tinkered with their vehicles across the yard. They used their wizardry in mechanics and panel beating to repair the damage received when escaping the blazing mountains. They added a welded 90mm metal bull bar to the white Land Cruiser that Danny had taken the wheel of. They discarded the decal stickers that were attached, gave it a hard polish then painted the exterior trims, grill and bull bar black, to give the vehicle a meaner look, a job that both Razor and Drake were proud of.

Anton and Danny discussed whatever entered their minds, from the weather to individual history, from the present time to the ways they grew up with. They were getting to know one another and when Danny felt comfortable enough after swaying dialogue his way, he asked Anton the question on why he hadn't made the call to cash in on the reward money that was on offer for his apprehension.

'You're a friend of Drake's. So why would I go and do a thing like that?' he said. 'He likes you! He respects what you've done and who you are. Although Razor thinks you're one of the craziest bastards he's ever come across!' He laughed. 'I suppose that's his way of respecting you as well.'

Danny welcomed what his new comrades had to say about him. It relaxed his lessening paranoia somewhat as Anton combed back his thick mop of sandy blond hair and continued in his laconic way.

'Look around,' he sighed. 'What would I do with the money anyhow? I've got everything I want right here,' he continued as he sipped on his whiskey, simultaneously waving his arm towards his animals and the outlook. 'I prefer this new world. It's more peaceful. No stress, no demands, no one telling me what I should say and do. It was a toxic world before, Danny. That social media world was full of hate lies and hysteria.'

Containing his balance in his seat, Anton leant to his left side and pulled a drawer out from a cupboard that was pushed up against the side wall of the house. He grabbed two thick cigars from it, lit his own and offered the other to Danny which was happily accepted and lit without hesitation once Danny clipped the end off with his side teeth.

Anton continued while puffing on his cigar as Danny enjoyed his large intake, it had been a while since he had tasted the sweet flavour of a fine cigar.

'No electronic devices to numb people's minds anymore. No overboard political correctness anymore. No more people hiding behind a keyboard. People actually have to confront a creature if they've got a beef, god forgive!' Anton mocked with delight. 'People are actually learning the art of communicating face to face again,' he excitedly mused. 'Nah, too many people had a say in what you did or said before.'

Anton took a large suck on his cigar then blew the exhaling smoke above then continued, 'So, I don't need any money. I've adjusted well, and so could others if they just made a few sacrifices. I've got my animals, I've got my house, I've got the river at the back of my property, so no amount of money would make me a happier man, let alone blood money!' He winked.

The gesture was received with a cheer from Danny's glass. 'Nah, I wouldn't change this for anything in the world,' Anton finished as he panned around his property.

Danny nodded his head in satisfaction. He envied Anton's attitude, he agreed with most things he said, however, adjusting to the new life that had been forced upon society was something Danny couldn't adapt to as well as Anton had, no matter how hard he tried. Nevertheless, he enjoyed his one-on-one talk and thanked him accordingly for giving him sanctuary.

Other times during the week, he would spend with his female companions, taking pride when he would complete a conversation in sign language with Maddy without the helping translation of Zoe. Each finished dialogue would be met with high fives and fun-loving cuddles by his little blonde smiling sidekick, whilst Razor and Drake, with the help of Anton, went about arranging plans for their escape to the Northern states and Danny's heaven.

Danny hoped that Razor's logistical wizardry would come to the fore and be successful in negotiating a safe passage for their vehicles to be transported. Razor was using the proceeds from the robbery to bribe and buy information and try and secure a spot on either a trailer or container on the twice a week diesel powered locomotive that was destined for the Northern states.

Danny was hoping to be on the one that was to leave at noon on the Friday. Interstate passenger trains ran only three times a week compared to daily running's of the cargo and goods trains as precious fuel supply could only be distributed so far. Imports and exports between states was top priority and getting a seat on an interstate passenger train came at a high cost to the pocket of those who boarded.

The more time Danny would spend with the two estranged bikers, the more his paranoia would drain. Drake and Razor were including him in all their plans and problems, asking for his own input when discussing them. Although the two Vice Presidents would come and go from Anton's property, Danny's confidence was growing that anything they were up to away from him was to his benefit and not only their own.

He was eager to keep moving, eager to find his heaven, however, he knew he had to be patient. It would be fool hardy to continue without a plan. He now relied on Drake and Razor heavily, they were experienced men when it came to the art of subterfuge and Danny would have to fight his whims if he was to make it a certainty to be with his family once more.

On the second evening after they arrived, Anton had led Drake to a phone at the Riverside hotel, a 30-minute ride on horseback from his property. It was a venue where Anton had close connections with the proprietors and called in a favour to allow Drake access to the confidential and in-demand landline. The local waterhole was a single-storey brick and timber establishment with a public bar on one side and a large bistro on the other which led out to an even larger deck that overlooked the mighty Alpine River. Sixteen motel rooms were adjacent to the hotel with camping grounds behind it closer to the river, most of them were occupied.

It was here where Drake contacted Mia at the Graceville hospital at 6.30 pm, knowing she took her coffee break at that time, three and half hours after her shift started. He was fortunate to have Mia's close friend Kristy answer the call in the nurse's quarters and soon he was putting his wife's stress at ease, informing her that he was alive and well, the company he was with and what plans lay ahead.

Mia had been fretting profusely on the whereabouts of her husband, not knowing whether he had been caught up in the tragedy of the inferno and she was quick to inform Razor's wife Candice on the men's well-being after the secret phone conversation had finished, but not before she informed him that Barny had survived the siege. It was news that Drake took great pleasure in relaying to the guilt-ridden Danny when he arrived back at Anton's.

Danny was over the moon with joy that Barny had made it out alive. He would tell all those who were with him that he knew that Barny's Lord would spare him, Drake and Razor pleased that they could lessen the hardship that Danny was enduring. Although they advised him at the time that Barny was still yet to wake from his coma and had a long recovery ahead of him, Mia's advice was that he was going to pull through okay; nevertheless, Danny was proud that his friend had survived.

However, after another pre-planned phone call 48 hours later, other news that Mia had gathered, as she stealthily listened into senior police who had occupied the hospital, had Drake's mind in overdrive. Much to his initial shock, Mia had informed him that the authorities had confirmed that his new partner in crime was dead, and although Drake had an inclination on the reasons why after some thought, he was looking forward to an in-depth conversation with Danny the following morning.

As Drake, Razor and Anton decided to push their drinking session at the hotel through dinner time and into the evening, Danny was spending time by the river with Zoe and Maddy. Both were strengthening their connection as they sat on the sandy banks, a connection that was growing as every day and hour passed. They watched with vigilant parent like eyes as Maddy kept herself occupied at the water's edge. They discussed with sadness how little Maddy couldn't hear the sounds of nature that surrounded them. The running current of the water, the chirps and squawks of the native birdlife and the sound of the leaves rustling on the gentle breeze, with Danny vowing that Maddy would receive the cochlear implant she so desperately needed, no matter what the cost.

Danny was shirtless and only wearing a borrowed pair of loose shorts from Anton with his sunglasses donned. It was the first time any type of gun or knife was not by his side since he was forced from his home. Zoe sat barefooted, attired in a newly acquired dark green summer dress which was wrapped up above her thighs exposing her long slender legs to the late sun's tanning rays.

Conversation was mostly happy and spontaneous, other times quiet and interluded and at one of these quiet times Zoe noticed Danny winced a little when he leant his arm on the sand.

'Still sore?' she asked.

'Not really! It's a lot better than yesterday,' replied Danny.

He was referring to the burns he had received to his right forearm and hand, along with the scalding his fingertips took. From the time they had arrived at Anton's, Zoe had happily attended his injuries, dressing and re bandaging whilst applying antiseptic cream to his skin. She took his arm and unwrapped the bandage around his forearm.

'It looks great. You're a quick healer,' she commented as she scanned his arm and fingers whilst gently holding his arm. 'I think we can get rid of these.'

Zoe rolled up the bandages and laid them at her side. Danny peered back across the river overlooking Maddy frolicking in the shallows, looking unconcerned at Zoe's doctoring observations. Another quiet interlude bestowed them, coaxing Zoe to raise some questions that she had been burning to ask.

'I saw you guys counting money in the barn the other morning,' she declared.

'Did you?'

'I thought Maddy was in there. I heard some noises and poked my head in. You were right. There is a lot more,' she facetiously commented.

'$487,625,' Danny succinctly said.

'Holy fuck!' she gasped. 'Really!' Zoe was staggered.

'That's what we said. You should've seen the look on our faces when we finished counting.' Danny laughed. 'We had no idea it would be that much. We calculated that it would only be a third of that if we were lucky, but I guess all the money came from the long weekend and all the celebrations along with the bookie money. We didn't even factor that in.'

'May I ask how you came across it?' she coyly asked.

Danny was blunt and straightforward in his answer. He told her in fine detail how it was all planned and executed, including the frenetic chase up the mountain which ended in the demise of Cribbs and Pringle, and it was leaving Zoe astonished and in awe.

'Is that why you were so desperate to get to the vehicles during the fire?' Zoe asked.

'Yeah! I wasn't going to let it burn. It's my only way out of all this shit,' he replied.

'You mean you had all that money in the vehicles as we drove up? I wondered what you had been up to that morning. I knew Drake and Razor weren't in the compound. Solomon was letting everyone know about that. I could hear him from my bedroom,' Zoe relayed.

Danny gave the reasons why he did it, and why Drake and Razor were partners in the heist, and as Zoe listened on in amazement, entranced at Danny's honesty, she raised the courage to ask him further questions after he had finished relaying the events of Monday morning.

She took a deep silent breath and turned the subject to a personal level.

'Razor told me that you're not the person I think you are,' she conveyed with seriousness.

'How do you mean?'

'He advised that it would be a good idea if I left you alone and that I shouldn't be hanging with you. He said that you're not a nice person inside and warned me to stay away.'

'Really!' Danny smirked.

'Yep, he told me that you murdered a couple of cops in the mountains, and I'm not referring to any of the Devlins. Is that true?' she enquired furtively.

'They weren't coppers,' Danny snarled. 'They wore a badge but that's as far as it got. One of them was a rapist, the other a wife beater. Sandilands tried to rape my wife while she was in the police station. He's raped others, girls as young as fifteen. He had to pay for what he had done. He was the lowest of scumbags, he deserved what he got,' Danny said with no regrets. 'I'll do anything to protect my wife, her honour. He was never going to get away with what he done, not this time. Anyways, he was going to kill me and the boys. I had to protect them as well, so I got in first.'

Zoe accepted Danny's reasons. Of all the criminals she had defended, the one client she never would represent was a rapist, and although at first it scared her that Danny could do such a thing without any sign of regret, the reasons behind his motives were clear and she felt somewhat proud of what he had done as she flirtatiously probed further.

'Would you protect me?' she dryly asked.

'Are you my wife!'

'No.'

'You may as well be with all these questions,' mused Danny.

Zoe chuckled at his comment as she adjusted her legs away from the sun. She took a swig out her water bottle and continued with her delving.

'You know what! I've dealt with the hardest of hardest men. I've represented murderers, drug chiefs, you name it. I've seen and met them all. I could write a book on the monsters and sadists I've met, men who have scared the absolute shit of me. But I must say, I've never met someone like you Danny Pruitt. You're one of a kind, very different.

'I knew it from the moment we met at the compound. On one hand you're a kind, loving, caring person. I know no one who loves his wife and kids like you do. You're so loyal to the ones you love. I see it every time I speak with you. The pain you feel over your friends, the love you had for them, it's amazing, not to mention the way you handle Maddy, it's beautiful.

'But on the other hand, and if Razor's right in what he tells me, and what I've read and heard myself, you're possibly more ruthless than any of them put together. The things you have done to survive, your quest to get to your place up north, it's extraordinary to me. Not to mention how you smoothed over Solomon, never seen that before,' she said.

'Stop it! You're embarrassing me,' Danny chuffed.

'But on the other hand,' Zoe smiled as she continued, 'the so-called experts have a name for people like you.'

'Yeah, and what's that?' Danny asked, interested.

'A psychopath,' she mocked.

Danny laughed at that suggestion. Although he was always trying to come to grips on the things he had done recently, things he never thought himself capable of, he chortled to himself that if he were ever caught and the experts labelled him with that stigma, he would have no problem living with it.

'So, do I scare you? Do you worry being around me?' Danny asked.

'To the contrary. From the night we spent together at the rotunda, I've never felt safer around anyone in my life,' Zoe confessed.

Danny could feel that she was leading somewhere, even if she didn't want to divulge it. Once again, Teeto and Barny's words were in his mind. The flirtation between them was unmistakable and Danny thought it time to see what her real intentions were.

He stood up from the riverside sandy banks and helped Zoe to her feet with his hand then looked into her lucent jade green eyes with intent.

'Why are you helping me? Why do you want to be around me?' he gently probed.

Zoe had no immediate answer. She looked quite dumbfounded, embarrassed. She shrugged her shoulders and looked to the sand beneath her feet and softly responded, 'I don't know! I really don't know!'

She childly played with the soft sand between her toes as a brief pause ensued then panned her eyes on Danny's once more as he ogled at her.

'Maybe I want to see your heaven. You talk about it so much. I might feel I've missed out on something if I don't get to see it with my own eyes,' she teasingly added.

Danny stopped short of any promises. He asked why she wouldn't want to go back to the city, after all, she had an important job and highlighted the fact that she would have clients wondering where she was, not to mention her secretary and work assistants who would be fretting on her whereabouts by now.

Zoe shrugged off his concerns.' I phoned my secretary from the post office when Maddy and I were in Twin City. Had to wait a little while, there was a bit of a queue, but I got through to her. Everything's sweet. My colleagues will handle what's on my desk. I'm due for a holiday anyway,' she insisted. 'I've never been to the Amber Coast; it will be fun.' Almost daring Danny to take her and Maddy with him.

Danny was thinking to himself on how he could be so naïve. Maybe he did know what was coming next but chose to ignore it, Barny did say to him that she had fallen in love with him overnight, a prophecy that he was now beginning to listen to, however, now was the time to slow things down as delicately as he could. The last thing he needed was another woman and child travelling with him. It was going to be hard enough by himself, let alone keeping an eye out for two more vulnerable companions.

'You don't want to come with me, it's too dangerous,' he subtly warned. 'What if someone recognises me! My face was planted all over the papers if you'll remember. What if I'm arrested, you'll be on your own and stranded. No, I can't risk that with you *or* Maddy. You asked if I would protect you, well, this is the way I'm doing it. You can't be around me, not now, not like this.'

Zoe took heed of what Danny said. She understood it completely, however, her own mind was confused and astray. Deep down, she didn't know what she wanted in her life anymore. It had been upheaved almost overnight, but she knew Danny was right in one thing, Maddy's safety was paramount, that she knew for certain for the little one had been through so much for a girl of her age.

They left the river before the night sky took over, leaving each other to their own devices. Zoe and Maddy helped Anton who had arrived back at his property to tend to his animals and livestock before sunset whilst Danny took solitude on his makeshift hay bale bed inside the barn. However, if he thought he had seen the last of Zoe before sunrise, he would have another encounter with her, an encounter he never saw coming. As he dozed off to sleep, none the wiser that on this same evening at the same time, his beloved wife back in Graceville was laying in her own bed with her two boys by her side, privately struggling to come to terms with the knowledge that her husband was in fact alive after being notified of his death earlier in the day.

It was 1.30 am in the morning and Danny was awoken once more by his nightmares. Real-time images of the Devlin brothers lying dead in his home yard obsessed him. Images of their older sibling dying in front of him at Tambourine Bridge. Images of Karl and the young Constable falling helplessly after he had his brains blown out by Pringle. Images of Sandilands and Slacek and the body of Ricky, his best friend, blood-soaked and lifeless.

It all banged away in his half sleeping brain, not to mention the vivid image of the burning runaway horse which was the chief protagonist in his sub conscious torment, it was all terrorising him again. He raised from his bed in a lather of sweat as if he were hit with an electric shock, his chest pumping in and out as he struggled for breath.

Inaudible words were echoing off the barn walls, all louder than previous nights which alerted Zoe from her sleep in the adjacent bungalow. Concerned and frightened, Zoe stirred from her bed, lit the candle inside her lantern and made the wary walk across to the barn.

She opened the side door and poked her head through. She saw Danny sitting up on the edge of his bed. The rubber underly and bedsheet ruffled from his tormented wrestle, the top sheet and blanket was crinkled up to his side.

'Are you alright? You okay?' Zoe softly asked as she laid the lantern on the table against the barn wall.

Danny stared back, surprised to see Zoe standing there. In his self-obsessed daze, he had failed to see her enter.

Zoe edged to the end of the bed and knelt before him; she could see the fear on his face.

'Oh my god! What's wrong?' She was worried.

'These fuckin nightmares. I can't get rid of them,' he quietly choked.

Zoe rested her hand on Danny's knee and advised him to take some deep breaths and to try and relax, however, Danny's emotions were in overdrive as his body began to tremble. He started to cry, everything he had held within was leaking out. Tears of suffering, tears of fright, tears of remorse, he couldn't control it as the sobbing intensified. Zoe raised from the floor and sat herself next to him on the bed.

She cupped her hands around his face then gave him a comforting embrace as Danny's head collapsed beneath her shoulder. She gently patted at his head repeating that all would be okay. He was like a little boy being cradled in the arms of his mother as his crying continued, he had never felt so meek and vulnerable.

Zoe fathomed what the nightmares were all about. She comprehended what he had been through and what he had seen and done, Razor did his best to assure her of that, factual or not, all she could do was comfort him and wait for him to regain his composure.

'These thoughts,' she said. 'You've got to try and get them out of your mind. Think only of the good things in your life,' she stated. 'Think of the good times, think of the future, forget about what's happened. Think of your heaven, Danny, the place you're going to, how beautiful it is and how wonderful it's going to be when you get there. Think of your family and how brilliant it will be when you reunite with them.'

Danny raised his head from Zoe's gentle motherly embrace. She rested her hands on his shoulders and wiped the tears from his cheeks with her thumbs. She stared him the eyes and continued to reassure him.

'Conquer your nightmares by listening to your dreams,' she affirmed. 'It's the only way to stop them.'

Danny sucked in a large breath and exhaled with gusto then clasped his hands to his face, wiping away the leftover tears that had finally stopped.

Silence briefly passed as Zoe hands continued to softly pat at his perspiring head. Danny released his hands away from his face and looked down, however, he was not expecting to see what his eyes had quickly became transfixed on. The thin shoulder strap of Zoe's black silk nightwear slip had fallen while she was comforting him, exposing her right breast inside the fabric as the candle and silhouetted moonlight flickered throughout the barn.

Zoe could see that Danny was absorbed and was immediately aroused by it. Time seemed to freeze for the two of them, they were both unguarded and over sensitive, held within the moment until Zoe cautiously escorted his hand and placed it on her breast. Their eyes met only inches away as Danny's hold on her breast tightened, softly caressing her now stimulated nipple that was between the inside of his knuckles. He wanted to let go but his hand was not reacting.

Danny awkwardly adjusted himself, gently manoeuvring his legs and hips, feeling embarrassed at the swelling movement from his crotch. Zoe looked down and saw that Danny was hardening. Instinctively, she lowered her right hand and released him from his underwear, stroking and caressing until he was fully erect. He wanted her to stop, his conscious was yelling inside but couldn't raise a voice, it was if he had no control of what was happening.

Bereft of thought, he turned his head and kissed her on the lips, softly at first, then immoral passion engulfed them both as the kissing became unrestrained. Zoe raised herself to her knees then slowly straddled herself across him, guiding him inside of her with her left hand. She slowly rocked herself back and forth as he slipped deeper inside. She clasped both her hands at his cheekbones as she started to sigh, pushing her chest into his face, then wrapping her arms around the back of his neck.

Rapid sensations were running through Danny's body he had no command over, and soon turned her around and forced her onto the bed. Zoe hastily removed her slip then looked up at Danny. Their eyes locked in pensive inevitability; it was if they were conceding they had no power over their actions. Danny began to move his fingers, lips and tongue across her now naked body. He started at her neck and breasts, then slowly lowered his head across her stomach until it sat between her legs.

His conscience was blasting it was wrong, but he couldn't stop what was happening. It was if he was having an outer body experience, looking at it all from above, however, the blatant physical feeling was telling him something else. Zoe's gasps of pleasure escalated as her back arched. She couldn't remember the last time she felt like this, if at all, Danny was pushing all her sensual buttons and more.

Bodily sensitivities she never knew existed were sending quivers throughout as he spread his left palm and fingertips erotically up and down the contours of her back while his right fingers and tongue tantalised away between her thighs. Zoe's body was almost erupting in trembling rapture. He then moved his body over the top of her, kissing and caressing on her naked body. He raised himself above and entered inside of her once more, slowing his penetrations as their desired filled bodies synchronised in rhythm.

Zoe was ready to orgasm at any moment as he increased his deep pulsations. Danny held her aggressively but tenderly as he tightly pillowed the side of her head against his cheek with his left hand, Zoe clasping her hands tightly to his arms, her fingernails scratching at his triceps in unabated desire. Their bodies interlocked and became one, the intimacy levels intensified to the point of no return as Danny's thrusts accelerated with every lustful moaning breath. They soon climaxed together as their bodies locked as one, Danny howling deeply in a mixture of anguished pain and ecstasy.

Both were gasping for breath as their bodies continued to shake in after pleasure when they exhaustedly collapsed to the bed in unison with immense iniquitous bliss. They would again make love once more during the night, and again, the physical and emotional feelings would be the same.

They never spoke a word as they lay, although their eyes told a myriad of emotions which words could not explain when they would intermittently anchor together. Zoe would leave Danny's arms at the first low gaggle of the kookaburra's morning call, she wanted to be back with Maddy before the little one awoke. Danny felt her departure, he was unmoved, silent and stared into the semi darkness.

The night would be become another rung on the step ladder of guilt that he was accumulating, only this one would stand atop of all others, relegating the rest of his blameworthy sins to the realms of insignificance, so much so, they would all seem to be so trivial.

Chapter 41

'Well, look here, it's a dead man walking,' Drake bitterly welcomed him to the breakfast table.

Bacon, eggs, sausages with assorted fruits was the morning diet that was being shared from the wood fired BBQ that Anton had control over.

Danny wasn't exactly sure on how to take the comment. Had he upset his new comrades in some way? Was it a threat? He didn't know as he panned around the large outdoor table. Razor sat at the end while Zoe and Maddy sat to together to the side. Drake was opposite the females as he sternly changed his demeanour.

Danny sat down nervously. Maddy jumped from her seat and gave him a good morning embrace; he was still her knight in shining armour. He composed himself again and gave Zoe a knowing smile. He was reticent to see her when he heard her voice resonating across the property as she spoke to those around. He had spent the early morning penning another letter to Greta. Regardless of the awkwardness over Zoe, he knew he couldn't hide in his bed all day, so eventually changed into his denim jeans, boots and customary black T-shirt and passively made his way out to the outdoor breakfast table.

Drake pushed a couple of newspaper across the table and placed them under Danny's eyes, one from the day before and the latest edition that Anton had obtained from his early morning sojourn to his local store.

Danny picked up a rasher of bacon from the sharing plate between his fingers, put it to his mouth and started to chew, trying hard to keep a cool and calm persona before he casually looked down on the print in front of him.

' You got an explanation for this?' Drake demanded.

'What am I looking at?'

Drake forcibly tapped his finger on the newspaper to grab Danny's eyes.

FUGITIVES DIE IN BIKER INFERNO, the headline read.

He perused down the article to see that his and Ricky's name were the ones the paper were referring to, informing readers that they had perished in the siege and following wildfire, along with the survival and arrest of a third fugitive, namely David Barnard (Barny). He read further to see that Harry had also been arrested. Police had acted on a tip and visited his elder sister's place in the suburbs of Marlboro where she had been harbouring him.

Harry surrendered peacefully and was now biding his time in a jail cell awaiting advice from an appointed lawyer. Danny read more about his supposed demise and the more he read, the more his inner smiles broadened, proud that his farfetched plan had fooled the establishment.

Drake gave him time to read through the article; however, his patience was wearing thin and after a few minutes began to probe Danny on why police believe they had his body.

Drake leant back on the bench seat and folded his arms across his chest and in mild frustration asked, 'They think you're Teeto, don't they?'

Danny raised from the table without saying a word, still chewing away on his breakfast and began to walk towards the barn.

'Where the fuck are you going?' Razor bellowed.

'I'll be back in a minute,' Danny calmly replied.

He entered the barn and rustled through his borrowed backpack next to his bedside until he retrieved Teeto's rings and wallet. He clasped them in his hand then walked back to resume his seat at the outdoor table as looks of frustrated bewilderment followed his every movement.

'What are these?' Razor asked suspiciously when Danny produced them onto the table.

'They're Teeto's! These might help in remembering him,' said Danny.

Razor took the rings off the table while Drake searched through the wallet. The only contents were a five-dollar note, a bit of change, a few receipts from innocent purchases and a photo of the child he never got to cradle.

At first, the men were grateful that Danny had retrieved them and more grateful for the gesture of handing Teeto's belongings over to them, albeit a little late they commented, however, an innocent question from Zoe would be the catalyst to retrieving the truth on why the law believed that Danny had perished, a truth that the estranged Vice Presidents already had their suspicions about.

Zoe noticed that Danny's fingers were bare, particularly his ring finger where his wedding ring used to sit. She knew it was missing, she had for days. Danny had showed it off to her on the night they spent together at the rotunda and unfortunately for her, it was a subtle reminder that he was a married man and her sharp eye caught that it was absent and thought this as good as time as any to enquire.

'Where are *your* rings?' she innocently asked.

Drake and Razor nonchalantly waited for the answer as they digested their breakfast, they already had their theories. They had discussed them at the Riverside Hotel the previous night as they scanned photographs and read about the fire devastation and loss of lives through the news print they had before them. This morning's paper only confirmed Mia's information that police believed Danny had been a victim of the mayhem.

'They're on Teeto's fingers. I swapped them over before I jumped into the cellar,' Danny sheepishly confessed. 'I was hoping that they thought it was me lying next to Ricky.'

It was what Drake and Razor had deduced. They didn't know exactly how he did it, but now their conjectures had been answered. They gave one another a look of annoyed validation. Zoe's mouth was agape, her eyes widened in disbelief. She was stunned, and somewhat in awe how anyone could think of doing such a thing in the life and death situation that they faced at the time.

She looked at the Vice Presidents expecting a tsunami of repercussions to come Danny's way, however, before they could react, Danny got on the front foot to justify what he had done. He stood from his seat and pleaded his case in a calm and firm manner.

'You know as well as I do that the bodies left inside the Manor would've probably been burnt beyond recognition, including Ricky's. You said it yourselves when we were at Bonnieview, and it says it here as well,' he said pointing at the article in the paper. 'You also said that no one would know who he was, but you do! You've got something to remember him by. You were his best mates, you know he died, you knew who he was, that's all that matters isn't it? 'Would you rather his belongings be left in lost property at a morgue somewhere never to be claimed, or in your hands, the people who really cared about him. I feel Teeto's loss too, it's a tragedy, but I've lost more, including my best friend and I'm just trying to retrieve what's left. I'm sorry for what I did, and know it would piss you off, but if they think I'm dead, so be it, it's the only way I can possibly have a chance to get my family back.'

Danny leant back on his seat holding back the emotions bought on by the thoughts of his family. His hands were shaking in tension and trepidation, waiting for the men's reaction, unsure how it would be as he kept his eyes firmly engaged at them. Danny knew he needed them on his side, if they turned on him now, his plans would be paralysed.

Seconds of silent tension passed before Danny lowered his head waiting for something to be said or done. Although Drake and Razor had a mountain of misgivings on what he had done with Teeto, his little declamation had got through to them. As late as last night, with the certain notion that Danny had tampered with Teeto's body somehow, they were ready to confront him which in no doubt would've ended up being an unpleasant experience for Danny.

However, the men decided to let a clear head rule their thinking instead of the alcohol, so decided to sleep on their deep agitation. Now that morning had broken and after giving deeper thought to the dangerous positions that they were all in, it became clear that Danny's perceived death could only work in their favour.

Both Drake and Razor let Danny know about the anger they had over disturbing the body of their endeared little brother; nevertheless, they had to move forward.

Drake spread his hands across the table as he stood, his tattooed muscled forearms and biceps tense as he stared Danny down. He thought the two hardened bikers may be about to use the weapons they had strapped to their side, a payback for the audacity he displayed towards Teeto; however, Drake's demeanour allayed his fear and Danny began to breathe easier.

'As much as we disagree with what you did, you do have a point about something,' Drake said with surety.

Danny lifted his head higher and asked what he was asserting.

'Well, if they know you're alive, they'll come after you. And if they find you, they find the money, and if they find the money, they find us, and that can't be happening, can it?' Drake urged with authority. 'We can't change what's done. We all loved Teeto, but nothing will bring him back.'

'Or Ricky,' Danny butted in.

'Or Ricky,' Drake repeated.

Drake took another deep breath, held it in and after a large exhale, advised all at the table that Danny must remain a dead man. Danny nodded his head in gratitude, he banked on Drake seeing his logic, however, Razor's animated exchange wasn't over.

'Don't get too confident,' he warned Drake. 'Just because they've got his rings and wallet doesn't mean they'll put it to bed,' Razor stressed as he glued his eyes on Danny.

'What about DNA, genius? What happens when that comes back? You know they'll get it, don't you! You ever thought of that?' he vigorously questioned.

'Never entered my mind, mate; we were in a bit of hurry if you'll remember. I'll worry about that later. At least this will give me time. I just wanna get up north ASAP, they'll never find me there,' Danny said.

'Didn't you say you had a deposit on it?' Razor interrogated, referring to his property called Heaven. 'There will be a paper trail somewhere.'

'I never signed anything. It was a handshake agreement,' Danny advised him, explaining that his trust in Steve was absolute, a detail which was enough to satisfy the angst of the men for the time being.

Drake turned to Zoe's experience in the process of DNA recovery. He was hoping that the knowledge she was privy with regarding how detectives and prosecutors worked would be of benefit.

'How long does the process usually take until they would get a result?' Drake asked.

'These days it could take up to a month to confirm compared to the 1-3 days of previous times in a criminal case. But because Danny's case is pretty high profile and what I know of Conroy and Vaccaro wanting to wrap it up, they would be wanting to finalise it as soon as they could,' Zoe advised.

The men knew time was of the essence if they wanted to stop any DNA samples being taken. They didn't know if it had already been done, a major problem which was now at the top of their headaches as they bounced scenarios around. They turned to Zoe once more and asked when Greta would've been informed of Danny's death.

'Probably yesterday. Going on reports here in the paper,' she advised. 'Oh shit!' Zoe stopped.

'What?' Danny asked as she turned to him.

'Your wife! She probably thinks you're dead,' Zoe fussed. 'Oh my god! She must be going through hell right now.'

Danny tried to get some reassurance from Drake. He asked him to reiterate that Mia saw Greta visit Barny after she had passed on the note to him. Drake confirmed it once more and Danny was confident that his wounded buddy would've somehow informed her that he was still alive, that he was certain of, and added that she would know soon enough if that wasn't the case when she received his letters.

Drake refocused on the conversation at hand and followed up with the question on what the usual time frame would be retrieving DNA from next of kin.

'Probably a couple of days,' Zoe concluded. 'What is it, Friday! Maybe the weekend, but that would be unlikely. They always wait a few days for family to grieve before they ask for a sample, so at a guess, I would probably say Monday. They don't work too quick these days,' she smirked. 'But as I said, I know Conroy's in a hurry to wrap it up.'

Danny, Drake and Razor, and with input from Anton, procrastinated over ideas on how they could prevent the DNA testing from happening as Zoe continued perusing through the papers, becoming more disturbed as she read about the destruction they left behind. The men covered a myriad of scenarios, from the ridiculous to the reasonably thought out. Anton even suggested to steal Teeto's body from the authorities, an idea which was met with sarcastic mirth from all.

'What if Greta refused a sample being taken?' Danny asked. 'If she knows I'm alive, she won't let it happen,' he assured them.

'They would go and get a court order if she refused,' Zoe counteracted.

'At least that would give us more time,' Danny surmised.

The men were at a loose end. Silence gripped around the breakfast table; no solution was entering their over loaded minds until Zoe's speculative brain raised the name of Teeto once more.

'What about him?' Drake and Razor responded in unison.

'Doesn't he have a boy?'

'Yeah, so what?' Drake asked.

'Your wife Mia! Doesn't she do house calls to Teeto's son?' she quizzed.

Mia, along with a small group of nurses around the district, went out of their way to help the needy and poor who couldn't afford any medical assistance. They volunteered their time and services without the hospitals knowledge to visit the unfortunate, checking in on the health of single mothers and their children around Graceville. They would distribute aide from simple bandages and paracetamol tablets to antibiotics and medical advice. It was all done on the quiet for if anyone from the hospital found out that they were confiscating valuable stock, it would undoubtably mean instant dismissal, if not criminal charges. As it was, the mother of Teeto's child happened to be one of the needy who Mia made regular visits to.

'What are you getting at?' Drake queried.

'Well, it's a long shot, but what if your wife makes a visit to the mother. Maybe she can get a sample off Teeto's boy. I know they keep retrieved samples at the Graceville hospital before they transfer them down to the labs in the city. If she could get a swab off Teeto's son, maybe she could make a switch from the sample they get off Danny's boys. If that could happen, they will have a match, and our friend here will be officially dead,' Zoe chuffed, patting her left hand gently on Danny's shoulder.

'I don't want to involve Mia,' Drake cautioned. 'It would be too risky for her. If she were to be caught, it would open a whole lot of other questions, questions that we don't want answered.'

Drake paused for a moment and thought further. 'I'll call her again from the Riverside at the start of her shift and discuss the risk assessment with her,' he said, not dismissing the plan yet.

Mia had done some secretive and manipulative things for her husband and club previously when it came to the Graceville hospital, successfully at that, but nevertheless, Drake affirmed again that there would be no pressure put on her if she thinks it cannot be done.

For the time being, it was the only solution they had to keep Danny a dead man and the more they discussed the danger, the more they concluded that it might be good idea that they too somehow become anonymous. Along with the carnage of the fire, the paper had also written about the siege before it, and with it came information about the arrest warrants that had been issued.

The authorities had the body of the President, but nonetheless, the Vice Presidents and all surviving senior members of the Sultan MC were still high on the police target list to answer the charges against the club, impending charges that instigated the raid in the first place. However, the one thing Drake and Razor did have on their side was time, albeit limited, as forensics were still processing through the remains of the victims, not knowing yet whether the two Vice Presidents were among them.

Regardless of their concern being on the police target list, the danger that gave them most angst was knowing that Crow was still out there, and their co-Vice President wouldn't take too kindly knowing his two cohorts had absconded from the Club in its most demanding and desperate hour. Drake and Razor were hoping that the law would catch up with him before he would catch up with them, as they had already conceded that Crow would surely come after them once he had spoken to surviving members and contacted other chapters of the club.

Razor grabbed a backpack from off the ground and laid it on the table. He produced three train tickets out of it, flicked one of them to Danny and two to Zoe.

'What this?' Danny asked.

'It's your ticket to freedom,' Razor proudly informed him.

Danny raised his eyebrows and perused the ticket. One-way to Burbank, it read, the capital city of the Northern State of Capricornia. 340km north of their lay his heaven. The time had come for him to take the final journey.

As Danny pondered over his train ticket, Razor suggested to Zoe that she could try and provide them with more information on anything concerning the investigation regarding the Sultans MC when she returned to Marlboro, calling from the phone inside her office building.

'See what you can find out for us. We'll set up a time and we'll call you from here,' Razor said.

Zoe was annoyingly bemused by Razor's carefree insistence. He wasn't asking her, it seemed he was demanding her without a thought on what she was going to do with herself. She was only there through circumstances, circumstance beyond her control, and now Zoe was asking herself what the hell has she got herself into. 'Am I a part of their group now?' she dwelled. 'Aiding and abetting wanted men! That really would be detrimental to my career, a disbarment for sure.' However, that wasn't the main shock that was troubling her at this instant, it was the train tickets that lay before her.

It was now 9.30 am and Razor advised that she needed to pack her belongings as her and Maddy were on the next train back to Marlboro at 12.45 pm, fifteen minutes before Danny would be on the one heading North in the opposite direction. Razor also suggested that Danny start packing himself.

Zoe was speechless. Naively or not, she never gave it a thought over the last few days that this would be coming. She twirled the tickets in her hands as an empty forlorn look encased her face. She was waiting for Danny to say something, anything! Anything that would include her name; however, no comment would be coming from him. All he did was furtively search for a reaction from her as she concentrated on the tickets in her hands.

Although he had warned her off about traveling with him, he also knew that he hadn't totally convinced her, and the abrupt arrangement would be a punch in the stomach to her. The one thing he did know is that he couldn't fight for her, and it was a realisation that Zoe quickly fathomed also. To do so would give a hint of what happened between them last night, and that could not be disclosed to present company, it could not be disclosed to anyone.

He knew Razor was a man of high moralistic values, that he had made clear to him over the preceding weeks despite his dealings in club business and Danny couldn't risk provoking what would be his certain reaction. Danny deduced that Razor would probably cut him loose right there and then if he knew of his infidelity, and the silence from Danny only made Zoe turn her head towards him with a conceding blank stare. It seemed that both their destinies had been made up for them.

Zoe turned her back on Danny and communicated with Maddy. The little one was oblivious to what was being said although she knew it was important going by the facial expressions and demeanour that the adults displayed as she continued to chew and digest her breakfast. Danny couldn't make out was relayed between them but soon Zoe was up on her feet and taking Maddy by the hand.

'Okay. We'll go and pack then,' Zoe said with sufferance.

She left the breakfast bench and led Maddy towards their bungalow, keeping her head high as her earrings bounced on her elegant strides. Danny was hurting for her. In a perfect world, he would've loved for her to travel with him. In a perfect world, he would never have had sex with her. In a perfect world, the Devlin brothers wouldn't have come visiting, and in a perfect world, he would still have his house, his best friend would still be alive and his wife and children would be by his side; however, in Danny's new world, nothing would ever seem perfect again.

As Zoe and Maddy made their way inside the bungalow, Danny posed the question on what the men's plans were, now knowing that the only train ticket going North was his.

Razor replied that once they had the assurance that all problems and plans were settled in Graceville, they were going to wait for their loved ones to join them at Anton's. Both had passed the idea that they too would travel North with Danny. Razor had travelled to the Amber Coast and was very fond of the place and it wasn't taking much to twist his arm.

He had even spoken about settling there after Danny had conveyed the knowledge that property was very cheap in these economics times and as it was now, money would be no problem for either him and Drake to relocate their loved ones and leave their present life behind.

Both explained to Danny that it was impossible to get a freight cart on the train for their vehicles despite Razor's best efforts. There was just no room, not even an offer of doubling the price could get them space. They had left it too late and both made it clear that the vehicles were too valuable for them to leave behind. They made the decision to wait another week for their wives to join them. Danny's perceived death had changed everything.

Drake and Razor were not men to leave any loose ends lying about and the realisation of themselves now having warrants hanging over their heads only strengthened their resolve to make sure that no trail would be left concerning their movements. They needed to resolve the problem one way or another and they could only do it with the help of Mia and Zoe, so staying close to a phone to enable Drake to contact his wife was paramount.

They had already sent out communications to their contacts to establish falsified identifications papers, not only for themselves, but for Danny and his family also. It was a mission that they needed the help of Zoe Valetta, as the same contacts they were using were the same people that the esteemed lawyer had previously represented. Although Zoe didn't know it yet, she was going to become the conduit between them, the vital cog in the wheel to achieve the liberation that they now desperately required.

Danny was taken aback on how the men were working for him. They were going out on a limb, above and beyond what he had ever expected. He was overwhelmed by it and deeply expressed his gratitude.

'As you said to us one time. We need you as much as you need us,' Drake affirmed as both promised that they would do everything in their power to help Greta and his sons after Danny raised his concerns over them.

'We will get them to you,' Razor vowed with authority. 'Once we know it's safe for them to travel. We'll make sure they're on the train to your stupid heaven.' He smiled. 'You'll just have to give it a few weeks.'

The forceful sincerity emanating from the two ex-Vice Presidents was putting to bed any paranoia and mistrust that was still lingering over his two new partners. Danny had lost two close friends, one he would probably never see again, the other he *knew* he would never see again. Conversely, he had gained another two, two who he could finally put his utmost faith in, and it was a faith that he had no other option other than to believe in.

He had only known them for less than a month but his trust in them now was absolute. They had a lot in common and it was only a matter of time before it came to the surface on either side, with the last ten minutes of conversation only cementing their pact in stone. Danny walked to both and shook their hands vigorously. It was a show of unification amongst them and when Razor pronounced, 'Welcome to our new club. It starts with the three of us.' Danny had a steel of determination inside that he could now overcome all that lay ahead of him.

Drake and Razor left him alone at the breakfast table to talk with Anton over the availability of using the Riverside Hotel phone in the afternoon. It was then that Danny delved deeper into the events that they had left behind from the newspapers in front of him. He read with contrition at the loss of life and properties due to the wildfire, totally relieved that his hometown of Graceville avoided the firestorm. The newsprint pinpointed the ignition point and cause to a single car accident on Syrian Creek Road. The article printed that a body was found inside the burnt-out wreck, that of a not yet named police officer. He wondered why they never mentioned the second occupant.

'Maybe the authorities would be too embarrassed if the media and public got hold that John Pringle had escaped their clutches. Imagine the repercussions of that. Yeah, they wouldn't want that getting out. That would be the reason,' Danny assured himself.

He again focused his reading on the fire and the blame for its ignition, and despite what was written, Danny knew better than what was printed. He cast his mind back and beheld that he had the chance to distinguish the threat. Instead, he allowed his self-absorbed rage to ignore the danger and the result was catastrophic. It was another rung added to the ladder of guilt and it would be another secret he would keep deep inside.

He adjourned to the barn and began to pack his belongings, minus his little array of armoury. Anton warned him that security at the train station was as strict as ever with portable metal detectors scanning both person and luggage before they could board. They would be in another state when they crossed the Alpine River to the Twin City railway station and the lax of the law that Danny was used to in the Hexagon Valley Shire under Johnston's rule was not how it was in other parts of the country. Danny heeded Anton's advice and went without any protection on his body.

However, as he packed, Solomon's words echoed in his thoughts—there's no more a frightening feeling than a man with a gun, other than knowledge of being without one. A philosophy the President passed in conversation during his stay at *La Fortaleza*, and not being able to carry any safeguarding measures was adding to his already travelling apprehensions.

Anton helped with a suitcase that had thin inner hardened plastic liners that he could stowaway his money, hidden and unnoticeable underneath the little amount of clothes and belongings he had packed. The men had split the takings from the robbery with Drake and Razor reaping $100,000 each, the rest Danny would carry North with him which included Barny's percentage.

It was his problem on how to get it to his buddy in the future, so for now, Danny would be guarding every cent with his life. He wrapped the cash in black plastic and tied it with tight fitting rubber bands. Each wad was secured in $10,000 increments, the gold coins were covered in a silicon compound and adhered flat together in two-inch high bundles then spread out in the same rectangle shape and size the cash had been wrapped.

Danny was all ready for the trip into Twin City, they had to arrive at least thirty minutes prior to departure and time was now ticking on. He sat on the edge of his bed, restlessly and hurriedly questioning himself as he pondered his uncomfortable situation with Zoe.

Have I got some type of commitment to her now? Am I now somehow responsible for her after what happened between us? He didn't know how to react. Since the day that he had first laid eyes on Greta, Danny had never even touched another woman, let alone made wild passionate love to one and he was at a loss on what to do or say. Both Zoe and Maddy had kept him sane over the last week, gave him support, gave him solace, gave him laughs, but more importantly, gave him something for his overprotective instincts to worry about, keeping his pain and anger constrained somewhat.

Nevertheless, no matter how much affection and attachment he had towards them he had to remain focused on what lay ahead, he couldn't jeopardise it all now.

As he fixed his blank gaze into his suitcase, arms outstretched, resting his fists on the bed while he sat, wondering if he should confront Zoe before they left, a realisation began to overwhelm him. From the moment he was forced from his home, the burning knot in his stomach had never ceased and at times the pain was unbearable. Every day on the run, every muscle in his body had been aching. He had to endure a constant banging in his head, he guessed it was through lack of sleep.

This morning, however, it was all gone, and he didn't understand why. Danny felt good. He felt relaxed, at ease, there was no pain to wince at, physical ones anyway, it had all disappeared. He pondered deeper into the reasons why all his ails had left him. He then smirked to himself that maybe he released all the demons out of him last night, he just hoped that he didn't put one of them inside of Zoe.

Danny let out a big sigh and stood from his bed. Movement caught his eye through the window of the barn. It was Maddy walking across towards Anton's livestock that were meandering around the grounds. Zoe had suggested it may be a good time for her to say goodbye to her favourite animals situated around the property, chiefly one of the goats that had taken to Maddy while she was there, always following the little one around no matter where she went. Maddy loved it, and it would put a smile on everyone's face to see her interacting with the placid young doe.

After he had moved to the barn door entrance, he caught her eye as she walked. Maddy stopped, her eyes looked saddened when she began to approach him. She halted at Danny's feet then gave him a light embrace. He immediately noted that it wasn't with the same enthusiasm that she would normally give him, however, he kept up his smile as she moved away. As Danny watched Maddy walk towards the young doe, the sound of the bungalow door closing grabbed his attention.

Zoe had seen the silent hug between them. She laid the suitcases at her feet, one larger than the other. Thanks to her little shopping expeditions, Zoe had a bit to pack and was grateful that Anton had given her a suitcase large enough to hold her newly attained possessions. The smaller case was Maddy's, she had wasted no time in tidying away her limited belongings. Zoe slowly walked towards where Danny was standing, He moved away from his barn door and stepped closer to where she was coming from.

Zoe watched with a heavy heart as Maddy interacted with the animals.

'She asked me if you were going to be her new daddy, you know!' Zoe expressed.

'I can't even be a parent to my own children!' Danny said, exasperated.

They both looked at the young one from a distance, wondering what may become of her. It was then the penny dropped in Danny's mind on how much of an impact he had over his two female companions but as long as he was breathing, he never really would understand the effect he had over the woman standing next to him, and of all the people who had been entangled in the spiralling web that was Danny Pruitt, Zoe Valetta would pay the highest emotional cost.

He asked what her reply was to Maddy's vexing question.

'I told her the truth. That you already have a family. Two sons, a wife! And that you will be back with them soon. So, I told her that's it's just her and me for the time being, kiddo,' Zoe replied.

Danny could sense that Zoe's persona had changed from when they were at the breakfast table. He deduced her voice seemed a little broken when she spoke and whilst she was packing away inside her bungalow, Maddy sensed the sadness in Zoe's demeanour also.

'You love him, don't you?' she had asked.

Zoe was taken aback from the startling question; she could feel herself blush.

'Don't be silly. I love him in a different way to what you're thinking. He saved my life. He saved yours. Three times! I'm just going to miss him, that's all.'

Zoe then turned back to her suitcase and it was then that it all hit her like a sledgehammer. The same feelings she had when she entered *La Fortaleza* to find Danny was no longer there—foolishness, embarrassment, self-anger—only this time it was tenfold; the self-abasement was overwhelming.

She so much wanted to tell him how the last week had been the most exhilarating time of her life, despite the horror that she had seen. How listening to his escapades was so exciting to her. How his company unwittingly set free her true nature, fun loving, adventurous, relaxed. Traits that had been kept inside through the demands of her work and loneliness away from it. She had shut off the little voice inside of her head that had repeated over and over that it was foolhardy and lunacy to open her heart to him.

Danny had saved her life, and that she owed him everything she believed, and in those few hours she laid in his arms, she had never felt more protected and contented, sadly, she knew by heart it was a yearning that could not be reciprocated. Her emotions were running high, she didn't want to speak about how she truly felt. She was sure it would be too humiliating and embarrassing for her, luckily, Danny was about to ease her anxieties, slightly as it maybe, but enough to ease the lump in the throat that was preventing her from talking.

'I want to thank you for being there for me. Helping me through all this!' he said. 'Including last night,' Danny added with mixed emotions.

Zoe shook her head in sombre disagreement.

'I feel like I seduced you, took advantage of you. I'm sorry. I never meant for it to happen,' she guiltily apologised. 'You've got enough problems without me adding to them. I'm so embarrassed, sorry,' she again added with contrition, knowing that Danny would be holding a mountain of guilt himself.

'Don't be sorry. It was what I needed, believe me,' he reassured her, then jestingly related his theories on the exiting demons. It was a prognosis that Zoe grinned at with confused satisfaction.

'Alright! Time to get moving,' Anton called across to his visitors.

Drake and Razor had helped him harness up the rickety old carriage that Anton had built himself during his days of boredom and duly relayed to their guests that all was ready for them to depart to the station. The passenger cart doubled as a carryall and was made from a mix of timber and metal. It had a front bench seat that could sit three across with a small wooden partition separating the open 2.0m by 1.5m tray behind that had wooden bench seats to each side. Anton helped with the luggage and wryly informed Danny that there was a collared dark blue shirt waiting for him in the loungeroom of his house.

'Why do I need a shirt? What's wrong with what I'm wearing?' Danny asked.

'You're traveling first class. I got a single-berth sleeper for ya. Probably better than what you've been sleeping in this week. You gotta at least look the part,' Razor laughed as he joined them.

'First class?' Danny said surprised.

'Didn't you read your ticket?'

He scrambled his ticket out from his pocket.

'Shit! Okay then,' he mused. 'Never done that before.'

'It was the only ticket on the train that was available. All others were sold out,' Razor said.

'What about me?' Zoe asked, wondering if she would be given the comforts.

'Don't worry, you'll be travelling first class as well,' Razor eased her concerns.

'So I should,' she quipped.

Danny took his position on the front bench seat next to Anton. Zoe and Maddy sat opposite each other in the rear of the open carriage, cushions gave them comfort for their rear ends.

Drake and Razor stood by and with the guarantees, promises, handshakes, along with hugs from little Maddy, wished them luck on their journeys. They assured Zoe that she was now free of Solomon, free of the club, and also free of them if she helped with one last mission and duly gave her a wad of money to pass onto their wives to use for their plans in any way appropriate. Before they would leave however, Danny had to satisfy his curiosity on something that was bugging him from the time he entered *La Fortaleza*.

'I need to know something before I go,' he asked.

'Shoot,' said Drake.

'I need to know your real names.'

There was a brief pause of silence as Drake and Razor scanned each other.

'Just in case I read them in the obituaries, so I know it's you,' Danny shrugged with a smirk.

The stares of silence continued between the two until Drake drolly gave Danny his reply.

'We'll keep that information to ourselves until we meet again, my friend.'

Danny nodded back with a smile. He knew he probably wouldn't get an honest reply, nevertheless, he had to try.

As Anton flicked the reins to move through the gates and now out of earshot of the two men, Zoe whispered into Danny's ears that she knew the real names of his two comrades.

'I was banking on that,' Danny whispered in reply.

'Do you want me to tell you?'

'Nah, keep them to yourself for the time being. If I don't lay eyes on them within the next few weeks, I'll be calling you.'

'I'm sure you will.' Zoe smiled.

Under clear blue skies, they began the journey to the train station, traveling through the back roads that snaked into town adjacent to the Alpine River and soon Anton had steered his horse over one of the less busy bridges that crossed the river and over the border into New Banksia. Danny wanted him to take the less travelled roads, the less eyes, the less chance of recognition he figured but he was not going to get his wish.

To reach their destination, it was unavoidable to bypass the main roads that sat in the heart of Twin City. The wide-open rural city roads were busy with a frenzy of pedestrians, bike and horse riders, carts, carriages, trishaws, and rickshaws, along with the occasional automobile, all pushing and shoving around one another on their daily business.

Over enthusiastic pushbike riders were spooking horses as they dodged and weaved in front of carriages and coaches in their haste, which in turn would cause a lot of angst to the ones holding the reins. Foot patrolling and mounted police presence were noticeable as they took care of any escalating arguments that seemed to be the norm these days on the free for all roads that were travelled. Danny kept his head low and cap pulled down, touching the rim of his sunglasses.

The crowds that he wanted to avoid were in their hundreds as they reached the end of the road where Anton could go no further. A tiled and cement laid promenade nearly 400 meters long was the only path to the entrance of the train station. The picturesque streetscape had cast iron solar powered lamp poles that adorned the sides and middle of the walkthrough. Planter boxes and assorted tables and chairs sat around them.

Single-storey shops with wide glass frontages were either side of the enclosed walkway. Temporary open canvas tents of all sizes sat between the shops for pedestrians to walk through, selling anything from clothes and jewellery to furniture and tools. Danny had no option but to the run the gauntlet through the hordes of people who were either looking for a bargain from the many stalls, or vendors trying to sell a myriad of merchandise to incoming and outgoing passengers who they perceived had the money to spend. It was a hub of activity and the outlying areas of the train station was the most popular marketplace in the heart of Twin City.

Danny again lowered the peak of his cap and made sure his sunglasses were on tight before he exited his seat to give Zoe and Maddy a help down from the cart. He was taking no chances of anyone recognising him from his photo in the papers.

'Don't worry,' giggled Zoe. 'It will be okay,' she said, easing his paranoia. 'The pictures released had you clean-shaven and longer hair, not short back and side and a goatee beard, what you have now. Relax, it would be far more difficult to find one face amongst a thousand than it would be amongst ten,' she relayed with confidence.

They relayed their sincere thanks to Anton for all he had done over the last week. The gentle giant gave a wink and a salute before turning his carriage around and quickly disappear into the crowding distance.

As soon as they turned and began to walk, they could smell an extravagant array of food aromas that wafted on the breeze from the different stalls that cooked away inside the mini cafes and temporarily installed open deli annexes. Exotic cuisine smells from all over the world could be sensed up their nostrils from the multi-cultural gatherings, all simmering and cooking away over the wood and coal fired burners.

Danny started his walk towards the heritage listed railway station at a brisk pace ahead of Zoe who held Maddy's hand as the crowds thickened with every step they took. Noticing they were falling behind, Danny stopped and laid his suitcase on the ground, slung his backpack over his left shoulder then hoisted Maddy up with his right arm. Maddy adjusted herself across his back, riding piggyback style.

She knew what to do, it was the way Danny had been carrying her around at Anton's property over the last week, allowing him to have free arms as she wrapped her legs tightly above and around Danny's hips. Maddy smiled as she clasped her arms around his neck from behind. Danny was in protective parenting mode, guarding the little one from being knocked over from the hustling hordes. He immediately got flashbacks to when he would do the same with his own two boys with Greta in hot pursuit when they visited the Graceville markets or at a venue with large crowds.

Mercifully for Danny, only having one little monkey on his back was far easier work than having his twin male monkeys wriggling and pushing at each other as they almost strangled him in the process.

Progressing up the promenade, the tightness of the people moving in both directions forced them to turn their bodies sideways at times, evading chairs and tables strewn outside each food stall they passed. Danny moved as quick as he could, lugging his case with his left hand while Maddy bounced on his back from his hasty twisting and turning. Frustrated at the pace Danny had set and struggling with her inch and a half boot heels and large suitcase that she towed behind her, Zoe laboured to keep up.

Her attention would be taken by the scents and aromas from the perfumes and incense from the nearby stalls across the promenade. At times it would overpower the array of flavours that the many different food types gave off and the more she looked to where they were wafting from, the more she lagged behind until eventually, to her surprise and gladness, Danny suddenly stopped.

What Zoe couldn't see was Maddy pushing at Danny shoulders pointing to a food stall to their left. Danny turned his face to the little one and couldn't resist her smiling pleas to indulge in the edibles that were on offer, particularly the crispy fried chicken pieces that sat behind the glass of a Bain-marie.

Although Maddy couldn't hear, she could certainly see, and she could certainly smell, more so than the average person, and Danny thought that she was a girl of his own heart when she sniffed out the fried chicken.

He was always a sucker for some crispy southern fried chicken pieces. It had been a while since he chomped down on some greasy crispy fowl, and thanks to Maddy, he was not going to let this opportunity pass. The giant fast food chains such as KFC and McDonalds had closed their doors long ago, much to the enormous mortification of the masses who relied on the fast food outlets in their once busy and self-absorbed lives. Although Greta could cook up Danny his favourite fried chicken as good as anyone he knew, he would secretly joke to his friends she had nothing on the secret herb and spices that KFC produced, his favourite vice when it came to fast food.

Without hesitation, he lowered Maddy to the ground, delved deep into his pocket for some change and bought five pieces of the spice and seasoned covered chicken that was returned in a large brown paper bag. They both chowed down on their pieces with delight, Zoe declining an offer from Danny to nibble on a piece herself as she watched on confused, knowing that he was on a mission get to the platforms as quick as possible, yet now taking the time to stop for something to eat. The smiles of pleasure that consumed both Danny and Maddy's faces as they proudly scoffed down their delicacies was a sight to behold and made the unannounced break more than worthwhile for Zoe.

Happily wiping away their greasy fingertips on the side of their pants, content that their taste buds had been satisfied, the trio continued through the hustle and bustle for another 100 meters until they reached the large roundabout at the base of the station building at the top of the promenade. Inside the roundabout was a garden bed full of many different colours of roses, along with lavender plants sprawling across the foot of the bed, another cast iron solar powered lamp pole stood in the middle.

The crowds had thinned out and Danny could see that the uniformed station guards were to the fore assuring that no vendors, buyers or any undesirables such as beggars and vagabonds would impede or annoy the valued travellers entering in and out of the station. Danny lowered Maddy to the ground again as he observed the surroundings with his cautious and mistrustful eyes.

The exterior of the Twin City railway station was grand Victorian style that had many restorations over the years. It had a large central clocktower with four covered projecting verandas either side with single storey buildings attached at the ends. The building was made from large cream and dark red bricks supported by double cast iron columns. Inside, its awnings covered the length of the 450m platforms on both sides, a pedestrian overpass crossed the rail lines 50m down from the entrance to board the north bound train.

Security was at the ready as the three walked up the half dozen steps to gain entry to the platforms. Groups of people were to the front and behind as they approached, Danny trying to be casual as he could be, small talking with Zoe. With sunglasses on, he took off his cap and gave a nod of respect towards the standing guards. He immediately noticed that the holster on one the security guards was unclipped. He zeroed in on it, if he were to be recognised in any way and the situation were to deteriorate, it was what he would go for, he was not going to be taken.

Danny silently breathed a huge sigh of relief when the first two security guards let them pass without incident. They passed another duo of guards atop of the stairs at the station house entrance without so much of a look, then quickly found themselves at the window to have their tickets stamped. So much for the warning that Anton gave them about strict security. Maybe it was the company Danny was with that let him pass, a beautiful elegant woman with a young child, or maybe it was Anton's lovely borrowed collared shirt that made him look like he had never committed a misdemeanour in his life. Whatever it was, Danny didn't care, as long he passed.

The platform was busy with arriving passengers and station workers passing by with trolleys and carts loaded with goods to be re-stocked as both north and south bound trains sat idling before resuming their trips. They slowly walked down until they found the number of the carriage that Zoe and Maddy would board, first class number XPT004, fifth carriage down from the front of the diesel-powered engines.

'Well! I guess this it then.' Zoe sighed.

'Yep, I guess it is. Everything secured?' Danny added, referring to the large amount of money he gave her for safe keeping when the time came to help with

Barny and Harry's legal defence and any costs to do with his family. But just as importantly, the funds to get Maddy her much needed cochlear implant. Danny's enquiry was answered with assurance from Zoe that he needn't worry, all was safe and secure.

'There's something else,' he sheepishly asked.

He pulled out four envelopes out of his front pocket.

'I suppose you want me to get them to your wife?'

Zoe knew that they were letters to Greta. She was wise to the fact he had been writing to her all week and knew that he was wanting her to deliver them. It was a task that she had no misgivings about previously, however, after last night's steamy rendezvous, she hesitantly replied that it might not be a good idea under the circumstances.

'I don't want to meet your wife. I could never face her. I'll take them, but I'll give them to Mia to pass on,' she strongly suggested.

'Okay,' nodded Danny. 'I understand. But I thought lawyers of your ilk didn't *have* a conscience,' he mockingly added.

'How dare you!' Zoe smiled agape, greeting the comment with a light slap to his face.

It was hard for Danny to say goodbye, more so for Zoe, and even harder for Maddy. As the adults quietly discussed what may lay ahead for them, Zoe looked down to see Maddy had saddening tears in her eyes. She knelt to communicate with her as Danny watched on, naïve to what was being translated.

'What's she saying?' Danny asked as Zoe stood upright, worried by the look Maddy portrayed.

'She's afraid she will never see you again,' Zoë lamented.

It was a striking bolt that immediately pulled on Danny's heartstrings. He instantly felt guilty sadness for Maddy. He knelt before her, held her hand and with help from Zoe communicated with a brave face.

'It might take one week, it might take one month, it may take one year, but I will see you again, Maddy. You are the bravest and most beautiful young lady I have ever met and until that time, you will always be here,' Danny expressed, bringing his fist to his heart. 'I will always remember you, no matter what!'

He reached into his pocket and produced a gold coin then took Maddy's right hand. The coin was the first he had taken from the strongboxes that were taken in the heist when they began their counting. He would have it with him always, inscribing miscellaneous shapes that meant nothing to him into the bark of trees or on top of wooden tables and logs, or subconsciously twiddling with it between his fingers, a habit that both Zoe and Maddy had often joked around with him during their time together. To Danny, whether he knew it or not, it just made a useful replacement for the rings that were no longer on his fingers when he would get nervous or fidgety.

'This is my lucky coin,' he said to Maddy. 'I take it everywhere with me. Without it, I would be lost, and we would've never become friends.'

He laid it on Maddy's palm and closed her fist around it then wrapped both his hands over hers.

'I want you to take it. I want you look after it until I see you next. It's know you're lucky coin, okay!' smiled Danny.

He embraced her as tightly as he could. Of all the tragedies and turmoil that had been bestowed upon him over the last month, the sorrow he felt in his heart made all that had preceded him be forgotten as tears welled in his own eyes. He disentangled himself from the elongated embrace as the call came over the loudspeakers for Marlboro bound passengers to board. He looked at Zoe with yielding eyes and gave her a light hug and thanked her once more.

'You know the address up North. Write to me,' he softly said.

'I will.' Zoe nodded. 'Good luck. I hope everything turns out for you, Danny. I'll be praying for you,' she softly spoke, refusing eye contact with him as she ran her palm across his cheek before entering the carriage.

Danny slung his backpack on and grabbed the handle of his suitcase. He gave the same wave to Maddy as the one she gave him the first time he laid eyes on her the morning after the storm. Danny turned away with empty feelings encumbering him as he made his way to the overpass that crossed the rail line to board his northbound train.

Within 20 minutes, he found himself in his single-berth sleeper, ready for the eight-and-a-half-hour journey to the city of Newhaven, the coastal capital of the state of New Banksia. There he would have to wait another four hours while passengers disembarked, and others boarded before the train resumed its journey. It would then be a fourteen-hour trip further north until he arrived mid-afternoon in the northern state of Capricornia and the city of Burbank, twenty-six hours after he first stepped foot on the interstate locomotive.

From there it was up to him to figure out how he would travel the extra 340km to his heaven. It was an unknown burden he accepted as long it got him as far away as possible from the Venturian police force and Assistant Commissioner Martin Conroy.

After being shown the amenities and fittings in his sleeper berth by a young well-groomed gentleman who was employed by the rail company, Danny took his seat inside and nervously pondered what lay ahead. His thoughts were interrupted as the sound of blaring horns echoed throughout the station as the southbound train slowly exited on its way to Marlboro with Zoe and Maddy on board. He hoped and stressed that all would work out for them, for all their sake.

Within fifteen minutes, he was northbound himself and off into the unknown and although his quarters were tightly spaced, he was impressed by his surroundings. He had his private bathroom which included toilet and shower, with the latter he was looking forward to standing under. His room had a large comfortable couch that was covered in plush blue upholstery, which doubled as his bed.

Storage compartments sat above and opposite where he could lay his suitcase and light switches that were powered by the train's generators. He playfully switched them on and off, remembering the good old days when they used work in his own home. 'Thanks Razor. You done good,' he smirked with satisfaction.

The cabin's door could be locked from the inside with curtains that could be drawn when you needed privacy, a sure thing for Danny. A dining room awaited down the corridor if he chose to indulge, all paid for by the ticket that his comrade had purchased. It was a far cry from what he had been used to over the last month, swapping between the earth, sleeping bags, stretchers and hay filled mattresses trying to get an ounce of sleep.

Danny was content with his traveling quarters; he pulled out a 500ml bottle of whiskey from his suitcase that Anton had gifted him and added some ice and cola that was in the bar fridge. He made himself comfortable on the couch, pulled out an arm rest and took a swig from his glass, acknowledging inside that his goal was within grasp.

Pensively, he also knew that his personal battle of survival was only half completed and his fight for freedom would not be won until he had his wife and sons by his side in a place called Heaven. Until then, he would be on full alert, never letting his guard down, with or without a weapon by his side, as the next person who passed his presence, could be the person that could bring it all tumbling down.

Zoe and Maddy's quarters were similar, except for the double bunks which expanded out of the side wall. Maddy was happy with the facilities as she made herself comfortable on the top bunk for their six-hour trip, reading and drawing on some magazines that her unofficial guardian had purchased for her. Zoe sat below her on the bottom bunk. She had her back up against the wall with her knees folded up to her chest. She had flicked her heeled boots off and twirled her toes. She looked at her handbag which contained Danny's letters to his wife, one of the envelopes was protruding out of the unclosed zip.

'Should I look?' she pondered. 'No, I shouldn't! They're private.' She looked at them again. 'No, it would be wrong!' However, her curiosity was overpowering when it came to Danny and when she looked again a few seconds more, she couldn't resist.

She opened the last writings that Danny had enveloped and started to read his words with adoration. The unadulterated and pure emotion that Danny expressed to Greta was compelling to her. The outpouring of love, commitment and loneliness that his words relayed touched Zoe immensely the more she would read, and when she read Danny's line to Greta on how he had felt her last night, the tears started to filter down her cheeks. She didn't know whether she was crying for the separated love they both shared, and whether she was crying for herself, knowing it was a love she could never have.

She didn't want her time with Danny to be just a memory, she wanted more, she needed more. Even though it had only been the shortest of time, no one had ever affected her like he had done, and the truth of the matter was she could never divulge her time with him to anyone. That would give away her involvement. Maybe she could tell her mother about it, she was always there for when she had to destress over love and private work-related issues, but this was something entirely different, one which she had to keep within herself.

However, if it wasn't clear before, the words she was now reading left no doubt that she could never have what she desired. No matter how hard the emotions wretched away inside of her, she had made a commitment to him, and it was a commitment that she would follow through. She believed in him, his crusade, his narrative, and she would do everything in her power to see that Danny Pruitt would live a long life with his family.

As she looked through the windows of the train before they departed and saw him take the steps up and over the station overpass, she surely believed it would be the last time she would ever lay eyes on him again.

Chapter 42

'This is it!'
 'Number six?'
 'Yeah.'
 'I hope she's alone.'
 'Looks pretty quiet.'
 'What if she's not home?'
 'She will be. She hardly goes outside anymore apparently.'
 'Don't blame her! I would hate to be in her shoes.'

Mia and Candice had just arrived at the top of the street, they were in search of Greta. They arrived on a single horse-drawn two-seated buggy and were nervous about meeting the wife of their husbands' new ally. Mia had arrived at work at 3.00 pm for her duties at the hospital only to immediately answer a phone call from her husband.

She instantly informed her superiors that her son was ill, a lie she told to enable her to exit and carry out the instructions given by Drake; her nursing friend Kristy would cover for her. Both Mia and Candice, who had been taking care of Mia's son, had been paid a visit again by the police earlier in the morning. Inspector Vaccaro was again probing on the whereabouts of their Vice President husbands as nothing had pinpointed them to be amongst the victims at la Fortaleza as investigations continued.

An attractive lady with large smiling brown eyes, Candice was now five months pregnant with Razor's child. She had long dark hair with a deep crimson tint across her wavy fringe and tips. She had jewelled piercings that ran up the entire rim of her left ear to go with several in her right. Candice would always put on a smiling friendly persona to everyone she would meet; however, it belied the fact that on the interior she was as tough as nails who had a hard core to her. She was as loyal to her husband as a wife could be and when the police came visiting once more, the Inspector and his partners saw first-hand that Candice was not always friendly and affable.

'You tell me where they are?' she roasted. 'We haven't seen them. Do your fuckin job and we'll all know if they're alive or not?'

With help from Mia, they were convincing in their masquerade that they were two wives who were agonising over the unknown. Their façade was enough to satisfy the Inspector that they were none the wiser when it came to the whereabouts of their husbands and couldn't help with their investigations as there were still over a dozen bodies yet to be identified from the aftermath, a reality that Vaccaro respectfully informed the ladies about, along with the possibility that the bodies of the two Vice Presidents may lay amongst them, so until then, Inspector Vaccaro had no option but to believe what the women angrily relayed.

It was 5.30 pm when Mia and Candice arrived atop of the street. Mia's elderly female neighbour would take care of her son until they returned. The smoke haze that had descended across Graceville in the benign conditions since the fire had all but disappeared thanks to a brisk southerly breeze which blew it back over the mountain ranges. Nevertheless, townsfolk were still wary of the fires in case the temperature and winds predictably started to rise again, so in the meantime, as weather conditions suited, fire crews and volunteers were hard at work doing their best to stamp out any potential flare ups.

Mia gave a flick of the reins and started their slow travel towards Corey and Sarah's house and within a few strides halted the horse once more when they noticed movement outside of the house.

Greta was taking advantage of her solitude as well-wishers were no longer descending on the house after hearing that Danny had perished. It had been over twenty-four hours since Sgt Dane Grainger came visiting and it didn't take long for the news to spread that lives had been lost up in the mountains, the outlaw Danny Pruitt being one of them.

People had been coming and going since lunchtime to give their condolences, friendly and respectful measures that Greta was struggling with, trusting that Danny was far from dead. She deduced that the more she spoke or faced her supporters, the more chance she might give away what she really knew, and she was taking no risk on anyone becoming remotely suspicious.

Those who politely questioned her reaction were told by Sarah that there was nothing in the textbook that tells you on how to grieve for a loved one. Greta would quickly accept the visitor's sympathies and condolences then quietly adjourn to her room with her sons as Corey and Sarah entertained the well-wishers.

Greta had kept both Darcy and Daniel at home, regretting she ever allowed them to go to school the day before. With so much on her mind, it never dawned on her that her two boys may be victimised because of the events over the last month. Their first day at school was met with whispered comments and stares from teachers and adults alike with the teasing and taunts from the children about their murdering and outlawed father. The boys arrived home after school in tears, not understanding what was being said about their loving dad, and by the end of the day, tormented that their daddy had been shot and burnt, were almost inconsolable. Kids can be so cruel.

Greta had a long and tearful night protecting and reassuring her vulnerable young sons, passively enforcing that all that was said was just lies and vicious stories that people had made up, continuing the line that Daddy had just gone away for a while. With all the mothers love she had within, she cradled and cuddled her boys until they finally fell asleep beside her. As morning came with all the well-wishers, she had to protect the boys from hearing what was being said about their father. She demanded Corey and Sarah not to mention Danny's name in front of them and made sure that both Darcy and Daniel were away from earshot and enclosed in her bedroom away from the mourning visitors.

Greta needed some fresh air and whilst Sarah cared for her boys, decided to walk across to the adjacent parklands to gather her thoughts. Mia and Candice slowly edged their way in the direction where Greta was heading after they saw her exit the front yard. Greta crossed the road, walked through the grassy paddock of the park then took her position alone on the swing set. The ladies stepped down from the buggy, tied the reins to a gumtree on the edge of the park and started to walk towards where Greta was seated. Her hair was out, flowing on the stiff breeze across her face. She wore jeans, a dark sweater and her favourite fawn strapped sandals. She had her feet on the ground, hands clasped together on her lap and head down, slowly pushing herself back and forth in another world, she didn't notice that she was about to have company.

'Excuse me!' said Mia.

Greta looked up surprised to see the two ladies standing there. Mia wore a long dark blue woollen overcoat jacket to cover her nurses' uniform. Candice was wearing thick black leg ins, a light-coloured T-shirt with an open leather jacket, well-used work boots on her feet.

'Hi, my name is Mia. This is Candice.'

Candice leant over and shook Greta's hand.

'Yes, I've seen you. You're a nurse at the hospital, aren't you?'

'Yes, that's right.'

Greta stood to her feet.

'Can I help you with anything?' she asked.

Mia was straight to the point. 'I saw you visit Barny yesterday,' she said.

'You know Barny?' Greta quizzed suspiciously.

'Only recently.'

'How do you know him?

'I met him through your husband.'

'How? How do you know Danny?' Greta delved, concerned in what direction the conversation was heading.

Mia could sense the agitation in Greta. She had to be blunt and honest from this point on if anything were to be achieved. With subtlety, she said that she had first met Danny up at La Fortaleza while mending his wounds and that she had also met Ricky and Harry.

The women now had Greta's full attention as her memory twigged through Danny's personal written accounts.

'We need to know what Barny said to you,' Mia continued.

'he told me Danny's dead. Shot, then burnt in the fire. What do you think he told me!' defied Greta.

'He didn't tell you anything otherwise. I visited him before you did and gave him some information.' Mia coerced, tilting her head to the side in a pleading motion.

'What's this all about?' Greta asked. She could sense that the women knew more than what they were telling. Her heart started to pound nervously.

'Please! If he said anything else, we really need to know. If not, we will walk away. But if he did, you need to tell us now,' Candice subtly enforced.

'Who are you?'

'My husband is Drake; Candice's husband is Razor.'

'This means nothing to me. I don't know them!'

'They're the Vice Presidents of Sultans. I'm sure you know where your husband has been recently. I'll say again. What did Barny say?' Mia repeated.

'Please,' Candice urged. 'Time is very crucial here. We need you to be honest if you ever want to see your husband again.'

'You know he's alive?' Greta asked, wide-eyed and nonplussed.

'Yes, and so do you. Is that what Barny told you?'

'Yes,' confessed Greta. 'Where is he? Where's my Danny?'

'Your husband's been with ours for the last week. They've been up on the border. I was the one who informed Barny that your husband was alive,' Mia affirmed. 'Your Danny is on a train heading North as we speak.'

Greta's knees weakened. Everything was surreal to her. It was if the world had been lifted off her shoulders. Although she believed what Barny had told her, there was still a lot of doubt that circled in her mind, however, with the sincerity of truth coming from Mia and Candice, an overwhelming feeling of relief and delight started to consume her.

Mia explained that she had spoken to Drake only hours before, and with a smile, knowing what it would mean to Greta, again confirmed that Danny was on his way to a place called Heaven and that she would be with him soon. Continuing in a serious and important tone, Mia advised that before the reunion could happen, there was something that had to be accomplished.

She asked Greta if the authorities had come to retrieve any DNA yet.

'No, not yet. Dane, the Sergeant, he's a friend of ours. He told me this morning that they will be here tomorrow lunchtime.'

Mia and Candice gave each other a relieved and hopeful eye. They were to meet Zoe tomorrow at 12.00 pm at the Hillwood train station, the halfway point on the rail line between the city and Graceville. All going well, they would be back in town by 1.00 pm. With them on return would be the cash that the men had given to Zoe to help with the impending payoff to make the DNA switch possible.

'Good!' said Mia. 'Don't change anything. Let them take it. We'll take care of the rest.'

Greta didn't understand. The DNA retrieval had her worried no end. If Barny was right, whose body did they have? She worried it would all be exposed when the sample came back, however, the reassurance she received from the Vice Presidents wives would allay her fears. Mia and Candice jointly advised that the men had a plan, and she was not to worry about a thing. The less she knew the better they urged, and gently enforced she had to trust them if she and her two boys where to see Danny again. It was stern council that Greta excitedly accepted without hesitance.

The women could see that Greta was worried and confused. They felt for her immensely, all the tribulations she'd had to endure.

'I know this is hard for you,' Candice consoled. 'I know we've only just met but we're all in this together. *Our* husbands are under threat as well. We've been wanting to get away from the club for a while now and your Danny has given us that opportunity. They're working as a team and so must we.' She smiled.

Greta nodded her head. She could feel a sense of ease towards the women, a sense of trust, something she hadn't felt since her husband's dramas began.

'We're meeting Miss Valetta tomorrow at Hillwood,' said Mia. 'My husband said that Danny was going to give some letters to her to give to you. I'm sure he'll explain everything in his own words when you read them.'

Greta was overjoyed to know that she would be reading Danny's words again. Her eyes lit up upon the news, in turn raising smiles to both Mia and Candice. Her curiosity did get the better of her though about who this Miss Valetta was and asked appropriately.

'She's the club lawyer. She's been with the men since they escaped the fire with a little girl called Maddy. Drake said the club had her locked up in one of the bedrooms. They were going to leave her to die in the fire, but your Danny saved her, *and* Maddy apparently. Bit of a hero, your husband!' Mia said buoyantly.

'So I've heard,' Greta proudly replied.

Greta's memory was jolted on who Zoe Valetta was after she remembered her conversation with Inspector Vaccaro when he visited several nights ago and relayed her knowledge to the women.

'Can we meet you here tomorrow?' Mia asked.

'No. I won't be here. I'm moving to my sister-in-law's,' Greta informed. 'I was going to wait until they collected the DNA, then go to Kate's place.'

Greta didn't want to face anymore well-wishers, she needed to get away from the visitors knowing her inability to deceive would be too risky for her to carry on with the deception. She advised the ladies that she would be there by 1.00pm and passed on the address to them. Although Greta was eternally in debt to the kindness and friendship that Corey and Sarah had given her during her neediest hour, it was Kate whom she had to be with.

She was Danny's only next of kin. Kate needed to know he was alive, she deserved to know. She was just as devasted as Greta was on losing her older brother, that she knew, and there was no doubt in her mind that her sister in-law would keep the secret well and truly embedded. It would also give Greta the colossal opportunity to release her own relief and excitement of the imposing burden that she had been carrying, and within twenty-four hours, Kate's world, just as Greta's had done, would be turned upside down all for the better.

Greta had a bounce in her step as she returned to the house. The lingering doubts that plagued her had been put to bed by the meeting with the Vice Presidents' wives. Naively or not, she could finally foresee an end to the nightmare that had taken over her life. She left the ladies with more than appreciative gratitude and thanked them accordingly.

Mia and Candice were all too pleased to be the bearer of good news, also thankful themselves that they got to Greta in time. Greta entered the house and gave her twin boys the tightest loving squeeze a mother could give before retiring to her bedroom as Corey and Sarah looked on bewildered at her noticeable change, to afraid and reluctant to ask the reasons why. Being in mourning can work in mysterious ways they pondered to one another as they watched Greta disappear to her room.

Mia and Candice returned to their buggy, happy that the first part of the elaborate plan had been fulfilled and soon Mia had dropped off Candice to retrieve her son.

'I'll be about an hour. Meet you back at my place,' she said.

'Good luck,' Candice replied. 'See you then.'

Mia was off to execute the second part of the plan, a visit to the mother of Teeto's son. After a twenty-five-minute journey she found herself in the worst part of town, the very so-called slums that Danny had taken his buddies through on their way to the Depot hotel over a month ago.

She nervously alighted the buggy and tethered the reins to the single birch tree that gave shade over the nature strip. Car bodies, pushbikes and disposed household rubbish cluttered the surroundings. Two under nourished horses were stabled in the open carport adjoining the house, the stench was noticeable from the manure and rubbish.

Mia approached the door with her carry bag over her shoulder. Inside was her medical equipment along with personal items. She knocked on the door to be greeted by Issy, a twenty-year-old ice dependent user who was not looking her best at this time. With her inside the house was her mother, her grandparents, two sisters and three other young children other than her own. Issy was surprised to see Mia at the door, she wasn't expected until the end of next week for the children's regular check-ups and asked what she was doing at the house.

'Sorry to bother you, Issy,' Mia politely said. 'I'm just following up from my last visit. There's nothing to worry about but I would like to take some blood from young Tommy just to put my own mind at ease. I'm sure he's okay, but I want to make sure.

'A few children around town have been diagnosed with some type of new virus. The early symptoms were similar to what Tommy was going through the other week so I thought I would do the right thing and give him a test to clear him if it's okay with you. I think it's important to get it done, but as I said, nothing to worry about, it's just to ease both our conscience. We've got lab technicians at the hospital next week so I thought I would make the most of it. We should have the results by next Wednesday or Thursday.'

Issy allowed Mia inside without hesitation. She was always appreciative of the nurses helping with the children and mustered her son to the loungeroom. With help from Issy, Mia, with all her nursing experience, cheerily explained the procedure to the half-frightened young child and within a few minutes had a sample secured in her blood vial, and when Issy ventured to the kitchen and offered Mia a cup of coffee after her son nonchalantly asked if it was all over, Mia seized the chance to gain a mouth swab from the inner cheeks of young Tommy before anyone inside the house would notice.

    She quickly stored the two vials in her medical bag then patted the young fellow on the head and joined Issy in the kitchen. Mia quickly sipped down her coffee and politely made an excuse to depart the premises, proudly, but nervously content that the next step had been completed successfully. Mia knew though, it would all mean nothing if the next mission were to fail, and that she would have to wait until tomorrow.

Chapter 43

'Excuse me, mate! How long until we get to Burbank?'
'We are right on schedule, sir. We should be there right on 2.00 pm.'
'Thanks buddy!'
'Is there anything I can help you with?'
'Nah! All good.'

Danny closed the door to his sleeper, sat back on his seat and poured the last contents out of his whiskey bottle into his glass. He peered out the window of the fast-speeding train and saw billboards welcoming people to the state of Capricornia. Twenty-four hours had passed since the train had left Twin City and Danny was almost at the end of his journey. He had hardly left his quarters during that time, only once venturing out to the dining carriage for dinner the previous night and for a quick breakfast this morning.

He enjoyed a T-Bone steak with mash and vegies topped with mushroom sauce the night before as he sat alone on a table for two hidden away in the corner of the carriage. A widescreen television was operational inside the diner which had most people's attention, a sight that Danny had not seen in nearly three years. Travelers entranced themselves at the screen as they watched and listened to the news bulletin.

Talk show hosts were interviewing guests from government and infrastructure on the ongoing and future plans along with the progress of works taking place around the nation, Danny happy that no glancing peers were coming his way. The outlook was overwhelmingly positive the television news hosts conveyed which was sending a buoyant mood throughout the dining guests. There was no mention of the Syrian Creek fire or the shocking siege at La Fortaleza, the only news that Danny was concerned about.

He'd had plenty of time to think on his travels as he watched the landscape pass by his window, never really taking in the countryside's scenic beauty. From the tall mountain ranges in the distance to the river crossings and to the large rural towns and the vast expanses of grazing and pastural lands.

He spent the four-hour stopover at Newhaven in his sleeper, only venturing out amongst the peoples to have a cigarette or two in the smoker's area of the undercover platform, trying his hardest not to converse with anyone. During his nighttime sleep he tried to take Zoe's advice on concentrating on the good things, instead, the toll of listening through the silence of the bush as he strived to outwit the law, the screeching and roaring sound of the wildfire and the sounds of gunshots still echoed across his sub conscious before two hours of sleep would pass.

Although the chilling sweats were no longer with him, he continually awoke from his interrupted sleep. Tears of loneliness would come and go as he grappled with the perception that he was in a world of nowhere. He ascertained he no longer had any friends. The ones he left behind could never know he was alive and the ones he may make in the future, if he still had a future, he would have to live a lie to. He thought of Sarah as it all started to sink in.

They were as close as a male and female could be without the intimacy, she must be feeling devastated on hearing the news that he had died, not to mention Kate, his beloved younger sister. He thought of Corey, he forgave him for what he had done and completely understood the circumstances that involved his close friend in the re-po squad, how would he be feeling Danny thought with sadness. He thought of Damien, Benny, and all the others who had helped in his plight, deeply annoyed that he would never be able to thank them in person. What ate at his soul the most was that he no longer considered himself to be the loyal and faithful husband. Because of things he had done, he foresaw with angered sorrow that he could he never again look Greta in the eye.

What example had he set for his two boys, he lamented. What if they read about him in the future, surely, they would retain memories of what had transpired over the last month, and what about the psychological stress they would have to endure if they were forced to change their names, they would want to know why wouldn't they?

He bashed himself that Greta could never know about his night with Zoe. If she found out, he couldn't live with himself, it would give him reason to end it all. He conceitedly fathomed that he was the only one capable of doing it, everyone else's bullet couldn't do the job, they weren't even capable of grazing him. He gave deep thought to the slayings of all four of the Devlin brothers. No matter how hard he pushed himself to feel repentance, he would feel no remorse, the same with Sandilands and Slacek, the road to purgatory would never be travelled because of them. He stared into empty space around his sleeper and serenely calculated that maybe he *was* the cold-blooded killer Solomon and the Minister's press release made him out to be.

Danny's was equal to his lowest ebb emotionally as he pondered his future. Irrespective of what bombastic negative thoughts that entrenched his idle mind as the train neared its destination, 1400km away to the south of him, things were in motion that, had he known, would instantly reverse his state of mind.

Mia, in the company of Candice had already arrived back in Graceville from their planned meet with Zoe at the Hillwood railway station. Maddy and her had arrived in the city the previous evening, nervous but unscathed, and happy to be back in familiar surroundings, Maddy bunking in Zoe's spare room in her apartment. Zoe played the role of both friend and counsellor as Maddy tried to come to terms with the loss of her father.

Although Zoe despised Solomon, she knew that he loved his daughter as any doting father did; nevertheless, she was still angrily trying to comprehend how he could've put Maddy at risk the way he did. This was despite the ringing words still lingering in her ears from the Presidents tirade that it was her that put her in danger by arriving at the compound in the first place. After a lot of tears and cuddling before sleep the night before, both Zoe and Maddy were up early the following morning and dashing off to her office to show her face to her colleagues and get a catch up on work issues before she would make her way to the central station and board the outgoing train with Maddy by her side.

The three women had only ten minutes to converse when they met after arriving at the Hillwood Railway Station. The City and Graceville bound trains sat idling, waiting for the driver and carriage security changeover and safety checks to proceed before they would swap trains and venture back from whence, they came. If they happened to miss it for any reason, both parties would have to wait a further 90 minutes before the next crowded trains passed so the urgency of the conversation was sharp and to the point. They met in the busy pedestrian tunnel underneath the rail line that gave access between platforms.

Mia had met Zoe on more than one occasion when up at la Fortaleza or at brief meetings on behalf of her husband regarding legal matters. She was also familiar with Maddy and was pleased to see the little one. As for Candice, it was the first time that she had met the reputable lawyer as Razor was insistent that he keep his wife away from club business, and on first impressions, Candice begrudgingly mused to herself on the reasons why the club used her talents.

Zoe handed over the correspondence entrusted to her by the men along with Danny's letters to Greta. Also changing hands at the bottom of a zipped up small brown leather handbag was several wads of cash wrapped tightly in black plastic. Zoe did her best to answer questions from the ladies regarding the welfare of their husbands in the short time they had, advising the ladies that all they would want to know would probably be in the letters they now had with them. Zoe wanted the meeting to be over as quickly as possible. She wanted to put any public association with the Sultans MC behind her and relayed that her and Maddy were thankful their ordeal was finally over. Her only priority for the time being was to look after the wellbeing of her little friend, and of that, she was far from being sure on how to progress with.

Mia and Candice were both back in Graceville by 1.00pm and were hurriedly heading to Kate's house as time was now of the essence. On arrival at the station, they retrieved their horse and buggy from the recently built nearby stables where station attendants had been looking after them for a small fee while they were gone. Once they were back in the seats of the buggy, they had soon arrived at Kate's hoping that Greta was true to her word and had relocated to her sister in law's abode.

Their nervous angst was put at ease when Greta walked from the front door to greet them before they could exit the buggy, the excited anticipation of hearing from Danny was glaringly obvious across her face. Greta had spent an anxious morning waiting for Dane and Inspector Vaccaro to arrive to retrieve the DNA samples. They were in the company of the lead Detective appointed from the city office who had taken over the taskforce that oversaw the aftermath at La Fortaleza.

Young Daniel would be the test subject selected for the forensic representatives. They arrived at midday as Dane had promised and from the time they arrived and departed, the process would take no longer than fifteen minutes. Greta stood around quietly throughout, arms folded, fidgety and restless, reticent to engage in conversation as the visiting party relayed and repeated their condolences and apologies as they waited for the samples to be taken. The only time she spoke a sentence was to reassure her son.

Earlier she had informed Corey and Sarah of her decision to move herself to Kate's, reasoning that she no longer wanted to be seen by well-wishers and gracefully asked not to divulge to anyone where she was going. Both Corey and Sarah found it hard to feel anything else other than their declared deception and involvement in the repossession squad being the purpose for her departure.

'Did you meet her?' Greta asked with bated breath.

They gave a smile of acknowledgment as they moved towards her. Mia then delved into the small handbag and retrieved a handful of envelopes that contained Danny's letters along with one of the plastic wrappers that contained some cash.

'These are for you,' Mia smiled broadly.

Greta quickly broke the seal of one of the envelopes and raised the folded paper to get a glimpse, she immediately recognised that it was Danny's handwriting. With blissful tears welling in her eyes, she gave both Mia and Candice an embrace full of gratitude. 'Thank you, thank you,' she whispered as she held the writings in her hands.

As much as Mia and Candice wanted to share Greta's joy, they subtly warned that there were still more things that had to fall into place before a reunion would be possible, advice that Greta undoubtably knew herself.

With a truckload of anxiety, Greta asked what was to happen next.

'You do nothing. As we said, the men have a plan and we have to trust it, and it's what I'm going to help with right now. In the meantime, just go about being the grieving wife and we'll be in touch during the week. I know you want to be with him, but you must remain patient. You've waited so long, I'm sure you can handle another week or two. I'm sorry, but it's the way it's got to be!' Mia answered with sympathy.

As Mia finished her reply, both Candice and she noticed that Kate was exiting her front door about to join them. They took it as their cue to depart.

'Hang in there, Greta,' Candice smiled, 'we'll be in touch soon.'

As the women departed, Greta led Kate back inside the house after she suspiciously asked who their visitors were. After taking a minute for herself to partly read one of the letters, confirming in her overstrung mind that they were no doubt Danny's words she was reading, Greta disclosed to Kate who Mia and Candice were, and why they had paid the visit.

Greta and Kate excitedly read through Danny's heartfelt words and faithful instructions relating his absolute trust in Mia and Candice, stressing in words that she must follow their lead in whatever they do and ask of her. During this time and unbeknown to them, Mia had arrived at the Graceville hospital; the last leg of her mission was about to be put into action.

With the lure of $5,000 cash, Mia confronted Jimmy, the twenty-year veteran of Graceville hospital security and now leading operator. One of Jimmy's tasks was to oversee the entries and exits of the laboratory that stored medical evidence, equipment, drugs, and more importantly, DNA vials. Through gossip and not so hidden paperwork, Mia had found out that the Pruitt's were not the only one that the forensics team were in town for. Families of the deceased from the raging inferno, not only from MC members from La Fortaleza, but other parts of the ravished district who were unfortunate enough to be trapped by the wildfire, were also to be paid a visit for identification purposes.

The protocol was that for after each individual sample was taken, it was to be escorted by police back to the hospital lab for preservation and security measures. Mia knew that the first port of call was going to be Greta and it would take the best part of the afternoon for the rest to be gathered. Jimmy was well liked by hospital employees, particularly the nurses, whose safety depended on him from the drug-fuelled angry visitors and patients which was very much the norm these days.

Jimmy was an acquaintance of Drake and held the Vice President in high esteem. They talked often when he would visit his on-duty wife regarding his employment tasks as Drake had experience in the field. Jimmy's appearance belied his age. He was 43 years with an already greying beard and sides. He had a wrinkled face and stooped shoulders which made him out to be a lot older than what he was.

Mia had formed a firm relationship with the lead security officer and Jimmy would often speak to her about his torment and anguish on how his wife suffered a debilitating and chronic back condition. Mia could see the sorrow in his eyes when he spoke on how useless he felt not being able to help his wife. A simple operation was all that was needed to bring her back to 100% health, an operation that required $4,500 up front, money that Jimmy and his family simply did not have.

He was one of many that made ends meet on a week-to-week basis and he was grateful that he was lucky enough to remain employed. His wife was on a waiting list that could take up to three years, time they didn't have as her condition was deteriorating as every week passed, however, if they had the money forthwith to pay for the operation, it would sky rocket them ahead of the queue and as discussed with Drake over the phone days before, Mia was going to prey upon Jimmy's vulnerability.

All Jimmy had to do after police had delivered the first vials that came to the hospital laboratory was corrupt the hallway security cameras, leave the lab door unlocked and vacate his post for no less than three minutes. If he were to accept the dangled carrot and ask no questions, his wife would be on the operating table within weeks.

As events were colluding to aide Danny in his quest for freedom in Graceville, he had alighted from his train in the city of Burbank and in a world of worry on how to achieve the final leg of his journey.

Maybe there's a stagecoach or similar I can get a ride on? He pondered. 'Maybe hitch a ride on someone's horse and cart. There might be another train, a sugar cane one perhaps. A pushbike? Nah, I couldn't see myself riding that far,' Danny flustered.

In the end, it didn't bother him how long it would take, three days, one week, two weeks, he didn't care as long as he got there. But there was one way he was not going to go by and that was on horseback, he would rather die than put himself through that. He was still feeling lingering effects from riding big black whenever he sat down and was never going to consider the risk of sitting on another nutcase such as his old equine friend. As luck would have it, and as things had conspired for Danny in the past, the stars were about to align for him once more.

'Excuse me, mate!' he asked a station attendant as he exited the platforms 'What's the best way to get up to the Amber Coast? Is there a smaller train I can take, a stagecoach or something?'

'Your best bet is to get the bus, sir,' he replied.

'A bus?'

'Yeah! You can try your luck with that. The bus to Kingston leaves in about 20 minutes. It's parked down in the bays about a five-minute walk in that direction,' the attendant said as pointed his finger westerly.

'Since when have buses been back on the road?' Danny asked perplexed.

'Since Christmas, sir. The state has added them to the essential services list. They've been running them around city locations and major regional areas. One comes down from Kingston in the morning and then returns in the afternoon daily since then. The state has allocated more fuel rations to get things moving again, but you better hurry if you want a seat. As you can imagine, they're pretty much in demand, and if you've got the money to pay for it?'

Oh, I've got the money, Danny quietly thought. 'Where can I get ticket?' he asked.

'Keep walking that way and you'll see the office. Coastal bus lines it is.'

Danny thanked the stranger and walked hurriedly down the palm tree lined foot path towards the bus line office. To the left of him as he walked were shops and business offices, some open, some not. To the right lay multiple parking for horse carriages and coaches, in amongst them laid several solar powered and electric vehicles, along with the odd fuel driven automobile. Large sail annexes provided shade for the numerous horses.

The first thing he noticed was the humidity in the air as the sun beat down on him when he strode. It was different to the southern states, the air a lot thicker in the sub-tropical climate and Danny was given a quick reminder of it as soon as he quickened his steps as he switched his cap around, removed his sunglasses briefly and wiped the beading sweat forming on his brow.

As he neared the coastal bus line offices, he noticed up to a dozen buses idling away in the diagonal bays on the large bitumen car park opposite and could see the illuminated electronic destination signs above the driver's head. The bus in the third bay read Kingston, the one he would be boarding if he could grab a ticket. Also, to his chagrin, was a metal and canvas barrier walkway that passengers were filtered through before they boarded.

At the entrance stood two armed protective services officers with yellow fluoro jackets over their uniforms scanning for any weapons. Black caps and dark sunglasses gave them a look of utmost seriousness. More officers stood at the front of each bus ensuring that no suitcase luggage was bought onto the bus.

Danny would soon overhear that the reason for their presence was because on the third day of operations, the very bus that Danny hoped to board was hijacked at gunpoint by two desperados. They offloaded the driver and passengers shortly after departure and stole the bus. They were apprehended several days later 300 kms away inland and since that day, security had been updated to what it was today.

Kingston was a large town 355km north of Burbank situated in the heart of the Amber Coast, given its name because of the colour the sand portrayed as the sun rose, illuminating an amber hue along the coast's extensive beaches. Kingston's population was nearing the 150,000 mark and people considered it the gateway to the world heritage pristine tropical rainforests and beaches of the far north.

The small village of Port Denning, where Danny's heaven was, was situated a small distance before, was directly on route to it. If he couldn't get off there, then the minor city of Kingston was going to be good enough. It was a hell of a lot better than tracking the 340km some other way, and the thought of being in the air-conditioned comfort of the Mercedes irizar i6 57-seat bus was more than appealing to him.

He waited impatiently in line. Two female staff members attended those with inquiries, Danny listened intently if any of the customers ahead of him were purchasing tickets, so far so good. He impatiently looked at the clockface above the staff members, it showed he had only ten minutes before the bus was scheduled to leave. Finally, the elderly couple ahead of him had finished with their enquiries. Danny didn't see them purchase any tickets, maybe they already had them, he didn't know, however, one way or another, he was about to find out if he was to able purchase one himself.

'Hello. May I help you?' the attractive uniformed young blonde female enquired.

'Yeah, hi. Is it possible to get a ticket on the Kingston bus that's about to leave?' Danny asked.

'It certainly is!' She smiled. 'There are three seats left. You got here just in time. We had a cancellation. How many are you after?'

Danny internally breathed the hugest sigh of relief that was possible. 'Only the one,' he happily replied. He passed over the $125.00 that was required, a mixture of large and small notes out of his wallet, a lot more expensive than it was, he thought with raised eyebrows. He accepted the stamped paper ticket off the young lady, hurled his backpack on, picked up his suitcase then made the short walk across to the carpark through the security check. He nervously went through unhindered to where the driver stood outside the bus door with a clipboard in hand, the bus security officer watched over proceedings in silence.

'How are you going, mate?' the driver welcomed.

'Yeah, good thanks.'

'Heading to Kingston?'

'Yeah.'

'Grab the last ticket, did ya?'

'Yeah.'

'You're a lucky man. Usually they're sold-out days before.'

'Yep, the luckiest son of a bitch you'll ever meet,' Danny laughed with built in sarcasm. 'Didn't even know the buses were running again,' he added.

'It's great for me. I've got my job back again,' the driver enthusiastically replied.

The driver relieved Danny of his suitcase to put into the underneath bins with the rest of the luggage and asked him where he had come from.

'Down south,' Danny only divulged.

'That makes sense,' he said. 'You guys down there are a bit behind compared to us. Yeah, we're showing you the way on how to get things up and running again aren't we. And you thought we were the backward state,' he happily jibed. Danny jovially replied that it didn't bother him at all as he had no intention of returning south for some time yet.

'Anything valuable in here I should know about before I stack it?' the driver asked as he was about to load the suitcase.

'Only a quarter of a million dollars in cash.' Danny winked.

The driver laughed at Danny's comment. 'I wish,' he cackled back as he loaded the case then shut the bin door while the protective security officer's head turned at the comment. The driver introduced himself as Bob. He was a stocky built man with a muscular neck to go with his arms and thighs, probably in his late thirties, Danny thought. He was clean-shaven with a rounded face and short dark hair. He wore black shorts, grey socks with shiny black shoes and a white shirt with company green logo epaulettes on his shoulders.

Danny hesitated when Bob reached to shake his hand. He didn't want to give his common name out, so introduced himself as Daniel.

'Do you stop anywhere near Port Denning?' Danny asked.

'Yeah, we do. We stop at the marina there. Is that good enough for you?'

'It certainly will be. Good one. Thanks Bob.'

Danny couldn't believe his luck. 'This is meant to be,' he affirmed to himself, and with his confidence growing that all would work out, he boarded the bus and made his way down the aisle until he found a spare seat three quarters of the way down. He positioned his backpack in the racks above and took his aisle seat next to a young lad in his teenage years. Another two more passengers boarded as Bob took his position in the driver's seat.

The bus was now fully loaded, and Danny was blessing himself that he got there at the time he did. After a few long minutes, the security officer gave the okay for the bus to depart, on time and with no obstructions. With sunglasses still attached, Danny perused the passengers on board to see if any prying eyes were glancing in his direction as the bus slowly made its way out of the busy station precinct.

People seemed to be minding their own business as they quietly chatted away which made Danny relax a shade. The bus meandered through the main arterial streets of the city, stopping and moving through the traffic controllers who were directing traffic with octagon stop and slow signs, ensuring no major incidents occurred as the bus negotiated through the abundance of transport methods. The driver engaged the horn at regular intervals to warn that he was approaching. Thirty minutes after departing the station at Burbank, the bus reached the on ramp of highway number one, the road to heaven.

The bus would slowly increase its speed as it ventured up the three-lane freeway, the outer lane reserved for buses and fuel driven vehicles separated by large reflective orange bollards to prevent lane changes for safety. As the bus travelled further and traffic lightened on the once busy highway, it would reduce to two lanes and eventually one in each direction with overtaking lanes every 5km or so.

Danny kept to himself, only leaving his seat to fetch a drink or food rations out of his backpack, he hadn't eaten since breakfast. The other times were to take advantage of the two short toilet stops, lighting up a private cigarette. He took in the views along the way and remembered several spots from the previous time he was up this way. He took in the magnificent scenery of the mountains and hinterland to his left as they left the city of Burbank behind, together with the beautiful ocean views and beaches to his right on the occasions when the highway drew near to it and after nearly five hours of traveling and several passenger stops along the way, the bus turned right off the highway and down a well maintained road that lead to the small tourist and fishing village of Port Denning, three kilometres off highway number one. The bus stopped at the picturesque marina where Danny would finally disembark.

He was last to leave the bus, ahead of him five people alighted at the same destination as another three waited to board. Danny waited his turn before he thanked Bob for his help and friendliness as he lifted the bin doors and retrieved Danny's case for him.

'Spend that quarter of a million wisely,' Bob joked as they shook hands.

'You betcha. I've already got plans for it,' Danny cheerfully replied. If only he knew!

Danny gave him a wave as the bus continued its journey through the roundabout to make its way back to highway number one and complete its trip to Kingston a further 15km north.

Danny took a moment to gather his thoughts. He looked around at the once vibrant coastal town. A few people meandered around the marina where a plethora of boats were moored, assorted flags swung gently from the poles on the timber pier boardwalk.

The seaside village of Port Denning laid on a small peninsula which gave access to a scenic little harbour that gave protection from the ocean swells and weather. A lighthouse stood proud and tall at the furthest and highest point of the bluff amid the tropical trees and shrubs. The town had a regular population of around 1000 people, which would grow tenfold during the winter peak time as southerners flocked to the holiday area due to its warm climate, magnificent nearby rainforests, pristine surf beaches and ocean reefs a short distance further to the north.

Akin to many towns of similar ilk on the Amber coast, they relied heavily on the tourist dollar and as the visitors dried up, so too did the economy, and a big percentage of locals went looking for greener pastures. Resort style living was the main attraction, and many apartment retreats lined the ocean strip in amongst the giant palms, fig trees and Rosewoods, but now, as Danny would see, most resorts were dormant and empty.

Danny wandered over to the general store and purchased some readymade sandwiches and immediately nourished his empty stomach as he made idle chat with the middle-aged female proprietor. He also grabbed a loaf of bread with assorted spreads off the shelves and four water bottles together with some fruit, potato chips and bags of assorted nuts, the used by date didn't bother him. He stacked them into his suitcase after he paid in small notes and coins from his loot.

'Is the beachside walking track still accessible to the horse stud road?' Danny asked the lady.

'Yeah, it is. But you better watch for horse riders. They use it all the time now.'

'Thanks for the tip,' Danny nodded.

'Passing through or visiting?' she asked.

'Don't know!' shrugged Danny. 'Haven't made my mind up yet. We'll see what happens hey!' he smiled.

He politely said his goodbye and thanked her for the service and started the 6km walk to the property he had planned and sacrificed so much to arrive at. He avoided the main street that sat several blocks away from the marina, it was evening time, and the sun was beginning to lower and Danny reasoned he had no time for sightseeing as he wanted to get to his heaven as soon as time would allow.

He threw his backpack on once more and flicked out the handle of his suitcase and started to lug it behind him after he finished his sandwiches sitting by the curb and channel of the road. The chicken and salad agreed with him immensely as he wiped his lips with his fingers to get the last dregs of mayonnaise into his gullet.

A typical seasonal early evening storm was about to greet him as he continued down the sandy floor of the beachside trail, the gentle ripples of the ocean surf lapping at the shore kept him company for the entire length of the track, coconut palms lined the edge of the sand. The rain began to pelt down as light rumbles of thunder echoed in the distance. As wet as it was becoming, Danny didn't mind one bit. He enjoyed walking in the rain, it was cooling him down, his only concern was how waterproof his suitcase was. When the rain was at its heaviest, he sheltered his body over the top of his case to see if his wads of money were not being affected by the moisture and to his delight, everything was still dry as a bone including his spare clothes.

After nearly an hour of walking and being drenched in the downpour, he finally made it the end of the trail. The undulating lush green agistment paddocks of the horse stud greeted him opposite the entrance to the road. He now knew he wasn't far off. Danny turned right and walked another kilometre, the road dipping into a cutting, the paddocks of the horse stud giving way to low dense forest of local eucalypt and mangrove trees mixed in with thick dangling vines. He arrived at a fork in the road and veered left onto the gravel road.

A shallow rise greeted him as it sharply turned left again, the rains above suddenly halting as if it were shut off by a turn of a faucet. To his left the forest lingered, however, appearing again on his right was the beautiful green rolling hills and pastural lands of the thoroughbred. With excitement and a stomach full of nerves, he ascended the rise and stopped to take in what his eyes could see, releasing a huge smile of relief as he saw a familiar property ahead.

White ranch-style fencing surrounded the paddocks and lined the roadside. He walked slowly, never taking his eyes off the house he could see in the distance. He neared the entrance to the property. Large Alexandra palm trees lined the dull white crushed rocked driveway on either side. Two magnolia trees sat majestically near the pitched roof of the open two-bay carport, the concrete floor looked clean and empty. Another two magnolias sat below the stairs that rose to the entrance to the house, they'd grown a lot larger since Danny was there last. More palm trees of different species swayed on the wind across the surrounding lawns.

He noticed that the fencing had increased since he was last there nearly a decade ago, maybe Steve had sub-divided the land Danny mused. Steve's house was over the next rise, and he wondered if he had done the same. He wondered if he had received his letter, he wondered if he was still there. Danny arrived at the entrance of the driveway.

There was no sign of activity other than a group of horses grazing in a distant paddock. Other than the fronds and leaves swaying in the breeze, an eerie silence entranced him. The house he had pictured and dreamt about for so long looked empty as Steve had said in his last correspondence. Danny released his grip on the suitcase handle then shouldered off his backpack. The lowering evening sun reappeared, casting long shadows, glistening the moisture and raindrops off the surrounding trees.

He looked up at the arched metal gateway sign above, and with a broad smirk across his face read the word, H*E*A*V*E*N.

Chapter 44

It was Friday morning and Sgt Dane Grainger came visiting Kate's house with envelope in hand. It had been six days since he and Inspector Vaccaro had gained the DNA samples and the previous week had become one of the longest in Greta's life.

The Sergeant personally delivered the official letter as Greta no longer had a fixed address, thanks to the crimes of the Re-possessions office. All her mail, if any, now had to be picked up at the post office in town. The Sergeant was sanctioned to deliver the news; and Dane was already privy of what information was within. If it were anything else, he, along with every police officer in the state would have been notified before the results were returned to the Graceville police station, courtesy of Assistant Commissioner Martin Conroy.

The ladies welcomed him in after he tied the reins of his horse to a low branch of the one of the bushy trees that grew in Kate's front yard. Dane stated the reasons why he was there as he entered and handed the envelope over to Greta explaining who it was from. Greta opened the letter and read over its contents. In it was a brief letter outlining the process that was taken with signed condolences from the Assistant Police Commissioner. An enormous surreal feeling came over her as she held the second piece of paper, the official death certificate of Daniel James Pruitt, with the word *DECEASED* stamped across the bottom of the page.

The elaborate and precarious plan to deceive and outwit the authorities was now complete. For all intents and purposes, Danny Pruitt was dead.

'I'm sorry, Greta,' consoled Dane.

'It's okay, Dane. It's what we all knew anyway, wasn't it?' Greta contritely replied as she laid the envelope down on the loungeroom table.

'Danny's body is at the Graceville morgue,' Dane solemnly relayed. 'It's ready to be released into your hands. The coroner's office is waiting your instructions on how you would like to proceed with retrieving it.'

'You take it to the crematorium. They'll be expecting him. I want it done as soon as possible,' Greta advised with staid emotion.

Under the instructions of Drake passed on through Mia, the body was to be taken to the Harrison funeral parlour for cremation, when and if the time came to claim it. The strategies that lay ahead and the orders from Drake to burn the body could not have been clearer to his wife. A cremation would solve two problems for them. One was that the authorities would never have a body to exhume in the future, if for any purpose they needed to do so, and two, and more importantly, was that they would receive the ashes of their little buddy Teeto, and a chance to give him a proper farewell. Greta and Kate had visited the crematorium during the week and had arranged with the parlour to receive the body, hoping it would be sooner rather than later and their nervous and burdening wait was about to end.

Dane was a little dumbfounded at Greta's instructions. It had a coldness attached to it; one he was taken aback with. The Sergeant had previously visited her when off duty at least five times during the week. Not only for Greta's sake, but also for Kate's. He also worried for her and the separation from Ryan, not to mention that they were two ladies living alone without any male protection and Dane fathomed that it was his duty to look in on the girls as often as he could.

He was caught between a rock and a hard place when it came to Kate and Ryan. Who to console? Who to speak to first? Whose side, if any, would he take? The decision was made for him as he hadn't seen or heard from Ryan since he left town. He knew Ryan's state of mind was not in the best place after what they had been through on the hunt for Danny. He had been asking after his wellbeing, worried that he might be losing another pal on top of Karl, his two young constable friends and now Danny.

Kate had been blunt in her assessment of her estranged husband during his visits, harshly informing Dane that the last she knew was that Ryan was still at his parents' home and she too had not heard from him, information that was relayed without any noticeable compassion.

Notwithstanding his care for Ryan and Kate, Greta and Danny were where Dane's main concerns lay. He too wanted to mourn the death of his pal, to toast his life, however, on all visits during the week, it seemed to him that all he was receiving was the cold shoulder from both the ladies. Their reactions were strange to say the least, he reflected inside, but he wouldn't push his feelings towards them.

He convinced himself it was their way of holding the grief over Danny's death and kept his silence on his worries. For all the sympathy he held however, to hear that Greta wanted Danny's body cremated signalled alarm bells as it was against Greta's religious belief. A burial was the traditional Christian way, all of Greta's and Danny's deceased family members had always been buried inside the coffin, a fact that Dane was aware of.

When Greta insisted that there would no ceremony to coincide with the cremation, Dane's furtive instincts were being challenged. But no matter what misgivings churned inside of him, he too wanted closure to the whole tragic saga and would show quiet respect and adhere to Greta's wishes.

'What do I have to do to get it, I mean him, Danny!' Greta adjusted her tongue.

'Do you want me to meet you out front of the hospital?' Dane offered.

The Sergeant had experience on what the protocol was when it came for next of kin retrieving the body of their loved ones, he had become accustomed to it lately, and offered to help Greta with the process. Greta accepted his kindness and within the hour she would meet him outside the doors of the hospital while Kate tended to her sons.

Greta rode the back streets of Graceville on her way to the hospital; she had no desire to interact with anyone. The pedestrians, riders and cyclists she did happen to pass were strangers to her, but even so, she no longer cared if they did observe who she was. She tethered her horse to the barrier poles at the newly constructed hospital stables on her arrival. A row of gum trees gave shade to her plain bay mare amongst the other waiting equines, troughs of water gave them hydration if necessary.

Greta attached her skull cap to the saddle and adjusted her herself. First starting with her denim pants and dark chequered flannelette shirt before running her hands through her hair then tying it back again. She was deeply flustered internally as she walked to the hospital entrance. The deception and lies were slowly taking its toll on her over tired body, though externally she was determined to remain steady and resilient as she walked through the well-kept hospital grounds. She hurried up the concrete path, assorted rose bushes were in full bloom on either side of her before she would cross the circular driveway to the main entrance and meet up with the Sergeant who was in waiting.

Dane guided her inside the hospital doors then to the reception desks to meet the proper authorities and sign the release forms for the body. Thirty anxious minutes would pass until all the registered authorities in charge had signed and dated the release forms. When the paperwork was completed, two men employed by the hospital morgue greeted Greta and Dane in the waiting room of the office foyer. They introduced themselves and asked Greta on where and how she would like the body to be transferred, advising she had a window of 48 hours to take control of the deceased otherwise it would have to be transferred to the city's larger morgue to continue preservation.

Greta advised them that the Harrison funeral parlour would be expecting the body and that she would be grateful if they could transport it to their premises as soon as possible. The hospital employees nodded in respect and arranged the transportation immediately and soon the presumed body of Danny Pruitt would arrive at the funeral parlour to be readied for cremation at 9.00 am tomorrow, a week to the day that young Daniel gave his samples of DNA to the authorities.

'Thank you for your help,' Greta acknowledged. She gave Dane a light embrace, keeping her head low and to the side, she restrained from making eye contact. She exited the hospital foyer, leaving Dane bewildered and frustrated by her demeanour. Greta needed to get to the shelter and security of Kate's home as fast as she could. The stress from the lies and deception were starting to overpower her. Her stomach was churning as she approached her horse, she felt she was going to vomit through nerves alone.

Treating Dane in the manner she had was unavoidable, it still didn't change the enormous empathy she felt for him. He was part of the collateral damage, and a large piece at that, more so with Sarah and Corey, who she was trying to avoid the most as she knew she would never be able to hold onto the lie if ever Sarah, as expected, would start probing her decisions. Nevertheless, Greta was resolute that respected long standing friendships could not stand in the way of piecing her family back together.

Regardless of the recognition of Greta's strange decisional behaviour and demeanour, Dane was not going to let sleeping dogs lie. He needed to let off a bit of steam himself and earbash a few friends on the pressures and suffering that had surrounded him regarding his friend Danny, and his own tribulations were not going to go unrecognised. Dane had the understanding and respect of all who were associated with Danny and wasn't going to let the passing of his friend go without some type of wake or memorial drink, with or without Greta and Kate being involved.

Friends and associates of Danny's had already been asking about funeral details. They all thought the Sergeant was the go-to man regarding matters throughout their large friendship group. Dane could only say that they were still waiting on official notification before anything could happen, but now that his death was confirmed, he was going to commiserate and celebrate the life of the late Danny Pruitt.

After Greta had left him at the hospital, and also after deep and concentrated thought he changed into his civilian clothes after his shift finished at 3.00pm. His aim was to visit the local drinking holes and pass on the word that a wake would be held for Danny at the Depot hotel tomorrow afternoon on the Saturday, and all who knew him were cordially invited to attend.

The following day Sarah received the news at lunchtime as she worked her shift at the Graceville hotel when Dane paid a visit before the wake. She was shocked and angered at the secrecy and decisions that Greta had made. She promptly had her shift covered for the afternoon and still in her work uniform, hastily strode the 30 minutes to Kate's house to confront Greta.

'Where's Greta? I need to speak to her,' Sarah huffed.

'She's not here,' a still unforgiving Kate replied.

'Where is she?'

'Gone! She's left town,' Kate said abruptly.

Sarah was angered and bewildered. *How can she leave without telling me?* She frustratingly asked herself. 'Where has she gone?' she asked.

'She left this morning straight after the cremation. Only Greta and I were there. This will explain why.' Kate said as she passed a letter to an agitated Sarah before any argument could escalate.

'What's this?' Sarah snatched.

'She left you a letter through respect. Read it!'

Sarah immediately opened the envelope.

It read:

Dear Sarah.

I am so sorry I've had to leave the way I have without saying goodbye. I don't think I would be able to cope if Danny were to have a proper funeral. The hysteria, friction and media surrounding him is a situation I cannot put myself and sons through. I am leaving for my sisters to get some peace and solitude and regain my life.

I cannot thank you enough for what you have done for my boys and me and will forever be indebted to you. I hope you can understand what I have done. I will be in touch when my mind is in a better place. Please do not try and contact me as we need time and space away from Graceville.

Love always,
Greta.

Sarah began to wipe away the forming tears from her eyes.

'Can you see why she has left?' enforced Kate. 'She didn't want to cause any more chaos. She's had enough.'

Kate was referring to several incidents that had been occurring around town, and it was the perfect alibi to use for Greta's sudden departure and Danny's non farewell. Numerous fights had broken out in and around the drinking holes of Graceville since Danny's death which had resulted in three more deaths when guns were drawn during the melees.

Devlin sympathisers, along with a minority of police members who were directing blame straight at Danny Pruitt for their lost colleagues, were still looking for vengeance any way they could, and Pruitt allies were number one on their list when the availability and opportunity arose. Emotions were high and the new interim Minister had his hands full in trying calm the anger on both sides as the truth started to trickle out on the real events that occurred at *La Fortaleza*.

Police were now ruthlessly enforcing the law banning any carrying of weapons, relentlessly stopping and searching anyone whom they thought had a history of such a thing and overcrowding of jail cells was no longer a concern to authority.

Sarah bowed her head into her chest. She started to sob. She understood Greta's decision; she struggled to accept it, but she understood it. She also understood what might occur at a proper funeral service if it were to happen as she was also alert to what was happening around town. Her emotions were now ready to be released as her sobbing became uncontrollable. She had been stoic and caring since the day Danny went missing, stoic for Greta, stoic for Corey, for all the children. She had now lost two of her closest friends, one through death, now one through absence.

'You, okay?' asked Kate.

'I hate it. I just fuckin hate everything,' Sarah quietly wailed.

Kate had treated Sarah awfully since it was known about the re-po squad, finally, it was now time for forgiveness. She knew Sarah loved both Danny and Greta dearly. Her empathy surfaced as she softly embraced her.

'None of this is your fault. We all hate it. Go home. Be with your family,' she comforted.

Sarah regained her composure and then sadly and staidly said her goodbyes to Kate, who in turn was relieved that no further unwanted enquiries were to come from her. If it fooled Sarah, it would fool everyone else. It was up to Danny in the future if he wanted to let her know that he was alive or not, and Kate was gaining confidence that Sarah had believed what was read and accepted the circumstances and reasons why Greta had to leave without any goodbyes.

Unbeknown to her friends, Greta and her two boys were met by Mia and Candice at Kate's house as soon as the cremation was over, and with her sons, was aboard a Sultan owned stagecoach that had been sitting idle in Drake's garage. The reins were taken by a young tattooed clean-shaven club prospect who went by the name of Kel, who happened to be absent from La Fortaleza on that fateful Monday. More importantly, he was still loyal to the Vice Presidents and their lady partners.

The four-horse-driven carriage was bound for the Lyndale train station, the penultimate stop for the Graceville bound trains from the city, 18 kilometres away and a 90-minute journey southwest of town on the single lane rural highway. A course taken to avoid detection from Graceville locals who would no doubt recognise Greta if she were ever to board a train from her hometown.

After painstakingly overseeing the cremation, Greta arrived back at Kate's house and hurried her way straight to the bathroom, ignoring her boys who were being looked after by Mia and Candice for the short time they were away. She stared blankly into the mirror at her reflection, trying to take in all that was happening in her life. She had no idea whose body went into the furnace an hour before. No idea on what lay ahead from this point on. No idea why she had taken faith in Danny's written words to be totally reliant on two women she had only just met. She glared into the mirror, questioning if she knew herself anymore.

Greta released her hair from the plaited ponytail and roughly spread her fingers through her long waves in frustration. She looked down and saw a pair of scissors lying on the vanity basin. She clasped them in her right hand and in an instant began to cut. First snipping off an inch, then another, and then another as she clasped her hair in her left hand. The snipping quickly turned to frantic hacking, not finishing until the aggressive cutting left her thick dark strands sitting halfway up her neckline. She had never trimmed her hair as short since before she had met Danny. He adored the length and bounce of her hair and always encouraged her to keep it that way, he was proud of the way she looked.

She had no reason to cut it off, no premeditated thoughts of doing it, it just happened. Maybe it was the idea of trying to disguise herself, maybe it was all the stress that forced her to do it, maybe it was her deep seeded anger that festered inside towards her husband for tearing her life apart. She furiously dispensed the offcuts away as she continued to cut, not stopping until her reflected dark brown eyes demanded her to do so.

She angrily threw the scissors across the tiled bathroom floor, leant both her arms on the basin before wetting her face and head. Greta took a deep breath, towelled herself down then exited the bathroom as if nothing ever happened where she was greeted with silence. No questions were asked of her, only strange and surprised looks came her way from those around.

Greta conveyed her eternal gratitude and heartfelt goodbyes to Kate, it was as emotional as could be, both not knowing when they would see each other again, a sacrifice that had to be taken. Greta then took her seat inside the waiting carriage and comforted her twin sons seated beside her. Candice and Mia and her son sat opposite.

As the carriage began to exit through the outskirts of town, the sound of hooves on the bitumen echoed passed her ears. Oblivious to the conversation being held between Candice and Mia, Greta peered out of the coach's windows. It would be another fragment that would be ripped from her soul.

She was born and bred in Graceville, had lived there her entire life, married and given birth there. Her most cherished and happiest memories had taken place in the beautiful, picturesque town, yet, as she pushed further and further away from her home, she knew by heart that it would probably be the last time that she would ever grace its boundaries.

Chapter 45

Nervous and mindful of the reason for fleeing her hometown, Greta's restless transfer from carriage to train went unhindered and within three hours of departing Graceville, she had arrived in the metropolis of Marlboro. The three ladies and three children hastily made the 20-minute journey by foot from the Central station to the Princeton Towers hotel where they had pre booked two rooms for two nights on the 7th floor, one for Greta and her boys, the other, Candice, Mia and her son would occupy.

The 21-storey apartment and guest building were in the heart of the theatre precinct of the big city that had been restored with electricity since the New Year which in turn gave easy access to the upper apartments and hotel rooms with the elevators now operational. Despite the power being available, supply was being rationed to avoid grid overload until the system could be bought up to full capacity. 6.30 am to 9.30 am and again in the evening from 6.30 pm to 9.30 pm were the allocated time slots for electricity for the city blocks where the Princeton Towers was located, so if guests wanted to use the elevators, those selected times were the only chance to do so, otherwise it was a long and strenuous walk up the stairs to your apartment/rooms if it was on the upper floors.

Air conditioners were also functional during these times which Greta was thankful for when evening came. The ladies were grateful to have a room in the building. It was only thanks to the contacts of Zoe Valetta that they had acquired it, and the money received from Danny's heist. It had been booked out for the last three weeks and it was a similar story with other accommodation centres and buildings around the city, a sure sign that the economy was stimulating for the better as small businesses in and around the CBD started to reopen.

The ladies would not travel far from their temporary abodes, if at all. The low profile had to be kept allaying any fears of their whereabouts. Mia and Candice had left their rented properties in Graceville without telling a soul. They knew the police would soon come knocking again and when the time came, they wanted to be as far away as possible, and come visiting they did, only to be told by the landlord that the occupants had left without notice.

The 48 hours at the Princeton would mostly be restricted to the confines of their adjacent apartment rooms until they would meet with Zoe Valetta early Monday morning, two hours before they would board the interstate train to Twin City. The prearranged meeting was one that Zoe was not looking forward to at all, so much so, that she would change the rendezvous point from her private apartment to the foyer of the Princeton Towers hotel in an effort to avoid any contact with Greta.

Zoe had left a message for hotel management to pass onto Mia about the change of plans the previous day and at 6.33 am on Monday morning, short of two and half hours before their train was to depart, Zoe entered through the large revolving doors of the ground floor to see that Mia was already in waiting. She sat alone on a plush beige leather dual seat; more seats surrounded a long table with thick short legs to the side of her that were centralised in the open foyer. Hotel paraphernalia and magazines sat neatly on its glass surface.

To the front of Zoe as she walked in was the large, polished timber semi-circular reception desk where the three receptionists were busy with their morning paperwork and phone calls. To the right side of reception were large timber framed glass doors that led you into the conference room. The foyer's carpet was of deep red with small black and silver silhouetted diamond shape trimmings through it. Four large chandeliers hung from the ceiling which now were in full light as power was engaged to the building.

To the left from where Zoe slowly made her way to Mia were the elevators while to the right of the reception desk were the hallways to the toilets and a snack and coffee bar. At the forefront and right of the entrance was the dining room, candlelit for the early morning breakfast guests who had views of the street beyond.

Zoe was dressed in her business attire. Dark slacks, heels, tight fitting black halter top with jacket, her silver earrings dangling as usual. Maddy was by her side as she approached Mia who stood to greet her.

'You got my message then?' Zoe confirmed.

'Yes,' said Mia as she gave a friendly light embrace to Maddy.

Zoe delved into her office carry bag and retrieved an envelope.

'These are your train tickets,' she said.

All of them were one-way to Twin City. The group of six would sit together in an open six-seat section of the passenger train. A table would sit in between the three adjacent and adjoining seats. There would be luggage racks above them, their personal bags and backpacks would have to be at their feet for the ensuing five-hour journey.

Zoe then handed over an array of sealed envelopes, some of normal postage size, others larger.

'Everything that Drake and Razor wanted are all in these. Birth certificates, tax file numbers, healthcare details, licences, bank accounts, it's all in there,' Zoe affirmed.

She then handed another normal-sized sealed envelope to Mia.

'This one is for Danny when and if you get to him,' she impressed.

'I'll give it to Greta to pass on. She'll be down soon. I told her that you would be here. She's got some questions she wants to ask about your time with him,' Mia replied.

Time spent with Danny! The only thing that came to the forefront of Zoe's mind was their night of passion together. She had to think quickly, to divert the subject away.

'I have no time. She can wait until she meets up with him, I'm sure he will tell her everything she wants to know. And I would prefer if Drake or Razor handed over the letter to him,' Zoe passively demanded.

Mia reluctantly accepted her succinct response and lodged all envelopes safely in her carry bag. She then thanked Zoe for all that she had done.

'Good luck on your travels,' Zoe said. 'The men know how to contact me if need be.'

Mia secured the contents in her bag as Zoe took Maddy by the hand. She was about to leave when Mia asked with genuine concern if all was okay with her.

She seemed nervous and agitated in Mia's perception, not the usual self-assured and confident woman she had previously met. Her eyes were darting across the foyer and was fidgety in her actions.

'Are you okay?' Mia asked concerned.

'I'm fine. Why do you ask?'

'You look, I don't know? Flustered, that's all.'

'Do I?'

Mia paused for a moment. Her work in the health industry was alerting her senses to what maybe be discomforting her.

'Have you seen anybody?' Mia softly delved.

'What do you mean?'

'I have a pretty good idea of what you've been through. Drake said it was pretty horrific. What Solomon did to you, the siege, the fire, seeing Teeto and the others the way they were. It must have been terrifying, not only for you but for Maddy as well. It might pay to talk to someone. To get things out, it's not good for your health if you keep things bottled up inside,' Mia advised.

'I've had no time for that. I've been too busy running errands for all your husbands, haven't I?' Zoe snapped back with a contorted smile. 'This is not the time anyhow,' she spoke under her breath. She eyed towards Maddy and advised Mia that the little one was only deaf, not stupid, and relayed that all she was worried about at this time was keeping Maddy safe and loved.

'Sorry for intruding,' Mia replied.

Zoe was in a hurry to depart the premises. Not only did she want to see the last of Mia and Candice, but she also sure didn't want a face to face with Greta, and the quicker she could leave, the better she would be feeling.

'You need to prepare for your train, and I need to get to my office, so I'll leave you with it; as I said, everything they require is in those envelopes. Don't lose them. Your husbands know where to contact me if they need anything else. I'll keep my ears open for anything that might concern them. Good luck with everything.' Zoe nodded.

She again took Maddy by the hand and began to exit the lobby when the arrival bells of the ground-floor elevators attracted her attention. She instinctively looked towards the opening doors. Fleeting seconds passed before the occupant and her eyes locked on one another. Zoe's stomach erupted in fluttering nerves.

Danny's sons were exactly how he described them. She thought she knew them already by his proud and constant adoring's of them, however, it was the mother of whom she was fixated with. Despite the absence of her long dark crinkled hair in which Danny had given her numerous mental pictures of, Zoe was in no doubt of who her eyes were now instantly glued on.

Greta was wearing a loose-fitting black casual singlet that exposed her blue sports bra at the sides. She wore an above the knee dark blue and white shaded summer skirt and had black ankle boots on. Her chained blue sapphire-studded earrings that she had borrowed from Candice dangled freely. Her heavy black eyeliner along with her new ragged looking haircut, extenuated by her uneven fringe, topped off with her dark tanned skin gave her an exotic and free-spirited look that Zoe was errantly enhanced by, and to her, Greta was more beautiful than Danny had ever described.

Zoe's brief frozen stupor was only interrupted by Maddy tugging at her arm. The little one had also been ogling at the stranger and signed to her guardian on who the lady was, now staring back at them.

'I don't know,' she communicated. 'C'mon, we have to go.'

Greta watched on suspiciously after Zoe smiled in her direction then exited through the hotel doors with Maddy tightly clasping her hand, struggling to keep up with the pace that was set as the little one continued her glare back at Greta. As they disappeared through the revolving doors and out to the sidewalks of the city, Greta made her way to Mia, curiously asking on whether the visitor was Zoe Valetta or not.

'Yes, it was,' Mia answered, still perplexed at the sudden rush to exit.

'Did you say I wanted to talk to her?'

'Yes, I did.'

Greta gestured at Mia, wanting her to elaborate more on why she had left before she had a chance to speak to her. Mia agreed that it seemed strange to her as well, explaining the reasonings that Zoe had given, words that Greta found a little curious herself. A brief pause ensued as both looked towards the now vacant doors.

'She certainly wasn't what I expected,' Greta declared.

'That's what they all say,' Mia mockingly sighed. 'There's not a man I haven't seen drool over her.'

'Hmmmmm,' grumbled Greta.

Although Greta had no preconceived idea on what the mysterious lawyer may look like, in fact, it had never entered her mind with everything that was going on in her life. Nevertheless, it did take her by surprise to see a woman of Zoe's ilk and knowing that she had spent a full week with her runaway husband did silently take her breath away.

Bitterly disappointed that her meeting with Zoe Valetta never eventuated, Greta couldn't understand why the evasive lawyer never gave any of her time. She was desperate to find out more on her husband from someone who had been with him. How he was feeling, what he had been doing, what was his true state of mind. It was a missed opportunity Greta silently cursed, nonetheless, she couldn't dwell on it.

What lay ahead was far more important and boarding that train and leaving the city was now paramount. She helped her sons with bowls of cereals at the breakfast buffet, nibbling on some buttered toast with jam spreads herself, washed down with a large cup of black coffee with three sugars, shrugging off the uneasy negative thoughts of Danny and Zoe being alone together.

Within the hour, the three ladies and the children were packed and on their way to Central station by the horse driven carriage taxi that was organised by hotel staff and ready to board the interstate train to Twin City. The boarding procedure went smoothly amongst the hordes of people congregated in and around the station precinct and by 8.35 am, they were all in their seats ready for departure.

9.00 am ticked over and the whistles and horns blared throughout the undercover station as the train slowly exited, gathering momentum as it sortied through the suburbs. Daniel and Darcy were excited. Not only was it there first trip in an interstate train, but the real excitement was also the anticipation of reuniting with their father in the days to come.

After incessant questioning of why and where they were travelling, Greta finally relayed to her boys that they were on their way to surprise Daddy. She swore them to secrecy, using the pretence that their daddy had a lot of friends everywhere and if they were to tell anyone, he was sure to find out and spoil the surprise they had waiting for him. All along since their Daddy went missing, Greta had assured them that their father was only away on a trip and that they would be together soon.

Despite what other stories they had either been told or overheard, the two six-year-old twins had always believed what their mother had told them, keeping the same faith as their beloved mother had entrusted within herself.

Greta had begun to smile and laugh. Not only with her boys, but also with Candice and Mia. As the train tracked its way through the outer suburbs, then picking up speed as the rural surroundings started to overtake the vista, the more she was feeling at ease. It was the first time since that fateful day when she visited the market that she had instinctively smiled or giggled as the ladies' swapped opinions and anecdotes on all the miscellaneous subjects that arose.

The three had a lot in common, from child raising, to marriage and husbands, to their similar beliefs and credos, to what them made them laugh and to what made them curse. Mia divulged the intricacies of the DNA swap with her son and how the highly risky plan had worked, informing Greta that it was all for her protection that she was kept out of the loop, stressing that they were the instructions that had come from the men. Mia and Candice went about answering any questions that Greta could throw at them, from being ladies of the Sultans MC to what they had been told about Danny, both reassuring her that their husbands held him in the highest of regards.

If Greta hadn't realised before that she was now amongst strong allies, she was certainly aware of it now after the first few hours of travelling passed, and by the time they would arrive at Anton's, the days spent there would only enhance her belief that Mia and Candice were good friends that she just hadn't met yet.

The three ladies were halfway into their travels, engaging with the past, present and future expectations and hopes when Mia searched through her fully loaded carry bag that was laying at her feet. She was trying to expunge some lip balm to soothe her drying lips as Mia would quite often bite down on them, a jittery habit that Greta noticed from the first time they met. The children had moved away to the next six-seat booth adjacent to them which was vacant, a strange occurrence, the ladies commented, being that the passenger train was supposed to be fully booked.

Nonetheless, they made full use of it as the children played away from them. The ladies kept a close eye as the young ones occupied themselves with books and assorted toys. It was a chance for the girls to talk freely, unhindered by prying little ears. The conversation continued to be informative as they learned more about each other when Mia reached for her lip balm from her bag. She undid the zip atop of her bag as she lifted it when the bundle of envelope's she had received from Zoe fell across the floor at their feet.

'Are they the docs and letters from Zoe?' Candice asked, confident of what they were.

Mia arched her head at Candice, still bent over the contents that had fallen on the carriage floor. She detailed a look of concern, worried that Greta might start asking questions on what was in them and with the strict instructions from Zoe at the forefront of her mind, was hoping that their new friend wouldn't probe. To Mia's dismay, Greta's eyes didn't miss what fell out of the bag.

'Is there one for Danny?' Greta quizzed with optimism.

Mia and Candice exchanged sheepish looks at one another. Mia positioned the letters back in her bag and leant herself up against the back of the seat.

'They're for the men. We can't open them,' she said.

With friendly overtures, Greta insisted. 'If there's one for Danny, I want to read it.'

'It's not my place to pass them on,' Mia replied. She repeated that they were strictly for the men, and they wouldn't be happy if they saw them opened. Greta politely professed that her husband does not belong to the code of an MC and that it wouldn't bother him one bit if she opened a letter that was for him.

'What's mine is his, and what's his is mine. Always has been, always will be,' Greta said proudly.

Mia dallied hard inside on whether to concede to Greta's graceful persuasion. She fell silent, mulling on what to do when Candice interrupted with her own thoughts.

'Fuck 'em,' she spurned. 'The men are always keeping shit from us. Give it to her. It might be good news.'

Candice widened her smiling eyes at Mia then shrugged her shoulders.

'Okay,' agreed Mia. 'But don't blame me if it's something you don't wanna hear.'

She retrieved the letter out from her bag. 'It's the only letter for him, it's from Zoe Valetta,' she said as she handed it over to Greta.

'Oh!' Greta said with raised eyebrows as Candice gave Mia a friendly pat on the leg to motion, she was doing the right thing. Greta unsealed the envelope with her fingernails, pulled the pages out then made her herself comfortable in the corner of the seating. She started to read.

Dear Danny.

If you are reading this letter, I am assuming you have made it to Heaven. If anyone would have made it, I am certain it would be you, that I have no doubt of. I hope you are in good health and above all keeping safe and out of trouble and enjoying the sun and palm trees. By the time you would have received this letter, you will have now discovered that our plan came to fruition, and you are now officially deceased.

All the documents and related paperwork to assist you in the future are with Drake and Razor, which Mia would have delivered. Our plan would not have been possible if wasn't for the help that Mia and Candice provided and the sacrifices and secrecy that your wife had to take. You owe them all a big hug.

I hope the guilt and sorrow you felt over Ricky has eased a little and I say again, you shouldn't hold any blame over what happened. None of it was you're doing. I hope and pray that you do not punish yourself any longer.

You asked of me to attend to some tasks that you required and am pleased to inform you that most have been completed.

I will start with Barny.

I tracked him down to the Royal Saints hospital and he is recovering well. He is still under police guard, of course, which made things difficult, though I managed to work around it. I've spoken to him several times during the week and informed him of our positions. His recovery from the shoulder and hip wounds are impressing the surgeons; however, his burns were quite serious, but he's in great spirits considering.

He's a positive soul, that Barny, and he was more than pleased to hear that you were on your way to heaven. I told him that I'll be representing him as you requested. They had offered legal aid to him, but I nipped that in the bud very quickly. I'm pushing things as fast as I can. I'm hoping to have a bail hearing by the end of next week. I'm confident we'll get it.

Not that he can leave hospital straight away after but at least the police won't be sniffing around his ward. All in all, Barny is in good spirits and appreciative of what we are doing for him. I passed on an envelope containing cash to pay for Ricky's funeral costs. Barny said that his sister Janelle had visited; so, hopefully, he can get the money to her when she visits again. He said he will take care of any questions that would come from her regarding where it came from.

I was lucky enough to also track down Harry using my police and legal contacts. Unfortunately, Harry is in a holding cell at the City West police block. Along with Barny, he's facing a few minor charges, but I'm told they're soon going to add the murder of Constable Dukes to both as Conroy wants someone to go down for it. I look forward to ripping their case to shreds if that were to happen as we know neither of them pulled the trigger. I had a private sit down with Harry and spoke to him for nearly an hour. He wasn't in a good place at first; however, I think I convinced him that it will all be okay for him after detailing that I would be representing him as well.

He assured me that he hasn't signed any statement and added that he has denied involvement with any of the crimes he's been accused of. I told him not to speak with anyone unless I am present from now on. Hopefully, I'll be having his bail hearing at the same time as Barny's and relayed my confidence of freeing him. I will keep visiting him as much as possible to assist in his welfare.

At your request, and with Barny's agreement, Harry still believes that you perished in the fire. He is terribly upset at the loss of Ricky and yourself, but I do think him being none the wiser of your existence was the right call to make as he's in a fragile state of mind and could be a risk if he knew the truth. The money you have given me should be more than enough to help them with bail and any procedures that may arise.

I hope this news on your friends allays any worries you may have over them and as I promised you, I will do everything in my power to get them freed. They are in good hands, if I say so myself.

Candice could see Greta's stirring emotions as she read. She was keeping a secret eye on her as the pages ruffled in her hand.

'Good news?' she asked.

'it says here that Barny and Harry are okay. She reckons she might be able to get them bail,' Greta excitedly replied.

'See!' Candice nudged Mia. 'Good news.'

Mia accepted Candice's friendly play then added that if anyone could get them bail through bullshit and flattery, then it would be Zoe Valetta, that she had no doubts. It was news that made Greta even happier for Danny's friends. She flipped the page and continued to read:

Maddy misses you very much. There is not half a day that goes by that she does not mention her knight in shining armour. The coin you gave her never leaves her side; she treasures it very much. I am doing my best in caring for her. She travels with me everywhere I go and has become my capable new secretary. I have taken your advice and am taking steps to see if I can be her permanent guardian, YES, I will adopt her if all goes well. I have also made enquiries towards a cochlear implant and/or operation for her deafness. The feedback I am receiving has been more than positive and your money will also cover the expenses, fingers crossed.

Solomon's funeral is tomorrow, and I will be attending with her. Not that I want to be there, I hope he rots in hell for what he's done, however, Maddy has the right to be at her father's funeral. I am not looking forward to it. She understands what has happened to him and although she doesn't show too much emotion, I know she is hurting inside over her father. She doesn't know it yet, but Solomon dying was the best thing to ever happen to her. I know it's a cruel thing to say but I will never forgive him for all the lives he cost and put in danger, including hers.

I don't know whether you are receiving any news on what is happening down here regarding the aftermath of the siege and fire, but I can tell you it is still making the headlines. The powers that be have no inclination that I was anywhere near the club when it all went down so I am confident I can move forward without any repercussions.

At this point Greta asked the girls on who Solomon was. She tried to jolt her memory on what she had been told previously but needed affirmation from her friends. They replied in the best detail they could on who he was and what he had supposedly done, small information that Mia had pieced together from her phone calls with Drake. Greta then delved her eyes back onto the final page:

As for myself. I am still coming to grips with what has transpired in my life over the past two weeks. Sometimes I shiver to the bone recalling what had happened, but other times I smile contented thinking of the week I spent with you. I don't know how I would've coped without you being by my side. Our time at Anton's will never be forgotten. I do have my mother to talk and console with (she's such a sweet soul) which has been a great help but at this stage I have only told her a quarter of what we went through together. Maybe in time I will tell her all but at the moment Maddy (God bless her heart) is being my counsellor.

I don't know if I will ever see you again (it's probably best for all if I don't) or what the future holds. but I will always have that mental picture of your Heaven embedded in my mind that you continually described. I hope it is still as beautiful as you envisioned.

I also need you to know that words can never express how eternally grateful Maddy, and I are for all that you did for us. Both of us would not be alive if you didn't do the things you did. I could sit here for hours and put all my feelings down on paper, but I will not burden you any longer with my silly emotions as you have enough on your mind over what lays ahead for you. For the large peace of mind that both Maddy and myself require, we need to know if you made it to heaven and that you are safe so when and if you receive this letter, PLEASE reply to me as soon as you can as the unknown is already starting to eat away at us. You know how to do it.

I hope the reunion with your wife and children is everything you hoped for and that they arrive safely to your heaven. I wish you all the best in your new life and your secret will forever be held within both Maddy and I.

Always with you.

Regards,
Zoe.

    Greta folded the pages and softly re-positioned them back into the envelope.

    'All good?' Candice enquired. Even though Greta tried to hide it, she could sense that her demeanour had changed.

    'Yeah. All good news. She's just filling him in on what's happening. He'll be pleased to know I'm sure,' Greta smiled. 'She sure knows a lot. I hope she can keep her mouth shut,' she added sourly.

    'Drake trusts her. That's enough for me,' Mia assured.

    'And Razor. He's the last one to trust anyone, I can tell you that,' Candice supported. She then added with smiling sarcasm, 'If they're wrong, we'll all be single ladies then, won't we?'

    Greta accepted their guarantees on Zoe's commitment to them all; however, what she had just read was not feeling like good news to her. Externally, she wouldn't show her angst to the ladies, she was too proud for that, but internally, and reading between the lines, some words and sentences were a little too personal for Greta's liking.

    She knew that desperate and tragic events can bind people together, and loneliness even further. Disturbingly for Greta though, the grappling thought of her husband being with some sexy lawyer lady and tending to someone else's child, while she grieved his death and his own boys pined for him, was leaving a hole in her stomach.

    A myriad of negative thoughts stormed through her mind. How close *had* they become? Was this the reason why she didn't want to meet with me as she recalled Zoe's sheepish stare in the hotel foyer. How does she know so much about his personal life? What did she mean by their time together will never be forgotten? What did she mean by being contented? And what the hell did always with you mean when she signed off?

    Her inner battle continued as the train sped through the countryside. Time passed as she tried to keep in tune with the chit chat that progressed between herself and the girls. The talk of Candice's impending birth being the main topic, all going well, only another three months away, Greta's bodily instincts telling herself that she may be heading down the same path.

    Greta was smiling and responding to whatever arose, though her mind was somewhere else. She retrieved her shoulder bag that was beneath her feet and delved for a little plastic sealed bag. In it were Danny's rings. She took them out and straddled them across her fingers close to her own rings and softly twirled them around, subconsciously looking for some type of security.

It felt that another little piece of her heart had been taken from her, another hardening of her soul. But whatever she was feeling, the burdening questions for her husband had to be put at the back of her mind. She would wait for the right time and place, trying not to look to worried, just interested when that time would come. If Danny were to be lying about anything, she would know in a heartbeat, she was positive about that. So, for the time being, her focus would solely be on the long-awaited reunion that was hopefully forthcoming, and the questions would have to wait until they were settled into their new lives, if and when that would ever happen.

Amongst her rabid thoughts was also the burning mystery of the money that was mentioned in the letter. It too was eating away at her and was now at the forefront of her mind. Did Danny have a hidden stash that I didn't know about she quizzed herself. If so, how did he access it. Why would he use it to help others and not his own damn family? As the train continued to travel, a little gap of silence embraced the ladies and with that, Greta decided to throw caution to the wind.

'Do you know anything about this money?' she asked. 'In the letter, she was thanking him for the money she got to help with Barny, Harry and the little girl. I know *we* had nothing,' Greta stressed forcibly. 'Do you know how he came across it? Was it the club?'

Mia and Candice glanced at each other. They knew they were a lot privier to what had been transpiring than Greta. Together they thought it their duty, as woman to woman, and now friend to friend, to inform her of what they knew.

'It's the same money we've used to pay and bribe ourselves to where we are,' said Mia.

'What do you mean?' Greta replied.

Taking a deep breath, unsure how Greta would react, Mia leant forward making sure no over exuberant ears from nearby passengers could hear them.

'The money came from the Graceville Country Club! You heard about that, didn't you?' she coaxed.

'What? The robbery?'

'Yes. It was your Danny who pulled off the heist!' confided Mia.

'No way. He would never do that,' was Greta's instant response.

Mia gave her a staid look of certainty. Greta peered at Candice and received the same look of surety.

'Oh my god!' Greta paused. 'He did this with your husbands?'

'No. They weren't involved with the actual heist. Ricky and Barny were with him. Drake and Razor helped with the planning.'

Greta was shellshocked. Her heart started to beat unnervingly. Armed robbery! Danny! This is not him. He's not a criminal! However, it was all quickly coming back to her, the times that Danny spoke with jest about the Armaguard van. It was long ago, but it was all making sense. At the time when she heard about the heist, Danny did fleetingly enter her mind, but she quickly laughed it off, not even raising it with anybody. *How could it possibly be him anyway*! She determined, he was miles away in the mountains, of that she was certain.

Greta delved for more answers from the girls. How did they get so close to town? How much was stolen? How did they do it? How did they get away with it? Questions the girls had no answers to and truthfully promised they didn't have all the details. They would only know themselves when they would arrive at Anton's and be reunited with their own husbands.

Greta leant back in her seat. Her mind was now overloaded as she smiled at her two boys playing on the adjacent carriage table. The sound of the train's undercarriage pounded outside as she kept her thoughts to herself. As the silent gathering thoughts clustered in her mind, the words of her friend Sgt Dane Grainger began to ring in her ears. Maybe he was right when he said that Danny may have changed from the person he was. For what she had just been told was totally out of character of the man she married, or at least she thought so.

The train arrived at Twin City railway station on schedule and the five-hour journey was over. The women and children disembarked without disturbance and were met by Anton at the same point where he had said his goodbyes to Danny and Zoe, Drake and Razor insisting on keeping their low profile. Greta was anxious and worrisome, not only of what lay ahead, but also of the large population of people they had to negotiate through the market mall. She felt that she was fleeing the law with all the lies and deceit, and she was getting a first-hand feeling of what her husband must have had to endure. Putting her thoughts aside for now, she decided to just follow the lead of Mia and Candice who to her seemed confident and assured of what they were doing.

After endearing hugs of reacquaintance, Mia introduced her travelling party to the awaiting Anton. He was also gracious and pleased to meet the wife and children of his new friend Danny Pruitt. He commented with cheery respect that he felt like he knew them already, except for the haircut that Greta now adopted he drolly mused. Greta smiled and thanked him in return, proud and happy that Danny had boasted about his family.

The young boys were in awe of Anton's frame as he loaded the cases into the back of the cart. He gave them genial winks, alleviating any fears the lads held over the friendly giant looking character. Anton took the reins of the open carriage with Mia and Candice up front with him while Greta sat behind in the cart with the children on the bench seats, Anton providing cushions for comfort as he did for Zoe and Maddy over a week before.

Greta conversed with the young ones as she took in the fast-moving experiences of Twin City as Anton negotiated the horses through the busy streets. Soon they had crossed the Alpine River and further on were approaching the outside gates of Anton's property when two horsemen abruptly surrounded them without warning.

The unexpected intrusion and the shock surprise would soon turn to unbridled joy for the two ladies up front. They both jumped from their seats with unabated enthusiasm when Anton bought the horses to a halt, scaring Greta in the process. Two rough-looking tattooed men dismounted from their horses then wildly raced to embrace their absent wives; Drake and Razor couldn't wait any longer to see their ladies.

Greta's momentary fears were quelled as she watched the reunion, Anton happily assuring her of whom they were. Shortly after the delight of seeing their wives once more, Drake lowered his son Callum to the ground and approached Greta sitting up in the cart.

'Hello Greta,' he welcomed her with a soft handshake. 'I'm Drake. And this is Razor,' as he too sidled up to the cart. 'Don't worry, your reunion with Danny is not long away, that I promise.'

For the next three days, Greta would be overwhelmed and filled with embarrassed gratitude for the way she and her boys were treated. The anxiety over the contents in Zoe's letter waned significantly as she took advantage of the serene surrounds and the companionship that was gifted to her. The men had expressed on more than one occasion that they had taken an oath with her husband and that they would protect and look over his family, words that comforted her greatly. They added after Greta posed the possibility of Danny not making it to his destination by guaranteeing that they would find out one way or another, and if he wasn't in Heaven when they arrived, they swore that they would find him whatever the cost.

Greta made her temporary home in the bungalow, the same where Zoe and Maddy had slept, taking time out on occasions to lay on the makeshift bed in the barn after enquiring where Danny had rested. Her sons were happy during their stay, playing and tending to Anton's array of animals. Drake and Razor did their best to respond to the questions that would come from her, although when the topic became too hot for them to answer and respecting Danny's separateness, they would respectfully advise that they either didn't know or the answer she desired was for her husband to reveal.

As the time passed at Anton's, it was obvious to Greta that Danny had formed a tight bond with the former MC outlaws, not only through their tales of her husband, but also through the respect they showed when they spoke about him, revealing a lot of the traits, humour and ethics in Danny that she was already endeared to.

On the second day of her stay, she advised the group that it was her birthday and that afternoon Candice baked up a cake in the outdoor brick oven. She decorated it with homemade icing, creams and candles and surprised Greta with it, all singing a joyous rendition of Happy Birthday. Greta was thankful and wryly commented that Danny promised that they would be together by this time. She divulged that it was the only promise he had ever broken to her. 'I suppose I can forgive him regarding the circumstances,' she sighed.

Razor's logistical wizardry had finally come to the fore. Through a lot of hard persuading and secret cash payments to railway workers, he was successful in acquiring space for their vehicles on one of the two carriage trailers that the passenger train would be towing behind the main diesel locomotive. It was now Thursday morning, the fourth day of their stay and all were set to leave the following day at 12.15pm. Their seats and cabins would not be first class as Danny had travelled, however, the trip was going to be comfortable enough. Although each family would be on the same carriage, they would all be separated, having to share facilities with other travellers on the 26-hour trip to Burbank and the state of Capricornia.

Including the young boys, they all sat at the breakfast table enjoying the morning spread when Candice left Razor's side. Greta had abruptly left the table herself moments before looking for privacy at the nearby willow tree as the adult members at the table modestly looked on.

Greta was arched over with one hand on her stomach and gently wiping the bile and muck away from her mouth with the other.

'Welcome to the club,' said Candice.

Greta tilted her head and gave her an uncomfortable look, a mixture of fear and happiness. With her fingers, she kept the strands of her hair away from her cheeks. It was the third morning in a row that she had vomited during breakfast. She knew the signs, she knew her body, and with trepidation and excitement as Candice rubbed her back with comfort, Greta accepted the reality—she was pregnant.

Chapter 46

'What's it like out there?'

'Bloody beautiful.'

'Good sets?'

'More than enough for a rookie like me.'

'Cool, thanks bro!'

Danny nodded his head then continued to walk off the beach. The coastal patch near his property was the last surf beach along the eastern coast that riders could utilise for behind the next headland laid the village of Port Denning. Out across the seas from the town's harbour were the reefs and islands that stretched the remainder of the northern coastline, quelling any type of surf that board riders could exploit.

Danny wore black board shorts and had his sunglasses on. His towel was draped over his shoulder as he carried his surfboard underneath his armpit. The strangers he was talking to quickly changed and headed into the surf. It was early morning, an hour after sunrise and again he was challenging himself in the ocean. He didn't mind how many times he would be wiped out, the sense of freedom and seclusion he derived from the surf overpowered anything else that festered inside him. From the third morning he was there, he would spend the first hours of every dawning day in the water, if no one else was around, of course.

It was nearing the end of the second week since Danny had arrived at his Heaven and the stress and unknown concerning his family was nearing crisis point.

The morning after he had arrived, he was awoken by a growling Blue Heeler dog and a familiar face poking and prodding the tip of a loaded rifle into his sleeping body. Danny's head was on his suitcase, his softened backpack gave him cushioning for his head while a dark windcheater covered his shoulders and face. At first glance, according to the man with the rifle, Danny was just another vagrant taking advantage of the vacant house by sleeping on its veranda.

'Hey you! Wake up,' he repeated louder.

Danny turned and peered up with one open eye.

'G'day Steve,' he smiled.

'Jesus Christ! Danny. Is that you?' was Steve's astonished reply.

'Nice to see ya,' said Danny as he righted himself from the floor of the decking.

Steve ordered his dog Patto at ease. His four-legged partner then nestled quietly on his rear legs with his ears pricked then watched as the two long lost friends embraced each other tightly, Steve amazed, that his long-lost friend had made it to Heaven. They looked each other up and down with animated smiles. Both had changed a little since they last laid eyes on one another. Danny with his goatee beard and more muscular frame and Steve with an extra few kilos around the mid rift, along with a thicker and lengthened brown goatee beard of his own.

Steve Goulding still had his upright and confidence stance and his blue eyes still had that peering inspecting look about them. The two happily commented on their changed differences with Danny mocking Steve that he had taken on the cowboy look about him. Jeans, open collared shirt, dark boots, and wide brimmed hat as the pleasure engulfed them of seeing one another.

'Sorry about the rifle. I thought you were another drifter trying to break in again,' Steve apologised.

'It's alright. I didn't wanna break in. It looked too nice and clean inside to mess it up. The veranda was good enough. Anyways,' Danny quipped, 'I've been getting used to guns being pointed at me it over the last month or so.'

'So I've heard,' Steve drolly replied.

'We'll talk about that later,' Danny suggested almost shamefaced as he quickly changed the subject. 'Did you get my letter?' he asked.

'Yes, I did, but I've also been reading the Venturian papers Lisa has been sending up. So, you can probably forgive my shock at seeing you here. You've had an eventful new year, my friend.'

Danny rolled his eyes back and released a large sigh of agreement, acknowledging that Steve's comment maybe the greatest understatement he had heard.

'How's your wife? It's been far too long, mate,' Danny enquired, turning the attention away from himself.

'Lisa left me last March,' Steve replied. 'It was all too much for her. Don't blame her really. Surprised she lasted that long considering how everything changed. She took the kids and moved back home to be with her family, so I've been doing it alone up here ever since.'

Danny expressed his sorrow for his marriage break-up; however, Steve brushed it off immediately. He was more interested in Danny's trials and tribulations and was excitedly looking forward to hearing his friend's stories, especially how the hell he made it to Capricornia and Heaven itself. Danny light heartedly informed him that there would be plenty of time to hear his escapades as all he wanted to do now was enlighten his friend of his intentions.

'I've got something for you. Can we go inside the house?' asked Danny.

'Sure, no worries.'

Steve rustled a set of keys out of the front pocket of his pants then opened the door and allowed Danny inside ahead of him. All the furniture was covered in white sheeting. The spotted gum floorboards were immaculately clean and polished, the kitchen benches and idle appliances the same. Danny perused the open plan living of the interior, swirling his ahead above at the high ceilings and over hanging large fans. Steve walked from door to door and window to window to allow the fresh clean breeze to flow through and remove the hot musty claustrophobic scent from the house.

'Sorry for the smell,' he said. 'No one's been living in here for over twelve months. I used to rent it out to dudes who were working on the stud or the nearby orchards for extra income but as it is now, people have moved on to find employment. I had to let my own workers go. I couldn't afford to pay them anymore,' Steve lamented.

'What! You're here by yourself?' Danny asked, surprised.

'Yep. Other than Mitch, he's my only full timer. Nice guy. He's only in his early twenties but he knows what he's doing. He doesn't live too far off so he's pretty handy. I can only hire casuals when I've got the ability to pay them which is not that often, so I'm pretty bloody busy,' Steve laughed.

'Maybe I can ease your burden,' said Danny.

'That would be good!' thanked Steve. 'The stud is surviving on a shoestring, mate. Before the hard times hit, I had five stallions on my roster, over sixty broodmares, but now I'm down to one stallion only eight mares. As you probably read in my letters, I had to sell off stock and land to keep the vultures away,' rued Steve.

'I guess that explains all the new fences,' Danny said, confirming his assumptions.

'Yep! I had to sub-divide a great portion of the farm, including a large part of yours. It was the only option I had to keep the cash coming through the doors and survive. Don't worry,' Steve said after seeing Danny's face change. 'The contracts of the sale have got a covenant forbidding any of the new owners from building close to any of the existing buildings. The acre blocks that surround this house I kept. I use them for agistment, I don't charge too much but it's necessary. It's the only recent income I'm receiving other than trading and consultancy fees.'

'Shit mate! You must be heartbroken,' Danny said.

'It fuckin kills me, mate,' sorrowed Steve.

'Well, maybe this can brighten you up.'

Danny lifted his suitcase onto the black and white speckled marble kitchen bench then pulled back the zip. He felt around through his clothing until he grasped the black wrapping that contained his money. Steve's curious eyes watched on as Danny laid it on the bench then untie the wrapping and produce the first wad of $10,000. Then another, then another, and then another.

'So! What do I owe you for the rest of the house? Is this enough?' Danny nonchalantly said.

Steve looked on in amazement. It had been a long time since he had seen an amount of cash like this before. He had grown up in the electronic banking age, they all had, and to see the amount of paper money was an exciting eye-opener for him, but most of all, it was going to be a godsend to him.

Steve was flabbergasted and couldn't come up with an immediate answer to Danny's question. He was overwhelmed by the amount of cash that was produced before him. The gesture was over generous he confessed, however, instead of accepting anything at this point in time, with rugged sincerity, Steve enforced with goodwill there was plenty of time to work out the sum later because for the moment, catching up on each other's stories was far more important than settling a long-awaited debt.

The ensuing days were a mixture of inner peace and torment for Danny. Happy and contented to have survived and made it to his part of heaven unscathed, distraught and grieved of the unknown concerning Greta and his sons. He kept himself busy by helping his pal out on the farm. Steve informed him that he couldn't pay him, not that Danny would have accepted it anyway. His friend had given him a lifeline, and to that, Danny would be forever grateful, so if he could lessen the burden of work to be done, he wouldn't hesitate in giving him a helping hand.

On quieter times he would read the plethora of books left behind by tenants who had come and gone from the house. From miscellaneous sports magazines and fiction to biographies and history, he would peruse through them all at any opportunity to fill the void of anxiety and boredom. He would keep active by running around the property boundaries after his surfing and obsessed himself with exercise programmes, busting out repetitive push-ups and sit-ups.

He positioned a boxing bag inside one of the nearby horse stables and punched his anger and pain out to the point of exhaustion. When he wasn't pushing his body to the limit, Steve, with his dog Patto always by his side, would show Danny around the full extent of what land remained, from his cultivated vegetable patches to his small flock of sheep, dear and cattle. Danny did his best to tend the horses through Steve's coaxing; however, his deep-seated phobia regarding equine was still festering despite the animated stories he would relay to Steve about the big black gelding he befriended, so he refrained from jumping in the saddle if he could avoid it.

He spent time moving around the furniture inside the house to his liking, rearranging it on more than one occasion, picturing in his head how Greta would like it. He silently sang happy birthday to her, drunk, angry, depressed.

Steve would make the short journey back and forth from town to restock supplies when required, including one early trip to secure a sidearm weapon that Danny had requested. This was easily acquired through Steve's associates in the local farming industry. Danny was nowhere near confident, or stupid enough for that matter to show his face anywhere and wandered only in and around his Heaven. When the sun started to set and all the chores were done, the men would share beers and whiskey as they caught up on each other's life experiences they had missed out on since being apart.

At times Steve would listen agape as Danny recalled all the exhilaration, the tragedies, and the intoxicating adrenalin rushes that overpowered him while he was running and fighting for his life. Some tales would be told with excitement and laughter, some with anger and hatred, others with wrenching pain and tears. His night with Zoe would not be mentioned.

At the end of the first week the two men had come to an agreement that Steve had initiated, and which took some convincing for Danny to accept, as it seemed to him that he was getting the better end of it. In the end, and no matter how much Danny argued the point, Steve was having nothing else other than what he demanded.

Steve insisted that there was no need to pay him anything. He explained that if Danny had never given him a down payment, he would've had to sell it all and then be left with nothing. It was the down payment money that enabled him to survive and save the property and awkwardly confessed that there was nothing left, it had all been used up. The only thing Danny had to do to take full ownership of his parcel of land was to help Steve with the financials of maintaining the stud and farm, putting money in to help with machinery and shed repairs, along with feed and vet bills.

The real kicker for the deal that Steve wanted more than anything else to seal it, was to purchase a stallion that in his mind would return his stud back into the black, and for that to come to fruition, he needed Danny's money.

'It's bred in the purple,' Steve enthusiastically explained. 'His name is Master Ike. He won a Group one down in Burbank when he was an early three-year-old before he done a suspensory ligament and was retired. His sire is Lord Bruin who has produced multiple group one winners and his Dam is Miss Ellie May who comes from a Stakes winning family. Have you heard of any of them?' asked Steve.

'I have,' Danny responded. 'I know of Lord Bruin, he's a top stallion. But I'll take your word for it on the others.'

Steve knew Danny had a good insight of the racing game and loved the punt in the good old days. He would often talk to Steve about what was happening on the racecourses throughout the land but as Danny explained, his knowledge had waned somewhat since the hard times hit.

'He's only a second season sire but he's already produced a few two-year-old winners,' Steve continued. 'I reckon he will produce classic winners. You know, Derby, Oaks and Guineas winners. I reckon his progeny will get better with age. I'm sure of it.'

Danny could the see excitement in Steve's animated tones as he gleefully listened to his friend's sales pitch.

'Have you heard of Blue Acres Stud?' asked Steve.

'Yeah, rings a bell.'

'Yeah. It's one of the largest studs in the state. It's between here and Burbank. They're having a hard time holding onto their stock as well and they've put a few stallions up for sale, including Master Ike. And I want him,' said Steve vigorously.

'So what's the catch?' Danny shrugged.

'$40,000. The asking price is $40,000,' Steve's voice shallowed. 'You could put a few more zeros on that if it were a decade ago.'

There was a pregnant pause between the two as they sat on their veranda deck chairs overlooking the horses grazing in the foreground. Danny then shook the dregs of his 375ml stubby out over the edge of the handrails after he emptied the last swig into his stomach, knowing that Steve was awaiting his thoughts.

'Well! What the fuck are we waiting for? When do we pick it up?' Danny casually said, acting if he didn't know what all the fuss was about.

Steve was over the moon. It had been his dream to own a stallion of Master Ike's quality and was adamant that stud masters would be lining up to have their mares put to him in the spring breeding season. Steve knew his success wouldn't be overnight, nevertheless, it would keep the cash flowing through his stud, enough to keep him afloat. If he could survive another two seasons, the stallion would be the saviour of the stud and with Danny's money, that was almost a guarantee.

The men shook hands with jubilant force and cheered with their newly opened beers and after Steve had sculled down his ale, he was quickly on his horse and with Patto following was hi-tailing it into Port Denning. He stormed into the local post office and was on the public phone in a flash and ringing Blue Acres Stud to arrange the payment and pick up of his soon to be champion stallion.

Another week passed on and a Saturday afternoon had come around again and after attending all that needed to be done regarding the horses and property, Danny again resumed his seat on the deck chair overlooking the paddocks and entrance to his Heaven. Another restless and sleepless night had endured. He calculated that it had been 55 days since he last saw and touched his wife and 15 days since he had left Twin City.

He threatened to Steve on the morning rounds that if his family had not arrived by Monday evening, he was going to risk all and go search for them himself, a scenario that Steve greatly advised against. The point had come where he couldn't wait any longer. He had no idea where his wife and sons were. No idea that they knew he was still alive.

'They probably think I'm dead,' he gloomed. 'They'll never arrive here. It's all been a waste of time. Maybe it would've been better if I did die in the fire. At least it would've been closure for her,' he angrily remonstrated with Steve. His impatience was drenching him.

Danny's defeatist darkness would invade him as soon as his mind would rest, despite the vows and pledges that Drake and Razor had made. He concluded that anything could've happened to his family while he was escaping North. Every negative scenario rushed through his vulnerable brain and as time wore on, he was thinking that his Heaven was only turning into a waiting hell.

As evening approached, Steve laid his rifle by his side and with Patto resting at his feet, joined Danny on the veranda with a fresh bottle of whiskey. An empty bottle sat on the decking as Danny swirled around what whiskey was left in his glass. He was dressed in his casual black tank top and dark shaded cargo shorts with his bare feet resting on the vertical slats of the veranda as Steve positioned himself next to him. They re-filled their glasses and sat peering into the distance. Steve knew his friend needed company and although Danny was not in the talking mood, Steve thought it the right thing to do by being by his side after listening to his distressed worries during the day.

The familiar summer late afternoon storm clouds were gathering in the distance as the rolls of thunder started to echo over the surroundings. The escaping sunrays were breaching through the horse paddocks with the strengthening breeze swaying the Magnolias and palm trees that lined the long driveway. Both men sipped away on their whiskeys, relaxing with cigarettes and chewing and munching away on assorted peanuts and cashews, a vice that Steve was never short of.

Steve tried hard to get Danny's mind off the troubles that crazed him. He invited Danny to accompany him to the marina in Port Denning when night fell. Several music bands were going to be playing with food stalls and plenty of beers and spirits available. The small coastal community was celebrating the promised upsurge in the economy and travellers were already starting to filter through to the holiday village and Steve encouraged that it would be a great night for both.

His incessant friendly badgering parroted in Danny's ears as he procrastinated over his decision when Patto stood to his feet and let out a sequence of deep protective growls. Both men's attention was drawn to the dog and within seconds were alerted to what Patto was spirited towards, the sound of oncoming vehicles.

Danny quickly butted out his cigarette into the ashtray. Other than Steve's young farm hand Mitch, a single visit by the vet and a couple of deliveries by horse and cart, no one else had visited since Danny had arrived and the sound of vehicle engines approaching from the hidden distance were quickly making both men edgy.

'Are you expecting anybody?' Danny asked nervously.

'No. No, I'm not,' Steve succinctly replied.

The men stood to their feet, Danny resting his whiskey on the handrails. Steve retrieved his rifle from the deck and without hesitation, Danny hurried inside the house to retrieve his newly acquired semi-automatic handgun from his bedside drawers. They re-joined on the decking and listened to the sound of the nearing vehicles, Steve hushing his dogs now watchful barking.

The vehicles were still out of sight behind the thick forest ahead of their property, they would know soon enough if the vehicles were heading their way when they reached the fork in the road. If they drove straight ahead, they could relax, if they turned left, they were coming at them. They could hear the engines easing off as they approached the fork.

'Sounds like two of them,' said Steve.

The men's concerns jumped a level as the vehicles turned left at the fork. They were now coming their way and were soon heading up the gravel rise towards the stud's entrances; wind carrying the dust the heavy-duty tyres were jetting out and Danny's heart was starting to race as his stomach churned.

'Is it the cops?' he nervily asked.

'Don't panic yet,' Steve advised. 'Let's see if I can identify them first before we do anything. You better go inside, just in case.'

Danny opened the door to enter the house. As he held the handle of the fly wire door, he stopped and peered back to where the oncoming vehicles were approaching from. He looked past Steve who was vigilantly watching through the swaying magnolia and palm trees in the foreground and soon enough, both men were getting their first glimpse of the approaching vehicles. The unknown visitors began to level out from the rise and slowly neared the gates to Heaven. They came to a halt underneath the metal archway, but it wouldn't be Steve who would recognise them, it would be Danny.

He gently closed the fly wire door and slowly walked to the top of the outdoor staircase, feebly giving his handgun to Steve in the process as he passed.

'What are you doing?' asked Steve.

It was if Danny was in a trance, not hearing his friend's worry as again Steve asked what he was doing. Danny continued slowly down the stairs until he made it to the bottom step to where the gravel topped driveway uniformed with the entrance stairs, waiting for someone, anyone, to exit the vehicle. He was transfixed, it was like something was drawing him to a magnet, uncontrolled, unabated, as Steve casted a nervous vigilant eye over both his friend and the unannounced guests.

Danny continued his slow walk down the driveway as Steve again called his friend to stop what he was doing. Danny raised his right hand and gestured to him for calmness. He looked up at him on the veranda, turned his head again towards the vehicles then turned to Steve once more.

'It's the boys,' Danny breathed.

'What! What are you talking about?' Steve growled, confused.

'It's the boys! Drake and Razor!' he said more clearly.

The lead vehicle's distinctive bull bar and grill had instantly captured his attention from the moment he eyed them. It was black, the same matt coloured finish that matched the trims and knew for sure that it could only be Razor and Drake's chosen work. The engines were now shut off, echoes of thunder continued in the distance as the sound of swaying fronds and branches from the nearby trees wafted on the wind.

The silent vehicles were still 100m away. Danny stopped, searchingly staring at the reflecting windscreen, desperately trying to gather any movement from the occupants. He only wanted one thing to emerge out of it, and within an eternity of seconds the rear right door of the lead vehicle began to open.

The passenger descended her foot down onto the step plate then grounded both feet. She slowly moved away from the door and presented herself into the open. She wore cut-off denim shorts frayed at the hemline high up on her thighs, a loose white singlet and faded black work boots.

Danny fell to his knees. His body had slumped in euphoric exhaustion. After all what he had done, after all the sacrifices, after all the death and destruction, after all he'd dangerously risked and planned for, and after 55 days of never-ending pain, Greta now stood before him.

Greta walked to the front of the vehicle then stopped. She penetrated her numbing stare from afar. The lowering afternoon sun poked its rays through the distant storm clouds. Finally, she could see him. She was entrusted that he was alive, she was entrusted that he was in his Heaven awaiting her, but now she could see him, now she could truly believe. Greta cusped her hands to her mouth, the tears were already falling.

Frozen seconds passed for her, trying to believe that Danny was there, right in front of her. She lowered her hands away from her face and began to run to him. She needed to touch him, to feel him, to smell him, to extinguish her pining aching heart and mind. With every step, her momentum gained until she free fell into his arms, propelling both to the ground in unchained rejoicing. They embraced and kissed one another feverishly to all parts of the face and head as they rolled, ravishing the feeling of being in each other's arms again. They raised to their knees, grasping their hands to the side of each other's head.

Greta blissfully teared whilst they tunnelled into one another's eye's. It was if they were exploring each other, the changes, the differences, if any. She stroked her fingers through his thickened chin. 'You've grown a beard?' she happily cried.

Danny pinched her hair between his thumb and forefinger.

'You've cut your hair!'

Greta smilingly nodded then grabbed Danny's hand to her stomach. 'I'm pregnant,' she said.

The tears continued as a proud look engulfed his face. 'I'm happy,' he replied.

They were still on their knees as they secured each other in their arms again. Greta then eased away and delved her right hand into her hip pocket. With excited anticipation, dreaming of this precise moment, she produced Danny's rings, extended his fingers, then slipped them on. They continued their unabated embracing as Darcy and Daniel appeared by their sides.

The twins had scrambled their way out of the rear seats of Razor and Candice's lead vehicle and unsure what to do, made their way a short distance ahead of the bull bar and propped their awaiting eyes on their parents. At the same time as Razor and Candice stepped out from their front seats, Drake, Mia and their son Callum exited from the second vehicle.

They moved forward and gathered around the young boys and together watched the impassioned reunion. It was hard for them to not shed a tear, even for Razor and Drake, as hardened as they were, as the women interlocked their arms to them.

'What are you waiting for?' Mia and Candice goaded the twins with smiles. 'Go see your father,' they coaxed with a friendly push.

As soon as Danny saw them, the uncontrollable tears flooded out. He embraced them as tightly as a father's love could. With absolute devotion, he wretchedly repeated how much he had missed them. He unlocked his grip then ruffled their hair and asked if they had been looking after their mother as the overwhelming emotions absorbed them also.

'They've been my rock. Haven't you, my boys?' Greta assured whilst patting their faces. Another heartening family group lock ensued. Danny did not want to let go, he had lost them once, he was not going to lose them again. He softly wrestled all three in his arms as the consciousness began to sink into his soul.

He then looked down the driveway as he held his loved ones. He stood to his feet, still clasping his wife and sons as close as he could. He locked his eyes on Drake and Razor whilst looking over Greta's shoulder and gave them biggest heartfelt nod of gratitude he could muster. In unison, they both contentedly accepted his recognition with their own expressive nods then gave their own ladies a tighter squeeze with their arm, deeply satisfied that they had completed their mission.

Danny then turned to Steve who was taking in everything from his perched position on the veranda. His friend gave him a huge smiling thumbs up, took his whiskey from the deck table and raised his glass. Danny then returned his pacified admiring eyes into Greta's; he was now truly in heaven.

Chapter 47

'Please Daddy, please, please, please! Our friends are going to be there,' Danny's twin sons jumped at his feet, grabbing at his shirt, badgering, coaxing their father to join them.

Greta had already been in his ears for the whole day, and the previous one for that matter, joyfully pleading with her husband that everything would be okay, that he had nothing to worry about anymore. Going out for dinner would be the best thing for him, she playfully implored.

It was three days before Christmas, almost a year since Rosco and Billy Devlin came visiting the Pruitts' former home back in Graceville. Happily, this Christmas, Danny already had his children's presents wrapped and hidden, ready to produce on the day, including several for his three-month-old daughter.

Greta had given birth to Lani Jade, the name Lani being of Hawaiian origin meaning heaven or sky. She entered the new world at 11.34 pm on 28 September at the Kingston hospital. Both mother and daughter got through the proud event without complications; it was one of the rare times that Danny had left his own Heaven. Lani was born with the same deep brown eyes as her mother with an instant golden smile and weighed a healthy 7lb 8oz to go with her thriving set of lungs. It was a gift that her parents cherished with all their heart, a gift that Danny had never thought possible at the year's beginning.

The family had settled into the quiet lifestyle near the tourist village of Port Denning, his Heaven was now fully functioning the way he had always pictured. Steve had signed all the necessary paperwork to transfer full ownership over to Danny of the now four-acre property and house. Greta had found a job as a substitute teacher with the promise of a full-time position when school resumed after the summer break.

The twin boys had been enrolled at the local primary school under a different surname and Danny was happy, believing he was secure in his new environment. He kept himself occupied by working and helping with the decision making on the horse stud. Nonetheless, Danny's mind would never be at rest, always looking around the next corner for something to destroy and tear apart what had now been built. Although Greta had made an abundance of new friends through her work and new tennis club and frequently took journeys into town with her children, Danny's obsessive fears and paranoia would prevent him from travelling too often from his piece of Heaven.

The nation and the states within, along with the rest of the western world were on the upward spiral and as every month passed the economy and happier times grew with it. Government and large business had now become less reliant on fossil fuels. Renewable energies were now the way of the future, greener, more sustainable and laws were enacted to enforce legislation. Although times were still enormously tough for a lot of the population, hope was all that was needed for the less fortunate and it was obvious to all that what they were seeing was enough belief that prosperous times did lay ahead.

Automobiles were filtering through to the highways and byways again, electric and hybrid cars now outnumbering the fuel driven as the roads slowly became busier. Larger commercial and transport vehicles still relied on the proportionally rationed petrol and diesel fuels to keep the important freight moving. Internet services were becoming available once more and by the years end, most of population were back online. Mobile phone usage had begun to re-enter society as towers got the necessary upgrades and imported devices reached the shore again.

However, at first it would only be available to the well off and privileged until providers could supply and sustain the enormous demand. Until then, the general population would have a further frustrating wait before mobile phones, personal computers and laptops would become easily accessible to what it was previously.

Nirvana horse stud, which Steve and Danny renamed their small part of the world, installed their own fuel tanks to supply the previously dormant farm vehicles, an expensive cost for the day that was easily covered by Danny's gains. He advised Steve to install a large solar panel power system on the stud to cut future costs, all learnt from his days at *La Fortaleza*. By the year's end, tourists in numbers were starting to revisit the Amber Coast as domestic and international flights progressively took to the airways again, giving Port Denning the economic boost it needed.

Drake and Razor, with the absolute support of their wives, made the decision to make their home also in the northern state. Danny and Steve helped accommodate them in the first month of their stay but as Danny had promised them, it didn't take long for them to fall in love with the area and they soon acquired their own house and acreage nearby. Candice gave birth to a healthy girl, the proud parents naming her Samara, and by coincidence or not, Drake and Mia would again be joining the club as Mia was expecting in the early months of the new year.

Razor gained employment on the road maintenance crew, his expertise and experience made him an asset for the shire looking to fast track the backlog of work to be done on the deteriorated and neglected roads within the shire and by the time Christmas came around, he had already been promoted to a leadership role while Candice revelled in her role as a new mother.

Drake was also employed by the shire. His experience in the security business, not to mention his smooth tongue that could convince anyone of his wares whether it be true or not, enabled him to secure a job doing the rounds protecting shire assets. He was supplied with his own vehicle and although his shifts would vary, he embraced his new life with great enthusiasm while Mia didn't take long to land a job in the health care industry. As with Danny, both families would always remain aware of their surroundings and in which company they would socialise with as they knew that one careless or overconfident move or comment could bring all their worlds crashing down.

Courtesy of Zoe's documents and false identification papers, each family opened bank accounts under new pseudonyms. Within a month of arriving and inside a week of each other, they all travelled separately to the larger town of Kingston to secure health care cards and photo drivers' licenses. Not for one moment did they raise any suspicions as they successfully convinced government employees of who they were, including having their photos taken and being issued with new passports for any potential future travels.

They procured new ID cards using the same reasons as the tens of thousands of citizens throughout the nation used when they made their own visit to the appropriate government office. That is through disregard and hopelessness they had lost or destroyed their old cards. It was scenario that Zoe advised to take advantage of in her delivered documents, relying that the frustrated, workless, and penniless person thought they would never have to use them again.

They all took confidence in the lawyer's advice that the false tax file numbers and bank accounts they had at the ready was more than enough to put the three retreating families more than halfway across the line to secure the photographed plastic. While on their visit to Kingston, Drake and Razor found a tattooist to rid or cover any ink that would link them to the Sultans MC and with gentle persuasion and a financial incentive, they were confident that the owner of the parlour would quickly forget that they had ever visited.

Over the ensuing months, the three families would get together on a regular basis, rotating around each other's properties when they socialised and the more they did, the tighter the bond became, particularly for the women who couldn't go more than two days without some type of chat. Danny would retain his goatee beard, a facial feature that Greta took time to acclimatise to but soon would embrace. At Danny's loving request, Greta would slowly allow her to hair to grow towards its original length.

The men would try and avoid the drinking holes in Port Denning, if they did take a seat at any of the venues, it wouldn't be for long. Although as time passed by and their confidence grew, the possibility of the next touring customer being the one that could expose them was always knocking at the back of their minds. Steve would join them more regularly than not, forming a trust with the ex-MC outlaws and diverted the more prying questions from the locals and visitors with aplomb if anyone were to ask about his new friends.

Danny kept up his correspondence with Kate and Zoe and had them send their letters to a post office box he had set up in town. Greta would retrieve them for him; however, she was always wary of the ones that Zoe would send and discretely would ask of its contents, a soft demand that Danny would always oblige with as what was in them would cast no suspisions on their short relationship. He would read them first, of course.

Zoe kept him up to date on his pals' impending court case including the dismissal of any charges being potentially laid over the Tambourine bridge shootout and any occurrences that arose out of the siege regarding Barny. She was also successful in having more charge's thrown out on a technicality due to Minister's Johnston illegal manhunt before the trial would even commence. By late May, almost three months after the remaining charges had been set, she was pleased to write that both Barny and Harry had been acquitted on their most serious charges.

Zoe shot holes through the prosecution's case as she vowed. The trial lasted two weeks before the jury retired and after only 2 hours deliberation, they returned with a not guilty verdict. Barny and Harry took the stand and under instructions from their lawyer, the duo testified that they were nowhere in the vicinity when the shooting of Officer Dukes occurred, and neither was Ricky De Graaf.

The testimony was sanctioned by Danny, who didn't care if he were the only one connected to any of slayings, after all, he was dead, and it would be hard for anyone to prosecute an urn of ashes. They testified that they had only met up with Danny Pruitt inside the Kensington National Park. Zoe successfully argued that no one could possibly connect any of them to the shooting death of Officer Dukes. She proved that Dukes' fellow officer who in his statement said he saw the shooter, could not rightly identify any of the riders who were there.

The officer's time in the stand was an embarrassment to the prosecution's case as Zoe had a field day with him. The only people who could testify that Barny and Harry were riding with Danny Pruitt at the time of the shooting were the officers who accompanied Senior Constable Steve Sandilands down to the Watkins River before they botched the arrest and were tied up. But as luck would have it, officers Dawson and Bourke never got to the witness box.

As for Sandilands, it was also hard to get a statement out of a missing person, regardless of a signed statement from the now publicly disgraced vanished officer. Zoe successfully argued that the statement to be legally inadmissible due to other proven cover ups and crimes, not only from Sandilands but also from inside Minister Johnston's whole police force when it came to anything regarding the dubbed Graceville four.

Dawson's and Bourke's statements were never signed and no less than a month after the la Fortaleza siege and wildfire, they both had quit the force. Within days of the trial date being set, Dawson and Bourke had disappeared from the Hexagon Valley and the state of Venturia itself. They were warned off taking the stand by associates of an attractive female criminal lawyer, who, through her hired help, sternly advised that any testimony by them would be a testimony against the Sultan MC. This could be a future problem that could become very detrimental to not only to their own health, but also towards the health of their family. It was advice that both Dawson and Bourke readily accepted without argument. Danny's stolen gains had reached far and wide.

Although the DPP tracked down the Constable's whereabouts, nothing they could say convinced either of them to appear at the courthouse. Without their testimony, the most serious charges of facilitating in murder and conspiracy to murder to which the prosecution set their whole case around didn't have a leg to stand on.

Zoe Valetta was quick to discredit the oral evidence of any other witnesses bought to the stand, including one called Sgt Dane Grainger. She used her closing argument to plead with the jury that her clients were only scared and frightened men who not through their own doing got caught up in a whirlwind they could not escape, too afraid to surrender themselves due to an illegal hitman being hired by the government themselves, allegations that were already well and truly in the public domain after Minister Johnston's arrest.

She argued that it would have been foolhardy for them to come out of hiding while a gunman was hired to kill them. They were law abiding citizens she continued in her closing, with no criminal record, Barny a devoted Christian, Harry a clean and honest man just trying to eke out a living in the harshest of times, and it was a closing argument that the jury believed unanimously.

In the end, the only charges the jury found them found guilty of were firearm offences and with time already served, both Barny and Harry walked from court free men. It was another victory to Zoe Valetta and when she walked out of the courthouse, she couldn't have been more proud of herself to help acquit two honest and courageous men, not to mention the fulfilment of the gold-plated pedestal that Danny would elevate her on.

After the dust had settled on their acquittal and with Danny's instructions and approval, Zoe helped Barny set up several new bank accounts, accounts that would each open with $5,000. Five more deposits in each untraceable account would follow before the years end until the full $100,000 of his cut of the Country Club heist was settled.

Barny would retire to the quiet life, keeping his nose out of any trouble as he always did before he had met up with Danny almost twelve months ago. He used the money to purchase land where an old ruined and destitute church laid. It was close to the suburb he grew up in. In between the restoration of the old structure and living in the bungalow of his elderly parent's property nearby, he enrolled at a university to complete his theology degree. He hoped to take control of his own parish one day, whether it be on the land he is restoring or another. As Christmas rolled around, he was still yet to talk to or personally correspond with Danny. He sent a prayer for his buddy every single night in the meantime.

Harry was just so glad his nightmare was over. He still believed that Danny was dead, Barny never gave him reason to think otherwise. Mysteriously, $9,990 showed up in his own personal account. He discreetly questioned the bank on its origins, covering himself from any repercussions that may come his way if he didn't declare it, however, all he got in reply from the banks was that it was all above board and that it was a deposit made from an unknown account.

Barny advised him not to make anything more of it. He knew it was Danny's way of repaying the loyalty that Harry had given him. Harry found a job in manufacturing and would always speak proudly of the times he spent with his friends Ricky De Graaf and Danny Pruitt.

Zoe would pen her final letter to Danny in the second week of June after all had been settled with his pals. She sat in her private office den inside her inner-city dockland's apartment in Marlboro. It was drizzling rain and cold outside, the first real sign in the southern states that winter was upon them. Power was now restored twenty-four hours a day to the city precincts and its surrounds. Zoe kept herself warm by the small log gas fire. She had just finished showering and was dressed in a light dressing gown with her favourite furry mauve coloured slippers comforting her feet. It was an hour before midnight and under a solitary lamp she began to write.

She informed Danny that he had officially been exonerated of any guilt over the deaths of both Rosco and Billy Devlin as all statements and testimony's, including young Mickey Delvin's confessions of the true events, proved beyond doubt that the shootings were in self-defence. The case relating to the deaths of the elder Delvin's was still under investigation, news that Danny was none too concerned about.

Zoe likewise wrote that the investigation into the disappearance of Senior Constables Steve Sandilands and Victor Slacek was still ongoing, also informing him that police had firm suspicions on what had happened to them, again, news that Danny wouldn't lose any sleep over. To this day, the existence, or remains, of both were still unknown.

She wrote that she would continue to fight on his behalf to try and clear his name of any existing or retrospective charges that would be linked to him, it would be a fight that would occupy her for some time yet. She wrote about the happy revelations that surrounded the arrival of the adoption papers concerning little Maddy.

As of 30 June, Zoe would officially become her legal guardian and another six weeks after that, Maddy would also receive her long-awaited cochlear implant. Danny was overwhelmed with tearful joy when reading the news. He would feel proud that the promise he made had been realised and that he had played his part in giving Maddy the gift of sound and making her world a whole lot brighter.

As the clocked past midnight and after wishing him well with carefully chosen words she began to pen the last line of her final correspondence. With an accepting tear of closure dripping down her cheek, she wrote. *I know it will now be impossible to ever see you again, but I do know a part of you will forever be with me.*

Love Zoe.'

She laid her pen under the lamp and leant back on her office chair. With her right hand in a circular motion, she rubbed the growing bump in her stomach and with downward smiles whispered, 'How's my little demon going? Are you safe in there?'

Kate would set up a private post office box in Graceville so she could correspond with her elder brother without any fears. Nearly a month after Greta had left her side in Graceville, Kate had anxiously waited and worried on any news until she was be paid a visit by Zoe Valetta. Zoe had tracked her down for two reasons. The first and foremost was to retrieve the urn that contained Teeto's ashes so Drake and Razor could give their little buddy a proper farewell when they received them.

The second was to relay the news that her brother and sister-in-law had been successfully reunited, another request insisted upon her by Danny after Drake had spoken to her by phone shortly after their arrival. Although Kate knew of the celebrated lawyer and what role she had played in her brother's liberation, it would be the first and only time that they would meet face to face.

Their brief encounter was taken inside a coffee shop near the Graceville railway station with Zoe also discretely handing over some much-needed cash into Kate's hands, more would come later from her now distant brother. She was buoyantly expressive with her deepest gratitude towards Zoe on what she had done to help her family, totally unaware of how close her brother and lawyer came.

Without any family by her side now, Kate thought deeply about her life and was reconsidering building her relationship with her estranged husband. Unfortunately, tragedy would come calling once again in the form Sgt Dane Grainger. A day after the meeting with Zoe Valetta and ready to exit her house to catch a train to the suburbs to surprise Ryan, Dane was on her doorstep to relay the news that her husband had passed.

Worried about his friend's reclusiveness, Dane went to pay Ryan a courtesy visit at the home of one of his acquaintances where he'd been staying. Dane found him in his loungeroom chair with a gunshot wound to the head. Ryan's mental state had never recovered from what he saw at Tambourine Bridge and the aftermath that followed, including his separation from Kate. The black dog infested his soul and combining with his recent alcoholism, he took his own life in a drunken lonely depression. The shocking incident would now leave Kate with no family at all by her side and the grieving would be done alone.

She would write to Danny at every possible opportunity, cutting out articles from the papers that concerned him in any way along with informing him of the happenings of friends left behind and events occurring in Graceville. She wrote that she attended the wake in his honour that Dane had organised on the day that Greta had left. At first, she was not going to attend but, in the end, she couldn't resist not being there, curious to know what everyone had to say about her older sibling.

Upon arriving at the Depot Hotel an hour after the first drinks were toasted in the bar, it didn't take long for her to become the centre of attention. She took advantage of the well wishes and was coaxed to stand atop of a table and make a speech to toast her lost brother. With most of the gathering hanging on every word she orated, she took the opportunity to target anything government, police or re-po squad, and with venom, solely blamed the trio for her brother's demise.

With rousing enthusiasm, she expressed to the hoards on how Danny had stood up to them, on how his life was sacrificed in doing so. She enforced the gathering to take inspiration from him, to fight for what is right, to stand your ground, to raise your voice and don't let corrupt officialdom ever rule their lives again and not let Danny's death be in vain.

She received a raucous round of cheering and applause after she had finished toasting her brother. Dane made his way across the floor of the bar and softly grabbed her by the arm after she stepped away from the table. He whispered into ear before quickly moving on, sarcastically congratulating her on inciting the crowd, and incite them she did.

She had noticed Damien and Benny in the crowd from her elevated position whilst she was talking and afterwards thanked them accordingly, along with others who helped in Danny's cause. She had also noticed Corey while she spoke. By his side was another man of whom she didn't recognise and was interested in knowing the identity of. Kate stealthily asked around, avoiding any contact with Corey and Sarah and on hearing the name Brad Neilson, her blood began to boil, knowing that he was the only name on the re-po list that had evaded any sort of reprisal. Kate reasoned that justice still had to be served and with spite mixed in with anticipated smugness, sorted out the toughest and most vindictive men she knew that Danny was friendly with and relayed the news that one of the re-po squad was amongst them.

Brad Neilson came to Graceville looking for Corey and after hearing that he was at Depot Hotel, unwisely made the decision to pay the pub a visit himself. Even after Kate's fire and brimstone short eulogy and either through bravery or stupidity, Neilson decided to extend his visit and join in on the drinking session that ensued. He naively suspected that any repercussions regarding the re-po squad raid at the Pruitt's property had disappeared with Danny's death and unwittingly had no understanding that it was Kate who had held the list.

As the night sky descended upon Graceville and with drinks still being heartily consumed inside the hotel, Brad Neilson was suddenly ambushed upon leaving. He was dragged into a nearby alleyway by a vengeful drunken angry mob then beaten and stomped to an inch of his life. He would need permanent care for the rest of his living days.

As Danny and Greta were preparing for the imminent birth of Lani, a coronial inquest had begun in Marlboro on the events that led to the infamous *La Fortaleza* siege. Politicians in both government and opposition wanted answers on how it all went terribly wrong and why it cost so many lives. The inquest started with the illegal search of the Graceville four that culminated with the botched siege and devastating wildfire that followed.

Witnesses to every related incident that was of concern were to be subpoenaed before the court to testify. Justice Angus Spry oversaw proceedings and either listened or read statements from over 250 witnesses as weekly updates from Kate was sent to Danny's hands.

People such as Assistant Commissioner Martin Conroy and Inspector Vaccaro to SOG members and lower ranked officials such as Sgt Dane Grainger and employees from Minister Johnston's office appeared amongst other experts in their field. The inquest would last over six weeks and the coroners' findings would be scathing in some parts, particularly towards the decision making of senior police and the deep seeded corruption and misleading evidence that came from within the Hexagon Valley rule makers.

Captain Dennis Grundy who led the SOG incursion into the compound sat in the witness box for over two days being cross examined as he defended his actions while relaying his own version of events. He would eventually be discharged from the force without conviction.

By the year's end, numerous police and government officials had handed in their resignations because of the inquest with Inspector Vaccaro being one of them. He had retired from the force by mid-year, exasperated and stressed as his health began to deteriorate. The angst over his missing nephew Steve Sandilands, combined with his embarrassment and shame regarding the revelations exposed on the young Senior Constable's crimes would be a major factor in Vaccaro's wellbeing. The name Danny Pruitt would give him continued torment every time he would read or hear it mentioned.

Assistant Commissioner Martin Conroy would be promoted to the senior job under the re-elected Government of Premier Kendall in October, and together, they would relentlessly fight to rid corruption from their ranks.

Former Minister Colin Johnston's long-awaited trial was set down for 22 October; however, the disgraced politician would never step foot inside the courtroom. After being kept in protective custody since the day of his arrest, he arrived at the underground carpark of the Magistrates court in Marlboro on the first day of proceedings. Surrounded by police and protective service agents who clearly understood their prisoner had received threats to his life, Johnston exited the van in handcuffs only to be greeted by an awaiting gunman.

The credible threats to prevent him from appearing in court were taken seriously by police and the DPP, anonymous threats that could have originated from a plethora of sources. From fellow politicians, police or from disgruntled citizens, but also from people from the rife underworld of crime who were rightly afraid that he would incriminate them all to lesson his sentence. Former Government Minister Colin Johnston had only taken a dozen steps away from the presumed secured location before he was shot four times by the assailant. He would die of his wounds later that night.

There was not much public sympathy when the news of the shooting hit the streets. Nevertheless, it was another reminder to authorities they still had a lot of work in front of them to quell the blatant and brazen crime that had blanketed the times.

The gunman was shot by the protective entourage in the return fire and was killed instantly as he tried to make his escape. Authorities were privy to the fact that Johnston had made a lot of enemies on both sides of the law during his tenure and the list of suspects on the assassination was numerous. After the gunman's identity was discovered, one name on the list of potential suspects that raised more than a few eyebrows inside police rooms was John Pringle. He was a well-known associate of the deceased gunman and after several interviews after his own arrest, police knew that Pringle was gunning for the Minister.

The prosecution's proposed star witness in the case against Minister Johnston was last seen at the safehouse that was presumably protecting him, however, after his disappearance earlier in the year, in which the truth of his escape and those involved had now been established, there had been no siting of the notorious gun for hire. Senior investigators believed the most likely outcome for John Pringle was that his lifestyle had finally caught up with him.

After extensive heavy-handed threats and investigation by task forces, no police, politician, businessman or crime figure had any information regarding his whereabouts. In the end, authorities presumed the most plausible outcome was he too had met his maker from one of the myriads of enemies he had crossed from the underworld. Consequently, the theory of John Pringle's involvement waned as quickly as it was risen.

Although investigators had proven that Pringle was last sighted with Lucas Cribbs, no other body was discovered in the burnt-out wreck of the cruiser on that fateful Monday. One theory raised and seriously considered was that Pringle could've been so disorientated and injured after the crash that he may have wandered into the bush before falling down a ravine at an unknown location before succumbing to the wildfire.

Statements that two people were seen in the cruiser during the wild chase up the mountain had not been substantiated. Mixed accounts from witnesses was vague to say the least, from the cyclist's and pedestrians, to the victim of the horse carriage that was destroyed in the chase. Most of them could not give a 100% guarantee that there was a passenger or not, and along with other witnesses who stated that they had only seen the driver inside the cruiser, it was not enough evidence to convince any of the authorities that John Pringle was with Cribbs on that day. There were sightings of a third vehicle along Mason's creek road around the same time as the Armaguard van and cruiser, but once again, nothing was proven. Investigators concluded that if there were a third vehicle, it was most likely driven by locals who were crossing to and from private farm properties that were dotted along the road to Tangiloo.

As with the investigation into Pringle and Minister Johnston's assassination, the Graceville Country Club heist was also still heavily under investigation. What was established but not proven was that there were three known but unidentified accomplices. It was the only strong evidence the Investigators had to go on, supplied and substantiated by the guard that was overpowered, along with witnesses to the ensuing chase. Several lead detectives involved in the case were convinced that it was the Sultan MC who were the masterminds behind the heist and the perpetrators would've probably relinquished their lives in the inferno that followed. The belief was that they met the same fate as the van in which they had made their escape in and deduced that the money most likely disappeared up in flames.

The Sultan MC had been bought to its knees from a resulting combination of the siege, wildfire, and ensuing arrests. The fortress and surrounding lands that Solomon had built was quickly sanctioned back into government hands with outlying areas released as either National parklands or catchment areas. The club had lost forty members at La Fortaleza alone, though the real death count would never be known. Crow was arrested on the morning of Solomon Pike's funeral and being the highest ranked member of what remained of the club, the law came down on him with an iron fist.

Simultaneous raids throughout the city and suburbs led to further arrests and by the time police had finished, no one in authority was left to take control of the club's state chapter. Although interstate chapters had been building numbers in recent times, the state of Venturia and La Fortaleza was where the heart of club functioned, and it would take years to rebuild the notorious outlaw MC, if at all.

Crow was questioned heavily on the whereabouts of his fellow Vice Presidents as police were still to be convinced that they had perished in the wildfire. Although grossly charred remains had still yet to be identified from the carnage left in the mountains, the task force was leaving the investigation open until they had proof that the Vice Presidents were among the victims. Crow was adamant in his statements that both Drake and Razor had indeed perished in the initial incursion by the SOG, and the last he saw of them was when Solomon and five prospects took their bodies away to be buried with other club victims that had met their fate from the flying bullets of the raiding party.

Upon further questioning, Crow assured the task force that if they hadn't found his fellow Vice Presidents bodies it was because they were either still under ground at a place he could not confirm, or their remains were amongst those who hadn't been identified. Crow was steadfast and convincing in his lies that Drake and Razor were no longer amongst the living for he had his own reasons to mislead investigators. He was certain that they had been up to something in the lead up to the raid, actions that did not have club sanction which was severely against their code. He and Solomon had discussed their disloyalty during the morning siege.

Crow had already fled the compound before Drake and Razor arrived on their rescue mission and he was adamant that the two had deserted the club. The no show and silence since the siege was in his mind deafening and after hearing that their wives had disappeared also, it only confirmed his suspicions. The scorned Vice President wanted his fellow VPs for himself and was already planning on how he could implement his own form of justice, whether he was behind bars or not.

Crow would face the most serious charges thrown against the remaining members of the club. Drugs and Arms trafficking being at the top of the tree to go with manslaughter charges resulting from the siege. However, due to the backlog of the courts, he would not know his fate until well into the New Year, so until that time, Crow would remain on remand with no possible chance of bail.

Along with the coronial inquest and Minister Johnston's assassination, Barny and Harry's trial was heavily reported by the media, and one journalist from Graceville was at the forefront with her reporting. Impressing editors of Marlboro's largest selling newspaper with her expose on Minister Johnston, Valerie Corbett was head hunted by the paper to join their team of crime and court reporters, an offer she immediately accepted. Her journalism skills and sleuthing for a good story impressed the heads of the paper as soon as she was employed and quickly found herself spearheading the reporting of the high-profile cases.

Whenever the story of the Graceville four was raised or written about, Valerie would do her best in her reporting to ensure that Danny Pruitt and his partners were the real victims of the rife corruption throughout the Hexagon Valley government and police force, not the cop killing outlaws that was first reported. She would remain a stern close friend and ally of Kate and by the years end would help her find passage to the Northern state of Capricornia and Danny's heaven. It would be a secret that Valerie Corbett would guard with unconditional loyalty.

Sergeant Dane Grainger also resigned from the police force mid-year and turned back to his original trade of being an electrician as demand for qualified tradesmen increased with the rising economy. Of all the people that survived the whirlwind that surrounded Danny Pruitt, Dane would pay a mental price as high as anyone involved in the tragic saga. He had lost friends, good friends, that would take him a long time to get over the grief of. He had witnessed terrible events, incidents that the average police member wouldn't see no matter how long their careers spanned. Those shocking images would remain in his head and would have to take to his grave.

As much as Dane Grainger mourned the loss of his friend, he could not forgive Danny for the grief and personal pain that he had put him through. Dane needed to move on and once he saved enough money and was confident his family was secure, he decided to put the memories of Graceville behind him. As soon as the New Year ticked over, he had his bags packed and began to travel, finally settling in the northern city of Burbank to try and restart his life. Ironically, only 320km south of where Danny's heaven lay.

Nevertheless, whatever scars were left behind by the people who pursued him, Danny would have no sympathy for any of them. 'If they ride with them, they will die with them,' he had once enforced and held no regrets over the deaths that followed him. The only regrets he did hold was the mental strain that his friends had to endure while helping in his cause and what was left in the aftermath of the fire. As the months passed after his presumed death however, a few of them would learn otherwise than what was public knowledge.

You see, Danny Pruitt was, is and always will be an egotistical beast. Throughout his life, he never lacked confidence. He had his fair share of arrogance and nerve and with that combination embedded in his psyche, he couldn't resist the temptation of letting a few trusted allies know that he was too bold, too brave, and too smart, to ever let the villainous authorities incarcerate nor bury him. He chose two in particular, assured of knowing in his mind that if they ever spoke to anyone, it would only be incriminating themselves and Danny was positive that they would never risk such a thing.

He sent a letter to Damien with a wad of money inside, renumeration for the borrowed horse and to help with the setting up his wholesale nursery, a goal that

Damien had often talked about should the good times re-emerged. The letter was short and full of cryptic subterfuge. It only contained two sharp paragraphs, mainly about a relationship between a man and a reckless big black gelding and a hollow log near a river, enough for Damien to leave him in no doubt as to whom it came from.

Damien read the letter twice before he would shake his head in disbelief and with a smirk across his face, looked to the skies and wished his friend all the luck he could. Damien would spend most of the gifted money on the resurrection of his machinery and igloos which gave him a vital head start over his rival nurserymen in the valley. By the time Christmas came calling again, Damien was already set up to cash in on the economic revival.

Benny too received money to go with a letter that he found in his post office box. As with Damien's, it would be full of cryptic messaging. It took Benny a bit more time than Damien before he figured out what was meant to be said in the two paragraphs. All the same, when he did make sense of the words, he too smiled with content, knowing that his time and talents never did go to waste. Benny remained in the mountains until he was to be told by the lawmakers otherwise. He met up with Damien soon after receiving the letter and together, over a quiet and secluded drink, they discussed and cheered their friend.

Danny thought long and hard of sending a letter to Sarah and Corey. It played on his mind relentlessly, tossing up the pros and cons of doing so. In the end, he decided against it for if anybody in authority got the smallest notion that he was still in the land of the living, it would be their door that would be knocked on first. With care and protection at the forefront of his mind, Danny would have to mark another time in the future to reappear in their lives.

Only one other person would receive a letter, and it would make Danny giggle as he thought of the words to write. Making sure the origins of the letter could not be traced back to the area he now was secure in, and with Drake's help, he had all the letters sent to Anton's property who then re-posted them from a post office in Twin City.

No less than a week after the coronial inquest had finished and made public their findings, Dane Grainger sat on a log inside his property after chopping wood. It was a bright and mild sunny day when he was given a letter by his young cousin. Dane turned the envelope around to see where it had come from. There was no name to it. He looked at the stamp that was attached. *Hmmm, Twin City? I don't know anyone from there,* he silently posed.

With curiosity, Dane opened the letter intrigued to know of whom it came from. He took a swig out of his water bottle as he flicked the note open that was inside.

It read:
I'm sorry for a friend who laid under a horse.
a death that was a result from a gun, not mine, of course.
If only you stayed in town and not pursue
then many more would be alive like you
You were a mate who could be trusted

> but like so many beliefs, it would all be busted
> The arrow that passed your head that morn
> enabled the payback that I did warn
> Respect and esteem, I still have for you
> Enjoy your new life as I will do
> The support you gave to a widowed wife
> Will not be forgotten in this fucked up life
> The friendship we had still fills me with pride
> Till we meet again on the other side.

Dane slowly shook his head and spat to the side. A large reluctant smile started emerging across his face and with a mixture of admiration and irritation, he growled, 'I knew it. I fuckin knew it.'

Greta would know of the letters he sent; in fact, she was looking over his shoulders when he wrote. She was wary of the possible consequences if they fell into the wrong hands and protested strongly against sending them, but Danny would get his way even after he accepted and acknowledged her concern. He would explain to her what the cryptic messaging was all about, detailing the events that linked the words and what they meant. He would not elaborate on the payback of Sandilands and Slacek, only mentioning that they got what was coming. Danny feared what Greta's reaction would be if she knew exactly what he and Ricky had done in their then vengeful state of mind.

The first few months together were hard for Greta. Although ecstatic and thanking God in being reunited with her husband, she could see that he was not same man she saw last and it worried her immensely. She could see in his eyes that he held a lot of bitterness and anger. He was prone to fits of rage which she had never seen previously. His mind would sometimes wander whether it would be at mealtimes or just relaxing. She fathomed he needed help, maybe see a professional to ease the burden of what lay deep in his soul. Realistically, Greta knew that was not possible, so it would be up to her to nurse the scars that had been left.

As the months passed, Danny's nightmares would slowly diminish, except for the burning horse whose image would visit him on a regular basis. He would confide in his wife about his time away and detail the events as best he could as Greta delicately delved for answers. She never forced her curiosities on him, never sat him down and demanded that he tell what she craved to know. She would wait for the right time, whether it be lying in bed after being awoken from his restless sleep, out on the veranda in quiet times or over breakfast or dinner, she would wait for when Danny was ready to tell.

Sometimes it would be weeks in between when he would share his nightmares. She had no idea on what he had really been through, the countless times he avoided death, the characters he had met, the perceived sins he committed, along with the agony of losing Ricky, still angrily mourning that he never had the chance to say goodbye to him.

As Greta listened, she was at times frightened at some of the things he had done, frightened of the reasoning behind them. She privately questioned whether her Danny had changed for the worse as Dane had inferred back in her yard in Graceville eleven long months ago. She used Mia and Candice as sounding boards on subjects she couldn't bring herself to discuss with Danny, subjects that she was scared of, for the answer from him might leave her in absolute shock. She hoped the ladies' experience of being partners of men on the other side of law could shed some light on her worries.

The only story he would tell with any enthusiasm and laughter would be the times with his bull ants and scorpions, a tale he would share with anyone who would listen. To him, it was the greatest and most fascinating thing that occurred and repeated it often, chiefly to his sons. Greta would smile begrudgingly as he told the stories of his little bush gladiator, too polite to tell him that she had heard it all before.

Danny was a rock for her during her pregnancy though. He supported and cared for her as best he could, but Greta's anxieties over her husband would never wane. Remarkably as it was though, as soon as Lani was born, Danny's persona changed immediately. Greta noticed instantly when she arrived back home from her three days stay in the maternity ward that he was a different man from the previous months.

The random fits of rage seemed to have disappeared; if they still existed, he certainly kept them hidden from her. She silently and gleefully noticed that the coldness in his eyes had warmed and the bitterness within had soured. His sarcastic quick-witted humour had returned, he was making her laugh again. Greta was emphatic that his doting love of his new daughter was in no doubt the catalyst for the change around. Lani was a radiant new light in a previous dark world.

As the days closed in on a new Christmas, they were both as happy as they could possibly be despite the eternal danger that hung over their heads. They took no time in adjusting to the warmer climate and although they both missed Graceville, more so Greta, and its cold winters, Danny was more than happy that he didn't have to chop firewood through winter anymore to keep his family warm. He had been daring enough lately to take day trips with his family up through the nearby hinterlands and further north into rainforests to take in all the beauty his new home could muster.

He and his family took charter trips out to nearby islands and would spend the day playing on the pristine sands and snorkelling the reefs. Whether they travelled by horseback, carriage or by the Ford Mustang that he and Steve acquired cheaply and Drake and Razor helped in restoring; they were days in which Danny would forget what had transpired to put them there in the first place.

Not that Danny needed a forceful nudge, but Darcy and Daniel and a cheeky and happy Greta got their way and convinced Danny in joining their friends for the pre-Christmas dinner at a harbour side restaurant in Port Denning. Kate would also be by their side. Through a veil of secrecy and many change overs of transport, Kate eventually arrived in Danny's heaven a week earlier and the emotional re-joining of the siblings left both in tears of relief and happiness.

Kate made herself at home in the spare bedroom of Danny's house and settled in for her short stay. She knew it would be too high of a risk for her brother if she were to overstay her visit and had planned to return to Graceville after the New Year had greeted them. She and Danny made the most of their short time together, hardly leaving each other's side, recalling, and informing one another of their deeds through the tumultuous times that transpired, Danny in awe and so proud of what she had done for him.

Kate was so blessed that her brother and Greta had again found their happiness despite the lingering grief she still felt over the loss of Ryan.

The now family of six left their house for the one hour walk through the forested snaking tropical sandy beach tracks. Danny pushed the pram ahead of him as Greta linked her arms to his, smiling and interacting with the beautiful Lani, while Kate strode beside them as Darcy and Daniel rode ahead on their pushbikes.

As they neared the end of the trail, they would veer left and follow it towards the township at the base of the steep headland and mountainous bluff, blocking out the sounds of the last breaking waves of the Amber Coast before they'd exit near the marina, a short distance from the eatery they were to be dining in. Steve would join them at the restaurant as he chose to drive the Mustang. He couldn't get enough of being behind the wheel of a high-powered V8 engine again. He would drive Danny and his family back home after dinner, glad that it would take a couple of trips backwards and forwards to get them and their belonging's home.

It was a lovely warm evening with a pleasant tropical breeze wafting through the air to dull the humidity. They arrived at the carpark of the marina and met with Drake and Mia, Razor and Candice, along with their own children after they had parked their vehicles at the foreshore. They stopped and chatted for a moment, looking at the disembarking passengers of the idling twin hulled large vessels that had taken tourists out to the islands and pontoons floating above the reefs for sightseeing and scuba diving.

It had only been three weeks since the touring trips had been back in commission, much to the delight of the local population and increasing tourist. Sailing boats and yachts bobbed on the water between the pier boardwalks as their empty masts swayed to and fro in the lengthening sunset shadows. Even for a Saturday night, the streets of the coastal village were active as people went about their seemingly happy business as the three families continued their walk towards the restaurant, a further 500m down the Harbour Esplanade.

The restaurant was away from the main street of Port Denning where the other much busier and crowded eat ins and hotels were. Candice chose the licensed venue and had pre booked the tables and liked the fact that the venue was child friendly, the perfect setup for the group.

Greta was excited as they walked the remaining distance, Danny too was feeling comfortable and at ease with the surroundings as the self-admiration of connecting his family continued to fill his imperious pride. Greta couldn't remember the last time she had been out for dinner with friends and family, let alone with Danny. The mood was joyous as they arrived at the white coloured crushed rock entrance path to the restaurant. They congratulated Candice on her choice as they took in the vista and the rear views of the restaurant that backed onto the inlet which meandered towards the marina.

The restaurant had a predominantly outdoor dining area covered above by large canvas sails with wooden benched tables and seating positioned over and around the woodchip and lawn pathways. The internal section of the restaurant had assorted table and chairs that surrounded the large rectangular bar that was already busy with customers. Danny was at the rear as they approached to where the attendants would greet their guests. The path leading in was lined by assorted palms, bamboo trees and ferns, mixed with the native tropical grasses and plants.

Solar-powered Garden lights and citronella-scented torch lanterns were scattered throughout with the taller flame lit torches forming an aisle to guide guests to the reception entrance. Service staff were dressed in black shirts, black shorts/ skirts with a bright green restaurant logo patched over the front of their shirts and aprons as they busied themselves amongst the customers.

The atmosphere seemed cheerful and buoyant as laughter and a relaxing pre-Christmas vibe exuded from the venue. Danny grabbed a menu sheet from the stand as they waited their turn to be seated. He perused over the cuisine as the ladies ahead of him doted over the new-borns while the young boys stood to the side, giggling and gesturing about something no one knew. Steve had joined them with his date, eager and excited to show off his new ladylove as the introductions did a circle.

Small groups of people had congregated at the outdoor reception hub biding their time to be called upon to take their seats. There was an elderly couple along with a young family of four, all dressed in their casual summer attire which was the norm inside the restaurant. Not to look out place, Danny himself was dressed in summer casuals along with his party. The same could not be said of the group next in line to be seated which was made up of four adults, two of whom grabbed his attention.

The men were dressed in dark slacks, dark-coloured open collared shirts and were wearing shiny black shoes and had sunglasses resting on their foreheads. One busily had his face into a mobile phone, reading and replying to text messages as if his life depended on it. Each were clean shaven, well-built, and well groomed, the taller of the two with a shaven head, tattoos were easily sighted on both their forearms. They seemed a bit overdressed, out of sync and different compared to most diners at the venue Danny mused quietly to himself.

Drake, Razor and Steve tried to raucously discuss menu options with him, however, Danny's focus was elsewhere. There was a bespectacled middle-aged woman with the group standing next to a wheelchair-bound man who had his back towards them. Danny kept his nose in the menu, trying not to be noticed by the group ahead when the impaired man moved his wheelchair to the side then slowly turned his head in Danny's direction. Their eyes briefly engaged, Danny then submissively turning his away.

The stranger wore a cap and was dressed in loose dark slacks with his long-sleeved shirt buttoned up at the wrists and neck. A skin-tight white pressure garment was noticeable underneath his shirt. He wore skin-toned protective mittens over both hands and had a moonboot over his lower leg. Together with the glowing flickering bamboo torchlight and candle-lit lanterns at the reception hub, his face looked disfigured with the left side drooping significantly more than his right.

The tip of the man's nose seemed to be missing and his left eye socket, sagging and unsightly, looked be damaged severely. Danny wondered how he received his injuries and what would cause that type of disfigurement. He wondered whether his friends and family had noticed him also. Danny looked to get Razor's attention, but he was in deep conversation with Drake and Steve, still arguing joyfully over what meal was the better option on the menu.

Greta, the other ladies, and the children were further ahead of them and to the side. The man's uncomfortable stare continued in Danny's direction. Danny began to feel uneasy, impatient; he could feel the stranger's eyes squinting harder at him with every passing second, something wasn't right about this man his senses alerted, somehow, he was familiar. Danny could feel the man's scowl delving deeper and harder and instinctively turned his own eyes back at him. Both sets of eyes had now locked on one another, this time with more intent.

As Danny and the stranger studied each other, a waitress returned to the entryway and presented herself to the man in the wheelchair and with smiling hospitality greeted.

'Good evening, Mr Pringle, your table is ready.'

The End!

CPSIA information can be obtained
at www.ICGtesting.com
Printed in the USA
BVHW052305290123
657301BV00003B/124